THE GOOSE-STEP

THE
GOOSE-STEP

A Study of American Education

BY

UPTON SINCLAIR

AUTHOR OF

"THE BRASS CHECK," "THE PROFITS OF RELIGION,"
"THE JUNGLE," ETC.

REVISED EDITION

PUBLISHED BY THE AUTHOR
LOS ANGELES (WEST BRANCH), CALIFORNIA

CONTENTS

CONTENTS

CONTENTS

INTRODUCTORY

Six hundred thousand young people are attending colleges and universities in America. They are the pick of our coming generation; they are the future of our country. If they are wisely and soundly taught, America will be great and happy; if they are misguided and mistaught, no power can save us.

What is the so-called "higher education" of these United States? You have taken it, for the most part, on faith. It is something which has come to be; it is big and impressive, and you are impressed. Every year you pay a hundred million dollars of public funds to help maintain it, and half that amount in tuition fees for your sons and daughters. You take it for granted that this money is honestly and wisely used; that the students are getting the best, the "highest" education the money can buy.

Suppose I were to tell you that this educational machine has been stolen? That a bandit crew have got hold of it and have set it to work, not for your benefit, nor the benefit of your sons and daughters, but for ends very far from these? That our six hundred thousand young people are being taught, deliberately and of set purpose, not wisdom but folly, not justice but greed, not freedom but slavery, not love but hate?

For the past year I have been studying American Education. I have read on the subject—books, pamphlets, reports, speeches, letters, newspaper and magazine articles—not less than five or six million words. I have traveled over America from coast to coast and back again, for the sole purpose of talking with educators and those interested in education. I have stopped in twenty-five American cities, and have questioned not less than a thousand people —school teachers and principals, superintendents and board members, pupils and parents, college professors and students and alumni, presidents and chancellors and deans and regents and trustees and governors and curators and fellows and overseers and founders and donors and whatever else they call themselves. This mass of information I have turned over and over in my mind, sorting it, organizing it—until now, I really know something about American Education.

I do not intend in this book to expound my ideas on the subject; to argue with you as to what education might be, or ought to be; to persuade you to any dogma or point of view. I intend merely to put before you the facts; to say, this is what American Education now is. This is what is going on in the college and university world. This is what is being done to your sons and daughters; and what the sons and daughters think about it; and what the instructors think about it. Here is the situation: make up your own mind, whether it suits you, or whether you want it changed.

THE GOOSE-STEP

A Study of American Education

CHAPTER I

THE LITTLE GOSLING

Once upon a time there was a little boy; a little boy unusually eager, and curious about the world he lived in. He was a nuisance to old gentlemen who wanted to read their newspaper; but young men liked to carry him on their shoulders and maul him about in romps, old ladies liked to make ginger cakes for him, and other boys liked to play "shinny" with him, and race on roller skates, and "hook" potatoes from the corner grocery and roast them in forbidden fires on vacant lots. The little boy lived in a crowded part of the city of New York, in what is called a "flat"; that is, a group of little boxes, enclosed in a large box called a "flat-house." Every morning this little boy's mother saw to his scrubbing, with special attention to his ears, both inside and back, and put a clean white collar on him, and packed his lunch-box with two sandwiches and a piece of cake and an apple, and started him off to school.

The school was a vast building—or so it seemed to the little boy. It had stone staircases with iron railings, and big rooms with rows of little desks, blackboards, maps of strange countries, and pictures of George Washington and Abraham Lincoln and Aurora driving her chariot. Everywhere you went in this school you formed in line and marched; you talked in chorus, everybody saying the same thing as nearly at the same instant as could be contrived. The little boy found that a delightful arrangement, for he liked other boys, and the more of them there were, the better. He kept step happily, and sat with glee in the assembly room, and clapped when the others clapped, and laughed when they laughed, and joined with them in shouting:

Oh, Columbia, the Gem of the Ocean,
The—ee home of the Bra—ave and the Free—ee!

The rest of the day the little boy sat in a crowded class-room, learning things. The first thing he learned was that you must be quiet—otherwise the teacher, passing down the aisle, would crack your knuckles with a ruler. Another thing was that you must raise your hand if you wanted to speak. Maybe these things were necessary, but the little boy did not learn why they were necessary; in school all you learned was that things were so. For example, if you wanted to divide one fraction by another, you turned the second fraction upside down; it seemed an odd procedure, but if you asked the reason for it, the teacher would be apt to answer in a way that caused the other little boys to laugh at you—something which is very painful.

The teacher would give out a series of problems in "mental arithmetic"—tricks which you had been taught, and you wrote the answers on your slate, and then marched in line past the teacher's desk, and if you had done it according to rule, you got a check on your slate. You learned the great purpose of life was these "marks." If you got good ones, your teacher smiled at you, your parents praised you at home, you had a sense of triumph over other little boys who were stupid. You enjoyed this triumph, because no one ever suggested to you that it was cruel to laugh at your weaker fellows. In fact, the system appeared to be designed to bring out your superiority, and to increase the humiliation of the others.

In this school everything in the world had been conveniently arranged in packages, which could be stowed away in your mind and made the subject of a "mark." Columbus discovered America in 1492; the Declaration of Independence was signed on July 4, 1776; Switzerland was bounded on the north by Germany. This business of "boundings" appeared in little diagrams; Switzerland was yellow and Germany pink, and no one burdened your mind with the idea that these spots of color represented places where human beings lived. At this same time the little boy was going to Sunday school, where he learned something called "the creed," with a sentence declaring that "from Thency shall come to judge the quick and the dead." The little boy pondered hard, but never made sure whether "Thency" was the name of a person or a place.

Some thirty-five years have passed, but the little boy still remembers the personalities of these teachers. There was a middle-aged lady, stout and amiable, and always dressed in black; then one who was angular and irritable; then one who had pretty brown eyes and hair, but to the puzzlement of the little boy had also the beginnings of a mustache. Next came a young man with a real mustache, and pale, washed-out eyes and complexion; but he was dreadfully dull. The novelty had worn off the school by this time, and the boy had got tired of stowing away packages of facts in his mind. He had become so expert that he was able to do two years' work in one, and at the age of twelve was ready for what was called the City College. But he was judged too young, and had to take one year in the grammar school all over. The fates took pity on him, and gave him as teacher for that year a jolly Irish gentleman, so full of interest in his boys that he did not keep the rules. If you wanted to ask him questions you asked, and without first raising your hand; you might even get into an argument with him, as with any boy, and if he caught you whispering to your neighbor, his method of correcting you was novel, but highly effective—he would let fly a piece of chalk at your head, and you would grin, and the class would howl with delight.

In this strange, happy group the little boy went by the nick-name of "Chappie"; for the school was located on the East side of New York, and most of the boys were "tough," and had never before heard the English language correctly spoken by a boy. "Chappie" owned a collection of one or two hundred story-books which had been given him by aunts and uncles and cousins at a succession of Christmases and birthdays. The priceless treasure, when he left the school, became the foundation of a class library, to the vast delight of the other boys and of the Irish teacher. So the boy ended his grammar-school life in a blaze of glory, and went away thinking the public school system a most admirable affair.

CHAPTER II

THE COLLEGE GOOSE

The College of the City of New York at that time occupied an old brick building on Twenty-third Street and Lexington Avenue. It gave a five years' course, leading up to a college degree; but the first two or three years were the same as high school years at present. The boy went there, not because he knew anything about it, nor because he knew what he wanted, but because that was the way the machinery was built; he was turned out of the grammar school hopper, and into the city college hopper. In his earliest days it had been his intention to become the driver of a hook-and-ladder truck; later on he had decided to follow his ancestors to Annapolis; now he had in mind to be a lawyer; but first of all he wanted to be "educated."

Most of the students in this college were Jews. I didn't know why this was; in fact, I hardly knew *that* it was, because I didn't know the difference between Jews and Gentiles. They came from poor families, and most of them worked hard; they lived at home, so there was little of what is called "college life" about our education. There were feeble attempts made to get up "college spirit"; now and then a group of lads would run about the streets emitting yells, but their efforts were feeble, and struck me as silly. In the course of time one of the better dressed members of my class came to me with mysterious hints about a "fraternity." I didn't know what a "fraternity" was, and anyhow, I had no money to spare; I was living on four dollars and a half a week, and earning it by writing jokes and sketches for the newspapers.

I took six or eight courses each half year at the college, and as I recall them, my principal impression is of their incredible dullness. For example, the tired little gentleman who taught me what was called "English"; I remember a book of lessons, each lesson consisting of thirty or forty sentences containing grammatical errors. I would open the book and run down the list; I would see all the grammatical errors in the first three minutes, and for the remaining fifty-seven minutes was required to sit and listen while one member of the class after another was called on to explain and correct one of the errors. The cruelty of this procedure lay in the fact that you never knew at what moment your name would be called, and you would have to know what was the next sentence. If you didn't know, you were not "paying attention," and you got a zero. I tried all kinds of psychological tricks to compel myself to follow that dreary routine, but was powerless to chain my mind to it.

Then there was "history"; first the history of the world, ancient and modern, and then the history of England. I remember the tall, stringy old gentleman who taught us lists of names and dates, which we recited one hour and forgot the next. Here, if you were caught not paying attention, it was possible to use your wits and "get by." I remember one bright moment when we were discussing the birth of the first prince of Wales. Said the professor: "How did it happen that an English prince, the son of an English king, was born on Welsh soil?" The student, caught unawares by this singular question, stammered, "Why—er—why—his mother was there!"

Also there were the physics classes; rather less dull, because they included "experiments," which exhibited the peculiarities of natural forces—sparks and smoke, and noises of explosions major or minor. But why these things happened, or what they meant, was never understood by anyone, and whether an explosion was major or minor was entirely a matter of luck. I remember composing a poem for the college paper, dealing with the effect of physics upon a poet's mind:

> He learned that the painted rainbow,
>   God's promise, as poets feign,
> Was transverse oscillations
>   Turning somersaults in rain.

And then there was drawing. We sat in a big studio, in front of plaster casts of historic faces, and we made smudges supposed to resemble them. On this subject, also, I wrote some verses, portraying the plight of a student who forgot which cast he was copying, and paced up and down before them, exclaiming: "Good gracious, is it Juno or King Henry of Navarre?"

I studied a number of complicated technical subjects—perspective and mechanical drawing and surveying—though now, thirty years later, I could not survey my front porch. I studied mathematics, from simple addition to differential calculus. The addition I still remember; but if I were asked to do the simplest problem in algebra I should not have an idea how to set about it.

I remember with vividness the men who put me through these various torments; young men, some feeble, some impatient, but always uninterested in what they were doing; old men, kind and lovable, or irritable and angry, but all of them hopeless so far as concerned the task of teaching anybody anything of any use. Every morning we spent half an hour in what was called "chapel," and the old men, the members of the faculty, were lined up on the platform, and remain to this hour the most vivid line of human faces stored in my memory. It was their duty to listen to student oratory; and so perfect had been the discipline of their lives that they were able to sit without moving a muscle, or giving the least sign of what they must have felt.

Sooner or later we came into the class-rooms of these old men, and each in turn did what he could for us. I remember the professor of German, lovable, genial, highly cultured. During the two years that I studied with him, I learned perhaps two hundred words—certainly no more than I could have learned in two days of active study under an intelligent system. Little things he taught me that were not in the course, for example by a slight frown when he saw me trimming my finger-nails in class.

And then the professor of Greek, a white-whiskered old terror. For three years he had me five hours per week, and today I could not read a sentence from a child's primer in Greek, though I still know the letters and the sounds. I suppose there are Greek words which I have looked up in the dictionary a thousand times, yet it never occurred to any human being to point out to me that I might save time and trouble by learning the meaning of the words once for all. I marvel when I realize that it was possible for me to read "The Acharnians" of Aristophanes, line by line, and hardly once get a smile out of it, nor have it occur to me that there was any resemblance between what happened in that play, and the fight against Tammany Hall and the Hearst newspapers which was going on in the world about me.

And then the professor of Latin; he also was a terror,

though his whiskers were brown. He was a prominent
Catholic propagandist, editor of "The Catholic Encyclopedia," and conceived a dislike for me because I refused
to believe things just because they were told me. I can
see this old gentleman's knitted brows and hear his angry
tones as he exclaims: "Mr. Sinclair, it is so because I say
it is so!" Five hours a week for five years I studied with
that old gentleman, or his subordinates, and I read a
great deal of Latin literature, but I never got so that I
could read a paragraph of the simplest Latin prose without a dictionary. I look at a page of the language, and
the words are as familiar to me as my own English, but
I don't know what they mean, unless they happen to be
the same as the English.

And then the professor of chemistry; an extremely
irascible old gentleman with only one arm. There was a
rumor to the effect that he had lost the other through the
misbehavior of chemicals, but I never investigated the
matter. I learned that chemistry consists of mixing
liquids in test-tubes, and seeing that various colored
"precipitates" result. After you do this you write down
formulas, showing that a part of one chemical has got
switched over to the other chemical; but why these things
happen, or how anybody knows that they happen, was
something entirely beyond my comprehension, and which
neither the professor of chemistry nor his three assistants
ever explained to any member of my class. My most vivid
recollection of this class has to do with the close of the
hour, when a group of us would gather with our various
test-tubes, and each put up a nickel, and guess a color;
then we would mix the contents of the tubes in one big
tube, and shake them up, and the fellow who guessed the
right color won the "pot."

And then the professor of literature. Perhaps you
think I should have had some success in classes of literature; but that only shows how little you know about college. A new professor came in just as I reached this
class, and I learned in after years that he had got his appointment through the Tammany machine. A bouncing
and somewhat vulgar little man, he was an ardent and
argumentative Catholic, and his idea of conducting a class
of literature was to find out if there was anything in the
subject which could in any way be connected with Cath-

olic doctrine and history, and if so, to bring out that aspect of the subject. Thus I learned that Milton, though undoubtedly a great poet, had cruelly lied about the popes; also I learned that Chaucer was positively not a Wyckliffite. I had not the remotest idea what a Wyckliffite was, but got the general impression that it was something terrible, and I was quite willing to believe the best of Chaucer, in spite of his perverse way of spelling English words. As part of the process of disciplining our taste in literature, we were required to learn poems by heart, and this professor selected poems which had something to do with Catholicism. Seeing that most of us were Jews, this was irritating, but we got what fun we could out of our predicament. At that time there was a popular music-hall song, with a chorus: "Ta-ra-ra-ra-boom-de-ay"; so we used to go about the corridors of our college chanting to this lively tune a poem by Austin Dobson:

> Missal of the Gothic age,
> Missal with the blazoned page,
> Whence, O Missal, hither come,
> From what dim scriptorium?
>
> Whose the name that wrought thee thus,
> Ambrose or Theophilus,
> Bending, through the waning light,
> O'er thy vellum scraped and white!

I hope you know the tune of "Ta-ra-ra-ra-boom-de-ay," so that you may get the full cultural benefit from this recitation!

However, my little Catholic professor of literature did one thing for me; he let me know of the existence of a poet by the name of Shelley. We read "The Skylark" and "The Cloud" in class, and there came over me a realization of the ghastly farce I was going through in this college. I was near the end of my senior year, but my store of patience gave out, and I presented a letter to the faculty, stating that I was obliged to earn my own living, and requesting that I be allowed two months' leave of absence. The statement was strictly true, but the implication, that I was going to spend the two months in earning money, was not true; I spent the two months sitting on the bed in an eight by ten hall bedroom in a lodging-house, reading Shelley's poetry and Emerson's Essays and the prose of Ruskin and Carlyle. I went back to college and made up my lost months in a week or two, and passed my examinations without either credit or discredit—ranking just in the middle of my class.

I take it that the purpose of education is to discover the special aptitudes of the student, and to foster them. And here was I, a man with one special aptitude; here were a score of teachers, with whom I had been in daily contact for five years; yet I am sure, if these teachers had been told that one man in the class of '97 would come to be known throughout the civilized world in less than nine years, they would have guessed more than half my class-mates before they guessed me. I am not so egotistical as to imagine that I was the only man in that class who had special aptitudes; if few of the others have developed any, I think I know the reason—the machine had rolled them flat!

CHAPTER III

THE UNIVERSITY GOOSE

Columbia University at the time I went to it had just moved up to its new buildings on Morningside Heights. The center of the group was a magnificent white marble library, built almost entirely for display, and with but little relation to books and those who were to use them. But of this I had no suspicion; I had come now to the real headquarters of education, and I studied the fascinating lists of courses, and my heart leaped, because I was free to choose whatever I wished of all this feast. I was a proud "bachelor of arts," and declared my intention of becoming a still prouder "master of arts." To achieve the feat I must complete a year's course, consisting of a "major" subject and two "minors," and I must also compose a "thesis." To register for all this I paid a hundred and fifty dollars, earned by a newly discovered talent for writing dime novels.

My major subject was English; and as part of the work Professor George Rice Carpenter undertook to teach me the art of composition. This was an undergraduate course, taken by students of Columbia College, and so I had a chance to see how they were taught. To my dismay

2

I found it exactly the same dreary routine that I had been through at my City College. Our professor would set us a topic on which to write a "theme": "Should College Students Take Part in Athletics;" or perhaps, "A Description of the Country in Winter." My own efforts at this task were pitiful, and I was angrily aware that they were pitiful; I did not care anything about the matters on which I was asked to write, and I could never in my life write about anything I did not care about. I stood some six weeks of it, and then went to the professor and told him I wanted to drop the course.

So I discovered one of the embarrassments of the American college system. Students are supposed to choose courses, but no provision is made for them to sample the wares and make an intelligent selection. If anybody finds he has made a mistake, he is in the same plight as if he has married the wrong girl; he can not get out without hurting the girl's feelings, and I, unhappy blunderer in the undergraduate machine, had to hurt the feelings of Professor Carpenter. "I don't know what you want," said he, "or how you think you are going to get it; but this one thing I can tell you positively—you don't know how to write." To which I answered humbly, of course; that was why I had to come to him. But I had become convinced that I wasn't going to learn in that way, and my mind was made up to drop the course.

Also I took a course in poetry with William Peterfield Trent. The predecessors of Milton were the subject of our investigation, I remember, and perhaps they were uninteresting poets—anyhow, the lectures about them certainly were. I stood it for a month or two, and then we came upon a grammatical error in one of our poets. "You will find such things occasionally," said the professor. "There is a line in Byron—'There let him lay'—and I have an impression that I once came upon a similar error in Shelley. Some day before long I plan to read Shelley through and see if I can find it." And that finished me. Shelley was my dearest friend in all the world, and I imagined a man confronting the record of his ecstasies, seeking a grammatical error! I quit that course.

Also I had started one in French. It was the same dreary routine I had gone through for five years in Latin; translating little foolish sentences by looking up words in the dictionary. I seriously meant to read French, so stayed long enough to get the accent correctly, and then retired, and got myself a note-book and set to work to hammer the meaning of French words into my head. In another six weeks I had read half a dozen of the best French novels, and in the course of the next year I read all the standard French classics. I did the same thing with German; having already got the pronunciation, I proceeded to teach myself words, and in a year or two had got to know German literature as well as English.

Most of my experience at Columbia consisted of beginning courses, and dropping them after a few weeks. At the end I figured up that I had sampled over forty courses. I finished five or six, but never took an examination in one. And this was no mere whim or idleness on my part; it was a deliberate judgment upon the university and its methods. I had made the discovery that, being registered for a master's degree, and not having completed the necessary courses, I was free to register for new courses the second year, without paying additional tuition fees; and failing to complete the courses the second year, I was free to register for the third year, and so on.

Thus I worked out my system—education in spite of the educators! I would start a course, and get a preliminary view of the subject, and the list of the required readings; then I would go off by myself and do the readings. Almost invariably there was one book which the professor used as a text-book, and his lectures were nothing but an inadequate résumé thereof. At the beginning of his course on the drama Brander Matthews would say "Gentlemen, I make it a point of honor with you not to read my book—'The Development of the Drama,' until after you have finished my course!"

Brander Matthews was a new type to me, the literary "man of the world." His mind was a store-house of gossip about the theater and the stage-world, and I was interested, and eagerly read the plays. I knew that Brander was not my kind of man, that his world was not for me; but what kind of world I was going to choose, or to make for myself, I did not at that time know. As I dwell on these days, I see before me his loose, rather shambling figure, with a queerly shaped brown beard and a cigarette dangling from the lower lip. I do not know how this dangling was contrived, but I doubt if I ever saw the professor at a lecture that he did not have that cigarette in position as he talked. Brander is the beau ideal of the successful college professor, metropolitan style; a clubman, easy-going and cynical, but not too much so for propriety; wealthy enough to be received at the dinners of trustees, and witty enough to be welcome anywhere. He is a bitter reactionary, and has become one of President Butler's most active henchmen; his reputation as author of more than forty books is made use of by the New York "Times" for an occasional job of assassinating a liberal writer.

With Nicholas Murray Butler I took a course in the critical philosophy. At this time he was a modest professor, and his dazzling career lay in the future. I shall have many impolite things to say about Butler, so let me make it plain that there is nothing personal in my attitude; to me he was always affable. He possesses a subtle mind, and uses it thoroughly. With him I read "The Critique of Pure Reason" twice through and as a work of supererogation I read also the impossible German. I had had a little metaphysics before this, and was now pleased to have Kant demonstrate that I had wasted my time. I took seriously what I read, and assumed that my professor was taking seriously what he taught; so imagine my bewilderment when shortly afterwards I learned that Professor Butler had left the Presbyterian church, and had joined the Episcopal church, as one of the steps necessary to becoming president of Columbia University. It gave me a shock, because I knew he had no belief whatever in any of the dogmas of the Christian religion, and had completely demonstrated to me the impossibility of any valid knowledge concerning immortality, free will or a First Cause.

Another "man of the world" type of professor whom I encountered was Harry Thurston Peck, who gave me a course in Roman civilization of the Augustan age. It was so like America that it was terrifying, but Professor Peck I am sure was entirely unterrified. He was widely read in the literature of decadence, and from him I heard the names of strange writers, from Petronius and Boccaccio to Zola and Gautier. It was a world of grim and cruel depravity, but one had sooner or later to know that it existed, and to steel one's soul for a new endeavor to save the race. Poor Harry Peck was not steeled enough, and he broke the first rule of the "man of the world," and got found out. A woman sued him for breach of promise, and published his letters in the newspapers. There were some who thought he should not have been assumed to be guilty, merely because a blackmailer accused him; but the powers which ruled Columbia thought otherwise, and Professor Peck was driven out, and committed suicide.

It was a peculiar thing, which I observed as time went on—every single man who had had anything worth-while of any sort to teach me was forced out of Columbia University in some manner or other. The ones that stayed were the dull ones, or the worldly and cunning ones. Carpenter stayed until he died, and Brander Matthews, and Butler, and Trent, who purposed to read through the works of Shelley to find a grammatical error, and John Erskine, whom I knew as a timid and conventional "researcher," and who, I am told, has been chosen by Butler as his heir-apparent. But Peck went—and Hyslop, and Spingarn, and Robinson, and MacDowell, and Woodberry.

James Hyslop gave me a course in what he called "practical ethics," and this was a curious affair. In the first part he discussed abstract rules of conduct—regardless of the fact that there can be no such things. In the second part he attempted to apply these rules to New York City politics, explaining the methods by which Tammany politicians got their graft, and devising elaborate laws and electoral arrangements whereby these politicians could be kept out of office, or made to be good while in. The professor was a frail and ascetic-looking little man with a feeble black beard. It was painfully clear to me that the politicians were more clever than he, and would devise a hundred ways of countering his program before he had got it into action.

Now, as I look back upon this course, the thing which strikes me as marvelous is that never once in a whole year of instruction did the professor drop a hint concerning the economic basis of political corruption. The politicians got money—yes, of course; but who paid them the money, and what did the payers get out of it? In other words,

what part was Big Business playing in the undermining
of American public life? I took an entire course in "practical ethics" at Columbia University in the year '99 or
1900—two hours a week for nine months—and never once
did I hear that question mentioned, either by the professor
or by any of the graduate students in that class!

You would have thought that this would have made
James Hyslop safe for life; but alas! the poor man became too anxious concerning the growth of Socialism
throughout the world, and decided that the way to counter
it was to renew the faith of the people in heaven and hell.
You may find his ideas on this point quoted in "The Profits of Religion," page 224. He took to studying spiritual-
ism, and the newspapers took him up, and the university
authorities, who tolerate no sort of eccentricity, politely
slid him out of his job.

After his recent visit to the United States, H. G.
Wells wrote that the most vital mind he had met was
James Harvey Robinson, author of "The Mind in the
Making." Twenty-two or three years ago I took with
Professor Robinson a course in the history of the Renais-
sance and Reformation. It was a great period, when the
mind of the race was breaking the shackles of mediæval
tyranny in religion, politics, and thought. I read with
eagerness about John Huss and Wyckliffe, Erasmus and
Luther. I still hope for such heroes and for such an
awakening in my own modern world; meantime, I observe
that Professor Robinson, unable to stand the mediævalism
of Columbia, has handed in his resignation.

Then MacDowell, the composer. Edward MacDowell
was the first authentic man of genius I met; he is the only
American musician whose work has won fame abroad.
He was a man as well as an artist, and his courses in general musical culture were a rare delight. After much
urging, he consented to play us parts of his own works,
and discuss them with us. Needless to say, this was not
orthodox academic procedure, and the college authorities,
who do not recognize genius less than a hundred years
away, would not give proper credits for work with Mac-
Dowell. The composer's beautiful dream of a center of
musical education came to nothing, and he retired, broken-
hearted. As I described the tragedy at the time, he ran
into Nicholas Murray Butler and was killed.

Finally, George Edward Woodberry, who was in the field of letters what MacDowell was in music, a master not merely of criticism but of creation; also a charming spirit and a friend to students. He gave a course in what he called comparative literature, and made us acquainted with Plato, Cervantes, Dante, Ariosto, Spenser, and Shelley. He was a truly liberalizing influence, and so popular among the men that the Columbia machine hated him heartily. I was taking Brander Matthews' course at the same time as Woodberry's, and would hear Matthews sneer at Woodberry's "idealism," and at his methods of teaching. A year later Woodberry was forced out, under circumstances which I shall presently narrate.

CHAPTER IV

THE GOOSE-STEPPERS

In the year 1901 I was twenty-one years of age, and was ready to quit Columbia. The great university had become to me nothing but a library full of books, and some empty class-rooms in which to sit while reading them. No longer was I lured by elaborate prospectuses, setting forth lists of "courses"; I had tried forty of them, and knew that nine-tenths of them were dull. The great institution was a hollow shell, a body without a soul, a mass of brick and stone held together by red tape.

But before I went out into the world, I made one final test of the place. I knew by this time exactly what I wanted to do in the world; I wanted to create literature. I had an overwhelming impulse, so intense that it had completely ruined me as a hack-writer; my "half-dime" novels had become impossible to me, and the question of how I was to earn my living was a serious one.

And here was a great university, devoted to the furthering of all the liberal arts. This university had trained me to love and reverence the great writers of the past; what was its attitude to the great writers of the future? The university controlled and awarded a vast number of scholarships and fellowships in all branches of learning; that is to say, it offered support to young men while they equipped themselves to understand and teach the writings of the past. But what about the writings of the future?

What aid would the university give to these? I was planning to spend the summer writing a novel, and the idea occurred to me: Would Columbia University accept a novel as a thesis or dissertation, or as evidence of merit and of work accomplished, in competition for any fellowship or endowment under its control?

I made this proposition to the proper authorities at Columbia, the heads of the various departments of literature, and to the president's office as well; and I received one unanimous decision: there was no fellowship or endowment under the control of the university which could be won by any kind of creative writing, but only by "scholarship"—that is to say, by writing about the work of other people!

I was not satisfied entirely. It occurred to me—maybe there was some other university in this broad land of freedom which might have a more liberal and intelligent policy than Columbia; so I set out on a campaign to test out the question. I wrote to the authorities at Harvard, and at Yale, and at Princeton, and Cornell, and Stanford, and the University of Pennsylvania, and Chicago, and Wisconsin and California, and I know not what others. I did not let up until I had made quite certain that among all the hundreds of millions of dollars of endowment at the disposal of the great American universities, there was not one dollar which could be won by a piece of creative literature, nor one university president who was interested in the possibility that there might be a man of genius actually alive in America at the beginning of the twentieth century.

So I went out into the world to make my own way, and to fight for the preservation of my own talent. I had given the academic authorities nine years in which to do what they could to me, so I might fairly lay claim to be a completely educated man. I look back now, and see myself as I was, and I shudder—not merely for myself, but for all other products of the educational machine. I think of the things I didn't know, and of the pains and perils to which my ignorance exposed me! I knew nothing whatever about hygiene and health; everything of that sort I had to learn by painful error. I knew nothing about women; I had met only three or four beside my mother, and had no idea how to deal with them. I knew as much about sex as was known to the ancient religious ascetics, but nothing of modern discoveries or theories on the subject.

More significant yet, I knew nothing about modern literature in any language; I had acquired a supreme and top-lofty contempt for it, and was embarrassed when I happened to read "Sentimental Tommy," and discovered that someone had written a work of genius in my own time! I knew nothing about modern history; so far as my mind was concerned, the world had come to an end with the Franco-Prussian war, and nothing had happened since. Of course, there was the daily paper, but I didn't know what this daily paper was, who made it, or what relation it had to me. I knew that politics was rotten, but I didn't know the cause of this rottenness, nor had I any idea what to do about it. I knew nothing about money, the life-blood of society, nor the part it plays in the life of modern men. I knew nothing about business, except that I despised it, and shrank in agony of spirit from contact with business people. All that I knew about labor was a few tags of prejudice which I had picked up from newspapers.

Most significant of all to me personally, I was unaware that the modern revolutionary movement existed. I was all ready for it, but I was as much alone in the world as Shelley a hundred years before me. I knew, of course, that there had been Socialism in ancient times, for I had read Plato, and been amused by his quaint suggestions for the reconstruction of the world. Also I knew that there had been dreamers and cranks in America who went off and tried to found Utopian commonwealths. It was safe for me to be told about these experiments, because they had failed. I had heard the names of Marx and Lassalle, and had a vague idea of them as dreadful men, who met in the back rooms of beer-gardens, and conspired, and made dynamite bombs, and practised free love. That they had any relationship to my life, that they had anything to teach me, that they had founded a movement which embraced all the future—of this I was as ignorant as I was of the civilization of Dahomey, or the topography of the far side of the moon.

I went out into the world, and learned about these matters, by most painful experience; and then I looked back upon my education, and understood many things which had previously been dark. One question I asked myself: was all that deficiency accidental, or was it deliberate? Was it merely the ignorance of those who taught me, or was there some reason why they did not teach me all they knew? I have come to understand that the latter is the case. Our educational system is not a public service, but an instrument of special privilege; its purpose is not to further the welfare of mankind, but merely to keep America capitalist. To establish this thesis is the purpose of "The Goose-step."

And first a few words as to the title. We spent some thirty billions of treasure, and a hundred thousand young lives, to put down the German autocracy; being told, and devoutly believing, that we were thereby banishing from the earth a certain evil thing known as Kultur. It was not merely a physical thing, the drilling of a whole population for the aggrandizement of a military caste; it was a spiritual thing, a regimen of autocratic dogmatism. The best expression of it upon which I have come in my readings is that of Johann Gottlieb Fichte, Prussian philosopher and apostle of Nationalism; I quote two sentences, from a long discourse: "To compel men to a state of right, to put them under the yoke of right by force, is not only the right but the sacred duty of every man who has the knowledge and the power. . . . . He is the master, armed with compulsion and appointed by God." I ask you to read those sentences over, to bear them in mind as you follow chapter after chapter of this book; see if I am not right in my contention that what we did, when we thought we were banishing the Goose-step from the world, was to bring it to our own land, and put ourselves under its sway—our thinking, and, more dreadful yet, the teaching of our younger generation.

CHAPTER V

INTERLOCKING DIRECTORATES

The first step toward the intelligent study of American education is to consider the country in which this education grows. We are told upon good authority that men do not gather figs from thistles; we are also told that we cannot understand the cultural institutions of any country unless we know its economic and social conditions.

If you want to learn about America, the plutocratic empire, come with me and meet the emperor and his princes and lords; come to the Customs House in New York City, early in the year 1913. The memory of our busy age is short, so perhaps it will mean nothing to you if I say that the Pujo Committee of the House of Representatives is in session. They sit in a solemn row, eleven solemn legislators; and into the witness chair step one after another the masters of this plutocratic empire: J. P. Morgan senior, a bulbous-nosed and surly-tempered old man whom everyone in the room knows to be the emperor; George F. Baker, president of the First National Bank of New York, the second richest man in the world; William Rockefeller, brother of the richest man in the world; George M. Reynolds, president of the Continental National Bank of Chicago, the second largest bank in America; Henry P. Davison, Jacob Schiff—so on through a long list.

They are being questioned by a small, frail-looking Jewish lawyer named Samuel Untermyer. All his life he has been one of them, he has been in the game with them and made his millions; he knows every trick and turn of their minds, every corner where their money is hidden—and now he turns against them and exposes them to the world. They hate him, but he has them at his mercy, and step by step he shows us the machinery of our industrial and financial life, the thing which he calls the Money Trust, and which I call the plutocratic empire.

There is one phrase which makes the whole argument of the Pujo Report, and that phrase is "interlocking directorates." Interlocking directorates are the device whereby three great banks in New York, with two trust companies under their control, manage the financial affairs and direct the policies of a hundred and twelve key corporations of America. The three banks are J. P. Morgan and Company, the First National Bank, and the National City Bank; and the two trust companies are the Guaranty and the Equitable. Please fix these five concerns in your mind, for we shall come back to them in almost every chapter of this book. Their directors sit upon the boards of the corporations, sometimes several on each board, and their orders are obeyed because they control credit, which is the life-blood of our business world. Said George M. Reynolds, in his testimony, speaking of the control of American finance: "I believe it lies in the hands of a dozen men; and I plead guilty to being one, in the last analysis, of these men."

Such was the situation in 1913; and now, America has fought and won a war, and become the financial master of the world. The wealth of America was estimated in 1912 at a hundred and twenty-seven billions; in 1920 it was estimated at five hundred billions, greater than the combined wealth of the British Empire, France, Italy, Russia, Germany, and Japan. At the same time that wealth has increased, so has the concentration of its control. If the Pujo Committee were to conduct another inquiry in the year 1922, it would find exactly the same interlocking directorates, only more of them; and it would find that the financial empire controlled by three great banks and two trust companies has grown from twenty-two billions to not less than seventy-five, and probably close to a hundred billions of dollars.

Just how do these interlocking directorates work? A picture of their method was drawn in Harper's Weekly by Louis D. Brandeis, at that time an anti-corporation lawyer of Boston, and now a Justice of the United States Supreme Court. Said Mr. Brandeis:

Mr. J. P. Morgan (or a partner), a director of the New York, New Haven and Hartford Railroad, causes that company to sell to J. P. Morgan and Company an issue of bonds. J. P. Morgan and Company borrow the money with which to pay for those bonds from the Guaranty Trust Company, of which Mr. Morgan (or a partner) is a director. J. P. Morgan and Company sell the bonds to the Penn Mutual Life Insurance Company, of which Mr. Morgan (or a partner) is a director. The New Haven spends the proceeds of the bonds in purchasing steel from the United States Steel Corporation, of which Mr. Morgan (or a partner) is a director. The United States Steel Corporation spends the proceeds of the rails in purchasing electrical supplies from the General Electric Company, of which Mr. Morgan (or a partner) is a director. The General Electric Company sells the supplies to the Western Union Telegraph Company, a subsidiary of the American Telephone and Telegraph Company, and in both Mr. Morgan (or a partner) is director. The Telegraph Company has a special wire contract with the Reading, in which Mr. Morgan (or a partner) is a director—

So on to the Pullman Company and the Baldwin Locomotive Works. Mr. Brandeis points out how "all these concerns patronize one another; they all market their securities through J. P. Morgan and Company, they deposit their funds with J. P. Morgan and Company, and J. P. Morgan and Company use the funds of each in further transactions."

But Mr. Brandeis stops his story too soon; he ought to show us some of the wider ramifications of these directorates. He ought to picture Mr. Morgan (or a partner) falling ill, and being treated in St. Luke's Hospital, in which Mr. Morgan (or a partner) is a trustee, and by a physician who is also a trustee, and who was educated in the College of Physicians and Surgeons, of which Mr. Morgan (or a partner) is a trustee. He ought to picture Mr. Morgan dying, and being buried from Trinity Church, in which several of his partners are vestrymen, and having his funeral oration preached by a bishop who is a stockholder in his bank, and reported in newspapers whose bonds repose in his vaults. Mr. Brandeis might say about all these persons and institutions just what he says about the Steel Corporation and the General Electric Company and the Western Union Telegraph Company and the Baldwin Locomotive Works—they all patronize one another and they all deposit their funds with J. P. Morgan and Company.

Men die, but the plutocracy is immortal; and it is necessary that fresh generations should be trained to its service. Therefore the interlocking directorate has need of an educational system, and has provided it complete. There is a great university, of which Mr. Morgan was all his active life a trustee, also his son-in-law and one or two of his attorneys and several of his bankers. The president of this university is a director in one of Mr. Morgan's life insurance companies, and is interlocked with Mr. Morgan's bishop, and Mr. Morgan's physician, and Mr. Morgan's newspaper. If the president of the university writes a book, telling the American people to be good and humble servants of the plutocracy, this book may be published by a concern in which Mr. Morgan (or a partner) is a director, and the paper may be bought from the International Paper Company, in which Mr. Morgan has a director through the Guaranty Trust Company. If you visit the town where the paper is made, you will find that the president of the school board is a director in the local bank, which deposits its funds with the Guaranty Trust Company at a low rate of interest, to be reloaned by Mr. Morgan at a high rate of interest. The superintendent of the schools will be a graduate of Mr. Morgan's university, and will have been recommended to the school board president by Mr. Morgan's dean of education. Both the board and president and the school superintendent will insure their lives in the company of which Mr. Morgan's university president is a director; and the school books selected in that town will be published by a concern in which Mr. Morgan (or a partner) is a director, and they will be written by Mr. Morgan's university's dean of education, and they will be praised in the journal of education founded by Mr. Morgan's university president; also they will be praised by Mr. Morgan's newspaper and magazine editors. The superintendent of schools will give promotion to teachers who take the university's summer courses, and will cause the high school pupils to aspire to that university. Once a year he will attend the convention of the National Educational Association, and will elect as president a man who is a graduate of Mr. Morgan's university, and also a member of Mr. Morgan's church, and a reader of Mr. Morgan's newspaper, and of Mr. Morgan's university president's educational journal, and a patron of Mr. Morgan's university presidents' life insurance company, and a depositor in a bank which pays him no interest, but sends his money to the Guaranty Trust Company for Mr. Morgan to loan at a high rate of interest. And when the Republican party, of which Mr. Morgan (or a partner) is a director, nominates the president of Mr. Morgan's university for vice-president of the United States, Mr. Morgan's bishop will bless the proceedings, and Mr. Morgan's newspapers will report them, and Mr. Morgan's school superintendent will invite the children to a picnic to hear Mr. Morgan's candidates' campaign speeches on a phonograph, and to drink lemonade paid for by Mr. Morgan's campaign committee, out of the funds of the life insurance company of which Mr. Morgan's university president is director.

Such is the system of the interlocking directorates;

such is, in skeleton form, that department of the plutocratic empire which calls itself American Education. And
if you don't believe me, just come along and let me show
you—not merely the skeleton of this beast, but the nerves
and the brains, the blood and the meat, the hair and the
hide, the teeth and the claws of it.

CHAPTER VI

THE UNIVERSITY OF THE HOUSE OF MORGAN

The headquarters of the American plutocracy is, of
course, New York City. Here are the three central banks,
and here the hundred and twelve corporations have their
offices, and the interlocking directors roll about in their
padded limousines and collect their gold eagles and half-
eagles with the minimum of trouble and delay. According to the Pujo Committee, the banks and trust companies
of New York, all interlocked with the House of Morgan,
had over five billion dollars' worth of resources, which
was nearly one-fourth of the bank resources of the country. This did not include the House of Morgan itself,
which was, and is, a private institution. These figures,
of course, seem puny since the world war; in that war the
House of Morgan alone is reputed to have made a billion
dollars from its war purchases for the British government, and if the Pujo Committee were to inquire at the
present time it would find the banking resources of New
York City somewhere between fifteen and twenty-five billions of dollars.

It is inevitable that this headquarters of our plutocratic
empire should be also the headquarters of our plutocratic
education. The interlocking directors could not discom-
mode themselves by taking long journeys; therefore they
selected themselves a spacious site on Morningside
Heights, and there stands the palatial University of the
House of Morgan, which sets the standard for the higher
education of America. Other universities, we shall find,
vary from the ideal; there are some which have old traditions, there are others which permit modern eccentricities; but in Columbia you have plutocracy, perfect, complete and final, and as I shall presently show, the rest of
America's educational system comes more and more to be

modeled upon it. Columbia's educational experts take charge of the school and college systems of the country, and the production of plutocratic ideas becomes an industry as thoroughly established, as completely systematized and standardized as the production of automobiles or sausages.

Needless to say, the University of the House of Morgan is completely provided with funds; its resources are estimated at over seventy-five million dollars and its annual income is over seven million. A considerable part of its endowment is invested in stocks and bonds, under the supervision of the interlocking directors. I have a typewritten list of these holdings, which occupies more than twenty pages, and includes practically all the important railroads and industrial corporations in the United States. Whoever you are, and wherever you live in America, you cannot spend a day, you can hardly spend an hour of your life, without paying tribute to Columbia University. In order to collect the material for this book I took a journey of seven thousand miles, and traveled on fourteen railroads. I observe that every one of these railroads is included in the lists, so on every mile of my journey I was helping to build up the Columbia machine. I helped to build it up when I lit the gas in my lodging-house room in New York; for Columbia University owns $58,000 worth of New York Gas and Electric Light, Heat and Power Company's 4 per cent bonds; I helped to build it up when I telephoned my friends to make engagements, for Columbia University owns $50,000 worth of the New York Telephone Company's 4½ per cent bonds; I helped to build it up when I took a spoonful of sugar with my breakfast, for Columbia University owns some shares in the American Sugar Refining Company, and also in the Cuba Cane Sugar Corporation.

The great university stops at nothing, however small: "five and ten cent stores," and the Park and Tilford Grocery Company, and the Liggett and Myers Tobacco Company. I have on my desk a letter from a woman, telling me how the Standard Oil Company has been dispossessing homesteaders from the oil lands of California; Columbia University is profiting by these robberies, because it owns $25,000 worth of the gold debenture bonds of the Standard Oil Company of California. Recently

I met a pitiful human wreck who had given all but his life to the Bethlehem Steel Company; Columbia University took a part of this man's health and happiness. Crossing the desert on my way home, in the baking heat of summer I saw far out in the barren mountains a huge copper smelter, vomiting clouds of yellow smoke into the air. We in the Pullman sat in our shirt-sleeves, with electric fans playing and white-clad waiters bringing us cool drinks, but even so, we suffered from the heat; yet, out there in those lonely wastes men toil in front of furnace fires, and when they drop they are turned to mummies in the baking sand and their names are not recorded. Not a thought of them came into the minds of the passengers in the transcontinental train; and, needless to say, no thought of them troubles the minds of the thirty thousand seekers of the higher learning who flock to Columbia University every year. With serene consciences these young people cultivate the graces of life, upon the income of $49,000 worth of stock in the American Smelters Securities Company.

This University of the House of Morgan is run by a board of trustees. Under the law these trustees are the absolute sovereign, the administrators of the property, responsible to no one. They cannot be removed, no matter what they do, and they are self-perpetuating, they appoint their own successors. Their charter, be it noted, is a contract with the state, and can never be altered or revised. Such was the decision of the United States Supreme Court in the Dartmouth case, way back in 1819.

Who are the members of this board? The first thing to be noted about them is that there is only one educator, and that is the president of the university, an ex-officio member. Not one of them is a scholar, nor familiar with the life of the intellect. There is one engineer, one physician, and one bishop; there are ten corporation lawyers, and eight classified as bankers, railroad owners, real estate owners, merchants and manufacturers. Without exception they are the interlocking directors of the Pujo charts. The chairman of the board is William Barclay Parsons, engineer of the subway, and director in numerous corporations. The youngest member of the board is Marcellus Hartley Dodge, who was elected when he was 26 years old, and was a director of the Equitable

Life while still an undergraduate at Columbia; he is a son-in-law of William Rockefeller, and is chairman of the Remington Arms Company and Union Metallic Cartridge Company. He is said to have cleaned up twenty-four million in one deal in Midvale Steel, and in October, 1916, he is credited with making two million by cornering the market in munitions machinery. Frederick R. Coudert is one of the most prominent attorneys of the plutocracy, a director in the National Surety and Equitable Trust. Herbert L. Satterlee is a Morgan attorney and a Morgan son-in-law. Robert S. Lovett is chairman of the Union Pacific Railroad, and director of a dozen other roads. Newcomb Carlton, president of the Western Union Telegraph Company, guides the affairs of a great university in spite of the fact that he is not a college man. Reverend William T. Manning is an ex-officio member, one might say, being the bishop of the church of J. P. Morgan and Company. You must understand that Columbia is descended from Kings College, an Episcopal institution, and the bishop, and three vestrymen of Old Trinity are on its board. Pierpont Morgan, the elder, was on all his life, and Stephen Baker, president of the Bank of Manhattan and the Bank of the Metropolis, is still on. A study of those who have held office on the board of Columbia, from 1900 to 1922, shows fifty-nine persons classified as follows: bankers, railroad owners, real estate owners, merchants and manufacturers, 20; lawyers, 21; ministers, 8; physicians, 6; educators, 1; engineers, 3. The six physicians were on because of their connection with the College of Physicians and Surgeons, a branch of Columbia.

How rich in their own right are the particular Money Trust lords who run this great University it is not possible to determine, because these gentlemen, for the most part, keep their affairs secret. But in the list of those who have died during twenty-two years we have means for an estimate, for the property of many of these was listed in the probate courts of New York and appraised by the transfer tax appraisers. A study of these records has been made by Henry R. Linville, president of the Teachers' Union, and he has courteously placed the manuscript at my disposal. There are twenty-one trustees who have died and been appraised, and the list of their stocks and bonds fills a total of twenty-three typewritten pages, and shows that the total wealth on which they paid an inheritance tax amounted to one hundred and seventy-three million dollars, an average of over eight million each. I note among the list five members of the clergy of Jesus Christ, and I am sure that if He had visited their parishes He would have been delighted at their state of affluence— He could hardly have told it from His heavenly courts with their streets of gold. The poorest of these clergy was Bishop Burch, who left $37,840; second came the Reverend Coe, who left $80,683; next came the Reverend Greer, who left $172,619; next came the Reverend Dix, rector of Trinity, who left $269,637; and finally, Bishop Potter, my own bishop, whose train I carried when I was a little boy. in the solemn ceremonials of the church. I was duly awe-stricken, but not so much as I would have been if I had realized that I was carrying the train of $380,568. Such sums loom big in the imagination of a little boy; but they don't amount to so much on the board of a university where you associate with the elder Morgan, who left seventy-eight millions, and with John S. Kennedy, banker of the Gould interests, who left sixty-five millions.

You might possibly think that our interlocking directors would be so busy with the task of managing our industries and our government that they would not have time to superintend our education; but that would be underestimating their diligence and foresight. They do the job and they do it personally, not trusting it to subordinates. In the office of the Teachers' Union of New York I inspected a chart, dealing with the interlocking directorates of Columbia University; and except by the label, you could not tell it from the charts in the three volumes of the Pujo Reports. It is the same thing, and the men shown are the same men. They serve J. P Morgan and Company as directors in the coal trust, the steel trust, the railroad trust; they serve also on the boards of schools, colleges, and universities through the United States. You could not tell a chart of the Columbia trustees from a chart of the New York Central Railroad, or the Remington Arms Company. You could not tell a chart of Harvard University from a chart of Lee, Higginson and Company, the banking house of Boston.

You could not tell a chart of the University of Pennsylvania from a chart of the United Gas Improvement Company. You could not tell a chart of the University of Pittsburgh from a chart of the United States Steel Corporation. You could not tell a chart of the University of California from one of the Hydro-Electric Power Trust, one of Denver University from the Colorado Fuel and Iron Company, one of the University of Montana from the Anaconda Copper Company, one of the University of Minnesota from the Ore Trust. These corporations are one, their interests are one, and their purposes are one.

Evans Clark, a preceptor in Princeton University—until he made this survey—collected the facts as to the financial interests of governing boards of the largest American universities—seven of which were privately controlled and twenty-two state controlled. He found that the plutocratic class, or those intimately connected therewith—bankers, manufacturers, merchants, public utility officers, financiers, great publishers and lawyers—composed 56 per cent of the membership of the privately controlled boards, and 68 per cent of the publicly controlled boards. Says Mr. Clark: "Of the other two great economic groups in society there is little or no representation. The farmers total between 6 per cent in private and 4 per cent in public boards, while no representative of labor has a place on any board, public or private. And finally, no college professor is a trustee of the college in which he serves, while only fourteen out of 649 are professors in other institutions. Of these, six are Harvard professors on the Radcliffe board (the women's college connected with Harvard). We have allowed the education of our youth to fall into the absolute control of a group of men who represent not only a minority of the total population but have, at the same time, enormous economic and business stakes in what kind of an education it shall be."

And this condition prevails right through the list of our colleges, regardless of size, or where they are located or how financed. This was shown by Scott Nearing in an exhaustive study, reported in "School and Society" for September 8, 1917. He wrote to the governing bodies of all colleges and universities in the United States having more than five hundred students. There are 189 such institutions, and 143 of these supplied the lists of trustees with their occupations. The total number of trustees was 2,470. There were 208 merchants, 196 manufacturers, 112 capitalists, 6 contractors, 32 real estate men, 26 insurance men, 115 corporation officials, 202 bankers, 15 brokers, and 18 publishers, making for the plutocratic group a total of 930. There were 111 doctors, 514 lawyers, 125 educators, 353 ministers, 8 authors, 43 editors, 70 scientists, 13 social workers and 32 judges, making a total for the professional group of 1,269. For the miscellaneous group there were 94 retired business men, 3 salesmen, 123 farmers, 46 home-keepers, 3 mechanics, and 2 librarians, making a total of 271. For the purpose of this inquiry the lawyers belong, not with the professional class, but with the commercial and financial class, whose retainers they are. That makes a total of 1,444 of that class, or 58 per cent. In the state universities the commercial class had a total of 477 out of 776, or 61 per cent. And this, you will note, without counting the retired business men, who are certainly no less plutocratic in their mentality than the active ones; without counting the many doctors, ministers, editors, and educators who are just as plutocratic as the bankers. How plutocratic an educator can be when he is well paid for it is the next proposition we have to prove to you.

CHAPTER VII

THE INTERLOCKING PRESIDENT

We have investigated the governing board of the University of the House of Morgan. We have next to investigate the president they have selected to carry out their will. Naturally, they would seek the most plutocratic college president in the most plutocratic country of the world. They sought him and they found him; his name is Nicholas Murray Butler, abbreviated by his subordinates to "Nicholas Miraculous." I am going to sketch his career and describe his character; and as what I say will be bitter, I repeat that I bear him no personal ill-will. If I pillory him, it is as a type, the representative, champion and creator of what I regard as false and

right for a man to have a good time now and then." Of course, the Elks were disgusted.

In one of President Butler's published speeches I find him sneering at the progressives as "declaimers and sand-lot orators and perpetual candidates for office." What this refers to is men like Roosevelt and LaFollette, who go out to the people and seek election. It does not apply to those who go in secret to the homes and offices of political corruptionists and wire-pullers, there to plead, almost on their knees, for nominations and favors. A prominent Republican politician of New York said to me: "He begged in my office for two hours. He told me he had the support of this man and that, and then I inquired and found it was not so."

It is embarrassing to find so many people asserting that the president of Columbia University does not always tell the truth. It will be still more embarrassing to have to state that most of the presidents of colleges and universities in the United States do not always tell the truth. A curious fact which I observed in my travels over the country—there was hardly a single college head about whom I was not told: "He is a liar." I believe there are no effects without causes, and I have tried to analyze the factors in the life of college heads which compel them to lie. I shall present these to you in due course; for the present suffice it to say that a man who has held the highest offices in New York state told me how Butler had assured him that Pierpont Morgan had promised to "back Butler to the limit for President," and later this politician ascertained that no such promise had been given. Butler stated that he had the unqualified endorsement of another man; the politician questioned him closely—the matter had been settled only yesterday afternoon, so Butler declared. As soon as Butler left, this politician called up the man on the telephone, and ascertained that the man had not seen Butler for a month, and had made no promise.

Also, my informant had attended a caucus of the Republican party at the Republican Club in New York City, when President Butler was intriguing for the nomination for President. Butler came out from that caucus and was surrounded by a group of reporters, who asked him: "Was Theodore Roosevelt's name proposed?" Roosevelt, you understand, was Butler's most dreaded rival, and to

keep him from getting the nomination was the first aim
of every reactionary leader in the country. Said President Butler to the assembled reporters: "Gentlemen, you
can take this one thing from me—Theodore Roosevelt's
name was positively not mentioned in this caucus." But,
so my informant declared, Roosevelt's name had been
mentioned only a few minutes before in the caucus, and
President Butler had opposed it! It is worth noting that
Butler denounced Roosevelt and abused him with almost
insane violence; but when Roosevelt died he made lovely
speeches about him, and hailed himself as the true heir
of the Roosevelt tradition. He sought the support of one
of Roosevelt's close relatives on this basis, and the report
was spread among newspaper men that he had got it.

Nicholas Murray Butler considers himself the intellectual leader of the American plutocracy; he takes that
rôle quite frankly, and enacts it with grave solemnity,
lending the support of his academic authority to the plutocracy's instinctive greed. There has never been a more
complete Tory in our public life; to him there is no "people," there is only "the mob," and he never wearies of
thundering against it. "In working out this program we
must take care to protect ourselves against the mob."
Socialism "would constitute a mob." "Doubtless the mob
will prefer cheering to its own whoopings," etc.—all this
fifteen years ago, in one speech at the University of California. President Wheeler of that university remarked
to a friend of mine that this speech might have been made
by Kaiser Wilhelm; and Wheeler ought to have known,
for he had been the Kaiser's intimate.

And the fifteen years that have passed have made no
change in our miraculous Nicholas. As I write, Senator
LaFollette addresses the convention of the American
Federation of Labor, and says: "A century and a half
ago our forefathers shed their blood in order that they
might establish on this continent a government deriving
its just powers from the consent of the governed, in which
the will of the people, expressed through their duly elected
representatives, should be sovereign."

And instantly our interlocking president rushes to the
rescue. Before the convention of the New Jersey Bar
Association he exclaims: "Our forefathers did nothing
of the sort. They took good care to do something quite

different." And the Associated Press takes that and sends it all over the United States, and ninety-nine out of a hundred good Americans read it, and say, reverently: "A great university president says so; it must be true."

CHAPTER VIII

THE SCHOLAR IN POLITICS

What is the function of an American university president? Apparently it is to travel about the country, and summon the captains and the kings of finance, and dine in their splendid banquet halls, and lay down to them the law and the gospel of predation. I consult the name of Nicholas Murray Butler in the New York Public Library, and I find a long list of pamphlets, each one immortalizing a plutocratic feast; the Annual Luncheon of the Associated Press, 1916; the Annual Dinner of the Commercial Club of Kansas City, 1908, the Annual Dinner of the Pittsburgh Chamber of Commerce, 1917, the Annual Dinner of the Association of Cotton Manufacturers, Springfield, Mass., 1917, the Annual Banquet of the Chamber of Commerce of the State of New York, 1911, the Annual Dinner of the American Bankers' Association—and so on. In addressing these mighty men of money there is no cruelty which our interlocking president will not endorse and defend, no vileness of slander he will not perpetrate against those who struggle for justice in our commercial hell. "Political patent medicine men," he calls us; and he tells the masters of the clubs and bayonets, the gas-bombs and machine-guns that we seek our ends "by some means—violent if possible, peaceable if necessary"; he tells about Socialists "whose conception of government is a sort of glorified lynching."

And all this, you understand, not referring to the Bolsheviks; this in the days of the "Bull Moose"! In his speech before the Republican State Convention in 1912 President Butler portrayed the struggle with the Progressives as one "to decide whether our government is to be Republican or Cossack"! He discussed proposals to amend the constitution, saying it was like "proposing amendments to the multiplication table"! In the year 1911 we find him before the 143d Annual Banquet of the New

York Chamber of Commerce, stating that "our business men are attacked," and that this constitutes "civil war." Our political conventions are being besieged "by every crude, senseless, half-baked scheme in the country"—a terrifying situation, and what is to be done about it? The orator is ready with the answer: "Why should not the associated business men of the United States unite to demand that the next political campaign be conducted with a view to their oversight and protection?"

The associated business men of the United States thought this was fine advice, so through the agency of their Grand Old Party they nominated Nicholas Murray Butler for the office of vice-president of the United States. In that campaign Butler called one of his opponents, Theodore Roosevelt, a demagog, and the other, Woodrow Wilson, a charlatan; and he triumphantly polled the electoral votes of the states of Utah and Vermont, a total of eight out of a possible four hundred and ninety-one.

But did that end the political ambitions of our interlocking president? It did not. He gave an honorary degree to the senator who had helped him carry the state of Utah, and continued diligently to cultivate the rich and powerful. In 1916 we find him in the field again, and this time his ambitions have swelled, he wishes to be President of the United States. In 1920 he wishes it still more ardently; his campaign managers solemnly assure the world that he will take nothing less. The "Literary Digest" conducted a straw vote in the spring of 1920 to find out what the American people wanted; 211,000 of them wanted General Wood, 164,000 wanted Senator Johnson, 20,000 of them wanted poor old Taft, and how many of them do you think wanted Nicholas Miraculous? 2,369! But did that trouble our interlocking president? It did not; because, you see, he knows that the politicians nominate what the interlocking directorate bids them nominate, and the people choose the least bad of the two interlocking candidates—if they can find out which that is.

So President Butler's campaign continued, and with the help of O. L. Mills, the banker, and Elihu Root, the fox, and Bill Barnes, the infamous, he corralled the sixty-eight delegates of the New York state machine, and a few days before they departed for the Chicago convention we find President Butler giving them a dinner and making them a speech at the Republican Club. They went to Chicago, and in the hotel rooms where the wires were pulled President Butler argued and pleaded and fought, but in vain. One of the most prominent Republicans in the United States described these scenes to me, and told of the pitiful, impotent fury of Butler when finally Harding was nominated. He stormed about the room, denouncing this man and that man. "Look what I did for him, this, that and the other thing—and what he has done for me!" And when the delegation returned from Chicago, Butler received the newspaper reporters and poured out his balked egotism in a statement which startled the country. He denounced the campaign backers of General Wood, "a motley group of stock-gamblers, oil and mining promoters, munition makers, and other like persons." These men, he said, had "with reckless audacity started out to buy the Presidency." He went on to picture the New York delegation, the heroic sixty-eight who had stood by President Butler and saved the nation's honor.

Then, of course, there was the devil let loose! General Wood came out in the next day's paper, denouncing Butler's statement as "a vicious and malicious falsehood." It was necessary, said General Wood, "to brand a faker and denounce a lie." And also there was Procter, Ivory Soap magnate, and General Wood's principal backer, denouncing "this self-seeking and cowardly attack." President Butler was interviewed by the New York "Times," and was dignified. "I am sorry that General Wood lost his temper. It does not sound well." He went on to point out that the New York "World" had exposed the corruptionists who were putting up the money for General Wood; and this made lively material for the Democratic campaign—you can imagine!

There was a hurried session of the trustees of the University of the House of Morgan a day or two after that break of President Butler's. I have been told on the best authority what went on there; but you don't need to be told, you can imagine it. The interlocking president had denounced "stock-gamblers," and here on his board was one who had made two million by cornering the market! He had denounced "mining promoters," and here was a director in three mining companies! He had denounced "munition makers," and here was the chairman of Remington Arms and Union Metallic Cartridge! The trustees laid down the law, either an apology or a resignation; and so, a couple of days later, the New York newspapers published a statement from President Butler as follows:

"I am convinced that my word, spoken under the strain, turmoil and fatigue of the Chicago convention, and in sharp revolt against the power of money in politics, was both unbecoming and unwarranted and that I should, and do, apologize to each and every one who felt hurt by what I said."

The American people may have failed to appreciate the services of the president of their greatest university, but the plutocracy has appreciated him, and has showered upon him all the honors at its command. He has received honorary degrees from no less than twenty-five universities; he is a trustee of the Cathedral of St. John the Divine, and of the New York Life Insurance Company—the interlocking directorate! He is a member of fifteen clubs, and author of eight books of speeches. He has traveled abroad, and has been honored at Oxford and Cambridge, at Strassburg and Breslau. He is a Commander of the Red Eagle (with star) of Prussia, this honor dating from the year 1910.

In 1917-18 Nicholas Murray Butler was, of course, a vehement Hun-hunter; he was also vehement in denouncing American Socialists, on the basis of their supposed pro-Germanism. But let us go back ten years, to the time when the seeds of the World War were being sown. What then was the attitude of American Socialists, and what was the attitude of President Butler?

In the year 1907 the author of "The Goose-step" published a study of world conditions, "The Industrial Republic," in which he showed how the German Kaiser was drilling his people to make war on the world. The English edition of this book was barred from Germany by the Kaiser's government. The book showed how the German Socialists were struggling against their autocrat, and appealed to Americans to give their sympathy and support. I quote:

I do not think that we shall sleep forever; I do not think that the memories of Jefferson and Lincoln will call to us in vain for-

4

ever; but assuredly there never was in all American history a sign of torpor so deep, of degeneration so frightful, as this fact that in such a crisis, when the down-trodden millions of the German Empire are struggling to free themselves from the tyranny of military and personal government, there should come to them not one breath of sympathy from the people of the American Republic! And all our interest, all our attention, is for that strutting turkey-cock, the war-lord whose mailed fist holds them down! That monstrous creature, with his insane egotism, his blustering and his swaggering, his curled mustachios and military poses! An epileptic degenerate . . .

And so on. It was strong language, but it seemed stronger then than now. And let us ask, who were the American glorifiers of the Kaiser at whom these words were aimed? Head and front among them was Nicholas Murray Butler! In that same year of 1907 President Butler was spending the summer in Germany—arranging for the "epileptic degenerate" to send a "Kaiser professor" to Columbia University, to heighten his prestige with the American people! I have taken the trouble to look up this errand of President Butler in Germany, and I quote one sample of what our representative told the German people about their ruler. In the "Norddeutscher Allgemeine Zeitung," October 4, 1907, I read as follows:

A second more spirited honorer (Verehrer) of the Kaiser, Professor N. M. Butler, the president of Columbia University, returns home today, after a long sojourn in Germany. He explained among other things: "I was twice invited to the Imperial table, and I can only explain that the idea prevailing in America that the Kaiser is undependable is entirely erroneous. On the contrary, his personality has something uncommonly winning, and he possesses at the same time a democratic streak in his nature. The industrial and political activity, not merely of his own land, but of the entire world, awakens his most eager interest. He is a genuine statesman, and if he were not Kaiser he would surely become president."

And then President Butler came home, and when some one jeered at the Kaiser in the New York "Times," he rushed to the rescue with a letter full of glowing and eloquent praise; detailing all the virtues which a great ruler and statesman might possess, and pointing out the Kaiser as the sum of them all. It culminated with the sentence: "He would have been chosen monarch or chief executive by popular vote of any modern people among whom his lot might have been cast."

In enthusiasm for Wilhelm our Miraculous Nicholas had been forestalled by Harvard University, which had already established an exchange professorship, and had got another Kaiser professor in the person of Muensterberg, the eminent psychologist of the plutocracy, who used to delight his employers by analyzing labor agitators in jail, and proving by up-to-date psychological tests that they had done whatever crimes they were accused of. There was bitter rivalry between these two Kaiser professors, and still more bitter rivalry between the Harvard professor and the Columbia professor in Berlin. For, of course, these exalted scholars did not go to represent the American people, they went to represent the plutocratic empire, and they did not appeal to the German people, they appealed to the Kaiser's court. The wives of these two professors got into a scrap over the question of court precedence, and denounced each other in the newspapers, and a Frenchman, writing a book about Germany, described the Kaiser's court chamberlain as "bewailing in disgust the presence of increasing numbers of rich and well-gowned American women who got on their knees to royalty, and on all occasions betrayed their total lack of breeding and good manners."

But, you see, a German court chamberlain fails to realize the drabness of life in America, where the wives of eminent scholars have no way to demonstrate their superiority over one another, and when they come to places where there are courts and ceremonials they can hardly be blamed if the glory goes to their heads. We can hardly blame President Butler, because, after having had an eight-hour session with Kaiser Wilhelm, he hailed his host as one of the greatest statesmen of all time; but I think we may blame him just a little because he failed to imitate any of the good things which the Kaiser had done, and chose only the despotic things for his praise. For example, Kaiser Wilhelm had established old-age pensions and unemployment insurance in Germany, and had abolished child labor from the country; but President Butler came home and in a telegram to the Illinois Bankers' Association denounced the child labor law in such ferocious terms that even the interlocking directors were shocked, and refused to read the telegram at their meeting, or to give it to the press!

CHAPTER IX

NICHOLAS MIRACULOUS

We are now familiar with the social and political career of Nicholas Murray Butler; we have next to observe him as an educational administrator. We shall devote generous space to the study, for the reason already explained—that Columbia University is the largest and richest educational institution in the United States, and the model for all others that wish to grow large and rich. The author of its success is President Butler; and by observing him at work we learn how a university succeeds in the plutocratic empire, and what its success means to the faculty, the students, and the general public.

In David Warfield's play, "The Auctioneer," there is a scene in a second-hand clothing shop. The clerk comes up to the proprietor with a coat in his hand, and whispers: "How much?" "Eleven eighty-five," says the proprietor. But the clerk whispers, "Buying, not selling." "Oh!" says the proprietor, with a sudden change of tone. "Two dollars!" I am reminded of this when I follow President Butler from the great world of public affairs to the inside of his university. When he is interviewing political statesmen and millionaire backers and trustees, he values them at eleven eighty-five, but when he is talking to his professors and instructors, he values them at thirty cents. I have talked with some twenty men who have been or still are, under him, and I have their adjectives in my notebook—"hard, insensitive, vulgar, materialistic." "Insolence in conversation and letters" is the phrase used by Professor Cattell, while one of Butler's deans said to me: "Men of refinement cannot stand his air of extreme prosperity and power."

He rules the university as an absolute autocrat; he permits no slightest interference with his will. He furiously attacks or cunningly intrigues against anyone who shows any trace of interference, nor does he rest until he has disgraced the man and driven him from the university. His "Faculty Council" is a farce, because it has only advisory powers, and he overrides it when he sees fit. He makes promises to his faculty, to allow them this and that and the other kind of freedom and authority, but when the time for action comes he does exactly what he pleases.

One of his favorite devices is to use the trustees as a club over the heads of his faculty. Whatever is done, it is the trustees who have done it; but no one ever knows what Butler has said to the trustees, or what he has advised them to do. No member of the faculty has a seat on the board, or ever gets near the board except he is summoned to be browbeaten for his opinions. Says Professor Joel E. Spingarn, in a pamphlet on this subject:

Moreover, all the officers of the university hold their positions "at the pleasure of the trustees." This phrase has not as yet received final adjudication by any court of highest resort, but it is interpreted by the trustees to mean that the tenure of the professorial office is absolutely at their whim. No personal hearing is ever given by them to any member of the teaching staff, and a professor may learn of their intentions only after they have made their final decision of dismissal. This further increases the immense power of the president, since it is possible for him to prejudice the minds of the trustees against any officer toward whom his own feelings are unfriendly or of whom, for any reason, he entertains an unfavorable opinion.

And Professor Spingarn goes on to show how the problems of academic freedom are handled by a committee of the trustees, whose meetings only three or four attend. These are Butler's intimates, in one or two cases his creatures. Says Professor Spingarn:

Under such a system, it is small wonder that the president is surrounded by sycophants, since sycophancy is a condition of official favor; small wonder that intellectual freedom and personal courage dwindle, explaining, if not justifying, the jibe of European scholars that there are three sexes in America, men, women and professors; small wonder that permission to give utterance to mild theories of parlor Socialism is mistaken by American universities for superb freedom of action. But whatever may be the defects or the virtues of this system, it fails utterly unless the president is, as it were, a transparent medium between the teaching corps and the trustees. If he misrepresents the conditions of the university; if he distorts the communications entrusted to him for presentation to the trustees; if he uses his position to serve the ends of spite or rancor or his own ambition, hapless indeed (in Milton's words) is the race of men whose misfortune it is to have understanding.

The gravest offense which a man can commit at Butler's university is to interfere in any way with the administration, to criticize it even privately; the safe thing is to have no ideas about this or anything else, and to be a perfect cog in the machine. At luncheon, in the Faculty

Club, if you have criticisms you make them to your most intimate friends, and in whispers; and whoever and whatever you may be, you make your reports on schedule time, you perform your duly and precisely appointed functions. You are in a great education factory, with the whirr of its machinery all about you. It makes no difference if you are the foremost musician of genius that America has ever produced; you may be in the midst of composing your greatest sonata, but you must come at a certain hour to make your reports, and also you must not expect that an ornamental subject like music will be taken seriously, or its students granted full credits. If you protest about these matters you will receive cruel and insulting letters from the president, and if you don't like that, out you go.

Nor does it make any difference if you are a great poet, an inspired critic and teacher of youth, like George Edward Woodberry. You will be forbidden to give courses at convenient hours and on interesting subjects, because you will draw all the students away from rival professors in your department, who do not happen to be teachers of genius, but are henchmen and political favorites of the president. If you persist in having your own way, you will have your assistant taken from you and your undergraduate courses abolished; and if your students revolt and raise an uproar in the newspapers, the ring-leaders will be expelled. But you will not get back your assistant—no, not even though your students may offer to subscribe the money to pay for the assistant out of their own pockets! Not even though a Standard Oil millionaire may offer to endow the chair of the assistant in perpetuity!

Consider the experience of Professor Joel E. Spingarn, a distinguished poet and scholar, who took Professor Woodberry's place in the department of comparative literature, and filled it for many years acceptably. A member of the department of Latin, Professor Harry Thurston Peck, was sued by a woman for breach of promise, and his letters were given to the newspapers. Professor Peck declared that the woman was a blackmailer, and most of the faculty at Columbia thought that he should not be judged guilty until the charge was proven; but Butler got rid of Peck, incidentally publishing statements about him which caused Peck to sue him for libel. Professor Spingarn was outraged at Butler's proceedings, and introduced in the faculty of philosophy a resolution testifying to the academic services of Professor Peck, who had been twenty-two years with Columbia. This, of course, was a declaration of war upon the administration, and Butler made to Spingarn the threat: "If you don't drop this matter you will get into trouble." Within ten days thereafter he notified Spingarn that a committee of the trustees had voted to abolish his chair. Professor Spingarn published a pamphlet, in which he gave the history of the case, and the entire correspondence with Butler. I quote from his comments:

It would be disheartening to a proud son of Columbia to linger over all the details of official trickery and deception, of threat and insult, of manners even worse than morals; but it would be unjust to those who love Columbia's honor to hide from them the fact that, in the course of this single incident, the president of their alma mater told at least five deliberate falsehoods, broke at least three deliberate promises, and denied his own statements whenever it served his purpose to do so. It is without rancor, and with deep regret, that Professor Spingarn feels obliged to state these facts, and to express his mature conviction that the word or promise of President Butler is absolutely worthless unless it is recorded in writing and that even a written document offers no certain safeguard against evasion or distortion. It is to this executive, with this code of honor, that Columbia entrusts all avenues of communication between the subservient faculties and the governing trustees.

This is not a history or an estimate of President Butler's administration of Columbia; it is merely the record of a single abuse. But the record would be incomplete if it were not clearly made known that the facts, so far from being exceptional, are typical of his executive career. It is not merely that Columbia's greatest teachers, poets, musicians, have been lost to the university from the very outset as a result of his methods and his policies. The real scandal is worse than this. It is that in the conduct of its affairs a great university, so far from being above the commercialism of its industrial environment, actually employs methods that would be spurned in the humblest of business undertakings. Even the decencies of ordinary business are not always observed; and the poor scholar, unfamiliar with methods such as these, falls an easy prey. No device, however unworthy, is regarded as forbidden by custom or by honor. A professor may be asked to send in a purely formal resignation as a compliment to the prospective new head of his department, and then be dumbfounded to have his letter acted upon by the president immediately upon its receipt, and before the new head is actually appointed. A professor may be induced to come to Columbia by the assurance of the president that the usual contract, "for three years or during the pleasure of the trustees," involves an actual obligation for three years on the part of the university, while another professor holding the same contract with the university may find his chair abolished, on the recommendation of the president, at the end of two years. These are actual cases.

Shortly after this Spingarn incident President Butler completed the tenth year of his administration at Columbia, and a banquet was held at the Hotel Astor, attended by some two hundred members of the faculty. "It was an evening of much felicitation," the New York "Times" reported (May 16, 1911), but there were "almost imperceptible references" to the recent conflicts. The "Times" report goes on to quote some jovial remarks by Professor Seligman, head of the department of political science. I quote:

Prof. Seligman regaled the diners with some anecdotes of the days when Dr. Butler was an undergraduate. He told of a student to whom was spared the embarrassment of reciting by pulling the gong and getting the class dismissed. He said he did not know who that student was, but admitted that he had his suspicions, as he did in the case of the same student getting to the head of his class by making a ten out of his zero on the professor's record.

The above anecdote proves once more the ancient truth, that the child is father to the man; it would seem that by careful watching of one's classmates one can pick out those students who are destined to grow up into college presidents who do not always tell the truth.

CHAPTER X

THE LIGHTNING-CHANGE ARTIST

President Butler's career at Columbia has been like that of a drunken motorist in a crowded street; he has left behind him a trail of corpses. In the course of twenty years of office he has managed to expel or force to withdraw some two score men, including most of the best in the place. The cases of MacDowell and Woodberry occurred in 1902, the cases of Peck and Spingarn in 1910 and 1911. Beginning in 1917 there was a sudden series of casualties; but before these can be clearly explained, it is necessary that the reader should be made acquainted with another aspect of the career of Nicholas Miraculous —as pacifist and prophet of the Capitalist International.

Butler's friend, Carnegie, put up ten million dollars to establish a foundation in the cause of universal peace; and Butler became a trustee. The pointed question has been asked whether the Carnegie Peace Foundation pays for the elaborate banquets which President Butler serves to peace delegates in his home. Needless to say, when you have half a million dollars a year to administer, you can hire a great many secretaries, and print a great deal of literature, and give a great many champagne banquets, and make a great splurge in the world. Butler engaged a young man, Leon Fraser, to organize a peace movement in the colleges, and had him made an instructor in the department of political science at Columbia. We shall see in a minute what happened to this young man.

In the summer of 1914 Butler went to Europe to continue his peace work—but not with entire success. He came home in September, very much horrified at what had happened in Europe, and to the students at the opening of the university he made a speech in which you find him at his best, with his clear, keen mind and driving energy. He denounced the war-makers in language which left nothing to be desired. One thing this war had done, he said; it had "put a final end to the contention, always stupid and often insincere, that huge armaments are an insurance against war and an aid in maintaining peace. This argument was invented by the war-makers who had munitions of war to sell. . . . . Since war is an affair of governments and of armies, one result of the present war should be to make the manufacture and sale of munitions of war a government monopoly hereafter . . . . . How anyone not fit subject for a madhouse, can find in the awful events now happening in Europe a reason for increasing the military and naval establishments and expenditures of the United States is to me wholly inconceivable. Militarism —there is the enemy!"

Good for Nicholas Miraculous, you say! That is the sort of college president we want in America! But in the cold light of the morning after our pacifist orator thought it over. Perhaps he remembered his interlocking directorate—the grim-visaged, growling wild boar, old Pierpont Morgan, preparing to make his billion dollars out of the British government; young Marcellus Hartley Dodge, chairman of Remington Arms and Union Metallic Cartridge, getting ready to clean up his millions by cornering the market in munitions machinery! How awkward to meet Marcellus Hartley on the board, after talking about "the contention, always stupid and often insincere . . . . invented by war-makers who have munitions of war to sell!" Also, Butler was expecting to be Republican candidate for president two years from date; and it would not be easy to carry Elihu Root and Bill Barnes and Jim Wadsworth for a government monopoly of Remington Arms and Union Metallic Cartridge, to say nothing of Bethlehem and Carnegie Steel!

So President Butler sat himself down and edited his eloquence. The passages I have quoted are from the speech as given to the newspapers, September 24, 1914; but now see how it reads as published in Butler's book, "America in Ferment." "The contention, always stupid and often insincere," is softened to "the contention, always made with more emphasis than reasonableness." The argument which was "invented by the war-makers who have munitions of war to sell" now becomes an argument which was "invented by those who really believe in war and in armaments as ends in themselves." That lets out Marcellus Hartley, you see; in fact, it lets out Butler's friend the Kaiser, and everybody in the world since Genghis Khan. The proposed plank for the Republican party's presidential platform, providing for a government monopoly of the manufacture and sale of munitions of war, has been dropped overboard and lost forever; while the phrase about "increasing the military and naval establishments and expenditures of the United States" has been deftly turned into "asking the United States to desist from its attempts to promote a new international order in the world!" Let nobody expect that Nicholas Miraculous will abandon his charge of that half million dollars a year of Carnegie money!

After this you will be prepared for any amount of hedging. President Butler had for ten years been conducting with President Wheeler of the University of California an ardent rivalry for the affections of the Kaiser; but now the interlocking directorate is going to "can the Kaiser," and their university president is going to enlist in the speech-making brigade. Wheeler of California is three thousand miles away from the seat of authority, but Butler gets the "tip" in time, and saves himself by climbing out on the faces of those who took seriously his belief in universal peace.

For example, Leon Fraser, the young instructor who has been set to work organizing peace societies in American colleges, including Columbia! President Butler had sent a dean to ask Professor Beard to take Fraser into his department; now he sent the dean to ask Beard to drop Fraser again. Professor Beard, who has a capacity for indignation, told the dean that Fraser had done what he had been employed to do, and had done it sincerely and capably, therefore it was his intention to propose Fraser for a full professorship; and then Beard showed the dean to the door. Beard took the matter to the members of his department, and they agreed unanimously that Fraser should be promoted.

Knowing Butler as you now do, you will understand that he marked two more victims on his blacklist. One was Fraser and the other was Beard. Fraser was got rid of quickly; as soon as America entered the war, Butler announced that Columbia would not need so many professors, so he dropped three, Fraser among them. Subsequently he took back the other two; but Fraser meantime had enlisted. The dean remarked to a friend of mine, a Columbia professor, how fortunate it was that Fraser had gone to the war, so that a scandal over the question of his dismissal had been avoided. "Yes," replied my friend, "and wouldn't it be fortunate if he were shot to pieces, so that he could never come back and tell how Columbia treated him?"

The next experience in order of time is that of Professors Cattell and Dana; but since we have seen Beard put on the blacklist, perhaps we had better finish his story. Charles A. Beard is a sincere and determined fighter; incidentally, he is one of America's leading economists and scholars. There was an uproar in the newspapers over the charge that a labor leader, speaking at a civic center in a New York public school, had said: "To hell with the stars and stripes." He didn't really say it, as you may read in "The Brass Check," page 344. But the New York papers reported that he said it, so it was proposed to close all the civic centers in the schools. Professor Beard at

a public meeting stated that he did not think it was wise
to close all the schools to the public, just because one labor
leader was reported to have said, "To hell with the stars
and stripes." So next morning one of the New York
newspapers reported that Professor Beard of Columbia
University had defended a labor leader for saying "To
hell with the stars and stripes."

So now behold our professor summoned before the
interlocking trustees in solemn conclave! They demanded
to know what he had said, and he told them, and then,
thinking that the incident was closed, he started to leave
the room. But one of them called to him, and to the
consternation of this leading economist and scholar, he
was grilled for half an hour concerning his beliefs and
teachings, by two members of the board—Frederick R.
Coudert, lawyer, and director of a trust company, a safe
deposit company and a surety company; and Francis S.
Bangs, lawyer, and director in five express companies, a
trust company, a savings bank, and a water power corporation. They demanded his views on war and peace, on
Americanism and the constitution, on capitalism and the
rights of property; and when they had satisfied themselves
that he did not believe anything for which he could be arrested, they dismissed him, with orders to warn all others
in his department "against teachings likely to inculcate
disrespect for American institutions." Professor Beard
went back to his colleagues, and reported this extraordinary scene, and the members of his department burst
into roars of laughter; asking whether among the
"American institutions" for which they were to "teach
respect" the trustees included Tammany Tall and the pork
barrel!

Shortly after this it was announced that the trustees
had appointed a special committee to investigate the ideas
which were being taught at Columbia. "The Committee
on the State of Teaching," it was called, and its members
were four lawyers and one banker. The response of the
faculty was to meet and protest, and appoint a committee
of nine to defend themselves. The Faculty Council
adopted a very strong resolution on the subject of academic freedom—which resolution, be it noted, was afterwards suppressed.

The Columbia faculty at this time was preparing for real action, and Butler had his hands full smoothing them down. He sent one of his deans to see Professor Beard, and plead with him not to push the issue; the trustees had learned their lesson, said Butler, the incident would never be repeated. Also, if Beard forced the matter he would greatly inconvenience Butler, who was just then in trouble with his trustees because of his pacifist activities. No more professors would be dismissed from Columbia, except with the consent of their departments, so Butler promised; but he kept this promise no more than he kept others. Soon afterwards he got rid of Leon Fraser, and after that of another member of the faculty. Butler had promised that all nominations for promotion should come from the faculty; but soon afterwards he sent an ambassador to Beard, to say that a certain man whom the department proposed to promote would be refused promotion by the trustees; so the man was not named for promotion—and Butler was able to go on saying that all moves for promotion in Columbia came from the various departments! Professor Beard had had enough, and handed in his resignation, in which he paid his respects to "the few obscure and willful trustees who now dominate the university and terrorize the young instructors." Discussing the subject of academic tenure, he said: "The status of a professor in Columbia is lower than that of a manual laborer."

CHAPTER XI

THE TWILIGHT ZONE

A well known American scientist made to me the statement that there has not been a man of distinction called to Columbia in ten years, nor has one arisen there. To attribute so much to Butler and his interlocking trustees might seem to credit them with superhuman maleficence; but the scientist explained the phenomenon, as follows: American university teachers are greatly underpaid; there is no first class man who could not get more money if he turned his energies to other pursuits. If he stays as a teacher it is because he loves the work, and is willing to accept his reward in other forms—in the respect of his fellow men. But if he finds that he has no standing and no power; if he sees himself and his colleagues browbeaten and insulted by commercial persons; if he knows that all the world pays no attention to his opinions, assuming him to be the puppet of commercial persons—then the dignity of the academic life is gone, and nothing is left but an inadequate money reward.

What you have at Columbia is a host of inferior men, dwelling, as one phrased it to me, in "a twilight zone of mediocrity"; dull pedants, raking over the dust heaps of learning and occupying their minds with petty problems of administration. They have full power to decide whether Greek shall be given in nine courses or nine and one-half, also whether it shall count for four credits or four and a quarter. "And we love that," said one to me, with a bitter sneer.

The standing of Columbia University in the field of science under the regime of the interlocking president was interestingly revealed by a study published in "Science" in 1906, and continued in 1910: "A Statistical Study of American Men of Science," by J. McKeen Cattell, Professor of Psychology in Columbia University. It so happens that Professor Cattell has become President Butler's most vigorous opponent; but this investigation had no special reference to Columbia, and the method of conducting it was such as to preclude favoritism. A list of the thousand leading men of American science was obtained by writing to ten leading men in twelve different branches of science, and asking them to name the most eminent representatives of their science in the country. The one thousand leaders thus selected were studied from various points of view, their ages, the countries from which they came, the institutions at which they studied, the institutions with which they were connected. Of these leaders it appeared that thirty-eight had taken their doctorate degrees at Columbia, while 102 had taken their degrees at Johns Hopkins; 78 had studied at Columbia, while 237 had studied at Harvard. In 1905 Columbia had 60 of the thousand leaders on its faculty, while Harvard had 66 and Yale 26; but in 1910 Columbia had 48, a loss of 12, while Harvard had 79, a gain of 13 and Yale had 38, a gain of 12. In the listing of 1910 it appeared that 238 scientific men had gained a place among the leaders,

while 201 had lost their standing in that group. A study
of the institutions with which these men were connected
revealed an extraordinary state of affairs. Among the
Harvard men 22 had won their way to the first thousand;
among the Chicago men 13 had won; while among Columbia men, with a much larger faculty, only 8 had won.
On the other hand, 6 Harvard men had lost their standing,
and 3 Chicago men, while 12 Columbia men had lost—
more than in any other institution in the United States!
So much for academic autocracy!

Another table presented a study of the ratio between
the number of distinguished men at each institution and
the total number of the faculty at that institution. Disre-
garding fractions, it appeared that one man in every seven
at Harvard belonged among the first thousand, one man
in every six at Chicago, one in every five at Johns Hopkins, one in every two at Clark—and one in every thirteen
at Columbia! Taking the ratio of distinguished men to
the number of students, it appeared that there was one
distinguished scientist for every twenty-one students at
Johns Hopkins, and one for every ninety-six students at
Columbia. Considering the matter in relation to the
value of buildings and grounds, it appeared that Massachusetts Institute of Technology had a distinguished
scientist for every $53,000 worth of buildings and grounds,
while Columbia had one for every $259,000 worth. Con-
sidering the matter in relation to income, it appeared that
Johns Hopkins had a distinguished man for every $10,000
of income, while Columbia had one for every $45,000.
Before I finish with this book I expect to show you
that all the colleges in the United States are plutocratic;
but there are some which are less plutocratic than others,
and the above figures will show you exactly what the
plutocratic policy does, when it has its way completely, to
crush the life of the intellect, and turn a great institution
of learning into a thing of bricks and mortar without a
soul.

There are some fifteen hundred men on the Columbia
faculty; but you can count upon the fingers of one hand
the men of any originality and force of character. John
Dewey has stayed on; being the foremost educator in the
country, it would make a terrible fuss if he were to go.
Butler notes that Dewey takes no part in the internal

politics of the university, but politely resigned from a faculty committee to supervise expulsions, when he discovered that this committee was to have no power. There is one other professor at Columbia who is known to be a Socialist; a very quiet one, who has retired from the Socialist party, and is writing an abstract work on metaphysics. He is useful to Butler and the whole crowd of the interlocking directorate, because whenever the question of academic freedom is raised, they can say: "Look at Montague, he is a Socialist!"

Similarly, in the worst days of reaction in Germany, they used to have in their universities what were called "renommir professoren," that is to say, "boast professors," or, as we should say in vulgar American, "shirt-fronts." In the same way, whenever Bismarck was conducting his campaigns against the Jews, he was always careful to have one Jew in the cabinet. I count over these "renommir professoren" in American universities; two at Columbia, one at Chicago, two at Wisconsin, one at Stanford, and one at Clark, expecting to be fired; a very young man at Johns Hopkins, and two old ladies at Wellesley. That is the complete list, so far as my investigations reveal; ten out of a total of some forty thousand college and university teachers—and that shows how much American colleges and universities have to make a pretense of caring about freedom!

Exactly how does the plutocratic regime operate to eliminate originality and power? The process is perfectly shown in the case of Professor Goodnow, now president of Johns Hopkins University. Goodnow taught administrative law at Columbia, and when Professor Burgess withdrew, Goodnow was the choice of the faculty for the Ruggles professorship, one of the most important chairs in Columbia. Butler had promised the faculty that each department should decide its own promotions, but he was worried about Goodnow, because Goodnow had published a book in which he set forth the dangerous idea that the constitution of the United States as it now exists is not final. Goodnow studied the constitution as the product of a certain social environment, and that maddens Butler. "Don't you think there are some things we can call settled?" he remarked, irritably, to one of my informants. So the trustees, without consulting the faculty of political science, passed over Goodnow, and appointed one of the interlocking directors! William D. Guthrie, law partner of one of the trustees, a corporation lawyer, rich, smooth, hard, and ignorant, was selected to come once a week during half a semester, and give a lecture interpreting the constitution as the interlocking directorate wants it interpreted—a permanent bulwark against any kind of change in property relations. He did none of the work of an ordinary college professor, but conferred upon the university his plutocratic prestige for the sum of seventy-five hundred dollars a year.

Or consider the testimony of Bayard Boyesen, who was a member of the Columbia faculty for several years, and whose father was one of Columbia's oldest and most honored professors. Says young Boyesen, in a letter to me:

You speak of whispering at the Faculty Club. It was worse than that. I have on several occasions seen professors, after beginning luncheon at one table, rise and go to another because the talk had turned, not to radical propaganda, but to a purely intellectual discussion of such subjects as Socialism, Syndicalism and the like. I was on at least twenty occasions asked by different professors and instructors to hold as confidential the ideas they had expounded to me as their own.

To show the utter cowardice of many of the professors, I will relate a personal incident. During my third year as instructor at Columbia, I resigned in order to have all my time for other work, but was persuaded by a senior professor of my department to remain. He wrote me a very strong letter in praise of my work and guaranteed me a full professorship for the following year. When, however, I got into trouble with the trustees because of radical speeches made before audiences of laboring men, and because of a pamphlet I had written on education, the professor came to me and asked me to return the letter he had sent me. Very evidently, he feared that I might jeopardize his position if I quoted from it. And this man had told me that he could hardly see his way to remaining at Columbia unless I was there to help in building up a department sadly in need of rejuvenation.

An illustration of how Columbia gets rid of its "undesirables." I was told by Professor Ashley Thorndike of my department (English) that a charge had been preferred against me by Dr. Butler acting for the trustees, and that therefore I could not be recommended for appointment the following year. He refused to tell me what the charge was, on the ground that he was pledged not to reveal it. I thereupon wrote to Dr. Butler requesting an interview. His secretary wrote that the president was too busy to see me. I then threatened to bring the matter to court, for though an instructor's tenure of office is for one year only, I felt sure that the trustees had no right to make a charge of any kind against me without giving me an opportunity to answer it. After this, I obtained an interview with the president, during which he said that no charges of any sort had been made and that it was purely a departmental matter. He refused, however, to put this into writing, though he several times reiterated it. I returned to Professor Thorndike, and told him, as politely as circumstances would allow, that either he or Dr. Butler had "misinformed" me. He replied evasively that a man of my intelligence should have understood the whole matter from the beginning, and added significantly that I had been warned before in regard to my outside activities. I finally obtained from him an oral statement that there were no charges against me, as well as a grudging apology for the "misunderstanding."

CHAPTER XII

THE ACADEMIC DEPARTMENT STORE

I have several times mentioned in this narrative Professor Cattell and his opinions of Columbia. My story would not be complete without an account of his adventures, for he was the one man who gave the interlocking directors a real fight.

James McKeen Cattell was a teacher at Columbia for twenty-six years. He was the first professor of psychology in any university in the world; he is the editor of four leading scientific journals. Cattell objected to some of Butler's methods, such as the appointment of an unfit professor in his division, because this man brought with him a gift of a hundred thousand dollars. Cattell was left to learn of this appointment from the newspapers, and when he protested, Butler wrote him insolent letters, trying to force him to resign, as he had done with Mac-Dowell and Woodberry. But Cattell stuck, whereupon Butler took from him the use of six rooms, a laboratory of psychological research which had been built with funds obtained by Cattell. The income of a trust fund of one hundred thousand dollars, which Cattell had got "to increase the facilities of his department," was taken to pay Cattell's own salary.

Cattell then withdrew as head of his department, and took no more part in Columbia's politics. But he published articles criticizing the Carnegie pension scheme, in which Butler was a leading spirit. He showed how it was used to control the university professor, as seniority rights and pensions are used to keep employes in order. So in 1910 a resolution proposing to dismiss Cattell was before the trustees. In 1913 he published a book on "University Control," in which he demonstrated that 85 per cent of the members of college and university faculties are dissatisfied with the present system of the management of scholars by business men. In punishment for this the trustees voted to retire him on a pension—taking the step without the knowledge of the faculty. There was unani-. mous protest, and the trustees yielded. In 1917 Professor Cattell wrote a letter to members of the Faculty Club, referring to "our much-climbing and many-talented president." This, of course, was lese majesté, and for the third time a resolution proposing to dismiss Professor Cattell was presented to the trustees; but action was postponed, on the recommendation of a committee of deans and professors.

Nicholas Miraculous bided his time, and several months later came the chance to get rid of Cattell and at the same time to exhibit his new patriotism. Cattell wrote a letter to a congressman, in support of pending legislation exempting from combatant service in Europe conscripts who objected to war. The interlocking trustees, who had already conscripted themselves to make money out of the war, took the position that in writing this letter Cattell had committed a crime, and they suddenly dismissed him from the university. In spite of his twenty-six years' service, they did not even take the trouble to notify him what they proposed to do, but left him to learn of their action from a newspaper reporter who waked him in the middle of the night. The trustees declared that a professor could not take a stand on any public question as his own personal opinion; to which Cattell replied: "When trustees announce that no statement can be made by a teacher that is not affirmed by Columbia University, they challenge the intellectual integrity of every teacher."

These ferocious old men who had conscripted themselves to make money out of the war were not content to get rid of a too-independent professor; they wished to brand him for life, so they rushed to the press with a statement charging him with "treason," "sedition," and "obstruction to the enforcement of the laws of the United

States." And this although Professor Cattell was actively engaged in psychological work for the army, and his only son who was of war age had already volunteered! Professor Cattell, in his counter-statement, referred to the trustees as "men whose horizon is bounded by the two sides of Wall Street with Trinity Church at the end." He described the university as a place "overrun with intrigue and secret diplomacy." He said of President Butler: "He has run the university as a department store, playing the part of both proprietor and floor walker to the faculty, while an errand boy to the trustees."* Cattell brought suit for libel and threatened to sue for the pension to which he was entitled. The trustees waited several years, until the libel case was about to come up for trial, and then admitted their guilt by paying forty-five thousand dollars of the university's money,

With Professor Cattell there went out Professor H. W. L. Dana, a grandson of Henry Wadsworth Longfellow and of Richard Henry Dana; his crime was that he had belonged to the People's Council—with the knowledge of President Butler. Shortly after this went Beard, and Henry Mussey, one of Columbia's most loved professors; also my old teacher, James Harvey Robinson.

I write the above, and then the door-bell of my home rings, and there enters another man who went out—Leon Ardzrooni, an Armenian with an irrepressible sense of humor, who for two years was a professor of economics. I do not have to ask Ardzrooni about his success as a teacher, because his reputation has preceded him. He brought Columbia twelve thousand dollars a year in tuition fees, of which they paid him three thousand to lecture on labor problems; and every now and then they would send for him and make anxious faces over the fact that he taught the realities of modern industry. Professor Seligman, head of his department, heard the report that he made some of his young ladies—graduate students out of Barnard—"unhappy." "It would be all right for older

---

*The statements concerning Columbia University in the above paragraph were contained in a confidential statement sent by Professor Cattell to some of the Columbia faculty. In fairness to Professor Cattell, I wish to state that he did not furnish me with this statement, either directly or indirectly, and I have not asked his permission to quote from it.

people," said Professor Seligman; "but not for the young, who are so impressionable." Said Ardzrooni: "What's the use of teaching them when they're so old that I can't make any impression?"

The students asked him about an I. W. W. strike, and he told how such a matter appeared to the strikers. "Don't they get enough to eat?" asked one, a young army officer. "Yes, I suppose so," said the professor; "but so do the owners get enough to eat. That isn't the only issue." Professor Ardzrooni gave that answer at ten o'clock in the morning, and at twelve he went to the Faculty Club for lunch, and there on the faces of his colleagues he saw written the dreadful tidings—he had been reported! The busy telephone system of the university had informed the whole campus that the genial Armenian had been discovered to be a member of the I. W. W.; he had boasted to his classes of carrying a red card, and all his colleagues were so sorry for him!

Ardzrooni was summoned before Butler, and instead of taking it meekly, he demanded a showdown. Who was it that accused him of belonging to the I. W. W. and of carrying a red card? Butler refused to tell him, evading the issue, so the professor went on the warpath. It happens that he is a rich man, not dependent upon anybody's favor, so he went to Woodbridge, dean of the faculty, announcing that he was going to bring suit aganist the university that very day; he would put Butler on the witness stand, and find out whether a college professor has any rights, or can be slandered at will!

Instantly, of course, the whole machinery of intimidation collapsed; it had never occurred to anyone that a college professor might act like a man! They would drop the whole matter, say nothing more about the red card, give Ardzrooni promotion and increase his salary—anything to keep out of court! The professor of labor problems laughed at them, and following the example of all other self-respecting men, went out into the free world.

CHAPTER XIII

THE EMPIRE OF DULLNESS

Those who have stayed in the great academic department-store have stayed under the shadow of disgrace; branded as men who love their pitiful salaries more than they love their self-respect and dignity as scholars, more than they love the cause of democracy and justice throughout the world. They stay on the terms that the voice of democracy and justice is silent among them, while the voice of reaction bellows with brazen throat.

I have shown you the plutocratic president storming the banquet halls of merchants and manufacturers and bankers, pouring out what Gutzon Borglum, the sculptor, described as "his sweeping intolerance of free speech and of organization by those not of his belief." And everything in Columbia or connected with Columbia has been stamped with the impress of Butler's hard materialism, his cold and calculating snobbery. He uses the prestige of his university to confer honors on reaction both at home and abroad. In 1912 he honored Senator Underwood, praising him to the skies as the leader of democracy —this in the hope of keeping Woodrow Wilson from getting the Democratic nomination for president. In 1922 we find him glorifying an Episcopal bishop, the rector of Trinity Church, the governor of the Federal Reserve Board, a Belgian baron, a Portuguese viscount, the Chinese ambassador, and Paderewski, apostle of Polish militarism!

With the help of his millionaire trustees Butler has built up an alumni machine, and the alumni paper is the organ of his personal glory. He has built up a faculty machine, of men who understand that they are free so long as they agree with their president, and who go forth to carry out the president's will wherever the Columbia influence reaches—which is throughout the entire school and college system of our plutocratic empire.

Butler, you understand, was head of the department of education at Columbia; he fixed the policy of this department, making it a machine for the turning out of "educational experts," trained to see life as a battleground of money-ambition, and to run the schools as efficient factories. Butler edited the "Educational Review," and the present editor is a Columbia man, and his puppet. I shall take you with me before long for a trip over the United States, and show you the Tammany Hall of education; the league of superintendents, and the politicians of the National Educational Association, financed by the book companies and other big grafters, and combining with the chambers of commerce and professional patriots to drive out liberalism in education as in politics, and resist every new idea in every department of human thought and activity. They are backed by the political machines of special privilege, and protected and glorified by the "Brass Check" press; and everywhere you find Columbia men the leading advocates of routine, red tape, and reaction.

I turn over my notes; the people of New York are struggling in the grip of rapacious landlords, and here comes Samuel McCune Lindsay, Professor of Social Legislation at Columbia University, with a pamphlet to demonstrate that there is really no shortage of apartments, but on the contrary a surplus of thirty thousand. The Lockwood Commission puts the professor on the stand and draws out the fact that he was paid five hundred dollars by the Real Estate Board for the writing of this pamphlet. Samuel Untermyer, counsel of the commission, characterizes Prof. Lindsay's figures as "absurd," and forces the professor to admit that he made no actual investigation, and has "no practical knowledge."

I turn to another page. Dr. Albert Shiels is superintendent of the public schools of Los Angeles in the year 1919, and at the height of the White Terror in America he publishes in President Butler's "Educational Review" an article denouncing the Soviet government. At a mass meeting in Los Angeles the chairman states that he has made count of the errors of fact in this article, and they total one hundred and twenty-four. Louise Bryant, just returned from Russia, is at the meeting, and the audience votes to send a challenge to Dr. Shiels to debate with her. Someone in the audience puts up a two hundred dollar Liberty Bond to pay Dr. Shiels, and the audience contributes over twelve hundred dollars to give publicity to the debate. Dr. Shiels is invited to appear, and his answer is: "I believe it is contrary to good public policy to place Bolshevism and its practices on a par with debatable questions"—an answer which so delights President Butler that he calls Dr. Shiels to New York, to become Associate Director of the Institute of Educational Research of Columbia University!

Yet another case: The people of North Dakota are trying to take over the education of their own children and liberalize the school system of their state; and here comes George D. Strayer, professor of Educational Administration at Columbia University, addressing the legislative committee of the state educational committee, Minot, North Dakota, April 18, 1919, attacking the proposed new laws, and laying out a complete program of pedagogical toryism. No violation of academic propriety for a Columbia professor to take part in politics—provided it is on the side of special privilege!

Nor is it a violation of academic propriety if a Columbia professor rushes into the capitalistic press, provided he rushes in in defense of his masters. In the New York "Times" for May 22, 1922, I find Professor James C. Egbert, Director of University Extension and Director of the School of Business of Columbia University, spreading himself to the extent of three columns on the subject of "labor education." There was no slightest occasion for this professor to spread himself; nobody asked his opinion, he did not even have the pretext of a public address before some bankers' association. The only camouflage which the Times provides is the phrase, "in a recent interview"—that is, in this precise present interview with the Times! After which the Times goes on to publish nearly three columns of the professor's manuscript, with nothing but quotation marks to keep up the pretense that it is an "interview." Says the professor: "The educational system devised by the labor unions has virtually broken down"—which is a plain lie. The professor then goes on to say that the proper place for the labor unions to come for their education is to the established universities. I read the professor's three columns of eloquence, and realize that I learned the whole thing when I was three years old, in two lines of nursery rhyme:

" 'Won't you come into my parlor?'
Said the spider to the fly."

What is the final product of all this system we have been studying? It may be stated in one word, which is dullness. Some men are hired, and they are hired because they are dull, and will do dull work; and they do it. The student comes to college, full of eagerness and hope, and he finds it dull. He has no idea why it should be so; it is incredible to him that men should be selected because they are dull, and should be fired if they prove to be anything but dull. All he sees is the dullness, and he hates it, and "cuts" it as much as he can, and goes off to practice football or get drunk. I quote one more paragraph from the letter of Bayard Boyesen:

> There is nothing tending to make a teacher so enthusiastic and optimistic as any average class of freshmen, the great majority of whom come to Columbia eager, alert and responsive to every contact with beauty, nobility, aspiration and high endeavor; and there is nothing tending to make the teacher so disappointed and pessimistic as to see these same young men, after they have been blunted and flattened, go out with smiles of cynical superiority, to take their allotted places in the world of American business.

All this wealth, all this magnificence, stone and concrete and white marble—and inside it dullness and death! You read about the millions given for education, and rejoice, thinking it means progress; but all that the millions can buy is—dullness and death! Look at Nicholas Murray Butler, with a ten million dollar peace foundation, which he uses to finance the writing of a history of the war! Half a million dollars a year, donated to bring peace to mankind, and now, in the greatest crisis of history, Butler sets a man to writing a history of a war!

If you think I exaggerate when I state that the Columbia system means the deliberate exclusion of new ideas, and of living, creative attitudes, listen to our plutocratic president himself, laying down the law on the subject of education: "The duty of one generation is to pass on to the next, unimpaired, the institutions it has inherited from its forbears." Just so! To keep mankind as it has been, forever and ever, world without end, amen! Is it anybody's duty to discover new truth and complete man's mastery over nature? Is it anybody's duty to inspire us, that we may cease to be the bloody-handed savages that history has left us? Is it anybody's business to bring order out of our commercial anarchy, and use the collective powers of mankind for the making instead of the destroying of life? It is nobody's business to do these things; what we go to college for is to learn about our ancestors, and become what they were—the pitiful victims of blind instincts.

CHAPTER XIV

THE UNIVERSITY OF LEE-HIGGINSON

There is a saying that when you go to Philadelphia they ask you who your grandfather was, and when you go to New York they ask you what you are worth, and when you go to Boston they ask you what you know. We are now going to the hub of America's intellectual life, and make ourselves familiar with our most highly cultured university.

We shall begin, as before, by investigating those who run it; and straightway we shall get a shock. We shall find not merely the interlocking directorate—the princes, and the dukes, and the barons; we shall find the emperor himself, none other than J. Pierpont Morgan! I was puzzled when I studied the affairs of Columbia, for I knew that the elder Morgan had been on the board until his death, and I could not imagine how President Butler managed to overlook his son and heir. When I came to study Harvard I discovered the reason; the younger Morgan was graduated from Harvard in 1889. The purpose of such interchanges of royalty is, of course, to cement the bonds of empire.

The house of J. P. Morgan & Company is closely allied with the Boston banking house of Lee, Higginson & Company. Mr. Morgan was reelected to the Harvard board in 1917, along with Francis Lee Higginson, Jr., of Lee, Higginson & Company; Eliot Wadsworth, representative of Stone & Webster, an allied construction firm; Howard Elliott, then president and now chairman of the New Haven, a Morgan railroad; and, finally, a prominent corporation lawyer in San Francisco, representing the interlocking directorate in that city.

In his discussion of the Pujo report Justice Brandeis wrote that "Concentration of banking capital has proceeded even farther in Boston than in New York." He goes on to tell of three great banking concerns, with their interlocking directorates, controlling ninety-two per cent of Boston's money resources. These concerns competed in minor and local matters, said Mr. Brandeis, but they were all allied with Morgan. "Financial concentration seems to have found its highest exemplification in Boston." And exactly the same thing is true of the concentration of control of Harvard University and the Massachusetts Institute of Technology, and the group of smaller colleges located in Eastern Massachusetts. They are all "State Street"—this being the Boston equivalent of "Wall Street."

In 1916 the New York Evening Post, at that time in rebellion against the House of Morgan, published an interesting study of the financial connections of the governing board of Harvard. There are six members of the Harvard corporation, known as the "fellows," and these are appointed for life. In addition, there are thirty "overseers," elected by the whole body of graduates. The New York "Evening Post" examined these latter, and found eleven capitalists and seven lawyers, a generous majority for the plutocracy. Nor was there much danger to the plutocracy from some of the others; those classified as "public men" including Senator Lodge and F. A. Delano, ex-president of several railroads.

A year later the "Evening Post" made a further examination, considering not merely the fellows and the overseers, but the nine directors of the Harvard Alumni Association, the nine members of the Association's nominating committee, twenty candidates for overseers who had just been called, and six who had just been called as candidates for directors of the Association. That made a body of eighty Harvard graduates, forty of them Boston men, and twenty-nine of these forty being financial men, or attorneys for the State Street houses. All but six were connected with the three interlocked financial institutions; twenty were connected with Lee, Higginson & Company or its institutions—nine with the Old Colony Trust Company, the great Lee-Higginson bank, five with Lee, Higginson & Company itself, four directors in another Lee-Higginson bank, six directors in a Lee-Higginson savings bank, six in another Lee-Higginson savings bank, four in a Lee-Higginson insurance company, and six attorneys for these. "State Street," you see, is like Virginia; the old families have been intermarrying for so long that everybody is related to everybody else.

A Harvard graduate wrote to the New York "Evening Post," "Harvard has assets to be invested of about thirty-four million dollars. Is that the reason why practically five-sixths of the Boston business representation (of Harvard) is affiliated with investment banking concerns, or is it because they wish to use Harvard as a knighthood for their friends?" The "Evening Post" went on politely to say that it did not believe this was the case; the financial domination of Harvard had resulted by accident! But this bit of humor did not save the "Evening Post" from the wrath of the interlocking directorate. The paper offended also by opposing America's entry into the war—and so the valuable advertising business of Lee, Higginson & Co. was withdrawn, and shortly afterwards the owner of the paper was forced to sell out to Mr. Lamont, a partner of the House of Morgan. This story is in "The Brass Check," page 248. To complete it we should note the part played by Harvard in the swallowing. It was a Harvard overseer who bought the "Evening Post"; another overseer is now president and trustee of the "Evening Post" company, and a third overseer is also a trustee of the "Evening Post" company!

Also, it will be worth while to notice the Massachusetts Institute of Technology, until recently allied to Harvard. This is one of the most marvelous collections of plutocrats ever assembled in the world; it includes the president of the Powder Trust, and his cousin Mr. Coleman du Pont, who is emperor of the State of Delaware; also Mr. Eastman, the kodak king; two of our greatest international bankers, Mr. Otto Kahn and Mr. Frank Vanderlip; Mr. Howard Elliott, chairman of the New Haven, Mr. Elisha Lee, vice-president of the Pennsylvania; both members of the firm of Stone and Webster, with all of its enormous electrical interests; also nine other electrical bankers, two officials of the General Electric Company, one big electrical manufacturer, and six others who are interested in electric railways. Make particular note of this mass of electrical connections, because in succeeding chapters you will find several amusing instances of the influence of electric light and electric railway interests upon the policy and teaching of both Harvard and Massachusetts Tech.

As we have seen, the endowment of Harvard was estimated at thirty-four millions of dollars in 1917, and since then there has been a campaign in which nearly fifteen millions was raised. This money is under the direction of the Morgan-Lee-Higginson directorate, and needless to say is largely invested in Morgan-Lee-Higginson enterprises. We are told by some friends of Harvard that Harvard stands for "liberalism" in American education; do you suppose that Harvard stands for "liberalism" in American industry? Do you suppose that the votes of Harvard administrators are cast for policies of justice and democracy in the enterprises it exploits? If you suppose that, you are extremely naive. The Harvard votes are cast, just as any other votes of any other business concerns are cast, for the largest amount of dividends for Harvard. For example, Harvard owns twenty-five hundred shares in a Boston department store; has Harvard done anything to humanize the management of that store? It has not. Harvard likewise operates a mine. Harvard has a graduate business school and trains executives to run mines—on the basis of getting the maximum production at the lowest cost, and maintaining the present system of industrial feudalism.

I take these facts concerning the Harvard investments from a paper by Harry Emerson Wildes, a Harvard graduate. It is interesting to note that Mr. Wildes at the time he made this study was doing voluntary publicity work for the alumni group which was raising Harvard funds in Philadelphia; and Mr. Wildes was "dropped" immediately after this study saw the light!

We have seen how Columbia owns stocks and bonds in American railroads, public service corporations, and industrial corporations of all sorts. Exactly the same thing is true of Harvard. Says Mr. Wildes:

Twelve separate cities feed the Harvard purse from their traction lines, and more than half a hundred pay tribute from their lighting, heating, gas and power plants. Harvard has two million dollars in the traction game. The two-cent transfer charge on New York City trolleys goes to pay the interest on three-quarters of a million dollars' worth of traction bonds in Harvard ownership, and Boston ten-cent fare goes partially to Harvard's third of a million in Boston traction bonds.

Mr. Wildes goes on to study the effect of these investments upon Harvard, and the effect which Harvard, through the power of these investments, might have upon the industrial life of the country. I cannot present the subject better than he has done, so I quote his words:

With rapid transit lines throughout the nation in a state of rising fares, and continual labor strife taking place, the intervention of a conciliatory investor holding any such amounts might aid in bringing better harmony between the companies on the one hand and the public and the workmen on the other. But nothing has been done by Harvard University, nor by any educational body in the land, to work for the friendship of either public or labor towards the transit lines. . . .

How strenuously the influence of Harvard will be thrown on the side of limitation of armaments and the ending of war may be gauged by the total of more than a million dollars' worth of ordnance bonds and munitions stock owned by the corporation. And, as these are largely in great steel corporations such as Bethlehem, Midvale and Illinois, the attitude of the college heads towards the move for unionizing workers can be clearly understood.

When railroad brotherhoods put forth a plan for guild operation of the lines, they face a mighty opposition from security investors. The eight million dollars which Harvard holds in railroad stock and bonds would be affected by victory for the Plumb Plan. The professors of economics and particularly of railroad operation and finance can scarcely be expected to imbue their scholars with a holy zeal for the securing of the Brotherhood aims. . . .

Evidence of the patriotic ardor of the financiers directing Harvard's investments may be readily seen in the fact that only one per cent of the funds of the university is invested in the Liberty Loans. The total of United States bonds held is less than half of that spent for bonds of five foreign nations. Intervention in Mexico would perhaps be pleasing to the authorities, since they hold a total of nearly one hundred thousand dollars in Mexican government bonds. So, also, is the pacification of Central America through the stationing of American marines and blue-jackets in those lands. Meddling of our State Department in the internal affairs of Costa Rica, Honduras, San Salvador and the rest helps to uphold the value of another one hundred thousand dollars' worth of United Fruit Company bonds.* This company notoriously controls entire nations in Central America and sets up or deposes presidents at its whim. There is scarcely a large community north of Panama that is not in some degree tapped by the Harvard treasury. The American college is becoming the strongest single force in the world. Its management is almost entirely in the hands of international bankers or men dependent upon that group.

*These bonds have just been paid off, but the ability to pay them off was of course assured by American intervention.

Such are the business facts underlying Harvard University; such are the roots of the plant, and we shall now examine its flowers.

CHAPTER XV

THE HARVARD TRADITION

Harvard has a tradition, which is a part of the tradition of New England; it is one of scholarship, of respect for the dignity of learning. Money counts in New England, but money is not enough, so you will be told; you must have culture also, and the prestige of the intellectual life. More than that, in New England is found that quality which must necessarily go with belief in the intellectual life, the quality of open-mindedness, the willingness to consider new ideas.

Such is the tradition; and first, it will pay us to ask, how did the tradition originate? Was it made by Harvard University? Or was it made by Charles Sumner, antislavery senator from Massachusetts, who was found unfit to be a professor in the Harvard Law School, and wrote to his brother: "I am too much of a reformer in law to be trusted in a post of such commanding influence as this has now become." Was it made by Harvard, or by Wendell Phillips, who, according to his biographer, Sears, denounced "the restraint of Harvard, which he attributed to affiliation with the commercial interests of Boston, and the silence they imposed on anti-slavery sentiments." Was it made by Harvard or by William Lloyd Garrison, who was dragged through the streets of Boston with a rope about his neck, by a silk-hatted mob of State Streeters, many of them of course from Harvard?

Sumner, Phillips and Garrison were extremists, you may say; and the best traditions are not made by such. They are made by scholars, who lead retired lives and guide others by the power of thought. Very well; New England has had no more revered scholar, no more keen thinker than Emerson. Emerson was gentle, Emerson was dignified, and you will find Emerson a part of the Harvard tradition—one of its halls bears his name. So let us see what Emerson had to report about the Harvard of his time; how much credit he gives it for progress in the anti-slavery days. Writing in 1861, in "The Celebration of the Intellect," Emerson said: "Harvard College has no voice in Harvard College, but State Street votes it down on every ballot. Everything will be permitted there, which goes to adorn Boston Whiggism—is it geology, astronomy, poetry, antiquities, art, rhetoric? But that which it exists for, to be a fountain of novelties out of heaven, a Delphos uttering warning and ravishing oracles to lift and lead mankind—that it shall not be permitted to do or to think of. On the contrary, every generosity of thought is suspect and has a bad name. And all the youths come out decrepit citizens; not a prophet, not a poet, not a daimon, but is gagged and stifled or driven away."

And precisely that is what we have to report about the Harvard of the time of capitalistic reaction, which is 1922. For thirteen years Harvard has been under the administration of a cultured corporation lawyer of Boston, who has generally carried out the politics of his State Street associates in all essential matters, and has preserved just as much reputation for liberalism as can be preserved—safely.

A. Lawrence Lowell is not, like Nicholas Murray Butler, a climber and a toady; he could not be a climber, because he was born on a mountaintop, and there was no place to climb to—he could only stay where he was or descend. He belongs to the Lowell family, who are among the Boston Brahmins, and it would not occur to him that any millionaire could confer a favor upon Harvard University, or upon the president of Harvard University. On the other hand, it does occur to him that Harvard is a close corporation, a family affair of the vested interests of New England, which cover an enormous financial power with a decorous coating of refined exclusiveness.

Before the days of President Lowell, Harvard was presided over by Charles W. Eliot, a scholar who believed to some extent in a safe and reasonable freedom of opinion—using his own freedom to glorify the "great American hero" known as the "scab." President Lowell has inherited the Eliot tradition, and in my travels about the country I heard many rumors as to how he had stood by his professors in time of stress. When I got to Harvard, and turned these rumors into fact, I found an amusing situation. No circus rider who keeps his footing on two horses has ever done a more deft and delicate feat of balancing than President Lowell, with one foot on the Eliot tradition and the other foot on the House of Lee-Higginson.

They will tell you proudly that professors are not let out of Harvard because of their opinions; and that is sometimes true. One reason is, because the Harvard teaching staff is selected with meticulous care, and because, when the new man comes to Harvard he comes under the influence of a subtle but powerful atmosphere of good form. It is not crude materialism, as in Columbia; it is cleverly compounded of high intellectual and social qualities, and it is brought to the young educators' attention with humor and good fellowship. A friend of mine, a Harvard man who knows the game, described to me from personal experience how the State Street pressure operates. Somebody in Lee-Higginson calls President Lowell on the telephone and says: "How can we get So-and-so to put up the money for that chair, if young This-or-that gets his name in the newspapers as lecturing to workingmen?" President Lowell smiles and says he will see about it, and the young instructor is invited to dinner and amiably shown how the most liberal university in America cannot run entirely without money. The young instructor sees the point, and the president goes away, thinking to himself: "Thank God we are not as Columbia!"

Even down to the humblest freshman such pressure is conveyed. There are things that "are not done" at Harvard; and you would be surprised to know how minute is the supervision. You might not think it was a grave offense for a student, wearing a soft shirt in summer-time, to leave the top button unfastened; but a student friend of mine, who had ideas of the simple life—going back to nature and all that—was coldly asked by Dean Gay: "Is the button of your shirt open by mistake, or is the button missing?" And when he did not take this delicate hint, Professor Richard C. Cabot told another student that he might help the young man by advising him to close the top button of his shirt. I am advised that Harvard men will call this story "rot"; therefore I specify that I have it in writing from the man to whom it happened.

And if they are so careful about shirt-buttons, they would hardly be careless about public speeches. A couple of years ago the Harvard Liberal Club made so bold as to invite Wilfred Humphries, a mild little gentleman who served with the Y. M. C. A., to tell about his experiences in Russia; whereupon the president of the Liberal Club received a letter from the secretary to the Corporation of Harvard, politely pointing out that there was likely to be embarrassment to the university, and would the president of the club kindly call upon the secretary, in order to provide him with arguments, "in case the press takes the thing up in a way which might embarrass the progress of the Endowment Fund Campaign." Just as deftly as that, you see!

I found that Harvard's reputation for liberalism was based upon the custom of President Lowell to take into his institution men who had been expelled from other colleges. I was impressed by this, until Harvard men explained to me how it is managed. The basis of it is a painstaking inquiry into the character and opinions of those men, to make sure there is nothing really dangerous about them. In some cases they are men who have offended local interests, with which "State Street" has little concern. Others are men of ability who have offended religious prejudices in the provinces; the tradition of Harvard is Unitarian, and nobody is shocked by the idea that his ancestors swung from the tree-tops by their tails. The State of Texas has just passed a law providing for the expulsion of professors who teach that idea, so in due course you may hear of Harvard taking over some Texas scholar.

How men are investigated before they are taken into Harvard is a matter about which I happen to know from a man who underwent the ordeal. I will call my informant Professor Smith, and he was head of a department in a leading university. Appointed on a public service commission, he discovered that the local gas company was engaged in swindling the city. The facts got into the newspapers, and this public spirited professor was on the verge of being expelled by his trustees, several of whom were "in gas." Some friends of his put the matter before President Lowell, and Lowell made inquiry, and ascertained that Smith was a liberal of the very mildest sort, well connected and affable, in every way worthy to associate with the best families, and to train their sons; so Professor Smith received a letter, asking him if he would come to Cambridge and make the acquaintance of President Lowell. He made the journey, and found himself a guest at a dinner party in the home of one of the interlocking directorate. President Lowell was seated next to him, and they chatted on many subjects, but only once did they touch on the subject of Smith and his qualifications.

"By the way," said Lowell (I reproduce the conversation from careful notes). "I understand you had some little unpleasantness in your home city."

"Quite a good deal of it," replied Smith.

"I'm not quite clear about it," said Lowell. "It had something to do with the gas company, did it not?"

"Yes," replied Smith.

"It was merely gas? It had nothing to do with electricity?"

"Oh, no," said Smith. "Nothing whatever."

"You are sure the electric light company was not involved?"

"Quite sure. They are separate concerns."

"I see," said Lowell, and talked about the European situation.

So Professor Smith went home, and told a friend about the matter; the friend made him repeat it over, word for word, and then burst out laughing. "Don't you see the point?" he asked; but Smith saw no point whatever.

"Don't you know that gas companies and electric light companies are sometimes rivals?" inquired the friend. "You can light your house with either gas or electricity; you can cook with either gas or electricity, you can heat with either gas or electricity."

"Yes, of course," said Smith, still unenlightened.

"Well, you attacked the gas company," said the friend. "You did not attack the Edison Electric Company of your city, which happens to be a part of the electric trust which covers the entire United States. Harvard is all tied up with this electrical trust, and Massachusetts Tech still more so, and Lee, Higginson & Company are its bankers. President Lowell was perfectly willing for you to fight your local gas company, but he wanted to make sure that you hadn't trod on the toes of Harvard's leading industry! You will get your invitation to Harvard, I'll wager."

And, sure enough, the invitation came a few days later! To complete the humor of the story, the fact of the invitation became known at once among the faculty of Professor Smith's university, and had the effect of instantly killing the talk of Professor Smith's being asked to resign!

I tell this incident as it was told to me. Standing by itself it might not mean much; but before we finish with Harvard we shall have plenty of evidence to prove that when the electric men play a tune, the Lee-Higginson university dances. President-Lowell, I am told, did not know the difference between a mathematician and an astronomer; when Pickering died, he proposed to put in a mathematician, and was naively surprised when it was explained to him that modern astronomy has gone so far that an observatory cannot be run by a mathematician, however expert. But ignorant as our Boston Brahmin may be about the stars of the milky way, it is certain that he knows all about the stars of State Street, he has them carefully charted and plotted, and neither he nor any member of his faculty ever bumps into them.

CHAPTER XVI

FREE SPEECH BUT—

We have referred to the Harvard Liberal Club, an organization formed by some graduates who sympathized with the cause of social justice. This club brought speakers to Harvard, and got itself into the newspapers several times; for example, during the anti-red hysteria they heard an address from Federal Judge Anderson, who denounced the Palmer raids as crimes against the constitution. This caused President Lowell great annoyance, but he could not control the club, because it was a graduate organization. He demanded that it abandon the name Harvard, saying it might cause people to get a wrong idea of the university. Inquiries were made to ascertain if legal measures could be taken; and when he found that such measures wouldn't work, he came to one of its meetings, very courteous and deeply interested, trying to steer it into ways of academic propriety. "We are all liberals at Harvard," he said—an old, old formula! For a generation the British labor party has been hearing from the Tories: "We are all Socialists in England."

Just how much of a liberal President Lowell is, of his own impulse and from his own conviction, was shown at the time that Louis D. Brandeis was nominated by President Wilson for the Supreme Court. Brandeis is a graduate of the Harvard Law School, and was a prosperous corporation lawyer in Boston; a man of European culture and charming manners, he was the darling of Harvard, in spite of the fact that he is a Jew. The Lees and the Higginsons took him up—until suddenly he ran into the New Haven railroad! Then the other crowd, the Kidders and the Peabodys, took him up—until he ran into the gas company! After that everybody dropped him, and if he had not been a man of wealth he would have been ruined. When he was proposed for the Supreme Court, a committee of lawyers, with Austen G. Fox, a Harvard man, at their head, took up the fight against him in the United States Senate. This fight didn't involve Harvard, and there was no reason for President Lowell to meddle in it; but he made it his personal fight, and a fight of the most determined and bitter character.

In 1918 there was a great strike in the Lawrence textile mills, and this made a delicate situation, because Harvard holds six hundred thousand dollars' worth of woolen mill loans and mortgages, and an equal amount of bonds and stocks. It seemed natural, therefore, to the overseers that Harvard students should go out as militiamen to crush this strike; it did not seem natural to them that members of the Liberal Club should call meetings and invite strike leaders to tell the students of the university their side of the case. But the members of this Liberal Club persisted, and when the district attorney accused the strikers of violence, they appointed a committee to interview him and get his facts. They gave a dinner, to which they invited the directors of the mills to meet the strike-leaders; they appointed a committee to consider terms of settlement, and in the end they forced a compromise.

Things like this caused most intense annoyance to the interlocking directorate. This was voiced to a Harvard man of my acquaintance, one of the organizers of the Liberal Club, by a Harvard graduate whose father has been a Harvard overseer, and is one of Massachusett's most distinguished jurists. In the Harvard Club of Boston my friend was challenged to say what he meant by a liberal; and when his definition was not found satisfactory, the Harvard graduate exclaimed: "A liberal? I'll tell you what a liberal is! A liberal is a —— —— —— —— —— ——!" In order to reproduce the scene you will have to fill these blanks, not with the ordinary terms of abuse used by longshoremen and lumber-jacks, but with the most obscene expletives which your imagination can invent.

Such is the present attitude of the ruling class of Harvard toward the issue of free speech. The attitude of the students was delightfully set forth by an editorial in the Harvard "Crimson," at the time of the Liberal Club lecture of Wilfred Humphries, Y. M. C. A. worker from Russia. The "Crimson" was for Free Speech—But! What the "Crimson" wished to forbid was "propaganda"; and it made clear that by this term it meant any and all protest against things established. Said the cautious young editor: "Not prohibited by law, propaganda creeps in and is accepted by many as an almost essential part of freedom of speech!" This is as persuasive as the communications of the Harvard Union to the liberal students, barring various radicals from the platform, on the ground that the Union did not permit "partisan" speakers: the Union's idea of non-partisan speakers being such well-poised and judicious conservatives as Admiral Sims and Detective Burns! As the old saying runs: "Orthodoxy is my doxy, heterodoxy is your doxy!" There is a standing rule at Harvard barring "outside" speakers who discuss "contentious contemporaneous questions of politics or economics"; and this rule was used to bar Mrs. Pankhurst!

I tell you of these petty incidents of discrimination; and yet, if we are to keep our sense of proportion, we must state that in the totality of American universities, Harvard ranks, from the point of view of academic liberalism, among the three or four best. There was no interference with its professors during the war hysteria—and I found but one other large institution, the University of Chicago, of which this statement may be made. Also, Harvard has to its credit one post-war case, in which academic freedom was gravely involved, and in which the Harvard tradition proved itself still alive. This is a curious and dramatic story, and I will tell it in detail.

In the summer of 1918 the United States Army invaded Archangel in Northern Russia, and Vladivostok in Eastern Siberia, seizing the territory of a friendly people and killing its inhabitants without the declaration of war required by the constitution of the United States. This invasion was the blackest crime in American public history, and was denounced by many of our leading thinkers. Also it was denounced by five obscure Russian Jews, mere children in age, living in the East-side slums of New York City. Four boys and a girl printed a leaflet, asking the American people not to kill their Russian compatriots, and they distributed these leaflets in public—for which crime they were arrested, taken to prison, and beaten and tortured so severely that one of them died a few days later. The surviving four were placed on trial, and after a hideous travesty of justice were given sentences of from fifteen to twenty years in prison.

This is known as the "Abrams case," and it stood as one of our greatest judicial scandals. Among others who protested was Professor Zechariah Chafee, Jr., of the Harvard Law School. He published in the "Harvard Law Review," April, 1920, an article entitled "A Contemporary State Trial"; and subsequently he embodied this article as a chapter in his book on "Freedom of Speech." Dean Pound of the Harvard Law School, with Professors Frankfurter, Chafee and Sayre (President Wilson's son-in-law), also the librarian of the Law School, signed a petition for executive clemency in this Abrams case. These actions excited great indignation among the interlocking directorates, and Mr. Austen G. Fox, a Harvard graduate and Wall Street lawyer, drew up a protest to the Harvard board of overseers, which protest was signed by twenty prominent corporation lawyers, all Harvard men, including Mr. Peter B. Olney, a prominent Tammany politician; Mr. Beekman Winthrop, ex-governor of Porto Rico, and Mr. Joseph H. Choate, Jr., recently notorious in connection with the scandals of the Alien Property Custodian. The overseers referred the matter to the "Committee to Visit the Law School," which consists of fourteen prominent servants of the plutocracy, including a number of judges. The result was a "conference," in reality a solemn trial, which occupied an entire day and evening, May 22, 1921, at the

Harvard Club in Boston. Mr. Fox appeared, with a committee of his supporters and a mass of documents in the case; also the United States attorney and his assistant, serving as witnesses.

President Lowell's attitude on this occasion is described to me as that of "a hen protecting her brood against an old Fox." Professor Chafee himself tells me that President Lowell stood by him all through the "conference," and made Mr. Fox uncomfortable by well-directed inquiries. Mr. Fox's principal charge was that Professor Chafee had taken his quotations of testimony at the Abrams trial from the official record submitted to the Supreme Court in the defendant's appeal, instead of going to the prosecuting attorney and getting the complete stenographic record. And lo and behold, when Mr. Fox came to confront the fourteen Harvard judges, it transpired that he himself had committed a similar blunder, only far worse! He accused the five professors at the Law School of having made false representations in their petition to President Wilson; but instead of going to the office of his friend the government prosecutor, and getting a photographic reproduction of the petition as signed by the professors, Mr. Fox presented in evidence a four-page circular, printed by the Abrams defense, containing a fac-simile of the petition, with the signatures of the five professors; the statements which Mr. Fox claimed were inaccurate were printed on the reverse side of this circular. But it was easy for the professors to show that they had nothing to do with the circular or its statements. The document had been compiled by the Abrams defense some time after the professors signed the petition. Mr. Fox, champion of strict legal accuracy, had based his charge upon a piece of propaganda literature, for which the professors had been no more responsible than he!

It is interesting to note how the interlocking newspapers of Boston handled this incident. It was, as you can understand, a most sensational piece of news; but it was an "inside" story, a family dispute of the interlocking directorate. The only newspaper which gave any account of the indictment of the professors was the Hearst paper, which is to a certain extent an outlaw institution, and publishes sensational news concerning the plutocracy, when the interests of Mr. Hearst and his group are not involved. But no other Boston newspaper published the news about this trial at the time that it took place; the first account was in the Boston "Herald," nearly two months later, after the story was stale!

It was an amazing demonstration of the power of the Boston plutocracy; and it affords us curious evidence of the consequences of news suppression. I heard about the Chafee trial all the way from California to Massachusetts, and back again; and every time I heard it, I heard a different version—and always from some one who knew it positively, on the very best authority. These guardians of the dignity of Harvard thought that by keeping the story quiet they were helping the cause of academic freedom; but what they really did was to set loose a flood of wild rumors, for the most part discreditable to themselves. Of course, they may say that they do not care about gossip; but why is it not just as important to educate people about Harvard, as to educate them about the ancient Egyptians and Greeks?

CHAPTER XVII

INTERFERENCE

We have seen President Lowell's behavior when a group of Wall Street lawyers attempted to dictate to his university. We have next to investigate his attitude when it is his own intimates and financial supporters who are being attacked; when it is, not Wall Street, but State Street, which calls to him for help. Here again our Boston Brahmin has put himself on record, with exactly the same self-will and decisiveness—but, unfortunately, on the other side! We were promised some more evidence on the subject of Harvard in relation to Lee-Higginson and Edison Electric. Now we are to have it.

I am indebted for the details of the incident to Mr. Morris Llewellyn Cooke, an engineer of Philadelphia who was Director of Public Works under a reform administration. For a series of five years Mr. Cooke had been a regular lecturer at the Graduate School of Business Administration of Harvard University. He prepared two lectures on the public utility problem in American cities, which he gave at a number of universities, and was invited to give at Harvard. Mr. Cooke took the precaution to inquire whether he would be free "to discuss conditions exactly as they exist in the public utility field." The reply was, in the magnificent Harvard manner: "I am desirous that your lectures be both specific and frank. I am anxious for the students to see clearly the real relation of local public utilities to the municipalities, and vice versa, and am not considering whether your remarks may hurt any one's feelings."

Mr. Cooke came and delivered his two lectures, and was announced to give them again; but four months later came a letter from the dean of the Graduate School, saying: "Mr. Lowell feels, and I agree with him, that in view of the use you made of your invitation to come here this last year, we cannot renew the invitation." Mr. Cooke then wrote to President Lowell to find out what was the matter, and was told that he had violated academic ethics by giving to the press an abstract of his lectures. In answering President Lowell, Mr. Cooke pointed out that six weeks prior to giving the lectures he had written on three separate occasions to the Graduate School, giving notice of his intention to publish an abstract of his remarks, because officials in other cities wished the information on public utilities which he had accumulated. "Trusting that if this is not entirely satisfactory to you, you will so advise me at your convenience," etc. The reply from the Business School had been: "I note that you intend to publish these two lectures later, which will be perfectly satisfactory to us."

President Lowell now condescended to explain to Mr. Cooke wherein he had offended; he had violated "academic customs . . . not in the least peculiar to Harvard, but true in all universities." Mr. Cooke thereupon wrote to universities all over the United States; he obtained statements from a score or two of university professors, deans and presidents, showing that not only was there no such custom, but that it was a quite common custom for lecturers at universities to make abstracts of their lectures and furnish these to the press. The authorities quoted include the president of the University of Wisconsin, and a dean who is now president; Professor Dewey of Columbia, Hoxie of Chicago—and Frankfurter of President Lowell's own university! Theodore Roosevelt wrote:

Until I received your letter, I knew nothing whatever of any rule prohibiting the remarks of academic lecturers from being published in the periodical press or in other ways being quoted as material used in the lecture room.

If you really want to test the sincerity of President Lowell's statement, here is the way to do it: Imagine Theodore Roosevelt, distinguished Harvard alumnus, coming to his alma mater to deliver a lecture on "The Duties of the College Man as a Citizen," and preparing a summary of his lecture and giving it to the press; and then imagine him receiving from President Lowell a letter rebuking him for his action, and informing him that because of it he would not again be invited to speak at Harvard!

No, we shall have to examine Mr. Cooke's lectures, for some other reason why his career as a Harvard lecturer was so suddenly cut short. Mr. Cooke has printed the lectures in pamphlet form under the title "Snapping Cords." On page 9 I find a statement of the over-valuation of public utilities in Philadelphia, and note that the Philadelphia Electric Company has securities to the amount of over fifty million dollars upon an actual valuation of less than twenty-five million. And this is an Edison concern, allied with Boston Edison and Lee Higginson! I turn to page 12, and learn how the National Electric Light Association, the society of electrical engineers, is being used as a dummy by the electric light interests. I turn to page 14, and find the American Electric Railway Association shown up as planning to corrupt American education, creating a financed Bureau of Public Relations for the self-stated purpose of "influencing the sources of public education particularly by (a) lectures on the Chautauqua circuit and (b) formation of a committee of prominent technical educators to promote the formation and teaching of correct principles on public service questions in technical and economic departments at American colleges, through courses of lectures and otherwise."

The tactless Mr. Cooke goes on to examine the activities of "prominent technical educators" who have lent themselves to this program. Among the names I find —can such a thing be possible?—George F. Swain, professor of civil engineering in the Graduate School of Applied Science of Harvard University! Professor

Swain, it appears, has done "valuation work" for Mr. Morgan's New Haven Railroad—our interlocking directorate, you perceive! You may not know what "valuation work" consists of; it is the job of determining how much money you shall pay for your water, light, gas and transportation, and needless to say, the utility corporations want the valuation put as high as possible. Mr. Cooke, since the incidents here narrated, put through a rate case whereby the Philadelphia Electric Company collects from the city and the people of that city one million dollars *less* per year. So you see just what an ornery cuss Mr. Cooke is!

Professor Swain lays out "principles" for the doing of this ticklish "valuation work." * One of his "principles" is that when anything has increased in value, the increased valuation shall be allowed the corporations, but when anything has decreased in value there shall be no corresponding decrease in the valuation! (We used to play this game when we were children; we called it "Heads I win and tails you lose.") Another of Professor Swain's "principles" is that when states, counties or cities have helped to pay the cost of grade crossings, the railroads shall be credited with the full value of these grade crossings. (We used to play that game also when we were children; we called it "Findings is keepings.") Needless to say, a man who is so clever as to get away with things like that regards himself as superior to the rest of us, who let him get away with it. So, as president of the American Society of Civil Engineers, Professor Swain voices his distrust of democratic ideals, and informs the engineers that "present-day humanitarianism leads to race degeneracy."

And then I turn on to page 35 of the pamphlet, and stumble on still more tactless conduct on the part of this dreadful Mr. Cooke. He tells us about Dugald C. Jackson, professor of electrical engineering at Harvard University,† who also does this fancy "valuation work."

---

* See record of hearing, May 3, 1920, at State House, Trenton, N. J., before Governor Edwards, on motion of City of Jersey City for removal of Public Service Commission.

†Professor Jackson, in qualifying as an expert before the Pennsylvania Public Service Commission, introduced himself by the single statement that he was "professor of engineering at

Says Mr. Cooke: "Professor Jackson has never really been so much a university professor as a corporate employe giving courses in universities. While he probably receives five thousand dollars from his present teaching post he must receive at least four times this amount from his corporate clients—charging as he does one hundred dollars a day for his own time and a percentage on the time of his assistants!"

Mr. Cooke goes on to show that before taking up teaching, Professor Jackson was a chief engineer for the Edison General Electric Company. In 1910, while a professor at Harvard, he rendered a report showing that the Chicago Telephone Company was running behind over eight hundred thousand dollars per year; but two years later it was proven that the company could afford a reduction in rates of seven hundred thousand dollars per year! Again, Professor Jackson rendered a report showing that the Buffalo General Electric Company had a valuation of $4,966,000; but the state commission subsequently fixed the valuation at $3,194,000. He valued three thousand municipal arc lamps at $21.70 each, but the New York commission showed that the actual cost of these lamps was $13.53. Says Mr. Cooke:

"What constitutes being employed by a corporation? Professor Jackson is to all intents and purposes consulting engineer in chief as to rates and valuations to the entire electrical industry in the United States. He has made inventories of the Boston Edison Company and the New York Edison Company. He is now engaged in doing similar work for the Philadelphia Electric Company. These three companies have a combined gross annual income of thirty-five million dollars."

Do you see the "nigger in the woodpile" now? If you are a mine guard or strike-breaking gunman, experienced in shooting up the tent-colonies of striking miners, the corporations will pay you five dollars a day and board for your services. If you are a "prominent technical educator," with a string of university degrees and

the Massachusetts Institute of Technology and head of the Department of Electrical Engineering and professor of electrical engineering at Harvard University." It should be explained that he held the last two positions only ex-officio, by virtue of the affiliation of the two institutions which existed for a few years.

titles, who can enable the great corporations to swindle the public out of tens of millions of dollars every year, then you can command a salary of a hundred dollars a day, with a percentage on the time of your assistants. That is what a college education is for; and if you think that an over-cynical statement, I ask you to read the whole of this book before you decide!

And what is a college president for? A college president is paid by the interlocking directorate to take their "consulting engineers" and "valuation experts" and cover them with a mantle of respectability, enabling them to do their dirty work in the name of education and public service. And if any freak individual comes along, trying to break in and spoil the game, the function of a college president is to furnish what the college football player knows as "interference"—tripping the fellow up, slugging him, maiming him. In football there are strict rules against fouls; but in this game of plutocratic education "everything goes."

CHAPTER XVIII

THE LASKI LAMPOON

A more recent test of Harvard University was made by Harold J. Laski, a brilliant young writer whom President Lowell in an unguarded moment admitted to teach political science. Laski holds unorthodox ideas concerning the modern capitalist state; he thinks it may not be the divinely appointed instrument which it considers itself. Laski raised this question in his Harvard classes, which caused tremendous excitement in State Street. The Harvard "drive" for sixteen millions was on, and a number of people wrote that they would give no money to Harvard while Laski was on its teaching staff. On the other hand, a Chicago lawyer wrote that his son had never taken any interest in his studies previously, but that since he had come under Laski's influence he had become a serious student; this lawyer sent fifty thousand dollars to make up the losses. The controversy got into the Boston newspapers, and President Lowell stood by Laski; no Harvard professor should be driven out because of his opinions. "Thank God we are not as Columbia!"

I asked a Cambridge friend about President Lowell's heroism, and he took a cynical view of it. Lowell is the author of a book interpreting the British constitution, and has a reputation in England based on this book; he has received an Oxford degree, and hopes some day to be ambassador. In England people really believe in free speech, and practice their beliefs; and Laski, it happens, is a Manchester Jew, his family associated with the present ruling group in England. Also, Laski himself wields a capable pen, and is not the sort of man one chooses for an enemy. If Laski were to go home and state that he had been expelled from President Lowell's university because of disbelief in the modern state, what would become of Lowell's English reputation? Said my friend: "If Laski had been a German Jew, or a Russian Jew"—and he smiled.

As to the overseers and their handling of the case, Professor Laski writes me that they were very nice to him. "I was simply invited to a dinner at which we exchanged opinions in a friendly fashion. My only doubt there was a doubt whether the committee realized how very conservative my opinions really were in this changing social world. Like most business men, they had little or no knowledge of the results of modern social science."

The climax came with the Boston police strike in the fall of 1919. This was a very curious illustration of the part which the Harvard plutocracy plays in the public life of Boston, so pardon me if I tell the story in some detail. You know how the cost of living doubled all over the country, while the wages of public servants increased very little. The policemen of Boston were not able to live on their wages; they begged for an increase, and the police commissioner promised them the increase if they would wait until after the war. They waited; and then the police commissioner tried to keep his promise, and the mayor and the Democratic administration worked out a settlement. But the Harvard plutocracy, which runs the government of the state, decided not to permit that settlement, but to force a strike of the policemen, so that they could smash the policemen's union. The late Murray Crane, senator and millionaire, holder of a Harvard LL. D., planned the job in the Union Club of Boston, together with Kidder, Peabody & Co., the bankers. Governor Coolidge, the tool of Crane, upset the arrangements made by the mayor of Boston, and the mayor was so furious that he "pasted the governor one in the eye"— the inside reason why Coolidge disappeared so mysteriously during the strike. But the newspapers of the interlocking directorate celebrated him as the hero of the affair, and he became vice-president of the United States on a wave of glory!

The strike came, and according to the standard American technique of strike-breaking, hoodlums were turned loose at the right moment, to throw stones and terrify the public. The whole affair was obviously stage-managed; nothing was stolen, and no real harm was done. Insiders assured me that all the time the "riots" were going on, there was a safe reserve of police locked up in the police-station, waiting in case things should go too far. The Boston policemen were represented as traitors to society, and a wave of fury swept the country—including Harvard, which holds hundreds of thousands of dollars' worth of Boston city bonds, also securities of Boston public service corporations. These properties must be protected; so a "Harvard Emergency Committee" was formed, headed by the professor who had first reported to the overseers Professor Laski's too great zeal in outside activities. Needless to say, no one complained about the "outside activities" of this anti-strike professor; on the contrary, President Lowell issued a resounding call to Harvard men to help smash the policemen's strike.

Incidentally, Harvard men smashed Harold J. Laski, who had the temerity to interject himself into this class war. Laski went to Boston and made a speech to the strikers' wives, expressing sympathy with their cause; whereat all Boston raged. "I would like to ask you something, Mr. Laski," said President Lowell, at a dinner party. "Why did you make that speech?" "Why, Mr. Lowell," said Laski, smiling, "I made it because there is a general impression throughout the labor world that Harvard is a capitalistic institution, and I wanted to show that it is not true." Laski was only twenty-six years old at the time, and it took some nerve, you must admit. How to get this young incendiary out of Harvard was the next job of the interlocking directorate.

Meet Mr. James Thomas Williams, Jr., of Boston. Mr. Williams was graduated from Columbia University in the same year that I quit it; he then joined the Associated Press, and now serves the interlocking directorate as editor of the Boston "Evening Transcript," the paper which is read by every Tory in New England. You may learn more about this paper by consulting pages 284, 306, 307 and 379 of "The Brass Check." Also, perhaps I should tell you a little incident which happened after "The Brass Check" came out. Desiring to test the capitalist newspapers, I made up a dignified advertisement of the book—nothing abusive or sensational, merely opinions from leading journals of Europe. I sent this advertisement, with a perfectly good check, to the Boston "Evening Transcript," and the check was returned to me, with the statement that the "Transcript" thought it best not to publish the advertisement, because of the possibility of being sued for libel.

I was puzzled at first, wondering what paper might sue the Boston "Evening Transcript" for publishing an advertisement of "The Brass Check." Then I remembered that in the book I had accused a Boston newspaper of having shared in the slush funds of the New York, New Haven, and Hartford Railroad; also of having suppressed reports of Justice Brandeis' exposures of the Boston Gas Company, at the same time publishing page advertisements from this gas company; also of having published advertisements of "Harvard Beer, 1,000 Pure," at the same time suppressing news of the fact that the federal government was prosecuting the manufacturers of Harvard Beer for violation of the pure food laws. So I understood that the Boston "Evening Transcript" was afraid of being sued by the Boston "Evening Transcript."

Now behold the editor of this fine old Tory newspaper rushing to the defense of his interlocking directorate. Mr. Laski must be driven from Harvard, and Mr. Williams knows exactly how to do it. He interviews the editors of the Harvard "Crimson" and "Advocate;" finally in the editors of the "Lampoon," he finds a group who will carry out his ideas. The result is an issue of that paper, January 16, 1920, known to history as the "Laski Lampoon." If ever there was a fouler product of class venom, it has not yet come under my eye.

7

I have never had the pleasure of meeting Harold Laski, but I form an idea of him from a score of pictures in this publication. From a painting on the cover I gather he is a short, thin, naked young skeleton with a paunch; he wears large glasses, and has a fringe of whiskers, or long hair, and a red dawn behind him, serving as a halo. From another picture, a piece of clay modelling, I am puzzled about the whiskers, or hairs, because I do not know whether they are little worms or pieces of spaghetti. From other cartoons I gather that Professor Laski sometimes wears clothes, and does not wear them entirely in the Harvard manner; that is, his clothes do not fit him, and his hat has too broad a brim, and is not worn entirely straight on his head. I gather that he sometimes smokes cigarettes, a vice entirely unknown in refined undergraduate circles.

Also Mr. Laski is described to me in a hundred or so sketches, verses and witticisms. He is "the great indoor agitator"; he is "a member of the firm of Lenin, Trotski and Laski." This evil young man, you must understand, holds the idea that the people of Russia should be permitted to work out their own revolution in their own way, and that American troops should not be sent in to attack them in Archangel and Siberia without a declaration of war. This makes him a "Bolshevik"; this makes him "Laski de Lenin," and "Ivan Itchykoff," and the author of "The Constitution of the Russian Itchocracy," and of the "Autobiographia Laskivia." "Love had to go. One love was bad enough, but thirty or forty were insupportable. I had tried it and I knew." He is invited to "sing a song of Bolsheviks," and he tells us that "Comrade Lenin has a hundred and forty-eight motor cars, and Comrade Trotsky has fifty-two." He is "Cataline," and again he is "Professor Moses Smartelikoff"—the "Moses" meaning that he is a Jew, and the rest that he thinks differently from Harvard. Such thinking must not be allowed to get a start, say our cautious young undergraduates:

The moral, oh ye masters, is, without a doubt,
Stop infection early; kick the first one out.

And here are more verses, addressed to our unpopular professor:

As you sit there, growing prouder,
    With your skillful tongue awag,
As your piping voice grows louder,
    Preaching Socialistic gag—
Stop a moment, let us warn you,
    Nature's freak,
That we loathe you and we scorn you,
    Bolshevik!

Harold Laski was scheduled to give a lecture at Yale, and when he got there he found this copy of the "Lampoon" on sale all over town, together with a reprint of an editorial in the "Transcript" denouncing him. He was young, and rather sensitive, and naturally it occurred to him that he was wasting his talents upon Harvard. He would be allowed to stay there, he told a friend of mine, but he would never be promoted, he would have no career. On the other hand, the University of London offered him a full professorship at a higher salary, in a part of the world where men may think what they please about the capitalist state. Laski resigned; and so cleverly the job had been managed—he had quit of his own free will, and the great university could go on boasting that its professors are not forced out because of their opinions! As a commentary on this story, I am sure you will be interested in an extract from a letter from Laski, dated August 16, 1922:

The results of the American atmosphere are quite clear.

1. Many men deliberately adopt reactionary views to secure promotion.

2. Many more never express opinions lest the penalty be exacted.

3. Those who do are penalized when the chance of promotion comes.

I am very much impressed by the contrast between the general freedom of the English academic atmosphere and the illiberalism of America. Three of my colleagues at the London School of Economics are labor candidates; business men predominate on the governing body; but interference is never dreamed of. At Oxford and Cambridge the widest range of view prevails. But alumni do not protest, and if they do, they are told to mind their own business. In America, one always feels hampered by the sense of a control outside; in England you never feel that it is necessary to watch your tongue. No ox treads upon it.

CHAPTER XIX

RAKING THE DUST-HEAPS

We have studied the "Laski Lampoon" to see what we can learn about Professor Laski. Let us now examine it to see what we can learn about Harvard. You remember the student who was compelled to button his collar; so you would expect to find Harvard objecting to a radical professor who did not wear the right kind of tie, and did not get his clothes from the right tailor. The "Lampoon" refers again and again to this, both in verse and drawings; it speaks of Laski's "creed of charming untidiness"; and if you want to know about Harvard's creed of charming tidiness, turn to the advertising portions of this paper. One cannot publish an American magazine without advertisements, and the "Laski Lampoon" is almost up to the standard of the "Saturday Evening Post"—it has fifteen pages of reading matter and thirty-nine of advertisements!

Some of this matter we may assume was contributed as a means of helping to save our alma mater from Bolshevism; for example, the page of the Baldwin Locomotive Works, and the page of the United Shoe Machinery Company, and the quarter-page of the Boston "Evening Transcript," telling us: "This paper stands unflinchingly at home and abroad for 'straight Americanism,' for the cultivation of 'an American character,' which the First American called 'the Cement that binds the Union.'" But the rest are the advertisements of concerns which expect to sell things; and as they spend enormous sums in this way, they make it their business to get the returns, and know how to appeal to each group. So here we learn what Harvard men like, and why they did not like Professor Laski! "Follow the Arrow and you follow the style in collars," we are told, and on another page: "*Correctness* dominates the style policies of these stores." Here are the usual handsome, haughty young men in "the Kuppenheimer clothes," and here is the specially proper "Brogue Boot."

Wishing to see just what Harvard men spend their money for, I take the trouble to classify this advertising. There are seven and one-half pages devoted to clothing, three and three-fourths devoted to luxurious hotels, three and one-half devoted to automobiles, and three and one-half to investments of the interlocking directorate, including an invitation to gamble in German marks. One and one-half pages are given to tobacco, one and one-fourth to candy, one and one-fourth to games and sporting goods, one to jewels, one to movies, three-fourths to music, one-fourth to the "Transcript," one-fourth to art, and one-fourth to books. From the above we may reckon that Harvard students spend thirty times as much on clothes as they spend on books, and fourteen times as much on motor cars as on art. Such is the state of "culture" when teaching is dominated by a vested class, which fears ideas, and forbids all thinking save what is certified to be harmless.

It is a truism in the affairs of the mind, that when you bar one truth, you bar all; and when you refuse to permit students to use their minds, when you withdraw from them the vital stimulus of intellectual conflict —then they go off and get drunk. The last "senior picnic" at Harvard was "a glorified booze party," so I was told by several who attended. There was a ball game, and certain prominent residents of the "Gold Coast" amused themselves by circulating among the crowd, making filthy remarks to girls. Some of the students became indignant, and wished to take the matter up, knowing that the remedy for such evils lies in publicity. But Mr. Frederick J. Allen, secretary to the Corporation— the same gentleman who made the tactful inquiry about the Wilfred Humphries lecture—pleaded with them to spare the good name of the university. So of course there will be another "glorified booze party" next year; and, needless to say, there will be the useful efforts to make certain that Harvard men do not think any new or vital thought about the issues which are shaping the mind of the world.

Class ignorance, class fear, and class repression are written over the modern curricula at Harvard, as at all other American universities. It proclaims that it opens its doors to all classes of the community, and sets forth statistics to prove that it is not a rich man's affair; yet it has among its thirty overseers only three or four educators, not one woman, not one representative of agriculture, and not one of labor! The modern revolutionary movement is not explained to the students; and so they go out, ready to believe the grotesque falsehoods which are served up to them in the Boston "Evening Transcript" and the Providence "Journal"; ready to be led into any sort of lynching bee by the hundred per cent profiteers.

There was one young graduate of Harvard who managed to chop his way out of this glacier of cultured prejudice, and went over to Russia and gave his life for the revolution. His generous spirit will wipe out in Russian history the infamies committed by American capitalist government against the workers of Russia. He is in every way as beautiful and inspiring a figure as Lafayette, and he will live in the imaginations of the Russian people, precisely as Lafayette lives in ours. A hundred years from now he will be Harvard's proudest product; but what has Harvard snobbery to say about him today? During the endowment drive for sixteen million dollars, carried on three years ago, Harvard boasted of its "hundred per cent record" for patriotism—but adding three words, for which it will blush to the end of history: "EXCEPT JOHN REED."

No, the modern revolutionary movement is not interpreted at the university of Lee-Higginson. What is interpreted? I have a list of some of the titles of "theses in English," accepted for the Ph.D. degree by Harvard University in the last ten years, and representing Harvard's view of general culture. Slaves in Boston's great department store, in which Harvard University owns twenty-five hundred shares of stock, be reconciled to your long hours and low wages and sentence to die of tuberculosis—because upon the wealth which you produce some learned person has prepared for mankind full data on "The Strong Verb in Chaucer." Policemen who have had your strike smashed by Harvard students, rest content with your starvation wages—because one of these students has enlightened mankind on "The Syntax of the Infinitive in Shakespeare." Girls who work in the textile mills, who walk the streets of the "she-towns" of New England and part with your virtue for the price of a sandwich, be rejoiced—because you have made it possible for humanity to be informed concerning "The Subjunctive in Layamon's 'Brut.'" Men who slave twelve hours a day in front of blazing white furnaces of Bethlehem, Midvale and Illinois Steel, cheer up and take a fresh grip on your shovels—you are making it possible for mankind to acquire exact knowledge concerning "The Beginnings of the Epistolary Novel in the Romance Languages." Miners, who toil in the bowels of the earth in hourly danger of maiming and suffocation, be reconciled to the failure of a great university to install safety devices to protect your lives—because that money has gone to the collecting and editing of "Political Ballads Issued During the Administration of Sir Robert Walpole." Peons, who quiver under the lash of the masters' whip beneath tropic suns in Central America, be docile—because your labors helped to pay off the bonds of the United Fruit Company, so that a Harvard scholar might win a teaching position by compiling "Chapters in the History of Literary Patronage from Chaucer to Caxton."

CHAPTER XX

THE UNIVERSITY OF U. G. I.

Having visited the city in which they ask you what you are worth, and the city in which they ask you what you know, we have next to visit the city in which they ask you who your grandfather was. We shall find that in these modern days the purpose of the inquiry is to find out if your grandfather was rich. If your grandfather was poor, it will be necessary for you to become richer before you get what you want in that city.

In order to reach Philadelphia from Boston we take the New York, New Haven & Hartford Railroad, which is a Morgan road with a recent Harvard overseer for chairman, a Brown trustee for vice-president, a recent Yale president for director, and a member of the Yale advisory board, a Washburn College trustee, a Wellesley trustee, a Pratt Institute trustee, and two Harvard visitors for directors. The second part of our journey is on the Pennsylvania Railroad, which is a Morgan road and is interlocked with the Guaranty Trust Company, Massachusetts Tech, Johns Hopkins, Princeton, Yale, the University of Pittsburgh, the United States Steel Corporation, Bryn Mawr College, Wilson College, Carnegie Tech, the

Girard Trust Company of Philadelphia and the University of Pennsylvania. Or, if we prefer, we can take the Baltimore & Ohio Railroad, which has a Johns Hopkins trustee for president, and another Johns Hopkins trustee for director, a Pittsburgh trustee, a Princeton trustee, a Lafayette trustee, a Rutgers trustee, a Teachers' College and a Lehigh trustee for directors, also a Morgan partner and a First National Bank director and two Guaranty Trust Company directors and a trustee of the University of Pennsylvania. Or we can take the Reading Railroad, which is Morgan and University of Pennsylvania, University of Pittsburgh, Swarthmore and Pennsylvania State; or the Philadelphia, Baltimore and Washington, which is University of Pennsylvania, Equitable Life, and Johns Hopkins.

We arrive in Philadelphia, which means the City of Brotherly Love, and observe in every down-town city block its ideals embodied in especially large men in blue uniform, riding on especially large horses and carrying especially large clubs, also revolvers scarcely concealed. Philadelphia is located in the state of Pennsylvania, which means Penn's Woodland, and was named after a radical pacifist. All over these woodlands now ride the state constabulary, and club the heads of persons such as William Penn whenever they show themselves in action.

In the New York branch of our plutocratic empire of education we found the emperor, and in the Boston branch we found his son; in Philadelphia we find the eldest of the grand dukes. The office of J. P. Morgan & Company in that city is known as Drexel & Company, and Philadelphia's great university is presided over by Mr. Edward T. Stotesbury, head of Drexel & Company, and partner in J. P. Morgan & Company of New York. Mr. Stotesbury is the chief investment banker of that part of the country; he is president of three railroads and director in about twenty, also in about twenty coal companies, and as many financial institutions, banks, trust companies, safe deposit and insurance companies, also the Baldwin Locomotive Works and the Cambria Steel Company. The laws of the United States strictly forbid railroads to own coal companies, and vice versa, but the interlocking directorate has defied this law for a generation, and Mr. Stotesbury is one of the principal defiers.

This eldest of the grand dukes is active in their Grand Ducal party, having taken the job of raising the money to buy the presidency of the United States in 1904 and 1908. He is also a patron of the graces of life; he spent fourteen thousand dollars for a trotting horse in a city in which tens of thousands of little children go to school hungry every day; he is so little ashamed of this performance that he caused it to be embodied in his biography in "Who's Who." As second grand duke of his university, Mr. Stotesbury has the son of old "Pete" Widener, Philadelphia's traction king; as assistants on the board of this university he has a partner in his banking firm, and a choice assortment of plutocrats, totalling as follows: five bankers, three lawyers, two public utility officials, two corporation officials, three manufacturers, an insurance and coal mining man, a publisher, an architect, an engineer, two doctors, two judges, and a senator. It is difficult to classify these trustees exactly, because the functions of the various members overlap; most of the bankers are in the coal business, the lawyers are directors in banks, the architect is an ex-banker, the engineer is director of a power company and a trolley company, while the publisher is president of a steel company and a railroad, and director of a national bank. One of the public utility officials is the brother of Senator Penrose, one of the most aristocratic political corruptionists America ever had; one of the lawyers, Wickersham, was Taft's attorney general; the senator is George Wharton Pepper, chief lackey to the plutocracy of Pennsylvania. Another lawyer is general counsel and active vice-president of the United Gas Improvement Company; two of the bankers are directors in that company. Another of the bankers is a sugar smuggler, and one of the manufacturers helped in the effort to buy a presidential nomination for General Wood.

One could not get a more plutocratic board than this; and the significant thing about it is that they are nearly all of them active, hard-fighting plutocrats; no retired bandits fattening on their accumulated loot, but hard campaigners, living in the saddle, riding day by day to combat. They are the banking men, the coal men, the gas men, the railroad men, who are robbing the public and crushing labor hour by hour, and the control they exercise over their educational system is of the instant, vigilant, smashing kind which you would expect from military men on hard service.

It is a little difficult to find a satisfactory name for a university in which so many plutocratic interests are so completely represented. I might call it the University of Morgan-Drexel, or I might call it the University of the Pennsylvania Railroad, and be entirely just and exact. After studying its management and history, I realize that its most active single interest is the United Gas Improvement Company of Philadelphia, known as U. G. I. You must not think of this as a local gas company; it is a great chain of corporations, ruling over three hundred cities and towns, and with a total investment of five hundred millions of dollars. Of the seven directors of this concern, Mr. Stotesbury and two others are on the board of the university, and a fourth left only last year; also an attorney for the U. G. I. is on the board. Mr. Randall Morgan, vice president of the U. G. I., is chairman of the finance committee of the university, the all-powerful position.

Some eighteen years ago Lincoln Steffens described the City of Brotherly Love in an article entitled "Philadelphia Corrupt and Contented." He told how the political ring voted dead dogs and Negro babies at elections, and how they played poker in hotel rooms for the franchises and public privileges of the city. Philadelphia was corrupt in those days, but it was not really contented; for the people had assembled with ropes in their hands, to mob their city councilmen who were giving away a franchise to the U. G. I. But since those days the war has come, and taught our rulers how to handle social discontent. There was a general strike in the City of Brotherly Love, and it was smashed; the little Socialist bookstore was raided, the books burned and everybody who sold them jailed, and now Philadelphia is truly contented, and where the interlocking directorate used to plunder in tens of millions it now plunders in hundreds.*

*In April, 1922, all the officers and directors of the United Gas Improvement Company, and its subsidiaries, were indicted by the Federal grand jury in New York for criminal activities. This grand jury took testimony for over four weeks, hearing city officials from all over the Eastern and Central states. The charges listed in the indictment were that the U. G. I. "(1) insti-

From the beginning the U. G. I. has been vigilant in holding down the professors in its university. As early as 1886 Professor Edmund J. James prepared a paper in which he showed the excessive cost of gas furnished by private companies; for this he was severely mishandled. Later on, when a syndicate was formed to steal the waterworks from the city of Philadelphia, they offered Professor James twenty thousand dollars to keep still on the subject of municipal waterworks; and when he declined this most generous proposition, they let him go to the University of Chicago.

Next, in 1898, Professor Leo S. Rowe, now director of the Pan-American Union, published a paper on Philadelphia's experiences with its gas supply. Mr. Clark, one of the vice-presidents of the U. G. I., took great offense at these statements and made desperate efforts to compel Mr. Rowe to change them. Professor E. W. Bemis of the University of Chicago has stated over his

---

tuted and caused to be instituted unwarranted, vexatious and tortuous litigation against competitors for the purpose of injuring and intimidating them and preventing them from continuing to engage in the industry; (2) instigating the false arrest of competitors and falsely charged said competitors with counterfeiting trade-marks; (3) acquired control of competing companies wherever possible and operated said companies as ostensible but not real competitors of the United Gas Improvement Company; (4) secretly and fraudulently acquired stock control of competing companies and eliminated competition on the part of said companies; (5) entered or caused to be entered collusive bids for contracts for furnishing and maintaining incandescent gas street lamps by two or more companies belonging to the United Gas Improvement Company, each company falsely representing itself to be independent and not connected with any other company bidding for the same contract; (6) concealed and denied ownership of various subsidiary companies, and operated said companies ostensibly as competitors but in fact as unlawful instruments in accomplishing the objects of the combination and monopoly; (7) circulated or caused to be circulated false and misleading reports concerning competitors for the purpose of preventing competition; (8) molested, injured, and interfered with competitors for the purpose of intimidating and discouraging them and preventing them from continuing as competitors in the industry; (9) entered into contracts with competitors whereby said competitors agreed to refrain from competition." The prosecutions were called off by Attorney-General Daugherty, the particular government official whom President Harding has appointed for the protecting of big business criminals in the United States.

own signature as follows: "Failing in this endeavor, he, Clark, became much excited, and declared to me that if Professor Rowe did not change or withdraw the account, he would lose all social and scientific standing in Philadelphia and at the University of Pennsylvania. Mr. Clark added that he was positive of this, because he was in close touch with both the city and the university." Bear in mind, if you can, the name of this injudicious Professor Bemis, because we shall hear about him and his adventures at the University of Chicago.

A friend of mine in Philadelphia, who was in touch with this controversy, told me the curious experience of a young instructor, who is now connected with the State Department at Washington. This instructor dug out information concerning certain defects in the charter of the U. G. I.; and when the directors of the company learned what he had got, they treated him to "the finest dinner on earth." "One thing we want to suggest that you change," etc. "Well," said the young instructor, "I got this out of an ordinance." He went to his dean with the facts, and the dean found he was right and told him to stick by it. This dean was Lewis, another man who got into trouble in the university, and had a ten years' campaign to hold his job, because he persisted in taking part in the activities of the Progressive party. The young instructor turned his material over to Professor Rowe, and Rowe made use of it, and as a result his salary was held down for years; none of his young instructors could get promoted, and he was handicapped at every turn. Finally, when he was doing war work for the government, and Secretary McAdoo asked for further leave of absence, an ugly answer was returned by the university, and Professor Rowe was forced to withdraw.

Next came the adventure of Professor Clyde King, who in 1912 made the discovery that the U. G. I. was robbing the government of the city of half a million dollars a year, by delivering gas of less than twenty-two candlepower, the quality specified in its lease. They worked this little scheme through the chief of the Bureau of Gas, and the exposure made a terrific scandal in Philadelphia. This chief had ten thousand dollars a year for his department, and he himself drew fifty-five hundred of this, and had five assistants, and only one doing any work. Professor King took records as to the gas tests, and proved that the U. G. I. had notice in advance, by a secret telephone code, and they pumped in benzol vapor to improve the quality of the gas.* The president of the gas company, of course, denied that he knew anything about it. The vice-president and active head of the gas company, a trustee of the university, made desperate efforts to suppress this scandal, but he failed; and as a result of the exposure, the chief of the gas bureau was fired—and three months afterwards was given an honorary degree by Muhlenberg College, at Allentown, Pa.

You may have been puzzled as you read this book to understand why the plutocracy should be so anxious to own universities and colleges; but now you can understand. If you own a university or college, neither you nor your friends can ever be sent to jail, and no matter what crimes you may commit, you can always be made respectable again. This was proven in the case of the gas chief, for shortly afterwards the U. G. I. came back into control of the city, and the gas chief was reappointed to his office! It is interesting to note that the grand duke of Muhlenberg College who arranged this honor for the gas chief is Colonel Trexler, president of a lumber company, a cement company, a trolley company and a telephone company, and author of the wittiest remark now current in the educational world: "I believe that colleges should grow by degrees!"

CHAPTER XXI

STEALING A TRUST FUND

Before we go on with this story we should make the acquaintance of the executive head of the University of U. G. I., who bears the title of provost instead of president. From 1911 to 1921 he was Edgar Smith, a former professor of chemistry, who had been all his life an active henchman of the interlocking directorate and its political machine. He attended the Chicago convention in 1912 as a delegate from Pennsylvania, and voted for Taft as

* See files of Public Service Commission, City of Philadelphia.

a candidate. He was intimate with the contractor-politician who ran the political machine of Philadelphia; he defended this man in public, and freely defended other political crooks, while denying his deans and professors the right to take part in politics in opposition to such crooks. When he took office the trustees promised they would finance the university, but this promise was not kept, so he had to go to the politicians every year and spend weeks begging for a subsidy, and being scolded for the improper activities of his faculty.

In his attitude to his trustees this provost was the ideal of subservience. He publicly declared that he himself had "no policy"; he placed the responsibility of action on those who asserted the right and had the power to act—that is to say, the trustees. He referred to them always as "the administration," and in all public matters he took to them an attitude of touching deference. Thus, speaking at a banquet of the Pennsylvania alumni in New York, he said: "Tonight you will not expect me to occupy much of your time, for our trustees are your real guests, and you desire to hear from them." Needless to say, such a type of mind is religious, and wedded to all things dull. Provost Smith never wearied of telling his audiences that he was a believer in "an old fashioned education"—with "four years each of Latin, Greek and Mathematics, and from four to three years of English, French and German."

In administering the university, this aged-minded provost made it his function to carry to the trustees all manner of scandal concerning his radical professors—such as the fact that one of them was accustomed to dig in his garden on Sunday! Also he would bring back to the professors pitiful accounts of the embarrassments to which he was exposed. His attitude is illustrated by a statement he made to three professors whom he summoned to his office at the time the U. G. I. was under attack. "Gentlemen, what business have academic people to be meddling in political questions? Suppose, for illustration, that I, as a chemist, should discover that some big slaughtering company was putting formalin in its sausage; now, surely, that would be none of my business!"

Said one of the professors: "My answer would be that

if I were to find such a condition, I should have no right
to go to sleep until something was done about it."

As a result of this attitude, the dean who had charge of
these professors was allowed no funds at all; he would
have to go to the provost if he wanted to have a cupboard
built in some store-room, and whenever he went, he would
find his boss with newspaper clippings on his desk. "Now,
Young, how can we get any results with this kind of thing
going on?"

It so happened that fate had played upon poor Provost
Smith a cruel prank. Some forty years ago there lived in
Philadelphia a truly liberal capitalist, who in his will left
six hundred thousand dollars to found the Wharton
School of Finance at the university. He laid down what
the school was to teach as follows:

> The immorality and practical inexpediency of seeking to ac-
> quire wealth by winning it from another rather than earning it
> through some sort of service to one's fellowmen.
> The deep comfort and healthfulness of pecuniary indepen-
> dence, whether the scale of affairs be small or great.
> The necessity of rigorously punishing by legal penalties and
> by social exclusion those persons who commit frauds, betray
> trusts or steal public funds, directly or indirectly. The fatal con-
> sequence to a community of any weak toleration of such offenses
> must be most distinctly pointed out and enforced.

And then the shrewd old rascal, evidently knowing
his business associates thoroughly, added this amazing
provision.

> The grantees covenant that these things shall be done, and
> that the failure to comply with these stipulations shall be deemed
> such a default as to cause reversion in the manner hereinafter
> provided.

Now, you understand that the first principle of the
interlocking directorate is never to let go of money on
which it gets its hands. It is accustomed to misappro-
priating funds, and turning public funds to its own uses;
a little thing like a deed of trust would not stand in its
way. What it failed to realize in the case of this Wharton trust was the uncomfortable amount of agitation and
publicity which would be involved. If the trustees of
the University of U. G. I. had realized what was coming
to them, they would have made up that six hundred thousand dollars by raising the price of gas in Philadelphia.

For the effect of the deed of trust was to bring in a

number of ardent young teachers who took seriously the words of the dead founder, and believed they had rights in the place. They shamelessly attacked the U. G. I., as I have narrated; they attacked other interests of the interlocking trustees in the same reckless way. For example, Professor Thomas Conway proved how the street railways were being plundered and ruined. He was unanimously recommended by his faculty for promotion, but this recommnedation was held up for three years by the trustees. During these three years the trustees were engaged in selling a street railway at an inflated valuation to the New Haven, and were putting through another "deal" of the same sort in Indiana!

Or take the case of Dr. Ward W. Pierson, who showed before the public service commission how the coal companies were charging $1.70 per ton transportation charges on coal, whereas the actual cost was only 55 cents; and here was our university, with two-thirds of its trustees interested in the mining and transporting of coal! Here was a coal operator about to give a large sum of money to the university, and withdrawing it! Dr. Pierson also was recommended for promotion, and waited three years, and meantime the scandal bureau of the interlocking directorate was put to work on him, and he was charged with a grave offense. His colleagues investigated the charge, and proved it to be absolutely without foundation.

Next came the case of Scott Nearing, who had begun his career as secretary to the Pennsylvania Child Labor Committee. At this time Pennsylvania had more working children than any other state in the union. For example, there was Helen Sissack, a girl of twelve working in a silk mill, walking three miles from her home to start work at six o'clock at night, finishing work at six in the morning, and walking three miles back. Nearing became an instructor at the Wharton School, but went on opposing child labor, and the president of the Pennsylvania Manufacturers' Association attacked him, and the dean of the Wharton School was instructed by the provost of the university to instruct Nearing to stop his child labor talks. The university was scolded by a newspaper belonging to Joseph R. Grundy, woolen manufacturer and political boss, and this sent the provost into another panic.

After several years of strife, Nearing promised to be "good" for a year, and he was "good" for two years; that is, he made no outside speeches; but it didn't help him, because what he said in his class-rooms was reported by the students, and reached the ears of the interlocking trustees. The standard time for promotion in the Wharton School is five years, but Nearing waited eight years, and along with his promotion he got a notice from the provost that the period of his appointment was for one year at a time! Randall Morgan, vice-president of the U. G. I., and trustee of the University of U. G. I., remarked to a friend of mine: "He may stay until he's bald-headed, but he'll never get promoted." Another trustee said to Nearing: "We'll give you young fellows rope and you'll hang yourselves. There'll be no dismissals." This was E. B. Morris, president of the Girard Trust Company, a Morgan concern, with Mr. Stotesbury, the grand duke, for a director; also chairman of the Cambria Steel Company, of which Mr. Stotesbury is a director; also director of the Pennsylvania Steel Company.

The provost thought he knew how to handle this matter. He said to one of his henchmen: "Load him with administrative work, so that he can't lecture. 'Squeeze' him." This is a term which they understand at plutocratic universities; to "squeeze" you is to make changes in your curriculum, so as to make your courses less important; to take them out of the required list, or to give required French at the same hour, so that nobody will be free to come to your courses; or to put them at inconvenient hours, say at three o'clock in the afternoon, when nobody likes to come. If you are a professor, they will "squeeze" your young men; you will be unable to get promotions and proper salaries for your subordinates, or equipment or proper supplies for your department.

You may find the adventures of Scott Nearing set forth in a book called "The Nearing Case," by Lightner Witmer, a professor at the university. It is interesting to note that Professor Witmer paid for the publication of this book by being "squeezed" himself, and by having his young men "squeezed." Scott Nearing, ring-leader of the agitation, they kept on a salary of fifteen hundred

8

dollars—and at the same time they delicately called his attention to an opening which presented itself at another university, where he might get three thousand dollars! "What a shame about that nice young Nearing fellow!" said Professor Lingelbach of the department of history. "He might have been getting seven or eight thousand dollars now, if he had held his tongue!" But on another occasion this venerable professor argued in a faculty discussion that there was no suppression of free speech at the University of Pennsylvania. Somebody put to him the question, suppose he wanted to join in municipal research work, to take up gas or street railways. Yes, everybody present admitted, that might make a difference!

CHAPTER XXII

PROFESSOR BILLY SUNDAY

No study of the University of Pennsylvania would be complete which failed to mention that it was founded by Benjamin Franklin, and gave an honorary degree to Thomas Paine. Franklin's doctrines, political and religious, could not be taught in any university in America today, while as for Paine, he could not keep out of jail in any state of the Union. Theodore Roosevelt described Paine as "a filthy little atheist," which makes one think of Agassiz's student, who defined a lobster as "a red fish that swims backwards." There were only three things wrong with the definition, said Agassiz; a lobster is not red, it is not a fish, and it does not swim backwards. Thomas Paine was not filthy, he was not little, and he wrote: "I believe in one God and no more." Paine first proposed the Declaration of Independence, he saved the American Revolution by his eloquence, and he will come into his own when Americans are free men. Meantime, the great university which honored him would not dare to mention his name, and his place in the academic sunshine is taken by the Rev. William A. Sunday, D.D.

For the benefit of posterity, I explain that Sunday was an incredibly vulgar and blatant religious revivalist, who abused the labor movement and extolled the rich, and was used by the interlocking directorate to keep the eyes of the masses fixed on heaven. They carried him from one city to another all over the United States, and in Philadelphia they financed for him a four weeks' campaign. Sunday had already received the degree of doctor of divinity from one American college; he was now welcomed with open arms by the University of Pennsylvania, which had barred Samuel Gompers from speaking, and more recently has barred James Maurer, president of the Pennsylvania State Federation of Labor.

About the reception of the Rev. Billy, you may read in his biography, a chapter headed "A Wonderful Day in a Great University." "The greatest day of his crowded life," the biographer comments, and quotes a few samples of the eloquence whereby the great evangelist promoted the cause of culture and scholarship. "Oh, Jesus, isn't this a fine bunch?" he began his closing prayer. "Hot Cakes Off the Griddle" was the title of his address, and he portrayed the wife of Pilate—"one of those miserable, pliable, plastic, two-faced, two-by-four, lick-spittle, toot-my-own-horn sort of women"; and then Pilate himself—"one of those rathole, pin-headed, pliable, stand-pat, free-lunch, pie-counter politicians." Speaking in the largest auditorium of the university, before the assembled students and instructors, Billy Sunday declared that "Jesus Christ is either the son of God or the natural offspring of a Jewish harlot."

You will appreciate this even more when you learn that one of the underground charges laid against Scott Nearing was that he, when asked privately by a student for his opinion of the Episcopal Academy, had said that he would rather send a son of his to hell than to the academy. This shocked a trustee, Mr. Bell, Republican machine politician and ex-attorney general, who had never heard such language used in political life. But Mr. Bell did not object to the Rev. Sunday stating that ex-President Eliot of Harvard University was a man "so low-down he would need an aeroplane to get into hell." Poor President Eliot, it should be explained, is a Unitarian—that is the reason he gets cussed!*

---

*Ordinarily a man's domestic misfortunes are not proper basis for attack upon his ideas; but when a man sets himself up as a teacher of the young, when he claims that he has the one true and valid moral system, and pours out virulent abuse upon all who differ with his ideas—then it seems reasonable to call attention to the fact that the son of the evangelist, William A.

Mr. Bell is not the only pious politician on this pious board. Senator George Wharton Pepper is a devout Episcopalian, leader of the church of J. P. Morgan and Company in the City of Brotherly Love. Mr. Pepper is so pious that he does not believe in education, he believes only in religion. In his book, "A Voice From the Crowd," he says: "Subtract God and you get—not secular education, but no education at all." Again he says: "The teacher who interprets all of life in terms of brotherhood is responsible for leading the students to forget God." So, needless to say, Mr. Pepper was annoyed when Scott Nearing caused to be published in the Philadelphia "North American" a letter addressed to Billy Sunday, advocating the godless idea of brotherhood. Read Nearing's evil words:·

You have declared your interest in the salvation of Philadelphia.

Look around you and ask yourself what salvation means here.

The city is filled with unemployment and poverty; multitudes are literally starving; thousands of little children toil in the city's factories and stores; its workers, a third of a million strong, have no workmen's compensation law for their protection. Meanwhile the railroad interests which control the hard coal fields are reaping exorbitant profits; the traction company exacts the highest fares paid by the people of any American city; the manufacturers, intrenched at Harrisburg, are fighting tooth and claw to prevent the passage of up-to-date labor laws, and the vested interests are placing property rights above men's souls.

These monstrous offenses against humanity—this defiance of the spirit of Christ's gospel—exist today in the city which hears your message.

And further: the well-fed people, whose ease and luxury are built upon this poverty, child labor and exploitation, sit in your congregation, contribute to your campaign funds, entertain you socially, and invite you to hold prayer meetings in their homes.

These are they that bind grievous burdens on men's shoulders, that make clean the outside of the cup and the platter—the devourers of widows' houses, against whom Christ hurled His curses.

Here is Dives; yonder is Lazarus. And it is Dives who has made your campaign financially possible.

Sunday, Jr., has been arrested in the city of Los Angeles twice within the past fortnight. The first time he was fined two hundred dollars for reckless driving of an automobile; the second time his home was raided, and he and seven of his guests were arrested upon complaint of the neighborhood that they have been conducting drunken debauches for many weeks.

Make no mistake! The chief priests, scribes and Pharisees of Philadelphia will never crucify you while you deal in theological pleasantries. Has it occurred to you that their kindness is a return for your services in helping them to divert attention from real, pressing worldly injustice to heavenly bliss? Turn your oratorical brilliancy for a moment against low wages, over-work, unemployment, monopoly and special privilege.

Before you leave Philadelphia will you speak these truths?

We pray "Thy Kingdom come on earth." While men are underpaid, while women are overworked, while children grow up in squalor, while exploitation and social injustice remain, the Kingdom of God never can come on earth and never will.

It was after the publication of this blasphemy that our interlocking trustees decided that Scott Nearing must go. They knew that the young professor's colleagues were solidly behind him, and they also knew that there had been no room in Logan Hall big enough to hold the crowds of students who thronged to his lectures. So they must be cunning, and wait until both instructors and students had scattered to the country, and there was no longer a chance of organized action. On June 14 they voted not to reappoint Nearing, and the provost wrote him a brief note advising him of this action; at the same time the trustees voted privately that they would make no statement on the subject—regular gum-shoe work, such as they were accustomed to use when they put a bill through their city council, stealing the socks off the feet of William Penn's statue!

But some of the alumni got together and formed a committee, and wrote letters to all the trustees, and also wrote letters to the press, and before long the newspaper reporters were dogging the trustees, trying to "smoke them out." "Why should we make an explanation of what we choose to do as trustees?" demanded Mr. J. Levering Jones, trust company and street railway company and insurance company director and Republican machine politician. "The University of Pennsylvania is not a public institution." And then the reporters got after the pious Senator Pepper, who also denied that the university was a public institution. The people of the state were putting up a million dollars a year for it—they are now putting up a million and a half; but they have no say as to how this million dollars is spent! The professors of the university were in the same position as Senator Pepper's secretary, so this pious man declared; he had the same right

to discharge them, and they had no more right to demand
an explanation. Nor were the trustees obliged to pay
attention to the provisions of the Wharton trust deed—
in spite of the indignant protests of Mr. Morris, one of
the trustees of the Wharton estate.

The agitation continued, and little by little these
trustees were smoked out and forced to reveal themselves. Terrible rumors were spread as to what Scott
Nearing had done. He had questioned a student, the
son of a Philadelphia judge, and not liking the student's
answers, had sneered: "That is the kind of ignorance
you would expect to find in judicial circles." The above
statement being widely quoted by the trustees, Nearing's
colleagues produced a signed statement from the student,
that he had never met Professor Nearing or spoken to
him; he had sat in Nearing's classes, but had never been
asked any oral questions by him.

The real reason behind the whole proceeding was revealed by a legislator up in Harrisburg, who got drunk at
the Majestic Hotel and told how "Joe" Grundy, woolen
manufacturer of Bristol, and president of the State Manufacturers' Association, had fixed it up with Senator Buck-
man, his political boss, that the university should not get
its annual appropriation until Nearing was fired. So
Nearing was fired, and stayed fired, and that was the
end of it. Several of his colleagues quit the university;
the rest of them raised a fund to pay Nearing a year's
salary, as tribute of their admiration; but they themselves
stayed on and behaved themselves, and there has been no
more disturbance at the Wharton School. The University of Pennsylvania professors no longer go out and
lecture against child labor, they no longer serve on public
commissions—or if they do, their findings are what the
interlocking directorate wishes found. There are no
longer graft exposures in Philadelphia; as one professor
remarked to me: "It's all inside the heads of people who
don't tell!" And this same professor reported an excla-
mation which came from the lips of his dean: "Oh, how
I hate reformers!"

CHAPTER XXIII

THE TRIUMPH OF DEATH

What is the intellectual state of the University of U. G. I. at the present moment? I questioned four different professors about it—taking the precaution to meet each one secretly, not letting even the others know about it. Always I got the same report, frequently backed by the same anecdotes. Some one had gone to the head of a department in the Wharton School to say that the "Young Democracy" group of students wanted to arrange a debate, to have one of their professors answer the Socialist arguments of Scott Nearing. "I should like to do it," replied the department head. "It's just what I believe in, but I am very busy, and have plans to have my department expanded; I don't believe in pussy-footing, but there's no use throwing away a chance to get some good work done." In other words, this man did not even dare to debate *against* Scott Nearing, for fear of offending his trustees! In the Greek department a young instructor did not dare join the "Young Democracy" group, though this was an open forum, strictly non-political; he would give his money, he said, but not his name, it was too dangerous. "They never interfere with my teaching Greek," he added.

Keep hidden, that is the wise policy; keep your head down. Anything you say may get into the newspapers, and get in wrong. A leader of the striking longshoremen was arrested and clubbed, and a student tried to raise bail. "Penn Man Defends Radical," ran the scare headlines. And some one told me a mournful story, one that I heard over and over again in the colleges and universities I visited. You know in country settlements they have the traditional "village idiot"; likewise in every college and university they have some unhappy, beaten man, who made a mistake once in his youth, and has never been able to atone for it. At the University of U. G. I. there is a young professor, whose students wished to debate the McNamara case; they asked him for advice on each side of the debate, and he made suggestions, and tried to explain how the use of violence would appear to a labor leader. For this he was hauled up be-

fore the trustees and brow-beaten. He has never got beyond the rank of assistant professor, and is a broken
man. He was an active party Socialist, but now does
nothing, and if he writes a letter to a newspaper on a
public question, he dares not sign his own name to it.

The trustees may not pay much attention to the teaching of Greek, but they watch the economics and history
departments like hawks. A friend of mine, not a professor, told of taking a motor ride with one of these
trustees, who referred to a Wharton School professor as
"that pizen pup."

"What ideas of his do you object to?" asked my
friend.

"Oh, all kinds of ideas; that Ireland should be free,
for example. As near as I can get it, he believes just
what my cook believes."

Said my friend: "You are mistaken about the man.
He's really a lovable fellow; if you knew him you would
like him. But, naturally, you don't meet him. You
have an unwritten law—he would have to ask permission of his dean or of the provost before he met you;
otherwise he would commit an unthinkable offense."

"Well," replied the trustee, "he's unscientific, and anyhow, he doesn't get along with the boys."

My friend said: "But that's because his curriculum
was changed so that he can't get any boys."

"Well, anyhow," said the trustee, "he's not the calibre
of man we want for full professor."

A woman friend of mine was present at a tea party
where the head of a department in the University of U.
G. I. told about a proposed appointment in the political
science department. The man under discussion was connected with the State Department in Washington. He
was wealthy, said this dean, and had a good social position; his wife's mother had especially important social
connections. He was right on Russia, he was right on
Japan, he was right on reparations; he had written the
recent note of Secretary Hughes to the Bolshevist delegation at Genoa, and Hughes had passed this note with
only two or three emendations. Such is the atmosphere
in the high-up circles of our plutocratic education; such
are the standards of eminence! I am informed on the
best authority that this sturdy opponent of the Soviet

government in our State Department received three flattering offers from leading Eastern universities, as soon as it became known that he was the author of that Hughes note!

Such is the way the game is played. As one professor remarked to me: "Knowing the ropes as I do, I could get any sort of promotion, any sort of honors—and that not by worthy work, not by any true contribution to science, but simply by knowing the interests, and being unscrupulous enough. It is a situation which destroys the morals of every man who knows about it." And another said: "There is not a man in the Wharton School today who truly respects himself."

Such are the instructors; and the students are what you would expect. One professor said to me: "Not five per cent of my men are thinking about public questions. They take what I teach them as cows in the pasture take rain, something to be endured but not thought about. They come from high schools where they have heard no discussions of vital questions. I have talked with thousands of them; ask anybody in the university and you will get the same answer—their mental life is as dead as the tomb."

Another professor told how one of his colleagues had brought into his class a former lecturer of the Y. M. C. A. in Siberia, who described to the students the behavior of Semenoff, the Cossack bandit, one of the pets of our State Department. The lecturer had traveled in Semenoff's train, and had been invited to tea, and Semenoff came in with his tunic spotted with blood, explaining that he had just dispatched a carload of prisoners. He had shot them, one by one, with his own revolver, and left the dead for the American troops to bury. There had been some discussion of the incident in the class, and not a man there thought there was anything wrong about it. "They never batted an eye," said my informant.

Such are the triumphs of plutocratic education; and lest you doubt this, I mention that the students proved their convictions by action. They kidnapped a Russian student, a quiet and unobtrusive fellow, a Socialist, not a Communist; they carried him in an automobile some fifteen miles outside the city, beat him until he was helpless, and left him to get back as best he could. This was punishment for expressing the opinion that the Russian people should be permitted to work out their own destiny in their own way. For things such as this the state of Pennsylvania contributes a subsidy of a million and a half dollars a year!

The interlocking trustees are so sure of their power that they ventured recently to give to all the world a demonstration of it. The old provost retired, and they cast about for a new one, and offered to the American academic world the gravest insult it has yet sustained. You might spend much time searching through the names of prominent people in America, before you found one less fitted to be head of a great university than Leonard Wood; a second-rate regimental surgeon at the Presidio in San Francisco, who had the fortune to become the favorite of Theodore Roosevelt, and was by him rushed to a high command in the army, against the unanimous protest of army men. In 1920 he was picked out by a group of millionaire adventurers as their candidate for president; these men were shown by the New York "World" to have spent millions to buy him the nomination. They failed; and perhaps to soothe the general's wounded feelings the trustees of U. G. I. selected him for the highest honor in their gift. Also, Harvard has just made him an overseer—the interlocking process in a new form!

At the University of Pennsylvania the General receives twenty-five thousand dollars per year. He has not yet condescended to honor the university with his presence, but his duties are performed by an assistant provost, at six or eight thousand. As faculty men explained to me, the one thing which makes it possible to tolerate the indignities of management by business men, is the fact that the president is always a professional educator, a man who has been one of them and understands their problems. But here is a man who has never been an educator, and is not even a graduate of a university; a military autocrat, utterly out of sympathy with true ideals of education. So the professor is pushed one step lower in the social scale, his status of inferiority is fixed; and at the University of U. G. I. everybody sits still and holds his breath, waiting for the Grand Duke of Drexel-Morgan to die, and leave his millions to his dead university!

P. S. As this goes to press, General Wood resigns.

CHAPTER XXIV

THE TIGER'S LAIR

For four years during my early life as a writer I lived—first in a tent, then in a little cabin which I built, then in an old farm-house—in the wooded hills about five miles north of Princeton. I wrote "Manassas" there, and "The Jungle." For "Manassas" I used the Princeton library, so I spent a great deal of time about the place, and got to know it very well. I dwell on those days, and visions rise of elegant country gentlemen's estates, deep shade-trees and smooth cool lawns with peacocks and lyre-birds strutting about; and the campus, with elegant young gentlemen lounging, garbed with costly simplicity and elaborately studied carelessness. I remember the warm perfumed evenings of spring, with the singing on the steps of "Old North"; the bonfires and parades and rejoicings over athletic victories; the grave ceremonials of commencement, and the speeches full of exalted sentiments. I remember a tall black-coated figure —I never saw it without a shining silk hat—striding about the grounds, or standing on the steps of "Prexy's house," responding to a serenade, and reminding the students how they were destined to go out and be leaders in the battle for all things noble and true and grand.

Then I would go into the library and work for a couple of hours, and come out late at night, and see these same young leaders of the future come staggering out of their clubhouses to vomit in the gutter. The public was told that drinking was forbidden in these clubs; but I saw what I saw. I suspected that the tall gentleman in the black coat and silk hat must also know what was going on, and that therefore he did not mean his golden words to be taken with entire literalness. If only there had been some way by which I could have warned the world concerning this eloquent college president who did not mean his golden words—what a tragedy to mankind might have been averted!

I did not meet Woodrow Wilson at Princeton, but I met a good many of his professors. I called on his professor of literature, Henry Van Dyke, poet and scholar, a dear amiable gentleman who had about as much idea of the realities of modern capitalism as had the roses in his garden. I met some of his students—I took walks over the hills with one who had literary aspirations, and considered Tennyson's poems to Queen Victoria the highest imaginative flight of our age. This earnest young man discovered that I admired a disreputable English free-lover by the name of Shelley; and so our acquaintance died. Another time my family was away, and I lived in town in a student boarding-house; I turn weak even now when I think of those solemn, pale, black-clad young men from the theological seminary, eating their thin and watery meals, and living in a state of mind precisely as if the last hundred and fifty years had never happened to anybody.

The manners and traditions of Princeton are English; the architecture, the ivy, and the elaborate carelessness of the men's attire. Strolling about the campus you might be in the midst of one of those interminable English novels, in which the hero goes first through the public school and eats at "tuck-shops," and then meanders up to Cambridge or Oxford, and gracefully loiters for two hundred pages, punting on the river, reading a few random books of poetry, and seducing a girl or two. Princeton is the home of the graces, the most perfect school of snobbery in America. It is meant for gentlemen's sons, and no nonsense about it; no Negroes, few Jews or Catholics if they are known. The society clubs run, not merely the campus, but the faculty, and the endowment is presided over by the prettiest bunch of plutocrats yet assembled in our empire of education.

The grand duke of Princeton was, until he died last year, Mr. Taylor Pyne, numbered among a score of the wealthiest men in the wealthiest country in the world. Mr. Pyne was a director in the National City Bank, one of the three great institutions of the money trust; he was also a director of the Delaware and Lackawanna Railroad, and of the Prudential Life Insurance Company, one of the great honey-pots of Wall Street. It was on Mr. Pyne's cool green lawns that I watched the peacocks and lyre-birds, in the days when I had come back from the Chicago stockyards, white and sick with the horror of what I had seen.

The second grand duke of Princeton is Cyrus H. Mc-Cormick, head of the International Harvester Company, also a director in the National City Bank. The third grand duke is William Cooper Procter, the Ivory Soap magnate, who tried to buy the presidency of the United States for General Wood. Mr. Procter is also a director in the National City Bank—quite a smell of Standard Oil on the Tiger's coat, you notice! The fourth grand duke is Robert Garrett, the biggest banker of Baltimore, whose brownstone mansion was one of the wonders of my child-hood.

All the above are life-trustees of Princeton; and to assist them they have two more bankers, and a Philadelphia lawyer who is a director in the Pennsylvania Railroad, and in the Lehigh Railroad and the Lehigh Coal Company; a cotton manufacturer who is a member of the Republican Campaign Committee; a Pittsburgh merchant who is director in a national bank; the secretary-treasurer of the United Railroads of New Jersey; the president of the United States Trust Company; a publisher who is a director of two banks, a lawyer who is director of two insurance companies, and another who is chairman of a railroad, and another who is attorney for the Prudential Life. No unsound or subversive ideas need apply at Princeton! And the just reward of all this respectability was reaped when H. C. Frick, the steel king, died, and left a great part of his fortune to the university.

Woodrow Wilson made a lot of trouble for these super-plutocratic trustees. He saw that the club system was destroying the intellectual life of the university, and he tried to break it up and introduce a system under which the rich students would at least know the names of the less rich ones. He was bitterly fought at every point by the society group, led by Andrew West, head of the Latin department, and dean of the Graduate School, a college politician who is genial to people he can use, but is a bitter partisan of reaction. This Dean West had a vision of a hyper-exclusive school for graduate students, an ivory tower of classical culture, and he got Mr. Procter, who owns a tower of ivory soap, to offer half a million dollars for this purpose. But Woodrow Wilson objected to the plan and delayed it, and Mr. Procter became angry and withdrew his money—which caused a furious hullabaloo among the Princeton plutocracy, led by Mr. Taylor Pyne, the first grand duke.

For some time the conflict raged, and it was settled in a peculiar way. Dean West got somebody to offer three millions for the proposed school; and that licked Woodrow, and Woodrow bowed his head in submission. It had been possible to hesitate over half a million, but three millions—"flesh and blood cooden bear it!" I am quoting from the delightful scene in Thackeray's "Yellowplush Papers," where "Chawls," who is in the service of the Honorable Algernon Deuceace, is being tempted to do some rascality for "his Exlnsy the Right Honorable Earl of Crabs." At first he resists the temptation; but then his Exlnsy "lugs out a crisp, fluttering, snowy HUNDRED-PUN NOTE! 'You shall have this; and I will, moreover, take you into my service and give you double your present wages.'

"Flesh and blood cooden bear it. 'My lord,' says I, laying my hand upon my busm, 'only give me security, and I'm yours forever.'

"The old noblemin grin'd, and pattid me on the shoulder. 'Right, my lad,' says he, 'right—you're a nice promising youth. Here is the best security.' And he pulls out his pocketbook, returns the hundred-pun bill, and takes out one for fifty. 'Here is half today; tomorrow you shall have the remainder.'" And so Dean West became the master of the Graduate School of Princeton; according to the terms of the gift he and another man hold the purse-strings. Up with the aristocratic tradition, and good-bye to elegant and studied carelessness! Everybody in the Graduate School of Princeton must wear an academic gown for dinner!

They kicked Woodrow Wilson upstairs, and put in his place a Presbyterian clergyman by the name of John Grier Hibben, snob to his fingertips, a timid little man who compensates for his own sheltered life by being in his imaginings a ferocious militarist, clamoring for all kinds of slaughter. He is an active director in half a dozen organizations for the purpose of getting us ready for every war in sight, and only the other day he was calling at Commencement for us to "bring down our fist on the council-table of Europe" and to "take Russia by the throat"—using, by an unfortunate coincidence, the very same words that we heard a few years ago from Wilhelm Hohenzollern! President Hibben was educated at the University of Berlin; a curious fact which I note about one after another of these academic drill-sergeants —Butler of Columbia, Berlin—Lowell of Harvard, Berlin—Smith of Pennsylvania, Goettingen! These we have met so far; and next we shall meet Angell of Yale, Berlin—Wheeler of California, Heidelberg—Wilbur of Stanford, Frankfurt and Munich—everyone of them learned the Goose-step under the Kaiser!

CHAPTER XXV

PEACOCKS AND SLUMS

Evans Clark, now of the Labor Bureau in New York, was for three years a "preceptor" at Princeton, and tried to interest the young men in what was going on in the outside world; among other things he assigned them Walter Lippmann's "Preface to Politics" as a book to read. I remember that I made a diligent "go" at this book, to find out what Lippmann meant and what he wanted; but I never could, and I doubt if any Princeton under-graduate could do more. However, Professor William Starr Myers of the department of history, a popular orator at ladies' clubs, thought it was a terrible book, and pleaded with Clark that he was "taking an unfair advantage of immature minds!" A professor at another university, who knows Professor Myers well, tells me that "he is, next to Cal Coolidge and Ole Hanson, the most consummate ass on radicalism in the country. He is the lion of the afternoon pink teas."

As always, where you have smooth cool lawns with peacocks and lyre-birds on them, you also have vile and filthy slums, in which babies die of typhoid and dysentery, and little children grow up crooked and poisoned for life. In this elegant aristocratic university town are some of the worst slums in the world; the Rev. Edward A. Steiner, author of "The Trail of the Immigrant," was brought to Princeton to preach, and he inspected them, and writes me: "The housing conditions at Princeton were about as I have found in the most congested district of New York. Under the shadow of three million dollar dormitories were tenements of the worst type. They were occupied by colored and white help." *

There was a young social worker, Nell Vincent by name, who was called to act as secretary to the charity organization society of the town. Some common laborers, working on the college buildings, went on strike and began picketing. It was a spontaneous strike, by Italians and other foreigners, and Miss Vincent, who knew their wives and children, tried to organize them, and spoke to them at a meeting, urging them to refrain from violence and abide by the law. The news of this came to the charity organization trustees, and there was a terrible fuss; some of the prominent members of the faculty summoned Miss Vincent to appear before the board, and challenged her for stirring up trouble in the town. One charge they brought against her was that she had never been to church; another was that while living on a "good" street, she had invited the poor to visit her, and the wives and families of Italian laborers trailing up to her door had "lowered the social tone of the street." She had brought into Princeton a critical sentiment, which was most distressing to the authorities of a fashionable university. One professor's wife reported that the attitude of the Italians had entirely changed; she no longer had any pleasure in distributing charity to them, they did not love her any more. President Hibben finally succeeded in patching up the trouble; but he told Miss Vincent, referring to some of the university trustees who are members of the charity board, "You have no idea how I had to argue with them!" In a letter to me Miss Vincent uses the phrase, "the exquisite lie that is Princeton."

In connection with this strike Evans Clark tells an anecdote which throws a bright light on Princeton education. He was invited by a student to lunch on Prospect avenue, where all the rich clubs are. The strikers had quit work on a club building, and were picketing this

* "Some Unsolved Social Problems of a University Town," by Arthur Evans Wood, Assistant Professor of Sociology at the University of Michigan; a thesis of the University of Pennsylvania, published by C. W. Graham, Ann Arbor, Michigan, 1920. This document gives a detailed study of Princeton slums. On page 32 it appears that the infant mortality rate of Princeton in 1916 was 150 per thousand, as against 96 per thousand in New York City.

building, riding up and down on bicycles. "What are those men doing?" asked the student, and Clark explained—they were pickets. "What are pickets?" was the next question. They went inside, continuing their conversation at the club dining-table; here were a score of college men, and all asked questions, and hardly one knew what the word "picket" means, and hardly one knew there was a strike of the laborers working on Princeton's exclusive new club!

Six or seven years ago we had a chance to make war on Mexico; and the former president of Princeton took us part way in, while the then president of Princeton tried furiously to get us all the way in. It happened that Norman Angell, the English writer and pacifist, was invited to Princeton to lecture, and made some casual reference to the militarist propaganda against Mexico—and so got himself into a bewildering experience. Picture him, a foreigner from a land of politeness, an invited guest at a university supposed to represent culture and urbanity; and the president of this university, a clergyman of Jesus Christ, springs up in the audience and challenges him. "Do you believe in murder? Do you believe in allowing American citizens to be murdered in Mexico?"

The lecturer tries politely to answer, but is not allowed to finish. "Answer me, yes or no!" cries the president of Princeton. "Do you believe in murder?" And when the Englishman still fails to answer yes or no, the shepherd of Jesus shakes his finger at him, trembling with rage and screaming again and again, "Answer me, yes or no! Do you believe in murder?" Both Evans Clark and his wife were witnesses of this extraordinary scene, and described it to me in detail, not resenting my incredulity, but patiently assuring me that they were not exaggerating, it happened just so. And a letter from Mr. Angell substantiates it.

In the year 1916 arrangements had been made to have President David Starr Jordan of Stanford speak in a hall on the campus; but President Hibben, a life-long friend of Jordan's, refused him the use of the building, and he had to speak in the Presbyterian church. Two or three students had organized an anti-war society, and they invited Professor Henry Mussey of Columbia, but could

9

not get either a college hall or a church of Jesus Christ; they rented an obscure room in the labor quarters of the town, and here the lecture took place. It had not gone very far before Frank Jewett Mather, professor of art—sixty years of age, and old enough to know better, you would think—stuck in his head, and then slammed the door with a loud noise. Apparently he went off for re-inforcements, for ten minutes later he flung the door open, and entered with a professor of French and an-other professor. These three stamped over the hall, up one aisle and down another, shouting comments on the lecturer's remarks, and not stopping at personal insults. In order to appreciate the scene you would have to know Henry Mussey—so gentle and charming, rosy-faced, smil-ing like a cherub just arrived from heaven. And here was Evans Clark, a young preceptor, presiding, and he had to get up several times and ask three full professors of his university to behave themselves like gentlemen! Finally, they marched out, shouting "Vive la France!" "Was this before we went into the war?" I asked, and the answer was: "It was after Princeton went into the war, but before the rest of the United States did."

Also Mr. Clark's wife told me some of her adven-tures. She is Frieda Kirchwey, daughter of a former dean of the Columbia University Law School; she is one of the editors of the "Nation," and as lovely a person as you will find. But you know how it is with these proper society people, their imaginations always run to foulness concerning people who differ with them; they cannot see how anybody who refuses to believe in class privilege and wage slavery can lead a decent life. Before the Clarks had been at Princeton a few months, a head of one of the departments asked if it was true, as reported, that their marriage was a trial one! Then, in a rail-road train, sitting behind two socially exclusive professors' wives, Frieda Kirchwey became acquainted with Princeton ideas about herself. At this time she had a job in New York and commuted every day; the trip takes an hour and a half each way, and you must admit that a woman who stands that all the year round must love her hus-band a good deal. But here sat the two ladies, gossip-ing about pacifism, and the moral obloquy attendant thereon. "My dear," said one, "they say he's married, but nobody ever sees her; she doesn't live with him—except maybe on vacations, of course. Nobody knows where he picked her up."

To balance this, you should have a glimpse of the morals of Princeton's chosen ones. Let me remind you that President Hibben is a clergyman, and that Dean West of the Graduate School, who makes the students wear academic gowns at dinner, is a clergyman's son. Now read the following paragraph from a letter of Miss Vincent:

You of course are familiar with the time-honored custom of college commencements, class tents in and around which old grads let loose and get messed up generally, with booze and women. Well, in Princeton these tents are set up on vacant lots around in the town, and the townspeople feel that it is a most degrading influence upon their children, who hear the ribald songs and see sights that even grown people stay within doors to avoid if possible, during this grand and glorious reunion of the sons of Princeton. A protest as to this condition came up at a civic meeting. A committee of which I was chairman was appointed to meet Dean McClenahan of Princeton and the dean of the Graduate School. We met. The genial dean of the Graduate School after a few innocent questions said, "Why yes, Miss Vincent, you see we can't very well have the reunion tents on the campus, because it would reflect upon the university's good name, and would influence parents against it. But we do need to foster the reunions, because we need the support of the old graduates to keep up the college spirit."

You see, they are not really concerned about morality; like all the rest of the bourgeois world, they are merely concerned not to be found out; that, and to protect property. Above all things else, there must be no taint of social protest at Princeton. I have a rather pathetic letter from a young man who was a preceptor at Princeton for a year. He admits that he was dropped from the university because of his "radical point of view," but he asks me not to mention his name or to tell his story. He still holds to his Socialist philosophy, but he believes that his best work "can be done as a research worker rather than as a propagandist." He was only twenty-four at that time, and he was lacking in "tact and circumspection." He adds: "Of course I do not think that in justice I should have been dropped. Robert McElroy of Princeton has been guilty of more propaganda in recent years than I could put forth in a lifetime. He stayed because his propaganda was for hundred per cent Americanism." In order to make the significance of this clear to you, I mention that Professor McElroy is head of the Department of History and Politics at Princeton University, and at the same time was for three years educational director of the National Security League!

In the teaching of the social sciences Princeton is a perfect illustration of intellectual dry rot. One who has been through the mill tells me that it is "a combination of conventional history—anecdotes and dynasties— metaphysical economics, legalistic and scholastic political science, and no sociology worthy of the name." How much they respect the facts in history you may judge from a remark made by a Princeton professor to a friend of mine—that "Charles Beard is no gentleman to speak of the founders of the Constitution as he does!" Also from the fact that the professor of economic history is George B. McClellan, former mayor of New York City. Mr. McClellan bears a name honored in our history, and he was invited to lend this name to serve as a screen for the thugs of Tammany Hall while they plundered the people of the metropolis. He loaned it, and for seven years protected the keepers of brothels and dives, also the public service corporations which had put up the campaign funds to elect him; a form of public activity so much appreciated by Princeton that they gave him an LL.D., and made him a trustee as well as a professor!

I talked with the wife of a Princeton instructor, who was performing some clerical duties for her husband, and thereby had opportunities to "listen in" on Princeton education. She tells me of juniors and seniors in the great fashionable university, who would ask naive and childish questions about things that were going on in the world, revealing ignorance of which grammar school children would be ashamed. These elegant young idlers had been to college for three years, some of them four years, and had not learned to read a newspaper! Yet they were all eager to go to war, for a cause of which they understood nothing, and of which their leaders understood no more— as they proved to us before they got us out of the mess.

Two years later there came as it were a colossal volcanic eruption, whereby Princeton culture, Princeton ideals and Princeton pieties were exploded over the entire globe. At present writing it appears that it will take mankind a hundred years to recover from the disasters that resulted. You, plain working men or business men who glance at this book, and think that college stupidity and corruption does not concern you, take this one fact and ponder it: millions of German and Austrian babies are hopelessly deformed by rickets, tens of millions of Russian peasants have perished of starvation, three hundred billions of human treasure and thirty million human lives were thrown away to no purpose—because, forty-five years ago, one student of Princeton College, Thomas Woodrow Wilson by name, was studying Hebrew, Greek, and imbecile theology, when he should have been studying economics, geography, and social engineering!

CHAPTER XXVI

THE BULL-DOG'S DEN

A short journey on Mr. Morgan's Pennsylvania Railroad, with its Johns Hopkins, Princeton, Yale, Bryn Mawr, Wilson, Lafayette, Rutgers, Teachers' College, Lehigh, Pittsburgh, Massachusetts Tech and University of Pennsylvania directors, and another short journey on Mr. Morgan's New Haven Railroad, with its recent Harvard overseer for chairman, a Brown trustee for vice-president, a recent Yale president for director, and a member of the Yale advisory board, a Washburn trustee, a Wellesley trustee, a Pratt Institute trustee and two Harvard visitors for directors, and we find ourselves at the home of Princeton's age-long rival, Old Eli; another carefully guarded fortress of the plutocracy, a ruling class munition factory, turning out mental bombs and poison gas for use in the class war.

There was a time when Yale was called "democratic." This did not mean, of course, that the students had any use for the "muckers" of the town of New Haven, but merely that all the students knew one another; they were all bound for the top, and all stood together. But the secret societies came in, and now Yale is just what Princeton is, a place where the sons of millionaires draw apart and live exclusive lives. These secret societies run not merely the student life, they run the institution, through the alumni who belonged to the societies when they were undergraduates, and are now getting their sons and their friends' sons in, and doing everything to hold up the power of "Skull and Bones."

For this new imitation piracy the young fellows begin their training long before they see the college; there are eight or ten fashionable preparatory schools, which also have their fraternities, so that the lads are intriguing and wire-pulling and imitating one another's imbecilities before they get out of short trousers. It is a rigid caste system, a set of artificial ideals and standards—clothes, accent, athletic prestige, money-spending, all the arcana of snobbery. The older fellows are watching, criticizing, patronizing; you "make" the proper "frat" at your "prep" school, and then go to the great university, knowing that you are watched every moment by sharply critical eyes. For a year or two you bend every thought and effort to being just exactly what the great social leaders dictate; and then comes the day of anguish, when the "tapping" is done, and you are swept on to a lifetime of triumph, or cast down into everlasting humiliation.

The standards of these fashionable societies permit you to get drunk and to acquire your due share of venereal disease, but they do not permit you to wear the wrong color tie, or to use the wrong kind of slang, or to smoke the wrong tobacco. Needless to say, they permit no smallest trace of eccentricity in ideas, and here we have a mob sentiment which supplants all academic discipline. Fifteen or twenty years ago Alexander Irvine was pastor of a church at New Haven, and thrilled some students with visions of social reform. Jack London came in 1905, and gave his famous lecture, "Revolution," and prominent society students sat up all night to wrangle with him. But the war has swept all this away, there is no longer any trace of liberalism at Yale that I could find. Instead, there is discipline and herd sentiment. "This is the way we do it at Yale," and woe to the youngster who tries to do it differently!

One of its products of which Yale does not boast is Sinclair Lewis. (He ran away, and came to Helicon Hall to learn about Socialism!) He told me how the men in his class hated compulsory chapel, and proposed to organize and protest; they would get up early in the morning and march through the gateway, and defy the authorities. To a man they "cussed" the chapel; yet, so completely did the spirit of Yale conquer them, when they came to be seniors, and had to vote on college customs, they voted for compulsory chapel! "After all, it's a good thing, it helps to get the men together and make college spirit!"

Yale was founded on "the Bible, rum and niggers"—that is to say, the slave trade; and it stands today four square on wage slavery. It has an endowment of thirty-two million dollars; and needless to say, the interlocking directorate is in full charge. The board includes: the president of the New York Trust Company, who is a director in a trolley company, a fire insurance company, and a securities company; the president of the Merchants' National Bank of Boston; the president of the Title Guarantee and Trust Company of New York; the president of the Westinghouse Company of Pittsburgh; a Chicago dry goods merchant, who is a director of a great railroad system and a national bank; a silk manufacturer who is a bank trustee; the publisher of a leading newspaper, also a director of the Associated Press and two insurance corporations; another newspaper publisher who is a director in the Erie Railroad; the chief counsel of the Connecticut Trolley Company; and, to make the group entirely safe and conservative, four ministers of the gospel of Jesus Christ. Quite recently I saw a document which was sent out to the Yale alumni, asking their opinions on a group of candidates for the new elections; and at the top of the list stood the name of America's prize Tory, ex-President and Chief Justice of the Supreme Court William Howard Taft.

Taft is a Yale man, and is proud to boast himself a pupil of the late William Graham Sumner, professor of political economy, and a prime minister in the empire of plutocratic education. I doubt if there has ever been a more capitalistic economist than Sumner, a man who took a ghoulish delight in the glorifying of commercialism. He is the author of a book "What Social Classes Owe to Each Other"; reading this book you discover that what the rich owe is to enjoy their riches, while what the poor owe is to keep out of the way. Never that I know of has stark brutal selfishness been so deified, and covered by the mantle of science. "Every man and woman in society has one big duty. That is to take care of his or her own self." Such was the first commandment according to Sumner; and the second was like unto it: "Mind your own business."

Of course, to such a man there was no person so irritating as a "reformer" of any sort, and he never wearied of pouring out ridicule upon the man who imagined he could do anything to make society better. "Society does not need any care or supervision," decreed the all-wise professor, and that settled it; the hard young Roman rulers thronged to his classes, and absorbed his gospel of the wolf-pack, and went out with their minds encased in a triple-plated Harveyized steel armor of prejudice, ready to commit any crimes that might be necessary to the preserving of their privileges. Today the pupils of Professor Sumner are walking upon the faces of labor and stamping out the hopes of mankind in hundreds of the leading industries of the country, and in the highest posts of the government, from the United States Supreme Court down. Such a man is worth many billions of dollars to the plutocrats; they pay him a few thousand a year, and tickle his vanity with solemnly conferred degrees and an academic robe to wear, and at the end of his thirty years of service the editors of the "Yale Review" celebrate him in a series of articles as "Pioneer—Teacher—Inspirer—Idealist—Man—and Veteran."

Professor Sumner's place is now ably taken by one of his pupils, Professor Albert G. Keller, author of "Societal Evolution," which a well-known American sociologist describes to me as "a lengthy example of secondary rationalization to prove the immorality of social reform." In case you do not understand these scientific technicalities, let me explain that Professor Keller is employed by the New England plutocracy to act as intellectual night-watchman for their property; and that having got his orders what to teach, he then invents an elaborate set of reasons to convince himself and the world that this is the right thing to teach, and that in so teaching he is protecting society.

Meantime, what of the men at Yale who happen to have some vision of social service and human sympathy?

I managed to find one who had been there, and for a while thought he was going to make a success in the great university. He invented during the war a device to destroy submarines, and the United States government took it up. Word came to the interlocking trustees, and the secretary of the corporation, Mr. Anson Phelps Stokes, sent for the professor in haste. There was a story in this—some advertising for Old Eli! Simon Lake, a Yale man, had invented the submarine, and now another Yale man was to wipe it out! "For God, for country, and for Yale!" Mr. Stokes with eager fingers began turning the pages of an encyclopedia, to find out the date of Simon Lake's invention, and the date of his sojourn in the university!

But this bit of favor was quickly lost, when the professor took up the troubles of his colleagues, who found it impossible to exist upon their salaries, with the cost of living going up day by day. My friend had spent ten years preparing himself for university teaching; he had spent eight years teaching at Clark, at Harvard and at Yale, and now he was getting fourteen hundred dollars! He insisted that he and his colleagues should get more; and the secretary was irritated by this agitation. Mr. Stokes comes from a wealthy family himself, but believes that other people should wait for their rewards in heaven. He wrote my friend that college professors should not interfere with matters which are not their own business; also that he had never advised Yale instructors to get married!

What this means is that such universities as Yale, Harvard and Johns Hopkins rely upon their prestige to get them teachers, paying starvation wages, and tacitly establishing a celibate order in the service of the plutocracy. I note in my morning newspaper that Northwestern University, a great religious institution at Evanston, Ill., has come out into the open, and has refused to engage married men as professors, explaining that it cannot afford to pay a salary for two. So you see, we are literally realizing the sarcastic observation of Professor Spingarn, that there are three sexes in America—men, women and professors. There is only one step more to be taken, and I expect some morning to pick up my paper and read that the president of some great university has announced that, inasmuch as college professors who cannot afford to marry sometimes set bad moral examples for the students, it is now ordained that none but eunuchs need apply for jobs. If this arrangement has proved useful to the ruling classes of Turkey, and for the choir boys of the Vatican, why should it not be given a trial in our plutocratic empire?

CHAPTER XXVII

THE UNIVERSITY OF THE BLACK HAND

We have completed a survey of our five largest Eastern universities, Columbia, Harvard, Pennsylvania, Princeton and Yale; we shall now cross the continent, to the Western domains of our interlocking directorate. We may begin our journey on the New York Central, which is a Vanderbilt-Morgan road, and has a Columbia and a Cornell and a Rochester University trustee for directors, a recent Yale and New York University trustee for director, a Lake Erie College trustee for vice-president, and a Cornell trustee for vice-president, also a Guaranty Trust and two National City Bank directors; and continue it on the Michigan Central under the same auspices; then on the Illinois Central, which has a Columbia trustee and an Armour Institute trustee and a recent University of Chicago trustee, and a Knox and a Rockford College trustee for directors, and one First National, one Guaranty Trust, and two National City Bank directors; then on the Missouri Pacific, with a Brown University and a Vassar College and a Middlebury College trustee for directors, and a New York University council member for director and a Massachusetts Tech trustee for vice-president, and one Equitable Trust and two Guaranty Trust directors; finishing on the Union Pacific, which has a Columbia trustee for chairman, also a Rutgers College trustee and two Massachusetts Tech trustees and a Hebrew Tech trustee for directors, also two Equitable Trust, two Guaranty Trust, and three National City Bank directors. We may announce our coming by the Western Union, which has a Columbia trustee for president, and on its directorate two Columbia trustees, a Princeton trustee, a Massachusetts Tech and Hebrew Tech trustee, and

a recent Harvard overseer. Arriving in San Francisco
we shall be welcomed by the interlocking directorate in
charge of railroads, telegraphs, telephones, electricity,
land, water, gas—and education.

Across the bay from San Francisco, high up above the
city of Berkeley, stands the University of California, a
medieval fortress from which the intellectual life of the
state is dominated; and here also we find one of the grand
dukes of the plutocracy in charge—Mr. William H.
Crocker, whose father looted the Southern Pacific railroads, covering all California. Mr. Crocker is a "social
leader," and active head of the Republican political machine, which runs the government and is run by the
finance of the state. We shall feel at home with Mr.
Crocker, when we discover that he is a director of the
Equitable Trust Company of New York, one of the five
great banking institutions of the Money Trust, and that
he sits on this board with Mr. Coudert, attorney for
the plutocracy and trustee of Columbia University; also
when we learn that he was a director of the Parkside
Land Company, all of whose officers were indicted in the
San Francisco graft scandal.

Associated with Mr. Crocker in the running of the
University of California is Mortimer Fleishhacker, the
biggest banker in San Francisco, president of the Anglo-
California Trust Company, and first vice-president of the
Anglo and London National Bank. I can give you a
glimpse of this gentleman's activities, for the other day
I met a young newspaper man who had shipped on one of
the fishing vessels which constitute the "hell fleet of the
Pacific." Mr. Fleishhacker is vice-president of the Union
Fish Company, which is paying men $5 a ton for catch-
ing and salting cod, which are sold in San Francisco for
$160 a ton, the incidental costs being practically nothing.
Mr. Fleishhacker is also vice-president of the Alaska
Canning Company, whose workers are hired by a Chinese
contractor for $34 a month and board—which consists
of two meals a day of scurvy diet, and only one cup of
water a day. In the canning factories they work from
3 a. m. to 9 p. m., and they sleep in ramshackle bunk-
houses, with no heat, no light and tide water wetting the
floor. Eight of them died of small-pox while my friend
was there.

As aid on his university board Mr. Fleishhacker has his attorney, Mr. Guy C. Earl, vice-president of two power companies and two electric companies, and a very crude and subservient newspaper, the Los Angeles "Express"; also Mr. Dickson, proprietor of this same "Express." Also we find the president of San Francisco's gas company, Mr. Britten, an active enemy of every public ownership movement; Mr. Moffitt, vice-president of the First National Bank, an honest believer in capitalism at its worst, and a furious reactionary; also Mr. Bowles, president of the First National Bank of Oakland, and director in a railway, a water company, and a timber company; also Mr. Cochran, vice-president of the Southern California Edison Company, president of a life insurance company, a director in Mr. Fleishhacker's bank, and a director in half a dozen large financial institutions; also Mr. Foster, another director in Mr. Fleishhacker's bank. Mr. Foster lives in Marin county, just north of the university, and is known as the Duke of Marin; so you see these medieval titles are not entirely the product of my muck-raking imagination.

In addition to these seven, there are two wealthy corporation attorneys, one of them counsel for the Catholic Church, and for the grafters who were put on trial in 1910; a Catholic priest who is a close adviser of the archbishop who runs the San Francisco school system; and the wife of Sartori, one of the largest bankers in Los Angeles, who, as I happen to know, helped to finance the concession-hunting expedition of Vanderlip in Kamtchatka. These are the appointed regents; and in addition there are some who hold ex-officio—the Governor of the state, the Lieutenant Governor, the Speaker of the Assembly, etc. These do not matter, being merely machine politicians, selected by Mr. Crocker and Mr. Fleishhacker and two or three others in private conference, nominated by these gentlemen's newspapers, and elected by these gentlemen's checks.

Besides the state government and the university, and their own banks and railroads, Mr. Crocker and Mr. Fleishhacker control for the interlocking directorate a vast network of gas and electric companies, street railways, land companies, and power companies. The recent development of water power has made this the dominant industry of the state, and the means whereby the other industries are subordinated. Mr. Fleishhacker is president of the Great Western Power Company, and of the California Electric Generating Company, and a director in the Northwestern Electric Company; while his attorney, Mr. Earl, also a trustee of the university, is vice-president of two of these concerns. Eight other regents are active directors of such power companies; and we shall see shortly how they use their university as a propaganda department against power development by the state. Mr. Foster, the Duke of Marin, is president of the ferry company, and a director of the United Railroads of San Francisco, which has been a leading agency in corrupting the city for the past twenty years. Mr. Crocker is a director in the committee which is now trying to reorganize these United Railroads, after the looters have got through with them. We shall see how these gentlemen use their university as a strike-breaking agency for the benefit of their street railways, their ferries and their gas and electric companies.

One might think that the plutocracy of California ought to be content to leave its educational business in the hands of such a board; nevertheless, they have felt it necessary to organize an independent vigilance committee, to supplement Mr. Crocker and Mr. Fleishhacker. The prime mover in this action was Mr. Harry Haldeman, president of the Pacific Pipe & Supply Company of Los Angeles, a gentleman whose qualifications to direct the higher education of California were acquired while driving a stage. Mr. Haldeman founded what he called the Commercial Federation of California; later, learning from the war the advantages of camouflage, he changed the name to the Better America Federation. He went out among the interlocking directorate and raised the sum of eight hundred thousand dollars, to be expended for the purpose of keeping California capitalist. The Better America Federation is a kind of "black hand" society of the rich, a terrorist organization which does not stop short of crime, as I know from personal experience. It works in league with several depraved newspapers—the Los Angeles "Times," owned by Harry Chandler, speculator in Mexican revolutions, and co-partner with Mrs. Sartori's husband in the Vanderlip Kamtchtkan adventure; the Los

Angeles "Express," with two university regents in charge; the San Francisco "Chronicle," owned by Mike de Young, whom Ambrose Bierce pictured hanging on all the gibbets of the world; the San Francisco "Bulletin," whose bottomless venality has been revealed in Fremont Older's book. I have told in "The Brass Check," Chapter LXVI, the story of how "The Dugout," a returned soldier's paper in Los Angeles, was smashed because its publisher would not have it used as a strike-breaking agency. The secret service branch of the Better America Federation committed a dozen separate crimes in the doing of this job, and much of this was proved at the publisher's trial.

The Better America Federation investigates every person who runs for office in California, and black-lists him unless he is one hundred per cent capitalist. It browbeats public officials and slanders them in its newspapers; it causes the raiding of labor offices, and the jailing without trial of labor organizers; and among its other activities it runs the educational system of California, including the state university. The spirit in which it works is revealed in a bill which it came near to pushing through the last California legislature, providing for cancelling the license of any school teacher who, discussing the constitution of the United States with a pupil "shall express to such pupil any opinion or argument in favor of making any change in any provision."

How this organization puts pressure on university professors is a matter about which you do not have to take my word; you may have the word of Mr. Harry Haldeman, president of the Better America Federation. In the San Francisco "Call" for January 20, 1922, I find an article occupying the top of seven columns, "Aims of Better America Body Told Business Men of San Francisco." This is a report of a luncheon at the St. Francis Hotel, in which Mr. Haldeman explained his work to the president and vice-president of the Southern Pacific Railroad, and a group of such leading interlocking directors. Said Mr. Haldeman: "Through the children of the best business families throughout the land, who are attending universities, we are having students of radical tendencies watched. We are receiving reports of what is going on, both as to students and teachers that uphold radical doctrines and views."

So here is the spy system in our universities; college boys and girls set to tale-bearing on their fellows and on their teachers! On such ignorant and garbled reports professors in the University of California are black-listed for promotion; or they are quietly let out without explanation —or with just a lie or two. When they apply for jobs in other places, letters are written to keep them from getting those jobs. School teachers are black-listed over the entire state; students in the university who graduate with honors are unable to get teaching positions, because the employment system maintained by the university is under the control of this kid-gloved Black Hand.

The active manager of this organization until a few months ago was Mr. Woodworth Clum, a lawyer, author of a pamphlet, "America Is Calling," the substance of which is that America is calling her school children to mob their fellow students with whose opinions they do not agree. Mr. Clum was formerly secretary of the Greater Iowa Association, at a salary of ten thousand dollars a year; also secretary to the Iowa Commission to the Panama-Pacific Exposition. He left the state after a three years' controversy over the fact that this Commission had failed to file a proper statement of its expenditure of public funds with the state accountant, twenty thousand dollars being missing; also after a typewriter belonging to the Commission had been traced to the office of the Greater Iowa Association; also after Mr. Clum had walked across the street and brutally struck in the face a Civil War veteran, wearing a Grand Army button, because this old man was deaf and did not hear a band playing the Star-Spangled Banner some distance away, and therefore had failed to remove his hat.

Now, here is Mr. Clum's new organization, the kid-gloved Black Hand of California, working in close alliance with the "open-shoppers" and labor union smashers of the state, and holding over school teachers and college professors the lash, not merely of black-list, slander and starvation, but of sentence to fourteen years in prison. For you must understand that we have a "criminal syndicalism" law in California, and this is applied to you, not merely if you belong to a radical labor union, but if you take any action on behalf of the victims of the Black Hand. This organization has a private army of sluggers,

called the "citizens' police," which maintains a standing
offer of fifty dollars for every arrest of a "radical," and
three hundred dollars for every conviction. As I write
this book, one J. P. McDonald is arrested at Long Beach,
California, for asking signatures to a petition to President
Harding for the release of political prisoners—this petition being one which was signed by three hundred thousand American citizens and presented to the President by
a delegation of some thirty leaders of liberal thought.
Holding over this workingman's head the threat of prose-
cution for "criminal syndicalism," the police persuaded
him to plead guilty to vagrancy—though he had money in
his pocket and a job. They promised him he would get
thirty days, and the judge gave him six months, and
grinned at him. Such is California, described by Romain
Rolland as "Land of Orange Groves and Jails"; and
such is the atmosphere of espionage and terrorism in
which is conducted the University of the Black Hand.

CHAPTER XXVIII

THE FORTRESS OF MEDIEVALISM

My first visit to Berkeley was in the winter of 1909-10.
I had come to see a professor—I shall not name him, since
he does not welcome publicity; suffice it to say that he is
one of the world's leading scientists, and in any country
in Europe would be named among a dozen greatest contributors to advanced knowledge. He was educated in
Europe, and had come to the great California university,
thinking he would be welcomed as at home. Shortly after
his arrival came "Charter Day," and he was invited to a
grand academic banquet, a function which he described
to me with infinite amusement.

There was a table of honor across the front of the
room, raised above the others, and at this table sat
the president of the university, and on his right
hand the grand duke of the interlocking regents, and on his
left hand the second grand duke, and all the robber
lords and barons of the state carefully ranged
according to their financial standing, looked up in
the latest Moody's Manual, or Dun or Bradstreet, or
wherever it is that you find these things. At the other

tables, tapering away from the royal presence, were placed the deans and heads of departments, the professors, the assistant professors, the instructors, all graded according to the amount of their salaries, and any slightest variation in the order of precedence jealously looked out for and resented. My friend the scientist was put in his pecuniary proper place; the fact that he was a master mind who would have occupied the seat of honor at any function of any university faculty in Europe, made no slightest difference; he was not even asked to meet the interlocking regents, nor were they aware of his existence. The president met such great ones, and shook hands with them, for he was a fifteen thousand dollar a year man; but my scientist friend was only a four or five thousand dollar a year man, and was expected to stay with his own kind.

Also, while on this visit to Berkeley, I talked with the wife of a professor; the ladies, you know, have an especially acute sense for social matters, and often have a pungent way of expressing what they feel. This lady had been walking on the beach at Del Monte, the exclusive resort of the California plutocracy. Perhaps she wasn't meant to be there; anyhow, there came strolling toward her the president of the university, with two or three of the wives of his weathiest regents. They were coquettishly and elaborately got up, and he was indulging in elephantine playfulness, talking to them about "getting their tootsies wet"—crude efforts of a man of majesty and learning to descend to social dalliance. He stopped in front of the wife of his professor and spoke to her, but did not introduce her to the other ladies, a grave and intentional discourtesy. Instead of that, he looked at her sternly and said: "I wish you to know that I have no use whatever for science."

This, you must understand, to the wife of a man who was supposed to be discovering some of nature's most vital secrets! I asked in bewilderment just what could have been the motive for such a remark, and the explanation was that scientists sometimes think themselves of importance, and it is necessary to academic discipline that they should be put in their place. This same scientist was instrumental in bringing to the university half a dozen of the greatest men of Europe as lecturers—Arrhenius, de Vries, Sir William Ramsay. They were paid inadequately for

10

long journey, and my friend suggested that it might
good idea to reward them with an honorary degree.
President Wheeler, with instant decision: "I give no
ees to scientists!" "Whom do you give them to?"
l my friend, and the answer was: "I give them to peo-
f importance—to statesmen, public men, college pres-
ts." This was Benjamin Ide Wheeler, ex-professor
ie German Kaiser, and tireless singer of the Kaiser's
ses, holder of a Heidelberg degree, and of honorary
ees from all the great Eastern centers of the interlock-
directorate, Princeton, Harvard, Brown, Yale, Johns
kins, Dartmouth and Columbia. He called himself a
al, but never enough to offend Mrs. Hearst, who gave
university a Greek theater, with her son's name carved
ss the front of the stage.

While I was in Berkeley there was a scandal at the uni-
ity, because of the sudden appointment of a new pro-
or to be dean of the Graduate School. This was
id P. Barrows, now president of the university, and
rson whose career is of interest to us. He is a prod-
of the University of California, and was finished in
holas Murray Butler's educational enameling machine.
nce he went to be superintendent of schools of the city
Manila, and later on director of education for the Phil-
ne Islands. Having received a thorough training in
erialism, he came home to proclaim the gospel of the
led fist in our empire of raisins and prunes.

Dean Barrows was a fighting man, and became imme-
ely active in university politics. You may be startled
lear that anything so dubious as "politics" exists in a
rersity; but if you believe in applied imperialism, and
t to apply it to those about you, you are apt to find
le of them resisting, and you will have to put them
n, and put up others who are willing to obey you and
mote your interests. So Barrows became a tireless
rersity politician, and he and his subordinates also be-
le active in the outside politics of their city and state.
it happens, Berkeley had a large working class popu-
n, and a strong Socialist sentiment, and naturally
re is no higher duty that an imperialist college dean can
form than to crush Socialism in his home town.

I have described the university as a medieval fortress
a hill. You thought, no doubt, I was just slinging

language; but consider the situation. The university has nothing to do with Berkeley, it is not a part of the city, it pays no taxes, either to city or state; nevertheless, it lays claim to run the affairs of the city, and does so. If there are any charters or city contracts to be drawn, the university professors do it, and they do it in the interests of the university, and of the university's interlocking regents. If there is a school superintendent or a mayor to be selected, the university machine is ready with a university man. It is the established custom that one member of the school board of Berkeley shall be a university professor, and you always find this professor voting on the side of reaction and special privilege. For example, the law provides that insurance on school buildings be placed with the companies which make the lowest bids; the school board wished to violate this law, and a Socialist member of the school board fought for a whole day to prevent the violation, and was beaten by the vote of the university professor. When election time comes round, the university goes into the campaign as one man to "smash the Socialists." The university machine circulates slanders against the Socialist administration, and university students are registered and voted wholesale for the plutocracy. The university machine selects the local judges, and the Key Route, a street railroad, puts up the money to elect them—this money being voted by directors who are university regents. In one campaign Stitt Wilson, Socialist mayor of Berkeley, read from the platform the affidavit of a student to the effect that the president of the student body had stated that he had received five thousand dollars from the Key Route, to be used on the campus to beat the Socialist ticket.

Of course the Key Route expects to be paid back for this, and presents its bill whenever there is a strike of its workers. It would be too much to expect that the interlocking directorate should own and run a university, and then, in an emergency like a strike, should see eight or ten thousand young men sitting by entirely idle, except for fool studies. When strikes occur, the interlocking newspapers paint terrifying pictures of the public emergency, and the interlocking deans organize the students and give them special credits for the time they spend as "great American heroes." In 1913 came a gas and electric

strike, and the president of the gas company, a member of the board of regents, called on his university for help, and the boys from the engineering department were given credit for a full semester's work for their services as "scabs." After that, when the Socialists proposed a measure to have the regents elected by the people, the labor leaders of California said they weren't interested; working men didn't go to college, so why should they bother about such matters?

And just as this University of the Black Hand seeks to run the city, so also it seeks to run the state. Just now there is a bitter struggle under way, over a bill to enable cities and towns to combine and develop water power for their own use. The special interests of California are fighting this measure tooth and nail; and prominent among them are the ten university regents who are interested in power companies. Do these gentlemen fail to make use of their university in the struggle? If you expect such a thing, you do not know our empire of raisins and prunes!

The farmers of this empire are organized into farm bureaus at state expense. These bureaus are supposed to be run by the farmers themselves, but the university appoints "experts," and the state pays them to act as advisers and guiding lights to the farm bureaus. During this campaign it was observed that resolutions against the hydro-electric power bill kept coming in from the farm bureaus; which seemed unaccountable, because in the state legislature the farmers' bloc was unanimous for the bill. The mystery was traced down, and in every case it was discovered that the treacherous resolution had come from the "experts"—university men, appointed by university regents in the interest of their privately owned power plants! And at the same time in San Francisco, Mr. Crocker, grand duke of the regents, has just succeeded in getting Rudolph Spreckles, a liberal capitalist, out of control of the First National Bank, because Mr. Spreckles has committed the crime of supporting this power bill!

CHAPTER XXIX

THE DEAN OF IMPERIALISM

We return to David P. Barrows to follow his career as he rises to the heights of academic prominence and power. For seven years he stumped the state of California, proclaiming the destiny of the Stars and Stripes to float from the North Pole to the South. The world was to be divided up, it was our business to get our share; we should win because we were better organized, more efficient; the world would not tolerate small nations; strong men must rule. And presently came a chance for strong men to rule in Mexico; but the strong men had at their head a weakling by the name of Woodrow Wilson, who refused to act. You might think there would be some impropriety, some violation of military precedence, in a university dean's attacking a former university president, who had become President of the United States; but when Woodrow Wilson took Vera Cruz, and then refused to take the rest of Mexico, Dean Barrows rushed to the front, denouncing him before chambers of commerce, and being reported in the interlocking newspapers.

We shall note in the course of this book many cases of college professors forbidden to take part in "outside activities," and especially to get themselves into the newspapers. The professor's place is the classroom, we are told; and to this there is only one exception—when the professor is advocating more loot for the exploiters who pay him his salary. Shortly after this Vera Cruz affair the San Francisco "Star" published some revelations concerning our imperialist dean, stating that at the very time he was campaigning for intervention, he was vice-president of the Vera Cruz Land & Cattle Company. A friend who knows Dean Barrows well, defended him to me by the statement that his holdings in this company were not valuable. When I asked how valuable they might have become if the United States had conquered Mexico, my friend changed the subject.

The next part of the world to be divided up was Siberia, and our imperialist dean was made a colonel, and put in charge of the Army Intelligence Service. So far as I know, he has not told the full story of his adventures in

Siberia, but we may glean hints in the press of China and Japan, which charged that Colonel Barrows was an accomplice of Semenoff, the Cossack bandit, in a plot to separate Mongolia from the Chinese Empire and place it under the rule of Semenoff and the American concession-hunters. The situation in Siberia at this time was a complicated one. Kolchak was the official representative of the allies, fighting the Bolsheviki with American money and supplies. Semenoff revolted against Kolchak, and set himself up as an independent bandit, controlling a part of Mongolia. He was intimate with Colonel Barrows at this time, and a leading Chinese journalist wrote an article in "Millard's Review," in which he referred to Barrows as "an unscrupulous and unprincipled American adventurer." It was rumored at this time, and has since been thoroughly proven, that Semenoff entered the pay of the Japanese, and was used by them in their Siberian intrigues; Colonel Barrows himself admitted this in an interview published in the San Francisco "Chronicle," April 15, 1922.

Semenoff was in America at this time, backed by the Japanese intriguers, but supposed to represent the anti-Bolshevik cause. Naturally he was welcomed by his friend, Colonel Barrows, and ardently defended in the interlocking newspapers. Certain "Bolshevik" agitators pointed out that Semenoff had fired upon and murdered a number of American soldiers; and just what does our academic colonel think about the murdering of American soldiers by a Cossack bandit in Japanese pay? Our colonel declares that he investigated the matter, and that it was merely owing to "a misunderstanding"; General Semenoff wanted to move a train across a sector at Chita, where the Americans refused to let him go, and so he shot and killed a few American soldiers. That is all! The colonel describes Semenoff as "a man of iron, both in courage and military leadership. He was brave. . . . Semenoff did not thing (evidently a misprint in the newspaper) of which I disapproved. He accepted the help of the Japanese . . . but even in this he was helpless; when the allies refused their aid, he was compelled to accept Japanese assistance. . . . Whatever he did, it was with the sole aim of beating the Bolsheviki, whom he hated."

This was at the time that Senator Borah was exposing Semenoff's infamies. Borah read extracts from a speech by an American Railway Commission officer, who stated that Semenoff "carried with him on his so-called 'summer car' a harem of thirty of the most beautiful women I ever saw." Mr. Borah offered to show a picture of the car, and we wonder if this was one of the things which Colonel Barrows saw, when he saw "not thing" of which he disapproved! Colonel Morrow, in command of the American troops at Chita, stated that Semenoff's own Cossacks had estimated that Semenoff had slaughtered one hundred thousand non-combatants in Siberia. Colonel Morrow testified to "the extreme cruelty and wholesale murders" of Semenoff; this on April 12, three days before the Barrows interview. Also General Graves, commander of the American Siberian expedition, used the phrase "wholesale murderer," and described "grim murder trains, which took men out to be shot along the side track and buried in common graves; American soldiers ruthlessly murdered; an American lieutenant held virtual prisoner forty hours," etc. All this was fully reported in the press, and was in President Barrows' newspapers several days before he made his statement that Semenoff had done "not thing" of which he, Barrows, disapproved. To quote from the San Francisco "Examiner," April 13, 1922:

It is part of the testimony that prisoners captured by Semenoff's army in their raids upon villages were taken by trainloads to places which Colonel Morrow designated as "Semenoff's slaughter houses" and there shot down by the wholesale.

All this Colonel Barrows had every opportunity to see, and in it he saw "not thing" that he disapproved; so you see that our "dean of political science" is no fragile mollycoddle, no bespectacled professor living a closet life, but a real, red-blooded, two-fisted man of action. Coming back to California, fresh from "Semenoff's slaughter houses," Colonel Barrows proceeded to advocate the setting up similar establishments on the campus of his university. Speaking before a convention of the State High School Association, he advocated that the Bolsheviki should be stood against the wall and shot. "There is only one way to deal with Bolshevism—fight it. Force is the only way. The time has come to treat them with militarism; I believe in killing the Bolsheviki." Then Captain

Schuyler, one of the intelligence officers whom Barrows brought back with him, spoke his sentiments: "If a man stood before me and declared himself a Bolshevist, I would shoot him on the spot, like a mad dog."

Naturally, that made considerable fuss in Berkeley; for the city had a Socialist mayor and school board only a couple of years previously, and the chambers of commerce and the professional patriots were doing their best to establish the term "Bolsheviki" as including, not merely all Socialists, but everybody who believed in the initiative and referendum, or in government ownership of railroads. So the Socialists of Berkeley challenged Barrows to a debate. He accepted, and the Socialists tried first to get the university hall, and then the high school auditorium; but the president of the Berkeley board of education—a dentist, described to me by another school board member as rarely attending a session without the smell of liquor on his breath—opposed the use of the building, and advocated that all Socialists should be "driven into the bay." Finally, however, the use of the auditorium was obtained; it would only seat twelve hundred people, whereas between eight and ten thousand came.

This was July 30, 1919, at the time when "Bolsheviki" by thousands were being clubbed over the heads and thrown into jail all over the United States. The mayor and the chief of police of Berkeley sat on the platform, and two auto loads of secret service men attended; an effort was made to start a riot and raid the Socialists, a scheme which was averted by the quickness of Mrs. Elvina Beals, who presided at the meeting. Mrs. Beals was for many years a Socialist member of the school board, and the people of Berkeley know her. In the course of the debate, Dean Barrows advocated that the American government should conquer Siberia and Russia for Kolchak, and he asked whether the Socialists of Berkeley would support a strike to prevent the shipment of ammunition to Siberia. They answered with a roar that they would; and so Dean Barrows retired, and did no more debating with these Berkeley "Bolsheviki."

CHAPTER XXX

THE MOB OF LITTLE HATERS

President Wheeler having been intimate with the German kaiser, and ardent in his defense, the interlocking regents wanted somebody else to attend to their interests in war-time. What more natural than to turn to their Dean of Imperialism? They made him president, and he put "ginger" into the system of military training. Twelve thousand students get a free education, but must pay for it by taking two years of military training, fifty-five hours a year. A part of this training consists in learning to plunge a bayonet into an imitation human body, and you must growl savagely while you do this, and one student found it so realistic that he fainted and was dismissed from the university.

Under President Barrows' administration the best land of the university has been taken for an artillery field, and Strawberry Canyon, the one beauty spot available for nature lovers, has been taken for a million dollar "stadium," to be used for athletic tourneys. One professor resigned in protest against this vandalism; but President Barrows believes ardently in athletics, because it trains those strong young men who are to carry the flag from the North Pole to the South. He publicly stated that one advantage of having a big university is that you have abundant material from which to select athletic teams. In other parts of the world, when you hear of the "classics," you think of Homer and Virgil; but in California the "classics" are the annual Stanford-California foot-ball game, and the intercollegiate track-meet, and the Pacific Coast tennis doubles.

I visited the university this spring, and was invited to a fraternity house. These well-groomed young gladiators did not know quite how to talk to a Socialist author, so between courses of the dinner they relieved their embarrassment by singing, or rather shouting in very loud tones—and I observed that their songs invariably dealt with fighting somebody. I asked a student about to graduate what he thought of his classmates, and his answer was, "They are a mob of little haters. They hate the Germans, they hate the Russians, they hate the Socialists, they hate the Japs. They are ready to hate the French or the English any time they are told to; and always they hate Stanford."

Stanford, you understand, is a rival university, and they carry in triumph a battle-ax which they captured from this enemy many years ago; their military president and professors encourage this kind of play ferocity, as training for the setting up of slaughter-houses later on. These future world conquerors are pleased to portray themselves under the terrifying symbol of the Golden Bear. Almost every college is some kind of wild animal, you know; Princeton is a Tiger, and Yale is a Bull-dog, and they all sing songs about eating somebody up. At Harvard they tell you that the motto Veritas, means "To hell with Yale," and at New Haven they pledge their devotion in a carefully ordered climax, "For God, for country, and for Yale."

Needless to say, the university authorities see to it that no modern ideas get access to these young barbarians all at play. President Barrows' first act as president was to forbid Raymond Robins to speak at the university; he knew that Robins had been in Russia, and learned some things which President Barrows also learned, but did not tell. The kind of speaker Barrows wants for his students he found in General Joffre, whom he welcomed with open arms, making a grandiloquent speech about "a soldier president welcoming a soldier hero." The students thronged to hear the Marshal, though they could not understand him; and they mobbed poor Herman Meyling for offering Socialist literature for sale. "Intolerance is a virtue in war-time," says President Barrows; and, of course, all time is war-time to an imperialist.

The keen young commercialists of this school of hate are thoroughly imbued with the psychology of the dominant classes; even the boys who come from the working class are on the way to the top, and the quicker they learn to feel like gentlemen, the better fraternity they will "make." "I think organized labor should be killed," said one undergraduate to a friend of mine. So they are eager for strike-breaking expeditions, and their "soldier president" has kept alive this university tradition. When the electric workers went on strike, the mayor of Berkeley smashed the strike with university boys.

And then came the seamen's strike, which proved a more serious matter; it is a lark to run a dynamo or a trolley car for a few days, but to ship on a steamer is something you can't get out of, and some unfortunate boys who were trapped by the knavish university machine into shipping as seamen on the Matson Line and the Dollar Line paid for their blunder with their lives. Others of them came home thoroughly trained radicals—having learned more in a few months below deck on a steamship than they would have learned in a hundred years in the lap of their alma mater. Some of the steamships broke down at sea, and the capitalist newspapers were filled with scare stories about sabotage; but of course the real reason was inexperienced labor. On the steamship Ohio the chief engineer was a Washington athlete, the second engineer was a Boston dental student, and the third engineer an undergraduate student of the University of California!

All the time, you understand, the secret agents of the Better America Federation are watching the university. When they find the least trace of an unorthodox idea they report it, and the unorthodox person if he be a student, fails to pass his examination, or if he be an instructor he is let out upon any handy pretext. (All appointments in the university are for one year only; even the full professors have no tenure!). Take, for example, the case of three young instructors of English, whose conscience prompted them to sign a petition to the President for revision of the sentences of political prisoners. They were summoned before the acting heads of the university, and implored to withdraw their signatures. There was a bill before the legislature to increase the salaries of all professors, and loyalty to their colleagues should prompt them not to jeopardize this bill! One of them, Witter Bynner, the poet, asked if he might announce that the deans requested that he place the interests of the university above the interests of the country. Later, after Barrows had come in, it was intimated to these evil three that their contracts with the university would not be renewed. But this, of course, was not because of their unorthodox ideas; oh, no—they were not wanted because they had failed to qualify themselves for higher degrees by doing "research work!"

Just what is meant by "research work" in the University of California? It means the digging out of absurd details about far off and long dead writings, such as "the use of *tu* and *vous* in Molière." This is the kind of thing you must do if you want to rise to prominence in a university of the interlocking directorate. With what desperate seriousness they take such work you may learn from a program submitted to the department of English by the dean of the summer session. This program quotes the president of Northwestern University as follows:

> When you consider the value of your personal research, you will without any doubt regret that you have not paid more attention to this phase of your activities. You will discover that distinction in a professor is usually founded on successful research; that men for our faculty positions are selected largely on the basis of research ability; that the most essential credential is a research degree; that promotions within the faculty are based very largely on research accomplishments; that the only official record made by the university of the members of this faculty is the record of the publications of each member of the faculty; that the administration officers scan this list from year to year to see which men are engaged in production research; that research is looked upon with favor by every one of your associates.

So on through a long chant in praise of research, research, research. And the dean who quotes this adds:

> All this is absolutely true of the University of California. We may deplore this emphasis upon research, but it is a fact, a fact which must be reckoned with in our plans for ourselves, for one another, and for the department.

What the poor dean means when he says "it is a fact," is simply that it is the administration policy, and no one has the courage to oppose it. The authorities of the university know no vital thing for scholars to do, and are in terror of all genuine activities of the spirit; therefore they sentence men to spend their lives rooting in the garbage heaps of man's past history, while their students go to hell with canned jazz and boot-leg whiskey and "petting parties." Apparently some of the faculty are likewise not puritanical, for an undergraduate publication, "The Laughing Horse," remarked last spring that "the professors of Latin and Greek would much rather see a leg-show than the 'Medea' of Euripides."

There was one instructor at the university who made a real and successful effort to lift the thoughts of students above "leg-shows." That was Witter Bynner, one of our distinguished poets, and incidentally a most lovable and delightful human being. He was invited to the university as a special lecturer on poetry, and made an extraordinary success. But, alas, he was one of the men who signed the petition for the political prisoners; also he wrote twelve lines of rather stunning poetry, which you may find as a frontispiece to the volume, "Debs and the Poets." As Bynner says: "Certain eminent citizens demanded my dismissal and brought upon me attacks of every imaginable kind, personal, social and professional." Bynner's year at the university expired; and the authorities did not ask him to stay on. The students organized a class of their own, and begged him to meet them, outside the campus; also they issued a volume of verse in his honor. Come back to the University of California a hundred years from now and you will find that Witter Bynner has become an object of "research!"

CHAPTER XXXI

THE DRILL SERGEANT ON THE CAMPUS

These great military universities come to be run more and more on the lines of an army; everything rigid, precise and formal, all emergencies provided for, all policies fixed. The passion of the military mind for uniformity and regimentation is comically exhibited in an article published by President Barrows in the University of California "Chronicle," April, 1922, entitled "What Are the Prospects of the University Professor?" It was read before the Board of Alumni Visitors, who must have been edified, to note how completely the professor's life had been laid out for him by his thoughtful superiors. Colonel Barrows has a vision of the American college professor, taking in this country the place of the ruling classes of Britain, who govern "by reason of rank, breeding and traditional influence." With the idea of attracting that kind of man, President Barrows submits a schedule of his life, showing how much he will receive every year, when he will marry and have a family, when he will travel, what degrees he will get. The president does not specify what he is to eat, but he will assuredly not eat much, with a wife and "one or more children" on a salary starting at a hundred and fifty dollars a month.

One detail in this article intrigued me, so I wrote President Barrows a letter, as follows:

You state the salary of the young instructor, and say: "It has permitted him to marry and to provide for the birth of one or more children." The question which this suggests to me, and which you do not answer, is how many more children? Manifestly, the salary suggested would not make possible the raising of more than two, or three at the outside; but the young professor is 29 or 30 years of age, and he might have eight or ten children. What I should like to know is, what would happen to him if he did so? It is a fact that most of your professors don't, and there seems to be in your article the implicit understanding that they mustn't; so I am forced to assume that you favor what is known as Birth Control, and tacitly recommend it. I am one of those who believe that the methods of Birth Control ought to be made known, not merely to the cultured classes, but to the working classes, and I should like to know the stand of the president of the University of California on this subject. Will you answer for publication these two specific questions: First, do you recognize that your article implies the prevention of conception by the married instructors of your university? Second, would you advocate legislation to permit working class families to obtain a knowledge of these same methods?

President Barrows is usually rather free about taking up controversies, but on this occasion he for some reason thought it best to lie low!*

---

*When this chapter was published serially, President Barrows was interviewed by a reporter for the San Francisco "Daily News." He said: "As for Upton Sinclair, I received a lengthy letter from him not long ago asking me to debate on some very stupid subjects. As there seemed to be no sense in the letter, I paid no attention to him." The reader will be able to judge for himself whether there was any sense in my letter; also of the

Being devoted to the training of young aristocrats, this school of imperialism has no great fondness for the vulgar modern activities known as "extension work." "University extension," be it explained, consists in traveling about, giving education to tiresome common people, who had no leisure to get it when they were young, and so lack those British qualifications of "rank, breeding and traditional influence." At the University of California was a "regular" professor by the name of Ira Howerth, who was engaged in extension work, and took this work with plebeian seriousness; all over the state women's clubs and labor unions clamored for his lectures, and his efforts to comply with their demands led to endless conflict with the university authorities. The "consulting committee" did everything to handicap him; he was forbidden to address clubs in the city of Berkeley, and was refused the use of university rooms, and of the library. He could get no appropriations; and when finally the pressure of the people forced the legislature to grant funds, the authorities resented this, and blamed Howerth as the cause of money being "forced upon them."

In the year 1917, during the Charter Day exercises, Professor Howerth asked that some part of the time be given to the extension work. They gave him Friday night, the end of the week's activities, and on that night they arranged a big banquet in San Francisco, expecting to take all the people away. But Howerth invited President Van Hise of Wisconsin and Oswald Garrison Villard, and had the biggest meeting of the week. Of course, the university authorities were furious.

I can testify to Professor Howerth's competence as a teacher, for I had the pleasure of attending some of his lectures in Pasadena. They were given in the Board of Trade rooms, where to a large audience of mature men and women the professor gave intelligent explanations of the sociology of Lester Ward. Here

likelihood that President Barrows really thought there was no sense in it. For my part, I think the above statement puts President Barrows in the classification of those college presidents who do not always tell the truth.

we were on the home ground of the Black Hand, and it seemed to me inconceivable that the regents would permit this kind of thing to go on; and they did not.

In bringing an end to it, they chose the most insulting and humiliating method possible. Professor Howerth had his Sabbatical year, and while he was in Paris, eleven days before the end of his leave of absence, he received a letter from the president of the university, telling him that he was "fired." He made so bold as to return, and discovered that a report which he had prepared before leaving, describing the development of the extension work, had been taken over by another professor, and signed by that professor's name, and issued by the university, with no credit given to Professor Howerth. He made every effort to find out what were the charges against him, but could not get one word. He appeared before the finance committee of the regents—five of our interlocking directors, with Mr. Earl, attorney to Banker Fleishhacker, as chairman. Professor Howerth stated his case, asking what wrong he had done. Said Chairman Earl: "Has anybody anything to say on that?" No one had anything to say, and the committee went on with the order of business, leaving Professor Howerth standing there like a whipped school boy.

Such is the dignity of the teaching profession in the University of the Black Hand. And what is the standing of scholarship? On that point hear the weird experience of Professor Kiang, an eminent Chinese scholar, formerly of the University of Pekin, who was invited to teach his native language and literature to Californians for the munificent salary of eighty dollars a month. Professor Kiang presented to the university an extremely valuable library of Chinese books, which collection the university casually accepted. It happened that Witter Bynner was once asked by President Wheeler and Colonel Barrows whom he had found the most interesting man in the place. "Undoubtedly Kiang," responded Bynner; and the two gentlemen looked disconcerted. "Kiang?" exclaimed Wheeler, "Why he only gets eighty dollars a month!" Within a few days the Oriental professor's salary was raised to a hundred dollars a month!

Returning to China on a visit, Professor Kiang had an uncomfortable experience. On the steamer an American borrowed a hundred dollars from him, promising to return it at the journey's end. Later, in China, when Professor Kiang needed his money, the man turned on him with angry threats, saying that he was known to be living with a woman not his wife, and that the man would report him to the university and cause him to lose his job.

Now, the situation regarding Professor Kiang's wife was that for eight years his first wife had been hopelessly insane. In many parts of America you can divorce a wife who is insane, but in China you do not do this, because to divorce a woman is to inflict both upon her and her relatives a most dreadful disgrace. Insanity not being the woman's fault, nor the fault of her relatives, it is unthinkable in China to seek a divorce for such a reason. What you do is to avail yourself of the privilege of having a second wife. As a rule the Westernized Chinese have but one wife, but in a case such as this they would have two, and the second wife would be treated with especial consideration because of the particular circumstances. When Professor Kiang married again, the relatives of his first wife attended the ceremony, and this same attitude to the matter was manifested by everyone. Witter Bynner went to China with Kiang, to collaborate with him in translating Chinese poetry into English, and Bynner writes:

I can testify that the second wife has been signally honored; she was the first woman, for instance, to address a body similar to our chambers of commerce in the capital of Kiang's native province, and she broke another precedent by addressing, together with her husband, the officers of Wu Pei-fu's army. Wu Pei-fu is now, as you know, the Dictator of Peking and more or less of China. It will interest you to know that his general, Feng Yu-hsiang, being a Christian, was concerned to know whether there might be any conflict between Socialism and Christianity, and found them upon investigation to be expressions of the same thing. If there were any objection to Kiang's second wife, Feng Yu-hsiang, a Christian, might have been expected to feel it. Perhaps his being a Socialist, however, incapacitates him for true morality!

It had been understood that Professor Kiang was to return to the University of California; but now the Black Hand got busy. Not merely was there a flaw in Kiang's marriage certificate; also, he was a leading Chinese Socialist, one of the founders of that movement in his own country. So he received from President Barrows a cruel and insolent letter, informing him that he was not to return. It was practically the same thing as the Gorki story, and both Gorki and Kiang were enemies of the interlocking directorate. But Semenoff was their friend, so you do not find Colonel Barrows, in espousing his Cossack hero, mentioning the fact that Semenoff was traveling in America with a lady not his wife; still less do you find him mentioning those thirty most beautiful women in Semenoff's "summer car!"

Becoming aware of the Black Hand and its power in the institution, independent-minded men seek other occupations; the sycophants and the sluggards remain, and as a result, the quality of the teaching goes down. Every year the boys and girls pour in from the cities and ranches of California, and they are commanded to study dull subjects under dull instructors, and they prefer football and flirtation. In Berkeley there are twelve thousand, and in the Southern branch in Los Angeles four or five thousand more. Immorality is more common than scholarship; the conditions have become a scandal throughout the state, and our imperialist president finds himself with a peck of trouble on his hands, a board of quarreling regents who cannot agree what is to be done. There is a flaw, apparently, in Colonel Barrows' doctrine of the strong man; the strong man does not always rule—especially when he is a stupid man! So our "soldier president" has just asked to be excused from his job, and allowed to become once more a humble Professor of Political Ignorance.

P. S.—After this book has been put into type an interesting development occurs at Berkeley. The editors of an independent student publication, the "Laughing Horse," asked my permission to quote extracts from these chapters, and they printed six or eight pages in their issue of November, 1922. The publication created great excitement at the university, and a senior student by the name of Butler went to a magistrate and swore out a warrant for the arrest of Roy Chanslor, the "Laughing Horse" editor, upon the charge of publishing obscene matter. The pretext was another article in the magazine, a letter from D. H. Lawrence, the English novelist, reviewing and strongly condemning as immoral a novel by Ben Hecht. But the real reason was obviously the passages from "The Goose-step." The "Daily Californian," the student paper, gave the thing away, denouncing "the printing of disgusting articles by Upton Sinclair and other perverted 'knockers.' To jolt the university they hurled and blatted the most unprecedented compilations of lies that has (sic) yet found expression in these parts. At first the students rose in righteous wrath to 'tar and feather' the perpetrators of such foul, insane blusterings."

I am informed that the action against Chanslor was instigated by a high official of the university. The student, Butler, is a son of the president of the California State Bar Association; on the eve of the trial his father came to Berkeley and declared with indignation that his son was being made a tool of, and worse, was being made a fool of. The magistrate threw out the complaint, as it failed to contain the necessary legal technicalities. Chanslor was summoned before the Undergraduate Student Affairs Committee; he stood upon his rights, and a day or two later was summoned before President Barrows and expelled from the university. I quote an account of the matter, sent to me by one of the editors of the "Laughing Horse":

Barrows said he was doing so by a recommendation from the Student Affairs Committee, and gave as his reason not only the D. H. Lawrence letter but the poem by Witter Bynner, "Little Fly." He did not mention the excerpts from "The Goose-step." How Barrows can have the face to expel any student from the university for obscenity is quite beyond me! I, myself, saw Barrows sit through a "Smoker Rally" (the men's rally before the Big Game with Stanford), at which the football coaches and prominent alumni told the most vulgar and filthy stories that anyone ever heard. The speaker of the evening, an alumnus from Pasadena, told one story that I remember that one would hear only in the coarsest society. Moreover, the campus comic monthly, "The Pelican," prints thinly disguised obscenities of all sorts that are countenanced without a murmur. Yet Barrows solemnly upbraided Chanslor for printing this frank, straightforward and really highly moral letter. Apparently everyone has been cautioned not to let any indignation over your exposé creep into the case again.

I also quote one paragraph from a letter addressed to President Barrows, written by Roy Chanslor after his expulsion. I think it says about all there is to say on the subject:

You have apparently confused the sincere and fine and beautiful expression of a great artist and a brilliant and original thinker with the crude vulgarities and obvious obscenities regularly on tap at smoker rallies, and with the corrupt literature which I have heard is sold to those who desire it by bell-boys and train-boys. At the smoker rally held late in November, the night before the annual California-Stanford football game, it did not strike my attention that you did anything to stop the bawdy stories and the frankly vulgar exhibition of dancing which a student in black-face gave with a dummy stuffed to represent a woman, but it did strike my attention that you sat through the spectacle in a seat in the front row, tacitly, by your silence, countenancing the whole affair. This spectacle, which was frankly vulgar and obscene, apparently did not arouse in you any of the moral indignation which the letter of Mr. Lawrence did, a letter which I repeat is not obscene or corrupt or degenerate, but fine and sincere and beautiful.

CHAPTER XXXII

THE STORY OF STANFORD

Thirty miles south of San Francisco, sheltered behind the coast range of mountains, lies the great institution with whose students the "Golden Bear" does its fighting. Stanford University was founded by one of the "Big Four" railroad kings, who for forty years or more plundered the people of California. Like other railroad kings, Leland Stanford amused himself by purchasing race-horses and state legislators, but he differed from the rest in that he had a respect for knowledge. He wanted to be a trustee of the University of California, and when he failed, he decided to start a rival institution. When his only son died in early youth, the heart-broken old man chose this means of perpetuating the boy's name, and he pledged to Leland Stanford, Jr., University his land, his racehorses, and a part of his railroad stock; also a valuable asset in the form of David Starr Jordan, a scientist and teacher with some real interest in democracy.

Senator Stanford died in the midst of the panic of 1893, and his university was in a predicament; there was no money on hand, and it was impossible to sell any land, and parasites and blackmailers gathered in a swarm—relatives and friends, legislators whom the senator had kept on his payroll, newspaper editors and publishers he had

used. The editor of one San Jose newspaper sent in a
bill for twenty-five hundred dollars advertising—he had
printed news about the opening of the university! Senator Stanford left a hundred thousand dollars to every
relative he could find, hoping thereby to buy them off;
but within twenty-four hours of his death one of his relatives
in New York forged his name to a check for a hundred thousand dollars; another relative, a woman, was
shot by her husband, a gambler, because she did not get
her money quickly enough!

The only way to keep the university safe was to make
it Mrs. Stanford's personal property; all the professors
were listed as her private servants—a device which some
other presidents of universities might be interested to
make note of! For years the institution was supported
from Mrs. Stanford's income, eked out by the occasional
selling of a racehorse. The job of running a university
and a racing stable in combination offered a diversified
task for the widow of a railroad king and a specialist in
ichthyology. The senator had been offered a hundred
and fifty thousand dollars for "Palo Alto," a prize stallion; the offer was refused—and next year the stallion
died!

The university owned a fourth interest in the Central
Pacific Railroad, now a portion of the Southern Pacific;
the other fourths were owned by the Crocker estate, the
Hopkins estate, and Collis P. Huntington, the prize
grabber of them all, who resented the university as an insult to his lack of culture. He would "stop that circus
some day," he used to say; describing it as "putting a
two thousand dollar education into a two hundred dollar
boy." Some years previously he had proposed that in
order to determine the value of the Central Pacific stock,
each of the four holders should put some of it on the
market; this was done, and Huntington secretly bought
it all, and then turned Stanford out and had himself made
president of the road. Dr. Jordan described Huntington's
motto as: "Anything is mine that is not nailed down, and
nothing is nailed that I can pry loose." After Stanford's
death he tried to buy the university holdings in the railroad for three million dollars; but the university held on
—and had better luck than Johns Hopkins University,
which was left a big block of Baltimore and Ohio stock by

its founder, and was frozen out by the big fellows, and did not get a dollar. Ultimately the Stanford stock was sold to James Speyer for sixteen millions.

Many and curious were the efforts made to get Mrs. Stanford's money away from her university. A preacher came and delivered a sermon about her dead boy, in which he compared him to the youthful Jesus Christ—but he did not get her millions for Methodism! The Catholics came, and they deeply impressed the old lady's failing mind with their bells and incense and colored lights—but they did not persuade her to move the Stanford girl-students to their school at Menlo Park! Bearing in mind these trage-dies averted, we may forgive our ichthyological diplomat for some of the minor atrocities which he was unable to avert: for example, the great bronze statue of Senator Stanford, with his wife and son kneeling dutifully at his feet. This group is known to the irreverent students as the "Holy Trinity," and it used to stand in the middle of the campus; but the elements were also irreverent, and so it has been moved indoors, and fills the rotunda of the museum.

I do not know where in the world you can find a more curious and pathetic monument to human vanity than the family rooms of this Stanford museum; rooms full of great glass cases, filled with the domestic implements and the clothes, the toys and the trophies of the tribe of Stan-ford. Case No. One: The senator's uniform, his military vest, gloves, sword and pistols, which he never had occa-sion to use except on parade. Case No. Two: the crock-ery and lamps used by the Stanford family at all stages of its career. Case No. Three: the skirts and other wearing apparel of Mrs. Stanford's sisters—all these objects patiently classified and labeled in the old lady's handwrit-ing. Case No. Four: the photographs of the senator's racehorses, the cups they won, and the hoofs and ears of many of them. Case No. Five: sixty-two photographs of the Stanford family—this not counting the photographs in other cases. Case No. Six: the baby paintings, the chess set, and eight of the canes of the only begotten son. Case No. Seven: his baby shoes, toilet set, pens and cups. Case No. Eight: his boxing gloves, fishing lines, rifles, magic lanterns. Case No. Nine: his wood carvings and other apparatus. Case No. Ten: his toy boats and trains. Case

No. Eleven: his soldiers, cannon, drum. Poor, feeble lad, spoon-fed and coddled, he beat his little drum, but the drum-sticks fell from his nerveless fingers. If he had grown up he would have wasted the Stanford fortune, as the Pullman boys, and the Goulds, and the Thaws, and the Crokers, and the Whitneys, and the McCormicks, and so many others. Instead, he died, and the world has a university!

We continue our walk about the room. Case No. Twelve: the fans which Mrs. Stanford wielded in a lifetime of fascination. Case No. Thirteen: her souvenir spoons and necklaces. Case No. Fourteen: the senator's chair, and the canes which he carried, all carefully labeled as to where he purchased them and carried them. A plain and humble author, I have been able to go through life so far without ever owning a cane; but it appears that a senator and railroad king must have twenty-four elaborate and expensive ones; and posterity must have a fireproof building in which to preserve them, and great steel doors, such as you find in the vaults of a bank, to keep them safe from thieves. If you have not seen enough, come downstairs, and inspect more of Leland's toys, including his old-fashioned bicycle. The students declare that somewhere in this museum is hidden a model of Leland's last breakfast of fried ham and eggs; but this, of course, may be just youthful waggery.*

We are told not to look a gift-horse in the mouth, and the saying should perhaps apply to a university. We can hardly expect that a vain old lady, put in charge of an institution of learning for ten or fifteen years, would not busy herself to see that evil ideas were kept out of it. In the Bryan campaign of 1896, there rose up in the university a big bold fellow by the name of Ross, who actively favored Free Silver—which meant the cutting in half of the wealth of all the interlocking directors, except those who owned silver mines. Subsequently this bold bad man made speeches opposing oriental immigration, whereas he knew that Senator Stanford had been an ardent advocate of cheap Chinese labor. Also he said to some of his stu-

---

*A woman friend who has lived for sixteen years in Palo Alto swears to me that she has been shown, in the secret rooms of the museum, a porcelain plate containing a porcelain bologna sausage and a porcelain fried egg!

dents in the university that "a railroad deal is a railroad steal!" So Mrs. Stanford served notice on her president that Professor Ross must go; and this at the perilous time when the Catholic cohorts were gathering, with their bells and incense and colored lights and other magic spells! I could appreciate that President Jordan was speaking from the depths of his heart when he said to me: "The best thing that the founder of a university can do is to die and let others run it!"

The radical professor was let out, and there was a terrific uproar, and several others resigned. The controversy lasted all through the academic year. Professor G. E. Howard, head of the department of history, ventured to make a sarcastic reference to the incident in a lecture to a class, and some weeks later received a letter from the president, asking for his resignation; this was followed by a number of other resignations, chiefly in Professor Howard's department. This series of events caused so much injury to Stanford's reputation that the authorities made a desperate effort to counteract the effects. The story of what they did is told me by Professor A. O. Lovejoy, now of the department of philosophy of Johns Hopkins, and at that time professor of philosophy at Stanford. I quote from his letter:

Late in the academic year, near the beginning of which Professor Ross was dismissed, a statement addressed to the public and designed for signature by members of the Stanford faculty was drawn—by whom I do not know—and an attempt was made to secure the signatures of all members (I believe) above the rank of instructor. Each teacher was invited to come separately to the office of one of the senior professors, a close personal friend of President Jordan; was there shown certain correspondence between Mrs. Stanford and President Jordan, which had not been made public; and was thereupon invited to sign the statement—which was to the effect that the signers, having seen certain unpublished documents, had arrived at the conclusion that President Jordan was justified in the dismissal of Professor Ross and that there was no question of academic freedom involved in the case. It was perfectly well understood by me, and I think by all who were shown the letters, that we were desired by the university authorities to sign the "round-robin"; and it was intimated that if any, after seeing the correspondence, should reach a conclusion contrary to that in the "round-robin," they were at least expected to keep silence.

Because of this last intimation I myself for some time refused to have the letters shown me; and consented finally to examine them only after stipulating that I should retain complete freedom to take such action afterwards as the circumstances might seem to me to require. When I read the letters they appeared to me to prove precisely the opposite to the two propositions contained in the statement to the public. They showed clearly (a) that President Jordan—who under the existing constitution of the university was the official responsible in such matters—had been originally altogether unwilling to dismiss Ross, and had consented to do so only under pressure from Mrs. Stanford; (b) that the express grounds of Mrs. Stanford's objection to Ross were certain public utterances of his, and that, therefore, the question of academic freedom was distinctly involved. I drew up a short statement to this effect, and after the "round-robin" was published, communicated it to the newspapers, at the same time declining the reappointment of which I had previously been notified. I was thereupon directed to discontinue my courses immediately. About the same time another man—one of the best scholars and the most effective teachers in his department—who had refused to sign, and was known to disapprove strongly of the administration's conduct, but who had given no public expression of his opinion, was notified that he would not be reappointed; and it was currently reported in the faculty that the vice-president, then acting president, of the university, Dr. Branner, had announced a policy of (in his own phrase) "shaking off the loose plaster."

Professor Lovejoy goes on to tell how some years later, when he was visiting Palo Alto, "one of the signers of the collective statement to the public told me that he had signed with great reluctance, and with a sense of humiliation, but, since he had a family of young children, he had not felt that he could afford to risk the loss of his position. I cannot, of course, give this man's name." Professor Lovejoy calls attention to the fact that practically all the men who resigned were either unmarried or were married men without children. It might seem as if Francis Bacon, a scholar himself, had foreseen the plutocratic empire of American education when he wrote, three hundred years ago: "He that hath a wife and children hath given hostages to fortune."

CHAPTER XXXIII

THE WIND OF FREEDOM

The poor old lady died at last, but she did not leave her fortune to be adminstered by an eminent ichthyologist, badly tainted with democracy and pacifism. On the contrary, she left it to a board of fifteen trustees—the usual interlocking directorate. As first grand duke we find none other than Mr. Timothy Hopkins, son of Senator Stanford's colleague in the "Big Four." Mr. Hopkins is president of a milling company, and director in a trust company, an ice company, and a telephone and telegraph company. As second grand duke there is Mr. Frank B. Anderson, president of the Bank of California, the great Standard Oil institution of the state. I am told that Mr. Anderson is there to represent the Morgan interests. He is vice-president of another bank, and director in three gas and electric companies, and in numerous other great concerns, including the Spring Valley Water Company, celebrated in the San Francisco graft prosecutions.

Mr. Bourn, the president of this company, is also on the board; and Mr. Grant, described to me by a friend who knows him as "an idle millionaire, the son of an old money grubber"; but he can't really be so idle, being vice-president of a gas company and an oil company, chairman of a power company, director of the Bank of California, another bank, a trust company, another power company, a gas and electric company, another gas company, and a steel company. Also there is Mr. Nickel, "who married forty million dollars," and is a director of the Bank of California, president of an irrigation company, a live stock company, and of the greatest land company in California; also Mr. Newhall, the son of an old-time auctioneer, a dyed-in-the-wool reactionary, vice-president of a great land company. In addition to these, there are three prominent corporation lawyers, two judges, both very conservative, a banker, an insurance man, and Mr. Herbert Hoover, than whom the plutocracy has no more faithful servant in these United States. One of the corporation lawyers, T. T. C. Gregory, is that Captain Gregory who was Mr. Hoover's representative in Hungary, and used his control of the distribution of the relief funds and supplies furnished by the American people, for the purpose of breaking the revolution of the workers of Hungary, and bringing into power the infamous Horthy, who drowned the hopes of the Hungarian workers in a sea of blood. Few blacker deeds have been committed by American class-greed; but such is the state of our public opinion, that Captain Gregory came home and boasted of it in a series of articles in "World's Work," and Mr.

Hoover stood back of him, and the Stanford trustees
elected him to their exclusive board, and made him their
secretary!

Such are the men in charge of the Stanford millions.
David Starr Jordan has retired, and the great university
is governed from the cozy arm-chairs of the Pacific Union
Club of San Francisco. As president they have appointed
a physician, Dr. Wilbur, who learned the Goose-step at
two of the Kaiser's universities. He aspires to be, like
Colonel Barrows, "a man on horseback." In the days
before America entered the war some of the students of
Stanford were taking military training, and I am informed
by one who was present at the graduating ceremonies that
President Wilbur shook hands with all those who were in
uniform, and refused to shake hands with those who were
not in uniform. More recently, at an alumni reunion, he
gave a curious proof of the abject condition of spirit to
which the lackeys of the plutocracy have come. He was
describing how he went to the dock in New York to welcome Herbert Hoover home from abroad; said President
Wilbur: "I saw one of America's biggest bankers throw
his arms around him, and I said to myself: 'At last Stanford has arrived'!" The gentleman who tells me of this
incident, a scholar and a scientist, reports: "He said it in
sweet unconsciousness, and at least half a dozen of my
friends turned in my direction and gave me appreciative
glances."

Stanford was founded for the purpose of giving the
young people of California a free education; that was
the basis of its democratic spirit—but the interlocking
trustees have now decided to exclude all those common
people who cannot pay two hundred and twenty-five dollars a year. So the tone of the place is rapidly altering,
and on my recent visit one member of the senior class
remarked to me, "I have seen such a change in my four
years that I'm glad I'm through." Two years ago a group
of the students wished to start a liberal club for free discussion. A Chinese student writes me what happened, and
I quote from his letter, leaving his quaint English as it
stands, because the fine spirit of the writer shines through
it so very clearly.

Then we received discouraging advices from outsiders, prin-
cipally from faculty members. None was willing to encourage us

of such study. Occasionally individuals received discourtesy from their society, because of being connected to this movement. For instance, I was dismissed from a position soon after I was found out that I was "an ardent student of Socialism." Another illustration, I was short in finance once. Went to see the Dean of Man to ask for a loan from the university. Was at first refused this request because I was reported to that office being "socialistic in belief." Shortly after, a great majority of us left Stanford on account of their graduation, the movement died down gradually.

Now it is starting once more. I have a letter from another student, who is going to try again, in spite of warning from the older students that it may result in his not getting his diploma. The motto of Stanford used to be "the wind of freedom blows"; but this sentiment was expressed in German, and so a few years ago the trustees dropped it. Of course we know that talk about "freedom" nowadays is German propaganda, or else Bolshevik.

In the effort to introduce a little democracy into the faculty, President Jordan established an Academic Council, which was supposed to deal with questions suitable to the intelligence of professors. The educational affairs of the state were in a bad way, and some professors thought that was a proper subject for their attention. The Progressive administration of Hiram Johnson had just come into power, and the academic council adopted a resolution, favoring a commission to reorganize the educational system of the state. But the interlocking trustees would not stand for any dealings between their professors and a state administration which was pledged to put them out of politics. Grand Duke Timothy Hopkins came hurrying down, and ordered the Academic Council to withdraw their resolution—which they did. To one of the professors Mr. Hopkins made the grim statement, "We are coming back;" meaning thereby that the railroad and other big grafters were going to take over the government of California again—which they have done.

In her decree concerning the Stanford trust, Mrs. Stanford laid down the rule, phrased as a request, that no Stanford professor "shall electioneer among or seek to dominate other professors or the students for the success of any political party or candidate in any political contest." This rule, like all other such rules, is interpreted to mean that Stanford professors renounce their rights as citizens —when they do not happen to agree with the politics of

the plutocratic trustees.   Thus I note that no one makes
any objection when President Wilbur joins with President
Barrows of California in issuing a manifesto to the people
of the state, opposing some of the constitutional amendments now being submitted to the ballot.   Neither do the
Stanford authorities object that Professor "Jimmie" Hyde
spends two months campaigning with Mr. Moore, candidate of the power interests and other reactionary business
groups for the Republican nomination for senator.

I have shown you the University of California regents
dominating politics and finance through the great companies which turn water power into electricity and distribute it over the state.   I have shown you the University of
California helping these power companies to defeat the bill
for the public development and operation of hydro-electric
power.   And now we come to Stanford and we find one
trustee heavily interested in power companies, and several
others in electric companies, and others acting as bankers,
lawyers and judges for such companies.   And what does
Stanford have to say officially on the campaign for this
hydro-electric power bill?

There is in California a "League of Municipalities,"
an official organization of the communities of the state.
They hold a convention once a year; the officials of cities
and towns attend as delegates, and deal with all matters
concerning the welfare of their communities—sanitation,
health, paving, taxes, public utilities, etc.   This summer
Stanford University extended the hospitality of its buildings for the sessions of the convention, and of its dormitories as lodgings for the delegates; but the faculty of
the University and the citizens of Palo Alto learned to
their surprise that one of the sessions of the convention
was to be held at the Community House in the town of
Palo Alto, instead of being held in the university hall.   I
have a letter from a gentleman who was present as an
official guest at this session, and he explains the mysterious
change of location.

At its opening the President, Mayor Louis Bartlett, of
Berkeley, said that the delegates should be informed why this
particular session was being held in a different place from the
others, and then proceeded to read a letter from President Newhall of the Board of Trustees, asking them to omit the Water
and Power Act from their program in the University buildings,
as the university did not wish to be understood as taking sides,

162   THE GOOSE-STEP

and any action they might take might be interpreted, incorrectly, as being the action of the university. There appeared to be no objection to the danger of the university's being similarly misunderstood in regard to half a dozen other proposed constitutional amendments! The stupid officers of the League didn't take the hint, as gentlemen should, and drop the offending subject from the program entirely. They merely called the session meeting in the Community House in Palo Alto (which has nobly served as an open forum upon other critical occasions) and there we listened to a vigorous debate all afternoon, led by Rudolph Spreckels and Francis J. Heney on the one side and Allison Ware and Eustace Cullinan on the other, at the close of which a vote was taken which was unanimous for the Water and Power Act, with the exception of the vote of San Francisco, the most prominent figure in whose delegation was Supervisor (ex-Mayor) Eugene Schmitz—with some public corporation corruption record!

CHAPTER XXXIV

THE STANFORD SKELETON

I have referred to the dissatisfaction of Grand Duke Timothy Hopkins at the coming into power of a progressive government in California. This event was especially embarrassing to the Stanford trustees, because of a family skeleton which for many years they had been hiding in their academic closet. You understand that these high-up masters of finance have an elaborate system for plundering the railroads and public utility companies which they control. They have holding companies and investment companies and subsidiary concerns of various sorts, whereby they skim off the cream of the profits, without interference by public commissions. Nobody but a few insiders today can form any idea where the profits of an American railroad or public utility corporation are going, or what should be the income from any particular investment. And now, here are these same smooth gentlemen administering the investments of a university; what more natural than that it should occur to them to handle these funds in the same manner?

Apparently old Senator Stanford foresaw this, for his trust deed provided that the Governor of the state should receive a complete report each year upon the financial affairs of the trust. But the Governor of the state never received that complete report. For many years the faculty of Stanford, who were living on short rations, could get no statement whatever; the trustees allowed the university the lump sum of eight hundred thousand dollars a year, and no explanations. Finally, about 1908, after some years of agitation, a statement was prepared and circulated at a board meeting. It was the first financial statement which President Jordan had ever seen, and he badly wanted a copy of it, so he "swiped" it—at least so he told a member of the faculty, who told me. He called a meeting of the full professors, to whom he gave certain figures purporting to be the income of the university trust as communicated to him, but one of the professors who had made a detailed study of the court schedule of Mrs. Stanford's estate pointed out that the interest on the bonds there scheduled amounted to more than the purported total submitted by President Jordan—this not counting other sources of income. And Trustee Crothers, in a letter to me, admits that during the period he held the Pacific Improvement stock in trust the income from this one item amounted to two million dollars in thirty-one months, which is just about eight hundred thousand dollars a year! After that nothing more appears to have been heard or seen of this financial statement.

These facts are known to many who are interested in the university; they were known to Thorstein Veblen, who was a professor in Stanford for three years. In 1918 Veblen published a book entitled, "The Higher Learning in America," in which he referred briefly to this scandal. But his sense of politeness toward the university caused him to withhold its name—which got him into trouble with Professor Brander Matthews. If I tell you this story, it will lead us off the trail of Stanford for a page or two; but it will teach us about the prestige of universities and how it is maintained, and we shall thus be better able to understand the Stanford skeleton, and how it has been kept hidden all these years.

I am told by a person high up in Columbia University that it was Nicholas Murray Butler, sitting in his high watch-tower and keeping guard over his empire of education, who first saw this dangerous book of Veblen's, and turned it over to his henchman, Brander Matthews, to be "slated." Matthews wrote what was supposed to be a book review, but was really an assassination, and the New York "Times," which exists to perform these little services for the plutocracy, gave it prominence. Matthews found one trivial grammatical error in Veblen's book, and another printer's error which could be laid to Veblen; on this basis he accused of illiteracy the most brilliant economic satirist in the world! Because of Veblen's politeness in failing to name Stanford, Brander Matthews described him as "a creature who creeps up stealthily with a stiletto to deal a stab in the back." Says Matthews: "On page 67 and on page 70 Mr. Veblen seems to suggest that there are boards of trustees whose members make a personal profit out of the funds entrusted to them; the insinuation is hedged about with weazel words—i. e., 'instances of the kind are not wholly unknown, though *presumably* (!) exceptional.' "

To appreciate this extreme piety of Professor Brander Matthews, you would have to see him, as I have, dangling a cigarette from his lower lip as he lectures to his students, and causing these prematurely wise young men to chuckle at his worldly wit. For Brander is a club man and cynic, one of the very shrewdest, and he knows what butters parsnips. If in the bosom of the Century Club he and his friend, Nicholas Miraculous, were to hear a story about a member of a school board getting advance information and buying up real estate, or about a college trustee handling the investment of trust funds in such a way as to make "honest graft" out of it, the two of them would tip each other a wink. But when they are talking for publication—when they set out to assassinate a dangerous radical—the two cronies take on an air of innocent trustfulness which has not been met with in the world since Moses Primrose came home from the fair with his gross of green spectacles with silver rims and shagreen cases!

For my part I don't want to take any chance of being called "a creature who creeps up stealthily with a stiletto to deal a stab in the back!" Whatever my old friend Professor Matthews may say about me when he comes to assassinate this book in the New York "Times," let him at least put me under his other classification—that more respectable person "who comes straight at us with a bowie knife in his hand." Before I finish this volume I shall give Professor Matthews several cases of university and college trustees misusing funds; in a succeeding volume, I shall show him school board members getting commissions from book companies, and buying up land to sell to the public for school sites. If Professor Matthews will obtain a copy of a printed report made in 1908 to Mayor Taylor of San Francisco by a graft investigating committee, he will find it proven that one of the regents of the University of California invested university funds in a "French Restaurant" building on the corner of Geary and Mason streets, constructed by him with a view to its use as a house of assignation. And if that seems too far off for Professor Matthews, let him investigate the properties in New York City on which his own university holds its mortgages, and he will find that one of them at least was being used as a disorderly house last spring! Or let him run up to Rochester, where the university is moving out to a magnificent new site, furnished by Mr. Eastman, the kodak king, and all around that site he will find that members of the board of trustees and their relatives and friends have been making money buying up real estate on advance information. Or let him visit the Connecticut College for Women, at New London, and hear the story of Frederick Sykes, the recent president, who discovered that the trustees were stealing the funds of the college, even to the coal, and tried to interfere with them and was fired from his job! One of the trustees was a high school principal, and the board furnished him an automobile to go out and collect funds. He never got any funds, but continued to use the car, and when the scandal was exposed, it was explained that he had arranged to have the price of the car returned to the college in his will. The grand duke who ran this board of trustees was a multi-millionaire, who had set them a bad example by living a dissolute life. He wanted an inn-keeper's wife, and paid the inn-keeper forty thousand dollars to get a divorce from her; then the grand duke married the lady, and got an honorary degree from his college!

With this much of preliminary, we return to Stanford, to see just what this super-plutocratic board of trustees has done. To begin with, let me explain that the holding concern devised by the "Big Four" plunderers of the Central-Southern Pacific, for the purpose of skimming off the cream of the profits, was known as the Pacific Improvement Company. The affairs of this concern have been kept a dark secret; the holdings of Stanford in Pacific

12

Improvement stock were not made over to the Stanford trust by Mrs. Stanford, but were placed in the hands of Judge Crothers, a trustee, and by him turned over to the Stanford trust after Mrs. Stanford died. In the last annual report of the treasurer of the university, I find the value of this holding listed at one hundred dollars for twenty-five hundred shares, with "dividends from earnings" for the year of $2,482.44, and "liquidation dividends" of two hundred and seventy-five thousand dollars. That is a pretty good earning capacity for a hundred dollars' worth of stock, you must admit! You see how the big insiders operate—no one knows what this stock is really worth. In his letter to me Trustee Crothers admits that "there were a number of reasons why Mrs. Stanford did not wish the whole world, nor even all of the trustees of the university to know the terms . . . . of the Pacific Improvement trust." No probate courts, or inheritance tax appraisers, or other unfriendly investigators were ever to have a chance to stick their noses into Pacific Improvement!

Next, these super-plutocratic trustees turned over to Stanford University the sum of eight hundred thousand dollars a year, without explanation, and this sum of money was deposited in the Union Trust Company of San Francisco without interest. Let Professor Brander Matthews inquire around among his banker friends in New York, and find out how much they would be willing to pay him in the way of interest on a deposit account, amounting at its maximum to eight hundred thousand dollars a year! I am informed that when Mr. Anderson came into the board, representing the Morgan interests in the Standard Oil Bank of California, he pointed out that that arrangement was not a profitable one for the university. Also, I am told by a Stanford professor, in whose rigid integrity I have many reasons for trusting, that he once heard one of these trustees state angrily that the board had that afternoon made a loan of five hundred thousand dollars to one of their own members, at a ridiculously low rate of interest on the real estate security offered. Afterwards the trustee who had borrowed this money got into trouble, and no one knows how much money the university lost. In the last president's report I find a "capital decrease" recorded of $17,320 on Sacramento Northern Railway bonds. I also find an item, "Stock not recorded on books, when acquired in 1919 at Northern Electric Company reorganization." This is only one sample—nobody knows how many other items are "not recorded on books!"

There are other matters of record which can be verified by anyone. These trustees are the high-up members of the California plutocracy, the shrewdest business men the state possesses; they work diligently for their own financial interests, and have vastly increased their personal fortunes during the last thirty years. But what have they done for Stanford? They have made failures of the most important business transactions they have managed for the university. The president of the board of trustees is one of the richest ranchers in California, and there are on the board officials and directors of several of the state's colossal land companies; how comes it that men like Mr. Newhall and Mr. Nickel have never been able to tell Stanford how to make a success of its big ranches? The Palo Alto, Vina and Gridley ranches all failed, and the last two were finally sold at sacrifice prices. There were something like a hundred thousand acres, sold for about four million dollars, which is forty dollars an acre. The Gridley ranch was sold at a price so low that every piece of it was almost immediately saleable at an advance of forty per cent, without further subdivision; a great part of this land is now being held for two hundred and seventy-five dollars an acre.

And these same first-class business men have carried on elaborate building programs at the peak of high prices; they have leased a wonderful building site for a long term of years, with the privilege of buying at any time during the life of the lease, at a price set at the beginning of the lease! They have killed Stanford as a democratic institution, and brought it close to the rocks of bankruptcy, by starting a medical school in San Francisco, against the judgment of the best experts, and allowing the expenses of that school to swallow up the funds of Stanford. That they had doubt as to the success of the medical school was shown by their resolution in 1908, to the effect that this school should never be allowed to take more than twenty-five thousand dollars a year out of Stanford's funds. But in the last president's report I find the medical school with a minus balance of a hundred and nineteen thousand dollars—and this does not include the expenses of the instruction at Palo Alto, comprising the first four or five years of the course. For instance, the biological group alone shows a deficit of a hundred and thirty thousand dollars!

So much for the handling of the Stanford trust. If I had a life-time in which to study universities, I should like to see what care has been taken with the funds of the University of the United Gas Improvement Company of Philadelphia, and with those of the University of the Steel Trust, at Pittsburgh, and with those of the University of Heaven, at Syracuse, and with those of the Mining-Camp University at Denver. I should like to settle down in New York and make a thorough financial study of the University of the House of Morgan, and tell Professor Moses Primrose the names of all those trustees and professors who got advance news of the moving of the university to Morningside Heights; I should like to raise a fund and have a search made of the title records, and give him a list of the various lots and parcels of land which now belong to Barnard College, and figure up the total of the fortunes cleared by the insiders who purchased the old insane asylum which stood on that site! But maybe Professor Moses Primrose would call that "honest graft!"

CHAPTER XXXV

THE UNIVERSITY OF THE LUMBER TRUST

We take the Southern Pacific Railroad, which was plundered by the founder of Stanford, aided by the father of a Stanford trustee and the father of a California trustee, and which now has a Rutgers College trustee, an Equitable Trust, a Guaranty Trust, and a National City Bank director. We travel north for a day and a little more, and find ourselves in a country ruled with iron hand by three great lumber companies, and the interlocking banks which finance them. The headquarters of this oligarchy of the Northwest are at Portland and Seattle, and we begin with the former city. You expect, perhaps, to find a lumber country crude and wild; but you will find in Portland an old city with a long-established aristocracy, as much concerned with its ancestors as Philadelphia.

Fifteen years ago there was a strong movement for social justice in Oregon, led by reformers who fondly imagined that if you gave the people the powers of direct legislation they would have the intelligence to protect their own interests. We see now that the hope was delusive; the people have not the intelligence to help themselves, and the interlocking directorate is vigorously occupied to see that they do not get this intelligence. To this end they utilize two institutions, Reed College in Portland, which is privately endowed, and the University of Oregon, located in the neighboring town of Eugene. As we have seen with Eastern universities, it makes no particle of difference whether an institution is directly owned and controlled by the plutocracy, or indirectly controlled through the plutocracy's political machine.

The grand duke who attends to the education of Oregon is Mr. A. L. Mills, president of the First National Bank of Portland, and vice president of a trust company and an insurance company which handle the finances of the state. Mr. Mills is an active and efficient ruler; as his right-hand man he maintains a political boss, Gus Moser, and through him he beat the teachers' tenure law in Oregon, denouncing it as a move to establish a "teachers' soviet." He called in the Black Hand from California to his aid, and the pamphlets of Mr. Clum were distributed in Oregon, and a law was put through the legislature to compel teachers to take an oath of loyalty to the constitution, the flag, and the state. There is as yet no law requiring any oath of loyalty to truth, to freedom, and to justice.

In Reed College was a president, Foster, who had progressive ideas. He hired a liberal young professor who had just been fired from the University of Washington, Joseph K. Hart, now one of the editors of "The Survey"; and for three years the interlocking trustees fought to get rid of Professor Hart, and of Foster, who stood by Hart. Under such circumstances the regular procedure is to starve out the college; but they could not very well do it in this case, because they owned all the real estate surrounding the college, and the college was the main source of the real estate's value. Nevertheless, the editor of the Portland "Oregonian," the old Tory newspaper which manages the thinking of the people of Oregon, laid down the law that Reed College should get no publicity so long as Hart and Foster stayed.

The interlocking trustee who runs Reed College is Mr. James B. Kerr, who studied law in the office of an ancient reactionary, Senator Spooner, and is general counsel for Mr. Morgan's Northern Pacific Railroad Company. Mr. Kerr evolved from his legal mind a scheme to have a larger board of regents, taking in the former trustees, and making them a minority; so President Foster retired, and Professor Hart, who was away doing war work, was authorized to stay away!* A professor of history from the University of Washington was asked to become the new president, and when he was installed, Mr. Mills, in his role as general overseer of education, attended the ceremonies and made the principal address, in which he laid down the law to the new incumbent: "The business men of Oregon wish the youth of the state to become this and not that, we wish them to be 'shaped' in this way and

---

*One professor vigorously denies that this was the purpose of the enlarging of the board; but no one can deny that this was the effect. When I submit this comment to this gentleman, he tells me that it is "misleading." At the same time he gives me an opportunity to test his accuracy. He says: "It is my recollection that Mr. Hart was not encouraged by the council to expect the increased salary, which he demanded as a condition of his return." I submitted this proposition to Professor Hart, who replied:

"I hope Professor X's memory is usually more reliable than this. No question of salary was involved. Frankly, I do not *know* what was involved. I was on leave of absence, in the East. My leave of absence covered the academic year 1919-20. Toward the middle of the year, finding that I was anxious to remain in the East another year, I asked the college authorities for an

not that way." Educators who were present described to me the insolence, not merely of the grand duke's words, but of his manner. The board of regents of Reed College now consists of Mr. Kerr; Mr. Ladd, chairman of the Ladd and Tilton Bank; an elderly department store proprietor; a reactionary judge; and a retired clergyman.

Next for the state university. Here we have to deal with a "war case." I do not plan to make use of "war cases" as such, for I realize that intolerance in war time becomes what Barrows of California said it ought to be—a virtue. The only war cases to which I shall refer are those in which the war was a pretext, and the real motive was to get rid of an enemy of the plutocracy. My investigations indicate that this kind of war case constitutes one hundred per cent of the total. There may have been some professors in American universities and colleges who sympathized with the German Kaiser and desired to see him win; all I can say is that I have not come upon such a case.

At the University of Oregon was Mr. Allen Eaton, one of the most public-spirited young teachers it has been my fortune to hear about. There was an epidemic of typhoid in the town of Eugene, and eighty of the students were ill, and more than two hundred of the townspeople—twenty-two of them died within a fortnight. Mr. Eaton ascertained from the physicians of the town that the city water was contaminated, and so he published an article advising everyone to boil the water before drinking it. The water supply was controlled by a private water company, in which the banks were interested, also prominent members of the Eugene Commercial Club. Mr. Eaton's banker and others of these citizens undertook to "persuade"

---

extension of my leave for another year. You can see that that request involved no financial obligation on the part of the college, as I was on leave without pay and merely asked for a continuance of that status for another year. That was the whole question. Moreover, the college authorities were never courteous enough to tell me what had happened in the case. However, a friend in the faculty who knew of the discussions wrote me that the council felt that in view of the general situation it was best for me not to come back to the college, and that therefore extending my leave would be an empty form. Those are the facts."

him to keep quiet about the epidemic; "so much talk is giving the town a black eye." They made threats which forced the young professor either to "knuckle down" or to fight in the open. He chose the latter course, and he forced municipal ownership of the waterworks; a modern filtration system was installed, and in ten years there has not been a single case of typhoid traceable to the city water. We shall find in the course of this book many boards of trustees laying down the law that university professors are not allowed to take part in politics, but I think you must admit that in this case it might fairly be claimed that Mr. Eaton was forced into politics to protect his own self-respect.

He was six times elected to the Oregon state legislature, his chief local opponent being a hard-boiled politician in the hire of the Southern Pacific Railroad. Eaton made in the legislature an immaculate record; he exposed and abolished a wasteful type of road which the contractors were building in the state; he planned the Oregon building at the San Francisco Exposition, the most beautiful building on the grounds; he labored to introduce art into county fairs —and if you know what an American county fair is you can understand what a job the young instructor had! All this time his pay stayed low and promotion was lacking; nevertheless, he gave lectures for the people at the university and all over the state, and taught them what true art means—the people's own creation of beauty in their daily lives.

People who have lived all their lives in Oregon assure me that there has never been a man, either in the university or in the state legislature, who has done as much for education as Allen Eaton did. He undertook a campaign to increase the appropriation for the university; the governor of the state opposed him— this gentleman, being wealthy, sent his children to a fashionable university in the East. Eaton put through a bill to raise the appropriation from $47,500 to $125,-000, and when the governor vetoed the proposition, he directed a state-wide referendum campaign and carried the measure. He worked equally hard for the public schools; but at the same time he committed the crime of forcing the taxation of water-power sites, and advocating the direct election of United States senators. Still worse, he committed the crime of carrying to the Supreme Court of the state a case which kept the Southern Pacific Railroad from stealing sixty-six million dollars worth of timber-lands from the people of Oregon. Mr. Eaton is not a lawyer, but he got lawyers to help him, and he won the case; so the special interests of Oregon were out to "get" him at any price.

When the war came it happened that Allen Eaton was in Chicago, and he attended the convention of the People's Council. He took no part in the affair, not being himself a pacifist; but he wrote an honest account of the proceedings for the Portland "Journal," and so the large scale grafters got their chance. The Commercial Club of Eugene adopted a set of resolutions, bringing seven separate charges of disloyalty; the Spanish War Veterans endorsed the charges, and the regents of the university were summoned in solemn conclave, and Mr. Eaton appeared for trial, with the Portland Chamber of Commerce and the Commercial Club of Eugene as the prosecutors. Every one of the charges was disproven in every detail. The president of the university stood by Mr. Eaton, and the faculty of the university adopted a resolution in his support. The regents themselves admitted his innocence, for they stated that they "did not intend to accuse him of intending disloyalty to his government." Nevertheless, they accepted his resignation, giving him less than ten days' notice in which to shape his life plans— the Chamber of Commerce was in that much of a hurry!

Mr. Eaton ran for the legislature again, and among the super-patriots who set out to compass his defeat was a leading banker, who shortly afterwards was arrested for setting fire to a building in which he had stored a quantity of potatoes, held as an unsuccessful war-speculation; also a hundred percent sheriff, whose boast was that he had broken up a public meeting in defense of Mr. Eaton. At the very time he did this he had in his pockets forty-five hundred dollars which he had stolen from the county; a little later this was discovered and he was forced to leave overnight!

It might be worth while to mention that at the very time that Allen Eaton was fired from the University of Oregon, Professor Foerster of the University of Munich, an ardent pacifist, was denouncing the German government and being widely quoted by the allies; he was ostracized by the entire faculty of his university—nevertheless, the Kaiser's government let him continue to teach, because in Germany they really understand what academic freedom is, and stand by the principle. In all Great Britain there was only one case during the war of interference with academic freedom, and that was the case of Bertrand Russell, who was prosecuted and sent to prison for his pacifist activities. But in America, which understands no kind of freedom except the freedom of mobs to suppress anybody they do not like, I know of just two great universities in which some man or group of men were not hounded from their positions, for pointing out this or that unwelcome truth to the public.

CHAPTER XXXVI

THE UNIVERSITY OF THE CHIMES

We move a couple of hundred miles farther north to Seattle. It may be difficult to believe that there was ever a time when students in an American university took an active interest in the people's rights, and declined to receive favors from wholesale corrupters of public life; but such was actually the case ten years ago, at the height of the Progressive movement in the state of Washington.

The grand duke who ran the higher education of that state was Colonel Blethen, publisher of the Seattle "Times," an exceptional old scoundrel who had manipulated street railways in Minnesota, and then brought his fortune to Seattle and bought a newspaper, which he used for the rawest kind of blackmailing, by a "strong arm" advertising department. Colonel Blethen had been made a member of the board of regents of the university; and in the effort to rehabilitate himself and his family name, he spent twelve thousand dollars for a set of chimes, which he presented to the university with the stipulation that they were to be known by his name.

The students of the university did not feel grateful; fifty-one of them composed and signed a letter of protest which was inserted in the student daily, and put on the presses, when the printer "tipped off" Colonel Blethen's university president, and the presses were stopped. The students took the letter to the city and there printed it and distributed it. The editor of the college paper refused to publish again until he could publish the letter. When ordered by the authorities to issue the paper, he did so with a blank space where the letter had been!

Colonel Blethen's president was a gentleman named Kane—bear his name in mind, if you can, as we shall have some adventures with him at the University of North Dakota. President Kane accepted the chimes, and a solemn ceremony of dedication was performed—with the students distributing handbills of protest on the outskirts of the crowd! If you consider the coincidence of Times, chimes and crimes, you will understand that the young men were literally driven to writing verses. The ones they made strike me as exceptionally good, so I quote two stanzas.

ALL IS WELL

Recommended to friends of the University of Washington as a suitable Dedication Ode for the Blethen Chimes:

Clang the Chimes—clang the Chimes,
Help to glorify The Times;
And the fame to which it's heir
—All the sins that "dailies" dare—
Swell aloud from college walls;
Peal through all the college halls.
Slander's pence and scandal's dimes
Here transform to silver chimes
That shall tell, as they swell,
All is well; all—is—well. . . .

Champion of the den and sty!
Daily forty-page-long-lie!
Yet, despite its thousand crimes,
Praise The Times; clang its Chimes.
Let them charm the ear of Youth;
Let them swell its jeers at Truth
And in Truth's own court proclaim

Gold is power; brass is fame;
Watch The Times go on and sell
All the news that's fit—(for h—).
All is well; All—is—well.

The protest had been orderly and dignified—the only violence being committed by one of the regents, who had dragged a student about, trying to tear his papers away from him and denouncing him for what he was doing. The student body was thoroughly roused, and more than seven hundred signed a letter endorsing the protest. Blethen had come on to the campus to make a speech, and the students had heckled him and as one of them told me "had him on the run." The university authorities now barred all save invited speakers, and the president ordained that the teaching of progressive ideas at the university must cease, and there was to be no student criticism of president or regents, or their acts. The whole controversy was reviewed by the regents, who endorsed what the president had done.

We have spoken of Professor Hart, and how he was dropped from Reed. At this time Hart was at the University of Washington, and an incident will illustrate the feeling of all parties. Hart sat at luncheon in the Faculty Club, when President Kane entered and told of the action of the regents. Said Hart, "They think they can get away with it?" To which the president answered: "Aren't they the authorities?" Said Hart: "Do you realize that there are a thousand students in this university who have votes, and may hold the balance of power at the next election?"

Evidently the regents thought the same thing; it was the year of the Roosevelt revolt, and the Progressives were certain of carrying the state. A few days before the election, the Seattle "Post-Intelligencer," owned by the transportation lines and the Seattle National Bank, dug up a story to the effect that the Progressive candidate had divorced his wife. They mailed out ten thousand post cards to the women of the state: "Do you want a divorced man for governor?" As a result, the Democrats carried the election by eight hundred votes. They threw out two regents who had supported the students, and later on, as a result of the controversy, the governor turned out the entire board and put in four standpat business men, with a Catholic M. D. at the head. This gentleman made a desperate effort to have a Catholic chosen as president of the university, but finally compromised upon a High Church Episcopalian of Catholic extraction, a product of Nicholas Murray Butler's finishing machine.

Professor Hart was at this time one of the most popular members of the faculty with the students, a lecturer widely known throughout the state; he was now told that his inability to get along with his colleagues in his department was a reason for his dismissal. They gave him a year's leave of absence, though he did not want it; then they set out to find a substitute, and he applied for the job of substitute! Finally, they let out all three professors in the department, including Hart; a little later they took back one of them, the dean! A great many people thought this was a trick, and Hart's students protested bitterly, but in vain. They paid Hart an unusual tribute of appreciation, organizing a publishing company to finance his book on social service.

Old Colonel Blethen of the "Times" is dead, and the University of the Chimes now has as its first grand duke a gentleman who is president of a bank, a commercial company, an investment company, an irrigating company, and a mortgage and a loan company; he is assisted by a politician and lobbyist, chairman of the appropriations committee of the state legislature. In twenty-five years, I am informed, there has never been a farmer or a labor representative on the board! The university remains a place of low standards, no academic achievements, and perpetual cheap advertising by the administration. Three different men have written me to tell how they have been strangled—but always warning me not to use their names—not even to tell the details of their experiences! One writes about another professor, not in any sense a radical, but who tells the truth about public questions, and as a result has been an object of attack for twenty-five years:

Most of the time it has been under cover and has consisted in efforts to bring pressure to bear on the president and board of regents. But a number of times it has come out into the open. A governor some years ago in his inaugural address announced his determination to bring about the removal of Professor ———, and a few times an effort has been made in the legislature to make elimination of his department a condition of legislative support for the university. But while a good deal of publicity was given to these more spectacular assaults on academic freedom, they had little effect except perhaps to strengthen the administrative conviction that such departments were a good deal of a nuisance. Far more effective are the ever active forces which are working silently without any publicity upon those in control—president and regents. Nor does the failure to exercise power to remove indicate necessarily lack of real influence. There are many ways of disciplining an obstreperous faculty member without actual removal. A president in his control of salaries, distribution of library and other departmental funds may withhold from an offending faculty member opportunities accorded to those who have not incurred his displeasure. In the course of my experience as a faculty member I have seen a good deal of the sinister side of university control.

And peace reigns in the country of the Lumber Trust. Last year the big lumber companies cut wages, and on an investment of three millions they paid dividends of seven millions. At Port Angeles they are bringing in ship-loads of Japanese labor, in defiance of the law. The lumber-jacks and the blanket-stiffs work in hourly peril of life and limb; they sleep in filthy bunks and eat rotten food, and if they attempt to organize and better their conditions, their organizations are destroyed and their meeting halls sacked by mobs of business men. If they appeal to the public authorities they are laughed at; if they appeal to the public their voices are unheard; if they exercise the elemental right of self-defense, as they did at Centralia, they are shot, or beaten to death, or castrated with pocket knives and hanged, or tried before a mob jury and sentenced to ten or twenty years in jail. These things are done, not as acts of primitive barbarism, but as a business system; they are planned by the interlocking directorate, sitting in padded arm-chairs around tables in directors' rooms; they are carried out by efficient executives telephoning from mahogany desks. Such is the rule of the Lumber Trust; and at the University of the Lumber Trust the professors know all about it; they go to their classes and teach what their masters tell them to teach, and on behalf of justice and humanity they utter not one single peep.

CHAPTER XXXVII

THE UNIVERSITIES OF THE ANACONDA

We take the Northern Pacific Railroad, which has Mr. Morgan himself for a director, also two Morgan partners, one of them a recent Harvard overseer and a Massachusetts Tech trustee, and the other a Harvard overseer and Smith College trustee; also an Amherst trustee, a Hampton trustee, a Union Theological Seminary director, a Cornell trustee, and three First National Bank directors. We travel East until we come to the mining country; first, Montana, which has been swallowed whole by an enormous corporation, appropriately called the Anaconda. The people of this state maintain a university, scattered in four widely separated places, in order to please various real estate interests.

The State Board of Education, which runs matters for the Anaconda, contains the following appointed members: the personal attorney of Senator Clark, sometimes called the richest man in the world, and certainly the worst corruptionist who ever broke into the United States Senate; another attorney for big business, a hard fighting reactionary, who "grilled" a professor of the university law school for the crime of not giving his son high marks; another corporation lawyer, and a fourth lawyer who is a mild progressive; two merchants of the aggressive Chamber of Commerce type; one rich and conservative farmer; and one very subservient school principal.

The chancellor of the university up to last year was Edward C. Elliott, and he had to handle not merely this board, but the politicians of the Anaconda who run the state legislature; he had to go to them every year to beg for appropriations, and he had the bright thought that he would try to have an annual tax provided for higher education in the state. He suggested to Louis Levine, his professor of economics, to make a study of the whole tax problem in Montana. Professor Levine set to work—beginning with the subject of mining companies and their contributions, or lack of contributions, to the state taxes! In the course of the year 1918 occurred a state tax conference, and Professor Levine addressed it, and was furiously attacked by a representative of the Anaconda Copper Company, which had packed the conference with its lawyers and lobbyists.

Toward the end of the year Professor Levine completed his report on mine taxation, in which he proved that the great corporations paid only a small percentage of the taxes they owed the state. He submitted this report to the chancellor, who read it and had a desperate case of "cold feet." His contract was about to come up for renewal, and he decided that he had better shift the responsibility to the State Board of Education, which governs the university. Professor Levine agreed to this, but on the stipulation that if the board declined to publish the document, he should be free to publish it himself. He took the position that if he submitted to pressure in this issue, he would lose the moral right to lecture to classes of young people.

Now began a bitter struggle behind the scenes, with the governor of the state and a senator-henchman of the Anaconda striving frantically to keep the report from appearing. Finally the poor chancellor wrote to Levine, forbidding him to publish the report; Levine answered that there had been a definite understanding, made in the presence of President Sisson of Montana State University, that Levine was to be free to publish the report if he so desired. Accordingly he published it,* and the chancellor, in a rage, immediately "fired" him.

This was about as clear a case of the violation of academic freedom as had ever occurred in America. The matter created a great scandal, and this scandal caused pain to the faculty of the university. A committee of professors took the matter up, and reported, somewhat plaintively:

"It must have been foreseen that the enforcement of this order would lead to all of the undesirable publicity which has attended this whole affair, and which has brought down upon the University of Montana

---

*Taxation of Mines in Montana: B. W. Huebsch, New York, The book won the commendation of Professor Seligman of Columbia, America's leading conservative authority on taxation.

the condemnation of some of the most widely read newspapers and periodicals of the country, and which has made the university stand in the minds of people throughout the United States as a horrible example of narrow-mindedness, bigotry and intolerance. . . . Not only have the members of the faculty of the State University been made to feel that they have lost all independence of thought and action, which are (sic) absolutely essential to the maintenance of a university's morale, but the day is far distant when the University of Montana will be able to attract to its faculties broad-minded and eminent scholars of independence and initiative."

Also the American Association of University Professors took up the matter and sent out a representative to mediate. The State Board of Education could not face the public clamor; doubtless, also, they reasoned that the report was out, and their mining companies had sustained all the harm possible. They tactfully voted that both sides were right; the chancellor had acted properly in firing Professor Levine, but Levine should now be reinstated, and paid for the time he had been fired! The state legislature appointed a committee to investigate the university, and especially the teaching of "Socialism" in its economics department. This committee met privately in the empty bar-room of Helena's biggest hotel, and learned from Professor Levine that co-operative marketing by farmers is not the entire program of the Third International. After giving this information, Professor Levine resigned.

In the University of Montana law school was a young professor by the name of Arthur Fisher, son of the ex-Secretary of the Interior. He was a splendid teacher, popular with the students and with the faculty; but he associated himself with the Farmer-Labor movement, an effort of the people of the Northwestern states to take the control of their affairs away from the corporations. A former president of the university, who had been kicked out by the Anaconda, had started a liberal newspaper, the "New Northwest," and Professor Fisher became interested in this and thereby stirred the fury of the "Missoulian," a newspaper of the Anaconda, which discovered that

13

Fisher was a Bolshevist, and that he was "financing the paper with the street-car graft of his father"—Fisher's father being a man who had spent a large part of his life opposing the street-car graft in Chicago. In the spring of 1921 the "Missoulian" dug up the fact that Fisher had made a speech in Chicago during the war, urging that the United States should force the allies to define their war aims. That, of course, was "pro-German," and the American Legion—swallowed by the Anaconda—took up the issue, and demanded Fisher's scalp.

A faculty committee of the university spent a good part of the summer on this problem, and vindicated the young professor on every point; but the chancellor—who still had to get his appropriations every year from an Anaconda legislature—mutilated the report of his faculty committee before he submitted it to the state board of education; and he and his board and the attorney general of the state of Anaconda worked out a most ingenious solution—they gave the radical young professor a compulsory leave of absence at full pay; they forbid him to teach law at the university, but they pay him the state's money while he edits the "New Northwest!" And the interlocking directorate were so much pleased with this ingenuity of Chancellor Elliott that they called him to become president of Purdue University at a higher salary!

We move down to Moscow, Idaho, where we find another university of the Copper Trust. Five years ago this university had a president named Brannon, described to me by a friend as "a liberal conservative, an educator and a scientist." The politicians who run the state are the Day brothers, mining kings; they starved the university, and their henchmen, who controlled the school funds, refused to pay the university's bills. They tried to reduce the president's salary, though he had a contract; he resigned, but there was such an uproar in the state that they had to recede. Senator Day's whole family, including the ladies, now took up the intrigue against President Brannon; they caused an investigation of the bursar, and when the accounts were reported all right, they sent back their investigators with instructions to find something wrong. A prominent newspaper publisher served notice that he must have the university printing or he would make trouble; and it is reported on good authority that on this occasion President Brannon said a "cuss" word. Anyhow, he was forced to resign, though no charges had been brought against him. Dean Ayres, and another dean who had supported him, went at the same time. We shall meet President Brannon again before long at Beloit, and it will appear that he has learned his lesson; for this time, when the interlocking directorate gives him orders, he obeys!

The educational affairs of Idaho, both school and university, are in the hands of Dr. E. A. Bryan, chief administrative officer of the State Board of Education. I have before me a very sumptuous pamphlet, printed by this board a few months ago at the expense of the people of Idaho. It contains an address by Dr. Bryan, entitled "The Foes of Democracy," and has as a frontispiece the portrait of an exceedingly handsome but stern-looking hundred per cent American. Dr. Bryan has discovered four dangerous foes of democracy: first, the "reds"; second, the "radicals"; third, the "profiteers"; and fourth, the "robber barons." Just what is the difference between a "red" and a "radical" I do not know, and Dr. Bryan does not enable me to find out. Apparently a "radical" is a person who advises labor unions to use strikes to "injure the public." It is manifest that there can be no strike which does not injure the public; Dr. Bryan is a bit muddled, but it is clear what he means, that as strikes grow more big, they also grow more inconvenient. I find him equally muddled on the subject of the "profiteer"; because, while he tells us not to make "an excess profit," he does not tell us what "an excess profit" is, nor how there can be such a thing in a competitive world. Apparently it is the same thing as in the case of strikes: profiteering has got too big! But that big strikes might be a consequence of big profiteering has apparently not penetrated Dr. Bryan's handsome head.

Also I seek in vain to find out the difference between the "profiteers" and the "robber barons." All I can gather is that there are bad men in the world, and they abuse their power. It is Dr. Bryan's idea that they will read his pamphlet, and reform, and then all will be well. May I suggest that he send copies of his pamphlet to the Day brothers, and also to the Day wives, who run the mining and the education of Idaho?

The significant thing about the pamphlet, aside from its feebleness of thought, is the amount of space which it gives to the various kinds of evil persons. The "reds" get eleven pages, the "radicals" get four and a half, the "profiteers" get one and a quarter, and the "robber barons" get two and a half. I took the trouble to figure this out, and it appears that the head of Idaho's educational machine considers that eighty per cent of the perils to present-day American life comes from the poor, and less than twenty per cent from the rich. So I am not surprised to receive a letter from a university professor, telling me that "in Idaho, when a successor to President Lindley of the state university at Moscow was being sought, the state commissioner of education, Dr. Bryan, requested a Stanford professor to come and meet the regents. He did this and was *not* appointed, because of certain views in reference to the present economic order. Dr. Bryan told me this himself." I suggest that Dr. Bryan should issue a new edition of his pamphlet, listing a fifth variety of "foes of democracy," in the shape of university authorities who train the youth of the country to be henchmen and lackeys of the profiteers and the robber barons.

CHAPTER XXXVIII

THE UNIVERSITY OF THE LATTER-DAY SAINTS

We next take the Union Pacific Railroad, with its Columbia trustee for chairman, and a Rutgers trustee and two Massachusetts Tech trustees and a Hebrew Tech trustee for directors, two Equitable Trust Company directors, two Guaranty Trust Company directors, and three National City Bank directors; and find ourselves in Salt Lake City, in the domain of another group of mining kings, working in alliance with one of the weirdest religious organizations that have ever sanctified America, the Church of the Latter-Day

Saints. This is not a book on religion, so we shall merely say that the Mormons are hard-working people, who have heaped up enormous treasures, and have turned the control of these treasures over to the heads of their church. So here is a group of pious plutocrats, who run the financial, political, religious and educational life of the State of Utah.

Also, of course, they run the state university. Mr. Richard Young, the son of Joseph Young, was until quite recently chairman of the board of regents of the University of Utah, and also trustee of the Brigham Young University. He was a prominent stand-pat politician, and made it his business to see that the professors of his university said nothing impolite about the Copper Trust, or the Smelter Trust, or the Public Utility Trust, or the Latter-Day Sanctity Trust.

Seven years ago his activities culminated in a violent row. Two professors were fired without warning, and the resentment of the faculty was so great that sixteen others resigned, and the control of the university by the church and the corporations received a thorough ventilation. It appeared that professors had been admonished and punished for various strange reasons—such as mentioning the important part played by the English church in English literature; making a private criticism of a Mormon woman at a social gathering; or making an impolite remark concerning the cuspidor shown in a painting of Brigham Young, patriarch of the Mormon religion!

The two professors who had been fired were accused of criticizing the university president; also, it was charged that one of them had remarked in a private conversation: "Isn't it too bad that we have a man like Richard Young as chairman of the board of regents." The witnesses who told of the criticism of the president of the university were never called, and the president was never required to name them. The regents, in an elaborate public statement on the controversy, brushed this demand aside by saying that whenever there was disagreement between the president and members of the faculty, they would settle the issue by deciding, not who was right, nor who told the truth, but who was the most useful to the university!

This affair was investigated by a committee of seven professors, representing the American Association of University Professors, who issued an eighty-two page report, covering every detail of the controversy. From this evidence it appears that the charges against the professors were false; and it appears that the president was to be numbered among those many university heads who do not always tell the truth. A student at commencement had delivered an address, advocating "a public utilities commission, and investigation into the methods of mining and industrial corporations." The interlocking directors were furious over this, and the governor of the state set to work to find out what professors had approved it. The president of the university denied that the governor had engaged in any such activities; but the report produces a mass of evidence, making it perfectly clear that the president's statement was untrue.

Also, it appears that the interlocking regents were not above evasion of the truth. They denied knowing that the faculty of the university had adopted a petition for redress of grievances—and this although full details about the faculty action had been published in the newspapers nine or ten days before the regents met! By keeping at it, the committee of professors extracted a few admissions from these saintly plutocrats; thus, they got Chairman Young to admit over his own signature "that the president had warned a certain prominent professor that his activity in behalf of a public utilities bill might injure the university; that he advised an instructor against participating in a political campaign, and enjoined a partisan rally on the campus."

It must be a difficult matter, running a university in the capital of the Latter-Day Saints. You have to know that your wealthy regents are living in polygamous relationships, which differ from those maintained by wealthy regents in other parts of the country in that they are crimes under the United States law, but acts of holiness under the church law; and you have to know in just what ways to know about these semi-secret families, and in just what ways to be ignorant of them. Outside is all the world, laughing at you; and naturally you are sensitive to that laughter, and your professors are still more so. They cannot be entirely unaware of modern thought; and so you have to summon them to your office and plead with them, pointing out how certain regents object that they "have been teaching against the experiences of Joseph Smith." You have to get them "to bring into class discussions and explanations of the term God or deity, if they can conscientiously do so." You have to explain to them that unless they "can conscientiously do so," the legislature will withhold appropriations, and they will not get their salaries.

And then, when the Latter-Day Grafters put pressure upon you, you have to remove a competent professor from the head of your Department of English, and put in a bishop of the Mormon church, the distinguished editor of "The Juvenile Instructor, a monthly magazine devoted to the interests of the Sunday Schools of the Mormon church"; also author of "The Restoration of the Gospel, a volume of Mormon apologetics, consisting chiefly of lessons prepared for the Young Ladies' Improvement Association, 1910-1911, with an introduction by Joseph F. Smith, Jr., of the Quorum of Twelve Apostles, 1912." And when your professors object to things like this, your interlocking regents retire you, and put the brother of the Mormon bishop into your place!

That is what happened at the University of Utah; Mr. Richard Young, grand saint of the board of regents, put in as president of his institution Mr. J. A. Widstoe, M. A., author of "Joseph Smith, the Scientist," in which he proves that the Mormon founder anticipated all modern science—excepting only Darwinism, which is taboo by the Church! Now Mr. Richard Young has gone to his eternal reward as grand saint, and his place is taken by Mr. Waldemar Van Cott, attorney for the Rio Grande Railroad and the Utah Fuel Company, and the most active agent in the attack on the liberal professors. President Widstoe has been promoted to "apostle" of the Church, and his place as head of the university has been taken by Dr. George Thomas, professor of economics. What kind of economics they now teach at the university is summed up for me by a lawyer of

Salt Lake City, who was formerly on the faculty of the institution. He says:

"Let it be noted that the Mormon church is a business institution. It owns and controls properties, banks, commercial institutions and industries. It is conservative. It is a foe of all doctrines and plans that might weaken property rights. Also, let it be noted that the organization of the Mormon church is perfect and that those who hold power depend upon the doctrines of the church for their tenure upon power and influence."

And then I take up the catalogue of the university, to see what they are teaching their three thousand students, and I find that they are catholic in their tastes. As courses leading to university degrees, they include commerce and finance, commercial art, business bookkeeping and stenography, auto mechanics, carpentering and plumbing! Three professors at the university write me that conditions under the new administration are greatly improved. One professor asserts that there is now complete freedom. I trust he will not think me unduly skeptical if I say that I would attach more weight to his experiences if he were teaching, say economics, instead of "ancient language and literature."

CHAPTER XXXIX

THE MINING CAMP UNIVERSITY

We continue our journey on the Union Pacific Railroad, and come to the metropolis of the Rocky Mountains, a city entirely surrounded by gold mines, silver mines, coal mines and copper mines, and entirely controlled by hard-fighting piratical gentlemen who have seized these hidden treasures. Denver is only a generation removed from the mining camp stage of civilization, and mining camp manners and morals still prevail in its financial, political and educational life. In other portions of the United States you find the great captains of industry hiring politicians to run the state and city governments for them; but in Colorado up to quite recently they did their own dirty work —you would find the grand dukes of the interlocking directorate, Evans of traction, Doherty of gas and electric, Field of telephones, Cheesman of water, Guggenheim of copper, themselves the political bosses, hiring their thugs and repeaters and ballot box stuffers, and paying their own cash to their newspaper editors, clergymen and college presidents. These mighty chieftains used to fall out and quarrel and turn their scandal-bureaus loose on one another, so it was always easy to learn the insides of Denver finance, politics and education.

The leading prejudice factory of the State of Colorado has been the University of Denver, founded by the father of William G. Evans, traction magnate and Republican boss. Mr. Evans made himself president of the board of trustees of the university, and selected to run the institution an extremely venomous and abusive Methodist clergyman by the name of Buchtel. In running the government of Denver, Mr. Evans worked in alliance with the gamblers and the keepers of brothels and wine-rooms for the seducing of young girls; the violations of law became so flagrant that the political gang operating under Evans found its power threatened, and cast about for some candidate for governor to take the curse off them, and selected the Reverend Henry Augustus Buchtel, D.D., LL.D., chancellor of their university. As the Denver "Post" delicately phrased it, "They reached up in the House of God and pulled down the poor old chancellor to cover up the rottenness of their machine."

There was a meeting of the chancellor with Mr. Evans and his political henchmen. One of the purposes of his nomination was that his candidacy might aid Simon Guggenheim, head of the Smelter Trust, to buy his way into the United States Senate. The chancellor accepted the nomination, and invited all present to rise, join hands and sing: "Blest Be the Tie That Binds." You may find this anecdote in "The Beast," by Ben B. Lindsey, Judge of the Children's Court of Denver—that is, you may find it if you can find a copy of the book, which its publishers mysteriously ceased to push. Says Lindsey:

The tie that binds the Beast and the Church? Yes, and the Beast and the College! During the Peabody campaign (according to the "Rocky Mountain News") a young student named Reed had been practically driven from the Denver University because he criticized the corporation Governor. Later a university professor was sent to Europe to gather data which was used in the campaign against municipal ownership in Denver; and the professor was "exposed but not forced into retirement." Later still, Buchtel reprimanded a student named Bell for volunteering as a worker in one of our Juvenile Court campaigns. Mr. Evans was president of the Board of Trustees of the University, and the Reverend Henry Augustus Buchtel was his Chancellor.

The use of Buchtel in the campaign that followed was a huge success. Everywhere people said to me: "Why, the Chancellor will never stand for the sale of the senatorship to Guggenheim!" Or the "dear chancellor" will never permit this or that undesirable thing in politics. But Buchtel had already admitted to a ministerial friend that he believed Guggenheim ought to be elected—though he said nothing of it from the platform, you may be sure. After he was Governor, he not only endorsed Guggenheim but vigorously defended the Legislature for electing Guggenheim, honored Evans with a place on the gubernatorial staff, and gave a public dinner to the corporation heads who had most profited by the rule of the System in the state. They reciprocated by sending the Denver University handsome donations; Evans led with $10,000, and Guggenheim, Hughes and others followed with fat checks.

The keeper of a gambling hell, whom I summoned to my court and forced to make restitution to one of his victims, said to me: "I have some respect for Mayor Speer. He tells these preachers that he believes in our policy of open gambling. But I have nothing but contempt for that old stiff up in the State House who talks about 'the word of God,' and gets his nomination from a boss who protects *us,* and gets elected on money that *we* contributed to the organization!" It is one of the saddest aspects of this use of the Church that The Beast gains respectability thereby, and the Church contempt. . . . .

Buchtel was elected. His candidacy proved a successful disguise for the Guggenheim "deal," and the "church element" was used as well as "the dive element." A corporation legislature was put in power. It only remained for the corporations to deliver the United States senatorship to Guggenheim "for value received," and to betray the nation as they had betrayed the state.

Simon Guggenheim had no more claim to represent Colorado in the Senate at Washington than John D. Rockefeller has —or Baron Rothschild. He was the head of the Smelter Trust, and he had been financially interested, of course, in the election of Peabody in 1904, and the defeat of the eight-hour law and the suppression of the eight-hour strike. These things entitled him to the gratitude of the corporations only. He was unknown to the people of Colorado. He had never been heard of by them except in a newspaper interview. He had not, as far as I know, ever spoken or written a word publicly on politics. "I don't know much about the political game," he told one of his campaign managers, "but I have the money. I know *that* game." He does.

That was fifteen years ago, and they did their bribery in the old-style way. Guggenheim paid the campaign expenses of a majority of the Colorado legislators. At present the State of Colorado is run by Phipps, the steel king, and they do not have to buy the legislators, for it is the people who elect the United States senators, and they have bought up all the institutions upon which the people depend. They have bought the Y. M. C. A. and the churches by "donations," and they have bought the universities in Colorado by giving hundreds of thousands of dollars to them. Because Lindsey exposed this new style of bribery, the Phipps machine ordered all of Lindsey's child welfare bills killed by the state legislature.

And of course in their university they watch incessantly to make sure that no dangerous ideas reach the students. Last summer there was a meeting of all the clergymen of Denver on the campus of the university to listen to Dr. Harry Ward, general secretary of the Social Service Commission of the Federated Council Churches of America. The chancellor intervened at the last minute and forbade Ward to speak, denouncing him as "a menace to the present social order." Instead, he got copies of a report on the steel strike, which Judge Gary had had prepared by one of his kept clergymen, as a reply to the attack by the Inter-Church World Movement. Every member of the graduating class of 1921 received a copy of this report, being solemnly called in to receive it personally from the hands of the chancellor. A professor at the university, who had been scheduled to speak at the church of a Socialist clergyman in Denver, was called up and warned that if he wished to have a career at the university he must avoid that kind of thing. Shortly after this a representative of the Rockefeller education fund was invited to luncheon at the university, and the chancellor made a public appeal to him for funds, on the ground of his services in barring Dr. Ward. This was a trifle too raw, and the chancellor did not get his money!

The old man has just been retired; but the same gang still rules the board of trustees, with Evans the infamous as grand duke. As assistant he has an attor--

ney for the "Big Four" corporations which run the city of Denver, who spends his spare time leading crusades against the "reds"; also a prominent banker, a corporation lawyer, a real estate speculator, a capitalistic preacher, a corporation lawyer from Pueblo, a millionaire oil man and lawyer, a millionaire miner and banker—and finally, as Grand Duke junior, "Boss" Evans' son, John.

CHAPTER XL

THE COLLEGES OF THE SMELTER TRUST

The interlocking directorate of Colorado maintains also a state university at Boulder, on the Colorado and Southern Railroad; which road has a trustee of Williams College for president, and a General Theological Seminary trustee for director. The standards of academic freedom prevailing at the University of Colorado are very interestingly revealed in a case which occurred seven years ago.

During the coal strike of 1914, the operators and their militia set aside the constitution of the United States in the Southern counties of the state, and one professor at the law school took a stand against their action. The operators had burned and suffocated three women and eleven children at Ludlow, and Professor James W. Brewster accepted the chairmanship of a public committee to investigate the strike situation. In peril, not merely of his job, but of his life, he spent several weeks in the coal fields, questioning witnesses and bringing out evidence. He was the means of forcing an investigation by Congress, and he appeared and testified before the Congressional Committee. His subsequent dismissal from the university was investigated by the American Association of University Professors, and their report lies before me. I will state briefly the facts admitted, and the contentions of both parties to the dispute, and leave it for the reader to form his own conclusions.

Professor Brewster was nearly fifty-nine years of age, and the president of the university claims that on this account his appointment to the university had been merely temporary, and that this was fully made clear to Professor Brewster. Professor Brewster denies that he had any such understanding. It was admitted by both the president and the dean of the law school that Brewster's teaching was "entirely satisfactory." Says the report:

The testimony of students in his law classes is that Professor Brewster in the class room adhered strictly to the subjects he was teaching and made no allusions whatever to industrial questions. The courses that he was teaching did not in any way involve the issues that were then agitating Colorado. Immediately after Professor Brewster's testifying in December he was abusively attacked by several Colorado newspapers in unrestrained language and with the most unreasonable distortion and exaggeration of the tenor of his testimony. According to the testimony of President Farrand, E. M. Ammons, then Governor of Colorado, called up President Farrand by telephone soon after Mr. Brewster's appearance before the Commission in Denver, and urged the immediate dismissal of Professor Brewster because of his testimony.

The president of the university asserts that he refused the governor's request. That was in December, 1914; in May, 1915, Professor Brewster was invited to come to Washington, to give his testimony before the United States Commission on Industrial Relations. Professor Brewster went to the president of the university, and stated that he had been able to arrange for a colleague to take his classes for the few days of his absence. As to what happened next there is a disagreement. Professor Brewster claims that the president told him that if he went to Washington his connection with the university must cease at once. The president, in his statement to the committee of the association, gives his version of the interview as follows:

I told him that I regarded the publicity which had attended his former testimony as detrimental in its effect upon the university. In the inflamed condition of public sentiment in Colorado at that time it was exploited in a way which I regarded as unfortunate. His connection with the university was made prominent in the inaccurate publicity which resulted and the institution was drawn thereby into a controversy, and an attitude attributed to the university as an institution, which I regarded as unwarranted and unfortunate. In further discussion of this point and in illustrating the prejudice aroused by the testimony, I cited the feeling expressed by members of the Legislature and reported to me during the legislative session of 1915. I used some expression to the effect that his public statements regarding the industrial situation had been an obstacle in the university's effort to obtain additional support from the Legislature. I did not, as I recall it, lay any stress upon this and mentioned it incidentally as an illustration and matter of interest at the moment. I stated that in view of the inaccurate publicity and the involvement of the university at the time of his previous appearance before the Federal Commission, I thought it would be desirable, in case he decided to go to Washington, that a statement should be issued indicating the temporary nature of his connection with the university and that that connection would naturally terminate at the end of the academic year.

The outcome of the matter was that Professor Brewster decided not to go to Washington; nevertheless, he was dropped from the University of Colorado. It is interesting to note that among those who were retained at the University was Dr. John Chase, who will live in American history as the man responsible for the Ludlow massacre. He was adjutant-general of the Colorado militia at the time, and an unscrupulous partisan of the coal operators. Among the regents at the time was Mr. C. C. Parks, politician, banker, coal company director, and furious opponent of the strikers. Among the law faculty who fought Professor Brewster was Professor A. A. Reed, whose law partner was engaged in prosecuting a number of the former strikers. Professor Reed, a former bank president, was at this time an official of a national bank in Denver, and a director of the Colorado Fuel & Iron Company, Mr. Rockefeller's concern which put through the Ludlow massacre. I am interested to note that another member of the faculty who is not objected to is Professor L. W. Cole, director of the School of Social Service, who last summer recommended to the students of his summer school Vice-President Coolidge's magazine articles on the "Red menace," a farrago of foolishness gathered by the Lusk committee and their secret agents.

Also we ought to have a glance at Colorado College, located at Colorado Springs; a co-educational institution started by the Congregational Church, and now conducted by the interlocking directorate. They had a first-class business man for president, but there were brought against him "serious charges of indiscreet and improper conduct toward two women employed in the college offices." Now, of course, the business men who run the government of Colorado, in conjunction with the brothels and wine-rooms, understand that college presidents have to have their little pleasures in off hours; but some of the faculty thought that college presidents ought to have these pleasures somewhere off the campus. They endeavored privately to force the resignation of the president; whereat the trustees became furious, and fired a dean who had been active in the matter. When the students organized and protested, they contemptuously rejected the students' demands.

This matter likewise was investigated by the American Association of University Professors, and it happened that I studied their report before I knew anything about the trustees and their financial position. It was rather funny; I read what the trustees said to the professors, and how they behaved in the various conferences; I read their letters, and found myself thinking: this must be a rich man, and so must this; here must be the grand duke, the fellow who runs the place! Then I looked them up in "Who's Who," and, sure enough, there they were—Mr. Philip B. Stewart, mining and public utility magnate, an active Republican politician; and Mr. Irving Howbert, president of a bank, a gold mining company and a railroad, also an active Republican politician!

Would you like to hear one of these grand dukes addressing his college professors, gathered together to be taught their place? Listen to the affidavit of Professor George M. Howe:

> The meeting was opened by Mr. P. B. Stewart, chairman of the executive committee of the Board. Mr. Stewart berated us soundly for what we had done. . . . His mains points were that we had been guilty of sending libelous matter through the mail, for which we might well be sent to the penitentiary; that we had given the slanderous charges against Dr. Slocum into the hands of persons who should know nothing of them, since our letters would come into the hands of private secretaries of the men to whom they were sent; and that we had made the completion of the five hundred thousand dollar fund for the College impossible, since the Trustees, who were large contributors, would now withhold their subscriptions. His purpose was apparently to make us feel that our conduct had been thoroughly idiotic and ill-advised in every respect.

And then hear the summing up of the American Association of University Professors:

"The committee feels constrained to remark, further, that the attitude of the majority of the members of the Board of Trustees and of the Board as a body towards the faculty has been characterized by grave discourtesy, a lack of openness and candor, and an habitual disregard of the fact that the administrative officers and teaching staff of a college have large and definite moral responsibilities in relation to the internal conditions and standards of the institution with which they are connected."

The outcome of the whole matter was that the graduating class of the college fell off from eighty to twenty-six; but the interlocking trustees waited. They held the purse-strings, and they knew that the incident would be forgotten, and the students would come back—which they did.

Also the plutocracy of Colorado maintains an institution for training its engineers and mining experts; this is the Colorado School of Mines, located at Golden. Here also there was trouble, because on "Senior Day" some of the students got drunk and beat up a member of the faculty at a baseball game. Naturally, the president and the faculty resented this, and they suspended five of the students, and there was a great uproar, culminating in a student strike. This incident also was investigated by the Association of University Professors, and I studied the report before I knew anything about the various trustees. Here again I was able to pick out the grand duke by his bad manners, and by the way everybody cringed before him when he came down from Cripple Creek to deal with the row. He is Mr. A. E. Carlton, president of four banks and of several mining companies.

Naturally, so great a man realized the absurdity of suspending the sons of the plutocracy, merely for the beating up of a college professor! With the help of Captain Smith, another member of the board, he settled the strike by reinstating the suspended students and forcing the resignation of the protesting president. The board put in a former president of the college, who had been dismissed for cause, but who was exactly the sort of fellow they wanted, as you can see from the sworn testimony of seven different professors, to the effect that he had lowered the teaching standards of the college by insisting again and again that the sons of the plutocracy should be given passing marks after they had failed. The committee of university professors states that "Professor H. B. Patton, for twenty-four years a member of the faculty, informed the Committee that President Alderson condoned cheating on the part of a son of an influential Denver citizen." Says Professor Albert G. Wolf: "Many students at the school during Alderson's administration were allowed to pass, after having failed in their studies, because they were either athletes or relations of influential men of Colorado." Says Professor Stephen Worrell: "President Alderson arbitrarily raised the grades of some of the men I had either conditioned or failed. . . . . Subsequent investigation revealed that the men whose grades had been raised were relatives of prominent politicians in the State. I found on inquiry that the same thing had happened to other members of the faculty, but that they had all accepted the situation as inevitable."

This controversy was settled by the dismissal of several of the protesting professors, and by the appointment of a committee of the state legislature, which investigated the situation and reported in the following apposite words:

In conclusion, your Committee finds that the management and administration of the School of Mines is efficient, the trustees, officers, and faculty competent, well qualified, and trustworthy, and that the institution, members, officers, faculty, and trustees are entitled to the support, respect, and encouragement of the citizens of this State, the alumni of the institution, and the general public. Your Committee is of the opinion that the institution will flourish and its excellent reputation be maintained if it receives the encouragement and patronage to which it is so justly entitled.

CHAPTER XLI

A LAND GRANT COLLEGE

We travel Northeast, and leave the mining country. On the lonely plains of the state of North Dakota we find men toiling for long hours, and raising a hundred million bushels of wheat every year. They mill very little wheat, but ship it away to the "twin cities" of Minneapolis and St. Paul; and then import their own flour: which means that from the time the wheat leaves his land the farmer is paying tribute to a chain of exploiters—elevator men, railroads, speculators, millers, and the bankers who furnish the capital for these operations. The same situation prevails throughout the prairie states, and so here you have a well-matured class struggle between the dwellers in the country and the dwellers in the towns. Ever since the Civil War the farmers have been struggling to free themselves from the "money devil." Wave after wave of revolt has risen, and sunk again, but always the masters of credit have managed to hold on. They have done this by owning or subsidizing the newspapers, the agricultural weeklies and the general magazines, and also by controlling the schools and colleges in which the farmers' children are educated.

Writing in 1916, Gilson Gardner stated that the United States Bureau of Education had approximately two hundred employes, and out of this number one hundred and thirty appeared on the official rolls as drawing a salary of one dollar per year. "The source from which these men are paid is unknown. It is known in general, however, that some of them get their salaries from the Rockefeller General Education Board and some from the Sage Foundation or other endowments of private capital. The reports made by these employes go out as government experiment publications with the full prestige of official endorsement upon them."

One of the government employes who is not a corporation hireling is Professor W. J. Spillman, chief of the Bureau of Agricultural Economics, and editor of a farm paper. Professor Spillman states that a wealthy friend came to him, with a statement that the Rockefeller General Education Board was seeking to control the educational institutions of the country, to see that the men employed in them were "right." They had been successful with the smaller institutions, but some of the larger ones had held out, and Rockefeller was now adding a hundred million dollars to the foundation, "for the express purpose of forcing his money into these big institutions. He is looking for a man who can put this across. I think you are just the man for the place. There is a fat salary in it for the man who can do the thing," and so on. Professor Spillman expressed some doubt of the Rockefellers being able to accomplish their purpose, and the friend explained that the removal of the unsatisfactory educators would be brought about as the result of "local dissatisfaction."

You will call this a "cock and bull story"; but just notice—in the years 1915 and 1916 there were nine liberal presidents of Western colleges turned out of their jobs, and at least twenty professors, mostly of economics and sociology! Do you really think that the masters of the Money Trust, having bought up the last newspaper and the last popular magazine, would overlook your schools and colleges? If so, you are exactly the kind of foolish person they count upon you to be!

Most influential among the farmers are the so-called "land grant colleges," which, way back in the days of President Lincoln, received from Congress large grants of government land for their support. Much of this land was stolen outright by the grafters. I am told that in Maine large tracts of the most valuable timber land were sold for a mere song, and without advertisement; exactly the same thing was done in Michigan, Wisconsin, Minnesota and Oregon—these land steals form the basis of the power of those old aristocratic families whom we found running Reed College and the University of Oregon. From what I know of my United States, I feel quite sure that an investigation in any state between Maine and Oregon would reveal the same kind of thing.

Anyhow, here are these land grant colleges, some of them big and prosperous, educating the farmers' boys, and as yet not aspiring to the snobbery of the big universities. The interlocking directorate wishes to get hold of these institutions, and to see that dangerous thoughts are kept out. I purpose to show you what they did in one state; I bespeak your careful attention, because the story of one is the story of all, and in reading about North Dakota you will also be reading about Maine, Vermont, Michigan, Wisconsin, Kansas, Nebraska, Iowa, Colorado and Oregon.

John H. Worst, at that time lieutenant-governor of North Dakota, became president of the Agricultural College in 1895. It was a small institution at that time; by seventeen years of hard work he built it up until he had over twelve hundred students. Also he conducted, in connection with the college, a government experiment station, in which he had some devoted scientists. One of these, Professor E. F. Ladd, now United States Senator put in office by the Non-Partisan League, was a chemist, who became state pure food commissioner, and carried on a vigorous campaign against light weights and short measures, and the adulterating and misbranding of food. He went to the shelves of the grocery stores, and showed that the stomachs of the people of North Dakota were made a dumping-ground for timothy seed, gelatine and coal tar dyes. He exposed the use of dangerous poisons in patent medicines, and denounced the practice of bleaching flour—nor was he content to prove these things in his laboratory, he went out and taught the people of the state, and helped to put through laws against these practices. As a result, he incurred the mortal enmity of whiskey rectifiers, baking-powder manufacturers, paint manufacturers, the Beef Trust and the Milling Trust. I talked with Senator Ladd in Washington in June, 1922, and he told me that the last libel suit filed against him—for one hundred thousand dollars—had been dismissed on the fourteenth of the previous April; prior to that time, for twenty-two years he had never been free from libel suits and injunctions. At one time there had been six hanging over his head, and never one had been filed by a citizen of North Dakota, nor had he ever lost one.

Next, meet Professor H. L. Bolley, who is my dream of a scientist; a long, lean, keen old gentleman, a demon for the hunting out of knowledge, and an untamed champion of the people's cause. I met him in Fargo, and asked him if he would tell me his story, and there came a few more wrinkles on his thin face. "I have been in this for twenty-two years," he said, "and maybe it will be my fate to be kicked out for talking to Upton Sinclair!" Then the old professor thrust out an eager finger: "This is the question I am asking: Is a college professor a citizen? Or does he part with his rights, and become some kind of subject when he takes a college job? I made up my mind that I was going to stay a citizen, and exercise every one of the rights of a citizen, including the right to go out and talk to my fellow-citizens, to educate them, and organize them to protect their rights against all-comers. That is all there is to my story."

Professor Bolley is one of the leading plant pathologists of the United States; it was he who first discovered the causes of most of the diseases which plague the farms of North Dakota—of "rust" and "smut" and "root rots" in wheat and other cereals, of potato "scab" and flax "wilt"—and he worked out remedies for these troubles, and taught them to the people. He proved that "flax wilt" is due to "sick" soil—and that seemed a terrible thing to the land interests and the railroads, who were making money out of getting new farmers into North Dakota. These speculators were not interested in having Professor Bolley cure the "sick" soil; it paid them better if the farmers went into bankruptcy every few years. The discoveries of Professor Bolley were worth hundreds of millions to the farmers of the Northwest. He made discoveries about flaxseed, and the linseed crushers and paint makers tried to buy his services—they were used to buying professors. Bolley had them put the money into the institution, with the provision that it was to be employed for his researches. We shall presently see how his enemies tried to take it away from him.

Also, this professor-citizen took up the question of the grading of wheat, the sorest point with the Northwestern farmers. They are absolutely at the mercy of the elevator men and the millers, and the whole thing is one colossal swindle. Professor Bolley knows wheat as well as any other man in the world, and he showed the tricks to the farmers. In the first place, the wheat all gets mixed up in the elevators, and there is no way to tell Smith's from Jones's. Nevertheless, the farce of "grading" goes on, and its effect is to beat down the price to the farmer. The millers say they must have Number One Red Spring—but there is not enough of this produced in America to feed one big city! What determines the mixture is the percentage of protein, starch, and gluten, and they test the flour as it comes through the mill, and when this or that ingredient is needed, they let in wheat of a certain kind, regardless of its "grade." That which they grade as "D," and buy as "feed" wheat, just because it is shrunken, may be the richest of all in proteins, and be used in their best brands of flour.

It is a fact that a great part of the flour is made from "rejected" wheat; and the sole point of the rejecting is to lower the price. I asked, "What is the price of rejected wheat?" and the answer was, "It is a bottomless pit—you can buy it for anything." They reject wheat if there is water in it—but they have to put water in it themselves in order to mill it! They reject it for smut—but they use it just the same, because the brush that takes off the bran also takes off the smut! They even use the mouldy wheat, because they bleach it. Many times Professor Bolley found them rejecting wheat for smut, and he would go to that neighborhood and learn there was little or no smut to be found there, and the elevator men made no effort to keep the wheat with smut separate from the rest. The elevator and grading workers would tell him that they had received word—there was too much wheat on the market, and they were to buy only "rejected" wheat—as an act of charity to those poor farmers who had got smut into their wheat; but the effect of this action was to force more farmers into ruin.

Professor Bolley was invited to accompany fifty scientists, including some from Europe, to inspect the flour mills in the "Twin Cities." Here came the prize "boosters" of the millers, setting forth the wonders of the place and the extreme precautions they took to use only the very finest wheat—they were making their best flour. Professor Bolley dipped his hand into one hopper and then into another, and carried home samples of this wheat. Fifty per cent of it consisted of amber durum, which they rejected, seven per cent of another rejected kind, and the balance of a very inferior grade of winter wheat; no hard spring wheat in the sample! And yet the millers would invite Professor Bolley to the Chamber of Commerce, to tell them how they could teach the farmers to raise better wheat! Professor Bolley went to Russia and spent a year collecting hardy wheats; the Siberian wheat which he brought home thrived, but the millers said it was worthless—and they bought it cheap. Then the farmers stopped growing it; whereupon the millers suddenly decided that this Siberian wheat was good; the climate had changed it, they said!

Meantime, Professor Ladd had set up a model bakery and a flour mill at the experiment station, and on the basis of his demonstrations, President Worst was showing the farmers of North Dakota how they could save the sum of fifty-five million dollars a year, by setting up elevators and mills, and exporting flour instead of wheat. In this demonstration lay the beginnings of the Nonpartisan League movement, and the masters of the Money Trust perceived that they must crush these rebel educators. How they tried to do it is the story we have next to hear.

CHAPTER XLII

AN AGRICULTURAL MELODRAMA

In January, 1911, there was held in the Twin Cities a gathering of the interlocking directorate, called by A. R. Rogers, lumber magnate, Howe, the elevator man, and a group of the big bankers; afterwards they got in the late "Jesse James" Hill, the railroad king of the Northwest. These gentlemen worked out a scheme, and wrote their checks for five thousand each. One of them threw in a remark: "It would be worth twenty-five thousand a year of any man's money to get Bolley out of the state, or to keep his damned mouth shut."

They were going to "educate" the farmers of North Dakota, and they called their movement the "Hundred Dollar An Acre Club," subsequently changing it to the "Better Farming Association." They appointed an executive committee consisting of Rogers, the lumberman, Howe, the elevator man, one farmer, and eighteen North Dakota bankers, with the president of the First National Bank of Fargo at their head! These bankers were borrowing money in Wall Street at six per cent and lending it to the farmers of their state at ten per cent, which represented a profit of twelve million dollars a year to them.

As manager of their program of "education" they selected one Thomas Cooper, at a larger salary than any "educator" in North Dakota had ever been paid before. Forty-five thousand dollars a year was pledged, and Mr. Cooper set to work to "educate" the farmers as to the wickedness of Ladd, Bolley, and others. After three years the balance-sheet of the organization showed liabilities of forty thousand dollars, and assets of one brilliant idea. The bankers of the organization went to that other group of bankers who comprised the trustees of the North Dakota Agricultural College, and proposed that the college should take over Mr. Cooper and his salary and his deficit, and should give him entire control of the experiment station and extension division, and joint authority over the instruction division, with eighteen North Dakota bankers as an advisory board! This little job was put through in 1913, and the exact facts were hidden from the people of North Dakota, and two years later the Non-partisan League newspapers had to steal the documents in the case in order to make them known!

Now behold Mr. Cooper and his eighteen bankers in control of a state experiment station! The first thing they do is to lock Professor Bolley out of his laboratories, and the poor janitor is somewhat bewildered, not knowing whom to let in! They even take away from his department the research money which he had got from the linseed crushers! They forbid Ladd and Bolley to go to the state capital while the state legislature is in session. They issue a written order forbidding them to publish press bulletins or newspaper articles until these have received the O. K. of Mr. Cooper; and when Professor Bolley submits bulletins they chop them to pieces and publish them in such garbled form that they make nonsense. For four years they publish nothing at all of Bolley's work.

The brunt of the struggle fell on President Worst, not because he had done anything himself, but because he stood by his professors. In the fall of 1914 Worst was in Washington, attending a convention of the agricultural colleges, and the board passed a secret resolution promoting him to be president-emeritus—an honorary degree hitherto unknown in North Dakota agricultural culture. They had conceived the clever idea of putting Ladd in his place, because this would pacify the people, and they believed that Ladd would prove a poor executive, and would be unable to hold on. They came to Ladd and begged him to accept, and assured him that Worst had consented—which was not true.

When the governor of the state learned what they had done, he fell into a panic, and ordered them to rescind the action, and for a year thereafter they backed and filled and argued, trying to persuade Worst to resign and Ladd to take his place. In the following year Governor Hanna, himself a prominent banker and director in many corporations, appointed a new board of regents, with a banker as president, and another banker and his lawyer making the majority. To this new board President Worst protested against the disorganization in the institution, and proposed some division of authority. The interlocking newspapers lied about what he had said, and the board again got up the nerve to kick him upstairs. The students met, and in mass conventions denounced and protested, and the board spent three days badgering them trying to find out who had written an editorial of protest.

Finally, Worst went out and Ladd came in—on condition that he was to have complete authority, and that Professor Bolley was to remain. Senator Ladd tells me that as soon as he had been elected, and in the very room where these conditions had been agreed to, one member of the board asked him to get rid of Bolley, and called him a "damned fool" when he refused. After that there was never a single meeting of the board that they did not pick a row with him over this issue. Soon they began asking him to resign; at first they asked him to write his resignation, and later they wrote it for him—all they asked him to do was to sign it!

Also there were filed some forty odd charges of unprofessional conduct against Professor Bolley, whom they had now discovered to be "crazy." They gave this "crazy" man a busy time for several years. Two members of the board came to Fargo, to demand that Bolley should be fired; then an investigating committee of the faculty was appointed, which completely exonerated him. But the board insisted that this was a partisan committee; they appointed a committee of their own members, and this committee called on the chairman of the faculty committee, and abused him for not making a proper investigation; then they went to Bolley, and took up one question after another, and Bolley refuted each. After three hours one member of the board said: "Well, I think it's time to quit." The second said: "If you are satisfied, I am." The board received this report of complete exoneration from its committee, and decided they would have to discontinue the procedure—but they refused to exonerate Bolley! The controversy was carried to the national government, and the Department of Agriculture appointed a committee, which also investigated, and could find nothing wrong with the "crazy" professor.

This whole story of Bolley makes you think of the melodramas we used to see on the Bowery, where the heroine is tied to a railroad track, or tied on a log which is going into a saw-mill, and the rescuers come galloping up on horseback at the instant when the villain seems triumphant. In the fall of 1916 the Non-partisan League swept the State of North Dakota, and on January 1, 1917, Lynn Frasier came galloping into the governorship of North Dakota, and the farmers of the state got the results of Professor Bolley's experiments once more. Thunders of applause from the gallery!

CHAPTER XLIII

THE UNIVERSITY OF WHEAT

The state of North Dakota is small in population, likewise in its influence in the academic world; but its story is important, because its people have blazed a path upon which the rest of us are destined to travel for the next decade. What has happened in North Dakota education will happen in hundreds of our institutions, and therefore it is desirable that academic liberals should know the story.

The University of North Dakota is located at Grand Forks. The president from 1909 to 1913 was Frank L. McVey, who was chairman of a tax commission in Minnesota, and got in the way of "Jesse James" Hill, and was shunted off to North Dakota to get rid of him. That he was not a dangerous radical may be judged from the fact that in 1912 he objected to three of his professors taking part in the Progressive movement. In 1914 Professor Lewinsohn of the law school resigned his position with a dignified statement, and the president replied by a letter, in which he set up the contention that college professors are in the same position as judges.

The grand duke of the board of regents at this time was Judge N. C. Young, railroad attorney. Needless to say, Judge Young did not refrain from politics; on the contrary, he ran the Republican machine of the state— and incidentally never hesitated to denounce the liberals at his university. Judge Young's assistant was Mr. Tracy Bangs, aggressive attorney for the Northern States Power Company and the Northwestern Bell Telephone Company. Mr. Bangs defended in a murder case the son of a rich farmer, and got his client off on a plea of "self-defense," despite the fact that the victim, a farm-hand, had been shot in the back. Thereupon, several hundred of Mr. Bangs' fellow citizens, including many university professors, signed a petition to the grand jury, charging him with jury-bribing and demanding his indictment. One professor, A. J. Ladd, asked him to resign from the board of trustees while he was under this indictment. Mr. Bangs did not resign, but he bided his time, and as I write he is seeing to it that Professor A. J. Ladd is separated from the university!

In 1915, when the Non-partisan League was started, the university "opposed it by nature"—so a former professor phrased it to me. One man, Professor Gillette, consented to speak at the first meeting of the league, and his life has been one long struggle with the reactionaries ever since. In 1917 President McVey resigned, and the board hastened to nominate his successor, before the Non-partisans got in and appointed Frederick C. Howe! They selected President Kane of the University of Washington —upon the reputation which he had made for himself by forgiving the crimes and accepting the chimes of the Seattle "Times."

A professor at North Dakota, who got to know President Kane very well, describes him to me in these words: "He has less sense of honor than any man I ever knew." It was not long before he had proved his incapacity in North Dakota, and there was a storm of protest concerning him; by way of defending himself he set up the claim that the opposition was due to his refusal to appoint nominees of the Non-partisan League to posts as teachers. The statement was absurd on the face of it, because all nominations were made by the heads of departments; but it served to bring the support of the reactionaries. I am told on good authority that President Kane made a deal with the I. V. A.—"Independent Voters' Association," camouflage for big business—that he was to be retained and allowed to "swing the axe," in return for his using the university influence against the Non-partisan League.

The president had an organization all ready-made, in the fraternities and sororities; and in 1920, when the faculty petitioned for his removal, he and his reactionaries went to these groups for support. They incited a student rebellion—and I find this especially significant, in view of the insistence of all interlocking trustees and newspapers upon academic order and authority. What could be more shocking to a believer in propriety than for college students to organize and try to force the hands of their superiors? But of course that does not apply in a case where the sons of bankers and railroad attorneys and public utility magnates are endeavoring to cripple a political movement of "rubes" and "hicks" and "hayseeds."

The active agent in this student rebellion was the wife of an employe of the Grand Forks "Herald," whose owner, Mr. Jerry Bacon, represents the Twin City milling and railroad interests in North Dakota. Mr. Bacon had fought the movement for faculty control, calling it "sovietism in the university." I am told by one of his friends that in this matter of the student uprising he went up to Minneapolis and got his orders from Louis Hill, son and heir of "Jesse James." Whether he got the money from Mr. Hill I do not know, but I do know that the presses of his newspaper printed cards, supposed to be voicing the students of the university, urging the student-body to refuse to attend classes of those professors who demanded the president's resignation. A student strike to keep President Kane in office! It must have been much pleasanter for him than that other strike, back in Washington, when the students made rhymes denouncing the crimes and rejecting the chimes of the Seattle "Times"!

Last year, when the "I. V. A." came into power, the new Governor Nestos came to the university to deliver the Founders' Day address, and revealed the new scheme of his crowd—to "get" the liberal professors on the issue of religion. In the North Dakota legislature a representative of the "I. V. A." had proclaimed the terrible tidings that the state library was circulating "The Profits of Religion." He described the pages referring to the Catholic political machine as "so sacrilegious, so terrible, that I would not read it in this house or any other place." According to the Bismarck "Tribune," he "called the attention of every minister in North Dakota to this book"— apparently overlooking the inconsistency of asking the ministers to read the book, and at the same time forbidding the state library to furnish it to them!

Now came Governor Nestos, accusing the professors of "undermining the faith of the students"; and President Kane wrote letters to three of the liberals, O. G. Libby, A. J. Ladd, and Dean Willis of the Law School— several pages of virulent abuse, culminating in the announcement of their dismissal. Under the constitution, this matter should have been taken up by the dean, and the professors had the right of appeal to the university council. This council appointed a committee, consisting exclusively of Kane supporters; nevertheless, after hearing the evidence, this committee unanimously exonerated the professors, and the board of administration did the same. The board tried to settle the matter by requesting both Kane and the professors to resign, but the railroad attorneys who are now running the university will not permit that. The struggle is still on, and the outcome uncertain as I write. One man who has got away tells me how it feels to teach under the control of big business in North Dakota:

"It means the surrender, not merely of your mind, but of your character; a man who stands it for two or three years becomes wholly unfit to influence the young. It has been less than a year since I left, yet I have had letters from probably twelve men at the university, asking me to help them to get positions elsewhere!"

Finally, in justice to the liberal professors, I think I should state that no person now at the university has furnished me any information about it. Several were asked to do so, and declined.

CHAPTER XLIV

THE UNIVERSITY OF THE ORE TRUST

Let us continue East on the Northern Pacific Railroad, which has Mr. Morgan and two of his partners for directors, a recent Harvard overseer and Massachusetts Tech trustee for chairman, a Harvard overseer and Smith College trustee, a Cornell trustee, an Amherst trustee, a Hampton trustee and a Union Theological Seminary trustee for directors, also three First National Bank directors; and we come to the "Twin Cities," from which the Northwestern grain country is run. Here we are in one of the strongholds of the Steel Trust, also of the Lumber Trust and the grain speculators. Minnesota contains a great part of the iron ore of the United States, and the Steel Trust owns it all, and in alliance with the millers and the lumbermen, it runs the government of the state, and of course the state university. The university had a most wonderful endowment of government land, covered with the finest white and Norway pine. The Lumber Trust wanted this timber, and they got practically all of it. Likewise the Steel Trust wanted the ore that was under the land, and they got it; and sometimes it happened that the officials who sold this land at bargain prices were also trustees of the university.

For a generation the grand duke who ran the University of Minnesota was John S. Pillsbury, co-author with his two brothers of a famous work entitled "Pillsbury's Best," widely known all over the United States. I had better abandon this feeble jest and be explicit, stating that Governor Pillsbury belonged to a family of flour manufacturers, who knew that it pays to advertise. Governor Pillsbury himself went in more especially for lumber; he got fraudulent possession of more public lands than any other person in the state, and gave some of the profits to the university, and so is called the "father of the university." Now he is dead, and the grand duke of his institution is his son-in-law, Fred B. Snyder, president of a mining company and director of the biggest bank and trust company in Minneapolis. As his right-hand man he has Pierce Butler, railroad attorney, a hard-fisted and aggressive agent of the plutocracy, counsel for the Great Northern Railroad. As his assistants he has the vice-president of a national bank in Duluth, who is director of another national bank and a large owner of land and mines; the biggest dry-goods wholesaler in Minneapolis, director in the city traction lines; a water-power financier; the wife and daughter-in-law of two mining and lumber magnates; a physician, son-in-law of "Jesse James" Hill, the railroad king; and another very wealthy physician, on whose yacht on the Mississippi River the regents sometimes hold their meetings.

I remember Lincoln Steffens, telling twenty years ago of the Shame of the Cities, describing how the politicians in Pittsburgh would travel to Philadelphia, Boston, Cincinnati, and other cities, to find out the latest wrinkles in graft, with a view to applying them at home. It occurs to me that the interlocking regents of Minnesota must have sent a commission to study methods at the University of Pennsylvania; for when I asked Minnesota professors to tell me what happened to them, I heard the same story that I had heard in the Wharton School of Finance, told in the very same phrases.

If you displease your superiors of the Milling Trust, you may get no changes in your courses, but may have to teach large classes of freshmen, over and over again the same weary routine, until your heart breaks. You ask for more advanced classes, and you do not get them; you do not get promotions or increases in salary, and when you inquire the reason, your superiors are politely vague. If you still do not take the hint and abandon your independent manners and beliefs, the head of your department sends for you and tells you that he is very sorry, but there are a lot of cranks running the state just now. "Here I have a letter from the dean, who has it from the president, who has it from a regent." If your superior happens to like you, he offers you one more opportunity to recant, or he offers "to land you at Wisconsin"; he will give you "a bully recommendation," it will be "a fine opportunity for you." If, on the other hand, he does not happen to like you, then you pick up your evening paper, and read a scare headline on the front page, to the effect that you have been dismissed from the university for conduct unbecoming the academic profession.

There were some students who thought it would be interesting to have an "open discussion club." They were handicapped by many regulations; and, quite casually, the dean of student affairs would stroll in on their meetings, to keep watch over them. One of the students went to a member of the faculty, and asked him if he would come and explain to the students the doctrines of Karl Marx; the professor smiled, and answered that he wanted to stay at the university. I am happy to be able to say that the students were not so timid as the professor, and they now meet quite openly, calling themselves the "Seekers."

They have had several grave mishaps at this University of the Ore Trust. First, a man came and registered in the classes, and was discovered to be a Communist! The man had been brought to the United States when he was three years old, and so he was an alien, and was slated for deportation. But the government was in an embarrassing position; the man did not know what country to claim, and the government couldn't find out, and didn't know where to send him! Needless to say, however, the university got rid of him in a hurry.

They had for three years a Harvard Ph.D., educated in England; after the fashion of Englishmen, he was a member of the Fabian Society, and thought he had a perfect right to his political views, just the same as if he had been at Oxford. He began working for the Committee of Forty-eight, making speeches at other places, and so he got into the newspapers. The head of his department sent for him: "We have to keep out of the newspapers; look at me, I have been here twelve years, and I have never got into them!" But this instructor would not change his evil practices, so he too had to be got rid of.

Meet Professor John Henry Gray, one of the most distinguished economists in the United States. Professor Gray was for fifteen years at Northwestern University, and for fifteen at the University of Minnesota. He is not a Socialist, but an extremely mild liberal, a quiet man and a patient worker, who gets the facts on his subject and sets them forth regardless of consequences. He has been selected to represent the United States government on many economic commissions abroad—at the International Co-operative Congress at Manchester, 1902; at the International Congress on Insurance for Laboring Men, at Düsseldorf, and the International Congress of Commerce and Industry, at Ostend. He was appointed on a commission of the National Civic Federation in 1905, to study municipal ownership abroad; again, in 1911-1914, to investigate the regulation of public service corporations. He is associate editor of two economic journals—I might go on to give a long list of his honors and positions. But Professor Gray had the bad taste to become converted to the doctrines of municipal ownership, and the still worse taste, while working for the government in Washington during the war, to interfere with some of the interlocking directors from his home state, engaged in their usual practice of robbing the government. So Professor Gray's life at the university became a torment.

They removed him from the leadership of his department, saying that he had no executive ability and couldn't keep order. They would move him from one room to another, and subject him to every humiliation. He was sixty-three years of age, and would soon be entitled to a pension, so he held on; but he never got a "raise," and he was told that he never would get it, nor would any man he recommended ever get it. They brought in a subordinate from the census bureau in Washington, and paid this man $1,500 a year more than Professor Gray was getting. They "reorganized" his department, deposing him from the headship, and combining it with a "School of Business," and so finally succeeded in making him resign.

Or consider the strange experience of a young instructor of chemistry named Bernard Dietrichson. He had a dispute with his dean, and two members of the law faculty were appointed by the regents to make an inquiry. This committee reported that the department had been seriously mismanaged by the dean, and that Mr. Dietrichson "had done nothing to merit discipline or dismissal." This report was received by a committee of the regents, with Pierce Butler, chief bully of the board of regents, in charge. It issued a decision, stating that it had examined the findings of the investigating committee of lawyers, and that on the basis of these findings it held that there had been no mismanagement by the dean, and that Mr. Dietrichson ought to be dismissed! The regents' committee then suppressed the text of the findings of the investigating committee; but unfortunately for Mr. Butler, the document containing the suppressed facts came into the hands of Dietrichson, and he published it. Thereupon, the dean of the chemistry department was dismissed, and the department reorganized—a complete confession that Dietrichson was right. Nevertheless, he is still out of the university!

More money is appropriated for the University of the Ore Trust, more buildings are erected, more students come piling in; but the soul of the place is poisoned. There is no solidarity in the faculty, there is only intrigue, jealousy and fear. There is an elaborate system of outside spying, and no one knows whom to trust. If you go to the faculty club and listen to the gossip about your associates, and take part in the petty politics of your department, then you are respectable, and they let you alone; but if you don't do these things, then they know you must be some kind of crank, and it is the business of the spies to find out what you are doing with your spare time, and whether you have any dangerous ideas. If you make a public address, there will be volunteer patriotic organizations taking notes of your remarks, and a copy will be sent to the president of the university, or perhaps to the grand dukes of the board.

Meetings of the board of regents are by law required to be public, but they get around this by the simple device of having "executive sessions"—and once in a while a champagne picnic on Dr. Mayo's private yacht! A member of the faculty will be hauled up—he has never seen one of the regents before, and has no idea who has accused him, or what are the accusations. They do not scruple to ask him the most personal questions, not merely about his beliefs, but about his private life. Is it true that he is separated from his wife? Is it true that he took a young lady to dinner? They will call in his dean and his fellow professors, and if the charge is a serious one, he is decapitated in advance. Here sit the angry plutocrats, brutal, full of hate—"I understand this"—"Is it true that" —and so on. "Did you vote for Debs?" "Did you belong to the Progressive party?" "Do you believe in God?" "Have you studied the constitution of the United States?" "Do you believe in abolishing the capitalistic system?" "What church do you go to?"

Sometimes a professor gets "sore," and tells these mighty ones to go to hell; after that he can get no job in any American university. I was told of a leading authority on state government taxation and political science who is now making washboards. This man was listed as a "war case;" that is to say, he had served on a charter commission in Minneapolis, and had put through certain franchise provisions opposed by the public service companies; so when the war came he was called unpatriotic. He writes me as follows:

Usually the intimidation of a professor is so veiled and vague that he hardly knows what is wrong. A certain significant remark dropped at the right time, a certain coldness of attitude, failure to be included in certain social affairs, a certain slowness to get well earned increases, granted with gusto to others, many other little hints that his views do not meet with favor in certain quarters will serve to curb many a man with wife and babies to provide for. For instance, there were a score or more called before the regents at the time I was, every one of whom had opposed our entrance into the war and had not changed views as to the wisdom or justice of our going in, but they were willing to disavow their attitude, when confronted with instant dismissal. Some of these men told me they had to lie or starve their wives and babies, and they took the easier road.

Another man, a former professor, writes me of the present head of the university: "He does not hesitate to use the black-list to ruin a man's career." A professor now at the university writes me a long letter, telling me, among other cases, of a man summoned before the regents and later commanded to resign, for having stated in a private conversation to an old acquaintance that "now that the war is over, we ought to set the political prisoners free"; this man defended himself, and managed to hold on; but another instructor, an able man, was placed in peril of his job for having presided at a political meeting in his home ward, in favor of the labor candidate for mayor. This man was ousted a year later, under circumstances to be narrated.

You will wish to know something about the spy-system, maintained by the "Citizen's Alliance," with the cooperation of the trustees; so I submit a statement from Mr. Fred W. Bentley, who was for three years an instructor. His statement is dated August 20, 1919, and the essential parts of it are as follows:

One day last spring, I do not remember the exact date, I was called to the 'phone in my office, Room No. 111, Main Engineering Building, by a stranger who said his name was Miller. He first stated that he had a private matter to talk about, and asked if it were safe to talk to me where I was. I informed him that he could talk to me anywhere, that I had nothing to cover up.

He then told me that he was interested in a little enterprise and that some of my friends had recommended me to him as one who might help him a little financially. He said that he had never had the pleasure of meeting me but that he knew some of my friends. He asked me if I knew a man (I don't remember the name) who ran a saloon on Seventh Street, but I informed him that I did not. He asked me if I had seen the publication called "Hunger" and I informed him that I had seen someone selling it on the street but that I had not read it.

He said that they were trying to get out another edition and would have to have some machine (I don't remember what he called it) and asked if I would make a contribution toward it. I told him I didn't mind giving a dollar or two, and he asked me if I would leave it with State Secretary Dirba, which I promised to do.

A few days after that I saw Dirba and asked him if he had been approached in the matter and he said he had not. I told Dirba that if anyone did come to him to send the party to me, and thought nothing further of the matter until one day, sometime later, Dean Allen came to me in the drafting room and told me that the Board of Regents was meeting in the president's office and wanted to see me. I went immediately with Dean Allen to the meeting of the board, where I was informed that charges of disloyalty had been preferred against me. When I inquired what they were I learned that the above 'phone conversation was the basis for the charges.

After a few questions relative to the "Hunger" incident, President Burton and the members of the board proceeded to ask numerous questions as to my opinions on many topics, social, political and economic, all of which were none of their business, the more so since I was teaching Drawing, Descriptive Geometry, and Machine Design, and was never called upon to address the students on any other subject.

I cannot, of course, remember all their questions but some of them were as follows

Are you a Socialist? Do you belong to the Socialist Party? Have you attended any of the meetings at Commonwealth Hall? Have you ever belonged to the I. W. W.? Have you ever attended any of the I. W. W. meetings? Do you favor Trade Unionism or Industrial Unionism? Are there many Industrial Unionists in the A. F. of L.? Do you believe in bringing about the social change you advocate by education or violence? Do you believe in the confiscation of property? Have you read the constitution of Soviet Russia? Do you think it right that the employers of labor in Russia should be denied the right to vote? Are there many men of the faculty who believe as you do, etc.?

There is nothing to add to this, except that Mr. Bentley was not reappointed to the university—and was left to learn this fact by accident, from a friend! He had worked for three years at a very low salary, upon the promise that he would soon be made a professor; but now they dropped him—and so late in the year that he could not apply for a position elsewhere.

CHAPTER XLV

THE ACADEMIC WINK

They have had a series of presidents at the University of the Ore Trust. The old president was Northrop, an amiable gentleman, much liked by the faculty because he did not understand the modern card-filing system. Then came Vincent, one of the "go-getters." A professor whom he "got" writes me: "He apparently felt that he held a mandate to break the hearts of the men who had served under Northrop." As a result of faculty clamor, an "advisory committee" was established, but the method of appointing this was ingeniously contrived so that Vincent had the power to keep off any liberals. This committee met in secret, and my correspondent describes to me its operation:

A poor devil, Professor A, who had been teaching for a small salary in hopes of promotion, would receive some fine morning a notice from headquarters that his contract was terminated at the end of the year. Professor B would be advised that he had one year more to serve, during which time he had better be looking for a new place. Professor C would be notified that his salary would not be increased. Smothered with rage, disappointment and despair, he would rush to the president of the university to know in what particular he had erred or sinned. The president in his unctuous way would inform the professor that he was sorry for what had been done but could do nothing, because the matter lay in the hands of the advisory committee, with which he could not interfere. Our victim would then set out to find the advisory committee, but as it was made up of nine members and had adjourned, he could not locate it. He would continue his search, and perchance find one of the members of the illustrious committee. Upon his making inquiry as to why and to what purpose he would be assured of the member's sympathy, but would be told that there was an understanding among the members of the advisory committee that nothing should be said as to what was done in the sessions or how the members voted. The disappointed pedagogue could get nothing from anybody; there was no one responsible; he had been sandbagged in a dark alley, but who did the job he could not learn.

Vincent was called to become head of the Rockefeller Foundation. Then came Marion LeRoy Burton, a former clergyman, and president of Smith College for young ladies, a "booster" from way back, an inspirationalist of the Chautauqua school; the university gave him a grand reception, with bands and torches. He said in the hearing of an acquaintance of mine that he was going to make Minnesota a gentleman's school of the Yale type. What actually exists is a great academic department-store. Sinclair Lewis described it to me—"They sell you two yards of Latin and half a yard of Greek, and a bored young instructor hands it out over the counter." Lewis heard President Burton addressing a meeting of the plutocracy to raise funds, and telling the touching story of his life—he was a little boy who carried newspapers on cold mornings, and now he had fifteen thousand dollars a year, and a big house, and a retiring pension—a wonderful country is America!

Another friend of mine heard President Burton make a speech in Denver, before a gathering of business men called the "Mile High Club." He said that at his university the students were allowed to think, but they were "guided in their thinking"; and the business men got the point and chuckled. His speech was a series of cheap jokes and hackneyed utterances, delivered with fervid eloquence. His type of scholarship you may judge from the titles of some of the books which he has produced: "The Secret of Achievement"; "The Life Which Is Life Indeed"; "On Being Divine."

Last year President Burton got tired of his regents, and accepted a higher salary at the University of Michigan, where we shall meet him again. His place has been taken by one of the university's own professors, who was supposed to act as a rubber-stamp to the interlocking regents, but is now behind the scenes engaged in the usual struggle with Grand Bully Butler. President Coffman is not even allowed to make appointments to the university —to say nothing of allowing the heads of departments to do so. The names are brought up before the board of regents, and these wary gentlemen go over the man's list of degrees and his record, and then Grand Duke Snyder says: "That seems good, but is he all right generally?" meaning, of course, has he any "dangerous ideas."

In the fall of 1919 the inspirational President Burton delivered some of those wonderful high-sounding phrases, which are a part of our university swindle. He said that "integrity" must be the chief characteristic of university men and women. Whereupon a college paper, "The Foolscap," was moved to a little plain speaking. It said:

Academic freedom, to be sure, exists here at Minnesota as at other equally "ideal" universities. Our president has publicly announced that fact. Our faculty and the student body enthusiastically applauded that announcement. This academic freedom, however, is of so peculiar a nature that no one member of the faculty is free publicly to discuss it. The president may speak of it with an engaging boldness; the students may speak of it (and do) with a fine ironic scorn; but members of the faculty, those to whom is intrusted our instruction in "all forms of knowledge," those even whom we address as "Professor" and

"Dean," they dare not utter their true opinion concerning it; their mouths are effectually sealed. This the students know. They have seen the flush of shame and anger rise to the cheeks of embarrassed teachers who could reply to audacious undergraduate taunts of insincerity and dishonesty only with mortified silence. They have seen, at that moment when vigorous applause gave generous approval to our president's insistence on academic freedom, at that very moment when enthusiasm for truth was at its highest, at that very moment they saw instructors wink at their colleagues, and deans look meaningly at some understanding friend. Students, both inside and outside the class room, are particularly observant of the actions of their instructors. They know when deans applaud because they have to; when professors say things they do not mean. They know that even while they listen to talk of academic freedom they see men annually relieved of their academic burdens for having dared to utter what they deemed to be the truth. These students know the colleges from which such instructors were dismissed. They know the names of these instructors. They know the cause for which they were dismissed. They know, also, that such is the state of academic freedom at our university that, even as we go to press, at least one professor in the academic college—a professor, too, whose discreet devotion to facts, and whose cautious refusal to permit the slightest classroom interpretation thereof, make his potentially excellent subject an inexpressible bore—that at least this one professor is trembling with fear and anger because of official intimation that he had entertained opinions for which his institution did not stand.

This publication made a tremendous uproar in the university. For, of course, all university influence depends upon the keeping up of a pretense of freedom; the public must believe in these mighty captains of erudition and must not see them wink as they use their high-sounding words. A faculty committee of five members was appointed to investigate the statements made. This committee interviewed a great number of university people, members of the faculty of all ranks, both men and women, also students and alumni. They submitted a report, of which I quote parts. You note the carefully guarded phrases:

A great deal of evidence has been presented to your committee which indicates the existence in our academic community of a sense of restraint and repression of a kind and degree distinctly unfavorable to a sound and intellectual life. This is already indicated by the vote taken at the meeting of the faculty on February 16. The investigation of the committee has served to confirm and verify this impression of a condition that cannot be described as wholesome. Fears have been disclosed to the committee, which if recounted in detail might seem to many members of the faculty absurd and unbelievable, and which perhaps could not be entertained by others, either because of the possession of greater courage, or of a greater security of tenure, or because of the fact that their own convictions are in happier conformity with the ruling opinion. Nevertheless, the undoubted presence of these fears in the minds of many members of the faculty constitutes a psychological atmosphere depressing in its influence, and calculated to have a deleterious effect upon the sincerity and quality of the teaching done under a sense of it. . . . .

It has become of late a frequent experience that complaint on the part of some person or organization outside the university leads to an investigation, formal or informal, of the views or activities of some member of the faculty. Commonly, it may be taken for granted that the activities complained of are wholly within the discretion of a teacher and the rights of a citizen. The mere knowledge, however, that such complaints are under investigation, creates a sense of intimidation, felt most strongly, of course, by the more inexperienced members of the faculty whose academic tenure is less secure. . . . .

Much of the fear prevalent on the campus is due to reports of the manner in which investigations have been conducted by the regents, the attitude exhibited not always having been sufficiently clear and consistent to be wholly reassuring. Doubtless such impressions are sometimes due to mere inadvertencies; but the fact is that a member of the faculty, when summoned to answer charges preferred, frequently finds himself unjustifiably on the defensive. . . . .

Evidence has been brought to the attention of your committee which plainly indicates the use of espionage by external forces that continually attempt to exert pressure upon the authorities as to university teaching and personnel. Your committee is firmly of the opinion that such pressure is not in the public interest. The invasion by private detectives of the domain of academic life and thought is scarcely compatible with the maintenance of a sound and wholesome intellectual spirit. The methods and point of view of these people may be illustrated by your committee's own experience. Early in the course of this investigation, one of these agents sought and obtained an interview with a member of your committee, in which he volunteered the information that the "Foolscap" editorial (which, as it subsequently developed, he had not even read) was a piece of political propaganda, that he knew the particular party headquarters whence it came, and that it was certain he could discover the real author concealed behind the editorial screen. He offered, accordingly, on the assumption that your committee was interested, not in the question of fact raised by the editorial, but rather in the exposure and punishment of a quasi-criminal conspiracy supposedly involved in its publication, to worm himself into the confidence of the editor of the "Foolscap" and to procure for your committee by betrayal of this confidence the name of the guilty propagandist author. It is deplorable to note the constantly extending nets of private spy systems in civil life, and it is to be hoped that the threatened invasion of academic life by this sinister influence may be prevented. No thoughtful person can fail to see how blighting would be its influence, when once firmly established, in the destruction of mutual confidence, and in rendering impossible that frankness of discussion and opinion without which the intellectual life is not freely nourished and stimulated.

There remains only to state what action the faculty took in this matter. One member of the committee tells me about it:

They postponed action until such a time as the committee was ready to report again to a closed faculty meeting giving specific instances of lack of academic freedom, with names and dates. The committee, having decided to present three typical cases in detail to the faculty, asked the president to summon a meeting. He passed the buck to the committee of the deans known as the senate. The deans thought it inopportune to call the meeting at that particular time, it being just prior to the June examinations. Summer vacation ensued. In September, when college re-opened, one of the five committeemen had gone East for a year as an exchange professor; another had been retired as a Carnegie pensioner on account of his age; a third, though still drawing a salary as a member of the faculty, had received notice of his dismissal; and the other two saw the futility of trying to bring the matter up again.

Also I ought to add what action the regents took. They kicked out of the university the young instructor who had been most active in preparing the report. He has written me about the circumstances of his dismissal:

Nothing specific was sent to me. But, by what chain of circumstances need not be told, I saw with my own eyes a letter from Pierce Butler addressed to President Burton asking for my decapitation. The neatest thing you ever saw—not a direct order, and not even a request for my dismissal, but a carefully worded statement to the effect that it seemed to him (Butler) regrettable that the name of the university had been linked up in the press with the name of myself. That was all. But Burton sent it down the line of officials as a positive decree and my fate at Minnesota was settled. Usually, as you perhaps are aware, the thing is done by word of mouth only. Butler, of course, never imagined that this letter would reach my eyes.

Mr. Butler remains grand bully of the university; but here also we are at the "big scene" in the melodrama— the villain has the heroine helpless, but in the distance we hear the galloping hoofs of the rescuer's horses! The farmers of Minnesota with their Non-partisan League, and the workers of the cities with their unions, have got together into the Farmer-Labor party, and they have just elected their own United States senator. Before long they may also elect a governor of their state, and the University of the Ore Trust may become the University of the people of Minnesota.

P.S.—As this book is going to the printer President Harding, wishing to show the public exactly how contemptuous of public opinion it is possible for a public official to be, sends in the nomination of Grand Bully Butler for justice of the United States Supreme Court!

CHAPTER XLVI

INTRODUCING A UNIVERSITY PRESIDENT

From the University of Minnesota we take the Chicago and Northwestern Railroad, which has a Princeton trustee and a recent New York University and Yale trustee for directors, and two National City Bank directors. Overnight we come to Madison, Wisconsin, where for the first time we find an institution of higher education which has partly emerged from under the shadow of the White Terror. The reason for this is one man—Senator LaFollette, who for forty years has been fighting the battle of the people in his state. LaFollette has not always had his way; he has been in again and out again half a dozen times; but the thought of him is never out of the minds of the reactionaries, and many things they have wished to do in their university they have not dared to do. So at Wisconsin are two professors who are "rank" Socialists, and perhaps a dozen others more or less on the way to "rankness." Just now the state administration is LaFollette's, but the administration of the university is reactionary, a relic of the war hysteria.

The grand duke of the plutocratic element of the board is Mr. A. J. Horlick, whose contribution to American scholarship is a brand of malted milk, with a picture of a cow from which the commodity is understood to be derived. Quite recently the president of the University of Wisconsin announced that no one would be permitted to address the university who had not supported the government during the war. Mr. Horlick has proven his right to be numbered among the hundred percent patriots, the firm of which he is head having been indicted by the United States government and fined fifty thousand dollars for the hoarding of flour. (Query: Is malted milk made out of flour?)

The most active reactionary upon the board is Mr. Harry J. Butler, a railroad attorney of Madison; he is ably seconded by Dr. Seaman, a physician, anti-LaFollette candidate for governor last year; also by a wholesale grocer, a manufacturer of bathroom fixtures, two other attorneys, and a manufacturer's wife. For many years the university had a liberal president; since his death they have had an elderly zoologist of reactionary temper, who deftly dodges trouble by "passing the buck" to his board. The liberals, inside the university and out, are biding their time; they strengthened their hold on the state at the recent election, and now hope to get one or two more members of the board, so that when a new president is chosen he may be of their kind.

Last winter it was rumored that I was coming East, and the students of the Social Science Club asked if I would deliver an address at the university. Before I had time to answer, I learned from newspaper clippings that the president of the university had announced that I was not a proper person to be heard by the students, and would not be granted the use of a hall. I have to spend some time every day declining invitations to deliver lectures, and the elderly Wisconsin zoologist might have saved himself a lot of trouble if he had waited before he spoke. Of course, when he told me I couldn't come, I felt compelled to go.

President Birge had stated in the Madison "Capital-Times" that "Upton Sinclair's attack on journalism could only be fairly expounded if a representative of the Associated Press or other organized journalistic body were present at the same time to answer." Apparently it was the president's idea that I never talked on any subject but the newspapers, which of course was underestimating the range of my discontent. However, I wired the "Capital-Times," asking them to convey to their president the information, "I have been trying in every possible way to inveigle the Associated Press into answering 'The Brass Check' in any manner they might choose. I have publicly challenged them and their leading representatives a dozen different times. If President Birge will persuade the Associated Press to send a representative to debate with me, he will confer upon me the greatest favor I could name."

President Birge made no answer to this, and on Friday, April 28th, when I arrived in Madison, I learned that the students of the Social Science Club had arranged that the meeting should be held on the following Monday in the high school auditorium. I thought it would be interesting to collect a university president for this book, so the first thing I did was to go and pay a call on Dr. Birge.

I am told that in his own line he is a distinguished scientist, and his friends at the university explained that he is accustomed to being treated with extreme deference. I am sorry to say that I missed this point. I considered that I had been attacked in the newspapers entirely without provocation, and I was not willing to be content with polite evasions. In trying to get at the facts, I felt that I was acting in a public cause, and I was not thinking about the personality of a university president, any more than I was thinking about my own.

He is a rather small man, with small dark eyes, and he sat at his big desk, watching me uncomfortably. I asked him what reasons he had for pronouncing the ban upon me, and he could only say it was my reputation. I asked him where he had got his impression of my reputation, and of course he had to admit that he had got it from the capitalist newspapers. I asked if he had read any book of mine, and at first he said he had not, then he thought he had read "The Jungle," but had forgotten it.

"Oh, no, President Birge," I answered. "Nobody that has read 'The Jungle' has ever forgotten it." And I could see that this was not the answer he had expected.

I asked him on what he based his impression that I had exaggerated in "The Brass Check." He admitted that he had not read the book; whereat I remarked: "You have spoiled my score!" I explained that I had traveled from Pasadena to Madison, and stopped at nine cities on the way, and in each place I had talked to from ten to twenty educators—school teachers and college professors—and so far every person had read "The Brass Check." "I thought I was going to get to New York with a hundred percent record!" President Birge murmured sympathetically.

"You will realize," I added, "that it strikes me as significant that the one person who thinks the book isn't true is the person who hasn't read it."

I went on to tell about the many and various efforts I had made to lure the Associated Press into the arena. Before publishing the book I had submitted to Mr. Melville E. Stone, then general manager of the Associated Press, four questions for him to answer. He had previously written that he would be glad to answer any questions, but he fell silent when he read the questions I sent. I had written to Mr. Stone's assistant, now general manager, calling his attention to the book, and asking for an answer on various points. At the annual convention of the Associated Press, held in New York in April, 1921, after "The Brass Check" had been out more than a year, it was officially announced in the "Editor and Publisher," and also in the New York "Evening Post," that the Associated Press had a committee investigating "The Brass Check," and was shortly to issue a complete report upon the book. A couple of months later, when this report failed to appear, I wrote the Associated Press asking what had become of it, and when they failed to reply, I published my letter and sent a copy of it to the managing editor of every Associated Press newspaper in the United States—but without getting a reply from a single one!

Only a couple of weeks before I met President Birge, another annual convention of the Associated Press took place in New York, and I repeated my challenge to this gathering, and sent a copy to every managing editor, and also every publisher, of the thirteen hundred Associated Press newspapers in the United States. No attention was paid to these communications, and not one single Associated Press newspaper was willing to demand that the Associated Press should produce the report on "The Brass Check," which it had officially announced it was preparing.

I showed President Birge also how the students of his own Social Science Club had tried in vain to get the Associated Press to answer me. Their first request, that the Associated Press should send a representative to meet me on a university platform, had met with no reply; a second and very sharp letter had brought the response that no responsible newspaper man would be willing to meet me on a platform. Any newspaper man will realize the absurdity of this statement. The A. P. could find a man in any city—if they could furnish him with the facts!

Then I set forth to President Birge my qualifications as an orator in university halls; as it happened, I came within his specifications, in that I had supported the government during the war. I came of a long line of American ancestors; my grandfather and my great-grandfather had been captains in the United States Navy, and my great-great-grandfather had commanded the frigate "Constitution." I had had nine years of college and university life, and was a married man of good moral character. Also, I mentioned that it was not my intention to discuss the newspapers, but to lecture on "The College Student and the Modern Crisis." All these facts the elderly zoologist politely received, and told me that if I would embody them in a letter to him he would oblige me by a reply not later than noon of the next day.

I wrote the letter, and received the reply, which was that President Birge would not change his decision, but that if the board of regents saw fit to grant my request, they would be at liberty to do so. Thereupon I gave to the press my letter to President Birge and his reply, and also an interview in which I stated that the president had afforded me an exceedingly good example of my thesis "that educational institutions are controlled by special privilege," and that I would give up my intention of lecturing on "The College Student and the Modern Crisis" in Madison, and instead would discuss the subject of free speech in universities. The effect of which announcement was that the superintendent of the high school took fright, and withdrew permission for me to speak in his auditorium!

CHAPTER XLVII

INTRODUCING A BOARD OF REGENTS

On Tuesday morning the regents of the University of Wisconsin held a session; and I assumed that, having made the acquaintance of a university president, you might also be interested in interviewing a board of regents. I looked up the statutes of the state of Wisconsin, and ascertained that under the law all meetings of the board are public. So I went to the administration building at ten o'clock on Tuesday morning, the hour set for the meeting—and to my great surprise discovered the ladies and gentlemen of the august board meeting behind locked doors!

It appears that whenever they have a ticklish question to discuss, they evade the law by calling it a meeting of a "committee." I am in position to testify that the meeting of the "committee" was a meeting of exactly the same individuals as later constituted a meeting of the "board"; also I am in position to testify that they discussed exactly the same subject, because the anteroom in which I was invited to sit and wait was so near to the meeting-room, that I could hear the voices when they were raised, and I knew that they were discussing the subject of my proposed speech. I handed to the secretary of the board a formal request for a hearing, and then waited. At a quarter past ten, the secretary of the board came to the anteroom, which was occupied by myself and half a dozen newspaper reporters, and requested that we should go downstairs and wait, as it was not proper for us to be "listening in on the proceedings of the board." Naturally I was not gratified by this remark, as I had been sitting quietly in the chair which had been indicated to me as the proper chair for me to occupy, and I had not been told that it was my duty to stuff cotton into my ears.

However, I went downstairs, and waited another half hour, and then I wrote another note, stating briefly that I protested against the board settling a question in secret meeting, when the law required that their proceedings should be public. After that I waited another hour, and then the secretary informed me that the meeting of the board of regents was now about to begin, and that the "public" was welcome to enter. I entered the room where the ladies and gentlemen of the board had been violating the law of their state for an hour and three-quarters, and I was informed that the board would be pleased to give me ten minutes in which to present my case.

I have made it my practice to use most careful courtesy in dealing with my enemies, so as to put them in the wrong. I dutifully rehearsed to the regents my qualifications as a university orator, after which the board proceeded to question me, the two active questioners being Mr. Butler, the railroad attorney, and Dr. Seaman, the reactionary candidate for governor. The latter wanted to know if I had been correctly quoted in the newspaper interview, in which I had charged that President Birge "had been influenced by money" in his decision against me.

Pardon me if I go into details on this point. We have seen several university professors being cross-questioned by boards of regents, and it will be worth while for us to have exact knowledge of how these inquisitions are conducted. You would have thought that Dr. Seaman, being a man prominent in public life, would have taken the trouble to provide himself with a copy of the interview about which he intended to cross-question me; but he had not done so, and I, as it happens, do not go about with copies of my newspaper interviews in my pocket. I was embarrassed by Dr. Seaman's question, and could only explain that I had no recollection of having made any such statement about President Birge, and that certainly I could have no such idea about him. Newspaper reports were frequently inaccurate. What I had intended to say and should have said was that in his decision concerning me President Birge had "acted in the interest of special privilege." Later, when I went out from the board, and got a copy of the interview, I discovered that this is exactly what I was reported to have said, and that Dr. Seaman had been misquoting me in a public session of the board, with half a dozen newspaper reporters diligently taking notes!

President Birge arose and asked on what ground I could have made such a statement about him. My answer was that he had shown his attitude of sympathy with special privilege by many things he had said in our long interview; also he had shown a very strong prejudice against the enemies of special privilege.

"How, for example?" he asked.

I answered: "If I were a person disposed to take personal offense, I would have considered myself outraged by the remark you made to me, that without having read any of my books you had come to the conclusion that I was a person 'accustomed to pep up and exaggerate his statements in order to create a sensation and to increase the sale of his books.' " (I loathe the expression "pep up," and beg the reader to understand that I am quoting a university president.)

At this President Birge became much excited, saying that this had been a confidential conversation; he had given me his personal opinion of my reputation at my request, and I now proceeded to tell it in the presence of newspaper reporters—and he was a man old enough to be my father!

I answered that I did not see that age had anything to do with the matter, nor could I understand how our interview could be regarded as "confidential"; I had come to him, a public official, acting in a public matter. There could have been nothing "personal" between us, for I did not know President Birge, I had never even heard his name until I read his interview in a Madison newspaper, stating that I was an unfit person to address the university students.

Said President Birge: "I did not say you were unfit."

Said I: "I don't know what your word was, but your action was certainly to that effect."

Then Attorney Butler spoke up, and wanted to know if I had threatened that if I were not permitted the use of a university building I would attack President Birge and the university in some other hall. To this I said that my action followed automatically from the situation. I had come to Madison for the purpose of delivering to the students an address entitled: "The College Student and the Modern Crisis." If the university would permit me to deliver this address, I should deliver it. If they wouldn't permit me to deliver this address, I should naturally have to discuss the question of why they took such action. Mr. Butler's answer was that nobody should come to the university, with his consent, and try to bulldoze the board of regents by any kind of threat.

The board offered me an additional five minutes, if I

16

wished it, but I answered that the greatest virtue in an orator was to know when he had said his say. I thanked them and retired; and that afternoon they held another session, and Mr. Butler and Dr. Seaman, ably seconded by the bathtub manufacturer and the wholesale grocer, voted that I should be refused the use of the gymnasium. The seven other members of the board voted that President Birge should be requested to grant me the use of the gymnasium. President Birge himself did not vote, and I am sorry to state that the malted milk regent was absent and did not get recorded. Needless to say, all this publicity—it filled many columns of Madison's two newspapers for five days—resulted in the gymnasium's being packed on Wednesday evening. Some two thousand students heard my scheduled address, and asked me questions for an hour afterwards, and the walls of the building did not collapse, nor have any of the students since thrown any bombs.

Next afternoon I met the champion tennis team of the university, and played each of its members in turn, and beat them in straight sets; and I am told that the student body regarded this as a far more sensational incident than my Socialist speech. An elderly professor came up to me on the campus next day—I had never seen him before, and don't know his name; but he assured me, with deep conviction, that I had made a grave blunder—I should have played the tennis matches first, and made the speech second, and no building on the campus would have been big enough to hold the crowd!

CHAPTER XLVIII

THE PRICE OF LIBERTY

The University of Wisconsin has the reputation of being the most liberal institution of higher education in the United States, and on the whole I think the reputation is deserved. I have shown what a struggle it took to introduce one little impulse of new thinking into the place; and you must realize that every mite of freedom has been won by the same struggle, and the maintaining of it depends upon somebody's willingness to be disagreeable. I talked with one professor, who is known throughout the

United States as a writer and lecturer, not a Socialist, but a tireless advocate of social justice. This man has won, and he holds grimly the right to have his own say and his own way. He assigns to his graduate students "The Brass Check" as required reading, and as their thesis they make a study of some capitalist newspaper in its handling of half a dozen crucial public issues, such as the steel strike and Mexican intervention.

The rub comes when the professor goes outside and lectures to city clubs and chambers of commerce, and gets into the newspapers in favor of the recognition of Soviet Russia. Then all the reactionaries in the state clamor for his scalp. He said to me: "They say a fox learns to enjoy being chased, and in the same way I have had to learn to enjoy outmatching my enemies. I feel that I am being stalked by a band of thugs; I have to set out deliberately and consciously to build up my prestige throughout the state, to keep myself in the public mind, so that my enemies won't dare go beyond abusing me. Manifestly, that means that academic freedom is only for the man who has a tough skin and can be happy in a fight. The young man, also the weak man, is helpless; if he tries to tell the truth about anything, he'll have to go out and write life insurance for a living."

Such is the judgment, after nearly two decades' experience, of one of America's freest college professors, in America's freest university. That many men should fail in such a test is inevitable. There is another professor in the university, an elderly man, who began his career as a Socialist of the academic type; he is the author of standard books on Socialism, and all through the years when he made his reputation he recognized the unearned increment of land as a grave form of social injustice. He has now changed his views, and has become the tamest of conservatives, a pitiable figure. It happened recently that a friend of mine was in his office, and discovered an economic basis for this transformation. Some one wanted to buy some lots from the old professor; and the price was two thousand dollars each, he said. He listened to some protest of the would-be purchaser; then he said: "I know; the price was eighteen hundred a couple of weeks ago, but it has now gone up."

He hung up the receiver, and blandly explained to my

friend that he was the fortunate possessor of a tongue of
land between two lakes which blocked the development of
the city of Madison, and real estate values were increasing
there very rapidly! To a student of my acquaintance this
old gentleman recently made the statement that "one who
talks about unearned increment shows by that very act
that he has not brains enough to be a graduate student."
It is interesting to note that when the President of the
United States was appointing a commission to settle an
important public question, it was this man he selected to
represent the economists of the United States.

They had their war hysteria in Wisconsin, as everywhere. Senator LaFollette made a speech in which he
said we had "a grievance" against the German Government, and the Associated Press took out the word "a" and
substituted the word "no"—such a little lie, but it caused
the whole country to shriek for LaFollette's blood. A
petition for his expulsion from the senate was circulated
among the university faculty—the same thing the German
reactionaries did with their university professors at the
outbreak of the war. It is not recorded how many professors in Germany refused to sign; but there were six
courageous men at Wisconsin. One of these was Professor Kahlenberg, whose father refused military service in
Germany. Professor Kahlenberg lost the leadership of
the chemistry department, and most of his worthwhile
courses, and has not yet regained them.

Also, there was George F. Comings, a lecturer in the
Extension Department, who after the war advocated an
amnesty resolution at a meeting of the American Association of Equity, a farmers' organization. The resolution
was laid on the table; letters of protest were written to
the board of regents, and the lecturer was summoned to
appear before the regents to submit to a rebuke. He refused to appear, and was dismissed, and became candidate
for lieutenant-governor of the LaFollette party, receiving
the largest majority of any candidate on the ticket. When
Kate Richards O'Hare was refused permission to speak
in a university hall, Lieutenant-Governor Comings introduced her, and defended her from organized rowdies, at a
meeting in the assembly chamber of the state capitol. He
presided at a dinner of the Federated Press, at which I
spoke in Madison, and presented a resolution in favor of

free speech. It is interesting to note that while he was in the university his most ardent opponent was a very wealthy dean, who is interested in several banks and a power company, and sells stock to the other professors.

Some thirty years ago, during a controversy over academic freedom, the board of regents of Wisconsin adopted a resolution, as follows: "Whatever may be the limitations which trammel inquiry elsewhere, we believe that the great State University of Wisconsin should ever encourage that continual and fearless sifting and winnowing by which alone the truth can be found." A tablet containing this statement was presented by the class of 1910, but it was hidden in the cellar, covered with dust for many years, because the regents refused to allow it to be placed upon the building. It is now in place on Bascom Hall; and during the controversy over my address, the regents reaffirmed this motto as the policy of the board. But they refused to permit a committee of students and the faculty to determine what speakers should be heard. It appears that their understanding of freedom is the ancient one of freedom for those who rule.

I have referred to the fate of the weaker and the younger members of the faculty. Let me tell you one story; I do it with much hesitation, because the man who told it to me begged me not to repeat it, and I can only do so by taking care to give no hint of his identity. Suffice it to say that he is a young instructor, a self-made and self-taught man, who has worked his way up from bitter poverty in the face of severe physical handicaps. Life has meant continual suffering to him, but he is one of those natures which manage to use their trials as a means of self-discipline. He is one of the gentlest and sweetest natures it has ever been my fortune to meet. I wish he were a bold man and a fighter, but it happens to be the essence of his nature to shrink from strife and notoriety.

I introduce to you another gentleman, who loves attention, and does not hesitate to thrust himself forward—the Honorable David Jayne Hill, ex-president of Rochester University and ex-ambassador to Germany; a public personage of wealth and reactionary views, who founded an organization, the National Association for Constitutional Government, for the purpose of distributing his convictions to the people of the United States. The National Association for Constitutional Government, with David Jayne Hill as president, mailed out to all educators in the United States a pamphlet by David Jayne Hill, setting forth the importance of preserving those features in the constitution of the United States which enable the rich to become richer and compel the poor to become poorer. Along with the pamphlet went a personal letter, inviting the recipient to express his opinion of the views set forth in the pamphlet, and stating, among other things, that the pamphlet was not circulated for propaganda purposes, but purely to ascertain the views of others upon the question.

The young instructor received a copy of this letter; his opinion was asked for, and he gave it; he said that he thought the views expressed in the pamphlet were wrong, and he added: "When you state that you are not circulating it for propaganda purposes, I must say plainly that I think you are lying."

Let me point out that the young instructor did not rush to the newspapers with this opinion; he wrote it in a private letter, at request. He was specifically invited to say frankly what he thought, and he said frankly what he thought, to the organization which asked his opinion and no one else.

But, of course, he had insulted one of the great moguls of the plutocracy; he had committed lese majesté in its grossest form. It is easy to imagine what happened; the huffy mogul sent the letter to some mogul regent, or perhaps to a mogul administrator, and before many days the young instructor was summoned to appear before his mogul dean. Maybe you imagine that the dean pointed out in a friendly way that the youngster had been injudicious in using a short and ugly word, and ought to use longer words while he was connected with a state university. If that is what you imagine, you know very little about universities.

What actually happened was something I had to drag from the young man by half an hour of tactful questioning. It was evident that the experience had been a cruel one; he did not want to think about it, he could not speak about it without his hands trembling, and his voice also. He had been stormed at and denounced, he had been told that he was a fool and a puppy, and that he should there

and then take his pen in hand and write an abject apology
to the great mogul he had so insulted. And here was
a young man trying to exist upon the pitiful salary of a
university instructor, and with a young wife expecting a
baby. He demanded twenty-four hours to think it over,
and he went away and wrestled it out with himself. He
wrote the letter, and since that time has retired into his
own shell; he never thinks about public questions, he
writes no letters to anyone, he hardly even reads a newspaper, but lives and labors in a little specialty, where he
hopes to make some contribution to human knowledge.
Meantime, the dean who did this thing is one of the most
prominent and powerful persons in the university, in
charge of the moral destinies of several thousand future
citizens of the state of Wisconsin. And that is what
"academic freedom" means in America's freest university!

CHAPTER XLIX

THE PEOPLE AND THEIR UNIVERSITY

I do not want anyone who reads this book to get the
idea that I am so naive as to imagine that there is no
enemy of freedom of teaching save economic privilege.
I know there are others, and all I am doing is tackle the
biggest one first. If I work for the control of universities by organized farmers and labor unions, it is not because I am unaware that these groups have their interests
and prejudices, but merely because I believe that these
groups can learn to understand true freedom and justice,
whereas I know that a plutocratic class has never been
able to learn anything at any time in human history.

In the University of Wisconsin it is interestingly
shown that as soon as you break down the rule of special
privilege, you find yourself confronted by various kinds
of mass prejudice and group interest. The people of the
state consider that they own a university, and they expect
this university to do their way. The question arises—
who shall set the standards, the voters, or the faculty, who
think they know more? The Wisconsin farmer drives up
to Madison in his automobile, and demands an interview
with a dean, saying: "Here I am supporting this university by my taxes, and here you've gone and flunked my

son!" The farmers' organizations keep jealous watch over the percentage of "flunkings," and if it is too high, they say the university is being made into a place of academic snobbery. And maybe they are right—it is not so easy to say!

A former state superintendent of education in Wisconsin told me a funny story. It was proposed to have the normal schools teach engineering, but President Van Hise of the university said this was impossible; the university alone could teach engineering, it had mysteriously and mystically efficient methods of doing so. The superintendent met an instructor who had recently been taken on in this school, and thinking he would like to know about these special methods, he asked: "How did they tell you to teach engineering?"

"They didn't tell me anything," said the instructor.

"You mean they gave you no special instructions about how you were to teach?"

"Nothing at all," said the other; then he thought— "Oh, yes, to be sure, they told me to flunk one-third of the students and send them to the Agricultural School!"

Also there are the religious organizations, clamoring for their share of power. There is the so-called "Fundamentalist" movement in the Baptist church, an organization which combines theological with economic obscurantism, and wages vigorous war against the teaching of modern ideas. Professor Otto is giving a course on "Man and Nature," an elementary survey of evolution, the most popular course in the university. The Baptists denounce him as an atheist, and all the religious organizations have got together to demand that the university shall drop this course. The place is surrounded by a veritable fortification of religious establishments, all carrying on instruction of their own, and all trying to break into the state institution. There is the Wesleyan Foundation, which hires "student pastors," and is giving courses off the campus, and wants these courses to count as university credits. They have succeeded in arranging this at the University of Illinois; why not at Wisconsin? There are the Catholics, with a million dollar endowment, a chapel and dormitories, also clamoring for their share of university power and prestige. There is a Lutheran building, an Episcopal chapter-house, and so on. These religious movements are now opened with an official university convocation, and they are pushing, pushing all the time, trying to keep modern science away from the people.

Also, of course, the militarists have been lifted up by the war wave. Wisconsin is compelled to have military training, being a "land grant" institution. So the campus is troubled by the clamor of young men preparing themselves for slaughter. Officers strut about with artificial pomposity—I say artificial, because I suspect they are ex-real estate men and Rotary Club members. However, their disguise serves them with the khaki-clad sheep who rush here and there in response to barked-out orders, and have their photographs taken in long lines, to send home to mamma and papa on the farm. I wandered about watching them; and for variety I came upon a madman, standing all alone on the campus, leaping up like a jumping-jack, shooting his two arms this way and that, and making silence through a megaphone. I was puzzled, until I saw a moving-picture operator taking the scene; it was a "cheer leader" having himself perpetuated!

They have, of course, their athletic craze at Wisconsin, as everywhere else. Enormous sums are handled, and there is the usual graft; favoritism in jobs, free tickets and passes, and the "scalping" of these. There is the usual professionalism, with easy jobs for athletes pretending to go through college. There are the usual fraternities and sororities, organized into little snobbish groups, and busy with student politics, "log-rolling" and "back-scratching." If the purpose of the university is to prepare students for what they are to meet in outside life, these things, of course, have their place.

They have a daily paper, the "Cardinal," and I discovered that here also the students are getting a complete training in the ways of the outside world. The "Cardinal" is supposed to be the publication of the student body, and those who edit it are supposed to do the work for the honor and the experience. But large sums are taken in and no one knows where they go. There was an investigation by the student senate, and the findings were kept secret. One student on the board persisted in asking questions, and he was expelled; he ran for re-election, and on the very day of election the paper published an elaborate attack upon his integrity; his answer was published

the day after his defeat! The paper refused publication of
another student's article, demanding to know the circula-
tion of the paper and the salaries paid to the editors, if
any. It developed that the business manager had borrowed three hundred and seventy dollars from the paper
without security, and that there had been other such loans
not specified. A pretty complete training for capitalist
journalism and politics!

Here, as everywhere, it is the fraternity and sorority
groups which run the student body. They bring from
their wealthy homes the usual reactionary opinions; and
the last reactionary governor, Philipp by name, laid down
the ideal of a university a couple of years ago—the mothers
and fathers of Wisconsin might rest assured that their
university would send their sons and daughters home with
the same ideas they had when they came! I picked up a
couple of issues of the "Wisconsin Octopus," a humorous
monthly published by the student body. Here is a little
sketch, which might have been taken from the "Saturday
Evening Post," showing a long-haired student in spectacles, listening enraptured to a frantic Bolshevist orator on
a soap-box, while another figure, labeled "Stude Body,"
turns away in disgust. This heads an editorial, "Boost
Wisconsin." "Empty heads are the cause of mental revolution," says this wise editor—forgetting about stomachs.
He denounces "a small group, yet a very insistent and
annoying group," which is attacking its alma mater. "Wisconsin welcomes criticism, but criticism made in a holy
and healthy manner. Wisconsin has no room for knockers. They are not welcome. . . . . Let those with radical thoughts keep them to themselves."

I turn to the front cover of this satisfied publication;
it portrays a table in a lobster palace, with a semi-nude
girl-student at a supper-party with a man-student. There
is a quart bottle of liquor on the table, and another in a
bucket of ice beside the table, and the man-student has
fallen asleep, dead drunk. Such is student life according
to the "Wisconsin Octopus" for May, 1922. And in case
this issue be not representative, I take up that of January,
1922. This also portrays on the cover a semi-nude girl-
student at a "prom" with a young man-student, who can
scarcely be distinguished from the one in the "Arrow"
collar advertisement on the back cover. The frontispiece

of the issue consists of a drawing entitled: "The Clock Watcher," and we discover that a "clock watcher" is a man-student observing the ankles of a girl-student. On the next page we find a poem, which speaks for itself:

> Absinth makes the heart grow fonder,
> Makes the lights go blinking yonder,
> Makes one lamp-post seem like ten,
> Absent absinth, come again.

On the next page we find a cartoon, portraying a semi-nude girl-student, sunk in a lounging chair, smoking a cigarette; we are told:

> A good woman's a good woman,
> But a smoke's a smoke.

On the next page we find some sketches, seeming to indicate that the "prom" is a kind of college kissing game, and that at the end of this game the girl lies in a drunken swoon. Later on we find three drawings, "The Famous Prom Soak," which tell us in three funny ways that the "prom" is a place where both boys and girls get drunk and have a headache the next morning. A little farther on occurs an illustration of a boy and girl who are conversing:

> "I know something that beats the Prom."
> "What?"
> "Buy a car, and park some place."

A little later we learn: "If it's stag, it's a souse-party." A little later we see a girl walking on an electric-light wire, and it is explained to us, "A modern girl can't be shocked."

I think I have quoted enough. I leave it to the impartial reader to decide the question—whose heads are empty at the University of Wisconsin? Is it the little group of devoted idealists of the Social Science Club, who in the face of ridicule and scolding have brought a series of writers and public men, both radical and conservative, to discuss modern problems before the student body? Or is it the little set of snobbish fraternity men, who run the social and political life of the university, and edit its publications for the advertising of their own sensuality and cynicism?

CHAPTER L

EDUCATION F. O. B. CHICAGO

There was one American captain of industry with a monstrously developed bump of acquisitiveness; as he described himself: "I am a great clamorer for dividends." It was frequently charged that in the early days his clamoring—or at any rate that of his subordinates—did not stop at arson and burglary; it is certain that it did not stop at railroad rebates, "midnight tariffs," and numerous other violations of law. By such means he made himself master of the oil industry of the country, and was on the way to acquiring the railways and the banks and the Child's restaurants. He had made one or two hundred millions of dollars, and was busily turning it into one or two billions; but he found rising against him a clamor of public execration, and the poor rich man, whose second most conspicuous bump was of fear, began casting about for some way to take the curse off himself.

About that time he met an educator—one of these typical American combinations of financial shrewdness and moral fervor, a veritable wizard of a money-getter, a "vamp" in trousers, a grand, impressive, inspirational Chautauqua potentate. The old oil king was completely captivated. We can imagine him going home to the privacy of the royal bed-chamber, or wherever it is that oil kings and queens exchange domestic confidences. "Say, Laura, I met a fellow today—by crackie, he's a wonder! He's a professor of Semitics, or pyrotechnics, or something or other, I forget just what—but he knows everything there is, and he's going to build me a university and make me the greatest philanthropist in America!"

"Now, John," says the oil queen, "you better be careful and hold on to your money. The Lord is able to take care of people's souls, and they don't need this new-fangled modern learning."

"That's all right, my dear," says the oil king, "but every business has to advertise. I figured out that this is the cheapest yet. And, besides, I always wished I'd had an education, so that you and I might get invited out to dinner-parties, and not have everybody laugh at us the way they do."

This oil king had a pathetic trust in education, as something you could buy ready-made for cash, the same as a political machine or a state railroad commission. If anybody tried to put off on him an oil-field that had got salt water in, he would know the difference; but it did not occur to him that there might be fakes in education, or that a petroleum philanthropist might not be able to order the whole of the human spirit, F. O. B. Chicago, thirty days net.

I picture the educational "he-vamp," President Harper, calling into consultation some fellow-faker in the architectural line. Says the architectural wizard: "I suppose this old bird will want something plain and economical— the biggest floor-space for his money."

"Not on your life," says the educational wizard. "He wants something he never saw before; he's going in for culture. You know I specialize in these old things—Hebrew and Greek and Assyrian and Sanskrit and Egyptian——"

"How would it do to give him a row of pyramids?" says the architectural wizard.

"No," says the educational wizard, "he would think that was heathen. He's a religious old bird—a Baptist, like me; that's how I got him, in fact—met him at an ice cream festival."

"Oh, well then, it's plain," says the architectural wizard. "What we want is real old Gothic—stained-glass windows, mullioned, and crenellated battlements, and moated draw-bridges——"

"That sounds great!" says the educational wizard. "What does it look like?"

"I'll have one of my office boys get you up a sketch this afternoon," says the architectural wizard. "It's a good style from our point of view, because it uses about four times as much stone per square foot of floor-space, and stone is where we get our rake-off."

A thousand years ago, you understand, men rode over the earth, clad in heavy iron armor, like hard-shell crabs. Every joint had to be tightly covered, lest a flying arrow should pierce the crack; and when they built themselves homes they were moved by this same terror of swift arrows, so they made the windows narrow and deep. They built the walls of thick stone to withstand the pounding of battering-rams, and to hold up the enormous weight of the pile. Such was the origin of "Gothic" architecture; and I do not know any better way to expose to you the elaborate system of buncombe which is called "higher education" than to state that here in twentieth century America, where we know of bows and arrows only in poetry, and have the materials and the skill to build structures of steel and glass, big and airy and bright as day—we deliberately go and reproduce the architectural monstrosities, the intellectual and spiritual deformities of a thousand years ago, and compel modern chemists and biologists and engineers to do their research work by artificial light, for fear of arrows which ceased to fly when the last Indian was penned up in a reservation.

Not alone at the University of Chicago do you find stone towers with crenellated battlements—that is, notches through which arrows may be fired, and stones and flaming Standard Oil hurled down; you find them at college after college all over the United States. I look up some pictures I happen to have—here they are at Princeton and at Syracuse and at Colorado! You find Columbia University spending several millions for a huge Roman temple of white marble, called a library—a structure which is magnificent for picture post-card purposes, but which gives about ten per cent of the shelf-room that should have been bought for the money, and compels everybody in the main reading-room to use electric lights most of the day!

I recall one of my earliest radical impulses, derived from the spectacle I used to see when I stayed late in the afternoon in this library building. From regions unknown would emerge an army of old women with buckets and scrubbing-brushes; pitiful, wizened up old creatures crawling about the marble corridors on their hands and knees, mopping up the dirt of the students' feet and the spittle of their mouths. Manifestly, this cleaning might have been done by machinery, it might have been done by able-bodied men with mops; but women were cheaper, and there were those in charge of the university's affairs who cared more about money than humanity.

Of course, we know what such persons will answer; the old women were glad to get the work. In the same way they answer that chemists and biologists and engineers are glad to get a chance to do research work, even at cost of their eyesight. At the University of Chicago they discovered that men were anxious to get such work, even at the cost of their health. In his book, "The Higher Learning in America," Thorstein Veblen tells of an incident which happened in a certain laboratory "dedicated to one of the branches of biological science." Having been for ten years a professor at the University of Chicago, Professor Veblen felt under the necessity of withholding names; but I am not under the same necessity, and I make so bold as to state that it occurred in the Hull Biological Laboratory of the University of Chicago.

The building was supposed to be ventilated by a hot air system; fresh air was taken in from the outside, and warmed over steam coils, and distributed through the building. It began to be noted that members of the scientific staff were mysteriously falling sick. They would be forced to stay at home, or to take a vacation; they would get well, and then come back and get sick again. Finally, one professor went rooting about in the basement of the building, and made the discovery that the university authorities, in order to save the cost of heating, had boarded up the outside intake, so that the air which passed through the steam-coils was being derived in part from a manhole leading to a sewer. The great capitalist university had found it too costly to heat its Gothic halls—playfully described by Veblen as "heavy ceiled, ill-lighted lobbies, which might have served as a mustering place for a body of unruly men at arms, but which mean nothing more to the point today than so many inconvenient flag-stones to be crossed in coming and going."

CHAPTER LI

THE UNIVERSITY OF STANDARD OIL

Providence arranged it that soon after the University of Chicago was built, the oil king's digestion gave out, and he retired to the country to live on graham crackers and milk and play golf all day. The job of turning his two hundred million dollars into two billions was left to his efficient subordinates, and they were not so much interested in the old man's advertising ventures, so that the university was left to run itself. Veblen describes its spirit as "a ravenous megalomania." For years President Harper followed the plan of buying everything he wanted, and sending the bill to John D. But that was stopped, and now the running of the university is seen to by the usual board of interlocking directors, mostly elderly Baptists. They have had in past times some first-rate scientists; what they have now is a faculty of aged dotards, who set the tone of the place, and the young men try to act dotards to the best of their ability.

They are sensitive on the subject of petroleum at the university; they blush at mention of the word, and do not admit the conventional book-plates showing the lamp of knowledge. Some time ago a wag composed a "doxology" for use by the students, and the young radicals have fun with this—

> Praise God from whom oil blessings flow,
> Praise him, oil creatures here below,
> Praise him above, ye heavenly host,
> Praise Father, Son—but John the most.

I met one professor at the University of Chicago who insisted that teaching was entirely free. He added, with some asperity: "Of course you will do the Bemis story! We shall never hear the end of the Bemis story."

"Too bad!" I said, sympathetically. "I haven't heard that story; what is it?"

"Just a piece of slander," said the professor. "I know positively that the case of Bemis was not a case of academic freedom at all, and he himself admits it."

That was something definite. I ascertained that Edward W. Bemis is an economist and engineer, with offices in Chicago and New York, so I wrote and asked him about the matter. I quote his letter, and leave it for you to form your own judgment:

I was called from Vanderbilt University to the University of Chicago to the chair of Associate Professor of Economics and Sociology, at the opening of the University of Chicago in October, 1892. In March, 1895, President Harper informed me that the trustees had dropped me from the faculty the previous December, to take effect in July, 1895. He informed me then and in subsequent conversations that my attitude on public utility and labor questions was the cause, and that if he cared to talk about the reasons for my dismissal, I could not secure any other college position in the country.

A great deal was made of the matter in the newspapers all over this country, under the heading of College Freedom, and many papers took it up. I did teach after that, for two years, 1897-9, in the Kansas State Agricultural College, but, finding no openings in the larger universities, I turned my attention exclusively to the investigation of public utility questions, and to assisting states, cities and commissions in such matters. I found a congenial field as head of the Cleveland, Ohio, Water Department, under Tom L. Johnson, from September, 1901, to 1910, and have since then spent my strength on building up an organization of engineers and accountants devoted to assisting cities and states and other public bodies, including the national government, in appraisals and rate adjustments of public utilities.

I received no calls for teaching, save as above mentioned, since I was forced out of the University of Chicago, and for over twenty years have sought none. I have never been a Socialist, or an extremist along any line, but have investigated and to some degree favored public ownership of public utilities, and have had a friendly relation with the American labor movement.

My opposition to the efforts of certain Chicago utilities to secure lighting and street railway franchises, while I was at the University of Chicago, and the public address which I made during the famous Pullman strike in 1894, wherein I did not endorse the strike but did say that the railroads had often boycotted each other, violated law, etc., as well as had the men, were features assigned by President Harper for the opposition to me, resulting in my dismissal by the trustees of the university.

A professor at the University of Chicago who read this manuscript volunteered to get for me the university's side of the story, and he wrote me:

At the time of his "dismissal" Bemis was in the extension division. His appointment ran out and he was offered re-appointment, his remuneration to come from the fees of students. This action might, of course, be described in Mr. Bemis' phrase, "dropped me from the faculty."

I submitted that statement to Professor Bemis, who answered by wire:

My letter which you quote is absolutely correct. No proposition for continuance of my work, half of which was to advanced students within the university walls, was ever made to me.

Another of the casualties of Mr. Rockefeller's university was Professor Triggs, as I have told in "The Brass Check," and I gather they were not sorry when Veblen moved West. I was told that one professor had

17

recently been "on the carpet for excess of radical zeal," and I wrote to ask him if this was true. He answered that the trouble he had got into was for being away too much. Said he: "I have never known of anyone at Chicago being interfered with in any way 'for excess of radical zeal.' To be sure, no such excess exists." Which I find a charming reply!

To the same effect is the testimony of John C. Kennedy, formerly a professor at the University of Chicago. Questioned by Chairman Walsh of the Industrial Relations Commission, Professor Kennedy stated concerning the faculty: "A sincere desire to deal with fundamental conditions does not seem to be there in most cases. . . . . I think they are a poor crowd among which to look for leaders to bring about any fundamental change in social conditions." The reason for Professor Kennedy's discontent was that he had been engaged by the University of Chicago Settlement to make a survey of labor and living conditions among the Stockyards workers. He had prepared an elaborate and thoroughly documented report, which several of the packers found satisfactory; but Swift & Company—which has a member of the firm on the board of the University of Chicago—objected that Professor Kennedy had drawn "political conclusions" from his data; that is, he had suggested a remedy for the evil conditions in the Stockyards, for the workers to organize to protect themselves! These portions of the report were cut out before it was published, and the whole matter was hushed up, both by the university authorities and by the newspapers of the interlocking directorate in Chicago.

They have one "renommir professor" at Chicago, and are very proud of him. I don't think I exaggerate in saying that out of the score of faculty members I talked with on the subject of academic freedom, not one failed to mention Robert Morss Lovett as the university's certificate of emancipation from Standard Oil. Out of the warmth of his big heart Professor Lovett gives his help to Hindoo revolutionists thrown into jail, and to Russian sweat-shop workers clubbed over the head by the police. I asked him to read this manuscript, and he tells me that he thinks I am too severe upon the university. He wonders what I will have to say about places like Minnesota and Illinois, which are so much worse. To avoid misunderstanding, let me state that I have not been able to find a single one of the great American universities which is truly liberal or truly free; but there are degrees of badness among them, and the University of Chicago is one of the best. I have no desire to deny it due credit, therefore I note Professor Lovett's comment—that during the early days of the university President Harper stood for liberalism in religion, and thereby lost much Baptist money; also that the university made an enviable record during the war, in that there was no interference with the private views of any professor on this question.

Shortly after the war there developed a strong movement to refuse diplomas to about a dozen of the students who were accused of radical activities, but this movement was defeated at the last minute. I talked with several of these students, and with others who are now struggling to defend ideas of social justice at the university. They had a little paper, called "Chanticleer," and were so indiscreet as to reprint an article from the Seattle "Union Record" praising the paper. So the student daily hailed them as the "boy Bolsheviks" of the university, and both students and professors joined in a campaign of ridicule and sneering. The climax came with the fourth issue, containing an article by Clarence Darrow; not twenty students could be found to distribute this. Among the most active in attacking the little paper was a dean who has just died; he never lost an opportunity to denounce the radicals, and gave no scholarships or honors to such. I am presenting in this book many cases of college professors "let out" for speaking intemperately about conservatives; I am wondering if anyone will answer me by telling of a single professor "let out" from an American college for speaking intemperately about radicals!

I talked with another professor at Chicago, who does not want his name used. I asked him what he thought about the status of his profession, and he gave the best description of academic freedom in America that I have yet come upon. He said: "We are good cows; we stand quietly in our stanchions, and give down our milk at regular hours. We are free, because we have no desire to do anything but what we are told we ought to do. And we die of premature senility."

They have another professor at the University of Chicago who is not entirely satisfied with America as it is, and that is Robert Herrick, the novelist. He expressed the fear that I might try to write the same kind of book as "The Brass Check"; that is, to show direct pressure of financial interests upon college professors—whereas the way it is done is by class feeling, by the tradition of academic dignity, the prestige of old and established things, "the tone of the house." I took the liberty of telling Professor Herrick of a few cases I had collected, and he admitted that he had had no idea there were things like that going on.

Robert Herrick would, of course, never fail in urbanity and graciousness; but fundamentally, I think he is more pessimistic about American education than I am. He said: "Universities can't get money except by getting great numbers of students; so they dare not set any higher standards than rival institutions in the same neighborhood. So the American soul stays flabby; all that counts is show, and in every department you get by with superficiality. It is a lunch-counter system of education; read a novel and get a credit; then go out into the world, and use your college prestige to make a fortune; and then give your name to a college building. We do absolutely nothing for men and women who come to college, in the way of giving them true culture, higher standards of thought or conduct. I go to any university club and look over the alumni, and I see that we have given them no distinction—in dress, in speech, in morals, in ideas. You cannot tell them from the bathtub salesmen or the agents of barbers' supplies you meet in the lobby of the Blackstone Hotel."

The above is from a man who has been teaching for twenty-nine years at the University of Chicago; and you may compare it with the pungent remark of Professor Cattell, who was a teacher for twenty-six years at Columbia: "The average university club in America could more easily dispense with its library than with its bar."

P. S.—The remark on page 244, regarding the lamp of knowledge, was merely a joke on my part, but the publication of "The Goose-step" brought me a letter from a former Chicago student, as follows: "One fact you got, Lord knows how, I had straight from Dean Robertson (in an address in chapel); it is the matter of the rejection of the oil lamp as a symbol in the 'Coat of Arms' of the University."

CHAPTER LII

LITTLE HALLS FOR RADICALS

The touchiest problem with all academic authorities is that of "outside speakers." They can handle their own professors; by care in selecting instructors, and weeding out the undesirables before they get prestige, they can keep dangerous ideas from creeping into the classrooms. But it always happens there are half a dozen students who come from Socialist homes, and these get together and call themselves some society with a college name, and start inviting labor agitators and literary self-advertisers, to disturb the dignity and calm of scholarship. This puts the university administration in a dilemma; they are damned if they do and damned if they don't. If they refuse to let the radical propagandist in, there is a howl that they are repressing freedom of thought; on the other hand, if they do let him in, who can figure what millionaire may be led to alter his will?

There is always a little group of disturbers at every large university; and those at Chicago were moved to invite Upton Sinclair to come to their campus and repeat his Wisconsin performance. I was not present at the consultation between the president of the University of Chicago and his loyal and efficient secretary; but I have been able to imagine the scene. You understand, there isn't a particle of prejudice against radicals, and we have absolute freedom of speech at our university, we are willing for the students to hear anyone they wish; but we decide that we had better minimize the trouble by confining this literary self-advertiser to a small hall, so that students will not announce the meeting, and the newspapers won't hear about it, and the wealthy trustees and donors may not know that it has happened.

But the day before the lecture there is excitement in our president's office—Upton Sinclair has arrived in Chicago, and has telephoned asking for an interview. He comes; and we discover that he has shaved off the bushy black Bolshevik whiskers in which we had every right to expect to find him; also he has left off his red necktie, and has adopted a gentle and seductive smile—you know how cunning these Bolsheviks are! Our president's secretary tries to smooth him down—tells him what a great novelist he is, and how delighted we are to have him speak at our university, and how, of course, there is no particle of prejudice against radicals. Then he is taken into the dark Gothic chamber where our aged president sits by the dim light of arrow-proof windows.

Harry Pratt Judson has been at our university since it was founded thirty years ago, and is a holder of ten college degrees, and a high interlocking director in all the Rockefeller foundations for the guidance of American intellectual life. Also he is the author of a manual for college presidents entitled: "The Higher Education as a Training for Business," a book which deserves to be required reading for every course in educational administration, a standard guide to the art of persuading the rich to put up their money for mullioned windows and crenellated battlements and moated draw-bridges. There has to be somebody to keep the interlocking directorate aware of the importance of culture, and Harry Pratt Judson is the boy for this job; showing how a college education really does pay in dollars and cents, and putting it in language so simple that the basest pork merchant over at the "yards" can get the point. Says our President Judson: "Men buy and sell, not merely for fun, but for profit." And again: "A reputation for honest dealing with customers is a valuable asset." And again: "The habit of sustained mental application is got only by persistently applying the mind to work in a systematic way." Can any one deny these statements? If so, let him speak, or forever after hold his peace, while we, the administration of the University of Chicago, assert and declare that our Harry Pratt Judson is an educated educator and an inspired inspirationalist.

The Bolshevik author enters the presidential sanctum, still with that evil seductive smile. He explains that he has spoken to an audience of two thousand people at the University of Wisconsin, and fears that a hall seating only two hundred people will not accommodate those who wish to hear him at Chicago. He understands there is a large auditorium, Mandel Hall, which seats thirteen hundred——

"Ah, yes," says our president, with that urbanity which distinguishes him, "but we are accustomed to reserve

Mandel Hall for speakers who are invited by the university."

"Well," says the Bolshevik author—could anyone imagine the impudence?—"I should be perfectly willing to be invited by the university."

"I'm afraid that could hardly be arranged," says our president, as sweetly as ever. "Of course, Mr. Sinclair, you understand that we are quite willing for our students to listen to anyone's ideas; we have absolute freedom of speech at this university, but we have our established traditions regarding the use of our halls, and you could not expect us to make an exception in your case."

"Well," says the Bolshevik author, "it would seem, President Judson, that your idea of freedom of speech is that the radicals have a small hall and the conservatives a large hall."

But even that does not cause our president to waver in his urbanity. He is an old and wise man, accustomed to handling many crude people—you cannot imagine the things he has had said to him by pork merchants! He smiles his gentle, rebuking smile, and says: "You must admit, Mr. Sinclair, it would be better for you to have a hall that is too small than to have one that is too large."

To this the fellow answers that he is willing to take the risk. So our president sees there is nothing to be gained by prolonging the discussion, and tells him in plain words that the hall which has been assigned him is the only hall he can have.

The Bolshevik author goes out, and doubtless would like to denounce us in the newspapers, but our interlocking trustees have seen to that—they own all the newspapers in Chicago, and Upton Sinclair stays in the city a week, and not one pays any attention to his presence. More than that, we have got things so arranged all over the United States that Upton Sinclair can spend three months traveling over the country, stopping at twenty-five cities, and in all that time have only two newspaper reporters come to ask him for an interview! .

However, we know that he is a dangerous customer, and we watch with some trepidation to see what he will do. On the evening of the lecture we go to the hall, and fifteen minutes before the time set we find a state of affairs—truly, we don't know whether to be amused or irritated. We can't think how the students managed to hear about this unadvertised lecture, and it is a distressing thing to see so many young people with a craving for unwholesome sensation. They have packed the little hall; the aisles are solid with them; they are hanging from our mullioned windows, and blocking all the corridors outside the many doors. And all the time more of them coming!

The Bolshevik author arrives, accompanied by two or three professors. We have always said that these "reds" ought to be kicked off the faculty, and now we see the consequences of tolerating them! The author shoves his way to the platform, and—we tremble with indignation even now as we recall his proceedings—he tells the students about his interview with our august president, and states plainly that he thinks we have discriminated against him because he is a radical. He asserts, on the authority of several students, that no difficulty has ever before been raised about giving Mandel Hall for speakers invited by students; also he mentions that the university has barred Raymond Robins and Rabindranath Tagore. And we note that a large percentage of the audience laugh and applaud, as if they thought such fellows ought to be heard! He goes on to say that outside is a beautiful warm spring evening, and a quadrangle with soft green grass, and thick Gothic walls to shelter it from the wind. If they will go outside and squat, he will come and talk to them, and there will be plenty of room for everyone who wishes to hear his self-laudations.

The students laugh and cheer—what can you expect of young people, who have little sense of dignity, and think this is a lark? They troop outside, and more come running up from all directions. Never in the thirty years of our university has there been such a violation of propriety. For an hour the man delivers a rankly socialistic harangue to fifteen hundred students, and when he tries to stop, they clamor for him to go on, they crowd about and ask him questions, and he is kept talking until eleven o'clock at night, telling our young men and women about strikes and graft—all the most dangerous ideas, which we have been working so hard to keep away from them! Even things right here in Chicago—the fact that our biggest newspapers have their buildings upon land which they have stolen from the city schools; the fact that our school-board has been stealing several millions of dollars of the people's money, while a clerk of our city jail has got away with three thousand dollars belonging to his prisoners!

However, we are happy to say that some of our students resisted these Bolshevik blandishments, and gave proof of the principles we have instilled into them. We have a university paper called the "Daily Maroon," which the radicals impudently dub the "Moron." This paper next day had a report of the meeting, and it certainly was delightful the way they gave it to the oratorical author: "His talk was a more or less skilful combination of a frenzied street corner gathering (to be sure, there was no soap-box), and a lecture in Political Economy on capital and labor and the feudal system. All the old platitudes used for the last decade in liberal workmen's papers were repeated." You will not fail to appreciate the gentlemanly tone of that rebuke; and then, this most cruel cut of all: "One is tempted, too, to wonder what kind of novels Mr. Sinclair writes; if they are as full of mistakes in grammar as his address last night, his publishers must be gray around the temples." Reading the above, we were so much pleased that we sent marked copies to all the directors of the Standard Oil Company and the packers, so that our friends might have proof that the better classes of our students do not read socialistic books.

That was the end of the incident, except for a trick which the wretched Bolshevik played upon us. Would you believe it, he wasn't cowed by the rebuke of the "Daily Maroon," but actually tried to seduce our student body next afternoon by engaging in a tennis match with the champion of our university. Our champion beat him, though by an effort so mighty that it split his pants. But all the time the author was being beaten, he kept up a hypocritical pretense of good nature, intending thereby to win the regard of our young and unsophisticated undergraduates. In this purpose we are sorry to say he seemed to be successful, for next day the "Daily Maroon" appeared with a grave editorial, in which it took back at least a portion of the previous day's well-deserved rebuke:

Upton Sinclair plays tennis more pleasingly than he talks or writes. Although he lost two sets to Captain Frankenstein yesterday afternoon, he did it with a grace that does not characterize his books and speeches. He played and lost like a sportsman. He gave no evident sign of petty displeasure at being defeated. One admires manliness, and one finds far more of it in witnessing Mr. Sinclair on the tennis court than in reading one of his tearful harangues of the yellow press which, he declares, has hounded him, and suppressed his thoughts.

All we can say about that is, how fortunate that so few Bolsheviks take part in athletics!

CHAPTER LIII

THE UNIVERSITY OF JUDGE GARY

There is another great ruling class munition-factory in the vicinity of Chicago, Northwestern University, at Evanston, Illinois. It is one of those terrible places, of which there are scores in the United States, which began as little church institutions, and by the grace of graft have grown to enormous size. Northwestern is Methodist, and has some ten thousand strictly pious students, and over six hundred instructors, and not a rag of an idea to cover its bare bones. The man who was until last year its president fitted himself for that office by being the university's "Director of the Bureau of Salesmanship Research." The first vice-president of the university is the general counsel of the Illinois Steel Company; the third vice-president is vice-president of the Illinois Steel Company; while the grand duke is the very grandest of all grand dukes in the United States—that prince of open shoppers and potentate of reaction, Judge Gary, chairman of the United States Steel Corporation!

For many years previously the leading grand duke was James A. Patten, the grain speculator, whose million dollar corner in wheat was the sensation of my boyhood. Mr. Patten began life as a clerk in a country store, and his claim to direct a great educational institution is based upon his acquaintance with the grain commission business, one of the most thoroughly organized of American swindles. Mr. Patten is director of two national banks, a trust company, a grain company, and an Edison company. He is a malignant "open shopper," and during his reign at Northwestern waged incessant war upon two or three liberals who got into the place.

One of these men was Professor Gray, whom we have already met at the University of Minnesota. Gray managed to stick at Northwestern for sixteen years. He taught economics; a liberal colleague taught psychology, and the president of the university remarked to a friend of mine that these were the two hardest departments he had to administer, because one touched on religion and the other on the pocket-book! Gray was handicapped in the usual way by low salaries and lack of promotion for himself and his assistants. For many years he tried to get Harry Ward as assistant, but could never manage it.

Mr. Patten was twice elected mayor of Evanston, and when he ran again, Professor Gray, who was a Progressive, talked against him, and led the Progressive forces in the legislature that drove Patten's chairman out. Naturally, that caused Mr. Patten intense annoyance. He had given the university a gymnasium, and a generous share of the millions he had extracted from the bread supply of the American people. So he demanded that the president should support him; and the president sent for Gray, and proceeded to administer a rebuke. Gray asked: "Are you speaking officially or as an individual?"

The climax of the affair was that Gray asked to meet Patten and thresh the matter out face to face. They met at luncheon, and Patten presented his complaint. He was sore because Gray had quoted him as saying with regard to the pious students of the university—"it had cost more to get out the Bible vote than any other." "But," said Gray, "you did say that, didn't you?" Patten admitted that he had said it, so Professor Gray finally offered to settle the matter by writing a letter to both the Evanston newspapers, stating exactly what Mr. Patten admitted he had said, and exactly what he denied; but Patten was not satisfied with this settlement of the difficulty!

A little later Professor Gray was appointed by the National Civic Federation as one of a committee of economists to investigate municipal ownership in Europe. They were all supposed to be reactionaries, and their findings were supposed to be what they knew the National Civic Federation wanted; but Professor Gray had the wretched taste to become converted to the doctrines of municipal ownership by the facts he observed in Europe, and he so stated in his report. When he got a proof of this report he found that it had been doctored in the office of Mr. Ralph Easley, the very ardent "open shopper" and hundred per cent plutocratic secretary of that organization. The professor had to threaten a law-suit against the National Civic Federation in order to force them to correct the report.

Also, Gray had a "run-in" with Charles Deering, Harvester Trust magnate, the second grand duke of the board. Deering asked Gray to speak against a strike of the Harvester Trust workers, and said that he purposed to put this strike down with guns. "Yes, Mr. Deering," said the professor, "but suppose the day comes when you are under the sod and the other fellow has the guns." Needless to say, the authorities of Northwestern were glad when this too popular professor received an offer from the University of Minnesota, which had come for the moment under a liberal administration. A friend of mine was present at a private luncheon, at which Mr. Patten made the statement that he had got rid of Gray, and was now going to get rid of another man.

This especially pious university is the one we mentioned as having established a rule that only bachelors are to be accepted as teachers; also the one which we found officially declaring that excellence in a college professor lies, not in his being able to teach, but in his diligence in raking in the dust-heaps of history. Last spring they gave their grand duke the usual honorary degree, and took occasion to have him instruct their ten thousand students in the principles of American piety. A copy of the address lies before me, one of those beautifully but mysteriously printed pamphlets which bear the name of no publisher and no purchase price, but manage to get circulated by hundreds of thousands of copies all over the country.

The subject of Judge Gary's address is "Ethics in Business," and he begins by making some curious admissions. There was a time, "not many years ago, perhaps not much more than a score," when in American business "the rule of might over right prevailed. . . . . Competition was tyrannical and destructive. Weaker competitors were forced out of business, often by means not only unethical but severe and brutal. The graves of insolvents were strewn along the paths of industrial development and operation. The financially strong grew stronger and richer."

Of course you understand what all this means; it is an amiable preliminary to the statement which Judge Gary is going to make, that now all these evil things have changed, this wicked time has passed! But I would like to put to Judge Gary the question: how did it happen to pass? Who brought it about, and what were you, Judge Gary, doing at the time? Were you going about the country, telling boys and girls in colleges about the need of business reform? The question answers itself. At that time Judge Gary was head of the Federal Steel Company, and busily engaged in organizing the Steel Trust, the most perfect illustration in America of the evils he refers to. Also he was engaged in denouncing as agitators and disturbers of the public peace the very men, from Theodore Roosevelt down, whose labors on behalf of reform he now pretends to justify and accept.

In those wicked days, he tells the students, the masters of industry "did not give to employes just consideration. The wage rates were adjusted strictly in accordance with the laws of supply and demand. The welfare of the workmen was decided almost entirely from the standpoint of utility and profit." But now, all that is over. "The large majority of business men now conduct their affairs" on the basis "that employes are associates rather than servants, and should be treated accordingly. . . . . Conscientious treatment of employes which secures their respect and confidence will tend to increase their loyalty and efficiency." And this from the man who continues to maintain throughout the greatest industry in America a twelve-hour day, with a twenty-four-hour day once a week! Who uses all the power of his colossal organization to deny to his employes the most essential of all industrial rights—the right to organize for their own protection! Who, as an incident to this policy, maintains the most widespread and most infamous system of espionage and terrorism that has ever been known in an Anglo-Saxon country! This man, who pays more money to spies and provocateurs in one year than the czar of all the Russians paid in ten—this man, whose hands are slimy with the blood of union organizers shot down in cold blood, whose lips are foul with ten thousand lies, told about his wage-slaves during the last steel strike—this man has the insolence to stand up before a commencement audience at a "Christian" university, and declare that justice and kindness now prevail in American big business, and that wage rates are no longer "adjusted strictly in accordance with the laws of supply and demand!"

Such is the state of social conscience in the greatest educational institution of the Methodist church in America; but, thank God, the entire church no longer applauds this re-crucifixion of Jesus. The Inter-church Federation has issued a report on the steel strike; and if you want to know just how honest a man Judge Gary is, take the trouble to read their account of the handling of this strike by his Pittsburgh newspapers. After that you will be able to get the full humor of the comment of Bishop McConnell of the Methodist church upon the giving of the degree to Gary. At the "Evanston Conference" the bishop said that the conferring of this degree did not mean any intellectual attainments on the part of the recipient; "it merely means that for certain specific and well-known purposes you are giving him a degree." In other words, you are selling your soul for the price of a building!

CHAPTER LIV

THE UNIVERSITY OF THE GRAND DUCHESS

We take the Illinois Central Railroad, with its Columbia trustee, a recent University of Chicago trustee, a Knox College and a Rockford College trustee, and an Armour Institute trustee, and one First National, one Guaranty Trust, and two National City Bank directors, and find ourselves in the town of Urbana, where the state university is located. Here is another of these terrible mushroom places, with a thousand instructors, and ten thousand students exposed to all the ravages of commercialism. I first heard of this university after the publication of "The Jungle," when the Chicago packers flew to their interlocking regents for protection, and a committee of the university faculty was appointed to inspect the stockyards and report that everything was all right. In return for this, Mr. Armour gave some money for a veterinary college, and Mr. Armour's partner, Arthur Meek-er, was made a regent, and his portrait now hangs in the Sanhedrim where the interlocking regents meet.

This University of Illinois has made itself conspicuous in the glorification of trade; they have a whole college devoted thereto, with an especially large building, and ten years ago they had a solemn ceremonial in which they dedicated this temple to Mammon. The affair was known as a "Conference on Commercial Education and Business Progress," and doubtless it caused great progress in the business of getting contributions from the plutocracy and its politicians. It lasted two days, and was addressed by such dignitaries as the president of the Chamber of Commerce of the United States, the president of the Chicago Association of Commerce, the dean of the College of Commerce and Administration of the University of Chicago, and the President of the Board of Trustees of the University of Illinois, who was, and still is, chief operating engineer of Edison Electric. There was an invocation to the God of Commerce by the Reverend President of Knox College, and an address by the President of the Illinois Bankers' Association, who opened the Hall of Fame of the University by presenting a portrait of a lately deceased banker; then there was a prayer of dedication to the God of Bankers by the Reverend President McClelland; and on the evening of the last day there was a banquet tendered by the Commercial Club of Urbana, with all the big business potentates above-mentioned listed as "honored guests," and preceded by an invocation to the God of Gastronomy.

The university traditions thus established have been reverently cherished. In 1916 the college put on three lectures, under the auspices of the Chicago Board of Trade, dealing with the art of gambling in the staff of your life and mine. A gentleman living in Urbana writes me:

These lectures were illustrated by lantern slides, conspicuous among which was one giving the signals used on the Board of Trade in the rapid gambling when the Board is in session. This was minutely dwelt upon and the manual code of signs fully explained. After the close of the lecture I went to a fine old professorial acquaintance. I said: "I know now where my children are taught grain-gambling. If they are to be gamblers I want them to be first-class gamblers. Where do you teach poker, baccarat and other games?" He said: "Upon my word, I never knew any such thing was carried

on by the University of Illinois." He appeared much disconcerted, blushing greatly.

Needless to say, such an institution is profoundly and
reverently religious. It is at this place that the various
sects have been able to get credits for their teachings. The
laws of the state prohibit religious instruction in public
institutions; nevertheless, you can go to the University of
Illinois and study in the Bible classes of the Baptists, or
the Methodists, or the Lutherans, or the Campbellites, or
the Seventh Day Adventists—and some day, no doubt,
the Holy Rollers; you may learn about how Jonah swallowed the whale, and how David killed Cock Robin with
his little bow and arrow; and as a reward for these labors
you may receive a university degree—having just as much
cultural significance as if it were conferred by the king of
Dahomey.

I visited Urbana, and took occasion to inspect a file of
the student paper, "The Daily Illini." A Jewish student
had written to this paper a polite and respectful letter, suggesting that the university authorities should open the
libraries and tennis courts on Sunday, for the benefit of
such as might care to make use of them. The reply was a
letter from the "dean of men," a piece of insolent rude-
ness. With elaborate sneering he informed the heathen
student that he lived in a Christian community, and must
make up his mind that this community intended "to preserve the Christian traditions."

Of course, there would be no use talking about a little
thing like the constitution of the United States to so
mighty a person as a dean of men in a state university.
Nevertheless, I mention in passing that our forefathers
put into the constitution a provision that "Congress shall
make no law respecting an establishment of religion";
and this, it would seem, ought to serve as a guide for
state legislatures and all bodies deriving their authority
therefrom, including regents of state universities and
their presidents and deans. Perhaps it will be more
to the point if I quote the second letter of the Jewish
student, who suggested that the dean of men should investigate how students really pass their Sunday afternoons
and evenings at Illinois: "Shooting craps in the privacy
of one's room, playing cards amidst dense clouds of smoke,

or shimmying to the strains of some horrible piece of canned jazz."

The board of this university is distinguished in that it has a grand duchess, who makes her home in Urbana, and runs both the university and the town. She is Mrs. Mary E. Busey, wife of a former Democratic congressman; she is president of the Busey National Bank, and a large land-owner, and in the year 1913, while a regent, she sold a tract of land to the university for $160,000 or $1,000 per acre, while land adjoining the tract was purchased for $600 per acre. Mrs. Busey herself attended these meetings and voted for this purchase from herself. (Attention Professor Brander Matthews of Columbia University!)

For president of her university Mrs. Busey selected an aged and venerable product of the university's own regime, who began his career twenty-eight years ago as director of the School of Commerce. He is David Kinley, locally known as "King David." I am told by several who have been his victims that he never fails to question an applicant for a position as to whether he is a Socialist. "This is no time for disloyalty," he says; nor will it ever be such a time while King David reigns.

Before the war the university was not so careful, and agitators and disturbers of the academic peace crept in. There was one young member of the faculty who had acquired at the University of Oxford the evil habit of going without his hat, and in October, 1917, the dean of the Graduate School delivered an address to the graduate students, formally condemning this practice. Other members of the faculty were seen to be smoking on the street— whereas we have learned from the Jewish student that university smoking is done only at poker and jazz parties. Another member was reported to the president by the dean of the college, on the charge of having accepted an invitation to speak on the topic, "Philosophical Reasons for the Non-existence of God." Fortunately, he was able to prove that he had not accepted such an invitation; also that he had not received it.

Another member of the faculty received an elaborate letter from the head of the sociological department, reporting several evil remarks he was said to have made to other professors, regarding his having taken some whis-

18

key with him on a camping trip, and other such matters. This professor was placed on trial before his dean, and was acquitted of the evil remarks. Later there were dreadful allegations concerning members of the faculty having been seen to be drinking at a supper-party at the country club. All the servants of the club were interviewed by a faculty committee, and denied the charges, and the agitation died down. Nevertheless, the activities of the scandal bureau continued, and the grand duchess became fearfully wrought up. Another investigation was conducted, this time by secret service agents of the United States government. Five professors were summoned, one of them a lady, Miss Shepherd, and she was told that she was "a rank, rotten, vicious Socialist and Anarchist." Mrs. Busey was terribly upset, and wrung her hands, exclaiming, "To think that members of my faculty should behave in this way!" "My faculty?" questioned Professor Tolman. "Do you mean to say we are your hired servants?" "Well," replied Mrs. Busey, "you are in my employ!" This was one of the incidents I mentioned to Professor Robert Herrick, who lives in his ivory tower at the University of Chicago, only a hundred miles away, and thinks that college professors are controlled by "the tone of the house," and never get direct orders from the plutocracy!

The upshot of the matter was a formal trial before the interlocking regents, with the dean of the Graduate School presiding. A great array of witnesses were summoned, and several of the victims described the scene to me. The affair was carried through with the utmost solemnity; the master of ceremonies would enter and announce: "Two witnesses wait without." The two witnesses would be led in, and questioned as to what evil things they knew about the radical professors. One old lady, wife of a high-up faculty-member, had a dreadful charge: "Well, they sit next us in the Faculty Club, and it's very unpleasant; Mr. Stevens laughs a great deal!"

The ceremonies lasted from ten o'clock in the morning until ten o'clock at night, and every now and then the accused professors would demand a chance to cross-question this or that witness, and they would be told: "Wait; you will have your chance." Witness after witness testified as to their political and religious beliefs, but they themselves were given no chance to be heard, neither were they permitted to call any witnesses for their side. Late at night the proceedings were adjourned, and the chance they had been promised was never given.

Even with this one-sided procedure, nothing wrong could be found with them, and the report of the regents exonerated them completely. Nevertheless, two of them were let out at the end of the year, and a third, Professor Richard C. Tolman, resigned. It is amusing to note that the charge against him had been disloyalty to his government, and as soon as he quit the university he was taken by his government into its most difficult and confidential service—the Department of Chemical Warfare! Apparently he gave satisfaction, for his government made him a major, and later on put him in charge of nitrogen fixation work.

CHAPTER LV

THE UNIVERSITY OF AUTOMOBILES

We take the Wabash Railroad to Detroit, traveling under the protection of a Columbia University trustee; and from Detroit we take the Michigan Central Railroad, with a Columbia trustee, a Cornell trustee, a Rochester trustee and a recent Yale and New York University trustee for directors and two First National, two Guaranty Trust, and two National City Bank directors; and so we arrive at Ann Arbor, home of the University of Michigan. In the upper peninsula of this State are enormous deposits of copper, with a great trust, Calumet and Hecla, in charge of the region. We shall feel at home here, because the enterprise is financed by Lee-Higginson, and all the old Boston families, the Shaws, Agassizs, Higginsons and Lowells, got in on the ground floor. So now when strikers have to be shot down or kidnapped, we find highly cultured graduates of Harvard in charge of the job; when they have to be lied about, the Associated Press is ready, with a Harvard graduate as general manager—see "The Brass Check," pages 358-361.

In the lower peninsula are great manufacturing cities, including Detroit, headquarters of the automobile industry. The grand duke of the state university is Frank B. Leland, president of the United Savings Bank and brother of a great motor magnate. As his right-hand agent and local manager at Ann Arbor he has Mr. Junius P. Beal, former owner of the Ann Arbor "Times," prominent Republican politician, director of a bank and an insurance company, and owner of most of the saloon property in Detroit; also Judge Murfin, a leading stand-pat politician; a doctor, who is also an active politician; the manager of the Grand Rapids street railways, who is interested in banks; and a Bay City manufacturer, who is president of a national bank.

No account of education in Michigan would be complete which did not mention Senator Newberry, the especial darling of the plutocracy of the state. Newberry is the son-in-law of A. V. Barnes, president of the American Book Company, which is the school-book trust, the most important single agency in the corrupting of American education. We shall come to know this American Book Company intimately when we deal with our public schools. Suffice it for the moment to say that when ex-Secretary of the Navy Newberry bought his way into the United States Senate, he used money which had been pilfered from the school children of the United States. Mr. Fred Cody, henchman of Newberry, and convicted with him, is an American Book Company agent, while his brother, Frank Cody, is superintendent of schools in Detroit. You see what a tight little system they have in Michigan!

As president of the university they had until two years ago a native son, who began teaching there fifty years ago. He is described to me by one who had much dealings with him as a typical "go-getter," with the mentality of a hardware sales agent; very expert at getting money from the rich, but in the realm of the intellect "a bouncing old fool." A year or two ago they got in Marion LeRoy Burton, the great inspirationalist whom we met at the University of Minnesota. We saw him introduced there with brass bands and fireworks, and I have a friend who saw the same thing happen at Ann Arbor; these inspirationalists, it seems, live always in the glare of fireworks and the blare of brass bands—or else the sound of their own eloquence, which is the same thing.

The University of Michigan is another of these huge educational department stores, a by-product of the sudden prosperity of the automobile business. Its spirit was in-

terestingly revealed by the Detroit "News" of two years
ago, at which time the enrollment amounted to twelve
thousand. Said the "News:"

> Whether it is wise or best for the individual and society
> is difficult to decide; but it is true and very natural indeed
> that for nearly all of these young persons an education is not
> greatly worth while if at the end of the college course or soon
> thereafter it can not be translated into good pay and the ma-
> terial comforts of life. The old ideal of education as an end
> in itself, as the deepening and broadening of one's view of life,
> as the acquiring of a certain amount and kind of culture, has
> gone from among us.

At this university they have, of course, all the usual
paraphernalia of fraternities and sororities and "student
activities"; also they have an oversupply of what passes
for religion in a commercial age. There are five or six
hundred instructors, employed to prepare boys and girls
for money-making, and a few fond idealists, who struggle
to introduce a little understanding of the intellectual life.
At this, as at other universities, you hear wailing about
the impossibility of getting college students to study; so
you would have thought that when a man came along who
proved himself a wizard at that art, the harassed authorities would have grappled him to their hearts. I put it to
you, overworked and troubled college professor, in whatever part of America you may be: suppose some one put
to you the task of getting seventy-five college boys to come
to you, begging you to teach them in off hours, and outside
the regular classes, and without any credits; offering to
rent rooms for the purpose, clean them up themselves, buy
lumber and saw it and build benches with their own hands
—would you say you know how to do that? Suppose you
were asked if you could spend hundreds of hours in intimate association with such students, and never once hear
a dirty story, never once hear talk about football or society politics, never see a man light a cigarette—would
you say that any man alive could do such a thing? Suppose it were up to you to get yourself invited to the
toughest fraternity-house on the campus, to read the Bible
to the men between five and six o'clock in the afternoon,
and have everybody in the fraternity-house attend, and
even bring in crowds from the other fraternity-houses—
would you think that could be done in any American university? And if a man were doing all these things, would

you say that he ought to be made dean of men, and then, as quickly as possible, president of the university—or would you say that he ought to be fired from the university in disgrace? Of course it would depend; before giving your answer, you have to know whether the man is a Socialist!

He is; and so he was driven from the University of Automobiles. His story was told to me by some of his former students, who ask me not to use his name; he has another job, and might very easily lose that. So let us call him Smithfield. He began teaching at Ann Arbor fifteen years ago, starting in on rhetoric. Naturally, the way to make rhetoric interesting is to see how it is used by live writers; so Smithfield and his classes would read H. G. Wells, and the plays and prefaces of Bernard Shaw, and the essays of John Stuart Mill. He would set his classes interesting stunts to do; a passage from Wells to write over in the style of Milton, or one of Shakespeare in the manner of Carlyle. His classes grew, and when he turned them over to others they fell off. The head of the department brought him three boys, sons of the interlocking directorate, who could not pass; Smithfield taught them, and they passed. "It's a marvel," said the professor; "I don't see how you do it."

But parents began to complain. Their children were coming home with different ideas; they were learning real things about modern life, instead of the pretenses the parents were used to! A nephew of Mr. Henry Leland, of Lincoln Motors, brought to Mr. Bulkley, the banker, at that time a regent, the dreadful story that Smithfield was a Socialist; so the president of the university summoned him in haste: "My dear Smithfield," said he, "can't you see that if you were to divide everything up, it would not be many years before the more able people had got possession of everything again?" Such was the mentality of the aged native product; and he was backed by Mr. Beal, the resident regent, owner of banks and saloon real estate. The boys had to come to this latter to ask for the use of a hall for a lecture by some unorthodox person, and they would regularly be asked this question about dividing up!

Matters got so serious, with complaints of rich parents, that there was a formal investigation by a committee. Thirty students were corralled and questioned by five members of the faculty. "Have you ever read a Socialist book? Have you ever been to a Socialist lecture? Where did you get these ideas? Were you taught Socialism by Professor Smithfield?" One and all, the boys testified that Smithfield had never taught them Socialism; he had taught them to think. He had been tireless in impressing upon them that they should learn to hold their minds in suspense, and to judge for themselves; they should test new ideas, and accept what they found convincing to their reason. As a result of this investigation, one of the deans informed Smithfield that he had been suspended by the regents, but this statement turned out not to be true—not yet!

These professors were charming fellows in their social life; but when they were offended in their class prejudices, they became vindictive. They were incensed against Professor William E. Bohn, who was a candidate on the Socialist ticket, and made a speech at Kalamazoo, which was taken up by the capitalist press. Professor Bohn's manuscript showed that he did not say what the papers accused him of saying, and many members of the audience substantiated his statement, nevertheless he was fired. About this same time they barred Jane Addams from speaking in a college building; she was arguing for woman suffrage, and that was a contentious political question, unfit for student ears!

For thirteen years Smithfield was in perpetual hot water, being "called up" and cautioned and pleaded with by the authorities. "What is the matter?" he asked of his dean. "Can't I teach?" The answer was, "You teach too God-damned well." This was Mortimer E. Cooley, a high-up authority in the engineering world, one of those valuation wizards about whom we learned in our study of Harvard. Dean Cooley has been interested all his life in privately owned public utilities, and he stated his point of view to one of his professors: "An engineer owes his first duty to the man who employs him." In the pamphlet, "Snapping Cords," by Morris L. Cooke, of Philadelphia, it is narrated how Professor Cooley serves his masters; he went to the Worcester Polytechnic Institute, and told these students that "in 1911 the average rate of return on all the capital (of all utility corporations) was

but 2.3 per cent." Mr. Cooke cites a circular of Henry
L. Doherty & Company, New York investment bankers,
giving a table of net earnings of such corporations for the
ten years from 1902, to 1912, and they amount to: gas
and electric, 8.45; industrials, 7.79; railroads, 4.25 per
cent. Mr. Cooke adds the important note that the securities of such utility corporations are from fifty to one hundred per cent in excess of invested capital!

Dean Cooley was troubled, because he could not get his
engineering students to take any interest in ideas. They
ought to have a little more culture than the average business men, he thought; so he tried to get them to read
Shakespeare and Milton, but in vain; he tried to get
them to read Darwin and Huxley, but in vain. Chemistry
and physics they got in the laboratory, but they had no
biology and wanted none. Smithfield tried them on the
social sciences, introducing them to Bertrand Russell and
Bernard Shaw; and these hustling young engineers suddenly discovered that literature had something to do with
life. In six semesters this teacher had eight sections,
over two hundred students. But every bit of this was
abolished by the university authorities, under pressure of
the plutocracy of automobiles, railroads and banks.

It was then that Smithfield's students took matters
into their own hands. They asked if he would meet with
them for talks, and they started an open forum, renting
some rooms above a drug store, and doing all the work
themselves. They cut out smoking and drinking, and took
to debating social problems. As one of them phrased it
to me, "We let loose a spirit of real knowledge, and if we
could have gone on, we should have changed the social
order in ten years." But, of course, that is exactly what
the plutocracy of Michigan did not intend to have happen; they are going to keep the present social order—
which means that we are going to have civil war in
America, with the horrors we have seen in Russia and
Ireland.

Some boys came to Smithfield, saying they would
like to meet on Sunday mornings and study religion.
Smithfield thought he would like to know something
about religion himself; so they got together and began
to read the Bible. Of course they read it with their eyes
open; they studied the class struggle in ancient Judea,

the Hebrews enslaved by the plutocracy of Rome, the Hebrew proletariat enslaved by their own exploiters, with the help of priests and preachers of institutionalized religion. You can see the same thing in Ann Arbor and Detroit, so Professor Smithfield's boys discovered the Bible to be "live stuff."

Presently came the Y. M. C. A. hand-shakers, seeking to introduce Bible study into the fraternity-houses. They would select some fraternity man to read the Bible between five and six o'clock in the afternoon; and then it was the Alpha Deltas, who boast themselves the toughest bunch in town, came to Smithfield and asked him to read to them. All the other classes petered out, and came to nothing; and naturally the "Y" people were sore, because a radical was able to hold his classes while they could not.

Professor Smithfield's attitude toward the war was about the same as my own; that is, he swallowed the allies' propaganda sufficiently to think there might be a greater hope for democracy if the allies were to win. He made speeches, and sold Liberty Bonds, and his enemies could not get him on this issue. So the scandal bureau was put to work. Professor Smithfield's wife was a teacher of swimming in the public schools of Detroit, and presently it began to be rumored that she had had a red-headed baby. One of the students told me the origin of this red-headed baby story, but I forget it; maybe the wife had been seen to pat a red-headed baby on the street, or maybe she had taken care of a red-headed baby for some friend—any little thing like that will do for the scandal bureau. It happens that the wife is likewise a Socialist, and in 1919 she answered some questions which students asked her about the Newberry case. As we have seen, the superintendent of schools in Detroit is a brother to Newberry's leading henchman, so Mrs. Smithfield lost her position as a teacher of swimming.

Shortly afterwards her husband lost his position as a teacher of modern ideas. They did not notify Smithfield himself, but the newspapers got hold of it, and the reporters interviewed his dean, and also Regent Beal, and both declared the report was untrue, it was a mistake. The dean told Smithfield it was a mistake; but shortly afterwards Smithfield discovered that it was the truth. And if you want to know why college teaching is dull, and why college students drink and smoke and gamble and go to "petting-parties," you have the whole answer in this experience of one live and interesting teacher.

They have a newspaper at the university, the "Michigan Daily," and on Sunday they publish an eight-page literary supplement of very excellent quality. In October, 1922, a senior student, G. D. Eaton, published in this supplement a review of John Kenneth Turner's book, "Shall It Be Again?" an exposure of the dishonesties of the late war, based upon documents, and therefore not to be answered. The student who reviewed it had been an ardent patriot, and had endeavored to enlist; being rejected as under weight, he managed to get in by a trick, and performed his military duties competently. He was invalided, and is at the university as a ward of the Federal Board of Vocational Rehabilitation. Immediately on the appearance of his review, President Burton summoned the faculty members of the Board of Control of Student Publications, and directed this board to dismiss Eaton at once, the declared reason being one sentence in the review: "Most history professors are senile, simple and misguided asses." A faculty member visited the offices of all three student publications, and not merely forbade that Eaton should contribute to any of these papers, but forbade that the papers should mention his dismissal in any way. The Dean of Students endeavored to have the government withdraw support from Eaton, so that he would have to quit the university. Extraordinary efforts were made to keep the case from getting into the newspapers; but a month later the Detroit "Free Press" got hold of the story, and gave young Eaton a little course in practical journalism. They got an interview with him, and from this interview they cut everything that might be favorable to his case; as the rest was not unfavorable enough, they embellished it with fourteen distinct falsehoods, which Mr. Eaton lists in a letter to me. Also I ought to mention that this returned soldier was mobbed and badly beaten by the students for an article in the "Smart Set," discussing the university. His successor as editor has been forbidden to publish an article proving that freedom of opinion among the students is not desired or permitted.

CHAPTER LVI

THE UNIVERSITY OF THE STEEL TRUST

We set out for Pittsburgh; and we can take either the Baltimore and Ohio, with a Johns Hopkins trustee for president and another Johns Hopkins trustee for director, also a Pittsburgh trustee, a Princeton trustee, a Lafayette trustee, a Teacher's College trustee, a Lehigh trustee for directors, also a Morgan partner and a First National Bank director and two Guaranty Trust Company directors, and a trustee of the University of Pennsylvania; or we can take the Pennsylvania Railroad, which is interlocked with the Guaranty Trust Company, Massachusetts Tech, Johns Hopkins, Princeton, Yale, the United States Steel Corporation, Bryn Mawr College, Wilson College, the University of Pennsylvania, the Girard Trust Company, and the University of Pittsburgh. It is this Pittsburgh institution we are now going to investigate, and we shall have no difficulty in tracing its financial connections. As one of the professors remarked to me, "At Pittsburgh the plumbing is all open."

He might also have added that this plumbing has been "swiped." In other universities the members of the plutocracy who run things have put up at least a part of the funds; in Pittsburgh they have made the people put up the funds, while the interlocking directorate takes the honors and emoluments. We saw Judge Gary being made a learned doctor of laws at Northwestern University; and that was not so bad, because everybody understands that this particular title is merely a compliment for big-wigs and money-bags. But at the University of Pittsburgh they made him a doctor of science, which is supposed to be a real degree; and if you could plumb the depths of Judge Gary's ignorance on every subject except making money and killing men, you would appreciate the absurdity of this academic performance.

The grand duke of Pittsburgh is Mr. A. W. Mellon, Secretary of the United States Treasury, and reputed to be the third richest man in the country; he is president of the Mellon National Bank, and vice-president or director in a list of fifty-five great financial and industrial organizations. As second grand duke he has his brother, Mr.

R. B. Mellon, vice-president of his bank, and vice-president or director of fifty-six organizations—beating his brother by one! As active assistant they have Mr. Babcock, mayor of Pittsburgh, lumber magnate and director in a long list of corporations. There are twenty-seven other members of this regal board, and any time a full meeting was held, they could transact the business of most of the banks and steel companies of Allegheny county. The typewritten list of their directorates, which lies before me, fills ten solid pages. I know you don't want to hear it all, so I will just give a glimpse, here and there: a steel king, whose father left him sixty millions; the treasurer of the Pennsylvania Railroad, western lines; a coal operator, vice-president of a national bank; the chairman of the Pittsburgh Plate Glass Company; a steel magnate; a physician who married Standard Oil; the head financier of the Thaw family; the chairman of a foundry company; a president of seven oil companies; another representative of the Thaw family; the owner of several newspapers; the president of an electric company; the president of a foundry company; the manager of several aluminum companies, Mellon enterprises; the president of the Heinz pickle palaces; a real estate and coal man; the president of a national bank and three coal companies; the president of a Mellon trust company; a United States senator and Mellon attorney; a young steel magnate; the president of the Carnegie Steel Company; two corporation lawyers; the head of the Carnegie Institute, a Presbyterian clergyman, and the Episcopal bishop, who has just fled from the smoky hell of the steel-country to his eternal reward.

We saw at the University of Pennsylvania a peculiar arrangement, whereby a private institution, entirely controlled by private plutocrats, receives a subsidy every year from the state, and spends this money for anti-social purposes. At Pittsburgh we see the same arrangement; the state contributes nearly a million dollars a year to be expended by these steel and oil and coal and railroad and money kings. This means in practice that every year the chancellor of the university has to make a deal with the political bosses. Finding himself inadequate to the task, he has turned it over to a firm of lawyers, one member of which was speaker of the legislature, and afterwards candidate for the Republican nomination for governor. Those who put through the appropriation get ten per cent of it; this is known as the "cut," and is a regular custom—even the public hospitals in Pennsylvania have to pay such tribute. There is a network of graft, involving every kind of organization in the state; the saloons, the doctors, the fraternal organizations—anybody who wants special privilege or freedom to break the laws has to put up bribes. The lawmakers protest against this or that steal, but when the orders come, they vote. How big is the rake-off we may judge from the fact that the mayor of Pittsburgh put up six hundred and ninety-five thousand dollars to secure his election to an office which pays a salary of eleven thousand dollars a year!

The people are helpless; they have no idea what is going on, because they have no newspapers, the so-called newspapers of Pittsburgh being merely house organs of the steel companies. The papers have an association regulating their output and prices, also the number of editions. They have agreed to issue no "extras," and have put up a bond of ten thousand dollars, which they forfeit if they violate this agreement. At the time of the steel strike they flooded the country with hysterical lies about the strikers; the record stands complete in the report of the Interchurch Federation.

Pittsburgh University is another mushroom establishment, with five thousand students and no ideas. The steel kings condescend to run it, but they do not patronize it; the interlocking trustees send their sons, not to Pittsburgh, but to the big Eastern universities. "Pitt" is bitterly jealous of "Penn," which is old and aristocratic and athletic. For a time Pennsylvania refused to play football with them, and they went to the state legislature, seeking to have this made a condition of the state appropriations for their rival!

The chancellor of the university was a preacher named McCormick, but he failed to "get the dough," so he quit, and they put in ex-President Bowman of Iowa University, a product of the Columbia University educational machine. Bowman is known as "Mellon's man," but he also has failed as a "vamp." It appears that somebody tried to work a little scheme on Grand Duke Mellon; it was announced in the newspapers that he had made a gift of land worth two million dollars. The papers played it up, with pictures of the Mellon brothers and fatuous interviews with Chancellor Bowman. But Mr. Mellon came out with the statement that all he had promised to do was to put up a hundred thousand dollars to secure an option on the property. They are hard-fisted fellows, these steel men, and as the saying is, they "have to be shown." They can see that it is worthwhile to train experts in steel-making, so Carnegie Tech is taken care of; but when it comes to general culture, this Latin and Greek stuff and highbrow ologies—they let the legislature do it!

The professors tell a story about Mayor Babcock, lumber magnate and interlocking trustee. Chancellor McCormick wanted to advance a young man in the chemistry department over the head of his senior, who was a Jew. He explained in a meeting of the trustees that it would look all right, because the Jew was not a Ph. D. Mr. Babcock, deputy grand duke of the board, had fallen asleep, and now he opened his eyes suddenly. "Ph. D? What the hell's that?"

Needless to say, they don't waste much time fooling about academic freedom at the University of Pittsburgh. The nearest approach to a radical that ever got into the place is a professor at the law school, who made so bold as to sign some protest against Attorney-General Palmer's raids on the constitution of the United States. There was a terrible uproar in Pittsburgh over this. The professor received a letter of protest from the chancellor, and was called in for a long argument. The new chancellor came in at this time, and at the first meeting of the board he started his money "spiel." "Gentlemen," said he, "the first duty before the university is to raise six and a half million dollars." But Mr. Babcock thought that the board had another duty, which was to listen to him curse the radical professor. The secret service department of the Steel Trust was put to work, and there was a report on this professor, and he lost his chance to become head of his department. "We must lie low now," said the chancellor. "We have a big program ahead."

Needless to say, they are very devout at this University of the Steel Trust. One of their grand dukes was the elder Mr. Heinz, distinguished author of "Fifty-seven Varieties," and proud owner of sixty-eight pickle factories and forty-five branch houses. Mr. Heinz was an eminent Presbyterian, and head of the World's Sunday School Association, and left a quarter of a million dollars to Pittsburgh University for a building to teach Sunday School work. Naturally, therefore, it seemed a dreadful thing to the interlocking trustees that the church should turn traitor to their interests. Trustee Follansbee furiously attacked the Interchurch World Movement report on the steel strike; at a meeting in New York he said that it had set back the cause of Christianity fifty years. And when the United States Senate sent out a committee to investigate the strike—then suddenly the fighting steel kings discovered what a handy thing it is to own an educational machine! Mayor Babcock gave the senators a grand dinner-party, to which he invited his chancellor and some of his trustees and deans, and these eminent and disinterested gentlemen loaded the senators up with information concerning the Bolshevik uprising in Western Pennsylvania.

Needless to say, there are no liberal movements of the students at this university, and no "outside speakers" bringing them improper ideas. A recent graduate writes to me:

One cannot describe the stupidity and ignorance of the students. Most of them could never see beyond themselves; most of them attended school to avoid working, for the sake of the diploma which at least would give them more pay, if not secure them a better job, and some even because they could not think of a better, easier, and happier way to spend four years. The professors and instructors were even worse, there being hardly one who could inspire a student.

Also needless to say, there is no organization of the professors; the university has the "open shop" as well as "open plumbing." At the time of the Scott Nearing affair at Pennsylvania, there was a strong movement for faculty representation, and several of the men who stood for this movement were charged with insubordination and fired; others, who stood by the authorities in order to curry favor, got promotions. A University Council was established, but it proved a tender plant, and did not survive in the smoke-laden atmosphere of the steel country. Chancellor Bowman has now laid down the law, that all appointments are subject to annual renewal; teachers are no different from other employes, and he intends to run the university like a business concern. This is the sort of talk that brings satisfaction to steel kings!

I was told about a professor who was brought before the chancellor, upon the charge of having destroyed the religious faith of one of his students. The boy's father had complained, and it developed that the professor, in a private talk with the boy, had been asked and had answered questions about the divinity of Jesus. There was a solemn council of the chancellor, the dean, and all the professors in this department, and the chancellor drew up a statement for the professors to sign, to the effect that they would do everything in their power to avoid tampering with the religious faith of the students. They refused; the utmost they were willing to sign was an agreement that they would not go out of their way to tamper with the religious faith of their students.

These men, of course, are teaching the scientific method, which is incompatible with revelation; they know it, and the chancellor knows it; all he asks is to avoid trouble with parents and interlocking trustees who are making money out of the system of private monopoly, and wish to keep the thoughts of their wage-slaves upon their future heaven and off their present hell. A friend of mine tells me that, at the time of the Braddock shootings the Pittsburgh professors "talked like Bolsheviks"—but only among themselves! When it comes to public talking, that is attended to by people like Mayor Garland, a former trustee, who at a big meeting of faculty, students and alumni declared that "in a community like Pittsburgh, which depends upon a high tariff for its prosperity, it would be very wrong for any professor to advocate free trade." A friend of mine asks: "Was he joking?" I answer that one might as well expect to hear a convocation of Catholic prelates joking about the Immaculate Conception.

And while we are in this neighborhood we ought to make note of the curious experience of Prof. G. F. Gundelfinger, author of "Ten Years at Yale," who was assistant professor of mathematics at the Carnegie Institute of Technology, and wrote a personal letter to the president protesting against an indecent orgy of the students, publicly conducted and led by the president. The

letter was sent to the president's home, and was opened
by his wife; Professor Gundelfinger was fired a few days
later. He made a public fight, and the trustees dismissed
the president—but they did not take Professor Gundelfinger back!

CHAPTER LVII

THE UNIVERSITY OF HEAVEN

We travel to Buffalo by the Pennsylvania Railroad,
and from Buffalo we continue our journey by way of the
New York Central Railroad, which has a Columbia trustee and a Cornell trustee and a Rochester trustee for directors, a recent Yale and New York University trustee
for director, a Lake Erie College trustee for vice-president, a Guaranty Trust director and two National City
Bank directors; and so we arrive at the University of
Heaven, which has God Almighty for a director.

Thirty years ago there was nothing here; now there
are a score of elaborate buildings, and six thousand students. Never has there been such a series of grand dukes
and duchesses as at this university; Mr. John D. Archbold, president of the Standard Oil Company, and Huy-
ler, the candy king, and Samuel Bowne, the cod liver oil
king, and L. C. Smith, the typewriter king, and Mrs.
Russell Sage, the charity queen, and E. L. French, head
of Crucible Steel and the Halcombe Steel Company. At
present they have as their chief duke Horace S. Wilkin-
son, steel magnate, one of the leading powers in the steamship lines of the Great Lakes. As assistants there are
half a dozen prominent business men of the town, including the two leading merchants; a former brewer of New
York, who is head of a great asphalt company and a sugar
company; Mrs. Bowne, the widow of Samuel Bowne; Mr.
Childs, the coal tar king; Mr. Flaccus, the Pittsburgh
glass magnate; the Honorable Louis Marshall, millionaire
lawyer of New York; the Honorable Edgar T. Brackett,
leading politician of Saratoga Springs, headquarters of
New York state's gambling and political conventions; and
the Reverend Ezra Squier Tipple, D.D., Ph.D., president
of Drew Theological Seminary, professor of practical
theology, and author of the "Drew Sermons, Series One

19

and Two," and of the "Drew Sermons on the Golden Texts, Series One, Two and Three."

All this has grown out of the genius of one man, the Reverend James Roscoe Day, D.D., Sc.D., LL.D., D.C.L., L.H.D., chancellor of the University of Heaven. He made it, unassisted save by God.

What is Heaven—in the plutocratic sense? It is a place whose streets are paved with gold and flowing with milk and honey. It is inhabited exclusively by the elect, all others having been cast into outer darkness. It is a place entirely under the control of the "right people"; all unorthodox thoughts are barred, "chapel" is conducted every morning, and if anybody does not like the way we run things, he can go to hell.

Some time ago I made you acquainted with the ideal university president of the metropolitan plutocracy, Nicholas Murray Butler; a man of the world, dignified and urbane, his religion of the Episcopalian variety, reserved and proper. Compared with him, Chancellor Day of Syracuse University is provincial and naive, representing the adoration of wealth in its primitive, instinctive form. His emotions flow with child-like enthusiasm; his denomination might be described as evangelical Mammonism. His fervor is such that he is not ashamed to bear testimony before the world; to raise his hands in public and shout: "Money, money! Hallelujah! Amen!" This chancellor brings to the support of his plutocracy the direct personal revelation of the Almighty. When he makes commencement orations, or gives interviews to the interlocking press, or sends telegrams of congratulation to the murderers of strikers, he brings to their support the latest decisions and interpretations of the Throne of Grace. "God has made the rich of this world to serve Him. . . . . He has shown them a way to have this world's goods and to be rich towards God. . . . God wants the rich man. . . . Christ's doctrines have made the world rich, and provide adequate uses for its riches." These are from the chancellor's book, "The Raid on Prosperity"; you can find more of it quoted in "The Profits of Religion."

Recently he has published another book, "My Neighbor the Workingman," and in this book we find God in a bloodthirsty mood. It appears that the radicals are taking advantage of our courts, which "assume innocence until guilt is proved." There must be "a suspension of this order of things," God says; "we have found no foe more worthy of extermination." Strikes, God teaches us, are efforts to make labor superior to law; "the strike is a conspiracy and nothing less." Yet when labor proposes to use legal methods, God does not seem to like it any better; we find Him discussing the founding of the Labor Party in Chicago, and speaking of the delegates as "these Simian descendants"—and just after He has made His chief complaint against strikers, that they call non-union men bad names! God portrays the Socialist utopia: "The soap-box orators, in the tramp's unclean rags, will take charge of the banks, and the bomb-makers can be started to run the factories." Opposed to this is God's own utopia, and you may take your choice: "The rich and the poor dwell together. There is divine wisdom in the plan. They always have so lived. They always will so live. Noble characters are in both. It must be the divine order."

This chancellor of the University of Heaven was providentially equipped for his rôle. He stands about six and a half feet high, and broad in proportion, with the face of a Jupiter commanding the lightnings. He has a magnificent rolling voice, so that Jehovah's commands are heard as usual amid the thunders of Sinai. He is a masterful personality; he knows instantly what God wants, and he goes after the bacon and gets it for God, and every plutocrat, meeting him, recognizes him as the ideal person to take charge of the thinking of posterity.

No nonsense is tolerated at Syracuse; they know what truth is, and how it should be taught, and you teach it that way or you get out, the quicker the better. Early in the chancellor's administration he discovered that John R. Commons was tolerant toward free silver, and he fired him, giving as his reason that the professor was tolerant towards Sunday baseball! Every year he discovers that several others are tolerant towards something ungodly, and he fires them. There is no "tenure" or faculty control, or stuff of that sort; it is the chancellor who pays the salaries, and the chancellor who decides what the various men are worth—and he generally decides they are not worth much. He said at a faculty meeting, "You fellows needn't think you mean anything to me; I could replace you all in an hour and a half."

This is his regular manner toward his faculty; he subjects them to the most incredible indignities. For example, he gave the degree of doctor of science to one of his grand dukes, Mr. E. L. French, president of Crucible Steel. At a faculty meeting at which this project was brought up, one of the professors ventured to suggest that it might be better to make it an LL.D., which is generally understood as having an honorary significance, instead of an Sc.D., which is understood to indicate actual achievement in the scientific field. Chancellor Day pointed at the objector a finger which trembled with rage, and shouted: "Sit down and shut up!" This was Professor E. N. Pattee, and I find him still listed in the Syracuse catalogue as "director of the chemical laboratory," so I presume that he sat down and shut up as directed.

Several people described to me the eloquence of the chancellor's sermons, with the tremolo stop which reduces his auditors to tears. I asked one of them, "Does he believe in his religion?" The answer was: "No more than I do. He has no particle of Christianity or of faith; he uses it merely as a shield." To his faculty its purpose appears to be to beat down their salaries. If you go into his office to ask for a raise, he will glare at you and pound on the desk, shouting: "What's this I hear about you, John Smith? Do you believe in the divinity of Jesus? Have you been saying that you distrust the verbal inspiration of the Pentateuch?" Or maybe he will say: "I want you to understand, young man, I have been hearing reports about you. You were seen walking on the street with Professor So-and-So's wife!" Or maybe he will say: "I have taken the trouble to inquire, and I find that you subscribe to the 'Nation' and the 'New Republic.'"

Heaven, from the point of view of college professors, is an intellectual sweatshop. I was told of a professor of geology, who was there for twenty years, and finally got up the nerve to ask for a raise, and he got fifty dollars a year. Another professor asked for a raise, but the chancellor discovered that this man had written a book, and he said: "A man who has written a book ought not to expect promotion; it shows that he had spare time on his hands." All contracts with the university are verbal, and you take the chancellor's word for your fate. It may seem a dreadful thing to say about heaven, but the fact remains that a number of the chancellor's faculty, both past and present, unite in placing him among those college heads who do not always tell the truth.

A few years ago he got rid of his treasurer, Mr. W. W. Porter, who had served the university for nineteen years. The chancellor published a series of accusations against Mr. Porter, and the latter replied in a printed statement of twelve thousand words, which I have before me. It is a dignified and frank and convincing document. Mr. Porter bears testimony to that same "wrath and vindictive spirit and methods" upon which all authorities agree. He goes on to give the documents and figures of a series of petty grafts perpetrated by the chancellor: For example he states that laborers worked on the chancellor's farm, and were paid out of the university treasury amounts aggregating $710.82; also, that the chancellor sold this farm to the university "at cost," and when the treasurer asked for proper vouchers, "he immediately flew into a passion, stating that his word was sufficient"; also, that a member of the chancellor's family purchased a building, and leased it to the university, to be used as a book-store, at an excessive rental; also, that the chancellor sold his old automobile to the university at an excessive price; "the chancellor sold horses, wagons, harness, etc., at various times to the university, making out bills in favor of himself and receipting the same, acting as both seller and purchaser." We might go on to summarize twelve closely printed sheets of this kind of thing; but space is limited, so we content ourselves by stating that we know where this document is, and we will submit it to Professor Brander Matthews on demand!

CHAPTER LVIII

THE HARPOONER OF WHALES

For a score of years the worst scandal at Syracuse was a sort of Rasputin, whom the chancellor maintained at the university as his intimate and confidant. The man was a Nova-Scotia herring fisherman, originally hired by the late Dean French to split wood and mow lawns. It is generally whispered at Syracuse that he must have found out something about the chancellor; at any rate, he was suddenly promoted to become superintendent of buildings and grounds, and became the chief power behind the throne. Dean Kent of the Engineering College, the most distinguished man who has ever been on the Syracuse faculty, criticized the inefficient heating and care of the buildings, whereupon this man demanded his dismissal, and incredible as it may seem, secured it. The incident almost caused a strike of the students of the engineering school. One professor writes me:

No picture of the chancellor's regime would be perfect without the portrayal of a half-dozen or more prominent members of the faculty waiting in the ante-room outside the chancellor's office, having been told that the chancellor was too busy to see anyone. While they are waiting patiently, the chancellor's favorite struts through this room, dressed in a jaunty suit, jostles against members of the faculty in an arrogant manner without apologies, does not even knock at the door, enters and engages the chancellor in conversation, interspersed with ribald laughter, for an hour or more. This was almost a weekly occurrence for a generation.

And when someone made bold to criticize the chancellor for making an intimate of this low character, he flew into a passion and declared that anyone who so criticized him was criticizing Jesus; for had not Jesus chosen his friends among fishermen? So the intimacy continued; and last summer it came to a climax. The story is told in a letter from a friend at Syracuse, who is accurately informed concerning affairs at the university. I quote:

For some weeks Mr. Spencer, the manager of the dormitory grocery store, has been missing considerable quantities of groceries and meats. He made repeated complaints to the police, but nothing was accomplished. At length the situation became so bad that two detectives were stationed nightly at the store. Two weeks ago last Friday night about ten in the evening an automobile stopped about a block from the store, the driver then entered the building, and when he was well loaded with plunder, the detectives closed in. To their surprise they found that they had bagged the chancellor's favorite. He was taken to the police station and examined, and his house was searched, where more groceries were found. Hurlbut Smith, now president of the board of trustees, was sent for, and at his request the matter was kept out of the papers, because the pledges to the university emergency fund are being paid so slowly, that he feared the effect of such an incident. The chancellor and his favorite are now trying to bulldoze Mr. Spencer, manager of the store, into the statement that the chancellor's favorite often came to the store, took groceries and left a slip for them; but Spencer down to date has not made this statement, perhaps because he is not a liar.

Later: the board of trustees forced the "resignation" of the favorite. The chancellor stormed at the trustees, and two all-day sessions were held over the issue. His old legal supporter, Louis Marshall, tried all the wiles of a spell-binder on the trustees for over an hour, but could get only three votes for the chancellor's favorite. The chancellor has now made him his chauffeur and butler; but he will have to go down-town for groceries hereafter!

The chancellor's furious rages, the vileness of his language, and the slanders which he circulates about men who displease him—these things would be incredible, but for the fact that man after man unites in testifying from personal knowledge. Thus, Professor A. G. Webster, now of Clark University, tells of seeing the chancellor insult one of his professors on the campus; and subsequently Professor Webster mentioned this incident in a letter to the Boston "Herald," whereupon the chancellor wrote to the "Herald" in scathing terms, denying all knowledge of the incident or of Professor Webster. But, as it happened, Webster had in his files a letter from the chancellor, offering to appoint him head of the department of physics!

Dr. Homer A. Harvey, a physician practising at Batavia, New York, was a brilliant professor of Romance languages at Syracuse, and was studying medicine in his off-hours, taking various courses at the university. After two years the chancellor discovered this grave offense, and his first step was to deposit the professor's salary-check in the bank, short the amount of a recent increase in salary. The professor did not discover this until some of his checks were returned by the bank; then followed an interview with the chancellor, in which the young instructor was stormed at and denounced, and commanded instantly to abandon his studies at the medical college. He refused to do so, and resigned his teaching position. The chancellor flew into a dreadful rage, but the young instructor walked out, and completed his medical studies and got his degree. A year later he wrote to the chancellor about another matter, and received a suave and sympathetic letter, disclaiming all knowledge of the late unpleasantness. Dr. Harvey declined to accept this statement, whereupon the chancellor flew into a rage, and wrote a second and furious letter, bringing a great number of false charges against Dr. Harvey—and incidentally revealing a complete and detailed knowledge of the unpleasantness which he had just denied! Shortly after that Dr. Harvey learned that reports were being circulated at Syracuse, to the effect that at the time of graduation he had "been caught cheating at the finals, and had been brazen enough to boast openly of it." Dr. Harvey adds: "The source of that falsehood I have no difficulty in surmising."

And the same despotic methods which the chancellor applies to his faculty he applies to his students—to everyone, in fact, but his rich donors. A student who had been working in industry during the summer started a "discussion club" in one of the dormitories. It was only a few hours before he was "on the mat" before the chancellor. "Young man, study your books. Do what you are told at this university." Some of the students took to meeting secretly at the home of one of the professors, and they brought a Socialist from town to explain his ideas. The chancellor's spies brought word of this, and he stormed into a faculty meeting. "This place is honeycombed with sedition!" Still worse was the situation when they took a straw vote for president in 1920, and it was discovered that four of the students had voted for Debs. The newspapers got word of this, and shouted for blood.

Recently the University of Heaven had a sensational experience. An instructor became insane, and shot and killed the dean who had discharged him. Chancellor Day has long ago adopted the thesis, generally popular among the plutocracy, that all Socialists are lunatics; he now committed what his professor of formal logic would explain to him as "the fallacy of the undistributed middle term." He jumped to the conclusion that because all

Socialists are lunatics, therefore all lunatics are Socialists, and he trumpeted to the world the announcement that his dean had fallen victim to a Bolshevik assassin. To the bewildered editor of "Zion's Herald," a very pious Methodist paper of Boston, the chancellor announced that he had a right to "see red"; he had seen a pool of blood beneath the body of his slain professor!

The chancellor has personally excluded all radical and liberal publications from the library. Every book which deals with the subject of government ownership opposes that doctrine; all others have been systematically cleaned out. The chancellor even carries his hatred of labor unions to the point of crippling the university. Workingmen have been changed two or three times in one week; the chancellor set the maximum price that a workingman is worth at twenty-eight cents an hour, and as a result, the boilers of the heating plant were ruined, and the cost was four thousand dollars.

There is the same strenuous watching, with the help of spies and stool-pigeons, over the religious life of the university. Judge Gary was brought there last summer, to preach his piety to the students, who have chapel every morning, and "are expected to attend regularly the Sabbath church service of the denomination to which they belong." The chancellor received a protest from some minister, whose daughter had learned something about evolution, and he announced to the faculty: "You men are hired to teach your subject; don't try to teach theology." Then, observing a cold silence from this group of scientists, he added: "I don't expect you to change your opinions, but do, for God's sake, be as pious as you can!"

The old rascal is decidedly cynical among his intimates, fond of telling smutty stories, and willing even to joke about the educational game. His professor of psychology came to him, telling him about the wonderful new intelligence tests which some universities were using in place of examinations. "Fine!" said the chancellor. "We'll use them, but don't let them affect admissions. We want to give everybody a cheap education. Tell them it's a good one, and they won't know the difference." Confronted by the usual trouble of raising funds, he let himself be persuaded to try an appeal for small donations from a large number of the alumni; but the results did not equal the cost of the circulars, and the chancellor remarked at a faculty meeting: "I never went fishing for small fish with a net; I went out and stuck my harpoon into a whale."

In the days of his prime our vicegerent of Heaven was really a whale of a whaler; but he met with one great disappointment, which appears to have wrecked his career. He spent twenty years cultivating the president of the Standard Oil Company. He chiseled off the label of one of his buildings, the College of Liberal Arts, and labeled it the John Dustin Archbold College. He got Archbold to give him a stadium and a gymnasium, also a mansion to live in; but he hoped for more than that, and for ten years he whispered to his faculty: "Be careful now, behave yourselves, we have a great endowment coming." But Archbold died and left him nothing, and all the family could be got to put up was half a million dollars.

From that time on the chancellor's star began to wane. The university had been running into debt, and some time ago the banks refused to carry it any further, and the grand dukes refused to "come across." The alumni would do nothing, for they share in the detestation with which the chancellor is regarded by the faculty and students. In order to confound his enemies, the chancellor hired a firm of professional money-raisers, who undertook to get six million dollars in thirty-six weeks for Syracuse. But before they had gone very far they realized that no one would put up money, so long as the chancellor remained in office; they told him so, and he dismissed them for incompetence. They sued for thirty-six thousand dollars still due, and it was shown that the chancellor had spent a huge sum of the university's money on this fiasco, and without getting a penny of return.

The debts of the university now amounted to a million and a half, and so matters came to a head. The interlocking trustees had done everything they could think of to persuade the aged whale-hunter to resign, but all their efforts failed, so they worked out a most ingenious scheme. One morning the chancellor opened his copy of the Syracuse "Post-Standard" at breakfast, and there, to his consternation, he found himself confronted with an elaborate front-page article to the effect that he had resigned. There was his picture, and there were columns upon columns of laudatory articles about himself, written by his leading teachers and his leading grand dukes and duchesses. Never was there such a series of panegyrics of a triumphantly retiring chancellor!

All the Syracuse newspapers had it, and what was the poor man to do? Should he dump out all that milk and honey into the dirt, and make for himself a horrible scandal? He bowed to his fate, and the trustees appointed Dean Peck as acting chancellor; but shortly afterwards Dean Peck died of heart-trouble, and our whale-hunter moved back into his office. There was no one with authority to keep him out, and he set the university carpenters at work making alterations on his new home and made to his faculty the triumphant announcement: "You see, gentlemen, God has vindicated me; He has struck Peck down, in order that I may return to my position!" Such is the University of Heaven; and we close with the familiar comment: "Heaven for climate, hell for company."

P. S.—Through a peculiar dispensation of Providence, the Chancellor of the University of Heaven was taken to his final abode on the day this book was published.

CHAPTER LIX

AN ACADEMIC TRAGEDY

We continue on the New York Central Railroad to Albany, and then take the Boston & Albany, which is leased to the New York Central, and has a Harvard "visitor," a recent Harvard overseer, a Massachusetts Tech trustee, and a trustee of Clark University for directors. It is to this latter university we are bound, to study one of the tragedies of our academic history.

In the gold rush of '49, a hardware and furniture dealer of Massachusetts went out to California, and established a monopoly in his line and made a fortune. He came back home, expecting to be welcomed by the aristocracy of his state; but they snubbed him, and so he turned his thoughts to education. He endowed a university, and put at the head of it one of the most original and fertile minds that have ever appeared in the educational field in America. President G. Stanley Hall of Clark University has been interested in almost every branch of advanced science; he is the author of great works on adolescence and senescence, and was the first to introduce psychoanalysis into academic teaching. He brought Freud and Jung to America, and even made so bold as to apply the psychoanalytic method to Jesus Christ. Instead of making Clark the usual academic department-store, he made it a place where the most advanced men in every field of science found a home, and where students came to specialize in the highest and most difficult branches of knowledge.

The founder was a plain old boy, and gave them two plain brick buildings, modeled on his "Boston Store," the great retail establishment of Worcester. So undistinguished are these buildings that the story is told of a farmer driving by, learning that this was Clark University, and exclaiming: "Christ! I thought it was the jail!" Yet these brick buildings carried the name of American science all over the world. We saw in our study of Columbia University that the great home of the plutocracy had one distinguished scientist for every thirteen members of its faculty, whereas the poor and unpretentious Clark had the highest standing of any university in the United States, having one distinguished scientist for every two members of its faculty!

This was not what the old hardware and furniture merchant had wanted; he did not understand what was going on, and saw no sense in a professor of mathematics who filled six blackboards with a complicated demonstration, nor in a professor of chemistry who discovered substances with names that filled whole lines of print. He quarreled with President Hall, and cut off most of the funds of the university, and started a second institution, Clark College, where poor boys could get an education in three years; to this latter institution he left a large part of his money. Of course, there was no other plutocrat in America who cared for what President Hall was doing, so for a generation Clark University was starved for funds. Nevertheless, many of the scientists stayed, because it was a place where they could do their work in their own way. They were free not merely to teach their own specialties, but to help run their university. Never in America has there been such an unruly faculty; men would pound on the table, and shake their fists in the president's face, calling him a great number of impolite names, and threatening to resign; but he would argue it out with them, and they would stay on.

The strongest emotion which animated old Jonas Clark was a hatred of the plutocracy of Worcester, which had scorned him. More than anything else, he wanted to make certain that this plutocracy should never get hold of his university or his college. Concerning the university he laid down the law in his will:

> And I also declare in this connection, that it is my earnest desire, will and direction, that the said university, in its practical management, as well as in theory, may be wholly free from every kind of denominational or sectarian control, bias or limitation, and that its doors may be ever open to all classes and persons, whatsoever may be their religious faith or political sympathies, or to whatever creed, sect, or party they may belong, and I especially charge upon my executors and said trustees, and the said mayor to secure the enforcement of this clause of my will by applications to the Court as above provided, or otherwise by every means in their power.

Such is the purpose for which Clark was founded. Its founder is dead, and two years ago its great president retired at the age of seventy-four, and the tragedy of America's most intellectual university can be told in one sentence—the plutocracy of Worcester has got it!

There are eight members of the board of trustees today. The grand duke is Mr. A. G. Bullock of Worcester, chairman of a life insurance company, president of a railroad and a railroad investment company, trustee of a savings bank, director of the Boston & Albany Railroad, two other railroads, a gas company, a Boston trust company and a Boston security company. The second grand duke is Mr. F. H. Dewey, lawyer, president of the Mechanics' National Bank and of the Worcester street railways, president of five other street railway companies and a steam railway, trustee for a savings bank and a national bank, vice-president of a gas company and two railroads, director of three railroads, an investment company, an insurance company, and a telephone and telegraph company. The third grand duke is Mr. C. H. Thurber, business manager of Ginn & Company, school book publishers, the largest and most active competitors of the American Book Company. Mr. Thurber's political views are described to me by one who knows him well: "Anybody more liberal than ex-President Taft is a Bolshevik to him."

These three constitute the finance committee and run the university. As assistants they have Judge Parker, one of the most notorious of the aristocratic corporation lawyers of Massachusetts, counsel for the men who smashed the Boston police strike; Chief Justice Rugg of the Massachusetts Supreme Court, a former Worcester lawyer and a very conservative individualist; Mr. Aiken, a high-up interlocking director, formerly of Worcester, but now president of the National Shawmut Bank of Boston; a cautious young lawyer of Worcester, in partnership with Judge Rugg's son; and another young man, who has just been appointed to the board, and is expected to serve as another dummy.

This board is a close corporation, self-perpetuating, with no elected representative of faculty or alumni. For twenty years the finance committee has had charge of the investing of the endowment, and I should like to call the especial attention of Professor Brander Matthews of Columbia University to what they have done. I am not intimately familiar with the changing standards of American high finance, and I do not know whether the administration of this finance committee is what would be described in banking circles as "honest graft" or "dishonest graft." They have invested the funds of the university through their own banks, railways, trolley lines and gas companies, and have paid the university four per cent interest on the funds, while neighboring institutions have been getting five or six per cent. For example, the treasurer of Wesleyan University writes: "All the invested funds of the university netted us last year 5.71%. This will show you, of course, that we carry very small balances in our banks and make no investments through them." As we have seen, Clark University has been making investments through the banks, and it has thereby lost 1.71% on $4,700,000, or $80,370 per year for twenty years, a total of $1,607,400, which went to make fat the banks of Worcester instead of to educate the students of Clark. Also I took the trouble to inquire concerning the State Mutual Life Assurance Company of Worcester, and I find that for the year 1921 it realized 5.51% on its book

assets. Mr. Bullock is chairman of this concern, and his
son is vice-president and general counsel; and you see
how much better they do for themselves than they do for
Clark!

The treasurer of Clark is the head of a big Worcester
bank, and his reports of the university's finances were not
audited; this irresponsibility continued for some time,
and this year Chief Justice Rugg asked that the report be
audited in future. I am told by a former professor that
it is almost impossible to get hold of a copy of this treasurer's report, and when you do get it you find it a mass
of enigmas. Thus the university carries one large block
of New Haven stock at 200, and another at 110! Mr.
Dewey, the lawyer who handles the finances of the university, is one of the shrewd big business manipulators
of Massachusetts. He and Bullock were with the Mellon
crowd which manipulated the legislature, and Dewey was
head of the New England Investment Company, the holding concern for the New Haven Railroad, the device
whereby the big investors skimmed off the cream from
that huge system, and left the "widows and orphans"
hungry. It is only the peculiar workings of our system
of justice which enabled these able gentlemen to escape
the penitentiary; and you find that their university has
large holdings in all these half broken-down railroads—
the Boston and Maine, the Vermont Valley, the Norwich
and Worcester, the Providence and Worcester—and more
than a hundred thousand dollars in Mr. Dewey's gas
company!

CHAPTER LX

THE GEOGRAPHY LINE

Needless to say, Clark University had been for a generation a cause of indignation to the town of Worcester,
which is the largest manufacturing center in New England, and next to Pittsburgh the most notorious "kept
city" and "open shop" town in America. Clark regarded
Worcester as the Mammon of Unrighteousness, while
Worcester regarded Clark as a nest of atheism, infidelity,
and Bolshevism. An American university with no stadium, no gymnasium, and no chapel, no "eleven" and no

"nine," no rowing crew and no "petting-parties"! Obviously, no gentleman would send his son to such a place; it would be left for "muckers" and Bolsheviks. One of the trustees expressed his opinion of the matter to a student with whom I talked: "The college would fare better if it turned out a winning football team than if it had eleven of the most famous scientists in the country. That's what the public wants, and that's the way to get the money."

When President Hall resigned, the plutocracy of Worcester perceived that their chance had come. They arranged for the president of Clark College to resign at the same time, and they cast about for some man of their own type to take charge of both institutions. The selection was made by Mr. Thurber, business manager of Ginn & Company; and again I don't know whether I should describe it as "honest" or "dishonest" graft. One of the principal "lines" of Ginn & Company is the Frye-Atwood elementary school geographies, which are handsomely illustrated, and have been sold to the extent of over half a million copies to school boards throughout the United States. The author of these books was a professor of geography, first at the University of Chicago, then at Harvard. It occurred to Mr. Thurber what an admirable thing it would be, if, instead of advertising these geographies as written by a professor at Harvard, he could advertise them as written by the president of Clark University! Also if he could use Clark University as a place for tea-parties to entertain visiting delegations of school superintendents and teachers desirous of meeting the distinguished author of Ginn & Company's leading "line"!

Of course I don't mean literally "tea-parties"; in the educational world these publicity enterprises proceed under the decorous title of Summer Schools. Elaborate advertising campaigns are undertaken, the praises of this or that particular "line" are seductively set forth, and the schoolmarms flock from all over the United States—likewise the principals and the high-up superintendents—and they meet the distinguished authors of school books, and listen to their patriotic eloquence, and go home singing the wonders of the various "lines." Then when the new orders are placed for text-books, the enterprising salesmen are on hand to get the business.

Mr. Thurber announced that he had a new president for Clark College and Clark University; he announced it at the commencement dinner, and there was consternation on the faces of everybody present, because nobody had ever heard of Wallace Walter Atwood, professor of physiography at Harvard University, and author of "The Mineral Resources of Southwestern Alaska," and "The Glaciation of the Uinta and Wasatch Mountains." I am told that one of Professor Atwood's colleagues at Harvard, hearing the news, remarked: "I suppose Clark thinks it is getting a geographer and an educator; Clark will find it has neither." And Clark did! President Atwood may be a well-informed man in his narrow specialty; certainly he fulfils the ideal of the interlocking trustees, in that he is a hundred percent pious and a hundred percent patriotic and a hundred percent plutocratic. But when it comes to the administration of a university, and to broad questions of public welfare—I have cast about and tested all the terms in my vocabulary, but I have been unable to find any one word to describe the ignorant crudity and childish absurdity of this former Harvard physiographer.

He announced at the very beginning that he had no interest in being the president of a poor man's university; he was going to start a "drive" for funds, and make Clark a normal and respectable place. In an address to the students he set forth the advantages of a technical education, using the standard phrases of the "go-getters": "As an expert witness you can sometimes get as much as a hundred dollars a day." This to a group of men whose chief pride was that they had a real understanding of the intellectual life! One student came to him to ask for time to pay his tuition fee. "Why do you come here if you can't pay what you owe?" asked the president, sharply. On the other hand, to a famous athlete, member of a wealthy family, who had found it impossible to pass his examinations, he said: "Don't worry too much about that; we all get by in the end; it took me five years to get through myself."

At the formal inauguration ceremony President Atwood announced—doubtless with a sly wink at Mr. Thurber on the platform—that he was going to make Clark University the great center of American geographic and physiographic education. Now I have no desire to deny the importance of these subjects; they are interesting specialties and have their place; but when some one sets out to raise them into major sciences, we may be sure that we are dealing with a buncombe artist, and may look with certainty for commercial motives. In the Clark University bulletin we find the commercial ideal set forth in the plainest possible language: "Many of the universities and colleges of this country are now calling for trained geographers. Commissioners of education, normal schools, and high schools are looking for men or women who can serve as supervisors or as special teachers of geography. The large financial houses are endeavoring to train men in commercial geography in their own schools. The departments of the government are now using trained geographers, and the Civil Service Commission has recently recognized the profession of geography"—etc., etc.

Under President Atwood's regime the graduate work in mathematics and biology has ceased. The two best psychologists are gone, and the department has declined to nothing. The department of chemistry is undermanned and woefully deficient in equipment. History and the social sciences are even worse off, and no adequate work in government is offered, in spite of the fact that the will of the founder specifies the preparing of useful citizens as the first task of the university. Instead of that—we have geography! There is an independent "Graduate School of Geography," free from faculty control and headed by President Atwood himself, with a professor of meteorology and climatology, and a lecturer in anthropogeography—delicious mouthful for schoolmarms to take home to Main Street!—also four other professors and lecturers, and four more listed as "offering closely related work." There are twenty-one courses in this Graduate School, and a "special series" of six lectures, besides a program of anti-Bolshevik propaganda, described as a "Conference on Russian Affairs," with five lecturers, including Mr. A. J. Sack, ex-chief of Ambassador Bakmetieff's lie-factory! In addition to this, there is the Summer School, with only one course in psychology, and only two in education, and only two in social science—but with twelve in geography! And worse yet, there is to be a "Correspondence School," with endless courses in the Frye-Atwood geographies, for rural school and grade teachers, with the horrified and -agonized faculty of the university compelled to give university credits for this commercial work!

Men who can thus turn culture into cash are seldom permitted to hide their light under a bushel in capitalist society. President Atwood has also become editor of a magazine; or rather director of the "Institute of International Information," a contrivance for getting subscriptions to a magazine called "Our World." In its pages you may find a picture of our worthy physiographer in full academic regalia, holding one of his geography books, decorated with ribbons, clasped in his hands. For four dollars you may join this "Institution," and get the magazine for a year, and "have the privilege of asking any question of international significance, etc." The funniest thing about the proposition is that our pious and super-respectable president of a reformed atheist university is here working hand in hand with and advertised alongside of Mr. Arthur Bullard. Surely President Atwood does not know who this terrible creature Bullard is—an international revolutionary conspirator who, concealing himself under the alias of "Albert Edwards," endeavored to undermine American institutions by a Socialist novel called "Comrade Yetta," and a most shocking "free love" novel, "A Man's World!"

CHAPTER LXI

A LEAP INTO THE LIMELIGHT

The program of converting Clark University into an advertising department of Ginn & Company proceeded merrily so far as concerned Ginn & Company; but it caused great distress to the faculty of the university, which held a series of meetings and prepared a memorandum to the board of trustees, in which they bitterly denounced the new policy. Also there were signs of revolt among the students; even the Rotary clubs and other business organizations of Worcester began to tire of a diet of geography, fried, boiled and hashed for three meals a day. I have not been admitted to the inside of President

Atwood's psychology, but some of his professors suspect that he began to realize that something desperate must be done, and resorted to the favorite device of George M. Cohan, who, whenever one of his plays began to lag, would come dancing out on the stage with an American flag.

The students at Clark maintain a Liberal Club, and invite speakers of all points of view to discuss public questions before them. They are accustomed to question these men and tear their arguments to pieces, and if the men cannot thoroughly document their statements, they have an unhappy time. That the students really conduct an open forum is proven by the fact that they brought not merely Harry Laidler to defend Socialism, but the Reverend Murlin, president of Boston University, to speak against it. They invited Frank Tannenbaum to defend the radical movement, and they invited the Reverend Dr. Wyland of Worcester to denounce it. Dr. Wyland's point of view on social questions is sufficiently revealed by the fact that in the Worcester "Telegram" he referred to Scott Nearing's "licentious and seditious utterances"—and this without having attended Nearing's lecture!

It was early in 1922 that the Liberal Club announced a coming lecture by Scott Nearing, and obtained President Atwood's consent for it. A few days before the lecture President Atwood summoned the president of the club, and told him that there was to be a geography lecture that evening and asked that the Nearing address be shifted to a different and smaller hall. President Atwood himself, of course, went to the geography lecture; when it was over he came to the hall where Nearing had been speaking for an hour and a half to some three hundred people. I am told that on the steps of the building he met a high-up society lady of Worcester, wife of one of the interlocking directors. This lady was trembling with indignation, and told President Atwood about the horrible thing that was going on in the hall—a Bolshevist speaker was shamelessly defaming the American people.

President Atwood went in, and listened to the address for about three minutes. Scott Nearing was discussing the control of American intellectual life by the plutocracy, and, as it happened, he had just got to the subject of educational institutions, and was describing the contents of "The Higher Learning in America," by Thorstein Veblen—who happens to be Atwood's brother-in-law. Atwood listened, and his bosom swelled. Some poet has described Opportunity as a beautiful caparisoned white horse, which gallops by and stops for a moment in front of a man, and then gallops on. At this moment Atwood perceived that the steed had halted before him; here was the way to make the Frye-Atwood geographies known, not merely to all the schoolmarms of the United States, but to all leaders of patriotic thought all over the world! President Atwood leaped upon the horse—and rode into the limelight!

What he did was to rise up in the audience, and tell the president of the Liberal Club to stop the lecture. He had to repeat this several times before the bewildered student got his meaning; then the student went upon the platform and told Nearing to stop, and Nearing politely did so. In talking about the matter with Nearing, I told him that I thought he had made a mistake; he should have insisted upon his right to finish his lecture—and I was assured by students at Clark that if he had done this, the audience would have politely put the president of the university out of the hall. But it didn't happen that way; Nearing stopped, and President Atwood went to the front of the platform and informed the audience that the meeting was dismissed. He said this three times, while the amazed people stared at him. He turned and instructed the janitor to "blink" the lights, so as to compel the audience to leave.

There were half a dozen of the faculty present, also the venerable scholar, ex-President G. Stanley Hall. One of the professors came forward and remarked that it seemed rather late to dismiss the meeting. President Atwood answered: "We can't have these things going on here."

"Why not?" asked the professor.

"This is no proper audience to hear such remarks."

"But the audience consists of at least fifty percent college men."

"Yes," said President Atwood, "that's the worst of it." And he pounded on the wall in his excitement. "This kind of thing must be stopped! I am going to crush it with every means in my power!"

The author of the Frye-Atwood geographies was new to Clark University, and does not possess the mentality to understand the place; he was genuinely bewildered by the uproar which followed. The students called mass meetings of protest; they organized and appointed committees, and proceeded in vigorous and determined fashion to make good their right of free speech. The incident, of course, was telegraphed all over the country, and brought back upon the head of the unhappy physiographer a storm of ridicule and denunciation. He fled from it, and shut himself up in his house. The student committee could not get access to him; but finally they dug him out, and put him on the griddle.

I talked with a member of this committee, and he told me how the president had called to see him at a fraternity house, almost weeping, and saying that his life had been threatened. Next day he received a delegation from the student-body, and made them a prepared speech, in which he said: "I deeply and sincerely regret the dramatic manner in which I interrupted Dr. Nearing." But a day or two later he appeared before a mass meeting of the whole student-body, and read them an address entitled "Extra-Curricula Activities and Academic Freedom," in the course of which he said that Scott Nearing had "maligned the moral integrity of the American people," and added: "I know that I should have closed that meeting. I do not regret that I have shown in a positive way that I disapprove of such influences within the halls of the university." To a committee of the students he stated that he had evidence of "a world-wide plot to bring Bolshevism from the street corner into the colleges," and this evidence he intended to lay before the board of trustees. He intimated that the liberal professors at Clark were privy to this conspiracy; but when the time came for him to produce the "goods," all he had was the absurd magazine articles of Cal Coolidge!

You see, the poor fellow is utterly ignorant of the problems with which he is trying to deal; a child in his mentality, he was talking to students who had been trained in the social sciences, and were accustomed to do their own thinking, and to produce evidence for their statements. These students persisted in pinning him down as to what he meant by freedom of speech and of teaching, and they succeeded in extracting from him one extraordinary piece of obscurantist dogma. He said to them: "If, in teaching geology I had in my class Lutherans who believed in an actual six day creation of the earth, I could only state that scientists were aware that the earth is very old and it is our theory, nothing but theory, that it evolved through countless eons; but as to its actual creation, whether or not it took six days we do not know. I could say nothing which seemed to contradict the beliefs which they had gained in the home."

Another student who had a session with him made very careful notes, and has placed these at my disposal. Said President Atwood: "When I came to this college and found that you had no chapel, I was shocked to the depths of my soul. My father was a minister, and I regard religion as the fundamental basis of all education." The student replied by informing his president that the study of religion formed an essential part of all the sociology courses at Clark. Said the student: "Do you suppose that many members of the student-body agreed with what Nearing said?" "No," replied President Atwood, "maybe not, but they would have if they had a chance to hear him." The student laughed at this, and told him that if he had let the meeting alone and sat quietly, he would have heard Scott Nearing questioned and made to back his assertions, if he could. The president was told about the misadventure of the Reverend Wyland, who had come to talk against Bolshevism, without knowing a single thing about the subject; he had been questioned and backed into a corner, and when he got off the platform he was "as limp as a rag." But somehow that did not satisfy President Atwood!

How simple-minded he is you may perceive from the fact that he allowed a professor of his geography department, coming forward in his defense, to point out that Harvard, by holding on to Laski, had lost more than a million dollars! He went before the Rotary Club at Worcester, which received him with tumultuous cheering; he was their kind of man! Also the Reverend Wyland defended him—with the result that the student glee-club canceled a concert at Wyland's church. The clergyman gave out to the press a statement that the reason for the canceling was that not enough tickets had been sold! President Atwood called off the weekly assembly, because he dared not face the students; they might refuse to sing, he said. They used to cheer him on the campus, but now they passed him in silence; when he addressed them at the mass meeting, there were present not merely the state police, but a number of private detectives. The newspapers had scare headlines: "POLICE PROTECT COLLEGE PRESIDENT FROM STUDENTS."

An interesting aspect of this affair is the behavior of the kept press of Worcester. One of the students said to me: "I read 'The Brass Check,' and I couldn't believe it, but now I know it is true, because I saw the Worcester newspapers do practically everything that you told about." Throughout the whole affair the students were orderly and dignified; yet their local newspapers sent over the country wild tales about riots and threats. The Worcester "Telegram," in its first account of the incident, ran the headline: "S P E A K E R F L A Y S S C H O O L S, CHURCHES, GOVERNMENT"—whereas Scott Nearing had not once mentioned the government. Next day the "Telegram" quoted the president of the Liberal Club as saying: "If we could raise enough money we would engage Upton Sinclair." This anecdote is told in the "Clark College Monthly," a student paper, which declares: "This statement is without the slightest foundation in fact. Asked by a reporter if the Liberal Club planned to have any more radical speakers, as for example, Upton Sinclair, Fraser had replied: 'Why, he is in California'; and thus grows the mighty oak!"

One day more, and the "Telegram" buried the students' official statement in an obscure page, and ran the headline: "STUDENTS TALK STRIKE, PREXY SAYS, 'LET THEM TRY IT'!" The Springfield "Union" declared that the "notorious Scott Nearing was delivering an anarchistic lecture." Throughout the whole affair both these papers referred to the student-body by such phrases as "irresponsible college boys," "make-believe radicals," "children who should be spanked," and "sincere young people of an impressionable age"; entirely concealing the fact that the average age of Clark students, including the freshman class, is twenty-one years, while

the average of the Liberal Club members at the time of
the Nearing lecture was twenty-five and six-tenths years.

To conclude the story: the protests of the students
availed them nothing. The author of the Frye-Atwood
geographies announced his intention to oversee their activities and their thoughts; and he has done so. He did
not announce his intention to get rid of the professors who
had publicly opposed him, but he proceeded to make it so
uncomfortable for them that they would hasten to remove
themselves. The great tragedy of American academic life
is the lack of solidarity of the faculty. Even the more
courageous and public-spirited men among the Clark
faculty did not seem to feel that they owed a duty to the
institution and its traditions; instead of proceeding to
organize the faculty, and to stand as a unit against the
degradation of Clark, what has happened is that six of the
best men have resigned in as many months; they have
found congenial places in other institutions, and their
colleagues are left to their fate. As John Jay Chapman
puts it:

"The average professor in an American college will
look on at an act of injustice done to a brother professor
by their college president with the same unconcern as the
rabbit who is not attacked watches the ferret pursue his
brother up and down through the warren to a predestinate
and horrible death. We know, of course, that it would
cost the non-attacked rabbit his place to express sympathy
for the martyr; and the non-attacked is poor, and has
offspring, and hopes of advancement."

The students, of course, are helpless; no student-body
can ever control an institution, except for a brief period,
by some violent outburst. The best trained and most intelligent men go out every year, and a new crop of youngsters come in, who know nothing of the traditions of the
institution; nor can they find out what is going on in the
outside world, since the librarian of the university keeps
the "Nation" and the "New Republic" hidden away in the
basement, among the obscene literature which can only be
got by special signed request! So all that the interlocking
directorate has to do is to sit tight and hold on to the
purse-strings. In two or three years the last trace of the
Clark tradition will be forgotten, and the university which
stood at the head of America's scientific life will be one

more of the regulation standard educational department-stores—but distinguished by the fact that every summer it conducts geographical tea-parties, at which the distinguished author of the Frye-Atwood geographies tells the assembled fifth-grade schoolmarms that "the great object of you teachers is to prepare the minds of youth to stand firm against the great wave of radicalism which is sweeping American institutions off the face of the earth."

CHAPTER LXII

THE PROCESS OF FORDIZATION

While we are contemplating academic tragedies, let us take our familiar Baltimore and Ohio Railroad, with a Johns Hopkins trustee for president and another Johns Hopkins trustee for director, also a Princeton trustee, a Lafayette trustee, a Teachers' College trustee, a Lehigh trustee for directors, also a Morgan partner and a First National Bank director and two Guaranty Trust Company directors and a trustee of the University of Pennsylvania. We travel to Baltimore, where we shall find another university fallen upon exactly the same pitiful fate as Clark; save that the interlocking trustees have handled the matter more deftly, and have not made themselves a scandal in the newspapers.

Johns Hopkins University was founded by an old Quaker, who left three and a half millions to endow a university, with a medical school as an integral part. He had the wisdom to call in a great educator, Daniel Coit Gilman, who did in Baltimore exactly what Stanley Hall did at Worcester; the money, instead of being spent on buildings, was spent on men. I doubt if any institution in America has made as great a reputation with as miserable a physical equipment as Johns Hopkins University. Recently a friend of mine was walking down the street with a stranger to Baltimore, and my friend remarked: "There is Johns Hopkins."

The other looked, and thought my friend was joking. "Why, that must be a 'nigger school,'" he said.

"That is Johns Hopkins." And the other asked: "Where is the rest of it?" But there was no rest of it; these old buildings were the whole thing. But to this place came live young men of ability, some of them for almost nothing, because here the intellectual life was honored, and scientific investigators could do their own work in their own way.

The business men of Baltimore regarded Johns Hopkins exactly as the business men of Worcester regarded Clark. It was opened without prayer; therefore it was an atheist university, a terrible place. Now that the work is done and the reputation made, of course they are proud of Johns Hopkins, as well they may be, since it and the "Star-Spangled Banner" are Baltimore's only contributions to world culture—unless some day they count H. L. Mencken and the author of "The Goose-step," both of whom were born there!

Some twenty years ago Gilman retired from Johns Hopkins, to start the Carnegie Institution at the age of seventy. For ten years the university was administered by one of its professors; then the interlocking trustees cast about for some one of their own type of mentality, and pitched upon Professor Goodnow, formerly of the Columbia Law School. As we have seen, Goodnow did not get along with Nicholas Miraculous, but that was a long time ago, and the servants of the plutocracy gain in wisdom and caution as they grow older. Professor Goodnow had been legal adviser to the Chinese government, and had recommended that they should not attempt to found a republic—the last word of an American scholar to a people struggling for freedom! President Goodnow possesses a rather uncouth and forbidding personality, and I am told that he is a poor speaker, but he is a favorite orator at Merchants' and Manufacturers' Association banquets, because he tells them what they like to hear; also because he has set out to make John Hopkins what they like a university to be—an elegant country-club with athletics and "college spirit" and "rah-rah-stuff."

They have moved out to a magnificent new site at Homewood, and have fifteen million dollars, and all the beautiful buildings which are the price of a university's soul. The board of trustees has as its chief grand duke Mr. Daniel Willard, president of the Baltimore & Ohio Railroad. As president the board has Mr. R. Brent Keyser, copper magnate, and director of Mr. Willard's railroad, also of a bank. There is Mr. Levering, coffee merchant, and president of a national bank; also Mr. Blanchard Randall, a merchant, director of a national bank, a trust company, an insurance company, and a railroad, and reported to have made a million dollars out of one speculation during the war; also Judge Harlan, reactionary politician, counsel for a trust company; Mr. Woods, a steel magnate; Mr. Griswold, a prominent financier; Mr. White, another; Mr. Theodore Marburg, ex-minister to Belgium; and Newton D. Baker, who called himself a radical, but forgot it when he became a cabinet member.

Also I ought to mention one of the hidden influences in the university, Bishop Murray of the Episcopal church, a sort of pope of reaction in Baltimore, a bigoted mediaevalist who drove the Reverend Richard Hogue, secretary of the Church League for Industrial Democracy, from his pulpit in Baltimore, and broke up the church open forum by publishing in the Baltimore newspapers advertisements carefully veiled so as not quite to be libelous. Now the bishop is busy immortalizing himself by building a twelve million dollar cathedral; giving lawn parties to the rich, and making speeches explaining how the great structure is to be four hundred feet long and to have the highest tower east of the Mississippi. As a Johns Hopkins professor phrased it to me: "The church is running to plant; and so is the university."

Mr. H. L. Mencken, who lives in Baltimore and watches from a high tower, told me what has happened under the new regime. "It is a process of Fordization. The university has a campus, and the usual outfit of uplifters; it has a summer school, with advertising and journalism and gas engineering and folk-singing and pedagogy and counter-point taught in six weeks, and every known kind of Main Street stuff. It has gone flop at one crack to the level of Ohio Wesleyan; it is a technical high school for the manufacturing of ten-thousand-dollar-a-year Chautauqua fakers." Mr. Mencken insists that a student got his doctorate degree for marking on a curve the vocabulary of Latin students after six months' training. Also he told me the tragic tale of a professor of psychology, who "had a hyena of a wife," and some other woman made love to him, and his wife started a divorce suit, and he had to leave the new Baltimore Chautauqua. On the other hand, a gentleman who was for many years one of the most prominent members of the board of trustees held that position in spite of the fact that everybody in Baltimore society knew that he was living with another woman while he had a wife. He still holds a position on the bishop's committee to raise funds for the cathedral!

On the outskirts of Johns Hopkins hovers Miss Elizabeth Gilman, daughter of the former president, a gentle but indefatigable ghost, troubling the uneasy souls of the new Chautauqua-masters. Miss Gilman is a Socialist, and an ardent champion of starving wives and children of strikers. She sees her father's great university in process of being kidnapped, and now and then her distress breaks out into pamphlet or leaflet form. During a strike of the typographical union, Miss Gilman wrote to President Goodnow, protesting against the university's having its printing done in anti-union shops, but he coldly declined to have anything to do with "questions of that sort." I went to see Miss Gilman, to ask her to tell me about her experiences. She could not bring herself to do it, and, I think, in order to be fair to her, I ought to say that it is to others I owe what I have written here. I persuaded Miss Gilman to state over her own signature her opinion of the new Johns Hopkins, and this she did, as follows:

The university has been to me more like a sister than an institution. I gloried in what she stood for and in what she accomplished. During the last few years it seems to me that she has lost much of her intellectual leadership in America, at the very time when academic freedom and democratic principles need brave champions. The fine new buildings and campus have not to my mind compensated for a considerable lowering of intellectual ideals and accomplishments. Money getting is horribly dangerous to institutions as well as to individuals, and the Johns Hopkins University has been out to get money. It is true that this money has been given for education and not for profit, and yet even so, there may be the insidious temptation of adopting purely business standards. We need in Baltimore, as well as throughout the country, courageous, untrammelled leadership, as expressed in the motto of the Johns Hopkins University, "The truth shall make you free." My hope is that a new cycle may be at hand, and that the Johns Hopkins University will again lead in all that is best and highest.

I talked with three Johns Hopkins professors, and had a curious experience with each one in turn. Each told me of some feeble little effort he had made at liberalism, and how deftly and subtly he had been sat down upon by the university authorities. I made notes of the little anecdotes, planning to tell them here, without names, to show you how the proprieties are maintained by privilege; but to my great grief, each professor came to me in turn, or wrote to me subsequently, to ask that I should not use anything of what he had told me—the anecdote would certainly be recognized, and his career of usefulness might be hampered. Such pitiful little stories—and such pitiful little fears!

I found only one professor at Johns Hopkins who was willing to be quoted in my book. This gentleman I met at luncheon in the University Club of Baltimore, and he indulged himself in bitter sneers at the so-called "radical" type of professor. I myself could name about twelve really radical American college professors; but from the talk of this Johns Hopkins professor you would have thought there were thousands. To be a "radical" was the way to get promotion, said this John Hopkins man; to attract notoriety to yourself and make yourself somebody. Once you had got the name for being a radical, then the trustees wouldn't dare to fire you, because that would be a violation of academic freedom. I smiled gently, promising this sarcastic gentleman that I would send him a copy of my book when it was written, and let him see how his statements sounded side by side with the facts! How do you think they sound?

CHAPTER LXIII

INTELLECTUAL DRY-ROT

There are a few other universities, which in past times have established reputations in America; for example, Cornell University, located at Ithaca, New York, on the Lackawanna Railroad, with a Cornell trustee, a Columbia trustee, and a Princeton trustee; also on the Lehigh Railroad, with a trustee and recent president of Lehigh College, a trustee of the University of Pennsylvania, and a trustee of Lafayette College for directors. Cornell today has some six thousand students, and as choice an outfit of trustees as a plutocratic imagination could invent. The grand duke is Mr. George F. Baker, reputed to be, next to Rockefeller, the richest man in America. I might take a page of this book to list all the various institutions of which Mr. Baker is an interlocking director. He is president of the First National Bank of New York, one of the three great institutions of the Money Trust, and also a trustee of the Mutual Life Insurance Company, a great treasure-chest. He is director in a dozen railroads, and his son is director in many more.

Next to Mr. Baker stands Mr. Charles M. Schwab, president of Bethlehem Steel, and H. H. Westinghouse, chairman of the Westinghouse Company. It will suffice to indicate a few of the others—the head of the biggest bank in Ithaca; the head of a great machinery company, president of a national bank; a corporation lawyer and bank director; a metal manufacturer, director of many railroads; an ex-governor and prominent Republican politician; the chairman of the Bankers' Trust Company of Buffalo, president of a steamship company, a lumber company and a railroad company; the vice-president and counsel of the New York Central Railroad; a prominent corporation lawyer; a judge, ex-mayor of Ithaca, and director of a national bank; the president of a national bank and director of half a dozen others; the president of the Ithaca Trust Company, director of many other banks; an official of Mr. Schwab's shipbuilding corporation; the chief justice, and another justice, of the New York Court of Appeals; and, finally, that Major Seaman whose heroic defense of the Chicago packers you may read about in Chapter IV of "The Brass Check."

Not so very long ago Cornell had a famous president, Schurman, who had studied the Goose-step in three of the Kaiser's universities. I received an interesting account of him from Mr. W. E. Zeuch, who was on the Cornell faculty, when the Bolshevik-hunters got hold of some letters, written to him by another professor. This other professor was quite a "red," and Zeuch was trying to "tame him down"; the letters of Zeuch were not published, but he was represented as a Bolshevist, and his scalp was demanded. Cornell at this time was in the midst of a "drive" for ten millions, and a lumber magnate wrote to President Schurman that so long as Zeuch remained he would not lead the "drive." The economics department of the university appointed a committee, which endorsed Zeuch and declared that a contract had been made, and that the university should stand by a competent man. In twenty-five years the university had never rejected the decision of such a faculty committee; nevertheless, President Schurman proposed that Zeuch should resign from the faculty, and accept a position as a "fellow," to do the same amount of work and receive the same salary!

Also they had a flurry at Cornell over Thorstein Veblen three or four years ago. He had been scheduled for appointment; his courses had been listed, and the members of the economics department had sent out to various colleges a circular letter calling attention to the fact that Veblen was to come to Cornell, and that graduate students could get work with him there. But the interlocking trustees got busy, and the call was countermanded. Nevertheless, in the interest of discrimination it must be specified that Cornell is to be numbered among our less illiberal universities. One professor made so bold during the war as to advocate the financing of the war by taxation rather than by bonds. This would have meant that the plutocracy would have to pay at least a part of the costs instead of collecting it all by installments from you and me. The trustees of the university heard this professor explain his ideas; they did not take action to recommend this policy to the country—but they refrained from firing the professor. Also there is another professor, an elderly gentleman, who is a great favorite with the students, who take his liberal ideas with playful good humor. Several of this old gentleman's friends assured me that he would tell me the story of his twenty-five years' struggle for the right to think for himself; but apparently the old professor decided that he did not want to have any more struggles!

Hendrik Willem Van Loon, author of "The Story of Mankind," was also a member of this Cornell faculty, and gave me an amusing account of the atmosphere of the place. President Schurman was selling four hundred thousand dollars worth of education per year, "training boys to become superintendents of sewage disposal plants and presidents of Rotary clubs." Van Loon was gravely rebuked by Schurman, because of a humorous remark which created a scandal; he had been writing on the blackboard, when a thunderstorm had come up, and he playfully compared himself to Moses writing the Ten Commandments amid the thunders of Sinai. Van Loon swears it is true, and I am compelled to believe him— that when he asked to see the Dante collection they took him to inspect an electric manure sprayer! (A joke.)

Or take Brown University, located at Providence, Rhode Island, on the familiar New Haven Railroad. Here is an extremely wealthy institution, catering to the sons of the plutocracy, and almost as snobbish as Princeton. It was built in part out of Rockefeller money, and the man who has been its president for the last twenty-three years is a Baptist clergyman, for ten years pastor of Rockefeller's Fifth Avenue church in New York. For "chancellor" the university has an extremely wealthy cotton manufacturer, president of a bank; for treasurer it has the president of the Providence Banking Company, also treasurer of the United Traction and Electric Company, and of the Rumford Chemical Works. The three most active grand dukes of the board are Mr. Bedford, chairman of the Standard Oil Company, who represents the Rockefeller interests; Mr. Sharpe, head of the Brown & Sharpe Company, the largest manufacturers of tools in the United States; and Mr. Metcalf, a big textile manufacturer, president of the Providence "Journal" Company.

Also there is the manager of the Brown & Sharpe Company; the president of the Cadillac Motor Car Company; the head of a big New York banking company, president of a railroad and a coal company, director of three railroads, three trust companies, a milk company, a patent medicine company, and a brick company; a very wealthy manufacturing chemist; an influential New England textile manufacturer; a steel magnate; a lawyer, who is president of a land company and secretary of several railroads and trust companies; the treasurer of the largest textile manufacturing company in New England, who is director in half a dozen others, and in half a dozen of the largest financial institutions; another Providence banker; and, finally, Secretary of State Charles E. Hughes. Mr. Hughes first came under my observation when I studied the life insurance scandals in New York City. I noted that he sternly carried these investigations to the point

21

necessary to put Morgan and his group in control, and
stopped exactly at that point. For this service he was
awarded a national reputation and the governorship of
New York State. He has since occupied the Supreme
Court bench, and come within a few votes of being president, and is now guiding the foreign affairs of our country, making a desperate and almost a successful effort to
exceed the futility of the Wilson administration.

What happens to a great and wealthy university under
such a regime? Brown has a high tradition, derived from
Roger Williams, most famous of New England's religious
rebels. But in 1899 its president, Andrews, was ousted,
because he had dared to back Bryan in the campaign of
1896. Quite recently occurred a similar case, when William MacDonald, professor of history, was forced out, to
become one of the editors of the "Nation." Brown in its
day had such outstanding men as Lester F. Ward and
Meikeljohn, now president of Amherst; but those days
have passed, and there has followed a regime of intellectual dry-rot. It is a League of the Old Men, maintaining
a caste system, based upon seniority; any young instructor
who arises to suggest a new idea is quickly taught his
place. A professor who knows the situation intimately
writes:

In the fields of history, political science, economics and
sociology the policy under Faunce has been silent and safe
decay. These departments were once among the most eminent
in the country. Now they are absolutely dead. Except for some
formal texts by Professor Dealey no important publication has
come from these departments in over a decade. The economics
department is now being made over into a business school to
train men to make more money. The general educational
policy throughout the institution under Faunce has been that
of comfortable quiescence. With the exception of one man in
physics and three biologists there has been practically no intellectual activity or scholarly productivity at Brown for the
last fifteen years. This situation cannot be excused on the
ground of lack of resources. Brown has plenty of money and
pays very high salaries. It could get some of the best and
most productive men in any line of research and teaching if it
cared to do so. The decline of scholarly interests at Brown
has been accompanied by a parallel growth of interest in and
expenditures for the safer field of physical outlet, namely, athletics.

Under such a regime what becomes of the students?
Exactly the same thing as we found happening to stu-

dents at Harvard, Wisconsin, and California; they get drunk. In "The Book of Life," Chapter XXX, I discussed the morals of our young people, as set forth in an editorial in a student paper of Brown University. Said this student editor:

The modern social bud drinks, not too much, often, but enough. She smokes unguardedly, swears considerably, and tells "dirty" stories. All in all, she is a most frivolous, passionate, sensation-seeking little thing.

Let us move on to Wesleyan University, located at Middletown, Connecticut, also on the New Haven Railroad. Here is an institution with an old-time Methodist foundation and traditions of liberalism, and the usual board of interlocking trustees, the grand duke being a Philadelphia manufacturer of gas meters who is most versatile, being director in four large gas companies, two street railways, a bank, a trust company, four insurance companies, a publishing company, a sugar company, and a transfer company. Nine years ago his university began its downward course, with an especially notorious case of invasion of academic freedom. Willard C. Fisher had been a member of the faculty for twenty years, and professor of social economics for fifteen. He was one of those college professors who insist upon being a citizen; he served two years as councilman in the Middletown city government, and four years as mayor. He was not a Socialist, on the contrary, an active opponent of Socialism; but he considered himself a servant of the people, and did not hesitate to warn them of the economic waste and social peril of extreme inequality of wealth and the oppression of labor.

As a teacher in a Christian community, he considered it his duty to assert that industrial relations should be moralized. He organized the Consumers' League of Connecticut, and served it for many years as president. He developed the habit of attending legislative hearings at the capital, and speaking in support of progressive measures, such as workmen's compensation, income tax, industrial sanitation, factory inspection, and prison reform. And there, of course, he came into conflict with the interlocking trustees and the interlocking alumni. One influential alumnus, a wealthy manufacturer, was always a member of one House or the other, in order to watch out for the interests of industrial employers; and naturally it vexed him to be opposed by a professor of his own college. He declared this vexation openly; and also a group of Wesleyan lawyers declared their vexation, when the legislature employed Professor Fisher to write a workmen's compensation measure!

Also there arose an embarrassing situation, when Professor Fisher, as mayor of Middletown, discovered a trustee of the college to be delinquent with public school funds of which he was the custodian. (Memo. for Brander Matthews!) Mayor Fisher exposed this situation; nor did he consider it necessary to suppress his disapproval of President Shanklin's well-known habit of taking the thoughts and utterances of other writers and giving them to the world as his own. This president, who has been at Wesleyan for thirteen years, got his degree from the Garrett Bible Institute at Evanston, Illinois; but apparently a number of other college presidents have sympathized with his lack of distinction, because no less than ten of them have showered honorary degrees upon him!

Matters came to a head when President Shanklin started a drive for a million dollars. In a public discussion the president of a Hartford trust company asked Professor Fisher if he expected to go about the state speaking as he did, and have trust company presidents contribute to the support of the college in which he taught. It was widely rumored at Wesleyan that President Shanklin got contributions upon the condition that Fisher should be kicked off the faculty. A number of men of wealth refused to contribute on other terms; and so the president cast about for a handy pretext.

He found one. In the course of a public address, widely reported in Connecticut newspapers, Professor Fisher made the playful suggestion that it might be a good idea to close all the churches for a while, to give the people a chance to find out the difference between true religion and church formalities. Very soon thereafter Professor Fisher was asked to resign, and the president gave the reason—not the suggestion of the closing of the churches, but the broad publicity given to this suggestion by the newspapers! Professor Fisher might have stayed and made a fight, but he had been so humiliated by the changed spirit and atmosphere of Wesleyan, that he quit; and now the university is on the intellectual level of the Garrett Bible Institute of Evanston, Illinois!

CHAPTER LXIV

THE UNIVERSITY OF JABBERGRAB

Some fifteen years ago my postman brought me a puzzling communication from Sweden; a large and expensive linen envelope, carefully sealed with a great deal of red wax, registered, and addressed:

"Editor, Jabbergrab, Finanz-Lexikon, New York City." At first I could not make out why the missive was delivered to me, but then in one corner I noted "Jabbergrab is mentioned in Upton Sinclair's 'Industriebaron.'" I recognized "Der Industriebaron" as the German title of my story, "A Captain of Industry," written when I was twenty-two years old; it is a satirical biography of a great financier, and after his ignominious death the story quotes some eulogies of his career from an imaginary publication, "Jabbergrab: Heroes of Finance."

I made so bold as to open the envelope, and found several sheets of heavy foolscap paper, written in German in an exceedingly fine hand, and giving the data for a biographical sketch of a wealthy Swedish lumber magnate and financier. Here, in carefully tabulated and precisely ordered form, were the minute details of his life—the enterprises with which he had been connected, the offices he held, the properties he owned, the names of his children, the college degrees they had earned, the names of his race-horses and the prizes they had won, the names of his yachts and the cups they had won—all these items duly attested and signed by the great man himself.

Gradually it dawned over me what had happened. The man had read my satirical story, missing the point of the satire. He thought that I really felt all that admiration for a man of wealth and social eminence; and reading about Jabbergrab's "Heroes of Finance," the desire possessed him to have his own career immortalized in this biographical directory. So he had sat himself down, and painfully written out the data for the proposed sketch, and had sent it by registered mail to "Jabbergrab."

It is the Jabbergrabs of America who have created a good part of our "higher" education, and placed upon it the stamp of their crude and simple faith in material success. I have shown how the spirit of Jabbergrab has destroyed two shrines of American scientific life, Clark University and Johns Hopkins; I purpose next to show what that spirit does, when it has its way from the beginning, unhampered by any intellectual traditions. I invite you to visit New York University, an institution whose buildings are scattered about in various parts of the city, including an office building on Washington Square, in the heart of the clothing district, and another in Wall Street.

New York University has enrolled no less than thirteen thousand students, and is described to me by one who works in it as "an intellectual sweat-shop." As chancellor it has one Brown, who learned the Goose-step from the Kaiser, and as treasurer one Kingsley, a Wall Street banker, interlocked with the United States Trust Company, the Sixth Avenue Elevated Railroad, and the Union Theological Seminary. Last year Chancellor Brown published in the New York newspapers a series of thirty "advertising talks" on education, in the very latest "follow-up" style. These talks came to me in a little pamphlet, with a cover all printed over with photographs of newspaper clippings, and accompanied by a circular, carefully disguised to look like a personal letter, and beginning: "Dear Mr. Sinclair: You are one of the prominent citizens we had in mind when we prepared the enclosed advertisement. What we have learned of you encourages us to believe that this appeal of New York University must strike a responsive chord in you."

I may be over-suspicious, but I believe that these statements are not entirely in accordance with the truth; I believe that if they were made in accordance with the truth they would read this way: "You are one of the twenty-two thousand persons whose names we have got from 'Who's Who in America,' and we are taking a chance on being able to interest you in our university." These necessary differences between advertising and fact are understood and taught to the students in all university schools of advertising.

Chancellor Brown sets forth the fact that out of his thirteen thousand students, ten thousand are earning the money to pay for their education. I believe that every college student in the country should do this—my own son is doing it—so I should be the last man to sneer at New York University's lack of academic and social prestige. But here is the point: self-supporting students who go to night-school in New York go in order to increase their money-making capacity, and they judge the education they get by that criterion, and they irresistibly mold the educational standards of the institution they attend. So the spirit of education becomes that of Jabbergrab—ravenous greed, veiled by buncombe and hypocritical pretenses. That is what you have at New York University, and the fact is made clear in Chancellor Brown's own pamphlet. Talk Number Sixteen is headed: "Welcome to the Advertising Men." Says our Chancellor of Jabbergrab:

New York University is host today to members of the National Association of Teachers of Advertising, who are holding a sectional conference in this city while a similar conference for Western members is held at the University of Wisconsin. I am glad to welcome the members of this Association. Since I have been writing these little talks I have gained a feeling of warmer sympathy with all advertising men and their work. I have learned something of the fascinations—as well as the difficulties—of the profession.

So you see, our University of Jabbergrab has discovered advertising to be a "profession"; it takes its place alongside chiropody, palmistry and fox-trotting. If you want to know what these new "professors" are doing to American journalism, I invite you to read Chapters XLIII-XLVII of "The Brass Check"; I invite you to study the samples of advertising there quoted—one of which occupied a full page in all the most popular and respectable American magazines—and then come back to Chancellor Brown's pamphlet and read his statement: "Many advertising men, I am told, were formerly teachers. The two professions seem to me to have a great deal in common."

I should be sorry indeed to believe that about all American teachers, but I know it is true of some of the teachers who have been selected by the University of Jabbergrab. For example, consider Professor William E. Aughinbaugh, an editor of the New York "Commercial," a director in sixteen corporations, and for seven years "Professor of Foreign Trade" in New York University. He boasts of having crossed the equator thirty-six times on commercial missions, and he publishes through one of our most esteemed publishing houses, the Century Company, an elaborately got up book, entitled, "Advertising for Trade in Latin America." The price of this book is three dollars, and if you will study its maxims and apply them, you will find it worth all that. For example:

Latin-American advertisements are replete with the nude female form, which appeals strongly to all classes of readers. Due to the fact that a majority of the inhabitants are brunettes, or have Negro or Indian blood in their veins, the blonde exerts a stronger appeal to their imagination and for that reason should be employed when necessary or advisable to use such an illustration.

And so we know what the Chancellor of Jabbergrab means when he writes:

Advertising men have it in their power to educate millions of people not only in an intelligent use of commodities but in well-considered habits of thought and action.

Let us hear Professor Aughinbaugh again:

Reproductions of famous holy or religious paintings or scenes from the Bible may also be profitably used. . . . . It occurred to me that if a saint could be found whose special duty was to prevent loss of life during seismic disturbances, much might be done through his aid to bring calm into these regions of terror. I selected my second name, "Edmund," as the cognomen for the new assistant deity, added the prefix "Saint" to it, and wrote an appropriate earthquake prayer which was printed beneath the picture of the home-made saint. Of course each card contained our advertisement (of a patent medicine) which the supplicant for protection must have seen as he prayed.

And so we learned what the Chancellor of Jabbergrab means when he writes:

I can appreciate the reasons that impel any manufacturer to spread abroad through the columns of our newspapers and magazines the information about his worthy products. I can believe, too, that this information is often of real service to the public in guiding them to wise decisions regarding their expenditures and investments.

And again let us hear Professor Aughinbaugh on the subject of how to deal with the custom-laws of the countries with which you trade:

When I have decided upon an advertising campaign in any given Latin-American country, the requisite amount of cards, hangers, booklets, posters, banners, and other materials are boxed and shipped to the various ports, consigned to some man of straw. Upon their arrival at the local port they will be stored in the customs warehouse to await claim by the alleged consignee. At the expiration of sixty or ninety, or one hundred and twenty days, in accordance with the local laws, these goods will be advertised for sale to the highest bidder. By previous arrangement with your agent, or some merchant, who has been advised of the dispatch of these goods to his port, they can be bid in very cheaply and delivered to the person most concerned with their use. In Venezuela, for instance, on one shipment alone the duties would have amounted to much more than one thousand dollars, yet the local wholesale druggist bought the entire consignment at auction for eighty-five dollars.

And so we know exactly what the Chancellor of the University of Jabbergrab means when he says to the "Sectional Conference of Teachers of Advertising":

I believe, also, that the teachers of advertising can make a valuable contribution to the education of our future business men by teaching them how to use the force of advertising intelligently, effectively, and for the human benefit.

It happened that I saw Professor Aughinbaugh mentioned also as "Professor of Foreign Trade at Columbia University." Wishing to get the record straight, I asked my brother-in-law, who has been helping me get material for this book, to write Professor Aughinbaugh a note asking him where he was a professor. Thinking that possibly he might be away, or ill, or for some other reason might fail to reply, I asked my brother-in-law to write also to New York University for the information. The result was two letters: one from Professor Aughinbaugh stating that "for two years past I have held the same position in New York University and Columbia University. The work became too hard for me and I was obliged to resign my professorship at New York University, now devoting my time to Columbia University." The second letter was from the registrar of New York University, and stated: "Dr. William E. Aughinbaugh was, from October 11, 1915, to June 13, 1922, Lecturer on Foreign Trade at New York University. He did not, at any time, have professorial status."

Here was, obviously, a contradiction. Professor Aughinbaugh is listed in "Who's Who" as Professor of

Foreign Trade; and "Who's Who" states that it publishes no information except that furnished by the person concerned. Also, in a circular of his book, Professor Aughinbaugh is shown as "Chairman of Foreign Trade." Wishing to make certain about this matter, I dictated to my secretary a formal note, calling Professor Aughinbaugh's attention to the discrepancies, and asking him to state which title was correct. This note was signed by my brother-in-law and mailed, and no reply to it has ever been received.

But some three weeks after it was mailed, there called at my office in Pasadena a man who announced himself as an agent of the Department of Justice, and gave the name of "A. J. Taylor." He interviewed my brother-in-law, a young man of twenty-one, and stated that my brother-in-law had been writing letters of a "scurrilous and defamatory nature" to Professor Aughinbaugh; that he had asked questions such as he had no business to ask, that he had made "improper statements" about the wife of Professor Aughinbaugh, and that he was to "stop writing letters," or he would get into serious trouble. Subsequent inquiry of the Department of Justice in Los Angeles, of the United States Attorney for this district, Attorney-General Daugherty in Washington, and Post Office Inspectors of New York, Washington and Los Angeles, brought the positive statements that no such person as "A. J. Taylor" was known, and no investigation of any such matter had been undertaken. The Postmaster at Pasadena stated that he had received letters from private parties in New York, complaining of "blackmailing" letters written by my brother-in-law; and some ten days later there came a letter from Professor Aughinbaugh to me stating that he had learned from the postal authorities in California that I had written to him, under my brother-in-law's name, and asking what was the purpose of my inquiry. I replied, stating to Professor Aughinbaugh exactly what was my purpose, and asking him if he would in return answer some questions of mine, as follows:

1. Did you send this A. J. Taylor to see my brother-in-law?
2. Did you tell him to represent himself as an agent of the Department of Justice?
3. Did you make to him any statement which would have justified him in the wholly false and absurd assertion that my brother-in-law had ever mentioned your wife?

4. If you did send this "A. J. Taylor," who is he, and where can he be located?

5. If you did not send him, can you offer any suggestion as to how he learned about the correspondence between my brother-in-law and yourself, and what interest he had in troubling himself about the matter?

To these questions Professor Aughinbaugh made no answer, except to send me in an envelope three circulars of his book, in one of which he is described as "lecturer," in another as "instructor," and in another as "chairman." I wrote again, calling his attention to his failure to answer, but no further response came. From the publishers of "Who's Who" I learn that the lecturer-instructor-chairman-professor himself furnished them with the information concerning his status; also that he has recently written to them asking to be recorded as no longer "professor" but as just plain "lecturer!"

CHAPTER LXV

THE GROWTH OF JABBERGRAB

Modern industry is an enormously complicated thing, and specialized teaching of industrial processes is just as necessary as any other kind of education. I would not give anyone the impression that I object to the teaching of advertising or foreign trade or finance, any more than I object to the teaching of plumbing or manicuring finger-nails. My point is that all these arts should be taught in trade schools, and they should be taught *as trades*. For example, the International Harvester Company maintains an excellent school for training its employes; it does not pretend that this school is a "university," it does not call the turning out of harvester machines a "profession," and it does not constitute a high-speed steel worker a "doctor of science." It is when these schools of commerce and departments of trade crowd into universities, and take to themselves academic honors and dignities, and exploit themselves with high-sounding phrases of religion and social idealism, that I am moved to protest; as when I see some parasitic vine climbing a beautiful shade-tree, spreading out over the surface of the tree, blocking its light and air and choking it to death.

That is what is happening in the field of American higher education; it is happening not merely at New York

University and other great "intellectual sweat-shops," it is happening at practically every one of our state universities and at most of our great endowed institutions. It was Harvard which started this vile business, with a College of Commerce and Administration; Columbia followed suit, and the plague has spread from Maine to California. I consult a few college catalogues at random, and I find that at the University of Illinois they are teaching millinery, also at the University of Nebraska and the University of Southern California. At the University of California they have a "costume laboratory," also a course in "jewelry." At Boston University, made out of the millions of Isaac Rich, the merchant, and Lee Chaflin, the shoe manufacturer, they will teach you how to collect tips at summer hotels. The commercial men and women who specialize in such subjects come into the universities, and they bid against the professors of liberal arts for power and prestige and pay—and how much chance do you think a scholar or lover of belles-lettres stands against such people?

You understand that the president of a university, making up his salary budget, is like all other business men, he pays what he has to pay. And here is the Professor of Department-store Advertising pointing out that at Goldberg & Isaacstein's, in the shopping district, he can get fifteen thousand a year, and he has a letter in his pocket to prove it. He will come to the university for twelve thousand, because of his love of the higher things of life, but he won't take a cent less, and the president tries once or twice and finds out that he is not bluffing. For a year the president has been trying to get a first-class Professor of Commercial Correspondence, who understands the three varieties of "follow-up letters"; and the Director of his School of Business keeps telling him that any man who really commands that precious knowledge can get ten thousand a year. But who is there in the outside world that will pay anything to a professor of archeology, or to a man who can explain the Einstein theory, or a man who knows more about the life of Dante than anyone else in America? Such men have to take what they can get, and their salaries remain stagnant while the value of the dollar is cut in half.

At the University of Minnesota I was told about a

discussion at a meeting of the regents. The president of the university was very anxious to get Professor Stuart P. Sherman, well known as a conservative literary critic. Some one remarked that Sherman would want six thousand dollars; whereupon the grand duke of the board put down his fist on the table. "There's not an English man in America worth six thousand dollars!" he declared. I am sorry I cannot state exactly what value this gentleman sets upon the services of a grand duke of the plutocracy, but it is at least a score of times the sum of six thousand a year. But you see, this gentleman has all his life been buying men at their market price, and he knows that market price, and has no idea that they have any other value.

At the University of Chicago they have a School of Commerce, which is growing like the weed that it is, and in their advertising literature, with its variety of "follow-up letters," they tell you that after two years' training you can command a salary of twelve thousand dollars. This, of course, is the kind of talk that brings the business; these are the courses which the "he-men" take. And after they have got a degree, they become professors, and perhaps deans, and they run the university. If it is a question of starting a drive for funds, they are the ones who know how to get out the "literature," they are experts in the psychology of mendication. They understand the newspapers, and how to get favors from them; they understand the politicians and the big business men who run the politicians; they are the fellows after the trustees' own hearts, and when the time comes for the old president to be shelved, it is one of these "go-getters" who is in line for the place. We have seen that happen at one university after another; at the University of Illinois President Kinley was Director of the School of Commerce, and at Northwestern University President Scott was Director of the Bureau of Salesmanship Research.

Let us return to our University of Jabbergrab, where these new educational tendencies "rule the roost." Chancellor Brown sets forth that the "School of Commerce, Accounts and Finance" of his university contains six thousand students, and that from it has sprung a "Graduate School of Business Administration," also in the last three years a "School of Retailing." Twenty-two department-stores and other retail establishments in New York "have made direct connection with the university, and thirty-seven college graduates are each morning pursuing their studies in retailing in our class-rooms, and in the afternoon of the same day are receiving practical experience in the various operations of the stores themselves." I have not attended these classes, but I do not need to inquire what these students are learning; I can go to the New York department-stores, and see them displaying "marked-down" goods, which were marked up before they were marked down. I have only to read their imbecile advertisements in the New York newspapers, setting forth the latest fads and foibles of "Milady," and the latest "importations" of the latest "creations" of the keepers of French mistresses.

New York University's catalogue lists three professors of marketing, five professors of finance, four professors of accounting, four of business English, three of management, one of salesmanship, one of merchandising, one of foreign trade, one of life insurance—and a Director of the Wall Street Division!

Of course, this new kind of education is yet in its infancy, and we must not expect perfection. Pick up this university catalogue ten years from now, and you will find its deficiencies made up; you will find a Professor of Stock-watering and an Instructor in Political Manipulation. You will find an eloquent statement setting forth the fact that the handling of labor has now become an enormous American industry; that there are hundreds of large agencies for the putting down of strikes, and salaries as high as twenty and thirty thousand dollars a year are paid to competent masters of such work; therefore the university is establishing a Department of Strike-Breaking, with a Professor of Gunmanship and a Demonstrator of the Third Degree. Also there will be eloquent "advertising talks," explaining that business men now spend most of their time keeping agitators out of their factories, and that the secret service departments of great corporations have come to be the most important part thereof; so the university is now establishing a Department of Espionage, with a Professor of Varieties of Bolshevism, and a Dean of Deportation Proceedings, and a Special Lecturer on Attorney-Generalship.

CHAPTER LXVI

JABBERGRAB IN JOURNALISM

In all these new academic department-stores one of the leading departments is that of journalism. Here they teach you how to write for and edit newspapers; and needless to say, what the students want is to be prepared to fill positions on the capitalist press, and their judgment of a school of journalism is conditioned upon the salaries secured by its graduates. The first school of this kind was started at Columbia, with an endowment left by Joseph Pulitzer, the father of "yellow" journalism. Being curious to know what kind of ethics Mr. Pulitzer's school is teaching, I pick up a publication of the Alumni Association, "Clean Copy." The title page contains a list of officers, and I note the chairman's name, and his address—prepare yourself for a laugh!—care Ivy Lee, 61 Broadway, New York City! So we learn that the Columbia School of Journalism is preparing students to work in the offices of "Poison Ivy!" Its standards are such that it is willing for an employe of "Poison Ivy" to be chairman of its Alumni, and to advertise that fact in its paper!

When I first came in touch with Mr. Lee's lie-factory, he was press agent for John D. Rockefeller, Jr., at a thousand dollars a month; then he became prize poisoner for the Pennsylvania Railroad, and now he has in New York and Washington a great publicity bureau, serving all the railroads of the United States in their war upon the American people. What "Poison Ivy" gets for this work I have no idea, but it must be a generous sum; a friend of mine was looking for an apartment in New York, and entered one of those new palatial houses just off Fifth Avenue, and was informed by those in charge that the cheapest apartment in the place rented for twenty-five thousand dollars a year—and one of the tenants is Ivy L. Lee! It is interesting to note that it took a combination of our three most aristocratic universities, Princeton, Harvard and Columbia, to turn out this super-professor of prevarication!

Also the University of Wisconsin got in early on the journalism business. One of its professors got out a textbook, which was used until quite recently at Wisconsin,

and is still used at many other places; there are thousands
of practicing journalists in America today who got their
ethical ideals from Professor Hyde's text-book, which
advises students about dramatic criticism: "Very few
critics are so fortunate as to be able to say exactly what
they think about a play; they must say what the editor
wants them to say." . . . . The dramatic critic "must
praise more cleverly, and give his copy the appearance of
honest criticism."

Needless to say, they have a school of journalism at
the University of Jabbergrab. The director of this department is James Melvin Lee, who got his training for
the teaching of journalistic ideals on the staff of "Leslie's,"
the barber-shop weekly, and later for four years as editor
of "Judge," the bar-room comic. Concerning Professor
Lee's journalistic standards I have intimate knowledge,
derived from a protracted controversy over "The Brass
Check"; so here I can draw you a complete picture of
Jabbergrab in action.

A controversy with Professor Lee is a good deal like
fighting one of those enchanters you read about in the
fairy tales—your sword goes straight through him, and
leaves him the same as he was before. He made his first
attack on "The Brass Check" at the Brownsville Labor
Forum, and his cry was that he wanted definite facts—
there were none in my book! Again and again I supplied
him with facts, and discovered the curious phenomenon—
he paid not the slightest attention to any which I supplied;
he would come again, demanding the same ones! The
New York "Globe" saw in our controversy a good journalistic stunt, and they invited Professor Lee and myself
to row it out, and gave each of us a total of six columns.
And here in the "Globe," Professor Lee repeated one after
another all the various demands and challenges which he
had issued at the Brownsville Labor Forum—overlooking
almost all the data I had furnished him in the meantime!

For my first article in the "Globe," I took the trouble
to go over "The Brass Check" and count the number of
cases which give complete documentation—names, places,
and dates—and these came to a total of two hundred and
thirteen. In addition, there are perhaps a dozen or two
anecdotes which I narrate upon the authority of other
people, being in every case careful to name my authority.

Finally, there are half a dozen trivial incidents—such as the fact that an old college professor of mine fell down an elevator shaft in a department-store—which I did not document, for the reason that these incidents occurred to me in the final revision of the book, and I could not have the files of the New York newspapers consulted in time. Professor Lee's method of controversy was to pick out these few trifling incidents, and recite them to the Brownsville audience, and to the readers of the New York "Globe," with elaborate challenges to me to produce this information. Thus, to a single anecdote of Gaylord Wilshire being misrepresented by the Associated Press, Professor Lee devoted three paragraphs in the "Globe," demanding at great length the names of the newspapers and the dates; I supplied him with the names and dates of two newspapers—but to no result that I could discover.

Both in his Brownsville address and in the "Globe" controversy he took up my story of the Associated Press crimes in Colorado; but he was careful to confine himself to one detail, my telegram to President Wilson—because he was able to argue that this telegram was libelous and that it was "self-advertising." He made no mention of any other aspect of the whole series of suppressions which I proved against the Associated Press during that Colorado coal strike. Still more significant is the fact that nowhere in these controversies could I get him to mention the conduct of the Associated Press in the West Virginia coal strike. The reason was obvious enough; the Associated Press had here been so indiscreet as to come into court and submit its own dispatches in evidence, and its poisoning of the news was proved by its sworn official admissions. This was not the sort of "facts" that Professor Lee was looking for, and so he never let anyone hear about them!

Equally significant was his handling of the false report sent out by the Associated Press, to the effect that my wife had been arrested during our demonstration in front of the Standard Oil Building, New York, during the Colorado coal strike. I stated in "The Brass Check" that my wife notified the Associated Press of the falsity of this report, and demanded a retraction. In his first letter to me Professor Lee made the flat statement: *"The Associated Press does not have proof; it did not receive it."* In

22

my reply, I pointed out to Professor Lee the naïveté of
his own statement; how without one particle of evidence,
he accepted the word of the Associated Press, and turned
it into a flat statement of his own. My wife filed libel
suits against thirty Associated Press newspapers which
had published the false report, and the Associated Press
was liable for every dollar that these newspapers might
have to pay. Was it humanly believable that not one of
these newspapers would notify the Associated Press of
the filing of these suits? On the contrary, was it not certain that every one of these papers, under the advice of
their attorneys, would notify the Associated Press of the
filing of the suit, and of the paper s expectation that the
Associated Press would defend it? I sent to my New
York office a copy of a newspaper, containing an account
of the filing of the suit, and Professor Lee inspected this
evidence in the presence of my New York manager; but
did this make any difference to him? It made not a particle! When he took up the controversy in the New York
"Globe," he brought up the same argument again: "The
point at issue is whether such attention was called to the
Associated Press!"

Still funnier was what happened in the case of Professor Lee's demand that some one should name a newspaper which had suppressed the name of a department-
store in connection with a discreditable news item. Professor Lee, reading "The Brass Check," observed that
most of my anecdotes of this kind dealt with newspapers
in Philadelphia, Boston, Milwaukee and other cities.
Therefore, he phrased his challenge at the Brownsville
Labor Forum so that it referred only to *New York* newspapers; he called for names, places and dates—and of
course nobody at the Brownsville Labor Forum could supply such data. In the New York "Globe" he repeated this
challenge, very proudly and very confidently. But, alas,
right in the middle of the controversy, his friends on the
kept press threw him down! On June 27 he published in
the "Globe" his article headed, "Lee Calls on Sinclair for
Names, Dates, Places"; and nine days later the New
York "Evening Sun," in its baseball edition, Wednesday,
July 6, 1920, page two, column eight, published a story
about a man who had sued a department-store and col-

lected money from it—and nowhere in the article was the department-store named!

Also I ought to mention the behavior of this professor of Jabbergrab in connection with the New York "Times." This controversy, with all the documents, is given in a pamphlet, "The Crimes of the 'Times,'" which you may have for the asking. I will here mention only one or two details. The "Times" reported Professor Lee's Brownsville address to the extent of two columns, quoting mainly his defense of the "Times." I replied in a letter, and the "Times" did to this the most dishonest thing a newspaper can do—it refused to publish the letter, but discussed it in an editorial, and falsified its contents! I sent the "Times" a telegram, calling attention to the falsifications, but they refused any sort of redress. These falsifications stand in the files of the paper; they are listed in its index, found in every large library in the country. Students of "The Brass Check" will come upon those falsehoods; but they will know nothing about my answer, for my humble little pamphlet is not catalogued in libraries. I trust therefore that the reader will pardon me if I take two paragraphs of this book to state the facts; especially since every step of the controversy was a test, not merely of the "Times," but of the Director of Journalism of New York University.

The incident in dispute is told on page 77 of "The Brass Check," dealing with the publication of my novel, "The Metropolis." The New York "Times" had prepared a front-page news story about this novel, and the story was killed at the last minute by Mr. Ochs, publisher of the "Times." Professor Lee, in his Brownsville speech, declared that this narrative of mine was absurd upon its face. In my letter to the "Times," I put it up to the "Times" to say whether my narrative was true or false. The "Times," refusing to publish the letter, declared editorially that no such incident had occurred. Said the "Times": "Mr. Sinclair refers to this tale in his letter to the 'Times,' but with a shifting of ground. For his own positive statement in 'The Brass Check' he now substitutes the alleged statement of a 'publicity agent' of a publishing house," etc.

Now the facts were as follows: "The Metropolis" had been published in serial form in the "American Magazine"; and in "The Brass Check" I had stated that it was this magazine which had arranged for the story in the "Times." Subsequently I recalled that it was Moffat, Yard & Company, the publishers of the *book*, who had made the arrangements, and this correction I noted in my letter to the "Times." Manifestly, this made no difference, so far as concerned the "Times"; but you see what use they made of this "shifting of ground"! Their assertion, that I "relied upon the alleged statement of a publicity agent of a publishing house" was a flat falsehood; for in my letter to the "Times" I told them that "I saw the proofs of the proposed story with my own eyes." A day or two later I was able to telegraph them statements from the two gentlemen who had composed the firm of Moffat, Yard & Company, Mr. W. D. Moffat and Mr. Robert Sterling Yard, both declaring that they plainly remembered the preparing of the story by the "Times," and their disappointment when they found it did not appear as promised. The "Times" received this testimony, but refused publication to it, and paid no attention to my telegrams of protest!

And now, where was Professor Lee during this controversy? Professor Lee had furnished the "Times" with the ammunition to attack me; he had defended their journalistic practices, and they had published his defense. Here he saw them committing a piece of the baldest journalistic rascality—and what did he do about it? I telegraphed him again and again, asking him to take steps to induce the newspaper to correct its published falsehoods. Later on, I challenged him again and again to withdraw his published endorsement of the newspaper's ethical code. His reply was to go before the University Settlement, and repeat his attack upon "The Brass Check" and his defense of the "Times"—and the "Times" once more featured his address! To the manager of my New York office Professor Lee made the smiling statement that he was publishing a magazine for business men, and he did not care how much I attacked him in public—it would only help him with his business clients!

You have heard me protesting against the practice of covering commercialists and servants of privilege with the mantle of academic dignity; and here you see what it means, and why it is done. The New York "Times" did not dare to answer "The Brass Check" itself; for a year it had ignored the book—save to post in its editorial rooms a statement that anyone found with a copy in the office would be summarily discharged! But then came forward a personage with the high-sounding title of "Director of the Department of Journalism of New York University"; and the "Times" made itself into a megaphone, to carry this hitherto negligible voice to the farthest ends of the earth!

CHAPTER LXVII

THE CITY COLLEGES

There is another crowded institution in the great metropolis, the College of the City of New York, where I got the one degree of which I boast. I went back there this spring, after twenty-five years, and it was a curious experience. They have their new buildings, all in the venerable Gothic style, with arrow-proof windows; and in the faculty room I inspected a row of oil paintings of those old professors who had been the chief torment of five years of my youth. They were so lifelike it gave me a chill; I expected to see the old brown-whiskered professor of Latin, or the old white-whiskered professor of Greek, come down from his frame and denounce me for my twenty years of socialistic agitation.

This college has grown to enormous size, with some sixteen thousand students, and all the regulation "Main Street" courses; also there is Hunter College for women, with four thousand more. These are the only colleges in New York to which Jews can now get admission on their merits, and the student membership of "C. C. N. Y." is eighty-five percent Jewish; the Anglo-Saxons who constitute the interlocking trustees have a difficult time to keep down the active-minded East-side boys. One of them, Leon Samson, ventured to ask a question of General Webb at a "preparedness" meeting, and for this he was expelled. (He moved on to Columbia, from which he was expelled on the basis of garbled newspaper reports of a speech in opposition to the draft.) The students have not been allowed to have an open forum, and the list of speakers is sternly censored. Scott Nearing was barred, also the Reverend John Haynes Holmes, and a lecture by Bouck White was forbidden very dramatically an hour before it began. Incredible as it may seem, Glenn E. Plumb was not permitted to debate the "Plumb plan" before these students!

I found here all the regular methods for holding down the faculty. Said one young professor: "Our president commands a cruel form of torture; he sets you to teaching freshmen for the rest of your life." Promotion depends upon conformity, and dark secrets are whispered, and suffocation befalls those upon whom suspicion lights. I talked with one professor, a bit of a liberal, who gave me a curious picture of the operation of the academic terror. He had been recommended by the head of his department for promotion, but had been passed over; he went to his dean, and tried to drag out of him what was the matter. "Do you know?" Yes, the dean knew. "Will you tell?" No, the dean shook his head. "Will you tell me this, then? Does this reason, whatever it is, operate next year?" No, the dean wouldn't tell that. But for three years it did operate, and a live man was deprived of his right to advancement, and kept upon a dead routine until his spirit should be broken.

I sat with three of these young professors, and one after another they told me their stories, and I noted their phrases. "There is nothing brutal about it; we know our places, and we keep to them; but we think of things that we ought to be doing, and we don't respect ourselves; we invent sophistries to quiet our consciences, we build up a defensive mechanism." And one of the men told me how he had gone out during the summer, and had got a job as a salesman. "I was trying to get over my fear," he said. "I wanted to make sure that I could earn a living in the world."

"Did you earn it?" I asked.

"Yes," he answered; "but I didn't get over my fear. I don't want to be a business man and have to sell things!"

They told me of the efforts of various professors to introduce courses in literature, biology, political science. The heads of these departments are old men, some of them in office forty years; dull, timid, afraid of new ideas. To them everything since 1870 is worthless, and until quite recently they would not allow any modern courses, obviously in fear that if live teaching were introduced they would lose their students. I picture these poor pedagogues; I picture the other old men I knew on that faculty—exactly the same as all the other old men of all the other old faculties of all the other old universities. Modern life comes rushing down upon them like a storm, and they have no idea what to do with it, how to handle it. It is a hail-storm of boys and girls—thousands, tens of thousands, hundreds of thousands of them. What are they? What do they mean?—these strange, wild creatures, thrusting themselves forward, demanding their "rights," clamoring for new things never heard of by old professors! Despising Tennyson, and demanding Bernard Shaw! Doubting the Bible, disputing property rights, questioning marriage, discussing outrageous things —divorce, birth control—actually right out in public! I recalled Jack London's short story, about a group of old Indians up in Alaska, who saw the white men coming in and undermining their ancient civilization. These Indians formed a society to destroy the new intruders: "The League of the Old Men." And I thought to myself: that is what modern education is—a league of the old men to make the young what the old want them to be!

Colleges which are located in big cities have one advantage, in that the students more frequently live at home, and are less apt to develop that pest known as "college spirit." On the other hand, being in the midst of roaring commerce, they are even less apt to think about anything but preparation for money-making. Most of these "city colleges" and "universities" are nothing but trade-schools: for example, the University of Cincinnati, which boasts of four thousand students. The same men who control this place control the banks of the city; they took a professor of economics and made him president of a bank, raising him from four thousand dollars to twenty-five thousand—a lesson for all college professors to ponder! It was this institution which started the wonderful scheme of having students spend their mornings in college classrooms and their afternoons in factories, department-stores and banks. More than a thousand students are now following this plan, in some two hundred and fifty business places in Cincinnati!

Or take Washington University, in St. Louis, which

also has four thousand students. The trustees of this place were described to me by a member of the faculty as "hard-boiled, self-made millionaires." The university advertises in the newspapers for students, setting forth in plain language the increase in earning power attributable to a college training. The students here were forbidden to organize a liberal club; a young lawyer, a member of the faculty, is known as a Bolshevik, and when I asked him why, he said it was because, in a group of millionaires, he heard the opinion expressed that Judge Gary was the best man in the country for president, and he kept silence!

The other day I received a letter from a man in Philadelphia, sending me the advertisements of "Temple University"; I had never heard of such a place, but I looked it up—and behold, it has over eight thousand students, with a School of Theology, a School of Chiropody and a School of Commerce with courses in Salesmanship, Hand-lettering, Advertising Copy and Layout, Advertising Campaigns, Psychology of Advertising. The president and creator of this place is Russell H. Conwell, a Baptist preacher, one of Philadelphia's great men, described by John Wanamaker as "my yoke-fellow." He is the author of a lecture entitled "Acres of Diamonds," which up to 1915 had been delivered five thousand times, and had earned four million dollars. This, with a biography of the preacher and a history of his university, is available in book form; the most characteristically American thing which I have read since the autobiography of P. T. Barnum; a perfect product of that combination of commercial ecstasy and sentimental religiosity which is the soul of my country. The title, "Acres of Diamonds," is derived from the story of an Arab who went out to hunt for diamonds all over the world, and never discovered that he had acres of them on his own farm. Dr. Conwell has discovered that you can exploit the labor of your fellow man in Philadelphia just as well as anywhere else, and he pronounces the law of God that "to make money honestly is to preach the gospel." I took the trouble to go over the first forty pages of his lecture, checking off the words which refer to wealth in its many forms—money, gold, silver, diamonds, riches, millions, dollars, fortune, etc. You may think I am joking, but try it for yourself; in the first forty pages of the lecture I counted two hundred and eighteen such words! And each one of them spoken five thousand times—more than one million words of greed uttered to American audiences by one single preacher of Jesus!

Or take the University of Southern California, with nearly six thousand students, located in the heart of Los Angeles, metropolis of our "land of orange groves and jails." I have no words to describe the ravenous commercialism of this region, the earthly paradise of oil stock salesmen and "realtors"; its varied and multiple greeds affect my imagination like the sounds of a vast menagerie at feeding-time. Needless to say, the university of this outdoor stock-exchange has all the Jabbergrab courses: Feature Writing, and Advanced Advertising, Investments, Commercial Banking, Credits and Collections, Corporation Finance. The catalogue gives a list of commercial organizations which are called in to supervise various courses; for example, the course in business correspondence is under the patronage of the "Better Letters Association!"

The grand duke of this institution is Mr. E. L. Doheny, jr., whose father is the biggest oil magnate in the West, president of half a dozen bloated Mexican and California oil companies, of which Mr. Doheny, jr., is vice-president. Mr. Doheny, sr., boasts of owning the biggest private yacht in the world, and gives elaborate entertainments on this yacht, and has photographs of himself and his guests filling pages of our Sunday newspapers. Mr. Doheny has been vehement in support of intervention in Mexico, and fortunes of his money have been spent in intrigues to produce Mexican revolutions. Needless to say, therefore, he is deeply religious; appreciating the importance of all methods of holding down the masses, he gives a quarter of a million dollars to build a Catholic church, while his son is on the board of trustees of a Methodist "university."

The articles of incorporation of this institution provide that the trustees shall all be Methodists. They have a School of Religion, with a big foundation, and courses in such topics as "Personality in Missions," "Functions and Methods of Evangelism," and "The Pastoral Office under Modern Conditions"—which might be more briefly phrased as "How to Handle Doheny." As I write, the devout young Christian commercialists of this school engage in a mass riot with the students of the University of California's southern branch, and one of the students of the latter institution has the letters "U. C."—that is, University of California—branded on his forehead with nitric acid. This was supposed to have been done by the students of the rival institution; but investigation by detectives brought out the fact that it had been done by some of the student's own fellows. They did not like him, because he neglected student activities; also they wanted to discredit the University of Southern California, by putting the job off on it. You can learn everything at American universities—even the "frame-up"!

CHAPTER LXVIII

THE LARGE MUSHROOMS

America is half a continent, and its wealth is enormous, and there is a constantly increasing swarm of young people who want the social prestige which a college education gives. They have an opportunity to treat themselves to four years of pleasant idleness on papa's money, and they avail themselves of that opportunity. So all over the country spring up mushroom universities, swelling to unwieldy size, and making frantic efforts to accumulate traditions and reputation. We have visited a dozen of the great state universities, following our route along the Northern tier of states. To complete our survey we should also visit the prairie country, and see what this plutocracy of railroads and banks is doing to its young people.

Let us begin with the University of Nebraska, the dominant institution of the prairie country. This place contents itself with a small board of the big insiders— Mr. Hall, president of one of the largest banks in the state; Mr. Seymour, a banker of Elgin, and Mr. Landis, a banker of Seward; Mr. Judson, the largest retail merchant of Omaha, and Mr. Bates, wealthy rancher and insurance man. All of these gentlemen know money; they know nothing whatever about education, yet they guide the thinking of some eight thousand students. A study of promotions and salaries reveals the usual fact, that instructors who deal with commercial subjects have been advanced far beyond those whose humble task is the improving of the students' minds.

I am told of one professor who has been twenty years in the place, and who is a liberal, though in no sense a Socialist. Being a staunch believer in democratic institutions, he has criticized the anti-democratic elements in the university, and has been called into "conference" by those in control, and had the law laid down to him concerning his teachings. He has been held back upon what amounts to a starvation salary. Being an elderly man, he cannot make a change. Another, a professor of economics, a widely-known authority on matters of taxation, was appointed on a commission to study the revenue system of the state. He proved his competence so thoroughly that he was invited by the state legislature to appear before its committee on revenue and taxation, and give them the benefit of his knowledge. One of this man's colleagues describes to me what happened:

Back-stair influences were instantly mobilized. The professor was called into conference and warned not to meet with the committee, because it was not advisable for an instructor of the university to become involved in political questions. The professor insisted that he ought to give a law-making body the benefit of his own information. Suffice it to say, the professor never met with the committee, because it was hinted to him that dire consequences might follow. This man also is on a starvation salary.

Equally significant was the case of the gentleman who had charge of the dairy department of the University of Nebraska. The dairy business of Lincoln and vicinity is in the hands of a grasping corporation, which flagrantly adulterates its products; so the head of the dairy department conceived the idea of distributing the products of the College of Agriculture at a price much below that charged by the corporation. The dairy products of the university being genuine, there was great demand for them, and as my informant tells me, "the upshot of the competition on the part of the university led to a fight on the man who had charge of the dairy department, and ultimately resulted in his dismissal."

I explained my purpose to deal with "war cases" in this book, only when the war was used as a pretext to get rid of liberals. There was a series of such cases at the

University of Nebraska in 1918. Several professors were dismissed, but the records of the trial plainly show that they were dismissed because of economic unorthodoxy. One taught mathematics, and stated to the board of regents that he had not considered it his business to teach his students about the war. We have noted many cases of college professors being told that it is their duty to teach their specialty, and not meddle in public questions; now again we note that this rule applies only when they are advocating measures contrary to the interests of the plutocracy. When the plutocracy wants to go to war, then all professors have to teach war—even those who are supposed to be teaching mathematics!

An interesting demonstration of the policy of depriving college professors of their citizenship has just been given at the University of Oklahoma. Here is a state of oil speculators and starving tenant farmers. One of the products of their degradation is the squalid frenzy known as the Ku Klux Klan; and the board of regents has just issued a decree, declaring that the university must "keep the good-will of all factions and parties," and therefore members of the faculty are forbidden to take part in the controversy over the Klan. What this means is that they are forbidden to oppose it; I am told on good authority that the president of this board is a member of the Klan, as also the vice-president of the university, and about two-thirds of the faculty! The same decree forbids members of the faculty to take part in politics; but this does not interfere with five out of seven members of the board of regents being actively engaged in putting down the Farmer-Labor party by every means of intimidation and corruption.

Next let us glance at the University of Iowa, which has nearly six thousand students, and is controlled by the railroads which run this "rock-ribbed" Republican state. A member of the faculty writes me that its president is "politically a Harding Republican, and personally he has no curiosity about or sympathy with liberal thought of any kind. His attitude toward freedom of teaching in his faculty is a purely pragmatic one. Since his main job is to get funds from the state legislature, he does not propose to allow the 'indiscretions' of a professor to damage the cause of the university there. In

other words, a professor can say anything he wants to
in the class-room, if his students don't talk too much and
thus arouse sentiment in the state unfriendly to the university. An 'injudicious' remark might cost the university a half-million dollars in much needed appropriations." An excellent motto for this state of Iowa has
been composed by Ellis Parker Butler, as follows:

> "Three millions yearly for manure,
> And not one cent for literature."

Or take Ohio State University, with nine thousand
students. Here the president is a clergyman—"mission-
ary and pastor," he describes himself; also he is a coal
merchant and farmer, vice-president of a bank and president of an insurance company, and faculty committees
have to wait while he keeps his important business appointments. His professors are underpaid, and when
they get into debt, he doesn't increase their salaries, but
loans them money from his City National Bank at the
prevailing rate of interest. This, you perceive, offers a
quite unique method of controlling academic activities.
President Thompson, I am told, is frequently quite kind-
hearted to those who conform to primitive Calvinism in
their personal righteousness; but on the other hand, a
man who does not subject himself to the established order
is sternly disciplined—for his own good, of course, as
when a child is spanked. Ludwig Lewisohn was on the
faculty for six years, and tells me of one professor who
struggled many years to pay off a debt incurred for the
funeral of his wife; another, an excellent teacher and
scholar, who did not indulge in riotous living, but found
that with the increase of prices during the war his family
could hardly keep alive, delayed to pay a bill for a pair
of shoes, and the shoe store sent the bill to the president
of the university, and this guardian of the business proprieties fired the professor, stating that he "lacked integrity."

Lewisohn declares that at the faculty gatherings in this
university he never in his life heard a fundamental discussion of any subject; everything was "silence and
stealth." Another professor writes, describing the extreme patriotism prevailing: "A bugler plays taps every
Wednesday at convocation hour, and everyone is supposed

to stand still with bared head. The president is attended at all functions by his 'military staff.' All instructors must swear to an oath of allegiance in the presence of a notary before they can receive their salaries." This correspondent tells me how a member of the staff was forced out because he had separated from his wife; also how the "university pastors" on the campus are trying to establish a School of Religion, at state expense, and to get their courses listed for university credits. With a clergyman for president, this ought to be easy; especially when the president holds the opinion which President Thompson expressed in answer to a suggestion that his professors ought to have more opportunity to study and improve their education. He said that most of them held Ph. D. degrees, therefore their education was a closed matter, and their only duty henceforth was to teach, both in the regular session and in the summer schools!

A gentleman who was a member of President Thompson's faculty for more than ten years writes me about the place as follows:

"My personal difficulties were primarily with the head of the institution, who is a Presbyterian minister, a man who would not tell a lie, but a man whose word cannot be depended upon; very jealous, sensitive to criticism, apparently always your friend to your face and your bitterest foe to your back. My observation is that ninety per cent of the faculty at Ohio State are afraid to offend the president for fear he will make them suffer for it, either in failing to promote them or to raise their salaries. The result of this condition is a servile faculty that are working harder to have a good 'stand-in' with the president than they are to develop their subjects. I think another result of this condition is to make narrow-minded, selfish, self-seeking men. One of the reasons that prompted me to leave teaching was the little narrow-minded individuals with whom I was compelled to associate, men whose chief thought seemed to be, how can I get my salary raised. I am farming now, and I must say that I find the companionship of my cows and horses a great improvement over some of my associates in university circles."

CHAPTER LXIX

THE LITTLE TOADSTOOLS

So far we have been dealing with the great educational centres, which number their students in thousands and even tens of thousands; but for every one such institution there are scores of little places scattered over the country, with anywhere from a hundred to a thousand students each. In general, one can say concerning these little places that they try to be as much like the big places as possible. They get the local financial celebrities on their boards; they get the Gothic buildings with arrow-proof windows, and ivy of the quickest growing variety; they dress up their faculty in fancy robes, and their graduating students in caps and gowns; they have their fraternities and sororities, their full equipment of athletic teams and alumni boosters. And, just as in country villages you find more spying and more spite than in big cities, so in little colleges you find class greed and religious bigotry incessantly on the watch for any trace of a new idea.

To Beloit College, in Wisconsin, befell a singular fate—it got upon its faculty a young man of talent, who wrote a live novel. "Iron City," by M. H. Hedges, is a picture of life in a small college, located in a manufacturing town, and of the ferment of modern ideas trying to break into such a place. Mr. Hedges declares that he did not indicate Beloit especially, and has received many letters from professors in other college towns, saying that the cap fitted them. But the gossips of Beloit insisted upon riveting the cap upon their own heads, and there was a dreadful scandal.

Beloit is a town of twenty thousand inhabitants, its one big industry being the Fairbanks-Morse Manufacturing Company, the largest makers of scales in the world. Mr. Morse is the grand duke of the Beloit board, and has as his assistants Mr. Salmon, director of the Beloit Water, Gas & Electric Company, and Mr. Tyrrell, head of a great knitting works in an adjoining town; also a big Chicago wheat broker; the head of Montgomery Ward & Company; a great paper manufacturer; a leading Chicago insurance man; a local preacher; and a "special investigator" of the United States Department of Justice. So you see Beloit is fully equipped to install, not merely a college of commerce and a department of divinity, but also a school of spying.

With the publication of "Iron City" its secret service got to work immediately; I am told by one who was on the inside that three days after the book was out, one of the trustees called President Brannon on the telephone from Chicago, exclaiming: "I understand you have a novelist on your faculty. Why do you have people like that?" In less than a month the board of trustees had formally demanded Professor Hedges' resignation. President Brannon is a scientist, whom we saw kicked out of the University of Idaho by the mining kings; he had some liberal ideas when he came to Beloit five years ago. He liked his novelist, and tried to save him, calling him his best teacher; but the uproar was too great—the outraged townspeople stopped speaking to Professor Hedges and his wife on the street. Shortly after this, three liberal professors were driven from the institution, and the president pleaded for them also; it is said that he threatened to resign—but I note that they are gone, while he is still in office.

President Brannon had an interesting plan to remedy the housing shortage and improve the community spirit in this manufacturing town. He started a "chamber of commerce," for the purpose of constructing a million dollars' worth of homes on a co-operative basis, with the help of the labor unions. The banks, the utility company heads, and the Fairbanks-Morse people vigorously opposed the plan and tried to head it off; after it had got started they called up the local merchants and other members of the new "chamber of commerce" on the telephone, and ordered them to have nothing to do with so dangerous an undertaking, under penalty of loss of credit at the banks. So the "chamber of commerce" no longer exists.

There is peace now in Beloit and its college. The last danger passed when a student was expelled after publishing in the student paper a review of "The Brass Check"! The head of the local knitting works, one of the ultra-religious type of trustees, comes to the college and makes orations, being introduced as "a progressive

Christian employer"; whereas it is well known among the students that the white slave industry of the town is recruited from girls who cannot earn living wages in the knitting works.

These manufacturing towns are scattered over the Middle West, and they and their colleges are very much alike. Let us have a glimpse at Marietta College, in Ohio. The recent president of this institution was formerly editor-in-chief of the Chicago "Inter-Ocean," and championed the infamous Lorimer and the greedy Yerkes. A student with whom I talked was present in a class in sociology, to which President Hinman made the statement that preachers should not discuss social and civic problems. Some of the students took exception to this idea, and attempted to argue with him, whereupon he barred discussion in that class for the rest of the year. He fired a Y. M. C. A. secretary for the crime of having offered to a student a ticket to "Damaged Goods"—a play which had its opening performance in Washington, attended by President Wilson and his wife, and all the members of the cabinet and the Supreme Court.

The grand duke of this board was Mr. W. W. Mills, local traction magnate and capitalist, president of the First National Bank, interested in a cabinet company, a brick company, a bridge company, a chair company, a floral company, a paint company, and a street railway company. This versatile gentleman also controls the two newspapers of the town, and censors the proceedings of the state conferences of the Congregational church. His brother, also on the board, is director in the bank and president of the chair company. The rest of the board was made up of Mr. Mills' nephew, Mr. Rufus Dawes, a powerful millionaire of Chicago, president of a dozen different gas and electric companies; and his brother, Mr. Charles G. Dawes, president of the Central Trust Company of Illinois, and comptroller of the currency under President McKinley; a retired merchant, director in the Mills bank; a local railway attorney, related to the Mills; the president of the Mills paint company; the postmaster of the town, protégé of the Mills; an attorney for the Mills corporations; the pastor of the Mills church; a corporation lawyer, director in the Mills bank; and a retired minister, related by marriage to the Mills.

Professors Morse and Owens were let out of Marietta upon suspicion of liberalism, and in explaining the various reasons, the latter wrote: "Mr. John Mills expressed a sincere desire to wring my neck because I remarked at a dinner where he was present that the men in his mills are an unusually intelligent set." This referred to the chair company, in which conditions were especially terrible; there were cases of married men receiving as low as seven dollars a week in wages! Says Professor Owens:

We were urged to be Americans, and yet if we raised our wee small voice in favor of a wage that would enable the workers to live up to accepted American standards, we were at once regarded as dangerous anarchists. They were utterly blind to the fact that wages should be raised not only in the interest of justice but of efficiency. Repeatedly we stated that we were entirely willing to stand by each and every statement we had made. If we had lied we were willing to suffer the penalty. But we were denied every opportunity to present our view of the situation, denied a hearing which one of our by-laws said we were entitled to.

You remember Professor Bolley of the North Dakota Agricultural College, and his brave statement that a college professor is a citizen. For example, may a college professor become president of his local school board? Surely, yes!—you will say. But wait a moment; let me complete the sentence, "May a college professor become president of his local school board under a labor administration?" Well, now—of course—that depends!

At Rockford, Illinois, a manufacturing and commercial center, is a very exclusive college for young ladies, with a wonderful board of trustees, including a great agricultural implement manufacturer, another large manufacturer, and the widow of a third; the attorney for the town's principal industrial enterprise, also a large stockholder in the concern; the town's principal merchant, its principal lumber and fuel dealer, and the editor of its interlocking newspaper; a bank president, a steel manufacturer, a judge, and an ex-governor of the state of Illinois, a notorious corporation tool. May a professor in such a college accept any sort of office under a labor administration? Let us see!

President Maddox of Rockford College went in for

liberalism and the enlightening of the masses. He had got a very conscientious young teacher by the name of Seba Eldridge, and gave him a couple of impressive titles—"Head of the Social Science Department and Professor of Economics and Sociology." Professor Eldridge went out and did "social work," and presently the labor men of Rockford elected themselves a mayor, and this mayor appointed a school board. It would seem to have been of a representative character—a Catholic business woman of independent mind, a Socialist ex-teacher who was a good Methodist, a Swedish workingman, self-taught but of particular intelligence, a building contractor of large practical experience, and finally, as president of the board, Professor Seba Eldridge of Rockford College. Professor Eldridge had served on a local school board of New York City, and is author of two books, including a useful work on social legislation; the very man for the place, you would have thought. So thought the president of the college and the chairman of his board of trustees; and Professor Eldridge accepted the post.

But the business men of Rockford had still to be heard from! They had control of the board of aldermen, and they meant to smash this labor administration, so their aldermen rejected the board of education proposed by the mayor. Their newspapers fell to denouncing Professor Eldridge, and the big bankers made it plain that the city of Rockford could sell no school bonds until the board had a "business man" for its head. The interlocking trustees came round and interviewed the president, whereupon that gentleman suddenly changed his position, and withdrew his approval of Professor Eldridge's acceptance of the school board presidency. As the school board position paid no salary, and as the young professor had a family dependent upon him, he decided to let the mayor name a school board president who would be confirmed by the city council! He resigned from the college also and accepted a position elsewhere.

Mr. Fay Lewis, who lives in Rockford, has been kind enough to supply me with a file of newspaper clippings on this incident, which occurred in 1921. Among these clippings I find a curious illustration of the method by which the "Morning Star" of Rockford serves its interlocking directorate. There was a discussion before the

Rotary Club between the labor mayor of the town and a former president of the school board, representing the business men. The newspaper reports this discussion in full; that is to say, it quotes twenty-nine inches of what the representative of the plutocracy had to say, and two inches of what the labor mayor had to say in reply!

Also, I ought to give you a little glimpse into Williams College, at Williamstown, Massachusetts. It was originally established as an institution for poor boys. It has become the most exclusive country club in the United States, with the possible exception of Princeton. Like Brown University, it is a place of dry rot; the faculty is devoted to social life and respectability, and has been rewarded by Mr. "Barney" Baruch, who has established a summer school of politics for the purpose of promoting the "Bankers' International." The president of the University is Harry A. Garfield, son of a former president of the United States; and as I read the proofs of this book he rushes into the newspapers to set forth his ideas on the subject of a living wage. Unskilled workers, it appears, should not receive a living wage for their families, but only for themselves. Should the worker marry, the wife should help him to earn the household income until he educates himself out of the unskilled status—presumably by going to college and having President Garfield show him how!

P. S. to Third Edition.—I take this place in a much crowded book to insert an explanation which appears to be needed. I quote from a letter of my old professor, James Harvey Robinson:

I was astonished by the amount of material you managed to collect for "The Goose-step." And so far as I was able to check it up from personal knowledge it corresponded with my impressions. I have in press a little volume called "The Humanizing of Science," of which you will receive a copy before long. In it I refer to your book and Veblen's "Higher Learning" as the only ones that really deal with the actual controlling factors in our education. I was obliged to make a reservation or so in regard to your book, for I think that the policy of college presidents and trustees is a response to general unenlightened public opinion rather than a direct defense of particular economic interests. It may be the latter in some few instances. Some few trustees are just commonplace hysterical and panicky creatures. And they are just the ones who raise their voices in a crisis. Most of them are just "solid" citizens with the timidities and prejudices and ignorances of Main Street. Do you not think so? Good God man, I think education almost more of a farce than you appear to, but I cannot feel that the poor boobs who control it are worse than the generality of laity and clergy.

To this I replied as follows:

I have your letter, and I am certainly glad to know that you found "The Goose-step" interesting. I wouldn't expect you to agree with my point of view entirely; as a matter of fact, I think I agree with yours in this sense: I think that my point of view includes yours. I think that the stupidity to which you attribute college actions is an automatic product of the class point of view to which I attribute it. That is to say, I think that men's prejudices and preconceptions are the product in their minds and characters of the economic interests which have been operating upon them since the time they opened their eyes in the world. So they do certain things quite sincerely, believing that those are the right things to do, when as a matter of fact those things are merely the things which are advantageous and safe to them as the members of an economic group. Nearly everybody who reads my books gets the idea that I think that people act from definite conscious financial selfishness, but I don't mean that at all. I merely mean that their ideals and manners and customs and morals are all growths out of the soil of their class interests.

CHAPTER LXX

GOD AND MAMMON

I have tried in the closing chapters of "The Profits of Religion," and also in "The Book of Life," to make plain that I honor the religious impulse in its true form. But that does not mean that I owe respect to human systems which call themselves religious, and which make the spiritual needs of mankind a basis of enslavement. I can tolerate the business man who tells me that "money makes the mare go"; I can show him how, under a co-operative system, money would make the mare go faster. But I find it hard to tolerate those preachers of "personal righteousness," who keep the eyes of the working class uplifted to heaven, while their pockets are picked on earth; our modern Pharisees, who take the greatest of the world's proletarian martyrs, and bind him anew, and deliver him to be crucified upon a jewelled cross.

I make this explanation because we are now going

to have a glance at some of our "religious" colleges. Let us begin with Wooster, Ohio, an institution run by the Presbyterian church. We have seen how at Clark they are introducing a summer school, to make education pay; and we can see what that will end in, because the college of Wooster has for many years been run by its summer school: an absurdly crude, privately-owned, money-making institution, which draws schoolmarms by offering gold watches as prizes for those who bring in the greatest number of new students, and by advertising in terms of dollars and cents the amount of business done by its free teachers' agency. In country newspapers it advertises itself as "a School of Inspiration, Preparation and Perspiration." Fifteen hundred schoolmarms come each summer, and the local papers explain that they are "free with their expense accounts." The regular college, having only five hundred students, is relatively unimportant.

The active trustees, being local business men, naturally want to boost the summer school; whereas the faculty of the college have absurd notions of the dignity of true knowledge. Out of this grew a furious quarrel, which lasted for several years. The partisans of the summer school kicked out the excellent president of the college, who had spent sixteen years building it up from nothing. They brought in to replace him a shouting Y. M. C. A. evangelist of no college training, an utter ignoramus, and so many kinds of a liar that it would take the rest of this book to tell about it. The American Association of University Professors investigated the affair, and devoted a hundred and thirty-six pages to it, and the bulletin for May, 1917, is a study of the mental processes of a religious hypocrite, shouting about the love of Jesus, while stooping to every kind of vile and cowardly intrigue.

Also, while we are in Ohio, let us have a look at Muskingum College, at New Concord. We may see this through the eyes of Professor Arthur S. White, who was let out of the Department of Political Science and Sociology this year. The charge against him was that he had created "a critical attitude" among the students. The vice-president of the college charged him "with having taught the students to think, and that they were not thinking the right things." At the very beginning of his work, three years ago, he had explained to the students his dislike of "the compartment method of education," whereby students are crammed into a certain tight mold. "I remarked that such methods were destructive of personality, and must foster decay in our institutions. When I had finished the whole class applauded. At the end of the hour, some eight or ten waited to tell me that they were, and had been, victims of such methods, and that they hoped my work would be different." As a result of this, Professor White's classes in political science increased from twenty-seven to a hundred and forty-two.

There was no fault to be found with his character or personal conduct, nor is he a Socialist or propagandist of any sort. I quote again from his statement: "My method was to present all the facts on every question that were available; to analyze ideas, dogmas and institutions in the light of their original professions and accomplishments. I tried to respect the personality of my students, by insisting on their being free to make a conscientious choice of their loyalties." But, of course, this did not fit into a college whose dean phrased the duty of the faculty: "Our attitude toward the president should be that of the soldier to the general, it should be the attitude that he can do no wrong." Muskingum is a Presbyterian institution, and in order to get the financial support of the church, it advertises itself widely as a "safe" place for parents to send their children. Everything must be "in accordance with our tradition of ideals and customs." So, of course, the professor who taught his students to think had to move on.

Let us also move, to Meadville, Pennsylvania, where there is a little religious toadstool in the heart of the oil country, and with a Standard Oil board of trustees. On this Allegheny College we have a report of the American Association of University Professors, in the bulletin for December, 1917. The president (now president-emeritus) is a product of Judge Gary's Northwestern University, a Methodist clergyman, and trustee of the Carnegie Foundation. An alumnus who got to know him writes me: "Crawford is a man who has seemingly lost his moral perception, and throughout his stay at Allegheny was notoriously untruthful and untrustworthy." For fourteen years he had a professor of English literature by the name of Frank C. Lockwood, who was an ardent Prohibitionist, and came into conflict with the two local grand dukes of the board of trustees, political bosses and attorneys representing applicants for liquor licenses in Meadville. Professor Lockwood had the audacity to run for congress on the Prohibition ticket, with the backing of the Progressives; and, worse yet, although he himself was a Methodist minister, his wife joined the Unitarian church. The report does not make clear what the interlocking trustees expected the Methodist professor to do about this; they would hardly have been satisfied if he had divorced his wife for being a Unitarian; maybe they expected him to beat her until she reformed. Anyhow, the board adopted a resolution forbidding its professors to take part in politics by becoming candidates for public office; and, furthermore, it made clear its intention to drop Professor Lockwood at the end of the next year—so he quit. A college professor is not a citizen in Pennsylvania, any more than he is in Illinois!

Let us have a look at the prairie country, the "free state" of Kansas. At Washburn College, an institution of the Congregational church at Topeka, we shall again find the worship of God and Mammon perfectly blended. All the local plutocracy is represented on this board, and also a collection of clergymen, headed by the Reverend Charles M. Sheldon, famous throughout the Middle West as the author of "In His Steps." The president of Washburn is the Reverend Parley Paul Womer—I am aware this sounds like a novel, but it isn't. Washburn had been in financial need, and President Womer was called in as a "fund-raiser"; he being the perfect type of plutocratic piety, with knees calloused from constant worship before the altar of the Golden Calf.

His record also is set down in a report of the Association. We find him requiring one of his professors to promote a certain student, because his father was "a prominent and well-to-do man," and "had intimated that if Washburn would graduate his son he might do something handsome for the college in a financial way." We find him continually humiliating members of the faculty, by warning them not to do this and not to do that "which might conceivably be displeasing to any persons from whom we might hope for aid." We find him refusing all reforms in the way of faculty control, because "Washburn depends for its financial support on business men, men of large financial interests who would be quick to resent any appearance of Bolshevism in the administration of the college." We find him summarily discharging professors who opposed his combination of boot-licking and bullying, and then lying about these professors, and then asking that the committee of the Association should consider these lies to be "confidential"!

Finally, matters came to a head; more than half the faculty either resigned or were discharged, and the students rose up and began bombarding the pious president's house with rotten eggs. But did that make any difference to President Womer? It did not! The smell of rotten eggs evaporates quickly, but money endures, and he is the boy who gets the money. His interlocking trustees stood by him, and one month after the publication of the damning report of the Association, I find in the Topeka "Daily Capital" a front-page story about the culmination of President Womer's marvelous drive to raise the endowment of Washburn to eight hundred thousand dollars. He has raised three hundred and seventy-five thousand outside of Topeka, and three hundred thousand inside. Fifty thousand of this comes from Mr. Joab Mulvane, the grand duke of the city, and according to the newspaper, "the walls of the Chamber of Commerce shivered in the greatest uproar of applause they ever enclosed. . . . . President Womer received at last night's meeting a demonstration of cordial good-will and appreciation such as few public men hope for in a lifetime." "One of the greatest days in the history of Topeka," was Mr. Mulvane's own characterization of the event. There are two columns of this kind of rapture, with the names of all the donors and the "volunteer workers," and descriptions of parades, fireworks, dancing, brass-bands, and the singing of "Washburn pep songs."

Also the Methodists have their educational machine, and raise money from wealthy Methodists for the protection both of Methodism and of wealth. In the city of Washington they have a great central institution. An official of the United States Department of Education writes me:

I made a study of the American University in Washington not long ago. There are a number of wealthy men on the board.

They are obviously placed there for the usual purpose. Most of them never went to college themselves, and they know nothing about higher education in general or in particular. Now I saw no occasion to doubt their desire to do the best they know how for the institution. But some things they know about, from their associations, and others they do not. They simply cannot appreciate, for example, the fine zeal the founders had for the establishment of a great graduate university. They can see a considerable demand for education in law and business, and so they very naturally let the institution turn in this direction. Consequently a low grade law school and a lower grade business course are being established. The trustees can see some use in these courses and some demand. The need for a great graduate school, so patent to educators, the trustees are blissfully ignorant of, and I doubt very much whether on account of their limited educational experience they will ever be able to appreciate the need for such a graduate institution in Washington.

We move South to Durham, North Carolina, home of Trinity College, a considerable religious institution, founded by Washington Duke, the tobacco king. A friend of mine who knew the old gentleman tells me how he furnished his mansion, ordering the books for his library by the size and color of binding; and now his statue decorates a college grounds. The present head of the family is James B., locally known as "Buck" Duke, and it would be a poor pun to describe him as the Grand Duke of Trinity College. He and his brother, Mr. B. N. Duke, his wife, his son and his daughter, have all purchased the good will of North Carolina Methodism by making public gifts to Trinity, amounting to four million dollars; all three of the male Dukes are therefore on its board of trustees. James B. has just given a million to the endowment, fifty thousand towards a new school for religious training, and other sums for gymnasium and law building. So I note in the Greensboro "Daily News" an editorial headed: "The Duke Also Has Virtues."

Forty years ago "Buck" Duke could not borrow ten thousand dollars in North Carolina; today he boasts that he is worth four hundred million, beside what his father and brother have accumulated. Assuming that his services in providing the world with tobacco were worth a hundred dollars a week, it would have taken a hundred and fifty-four thousand years to earn his own share of this money. "Buck" is distinguished among interlocking trustees in that he has had a decision of the United

States Supreme Court on his money-making methods; the exact words are that he "persistently and continuously and consciously violated the law." The Supreme Court has not yet passed on the fact that a man who is worth four hundred million dollars pays only eight hundred and twenty-eight dollars taxes in the state where he lives in a magnificent palace!

The Methodist church is, as we know, violently opposed to the use of tobacco, but it applies the ancient saying of one of the Roman emperors, Pecunia non olet—money has no smell. Mr. Duke completed his purchase of the church by a so-called donation for the support of its superannuated ministers, and so his right to run both church and university is undisputed. He brought in a South Carolina minister of pliant principles, and made him president of the university, and this president never lost an occasion to chant the praises of his grand Duke. The grand Duke had this chief chanter made a director of his Southern railroad, and wanted to have him made also a bishop of the church, but for three successive years he failed; then he hired some regular lobbyists and sent them to the Methodist General Conference—and that was the way to do it. "Pecunia non olet"; and also, "pecunia parlat"; and also, "pecunia ambulare equinam fecit!"—if you will let me fix up the Latin.

CHAPTER LXXI

THE ORANG-OUTANG HUNTERS

There is a part of the United States which suffered for a century or two under the blight of Negro slavery; in consequence, from Virginia to Texas, the population still lives in the ideas of a hundred years ago. Here are communities which are not content to use religious dogmas as a shield for special privilege; they really believe the dogmas, and are willing to fight about them and to torture one another, as in the old days. In these states there has sprung up what is called the "Fundamentalist" movement, made up of seventeenth century Cromwellians in modern machine-made clothing; the only difference being that whereas the old Pilgrims wished to "come out from among them," the idea of these modern fanatics is to drive out the other fellow. They are carrying on an enormous campaign in the evangelical churches, seeking to keep out of the pulpits people who do not believe in the literal inspiration of Scripture—in Noah's ark, and Jonah and the whale, and Joshua blowing down the walls of Jericho; also in the virgin birth, and the six-day creation of man. They are especially indignant against "evolution," which means to them one thing, that man is descended from the monkey—something it does not mean to any scientist.

The leader of this new fanaticism is no less a personage than the Honorable William Jennings Bryan, the Peerless Commoner, who, having made several hundred thousand dollars out of lecturing, is not so keen for the breaking of the money power, but gives his time to the preserving of the ignorance of his forefathers. Mr. Bryan has used his enormous prestige with the legislatures of the Southern states; he came within one vote of putting through the Kentucky legislature a bill providing that no public appropriations should be used for salaries of employes who teach Evolution or Darwinism. Incredible as it may seem, he succeeded in putting through such a measure in the states of South Carolina and Oklahoma, and he expects to make a tour of the legislatures this winter and try with others.

These reactionaries are busy in all the Southern colleges, plying their brooms against the tide of modern thought. They succeeded in driving Professor Wheeler from the University of Mississippi, and Professor Rice from the Southern Methodist University at Dallas, Texas. Also they are strong among the Baptists, and at Waco, Texas, they have got possession of a large school called Baylor University. This place had a professor of sociology, G. S. Dow, who devoutly believed in his Baptist faith, and earnestly protested that he did not teach that "man came from another species"; but he published a text-book, "Introduction to the Principles of Sociology," in which he used some phrases of modern science, and the howling dervishes of Texas took it up. In Fort Worth is a Baptist preacher, who publishes a paper called the "Searchlight," and has grown rich out of waging war upon modern thought; in what delicate language his controversies are carried on you may judge from one sentence, referring to the expulsion of Professor Rice:

"While the Methodists have put their orang-outang out, we are keeping ours in!"

I really felt sorry for Professor Dow, as I read over a mass of clippings concerning his trouble; he is such a humble and patient Christian gentleman! But, you see, in his book he actually made reference to "primitive man," and we all know there was no such beast; says the "Searchlight": "Those of us who read our Bibles have always thought that he was made in the image of God." So Professor Dow was forced to resign, and he stayed resigned, in spite of indignant protests of his students.

The Baptists of Texas appointed a committee, which went about in these educational institutions, submitting to every instructor a questionnaire, and forcing the resignation of several who were too honest in their confessions. They held a "pastors' and laymen's conference," in which they laid down "uncompromising opposition to the teachings of Darwinian evolution, and the substitution of social service for regeneration." Reading their literature is to a modern man like having a nightmare; it takes you back three hundred years in human history, when they burned witches at the stake, and tore men to pieces on the rack. In Texas now they burn only Negroes; but the wretched, half-starved, rack-rented tenant-farmers and their wives are victims of the most degrading sort of terrors. In one issue of the "Searchlight" I find a portrait of a maniac with a big black moustache, cavorting with clenched fists on a platform, and advertised as "the man who preaches sin black, hell hot, life short, death certain, eternity long, and calls sinners to a blood-bought redemption."

In "The Profits of Religion" I have pictured the "Bootstrap-lifters," with their eyes uplifted to heaven while the agents of the Wholesale Pickpockets' Association are robbing them on earth. Just so it is with the "Fundamentalists"; while they were getting the professor of evolution fired from the Southern Methodist University, the public utility interests of Texas, camouflaged as the "Texas Public Service Information Bureau," have been poisoning the minds of the students. They have contrived a course of lectures, to be given by expert public utility pickpockets—the general manager of the telephone company, the president of the power and light

company, the general manager of the traction company—
so on through a long list.

Also these Fundamentalists are active in Tennessee,
where they brought destruction to an old friend of mine,
a thoroughly trained scientist and most humane and
charming gentleman, who was director of hygiene and
physician at the state university. They were cordial to
him in the first weeks, until he began attending the
Unitarian church; then a pillar of the rich Baptist church
in Knoxville refused to donate to the "Y" work at the
university "so long as they had Unitarians on the faculty."
In the hope of forcing my friend to withdraw, the president and dean proceeded to make him unpopular by requiring all freshmen to take a course of two hours a week
in "personal hygiene" with him—and receiving no credit
for the course! Still, the professor made a success of it,
and more students came to him for treatment than he
could handle; so last spring he was unceremoniously
dropped.

At Bethany, West Virginia, is a college of the religious body who call themselves the "Disciples of Christ,"
or "Christians"—to distinguish themselves from Baptists
and Methodists and Presbyterians and other kinds of
heathen. This institution is described as "a literary,
moral and religious school," and it now has some five
hundred students, and thirty or forty members of the
faculty. They got a young professor by the name of
Croyle, in the "Chair of Hebrew and Old Testament,"
and they kept him less than a year, and then summarily
fired him without notice. The professor put the case in
the hands of the American Association of University
Professors, which wrote to the president of the college
and proposed an investigation. The president's name is
Cramblet—again I have to explain that I do not make
these things up. President Cramblet replied to the effect
that he and his college did not want any interference
from professors' associations. "For the present we are
quite sure that we can make our own rules and conduct
our own affairs better than some people who are not able
to take care of their own business."

It is interesting to follow this story and watch the
slow process of the opening up of this religious hard shell.
It took the Association about a year and a half to do the

job; they kept boring away—a little publicity here and a threat of publicity there—until finally President Cramblet popped open and wrote a long letter, explaining the crimes of Professor Croyle, and agreeing to meet a committee of the Association and prove his charges. It appeared that Professor Croyle had come from the Union Theological Seminary, with his mind full of what in the West Virginia mountains is known as "destructive criticism." In one of his classes he had explained that maybe the story of God's plan to drown everybody in the world except Noah and his family was not to be taken quite literally; that night President Cramblet was called to the girls' dormitory, "because a number of them were weeping and well-nigh hysterical over this experience!"

It is interesting to note that the Professors' Association does not attempt to insist that church colleges shall maintain any standards of freedom of teaching or of thinking. All it lays down is that "church colleges should fully and unequivocally inform the public and their professors of all restrictions that their tenets impose upon academic freedom." And it notes that this "Christian" college has now taken out of its catalogue the statement that "Bethany seeks the latest and best results of modern scholarship," and that "the latest results of archeology are used in an attempt to understand the vitality of the Prophetic Activity!"

I close this chapter with the singular adventure of my friend, Harry Laidler, who went a few years ago to lecture at Emory and Henry College, one of the oldest institutions in Virginia. Laidler was secretary of the Intercollegiate Socialist Society, and the students had asked to hear him, and the president had consented. It chanced, however, that an itinerant preacher was present that morning, and he strongly disapproved of a Socialist lecture, and took occasion to save the students from the consequences of their wayward curiosity. He took the platform, and lifted his hands in invocation to the Almighty, imploring Him to protect these young minds from the heresies and false doctrines to which they were about to be exposed!

CHAPTER LXXII

THE ACADEMIC POGROM

It is natural that in a time of reaction such as the present, every form of organized cruelty and hatred should lift its ugly head; and so we have in our colleges not merely campaigns of religious bigotry, but also of race prejudice.

We know the ideal American college student. He comes from our best families, his figure is tall and straight, and his features regular and blank, according to the Gibson standard. He is perfectly groomed, in the Arrow collar and the Kuppenheimer clothes and the Brogue boot. He has always had plenty of servants to wait on him, so he does not know how to work. He is thoroughly skilled, however, in every form of play, and has been raised in a system of conventions which constitute "good manners." He comes to college to spend the four pleasantest years of his life in the company of his social equals. His father and big brothers before him have belonged to the right clubs, and are prominent in the alumni association. He goes in for athletics, and for the glee club, and gets a fraternity pin and a big Y, or whatever letter it may be, on his sweater; he becomes a leader of his class and a social favorite, and takes the college girls to dances in his big car, and now and then he takes one of the town girls out into the country on summer evenings, or to a road-house in winter. He is an expert in smoking tobacco, and connects up with the best university boot-legger—but all quietly, of course, and nothing to excess, except on football nights and special occasions.

There is only one thing wrong with this four years of paradise, and that is a lot of fool pedants and book-worms, who think they have something to do with running the college, and worry a fellow to death stuffing his head with old Anglo-Saxon roots and mathematical formulas, names and dates of dead kings and battles, and peculiarities of French and Greek irregular verbs. The young gentleman in college regards these pedants as his natural enemies, and the outwitting of them as one of his entertainments. If you have plenty of money you can hire sharp fellows to study examination papers and work out the science of "getting by," and two weeks before examinations you shut yourself up in your room, with a wet towel about your head and a pot of strong coffee on your desk, and you cram your mind with the necessary mass of facts, and so you pass. You understand the unwritten law of colleges—just as the old French marquis understood the heavenly system, when he said that God would think twice before he damned a gentleman like him. Make yourself a power in athletics and in social life, and pay a certain minimum debt to the thing called "learning," and you may be sure that no member of the faculty will have the insolence to "flunk" you. Such is American college life today, and when we read in college journals and in the capitalist press about the preservation of Anglo-Saxon traditions in our institutions of higher education, that is what we are talking about.

But now along come a lot of fellows—and worse, a few girls as well—whose features lack the regular vapidity of the Gibson type, but on the contrary, have been distorted by suffering and struggle. These people have for the last two thousand years been an oppressed race, and they display the painful qualities which oppression causes in human beings. Sometimes they cringe, and again, when they get power they may become insolent. For two thousand years they have survived in the world by two qualities, racial and religious solidarity, and commercial shrewdness. We in America are full of the raptures of dollar-getting; but here is a people who can make two dollars while we are making one, and can save ten dollars while we are squandering a hundred. Being people who have had to make their own way in the world, they are apt to be pushing and thick-skinned; they sometimes come where they are not wanted, and do not always take a hint to leave.

They try to break into "society"; that is, having acquired wealth, they assume they are entitled to the perquisites of wealth. But we bar them from our dinner-parties and our clubs, and sometimes from our hotels. Naturally their sons and daughters turn their eyes upon our colleges; and here is an atrocious situation. These institutions have established no social tests, but have left

24

their doors open for anyone who can pass an examination.
And these people take advantage of us—they actually
expect to break in among our sons and daughters, just
by learning more than our sons and daughters know!
That is easy for them, you understand; not being admitted
to fraternities and glee clubs, they have nothing better
to do than to sit in their rooms and read and study.
And what chance do our "Gibson types" stand against
such a proposition? They stand no chance whatever;
and so the Jews carry off the honors and the prizes—actually, if things were allowed to go on, they would become members of the faculty, and we should be sending
our future Anglo-Saxon conquerors to be taught by
Jewish scientists and men of letters!

Such is the problem faced by our interlocking
trustees and their faculties; it is an embarrassing problem, because, in the first place, the Jews are enormously
wealthy, and they stand together, and have not merely
financial but political power. Also, they take pride in
their culture; they point out that they gave the world
its first great literature, and have given to Anglo-Saxon
countries practically everything in the way of religion
which these countries consider divine. They have contributed their due share of scientists and writers and
statesmen of modern times; also they have given to the
world the religion of the future, through the labor of
Marx and Lassalle, Jaurès and Liebknecht.

In the light of these varied facts, we cannot come
out boldly and say that we refuse to admit Jews to
our universities; we find it easier to employ those peculiar talents for prevarication which our college heads
have developed. We invent what are called "psychological tests"; we fill our examination papers with "catch"
questions—little details of language idiom and social ob-
servance and historical tradition, with which the Jews
are less apt to be familiar. Or we conduct oral examinations, concerning which there are no records, and therefore no proofs of prejudice. By these means, in a
couple of years we cut down the percentage of Jews at
Columbia from forty percent to twenty-two percent, and
at New York University we cut it down from fifty percent to fifteen.

Our really aristocratic university, Princeton, has never

"made any bones" about it. Very few Jews and no Negroes have been able to pass the "examinations" for admission to Princeton. At Harvard it has always been possible to get in by passing a much stricter examination; but even by this method the percentage of Jews keeps creeping up, and when I was in Harvard last spring they were talking about introducing the "psychological tests," as at Columbia. One student reported a conversation with Richard Cabot, professor of "social ethics," who said that he did not object to the exclusion of Jews, but thought it should be done frankly. His idea prevailed among the overseers, and shortly afterwards a statement was issued which gives an amusing illustration of what Harvard regards as frankness. The statement set forth that there were more applicants for admission than Harvard was able to accommodate, and the governing body must take some action in the matter. Then: "It is natural that with a widespread discussion of this sort going on there should be talk about the proportion of Jews at the college." In the course of the "discussion" that followed, we find President Lowell deploring the growth of anti-Semitic feeling, and suggesting a marvelous plan to eliminate it from American colleges—let the Jews keep away!

And then the Negro question. They have a Memorial Hall at Harvard, and make much of their heroes who died to abolish Negro slavery. I have a cousin who went to Harvard twenty years ago, and though he is a Southern man, he was able to live comfortably in a dormitory in which there was a Negro student. But a year or two ago a student engaged a room in a freshman dormitory, and went to occupy it, and when they made the discovery that he was a Negro, they told him that a mistake had been made, they had no room vacant in that dormitory, or in any other dormitory. Not until they had been exposed several times in such evasions, did they come forward and announce that in future no Negroes would be admitted to freshman dormitories at Harvard.

We have mentioned New York University. During the controversy over Jews at Harvard, Chancellor Brown favored the press with the proud announcement that there was no discrimination against Jews at Jabbergrab; and a week or two later there was published in the "Nation"

(July 12, 1922) a letter from Mr. Joseph Girdansky, who made a reputation as an athlete at this place, telling about the experience of his younger brother, also an athlete, and presumably acceptable to his fellow students, since he was elected president of the junior class. When this result was announced, the faculty of Jabbergrab rose up and called off the election. First, it appeared, the officers elected were Bolshevists; second, there had been ballot-stuffing; and third, fourth and fifth, the elections were null and void. Several Jewish boys were threatened with expulsion for having been elected to class offices!

Mr. Girdansky went on to tell about his interview with Dean Archibald Bouton of Jabbergrab. This was two or three years ago, and the dean quite frankly admitted that it was a Jewish question. In the elder Girdansky's day, said the dean, the percentage of Jews had been from two to four, while now it had got to fifty. So the university was introducing what it called an "Americanization plan." Mr. Girdansky threatened to expose this state of affairs— right in the midst of Chancellor Brown's advertising campaign for funds! The dean begged him to wait until the fall, promising that the class elections would be settled satisfactorily. They were settled by a great number of the Jewish students leaving, and new class officers being elected, or appointed by the faculty—all the important ones being non-Jews!

At Barnard, which is the women's college of Columbia University, they have a committee on admissions, which in actual practice means the dean and the secretary, who decide upon the eligibility of girls who have passed the examinations. Highly competent graduates of New York high schools are left out, because they happen to be Jewesses; and in their place girls are taken from the fashionable "finishing schools," who are so poor in scholarship that they have to be conditioned. I was told of one case of a Russian Jewish girl who had been excluded and went to Hunter College and made a brilliant record. There was some agitation about this case, and the dean sent someone to look it up, and the report was that "keeping her out was a good job." The teacher who told me this story was interested in the matter, and went over to Hunter College herself to find out what was wrong about the girl. There were two things the matter with her:

first, she was a Socialist, and second, she had expressed her opinion in favor of the recognition of Soviet Russia.

Also at the University of Pennsylvania the issue has been taken up. The endowment drive was held up because the leaders wished to engraft upon it the verbal pledge to anti-Semitic contributors that Jewish enrollment would be curtailed. One seminary course at the university during the past year was largely devoted, under cover, to sounding out the views of the graduate students in economics upon the Jew menace. It was freely stated in that course that desire to reduce the high percentage of Jews in the Wharton School was the motive prompting the "intelligence test" requirement for admission.

Needless to say, the academic pogrom extends not only to students, but to professors. You may find this situation effectively set forth in a vital criticism of America, "Up Stream," by Ludwig Lewisohn. Mr. Lewisohn tells how he studied under the aegis of Nicholas Murray Butler, and made himself a master of English literature and English style. You do not have to take his word for this; he proves it in his book. Few indeed are the Anglo-Saxon professors in American universities who can demonstrate equal attainments! This German-Jew was poor, his family had made heavy sacrifices to give him an education; but he could get no teaching position, and for a long time the Columbia professors who had charge of his career kept from him the dark secret, that Jews are not employed to teach literature in American universities. Lewisohn was forced to do newspaper work, and not until years later did he get a chance to teach at the University of Wisconsin.

Also you ought to hear the experience of Professor Kornhauser of Denison University, at Granville, Ohio. He taught zoology, and was admitted to have one of the best departments in this Baptist institution; he was an active Y. M. C. A. worker, president of the Faculty Club, and commander of the American Legion post—it is difficult to see what more a Jew might do to take the curse off himself! He was offered an important position at the Battle Creek Sanitarium, and as the price of declining this, was made a full professor at Denison, and spent three years building up his department. But last April the president of the university asked him to resign, and stated as his reason that some of the financial supporters of the university objected to the presence of a Jew on the faculty. The students protested, and in the effort to silence them the president threatened that if they published anything about the case he would refuse to recommend Professor Kornhauser for a job at any other university. The senior class, by a vote of eighty to six, passed a resolution asking for the president's removal.

Also you should consider the experience of Professor Robert T. Kerlin, a high-minded and devoted Christian gentleman, who was dismissed from the Virginia Military Institute for having written a dignified open letter to the governor of Arkansas, protesting against the execution of some Negroes for the crime of having defended their lives against a mob. You may read his letter in the files of the "Nation," June 15, 1921.

And then, to return to the Jews, hear the strange experience of Mr. S. S. Catell, who was an instructor in accounting at the University of Oklahoma. Mr. Catell happens to be near-sighted, and was turned out upon the pretext that he was unable to teach properly on this account. He sent a questionnaire to his students, and out of a total of forty-nine, thirty said that his work was above the average, while eighteen said it was average; one was absent and did not reply. But this did not get Mr. Catell restored, and so he investigated, and discovered that the head of his department did not like Jews. The way in which the young instructor made this discovery would seem sufficiently convincing to anyone. He met the head of his department in the hallway of the latter's home, and the department head put to him a question: "Do you know who killed Jesus Christ?" Mr. Catell, in his letter to me, says that he contented himself with the answer: "I do not know, since it was so long ago!"

If I were a cultured Jew in America, I know what I should do. I should not flatter the race conceit of Anglo-Saxon colleges; I should make it my task to persuade wealthy Jews to establish an endowment and gather a faculty of Jewish scientists and scholars—there are enough of them to make the most wonderful faculty in the world. And then I should open the doors of this university to seekers of knowledge of all races—save that I should bar students who had anti-Semitic prejudice!

CHAPTER LXXIII

THE SEMI-SIMIAN MOB

Race prejudice is merely one side of the many-sided snobbery of college life. The college is the collective prestige of a mob of socially superior persons, and each and every one of them is interested to protect that prestige. I asked one of the most eminent of American scientists, a man who has lived most of his life in universities, what is the matter with these institutions, and his answer came in an explosion: "It is the semi-simian mob of the alumni! They have been to college for the sake of their social position; they have gone out utterly ignorant, and made what they call a success in the world, and they come back once a year in a solid phalanx of philistinism, to dominate the college and bully the trustees and the president."

"You don't think it's the president's fault, then?" I asked, and the answer was: "It is the alumni, that semi-simian mob!"

The problem of who is to blame, the president or the alumni, is like the ancient question: "Which comes first, the hen or the egg?" The president makes the alumni, and the alumni make the president, and the vicious circle continues ad infinitum. The alumnus who counts is the "successful son," and he values in his college those qualities which have enabled him to succeed. The college is to him a place where he can be sure of having his son made into the same admirable thing he knows himself to be. The college is an insurance agency for the business and social prosperity of his progeny. When he has got the youngsters into Groton, and then into Harvard, and finally into the Harvard Club, they will have made so many affiliations that nothing can hurt them; there will always be "openings," desirable friendships, quick promotions, favors and honors: there will be rich girls to choose from, a welcome in homes of luxury.

The college is to the alumnus a place in which he has invested four years of his life, and he wants to keep up the value of that investment. He welcomes everything which enhances that value—football victories, for example, which fill the columns of the newspapers, and enable him to swell out his chest and remember that he is a son of "Old Eli." On the other hand, if there are stories in the newspapers that his college has become a "hot-bed" of some kind, that is a humiliation, that is a diminution of his prestige; he calls up the president and trustees on the telephone, and wants to know what the hell does this mean?

College is the place in which the alumnus spent the happiest years of his life; it is the center of pleasant memories, about which to grow sentimental. He goes back to renew old friendships, to sing old songs, to feel tears in his eyes, delicious emotions stirring his bosom. And just as a shrewd mother of many daughters employs their charms and exploits the weaknesses of the male animal, so the college "alma mater" utilizes the tender emotions of her "old boys" to separate them from their cash. I have before me a begging circular of Yale University, got up in the best style of the schools of advertising, attractively printed in two colors on tinted paper. "Yale's power lies partly in your hands," we are told in red ink; and then in black ink: "An Endowment to Yale: Yourself. Interest on the Endowment: Whatever you can afford each year."

And when the time comes for a "drive," these herd emotions are whipped up to frenzy. We learned these tricks in the war days, and immediately after the war the colleges with one accord started to apply the technique: class quotas and sectional quotas, "follow-up" letters and daily "dope" for the press; the members of the faculty shutting their books and turning into "gladhanders"; "prexy" making speeches to the Rotarians and the Kiwanis and the Elks, and proving himself a "mixer." In 1920 I find Northwestern setting out after twenty-five millions, Pittsburgh after sixteen, Harvard fifteen, Princeton fourteen, Cornell ten, followed by Boston University, New York University, Oberlin, Bryn Mawr, Massachusetts Tech—a total of more than sixty institutions, demanding over two hundred millions of dollars. I have no objection to colleges getting money; I am merely pointing out the price of money in a class civilization—which is conformity to class ideas and ideals.

One of the most entertaining stories I heard on my tour of the colleges was told by a young congressman of the modern college type, who was graduated from one of the "little toadstools" in the Middle West. He is a handsome fellow, and made a reputation as a quarter-back, and was selected by his alumni association to lead a campaign for funds for a group of colleges which had combined together—Beloit, Ripon and Lawrence, all in Wisconsin. It was his duty to travel from city to city throughout the state; he would summon the "old boys," and rout out the football squads, and lecture at the Y. M. C. A.s, and call on the clergymen of the town for the names of the likely "prospects"; he would visit the homes of the rich, and make tennis dates with the sons, and take the daughters driving. All his expenses were paid; he was provided with the latest sport costumes, and automobiles without limit. He would be invited to dinner-parties, where he would talk about the institution, awakening tender memories in the bosom of the "old boy," and literally "vamping" him. He was furnished with a supply of fraternity pins, which he allowed the girls to extract from his necktie; needless to say, he was many times engaged. Sometimes, he told me, he even stooped to kiss the babies. He came back in triumph, with a total of three hundred thousand dollars to his credit. And one of his crowd made an even greater success—he not merely got engaged, but got married to the daughter of a multi-millionaire wheat speculator; the bride gave real estate and money to the institution, so the bridegroom's share of the loot was not begrudged him.

You thought perhaps I was exaggerating when I portrayed the childish pleasure of the oil king in his Gothic buildings, with crenellated battlements and moated draw-bridge. But that is the precise and calculated purpose of these trappings; they are part of the vamping equipment—they create an atmosphere and a glamour, they set the college apart from wholesale haberdashery, or hardware, or whatever may be the "line" of the successful son. This is the purpose of the ivy and the college songs, the sheepskins and gold seals, the gowns and mortar-boards and solemn processions. I have before me the picture section of the New York "Times," showing the installation of the new president of Yale. It is only a photograph, but if an artist had composed a picture of college flummery he could not have done better. In the background are the venerable buildings, with ivy-covered walls, memorial tablets, and huge iron gates; and here comes a procession, headed by a solemn young official in a long black night-gown, carrying a huge drum-major's baton, covered with filigree like a bridal cake—a mace of office, no doubt copied from the one used in the House of Commons. Behind him stride the outgoing president and the incoming president—a pair who might be labeled, like the patent medicine advertisements, "Before and After Taking." "Before Taking" you are a fairly capable and intelligent looking human male, but "After Taking" you have a large mouth, with jaw hanging down, and an expression of withered imbecility; in both cases you wear gorgeous colored robes, and immediately behind you, in frock-coat and silk hat, walks the grand duke of your board, grim-faced, solemn, and paunched. Next come half a dozen army officers, then a long double file of scholars in caps and gowns, the faculty, carefully ordered according to the amount of their salaries. On each side stand the rows of graduating students in their black nighties, their heads respectfully bared, their hands folded across their tummies.

This kind of monkey-business goes on once or twice a year in every American college and university. There is no "toadstool" so small that it does not hasten to get up such a performance, and to contrive itself a set of "traditions." There is none big enough or mature enough to put away childish things, to dispense with the tinsel and gold lace of the scholastic life. At Harvard they have a solemn commencement day parade, with the House of Morgan and the House of Lee-Higginson all in top hats and swallow-tail coats—the only sign of a sense of humor being that they forbid the taking of photographs! At Columbia, Nicholas Miraculous appears in a rakish tam-o'-shanter, which is of almost infinite dignity, because it signifies that he has not been content with a baker's dozen of honors from up-start American universities but has received the supreme academic accolade from Oxford.

We have heard the statement that "colleges grow by degrees." There is no law regulating the distribution of fancy names, and they serve just as peerages and lesser titles serve in England—to get campaign funds for the gang in office. Through the pages of "Who's Who in America" they are scattered as if with a pepper-box, and a study of them is an amusing revelation. Pick out the leading old tories in the United States, the blind leaders of the blind who have almost tumbled our country into the ditch; you will find everyone of them with a string of academic dignities tacked to his name. William Howard Taft has nine, Charles E. Hughes eleven, Woodrow Wilson ten, Leonard Wood nine, Henry Cabot Lodge nine, William C. Sproul nine, Robert Lansing six, Elihu Root sixteen, Herbert Hoover twenty-four. On the other hand, think of the men who have been struggling all their lives to make this country a little bit of a democracy: take the very truest and bravest of them—how many honorary degrees have they? How many has Louis D. Brandeis? Not one! How many has Robert M. LaFollette? Not one! How many have William E. Borah, Samuel Untermyer, Clarence Darrow, Lincoln Steffens, Fremont Older, Frederick C. Howe, John Haynes Holmes? Not one to divide among them!

No, the academic honors are reserved exclusively for the darlings of the plutocracy, the henchmen and retainers of special privilege. You remember the pious Senator Pepper, trustee of the University of U. G. I. Six colleges have honored him—including, of course, his own. Three honored Philander C. Knox before he died, and six honored Thomas Nelson Page. Four have honored David Jayne Hill, Col. George Harvey, Alton B. Parker and Frank O. Lowden; three have honored Judge Gary and A. Mitchell Palmer, two have honored Otto Kahn, four have honored Brander Matthews—including, of course, Columbia. We saw Columbia conferring a degree upon Paderewski; they also conferred one upon Miller, editor of the New York "Times," of whom Brisbane caustically remarked that the paper had been sold several times, and he had been sold along with it. Senator Depew, the aged buffoon, has one, Howard Elliott has one, Augustus Thomas has one; Owen Wister got one from the University of U. G. I., and Booth Tarkington one from Princeton—a little wee one, he being a mere writer of novels.

It is at the commencement ceremonies that these honors are bestowed; and always the president makes a speech, telling the great one how great he is. Sometimes the great one also delivers an address, and furnishes a copy to the newspapers in advance, and so the university becomes a center of propaganda for every form of class greed and cruelty. In the spring of this year, while I was touring the colleges, Judge Gary fed his pious poison to the graduating class at the University of Heaven. At the University of the Steel Trust they gave degrees to the president of Indiana University, and to an Episcopal clergyman, and to the chairman of the board of directors of the Standard Oil Company—a gentleman we met as one of the grand dukes of Brown University. "This highest honor of the university is appropriately bestowed upon Mr. Bedford in recognition of his activities in the development of the American petroleum industry," etc. At the Pennsylvania Military College degrees were conferred upon Secretary of War Weeks and the pious Senator Pepper. Mr. Weeks is described by the "Literary Digest" as "a banker and broker of high standing in private life," and he takes the occasion to give a boost to the liquor lobby, and recommend to these budding soldier-boys the return of Bacchus to America.

And while I am revising my manuscript for the printer, the college hordes reassemble, and the college orators remount the rostrum, and the broadcasting stations go into action. The world is informed by the president of Dartmouth College that too many students are trying to get an education in America, there is no use wasting our time on any but superior minds. And a few days later the new head of Colgate University, Dr. George Barton Cutten, repeals the Declaration of Independence and overthrows the political theories of Washington, Jefferson and Lincoln. Democracy is a delusion, "founded on a mistaken theory," and more than ever we must look to be ruled by aristocracy. "Manhood suffrage has been our greatest and most popular failure, and now we double it by granting universal suffrage."

With exceptions so few as to be hardly worth mentioning, the rule holds good that everywhere, in every issue involving a conflict between the people and special privilege, the universities and colleges are on the side of special privilege. In the San Francisco graft prosecutions the University of California was almost unanimous

in support of the grafters, so much so that when Rudolph
Spreckles and Francis J. Heney entered the University
Club in San Francisco, every man in the room would get
up and leave. On the other side of the continent the Harvard alumni machine fought almost to a man against the
appointment of Brandeis to the Supreme Court; and for
twenty-nine years this machine has voiced its political
ideals in the United States Senate through Henry Cabot
Lodge.

At the risk of boring you, I am going to take you to
just one of the meetings of these Harvard alumni. It is
a dinner, the fortieth anniversary of the class of 1881,
held in the University Club of Boston, June 22, 1921.
The principal speaker is a distinguished member of that
class, Mr. Howard Elliott, C. E. of Harvard, and LL. D.
of Middlebury College. Mr. Elliott was at this time a
Harvard overseer, and chairman of Harvard's favorite
New Haven system; he is now also chairman of Mr.
Morgan's Northern Pacific Railroad, and a trustee
of Massachusetts Tech. He is, therefore, the beau ideal
of the successful son, and what he says to his classmates
after forty years' experience in the outside world represents the very soul of the alumni. Mr. Elliott is naively
proud of his remarks, and has had them printed in a
pamphlet, which he sends about freely. Try to enter into
his primitive state of mind for a minute or two, and read
half a dozen paragraphs of his oratory:

There is a spirit of unrest, of discontent, of extravagance, of
idleness, of expected perfection, and impatience when we should
remember that perfection and success are not immediately within
one's grasp.

There has developed out of this a noisy effort by a relatively
small number of people to upset and dislocate the established order
of things and to "Fly to evils that we know not of."

What are called Radicalism, Socialism, Sovietism and Bolshevism are advocated, and too many people who should know
better lend a receptive ear to those foolish, yet dangerous, doctrines, and thus encourage the ignorant, the thoughtless and the
wicked.

In schools, colleges and even in our beloved Harvard, there
is some of this atmosphere, and it is disturbing many of the best
friends of education and progress in the country.

In giving young people their physical nourishment, we do
not spread before them every kind of food and say, "Eat what
you like whether it agrees with you or not." We know that the
physical machine can absorb only a certain amount and that all

else is waste and trash, with the result that bodies are poisoned and weakened.

In giving mental nourishment, why lay before young and impressionable men and women un-American doctrines and ideas that take mental time and energy from the study and consideration of the great fundamentals and eternal truths, fill the mind with unprofitable mental trash which, with some, result only in sowing the seeds of discontent and unrest? And which can result only in absolute life failure, spiritual and material.

The first thing we note from the above is, what an extremely low standard of English composition prevailed at Harvard from 1877 to 1881. The second is, upon what feeble intellectual equipment it is possible for a man to have charge of two great American railroads. The third is, why Mr. Howard Elliott declined an invitation to discuss the railroad problems of the country on the same platform with Glenn E. Plumb. The fourth is, why an advocate of special privilege tries so desperately to avoid giving the young people of the country an opportunity to compare his mental equipment with that of the radicals.

CHAPTER LXXIV

THE RAH-RAH BOYS

The most conspicuous of the activities of the alumni have, of course, to do with athletics; this is the part of college life which the students have made for themselves, and it *is* what college really means to the great bulk of them. Now, the sedentary life is one of the many evils invented by our civilization, and if college athletics meant that all the students in the institution, both men and women, were getting a thorough "work-out" three or four times a week, I should be willing to say that the athletics justified the colleges. But what college athletics really means is that two per cent of the students, or in small colleges probably ten per cent, get an excessive amount of exercise, sometimes to the permanent injury of their vital organs; while the great bulk of the students are surrendered to the mob-excitements of a series of gladiatorial combats and sporting events, which provide exercise only for the vocal cords and the gambling instincts.

College athletics, under the spur of commercialism, has become a monstrous cancer, which is rapidly eating out the moral and intellectual life of our educational institutions. College rivalries have been erected into the dignity of little wars, enlisting an elaborate cult of loyalties and heroisms. The securing of prize athletes, the training of them, the exploiting of them in mass combats, has become an enormous industry, absorbing the services not merely of students and alumni, but of a whole class of professional coaches, directors, press agents and promoters, who are rapidly coming to dominate college life and put the faculty on the shelf. "Drives" are instigated and funds raised for the building of "stadiums," and these, being a source of income, are a continual stimulus to new activities. So this evil, also, is one which breeds itself. The athletic alumni bring in new students for athletic purposes, and these students increase the athletic excitement while they are undergraduates, and go out from the institution to multiply the athletic alumni.

I am only stating what every insider knows perfectly well, that our college athletics today is almost universally commercialized. All the big colleges have "alumni committees," who are out scouting for the best athletic material; they are watching the athletic life of all the "prep" schools and other institutions where likely material is to be found—including steel-mills and lumber camps. They are offering husky men all sorts of inducements to come to the right college. The offering of money is supposed to be forbidden, but there are very few colleges today which do not regularly and systematically violate or evade this rule. There are many kinds of jobs in connection with the gladiatorial life which can be made available to the right persons, and which are or can be made into sinecures. There are tickets to be sold and accounts kept; there are duties as masseurs and attendants and janitors' assistants. I know of one case, of a student who managed the Intercollegiate track meet not so very long ago, who received eight hundred dollars for this small service. The athletic budget of Harvard is considerably over a million dollars a year, and football pays for it. First-class coaches claim twenty thousand a year and get it, and graduate managers also receive high salaries. There is a careful pretense kept up that this gladiatorial industry is managed by students, but in all the big universities this is a farce; the student managers are puppets, the real masters of the industry being the alumni —business men who bring the business point of view into sport. Anything to win!

Consider, for example, the athletic developments at Stanford University, which have played their part in the demoralizing of that great institution. There is a noisy bunch of alumni who have been called upon to raise money on various occasions, and who have thus come to power, and know it. They have cast out the honest but unpopular Rugby game, and brought in the American game of batter and smash. They run the annual contests with the University of California, working in alliance with the railroads, the hotels, the restaurants, and the "sporting-houses," which of course make millions out of the enormous crowds of free-spending people. The stadium at Stanford seats sixty thousand, at five dollars apiece, so you can see how much money there is at stake, and how quickly there grows up in the university a powerful group of students who are nothing but sporting promoters, with the point of view and the vices of the underworld.

Of course, everything depends upon victory, and to make certain of victory there are professional coaches— the alumni pay the Stanford coach ten thousand dollars a year, which is more than any professor has ever received in the history of Stanford, and twice the salary of the professor of clinical history. The alumni have raised a "yellow dog" fund, to bring in professional athletes, and of course these fellows know what they are there for, and do not waste much of their precious time upon studies. A Stanford professor assured me that many of them did not even bother to get text-books. The committee on scholarship was changed, because some professors had made themselves unpopular by refusing to lower the standards for these athletic idols.

Such was the story I was told at Stanford in April; and in July I read in my paper that Stanford's Board of Athletic Control is beginning the construction of a four hundred and fifty thousand dollar men's dormitory, to be built out of the receipts from athletic contests. This news appears on the "sporting" page of my newspaper, and is written by a "sporting" man, with a "sporting" point of view. Note the haughty tone in which the academic world is taught its place:

This would seem to be the correct answer to the row about taking in gate receipts by certain academic minded professors in the East, who charged "commercialism." The stadium cost Stanford approximately two hundred and five thousand dollars, and approximately one hundred and ten thousand was realized by Stanford as her share of gate receipts from the big game alone. A certain sum of money had already been advanced by the trustees to build the stadium. The crowd at this year's contests in the stadium is expected to be even larger.

And of course, if Stanford has a stadium, the University of California must have one. Her alumni and athletic boosters set to work to raise a million dollars, using the methods of intimidation they had learned during the war-time "drives." One member of the faculty, full professor and dean, became especially truculent about the meaning of "California spirit"—to be proven by putting up money for the stadium. Students were compelled to subscribe, and in the fall, when some of them found that they had not been able to earn money to pay their full subscriptions, they were refused admission to the university; that is, the university refused to accept their registration fees, until their stadium pledges had been paid!

Ex-President Jordan talked to me very emphatically about the athletic evil at Stanford and at other institutions. There was a famous coach at Stanford, who was taken to a university of the Middle West many years ago; he gathered in among his gladiators men who were too ignorant to speak English correctly, and some one paid them with cash, and with promises of college promotions, which the faculty duly delivered. Thus a certain famous football champion published in his home paper in California the statement that he had been offered fifteen hundred dollars and an education, to play football at this university. He went to the Law School, with less than a high school education, and he was graduated from the Law School the year he would only have entered Stanford. There was a gathering of college heads in Chicago, to consider the problem of professional athletics, and President Jordan was invited by a professor of the university in question to tell about his experiences with this coach. The result was that the alumni organized to demand the resignation of this professor. Concerning one of these gladiators President Jordan writes me:

"After leaving college, he used to stand in a San Francisco saloon where he collected small sums for letting men feel of his muscles. He is not now living." It would seem that one needs more than muscle to secure survival in modern society!

That was ten or fifteen years ago, and the exploiting of muscle has grown like all other kinds of American big business. At Princeton, which is especially notorious for the purchasing of athletes, President Hibben called a conference with the presidents of Yale and Harvard, to see what could be done about it; they solemnly passed a series of resolutions to the effect that the athletic managers must obey the amateur rules—which they knew all about and laughed at; they laughed none the less after this conference. I talked with a student at the Massachusetts Institute of Technology, who saw at first-hand the process whereby Princeton bought a champion hammer thrower and shot putter from that institution. It fell to my friend to answer the telephone in the athletic association office while the Princeton alumni were trying to get this man. The students at Tech are bitter about the way their athletes are bought or stolen—they haven't as much money as Princeton. Another all-around athlete was not allowed to run by Tech, but this did not worry him very much—because he had such a handsome offer from Bowdoin!

To get a famous athlete is the only way these little colleges know to "put themselves on the map." They make desperate efforts, and sometimes the results are comical. For example, in Kentucky is a little religious institution known as Center College. No one had ever heard of it before, but a couple of years ago it turned up with a carefully selected assortment of gladiators, and beat Harvard at football. I happen to know about one of the leading athletic lights who achieved this triumph; he was a pool-room hanger-on before he was brought to the college, and now that his brief day of glory is past, he is a farm-hand!

Everywhere these mighty men of muscle and money are coming to feel their power. Speaking at an alumni meeting of the University of Pennsylvania, a British rowing coach laid down the law to the vice-provost of the university:

You, Mr. Vice-provost, as representing the faculty, have told us that the university has added from eight buildings in '76 to eighty now; that the students have grown from one thousand to seven thousand, but what has made your university? Why, athletics. Athletics are the biggest advertisement for any university, and athletics have made Pennsylvania. What has the faculty ever done for athletics? Nothing. . . . . Get busy and alter it all. . . . . . Pressure on the faculty quick, and you can do it.

Thorstein Veblen, in his book, "The Higher Learning in America," gives an amusing illustration of the methods used to get these professional gladiators "by" in their classes. The athletic committee, casting around for "snap" courses, selected Italian as a likely one, and when examination time came round the gladiators were required to read a passage in Italian—the passage submitted being the Lord's Prayer! Professor Veblen does not name the university at which this happened, but I have ascertained that it was Mr. Rockefeller's University of Chicago.

A curious illustration of the operation of the athletic system in our smaller colleges is found in the January, 1922, bulletin of the American Association of University Professors, dealing with the affairs of Washington and Jefferson College, a religious institution located at Washington, Pennsylvania. All these little toadstools are trying to turn into big mushrooms, and there are two essentials to the procedure; one is—if you will pardon the mixed metaphor—the harpooning of whales, and the other is the winning of football victories. At Washington and Jefferson there was one member of the faculty, a professor of chemistry by the name of H. E. Wells, who failed to appreciate the supreme importance of football victories in college life. He had his mind set on the upholding of academic standards, and he ruthlessly "flunked" some prominent athletes, who had failed to make good in their class work.

Naturally, this roused the indignation of the athletic alumni, who were putting up their good money to pay the tuition and college fees, board and room rent of members of the football team. (This was proved by a committee of the trustees appointed to investigate the athletic situation.) The athletic alumni set out to "get" the cantankerous professor of chemistry, using for their purpose a man who was listed as "general secretary" of the college, but had been energetic and successful as a "field agent," recruiting students for athletics. This man, backed by the alumni, caused the publication in their interlocking newspaper, the Washington "Reporter," of an article attacking Professor Wells' record as a teacher, and presenting statistics as to the number of students he had "flunked." These statistics were entirely false, and Professor Wells sent in a correction—which correction was, as usual, buried in an obscure part of the paper. The American Association of University Professors points out the important fact that the college administration made no move to protect Professor Wells against these false charges; on the contrary, says the report, "the administration permitted a professor to be struck below the belt in such a way that his popularity with students and with alumni was extensively damaged." After that, of course, it was easy for a committee of the athletic alumni to appear before the trustees and charge that Professor Wells was "unpopular among the students." So Professor Wells was dropped by the trustees at three months' notice, without giving him a hearing, without giving him a right to face his accusers, in fact without his even knowing some of the charges against him.

Still more curious was the case of George Winchester, professor of physics. He had raised the money for the only first class laboratory at the college, and he had given more money than the majority of the trustees; but he committed the offense of putting studies above football, and for that he was punished. In March, 1918, the board of trustees granted to Professor Winchester "a leave of absence for the duration of the war, or so long as he remains in the service of the allies." After the armistice the board wrote to Professor Winchester, to ask him when he would be ready to take up his work again, and Professor Winchester cabled that he would be ready to resume work on July 1, 1919; after cabling, he went to Toulon to do work with the French Admiralty. Meantime, the athletic alumni got busy with the board, and the board summarily dropped Professor Winchester, and appointed his successor! Says the committee of the Professors' Association:

It would require stronger language than is suitable to this report to characterize justly the action taken. Regardless of any argument that might be developed to account for the extraordinary action of the board, it is sufficient to recount the bare fact that the board, after having granted a leave of absence, dismissed Professor Winchester in absentia, while he was in France on active service in the work for which leave had been granted, without a previous notification, without a hearing, without any redress whatsoever. It constitutes an act about which there can be no difference of opinion among right thinking men.

CHAPTER LXXV

THE SOCIAL TRAITORS

The failure of colleges to impart culture is a standard topic of our time, so I shall not dwell upon it. The theme of this book is something of far greater importance—the success of colleges in imparting a spirit of bigotry, intolerance and suspicion toward ideas. Says a teacher in a Pennsylvania college, who asks me not to use his name: "Our students are climbers, strangers to idealism, or at best mere dabblers at it." Or consider the testimony of Hendrik Willem Van Loon, who taught at Cornell, and later at Antioch, which is trying a novel experiment in combining education and everyday work. Van Loon declares that he found in the students of both colleges a profound and deeply rooted hostility toward originality, a personal resentment toward anyone who interfered with their standardized notions. They are taught from textbooks, and they follow the book, and refuse to think about anything that is not in the book.

To the same effect testifies Robert Herrick, after thirty years experience at the University of Chicago. Our colleges follow the English monastic tradition, says Professor Herrick; they pretend to watch over the morals of their students, but with the crowds now thronging in, the task is impossible, and the pretense is dishonest. No large university would today dare attempt any real control, nor would the parents support it; because fathers who send their sons to college with large allowances and high-powered cars know perfectly well that these young men go on "bats," and that they take girls out into the country in their cars.

What discipline they get, according to Herrick, they get from one another in their fraternities and clubs. They are uncritical, naive and barbarous, with herd feelings instead of ideas. The first requirement is that everyone shall be alike, a part of a mob. They teach the newcomer the rules; he must wear a freshman cap, and if he has opinions of his own they tell him he is too "tonguey," and proceed to knock the nonsense out of him. The faculty know of this, and think it is fine; they mix with the men, and join the fraternities, and help in the production of subservience and conformity. I quoted the above remarks to a professor in another university, and he threw up his hands. "My God!" he cried. "I am stupefied! My students accept everything that I say as gospel. If only I might once discover a crank in my classes!" And he quoted the phrase of William James, once of Harvard: "Our undisciplinables are our proudest product."

I have before me a letter from a professor in one of the "little toad-stools," Parsons College, Fairfield, Iowa. The Student Council passed a rule, which was later approved by the faculty, that all freshmen were to wear green caps. A hundred and fifty freshmen meekly submitted; but there was one "conscientious objector." My informant writes:

The upper classmen got together and announced that unless every freshman got a cap by noon of a certain day he would be subjected to the gauntlet of the paddling machine. I wish I could have gotten a picture of that mob of upper classmen on the campus of a "Christian" college, each provided with a club, as they lined up and forced Ball through the line of clubs, each taking as hearty a swat as possible—a fine specimen of the type of civilization we can expect from the leaders we are training in the Christian colleges today! What a new social order it will be! Through it all, the president has practically approved the whole procedure, from the chapel platform. Ball still refuses, in spite of a boycott by the student body, even his own fellow freshmen; and I understand a paper is to be read in chapel next week denouncing him, and calling for a boycott unless he submits. This is supposed to be the daily Christian religious service—the hour of devotion for the students!

Yet another professor compared his students to the crackers which are packed in tin boxes by the wholesale bakeries; all cut from certain patterns, and stamped with certain standard designs. We have sheltered them from realities, and kept them ignorant of the problems they are to confront. We have taught them a few formulas of morality, utterly unpractical and impossible to apply—as we prove by not applying them our-

selves. From their social life the students learn what the
real world is—a place of class distinctions based upon
property; they learn the American religion—what William
James calls "the worship of the bitch-goddess Success."
They throw themselves into the social struggle with ferocious determination to get ahead; and when they go out
into the world, they carry that spirit into the commercial
struggle.

In every profession they find, of course, that the way
to get ahead is to serve the powers that rule, and to betray
the general welfare. I could take you through the professions which are taught in our universities, one after
another, and show you how the prevailing ethical standards constitute treason to the human race. I could show
you in academic teaching how these same standards are
justified, in phrases only partly veiled. Take, Harvard,
for example, and the Massachusetts Institute of Technology, admitted to have the highest standards of any
engineering school in America; we saw the professors in
these institutions selling themselves to predatory corporations, and laying down high-sounding "principles,"
whose sole effect and purpose is to enable the Wholesale
Pickpockets' Association to plunder the public. I have a
letter from a high official of the United States Bureau of
Education, who tells me more about these engineering
traitors. He says:

> I recall one man, for example, who was called in by a water
> company for expert service in connection with the purity of the
> water, which was being questioned by the people. He contended
> with me that it was "his business" if he could find remunerative
> employment of that sort, and that he was under no obligation to
> give the public the benefit of his expert knowledge concerning
> the impurity of the water supply. But what aroused my ire more
> than anything else was the fact that he preached that kind of
> thing to his technical students as the standard of "loyalty" they
> should pursue toward the companies where they might be em-
> ployed after graduation. This man was a real scientist. He was
> so thoroughly interested in his subject that he was willing to take
> considerable personal risks in conducting experiments, but he was
> sadly lacking in that social and religious conception which makes
> us realize our mutual obligations and duties.

Or take the work of inventors; they have a man at
one of our greatest universities who is a famous inventor,
and he makes great scientific discoveries, and then he goes
to the big corporations and sells them—what? The right

to use his invention and spread it throughout the world for the benefit of mankind? No; he sells them the right to suppress the invention, and deprive mankind of the use of it for a generation or two! You see, a new invention may mean the scrapping of a great deal of existing machinery; if it falls into the hands of some independent concern, it may cost the big monopolists enormous losses. So they pay for the right to suppress it, and a great inventor is turned by the social system into a kind of scientific blackmailer.

Or take the lawyers; surely I do not need to prove to you how the lawyers are betraying mankind. A professor at the University of Chicago told me of attending a class reunion, where a group of high-up corporation lawyers got drunk and began gossiping about the tricks they had played in their profession, and, as the professor said, it made him physically ill. I also have heard these high-up lawyers talking; the late James B. Dill, who was paid a million dollars to organize the Steel Trust, spent many an evening in his home telling me the game as he had seen it, and it began with bribery of judges, juries and legislators, and ended with wire-tapping and burglary. The late Francis Lynde Stetson, one of the highest paid corporation lawyers in New York, went down to Trenton on the train with Judge Dill to beat some railroad rate law, and he opened his suit-case playfully, showing that he had fifty thousand dollars in new bank-notes. "That's a fine kind of work for a pillar of the church like you," said Dill, and the other answered, with a grin: "How do I know but that I may have to pay for my lunch?"

Or if you cannot believe Judge Dill, believe Judge Lindsey, who told me about a young man who came to Denver from the Harvard Law School, full of the fine phrases of altruism with which his teachers had filled him, and when he learned what he had to do to practice corporation law in Denver, he broke down in Lindsey's office, and buried his head in his arms and cried like a baby. Afterwards, so Lindsey writes me, "he capitulated and joined the gang."

Or maybe it is medicine the young man has studied. He has heard about the nobleness of the healing art, but he has to keep an automobile, and his wife wants to get into society, and competition is keen. There is one way a physician can make a thousand dollars by a few minutes' work, and any physician who is in touch with the leisure class has women on their knees to him every week, begging him to take their money. Dr. William J. Robinson estimates that there are a million abortions performed in the United States every year, so you see that our medical schools have not steeled all their graduates against this temptation. Now we have another one added—every physician in the United States is made by law a dispenser of joviality, the seneschal of the castle, the keeper of the keys to the wine-cellar!

Or maybe the graduate becomes a newspaper reporter. One of the oldest Wall Street reporters in New York talked to me last spring, telling me a little of the way things are going there. The newspaper reporters also are keepers of the keys of the wine-cellar; they have police passes, and some of them are running a bootlegging industry between New York and Canada! Others have gone into high finance on a large scale—because, of course, a financial reporter comes on information which is worth thousands, and sometimes tens of thousands. "Nowadays," said my friend, "when a Wall Street reporter gets a tip and rushes to the telephone, you don't hear him call his city editor; you hear him call his broker." I was told of one newspaper man who had the fortune to be called in when Mr. Charles Sabin of the Guaranty Trust Company gave out some news of the German overtures for peace, and this enterprising young man cleared fifty thousand dollars from the information.

Or perhaps the young man becomes a college professor; if so, he hides his convictions and makes himself a tight little snob and reactionary, to win the favor of the college machine. He hides the truth from his students, or he "shades" it, which is the same thing, and takes his pitiful little bribe in the dignity of a full professorship. He turns out class after class of young men, as ignorant of life and as helpless against temptation as he himself was once. So reaction rules in our country, and men who plead for social justice are slandered and maligned, and turned into criminals in the public eye; all the agencies of law and justice become mobs, and the Ku Klux Klan meets every night in lonely places, and lights its fiery cross and prepares for the wholesale slaughter of the future of mankind.

Just now the rich are having it all their own way; they can do the killing and the bludgeoning and the jailing—and it never occurs to them to think what an example they are setting to the workers, and what it will mean when the tables are turned, and the disinherited of the earth have their way for a while! It ought to be the chief function of educators to point out things like this to the public; but that would be "meddling in politics," and we have seen that politics in colleges is a privilege reserved to presidents and trustees. There are going to be ferocious attacks made upon this book, and this seems as convenient a place as any in which to explain what they mean. Faculty members will rush forward to defend their institutions; in some cases, no doubt, there will be resolutions of protest, with many signatures. They will have some ammunition; for, of course no one can write a book of this size,. full of such masses of facts, and not make a few slips of detail. These will be taken up and magnified into gigantic blunders, and denunciation of them spread broadcast in the capitalist press. When you read these things, bear one circumstance in mind: that any young professor who wants to become a dean in a hurry, who has a vision of himself selected as president in the course of a few years, will know that he can find no more certain way to win favor with his overlords than to find something wrong with this book, and then tell about it gallantly!

CHAPTER LXXVI

PREXY

I promised early in this book to consider how it happens that so many college presidents are men who do not always tell the truth. We have now seen far enough into the inside of colleges to understand the reason. The president of a college or university is the great reconciler of irreconcilabilities; he is the chemist who mixes oil and water, the high priest who makes peace between God and Mammon, the circus-rider who stands on two horses going in opposite directions; and all these things not by choice, but ex-officio and of inescapable necessity. The college president is a man who procures money from the rich, and uses it for the spreading of knowledge; in fulfilling which two functions he places himself, not merely in the line of fire of the warring forces of the class struggle, but between the incompatible elements of human nature itself —between greed and service, between hate and love, between body and spirit.

Consider the rich, how they become so. Either they or their ancestors before them have taken from others, and that which they have taken, the others have lost. The very essence of their richness is that there are many poor. If all were rich, there would be no sense in wealth, no power in it, for there would be none willing to serve. It is plain to anyone who can think that richness means possessing material things, and excluding others from possession thereof. Of such is the kingdom of Mammon.

And of what is the kingdom of God? In the region of the mind the situation is exactly the opposite; the wealth of one is the wealth of all, and the highest joy of possession is that the thing possessed may be shared by all and be of benefit to all, with no diminution to anyone. I am trying here to write a useful book; my pleasure is in communicating to you what I believe to be truth, and exactly proportionate to my success in spreading this truth is my own gratification. This applies to Shakespeare writing a play, it applies to Beethoven composing a symphony, it applies to Newton discovering a natural law; each gives something which all mankind may enjoy forever, and no one's pleasure in "As You Like It," or in the "Fifth Symphony," or in an understanding of the movements of the planets, is any less because at the same time millions of other people are having that same pleasure.

This fact determines the attitude to life of the true scientist, the scholar and the lover of the arts; it is as different from the attitude of the trader, the speculator and the exploiter as black is different from white, or night from day. There can be no greater irreconcilability conceivable to the human mind. But now comes a new species of superman, whose function it is to make peace between these two forces, to persuade the lion of commerce and the lamb of learning to lie down in the same pasture together! The name of this great American enchanter is PREXY.

How does he do it? I am moved to be blunt, and say in plain English that he does it by being the most universal faker and the most variegated prevaricator that has yet appeared in the civilized world. He does it by making his entire being a conglomeration of hypocrisies and stultifications, so that by the time he has been in office a year or two he has told so many different kinds of falsehoods and made so many different kinds of pretenses to so many different people, that he has lost all understanding of what truth is, or how a man could speak it.

The college needs money. Colleges always need money, because college students get three times as much as they pay for, and the hope of getting social prestige, to enable them to live easy lives, brings constantly increasing crowds each year to the college gates. So "prexy" seeks out possible donors; "prospects," as they are called in the slang of mendication. He cannot go to them directly and ask for money; the man who tries methods so crude is speedily eliminated from the list of college presidents. The successful one is the possessor of what is called "tact"; that is to say, he understands the weaknesses of human nature, he is an expert in the predatory psychology, a hunter who knows how to pierce the tough and scaly hides of old commercial monsters who have spent a lifetime watching people trying to get their money away from them, and have managed hitherto to resist all threats and blandishments.

The college president has to meet these plutocratic monsters socially; he has to be "human" to them—that is to say, he has to pretend to be interested in them, to admire them and their ways of life. He has to flatter their vanities, invite them to meals and find out what they like to eat, hold their overcoats and escort them to the motor-car, be gracious to their wives and a bit flirtatious to their daughters. After he thinks he has sufficiently gained their confidence, he begins a careful approach, to make these monsters realize the indispensability of propaganda to every ruling class. There is a battle of ideas going on in the world, dangerous notions are clamoring for attention, class hatreds and jealousies are raising their hideous hydra heads. What safety can there be for vested interests, unless they make it their business to see that the new generation is taught respect for the property clauses of the Constitution? There is no department of human thought into which this struggle with new ideas does not penetrate, there is nothing that universities do or teach that cannot be related, in the eloquence of college presidents hunting money, to the cause of law and order and safe and sane stagnation.

On that basis the college president does his "vamping"; and having got the necessary papers signed and witnessed before a notary, he gets a bath and a shave, and puts on clean clothes, and draws a deep breath, and expands his chest, and confronts the world with a proclamation of magnificent devotion to the service of truth and the welfare of mankind. These millions which he has just collected from the aged oil dinosaur, or steel megatherium, or beef pterodactyl, or whatever the beast may be—these millions he is now going to spend in a free and absolutely disinterested pursuit of understanding, with utter loyalty to scientific facts wherever they may lead, with complete trust in democracy and the wisdom of the people, with reverent humility before the God of Truth and Justice and Love. This that I am pronouncing you will immediately recognize as a standard commencement oration; delivered in the presence of a hundred plutocrats in decent frockcoats, and five hundred faculty members in caps and gowns, and a graduating class of a thousand young people; published next morning to the extent of four columns in all local newspapers, and relayed by the Associated Press to the extent of half a column to thirteen hundred morning newspapers throughout the United States. In the course of my trip among the colleges I was talking with a certain eminent scientist, and I spoke of the tragedy and horror that had befallen mankind through the failure of Woodrow Wilson to mean any of his golden words. "My God!" said the scientist. "Didn't you know what all that was? Haven't you been hearing that kind of thing for thirty years? Didn't you know that those speeches of Woodrow's were commencement orations?"

It makes no difference whether the college president is dealing personally with the interlocking directorate, as in privately endowed institutions, or whether he deals with the politicians who run the government machine for these same plutocrats. As a matter of fact, the college president who represents the so-called public institutions is in the more humiliating position of the two; for the free lance man has an open field, he can get himself invited to dinner-parties, and always has the hope that some day he may run into a politer plutocrat; but the president of a state university has no choice, he has to deal with the "boss" whom he finds in power. He will be snubbed and insulted until the tears run down his cheeks; and then he will go back to his deans and his kitchen cabinet and explain what it is that the political machine demands—the expulsion of this or that professor, the support of the university for this candidate or that bit of graft; and the president and his cabinet will work out the proper set of lies to tell to the discharged professor, or to the plundered public, or to both.

Thus the college president spends his time running back and forth between Mammon and God, known in the academic vocabulary as Business and Learning. He pleads with the business man to make a little more allowance for the eccentricities of the scholar; explaining the absurd notion which men of learning have that they owe loyalty to truth and public welfare. He points out that if the college comes to be known as a mere tool of special privilege it loses all its dignity and authority; it is absolutely necessary that it should maintain a pretense of disinterestedness, it should appear to the public as a shrine of wisdom and piety. He points out that Professor So-and-So has managed to secure great prestige throughout the state, and if he is unceremoniously fired it will make a terrific scandal, and perhaps cause other faculty members to resign, and other famous scientists to stay away from the institution.

The president says this at a dinner-party in the home of his grand duke; and next morning he hurries off to argue with the recalcitrant professor. He points out the humiliating need of funds—just now when the professor's own salary is so entirely inadequate. He begs the professor to realize the president's own position, the crudity of business men who hold the purse-strings, and have no understanding of academic dignity. He pleads for just a little discretion, just a little time—just a little anything that will moderate the clash between greed and service, the incompatibility of hate and love.

Either he succeeds in his purpose of persuading the professor to be less a scientist, a citizen, and a man of honor, or else he decides, in conference with his kitchen cabinet, that a way must be found to get rid of this unreasonable marplot. He and his cabinet now start a campaign of intrigue against the professor; they set going rumors calculated to damage his prestige; they contrive traps into which to snare him; or they wait until in the war between greed and service he gives utterance to some plain human emotion—whereupon they find him guilty of "indiscretion," and announce to the public that he has shown himself to be lacking in that "judicious" attitude of mind which is essential to those occupying academic positions. Or perhaps they find that they have too many men in that department; or they decide to combine the departments of literature and obstetrics. They have a thousand different devices, scores of which I have shown you in action. Always they tell the professor—with their right hands upon the Bible they swear it to the public and to the newspapers—that it is purely "an administrative matter," there is no question of academic freedom involved, and everyone in their institution lives, moves and has his being in the single-minded love of truth.

I have on my desk a letter from a Harvard professor, who tells me that my chapters on that institution are interesting, but he thinks I attribute too much cunning to the objects of my indignation. "These conforming preachers and editors and teachers are more of the genus Babbitt than of the genus Machiavelli." This is a question of psychology, which only the Maker of the creatures can decide. In any case it matters little, because my purpose here is not to apportion blame, but to point out social peril, and it matters not whether social traitors know what they are doing—the effect of their action remains equally destructive to society. I have called the American college and university a ruling-class munition-factory for the manufacture of high explosive shells and gas bombs to be used in the service of intrenched greed and cruelty. The college president is the man who runs this indispensable institution; and he is not one of the military leaders who sit in swivel chairs in city offices, he is one who sallies forth in person at the head of his armies, bravely hurling commencement bombs and Fourth of July torpedoes.

The college president is a human radio, a walking broadcasting station, a combination of encyclopedia and megaphone. He is that man whose profession it is to know everything; in his one mind is summed up ex-officio all the knowledge of all the specialties. He tells his professors what to teach, and how to teach it, and has little birds and whispering galleries and telepathic mediums to advise him if they obey. He is a human card-index, an information service bureau concerning the reputations of professors in all other institutions, and of promising undergraduates and Ph.D. candidates, and just what they are worth, and how much less they can be hired for. Or, if he does not possess all this knowledge, he possesses a perfectly satisfactory substitute—the ability to look as if he possessed it, and to act as if he possessed it. Such is the advantage of being an autocrat; criticism does not affect you, and whether you are right or whether you are wrong is the same thing.

The college president has acquired enormous prestige in American capitalist society; he is a priest of the new god of science, and newspapers and purveyors of "public opinion" unite in exalting him. He receives the salary of a plutocrat, and arrogates to himself the prestige and precedence that go with it. He lives on terms of equality with business emperors and financial dukes, and conveys their will to mankind, and perpetuates their ideals and prejudices in the coming generation. It is a new aristocracy which has arisen among us, and they all stand together, they and their henchmen and courtiers, against whatever forces may threaten. I have shown how they have invented a new set of titles of nobility, which they sell for cash, or use to exalt their patrons and overawe you and me. We shall find it worth while to turn over the pages of "Who's Who in America," and see what these mighty ones of the earth think of one another, and what they do to flatter one another's pride, and to keep their own order in the public eye.

"I do not give degrees to scientists," said Wheeler of California. "I give them to statesmen and college presidents"; which means that these gentry have a system of "you scratch my back and I'll scratch yours." Wheeler managed to get scratched no less than twelve times during his life, Eliot of Harvard eleven times, Shanklin of Wesleyan eleven times, Smith of Pennsylvania twenty times, Lowell of Harvard twenty times, Nicholas Miraculous twenty-five times. Descending in the scale of plutocratic importance we find Angell of Yale with nine honorary degrees, Faunce of Brown with nine, Schurman of Cornell eight, Judson of Chicago seven, Day of Syracuse seven, Burton of Michigan six, Goodnow of Johns Hopkins five. Jordan of Stanford got only four—you remember that our icthyologist and race-horse expert was tainted with pacifism and democracy!

You remember also the mushrooms and toadstools, and the absurdities we discovered at these places. I look up the present and recent heads of these institutions, and there is scarcely one who has not been able to get his back scratched. I find Crawford of Allegheny with seven degrees, Thompson of Ohio State with five, Mitchell of Delaware with three, Wishart of Wooster with three, Few of Trinity with three, Garfield of Williams with five, Conwell of Temple with two, Hixson of Allegheny with two, Brooks of Baylor with one, Buchtel of Denver with one, Parsons of Marietta with one, Goodnight of Bethany with one, Montgomery of Muskingum with one. Also, it is interesting to note, you will find all these presidents of little toad stools duly recorded in "Who's Who." You may look in that volume for the best minds in our country, the men who are serving as pioneers of social justice and democracy, and three times out of four you will not find their names, or, when you do find them, they are relegated, like the present writer, to a back volume. But all presidents of colleges, no matter how insignificant or absurd, take rank with senators and cabinet members and ambassadors and supreme court judges and admirals and generals, and go into every volume ex officio.

CHAPTER LXXVII

DAMN THE FACULTY

We have seen the successful sons returning to shed their glory upon their alma mater; and we have seen the successful grandsons enjoying their four years of play at learning and work at football. Let us now have a glimpse at the life of the scholar amid all this worldly pomp and gladiatorial clamor, the thunder of the foot-ball captains and the shouting of the cheer-leaders.

There are few more pitiful proletarians in America than the underpaid, overworked, and contemptuously ignored rank and file college teacher. Everyone has more than he—trustees and presidents, coaches and trainers, merchants and tailors, architects and building contractors, sometimes even masons and carpenters. A young instructor in a great endowed university, living on a starvation wage, made to me the bitter remark: "We are the fellows of whom the Bible speaks—we ask for bread and we are given a stone"—he waved his hand toward a showy new structure rising on the campus. I have before me a copy of "School and Society," for November 6, 1920, giving the result of an investigation: "How Professors Live." At the University of Illinois a hundred and sixty-seven men, or forty per cent of those at the institution, filled out a questionnaire. I quote a few paragraphs from those of the associate professors, each paragraph referring to a different man:

Old clothing is invariably made over for children. Have gardened a lot and kept chickens. Use butter substitutes. Wear clothing until frayed. Above expenses do not consider depreciation of furniture and household equipment.

Using vacations to earn money. Postponing dental services. Using inferior grades of clothing and using them when they should be discarded. Cut down food in quality and quantity.

We have no help, do our own washing and my wife makes all the children's clothes, etc.

Neglecting necessary repairs; inferior clothing, butter substitutes, etc. Almost no theatres, entertainments, travel or books.

Small apartment, clothing below standard of position, entertainment almost eliminated, etc.

General retrenchments (food, clothing, medical services, etc.) and the discontinuing of newspapers, magazines, all amusements, concerts, etc., that are not free. Am unable to subscribe to worthy causes (relief funds, etc.).

No vacation trips. Postponed dental attention. Inferior grades of clothing. Cannot wear as good clothes as I did when in high school and college. Have not spent as much on entertainment.

We use butter substitutes; I run a garden and sole the family's shoes; my wife makes all her own clothing.

Unable to take vacations or trips to relatives who live at distance. Buy no books, only clothing absolutely necessary. Self-denial in almost everything imaginable.

There you have nine little family tragedies, out of ninety I might have quoted from the article, out of one or two hundred thousand that exist in our country. So the poor professors and their wives and children live; and above them is the world of prominence and power into which they dream of climbing. The way of success is the way of toadying and boot-licking, of conformity and reverence for the gods established. Do you wonder that, as Harold Laski says, some men deliberately adopt reactionary ideas as a means to promotion, while others, whose brains do not permit them to be reactionary, conceal their real opinions? Do you wonder that the young instructor comes like the chameleon to take the color of the environment which surrounds him? However much he may be absorbed in his books, his wife knows about the world outside, and their children have to be reared in this world.

To show you how college professors are tempted, let me tell you an anecdote, the experience of a teacher of political science at one of our leading Eastern universities. I will call him Smith; and he was invited to meet the head of one of the largest universities of the Middle West, whom I will call Jones. President Jones had suggested that Professor Smith should come to his institution as head of a big department, and while Jones was in the East they met to talk it over. Said Smith, telling me the story: "This was a big chance, and I was disposed to accept it; but first I wanted to find out what would be my status. Of course, I could not ask the man directly: 'Shall I be free?' I might as well have asked: 'Shall I be allowed to commit rape?' What I did was to set a trap; I said: 'You know I teach a ticklish subject, public service work; the question is, should my teaching be administrative, or should it be policy-determining? My conception of the matter is that I should get the data, but not determine policies.' And you should have seen the man's face light up! 'That's it exactly!' he said. 'I'm so glad to have you make the distinction! That makes the matter perfectly clear.' And he went home and told his faculty that I was the best man they could possibly get!" While Professor Smith told me this story we were sitting at dinner in a restaurant, and he added: "It happened right in this room—at that table over there. I declined the appointment, of course. But you see how it is; when men face temptations such as that, it breaks down their characters in the end."

How much direct bribery of college professors there may be, I cannot say. A dean at the University of Wisconsin told me how a wealthy father had offered him money to "pass" his deficient son; and I suspect that kind of thing happens more often than it is told. But most of the time the thing is done through what I call the "dress-suit bribe." A college professor is human like the rest of us; he likes a good dinner and a good cigar; he likes to be invited to "nice" homes—and his wife likes it still more. I know a professor at a state university who "flunked" the son of a trustee—and this in spite of all kinds of pressure from those above him. But the average man can hardly be expected to jeopardize his career in a case like that. Where such temptations exist, it is a psychological axiom that many will fall.

I have heard faculty members—mostly very young ones, or else very old ones—assert that there is never any favoritism in college examinations; and I have contented myself with a gentle smile. Imagine such a situation as we saw at Columbia, when young Marcellus Hartley Dodge, heir to untold millions, was an undergradute. He gave to the university a building while he was still in college, and was prepared to make a still larger donation upon his graduation, and to become a trustee at the age of twenty-six. And now, some little whipper-snapper of an instructor of English composition, or of French syntax, presumes to "flunk" Marcellus Hartley, and subject that young prince of the plutocracy to the humiliation of stepping down among despised lower classmen! Let the whipper-snapper try it, and he would soon find out the meaning of that Columbia student-song whose chorus runs: "Damn the faculty!"

Sydney Smith made the remark that there was no use

expecting every curate to be a St. Paul; and we may say, quite as safely, there is no use expecting every college instructor to be a Charles A. Beard. Men who are trained in colleges of snobbery come out snobs, and if at the top of your educational system you heap all the honors upon wealth and all the humiliations upon scholarship, you will have at the bottom of your faculty young men who have learned what the world is, and have set themselves the task of getting up by the methods established. I assert that from top to bottom in our colleges and universities today wealth is replacing knowledge, and worldly-minded and cynical members of the faculty are catering to the rich among the students, knowing that when these students come back as "successful sons," they will be the persons whose friendship counts.

The students are organized into exclusive fraternities —perfectly ridiculous and perfectly banal things, and yet they run the social life of the colleges, and without exception they run the alumni association, and speak with the voice of the college in the public press. And do you think they fail to impress the faculty? Remember, the fraternity men are the ones with money and good clothes and good manners; they stand together and make a gang, they do "log rolling" for one another, they tip one another off to the "snap" courses and the "easy" teachers; they study the psychology of the various "profs," and advise one another how to "work" them. They frequently take faculty members into the fraternities, and thus get their backing for the system.

A professor at the University of Wisconsin told me a curious story. A group of boys had failed to get into any of the fraternities, and they had a bright idea; why not organize one for themselves? Somebody had organized every fraternity at some time past, and there were plenty of Greek letters still not taken up! So they proceeded to devise a new combination, and a mystic pin, and a set of pass-words and initiation idiocies; they rented a house, and invited some "goats" in other colleges to follow their example.

Now at this university there was a certain young professor whom I call Black, to distinguish him from my informant, whom I call White. Black was a country boy, who had worked his way through college, and had always

been a non-fraternity man. Now he came to White, very
much flattered, revealing the fact that he had been invited
to join a fraternity. White asked which one, and was
told—it was this one of which White had witnessed the
organizing only a year ago! It seemed just as good to
Black; and in a few years it would seem just as good to
everybody. But imagine the intellectual state of an institution when one of its professors, a mature man, a
scientist and master of an important specialty, could be
naively pleased at being invited to take part in flummeries
got up by a dozen boys not yet out of their teens, and
whose sole aim and ideal was to prove themselves superior
to a mass of other boys!

You miss the point of this story if you do not understand it as a symptom of the disease which is poisoning
our intellectual life. Every little "fresh water college" is
trying to "make" the big fraternities; every president of
every little toadstool is shaping his policy to such ends—
because that is the way to get the rich students, which is
the way to get the rich alumni, which is the way to get
the money. In the big Eastern universities, which are
the fountain-heads of this imbecility, the social competition amounts to a ravenous and frenzied war, involving
not merely the students, but the very mightiest of our
academic big-wigs. Look them up in "Who's Who," and
you find them solemnly recording their phi-beta-babbles
and their kappa-gamma-gabbles and their apha-apple-pies.

And when men of science and learning come down from
the thrones of reason and take part in the jostling and the
trampling and the climbing of this silk-hatted mob—then
you witness sights that make you despair for the human
race. Not so long ago the greatest thinker of our time
came to America—Albert Einstein, who happens to be a
Jew, and still more terrible to mention, a German. As
fate would have it, there came to our country at the same
time another distinguished visitor, the Prince of Monaco
—a mighty potentate, his bosom covered with various ribbons and jewelled orders. He is owner of the world's
greatest gambling-hell, at Monte Carlo, and keeps himself
out of jail just as do the gambling-princes of New York
—by owning the police.

Now the institution whose duty it is to welcome visiting scientists is the American Academy of Science; and

this institution prepared to welcome Einstein and the Prince of Monaco at the same banquet. But, horror of horrors, his Excellency, the Prince, refused to be received along with a German! There was terrible excitement in academic circles. The master of ceremonies was a high-up scientific snob, married to a member of the Morgan family, and a pet of Nicholas Miraculous. He decided that the invitation to Einstein must be canceled. But finally a compromise was arrived at; His Excellency consented to come, provided Einstein was put away in an obscure place at the foot of the table, and not asked to speak!

The greatest thinker of our time is a naive and child-like person, simple and human, and he apparently had no idea what was happening to him. He was not used to the world of what calls itself "science" in America, with its "pushers" and "tuft-hunters," forcing themselves to the front, while the real workers stay in their laboratories and do their work, suffering in silence "the insolence of office and the spurns that patient merit from the unworthy takes."

CHAPTER LXXVIII

SMALL SOULS

What every man and every organization of men in America want is to grow big. If you ask why they want to grow big they are puzzled, because it has never before happened to them to hear anybody question the moral axiom that bigness is greatness. An office building which is twelve stories high is twice as admirable as one which is six stories high; a city which has a million inhabitants is twice as important as one which has only half a million. It matters not that the additional population may be festering in wretched slums; whatever they may be, grafters and grabbers, drunkards and morons, a greater number of them is a thing to be boosted for and boasted about. The city grows big in body, but in soul it remains small.

And the same thing happens to the college. Every little college wants to be bigger than its neighbor, and looks forward to being the biggest in the state, and to that end employs the noisy arts of the real estate promoter and the circus agent. An article published in "School and Society," April 22, 1922, tells about the activities of "field secretaries" and "field agents" now employed by colleges. "According to the president of one of Ohio's state universities, only four or five of the forty colleges in the state are able to dispense with the services of one or more of these functionaries. Their use is apparently growing in favor. The dean of one of Ohio's strongest colleges confessed regretfully that the authorities in his institution are about to yield to the pressure being exerted within the institution to appoint a man to 'sell the college' to prospective students." Crossing the prairies I stepped from my train to get a breath of fresh air on a station platform, and found myself confronted by an enormous sign, hailing me in the breezy Western fashion: "Hello, this is Manhattan, Kansas, a Good Town, home of the famous Kansas State Agricultural College, 1400 acres, 50 buildings, 433 faculty, 3500 students. Free auto camping grounds."

The professor, needless to say, is expected to be a "good sport," and contribute his proper share to the "uplift" of his institution. Anything notable that he does is seized upon and exploited by the college press agent; and sometimes the efforts of publicity hounds to deal with unfamiliar sciences and arts produce comical results. Professor Jacques Loeb began to experiment in the artificial fertilization of the eggs of sea-urchins, and this was marvelous material for stories, it went all over the world. Hardly any of it was right, but that made no difference—not even in academic circles; Professor Loeb's star ascended, and so did his salary. He was invited to the University of California to continue his researches, and there he found the successful sons prepared to use him as they do the Mission bells and the Bohemian Club "jinks." They put a "booster button" on him, and got out picture post-cards of his laboratory, and a real estate firm started an advertising campaign to sell lots in his neighborhood. But when they found that Loeb resented this kind of exploitation, they lost interest in artificial parthenogenesis, and discovered that the professor was a godless materialist and a poor hand at teaching freshmen.

The average faculty member of course never scales the heights of fame, never sees his portrait on picture post cards. The college grows big in body and stays small

in soul; while the professor is apt to stay small in both
body and soul. His salary does not permit a generous diet,
and his work is confining and tedious. He teaches three
or four classes a day, and corrects compositions and test-
papers, and keeps records and makes out reports, and
obeys his superiors and keeps himself within the limits of
his little specialty. He leads a narrow life, withdrawn
from realities. He goes to lunch at the Faculty Club and
talks "shop" with his colleagues, men who live equally
empty lives and are equally out of touch with great events.
There is gossip and intrigue and wire-pulling; a professor at the University of Chicago heard his colleagues talk
for an hour about the fact that someone had got an increase in salary of two or three hundred dollars. A professor at Johns Hopkins compared his colleagues to the
lotus eaters: "Peaceful, endowed and dull."

As I write, Professor Frank C. Hankins, one of the
rebels at Clark University, hands in his resignation and
formulates his criticism of the teaching in our higher institutions:

The teacher of social science may treat his subject matter in
a purely formal manner, as is done in most high school courses in
civics, where attention is given to the powers and duties of Congress, the number of justices in the Supreme court, etc. This is a
pity; but the high school teacher and, unfortunately, a large number of college teachers of the social sciences must reckon with the
"man in the street," who would feel that "sacred" things were
being defiled if civics courses discussed the origin and development
of institutions, the relation of patriotism to war, or the relative
merits of individualism and collectivism in social life. It is a
real tragedy in the life of a teacher if he must squeeze all the
'juice out of his subject matter and give his pupils the dry pulp,
in order to hold his job.

And to the same effect testifies Ludwig Lewisohn, out
of many years experience at Wisconsin and Ohio State.
I jotted down his phrases in my notes:

It is like teaching from a cook-book. There are certain receipts which you follow. You try to explain the scientific spirit,
but you find that in college the word "science" means cut and
dried experiments without meaning. You teach the principles of a
subject, but you never apply them. You explain the "Novum
Organum," for example, but you don't apply Bacon's method to
the current formulas of capitalist imperialism. You explain the
relativity of morals according to Locke, but you never test present-day marriage and divorce, property rights and the duty of
obedience to the state.

And again, a professor now at Wisconsin: "You teach the facts, but you do not interpret them; and especially you do not deal with remedies. You teach details, not vision. You accumulate 'learning,' in the narrow sense of that word; raking in the dust-heaps of the past, and producing carefully documented treatises about absurdities." I have given a list of such topics in the chapter on Harvard; I ran into others here and there—Professor E. A. Ross mentioned two theses which won degrees while he was at Berlin—"The Linden Tree in German Literature," and "The Hay Supply in the Army of Frederick the Great." Or, if Germany is too far away, perhaps you would be interested in a Columbia thesis, composed by a man who is now a professor at Princeton: "Metaphors Concerned with Nature in the Prose of Aelfric"; or a Columbia thesis, by a professor who is now at Charleston: "The Dialect Contamination in the Old English Gospels." Said Neitzsche: "You beat them, and they give out dust like meal-sacks. But who could guess that their dust came from corn, and the golden wonder of the summer fields?"

Colleges are growing like those prehistoric monsters, the size of a freight-car, with brains that would fit inside a walnut-shell. And as they grow, there is more and more "administration," more and more red tape and routine; the professor is turned into a bookkeeper and a filing clerk. Writing in "Science," President Maclaurin of the Massachusetts Institute of Technology drew a picture of the adventures of Isaac Newton in a modern American university:

The superintendent of buildings and grounds, or other competent authority, calls upon Mr. Newton.
Supt.: Your theory of gravitation is hanging fire unduly. The director insists on a finished report, filed in his office by nine A. M. Monday next; summarized on one page; typewritten, and the main points underlined. Also a careful estimate of the cost of the research per student-hour.
Newton: But there is one difficulty that has been puzzling me for fourteen years, and I am not quite . . . . .
Supt. (with snap and vigor): Guess you had better overcome that difficulty by Monday morning or quit.

How can dull men, absorbed in dull routine, hold the attention of large groups of wide-awake youngsters? The answer is that they do not, and that is the failure of our colleges. The situation is summed up in a delightful anecdote, which was solemnly sworn to me by a college professor who dares not let me use his name. He was doing the customary "glad-hand" stunts at a reunion of the "old boys," and one of these successful sons came up to him, beaming with pleasure, and clasped his hand in a hearty grip. "Professor Smith! Well, well, Professor Smith, I sure am glad to see you! You have no idea what a good time I had in that English class of yours. We read 'Hamlet,' you remember, but we only got halfway through. I often find myself wondering how that play came out."

Or, if you cannot believe that story, take the testimony of Professor C. T. Titus of Whitman College, who tried the experiment of asking college seniors in what state the city of St. Louis is located. There were guesses as far apart as Louisiana, Kentucky and Tennessee! No wonder that Bertrand Russell remarks that "Education has been one of the chief obstacles to the development of intelligence."

CHAPTER LXXIX

THE WORLD OF "HUSH"

Knowing as I do the economics of our plutocratic empire, I had a general idea of what I should find in my tour of the colleges; but I had little idea of the details, and went with an open mind, prepared to follow the facts where they led. After I had visited a dozen colleges, I began to be struck by a peculiar circumstance; not merely was I encountering similar incidents—I was hearing the same phrases over and over! Certain expressions became familiar, and I would wait for them; if they did not come, I would suggest them, and note the instant response: "Yes, that's it exactly!"

I go over my note-book and cull out these phrases: "It is a slow strangling." "It is the wearing away of a stone by drops of water." "It is an intangible thing, an atmospheric pressure." "It is a question of good taste, of loyalty to the institution, to one's colleagues." So ran the story, over and over, all the way from California to Massachusetts and back again. I came to realize that the important fact about academic freedom in America is not the extreme and dramatic cases I have been narrating; it is the whole system of class prejudice and class repression, which operates for the most part without its victims being conscious of it.

I quote other statements from my note-book: "Our young instructors are weaklings, selected as such. They seek a comfortable berth, sheltered from the storms of the world." "They find that promotion depends upon conformity, and they conform." "There is a tremendous absence of freedom, but the victims don't realize it; they think they are merely being polite; before they know what has happened to them they have become small men." "No man who thinks can tell just when he will become a victim, or how he will be tripped up." "I can count an indefinite number of friends to whom I would express myself—up to a certain point." "You may stay in the place for years, and then some day discover one man to whom you dare to talk." "Those who go out have adventures, but pity those who stay." "The plow-horse does not feel the rein until he tries to step out of the furrow." "Yes, our men are free; they are horses that stand without hitching." Such statements, with varying phraseology, were made by scores of men, in as many different colleges and universities.

I sat in one group of faculty members discussing this subject, and the conversation took a humorous turn; they started making a list of the various offenses for which a man may be fired from an American university. You may be fired if you don't like your wife, or if your wife doesn't like you. You may be fired if you use the word revolution, referring to anything since the eighteenth century. You may be fired if you get into a fight with the janitor. "That happened to a very distinguished botanist of my acquaintance," said one professor. You may be fired if you go to church too little, or you may be fired if you go to church too much. I asked how the latter could be, and the explanation was that there are aristocratic universities like Harvard and Princeton and Pennsylvania, which follow the Episcopal tradition, and an excessive demonstration of piety would be highly offensive. You may be fired if you are near-sighted, and also if you are far-sighted. You may be fired if you are discovered to have Negro blood in your veins—an incident narrated by Alvin Johnson in the "New Republic," under a thin veil of fiction. You may be fired if you undertake to prove that a candidate of the Republican party for President has Negro blood in his veins—the singular experience of Professor W. E. Chancellor of Wooster. Of course you will be fired if you are discovered in any irregular sex relationship; also you may be fired if you discover the president of your university, or one of your prominent trustees, committing a similar offense. In general, you may be fired if you depart in any way from the beaten track of propriety— and this whether your motives be the lowest or the highest, whether you are subnormal or supernormal, a crank or a genius.

And here is the all-important fact; the decision in this difficult matter lies not in the hands of your colleagues, who know you, but in some autocratic individual who is too important to know you, and too busy. Says Professor George T. Ladd of Yale University, discussing the position of the college professor:

"His whole career, and the reputation and influence which he has won by a life of self-sacrificing labor, may at any moment be in peril through the caprice, or cowardice, or ill-will of a single man, or of a little group of men who have influence with that single man."

There are many college professors who have learned to adjust themselves to this situation, and make the best of it. They will call this book exaggerated and even absurd; but can they deny the statement of Professor Ladd above quoted? Can they deny that this is the situation in ninety-five per cent of American colleges and universities? The professors have no tenure and no security, save the kindness and good faith of those who hold the purse-strings and rule their lives. Says Professor Cattell in his book, "University Control": "In certain departments of certain universities, instructors and junior professors are placed in a situation to which no decent domestic servant would submit." If you will look up this book in your library you will find in it overwhelming evidence of the discontent of college professors with their status. Three hundred leading men were consulted, and out of these, eighty-five per cent agreed that the present arrangements for the government of colleges are unsatisfactory. Says

James P. Munroe, for many years a professor at Massachusetts Tech:

> Unless American college teachers can be assured that they are no longer to be looked upon as mere employes paid to do the bidding of men who, however courteous or however eminent, have not the faculty's professional knowledge of the complicated problems of education, our universities will suffer increasingly from a dearth of strong men, and teaching will remain outside the pale of the really learned professions. The problem is not one of wages; for no university can become rich enough to buy the independence of any man who is really worth purchasing.

Or consider the testimony of Professor E. A. Ross, of the University of Wisconsin, in the "Publications of the American Sociological Society," Vol. IX, 1914, p. 166:

> I agree with Professor Nearing; academic asphyxiation is much more common than is generally realized. President Pritchett's paper is, I think, far too optimistic. The dismissal of professors by no means gives the clue to the frequency of the gag in academic life. We forget the many who take their medicine and make no fuss. There, indeed, is your real tragedy. Don't waste any pity on the men who, despite repeated hints and warnings, go ahead until they are dismissed. They will generally prove to be able to take care of themselves. Pity rather the men who, without giving sign or creating scandal, bow to the powers above and cultivate a discreet silence. There are very many of them. I know it, for many of them have come and told me with bitterness and rage of the gag that has been placed in their mouths.
>
> Remember, too, that the source of danger is not endowment, at least if the donor has kept no strings upon his gift or is dead. It is not what has been given but what is hoped for that influences most the policy of university authorities. When a sizable donation is trembling in the balance, when an institution has been generously remembered in the will of some conservative gentleman who takes an annoying interest in the details of its life, how the governing board of the institution caters to the prejudices of the potential donor and how intolerable and unpardonable appear untimely professorial utterances or teachings which put the gift in peril!

I have before me a letter from Mr. Arthur E. Holder, who is not a college man, but a labor leader who had four years' experience with college men, as representative of labor on the Federal Board for Vocational Education. Mr. Holder writes:

> My conclusion after several years' contact with college professors and public school teachers is that the environment of school and college life is degenerating to the male species. Outside of a bare half dozen, these men seem to be afraid to say

that their souls are their own. They apparently admire boldness in others, and they applaud when another exposes the economic evils surrounding them. They do not hesitate to whisper as to their experiences; but it almost always is followed by a caution, "Don't say I said so," or "This is on the square," or "This is just for yourself alone," etc.

My experience in collecting material for this book brought out the academic situation with startling vividness. To begin with, I had the idea that if you wanted information on any subject you had merely to write to the people who had it. I collected from various sources the names of one or two hundred college professors who were supposed to be sympathetic towards social progress, and I printed a little circular outlining my proposed book, and asking them to tell me their experiences and conclusions. I mailed these circulars, and waited for replies; I waited two or three months, and the number of replies I received could be counted upon the fingers of one hand!

Of course, that might be because all these professors were satisfied with their position, and had no information to give. But I doubted that, and decided to travel over the country and talk personally with these individuals. I laid out a schedule and wrote again to arrange for interviews. Taught by experience, I explained that everything would be strictly confidential; but even on this basis I failed to hear from two-thirds of the men to whom I wrote. In various ways, through friends or colleagues, I would learn that this one or that one had thought it best to be able to say that he had never met me!

Still further insight came to me on the trip. I visited some thirty institutions, and met men and women who had taught in two or three hundred. Out of all these I should estimate that ninety-five per cent accepted my offer to consider what they told me confidential, and some even accepted my offer not to mention to their colleagues that they had talked with me. I would not need but one or two fingers to count the number of men and women now teaching in American colleges and universities who told me their experiences frankly, and stated that I might quote them by name.

Still further evidence: I came home after my seven thousand-mile journey, and sorted out my notes, and made a list of new names and new sources of information which

had been suggested. There must have been four hundred
such names, and I wrote a letter to each one, again enclos-
ing my little circular and making careful promises of
secrecy. Out of these four hundred I may have heard
from one hundred, and I should estimate that three-fourths
of these told me about the experiences of other men.
There are eight or ten who profess themselves fully satisfied with the conditions under which they work, but
even most of these do not care to be quoted. A number
avail themselves of my offer, not merely to consider their
communications confidential, but to send back their letters
after I have read them!

Another detail, even more significant: there would be
places in my notes concerning which I was in doubt, some
statement for which I wished additional verification, and
I would write to the people I had met. I recall them now,
one after another—men with whom I sat at luncheon or
dinner in a quiet corner in some restaurant, or in their
homes; some of them talked to me for two or three hours,
telling me their experiences and the experiences of their
colleagues, some shameful, some grotesque and absurd.
Many of these men promised me additional data, a clip-
ping or a letter or confirmation of some sort; and I write
to remind them of their promises, or to ask some new
questions—and there comes no reply! I write to some of
them two or three times before I realize what is the matter; these men are dead so far as concerns the mail! As
matters now stand, they can deny that they ever met me—
many of them told me that they would do that! But if
they should send me so much as a line of their hand-
writing, some day the Black Hand of the plutocracy might
raid my home and steal my papers—and then there would
be ruin for them and their families!

Can you think of stronger evidence of terrorism than
this? Out of not less than a hundred men who welcomed
me with every courtesy, who expressed cordial interest in
my project, and complete agreement with my view of the
academic situation—out of these hundred men I need
just the fingers of my two hands to count the ones who
have been willing to write and answer my questions under
the strictest pledge of secrecy! I take this occasion to send
my greetings to the others, and assure them that I do not
blame them too severely.

While preparing my proofs, still more evidence comes to me. In two different cases I sent a chapter of my book to university professors for them to revise, as they had offered to do. They dictated to their secretaries cold and stern letters, stating that they did not care to comply with my request; and along with these letters they sent me the manuscript, carefully and minutely revised! They understand that I will get the point; they have done what they promised to do, but at the same time they have protected themselves, and have a letter which they can display to college authorities, proving that they had nothing to do with my nefarious book!

Another case, still more significant: the liberal professors in one state university in the Middle West banded together and sent me a message through a former colleague, imploring me not to tell the story of their experiences in my book! The details of this controversy have been given full publicity in the press, and are public property; nevertheless, I am implored not to mention them, because it will stir up the reactionaries once more! Another professor in a great Eastern university, who told me how he took a public stand on an issue of academic freedom, telegraphs forbidding me to mention his name— and this though the story of his action has been publicly praised in the bulletin of the American Association of University Professors, and in several of the liberal magazines! A former professor in one of our largest Middle Western universities begs me to omit his name in telling his story—and this although I have newspaper clippings telling every detail! What am I to do about cases of this sort? Whom shall I consider, the individual professor or the public welfare? Read the man's pitiful words:

I realize the value to you of specific instances, and am well aware of how much I am asking when I request the omission of my name. But it means my livelihood! If I am again kicked out of educational work I shall never be able to accomplish such educational reforms as I have in mind for the future. Please don't put me in jeopardy! Sociological investigation often, of course, sacrifices the individual with perfect equinimity; but in this instance the individual is perhaps worth saving. Please let me know that you will spare me.

And here is another letter from a professor at another great state university in the Middle West:

27

I am greatly interested in the subject of the book which you are preparing, and I gladly give you my answer to the questions contained in your circular, with the definite understanding, however, that you will not mention my name as the source of information, or in any other way disclose my identity. The mere fact that as a matter of self-preservation and of protection to my family I feel compelled to make this proviso—disgusting as otherwise it is to me both as a man and a scholar—is proof sufficient of the control which special privilege exercises over educators in this country.

And here is one more letter, perhaps the most significant of all. The writer is a young scientist, who got his training at the University of Wisconsin, where for two years he took part in the activities of the liberal students. He tells me the effect which these two years have produced upon all his later career. Read his analysis of "academic freedom" among scientists; it covers the case completely, and every fairminded scientific man who reads it will be forced to admit that it is as exact as it is painful.

My position was student assistant, a half time instructorship. I stayed at Dr. P———'s house two years, and my relations with all the faculty of that department were intimate and cordial always, and still are. I was known as a rather harmless and intellectualized radical, and as rather a hard worker, one who spent long hours in his laboratory and applied himself assiduously: being especially useful around a scientific department by reason of ingenuity with apparatus. A sufficiency of all the technical virtues, you see, and the result was that I was very well thought of. A taste for sociology and radical discussion was looked upon as an amiable and altruistic weakness, which might serve to give my biology a humanistic turn. . . . .

No specific thing has ever happened since which I could lay against any of my professors at Madison. They have backed me cordially and enthusiastically whenever the occasion demanded. However, my reputation as a radical, still re-echoes through my career as a scientist; almost overshadows it. My chief professor, though he said I was the best man he had ever turned out, when I wanted a job, said also privately that he didn't think I would ever make a scientist, I was interested in too many other things. Another Wisconsin professor, when asked about me, questioned whether I would ever "settle down to a scientific career," though I had done absolutely nothing else for three years since I left there. A third expressed doubt, to me personally, that I would ever "accomplish anything." My reputation has followed me through two jobs, so that when considered for the one I now hold, the question of my radical proclivities was again raised. All these things, and many others, are hard to get at objectively; but they sum up to a condition in which an activity incidental to three years study on a Ph.D thesis appears still to be of more weight in the eyes of the men who pride themselves on being unbiased and liberal-minded scientists, than anything scientific that I may have accomplished. Every one of them would unhesitatingly state that a man's radical opinions were of no concern to them "if he did his work"; and no one of them would admit that any man would be "doing his work" if they knew he held these opinions. My own reaction is to pretend that I have lost interest in unconventional affairs, and to sedulously avoid any appearance of such interest in them in my professional capacity; in effect, I am one thing as a scientist, and another as a human being; I have dissociated most of my private concerns from my official ones; and the barrier between my school activities and any other intellectual interests is complete. I have two sets of ideas, two sets of friends, two modes of behavior, a regular double standard of morality, and I suppose I am only half a man in either capacity.

This is something of a tragedy to me personally, though that is not the interesting thing in general. The aspect of this that has struck me is, how perverted the whole unconscious thought of the academic institution is. As I have said, this is not evidence for a book. I might have trouble in demonstrating that my professors were not right about me. But one thing is certain; that I could have spent more than the amount of time and energy I spent on radical activities, on any of a number of more or less creditable things; on Wine, Women and Song, on student activities, golf, poker, or just plain idleness, and never have attracted any discreditable attention scientifically. Those things my professors and colleagues would disregard, provided I kept up a reasonable show of professional proficiency. There is only one realm of relaxation or dissipation which is recognized academically as a vicious incursion into scientific singlemindedness and assiduity; and that one is an intellectual interest in social unconventionality. That one distraction, and that alone, is recognized as an inherent and incontestible enemy of *scientific* right thinking. And the amusing part of it is that the scientists themselves fail to realize their own bias. For that is what it amounts to, even in the best of them; about one whole set of data, if they are not positively reactionary, then they not only have no positive opinions, but they impose upon themselves and others a negativity of opinion that amounts to a condition of **positive** prejudice.

CHAPTER LXXX

THE FOUNDATIONS OF FRAUD

I have taken you about from college to college and shown you the interlocking trustees, using the institution for the protection of their money-bags; also the successful sons, guarding the prestige and good name of their alma mater. To complete the picture I now draw your attention to the many organizations, national in their scope, which have been formed for the purpose of keeping our educational system in the capitalist fetters.

I begin with the Carnegie Foundation for the Advancement of Teaching, which was started seventeen years ago with a gift of ten million dollars. Its purpose was to provide pensions for superannuated college professors, and in his letter to the trustees Carnegie announced that "according to expert calculation" the revenue would be ample "to provide retiring pensions for the teachers of universities, colleges and technical schools in our country, Canada and Newfoundland." This statement was speedily shown to be absurd; the total cost of the system for Columbia University alone would have been twice the income of the Foundation, and the cost for all the country would have been two hundred times the income of the Foundation. So very speedily the Foundation was compelled to limit the institutions included in its list, and it began laying down rules for colleges, and assuming control of higher education. It refused pensions to professors in the University of Illinois unless the university would alter the conduct of its medical school at Chicago. In like manner the governor of Ohio was informed that the universities of the state must be "reconstructed" on lines laid down by the Foundation. Becoming still more embarrassed for lack of funds, the Foundation discovered that it was bad for teachers "to have the risk of dependence lifted from them by free gifts," and it proposed to have the professors begin paying for their own insurance.

Now, in the first place, a slight knowledge of economics will enable anyone to realize that a free gift of life insurance to professors at certain institutions would not permanently benefit the professors, because, under the stimulus of competition, this benefit would at once be taken into account in the salaries paid by the institution. So, what the Foundation amounts to is an endowment to certain privileged universities, with a highly autocratic control accompanying the gift. Under the plan as modified to compel the professor to pay for his insurance, the plan becomes a method of binding him to the institution and subjecting him to the administration. A part of the professor's salary is held out, to be repaid to him later on as a reward for good behavior. Says Professor Cattell:

"The professor who does not see eye to eye with Wall Street and Trinity Church may be compelled to sacrifice either his intellectual integrity or his wife and children. He is under heavy bonds to keep the peace; but it will be the peace of the desert."

If you are interested in this shrewd device for the enslavement of college professors, you are referred to Professor Cattell's book, "Carnegie Pensions," published in 1919. The new insurance organization is headed by Elihu Root and Nicholas Murray Butler, a sufficient guarantee of its character. That the sheep have learned to recognize these wolves in shepherd's clothing is shown by the fact that a questionnaire sent out by "School and Society" to a great number of college professors, asking for their opinions, brought a vote of thirteen in favor of the scheme and six hundred and thirty-six against it! The American Association of University Professors appointed a committee of twenty-four to study the scheme, and this committee submitted two elaborate reports condemning it.

The gentleman who was appointed by Mr. Carnegie to run this Foundation, and who worked out the scheme, is Dr. Henry Smith Pritchett; I look him up in "Who's Who," and find amusing evidence of what it means to have a strangle-hold over American institutions of learning. Dr. Pritchett goes about like an Indian war-chief with scalps at his belt—no fewer than eighteen honorary degrees from American colleges and universities! What the professors think of his administration you may guess from the comments on his last statement made by Joseph Jastrow, professor of psychology at the University of Wisconsin. "There is the same copious shuffling of the issues, the same lack of frankness, the same assumption of benevolence of motive, the same disregard of accepted principle as of actual opinion, the same aspersions and evasions."

The next great benefactor of our educational system was Mr. John D. Rockefeller, who has given one or two hundred millions of dollars to a foundation for the purpose of improving our schools and colleges according to Standard Oil ideals. The General Education Board has millions to give to those educational institutions which conform, and it holds over the head of every college and university president a perpetual bribe to sell out the interests of the people. Great numbers have accepted, a few have refused, and these have been the object of continual intrigue. Turn back to the chapter on North Dakota, and read the statements of Dr. W. J. Spillman of the United States Bureau of Agricultural Economics, concerning the efforts of these Rockefeller "educators" to dominate the land grant colleges. And let me call your attention to a speech delivered by this courageous public servant before the semi-annual conference of the National Board of Farm Organizations, February 11, 1919.

In order that you may understand Dr. Spillman's charges, I will first make plain the economics of the situation. After the war there was a frightful slump in values; the Federal Reserve Board, which controls our banking system, gave unlimited credit to the Wall Street banks, which they passed on to the big corporations, to enable them to get by the crisis without dropping the prices of their products. The farmers were left to "hold the sack," and they were ruined by millions—on my trip through the Northwest I was told of whole counties in which every single farm was for sale for taxes. The farmers wanted to know why the price of farm products should drop to nothing, while the price of manufactured articles was not affected. They wanted to know the cost of producing farm products, and they looked to the experts of the Department of Agriculture to get these figures. On the other hand, of course, big business decreed that the figures should not be got.

Their agent in carrying out this decree was the Secretary of Agriculture, David F. Houston, Harvard graduate, ex-president of the University of Texas, ex-chancellor of Washington University, and holder of seven honorary degrees; a member of the Southern Education Board, a subsidiary of the Rockefeller General Education Board; later chairman of the Federal Reserve and Farm Loan Boards, and now president of the Bell Telephone Securities Company. Dr. Spillman portrays Dr. Houston as lying, cheating and intriguing, resorting to every device in order to keep the facts about farming costs from being collected. Says Dr. Spillman:

I cannot give you the full facts about this matter without exposing honest and honorable men to the fury of this brutal autocrat, under whom they unfortunately have to serve. . . . . Early in his administration there was circulated through the department a typewritten sheet said to have been written by a member of Mr. Rockefeller's General Education Board, and which was said to represent Mr. Rockefeller's views, in which Secretary Houston concurred. This sheet purported to outline the duties of the department. It stated that the department should make no investigations that would reveal the profits made by farmers, or that would determine the cost of producing farm products. No representative of the department should ever under any circumstances even intimate that it is possible to overproduce any farm product. The entire business of the department was to teach farmers how to produce more than they now produce.

The General Education Board, you understand, possesses unlimited funds, it pays no taxes, and renders no accounting to anyone. Professor Cattell stated in "Science" that it "keeps for its own private use the information that it collects, and does not even publish the financial statements that should be required by law from every corporation, and first of all from those exempted from taxation." And these funds are used in paying fancy salaries to experts in all subjects, especially intrigue and wire-pulling. Dr. Spillman tells how this board got charge of the farm demonstration work in the South, and how he kept them from getting charge of the same work in the Northern and Western states. In order to hamper Spillman's work, "Mr. Houston issued orders to demonstration workers in the department not to co-operate with any outside agency except Mr. Rockefeller's General Education Board."

Soon after Mr. Houston became secretary he established an office in the department, known as the Rural Organization Service. The funds for the initiation of this work were furnished by the General Education Board. The important work of the Bureau of Markets was placed under this office, and Professor T. N. Carver of Harvard was invited to become head of the new bureau. He came to the department with real enthusiasm for his work, and at once proceeded to outline a series of important investigations on marketing of farm products, rural credits, and similar subjects. But when his plans were laid before the General Education Board by Secretary Houston they turned him down flat, with no explanation for their action. Professor Carver was much puzzled at this, and sought an interview with certain members of the board, for the purpose of finding out, if possible, why they had decided to discontinue their support; but he could get no information of any kind. He then told them in very plain language just what he thought of the General Education Board. Soon after this the newspapers carried a brief notice to the effect that Professor Carver had not found his work in the Department of Agriculture entirely congenial and would probably return to Harvard at the end of the year. He did return to Harvard soon thereafter. You will appreciate the gay humor of the fact that Professor T. N. Carver of Harvard University is named by Woodworth Clum, of the Better America Federation, the Black Hand of California, as one of two college professors who are heroically battling against Socialism in the colleges, and are deserving of the ardent support of all patriotic and liberty-loving Americans!

CHAPTER LXXXI

THE BOLSHEVIK HUNTERS

We shall next have a glance at those organizations and foundations which are frankly propagandist in their purposes, and which conduct departments of espionage and slander. We have already seen the work of the Better America Federation of California; there are a number of similar institutions which are nation-wide in their activities.

You remember, in the story of the University of Wisconsin, the young instructor whose career was placed in jeopardy by the National Association for Constitutional Government. This organization has been active in our educational centers, and among its publications is a pamphlet by a prominent corporation lawyer of Washington, advocating the establishment in all American colleges of a compulsory course in opposition to Socialism. Nicholas Murray Butler has actually established such a course at Columbia; it is required of freshmen, and is camouflaged under the name of "Contemporary History." The students have embodied their opinion of it in the phrase, "Contemptible History."

Also, the National Association of Manufacturers has been active. It was this organization which was exposed, in the famous "Mulhall" letters, as expending many millions in the bribing of Congress in the interest of big business. This organization has sent out agents to make propaganda in favor of commercial training in all colleges, and also to turn our public school system into an institution for the perpetuating of a class civilization. They call their scheme "vocational training," and they wish to educàte the children of the poor as workers, and to exclude them from general culture.

Also there is the National Security League, a high-up hundred per cent organization, whose active educational head received a three years' leave of absence from Princeton Univerity, to carry on propaganda on behalf of capitalist nationalism. In the beginning it was Hun-hunting, but later it turned into a Bolshevik-hunt, with Woodrow Wilson waging a private war in Siberia and Archangel, and Attorney-General Palmer's thugs clubbing the heads of men and women who dared to disbelieve in the divine right of the plutocracy. Just now this organization is carrying on a campaign in defense of the Supreme Court's right to annul acts of Congress, and defeat the will of the people in the interests of property. It has what is called a program for "economic education"; it proposes to have "the Constitution" taught in the public schools— meaning thereby the inviolability of special privilege. It sends out "dope" to the press of the country—and in this material I note an amusing concession to the well-known habit of newspapers to falsify. The "date line" of this press matter begins with the word "New York," and then a blank is left, so that newspapers may pretend to have received a long telegram from the metropolis!

There are such organizations as this in every section of our country. They call themselves merchants' and manufacturers' associations, chambers of commerce, citizens' alliances, national protective associations, home defense leagues. They do not deal especially with education, but when their attention is called to unorthodox teachings, or to "outside activities" of college professors, they intervene with authority. From the "National American Council" I have obtained a list of seventy-nine such organizations, all pledged to keep the American people in "blinkers." Recently a number of them—the National Association for Constitutional Government, the Public Interest League, the League for Preservation of

American Independence, the Constitutional Liberty League, the Anti-Centralization Club—have formed themselves into one super-organization known as the "Sentinels of the Republic." They intend to enlist a million patriots, their motto being "Every citizen a sentinel, every home a sentry-box." The object of this sentineling is to smash the Socialists, and among the organizers are of course David Jayne Hill and Nicholas Murray Butler.

Also, this chapter would not be complete without mention of that immortal committee of the New York state legislature, which has given to the English language a new word. The "Luskers" hauled radicals of all sorts before it, raiding their homes and offices, smashing their furniture and stealing their papers. It went particularly after the school-teachers, and we shall meet it again when we come to the schools. One of its chosen victims was the Rand School of Social Science, which is really a college, but modestly refrains from calling itself such. It is an institution in which students are frankly and shamelessly taught to think for themselves, and the politicians of the state and city of New York understand that their existence is jeopardized by such a place. The first steps taken against the Rand School were to raid the place and throw the typewriters and the teachers down the stairs. As that did not cause the pupils to stop thinking for themselves, the Lusk committee recommended, and the New York state legislature passed a bill, requiring that all institutions which carry on teaching in New York state shall have a license from the regents of the state education board; the intention, of course, being that a license shall be issued to all institutions in the state except the Rand School of Social Science and the "Modern School," organized by the followers of Ferrer.

The Rand School has refused to apply for a license under this law, and the Supreme Court, Appellate Division, has just ruled against the school, holding the act constitutional. The next step is to carry the case to the Court of Appeals, and after that to the United States Supreme Court. It is manifest that if this Lusk law is upheld, there will be no use talking any more about academic freedom, so far as concerns the state of New York. Common sense would suggest that the provision in the United States Constitution, forbidding the passing of laws interfering with freedom of speech and of the press, should cover this case; but when you investigate the subject you find that common sense and the plain words of the Constitution are not what count in capitalist law. There is a provision in our Constitution forbidding interference with "the right of the people to bear arms in time of peace"; but that right has not prevented the courts of New York state from upholding a law forbidding a citizen to keep a revolver in his home! It is pleasant to be able to record that Governor Miller, who signed these Lusk laws, was defeated for re-election in November, 1922, by a plurality of four hundred and ten thousand votes, the largest plurality ever cast in the history of an American state.

There are many other organizations watching our colleges. The interlocking newspapers are vigilant, and do not always confine their activities to their own locality. The Chicago "Tribune" has exposed and caused the expulsion of more than one college professor. We have seen in this book such activities on the part of the "Oregonian" of Portland and the "Missoulian" of Montana, the Seattle "Times" and the Boston "Evening Transcript," the Grand Forks, North Dakota, "Herald," the Rockford, Illinois, "Star," the Fort Worth, Texas, "Searchlight."

In Rhode Island is the Providence "Journal," whose publisher we have met as one of the three leading trustees of Brown University. The editor of this paper is a super-patriot, Mr. John Revelstoke Rathom, who is tireless in war upon "radicalism" in the colleges, not merely of his own state, but throughout New England. I find Mr. Rathom lecturing before the Liberal Club of Clark University—the same organization which was so bitterly denounced by the Worcester "Telegram" as Bolshevist! Mr. Rathom put no restraint upon his contempt for the parlor Socialists; he denounced them as "unsexed brains," and declared that he "would not pay them twenty-five dollars a week" on his newspaper—this being the final test of excellence in human brains. "Still," says Mr. Rathom, "they are permitted to teach our young students all this filth, this infidelity to country, this bestial doctrine." He declared that in many places "our public schools have become hot-beds of anarchy, instead of shrines of liberty."

Mr. Rathom's title to hundred percent Americanism is secured by his Australian birth and English education. In the days before America entered the war, this multiple patriot took up the task of bringing us in, and published in his paper an elaborate series of exposés of German intrigue in our country. It read like Sherlock Holmes, and was taken up by the interlocking press, and created an enormous sensation. Then Mr. Rathom started a series of articles in the "World's Work"—tales about German spies and bomb plots, and how Mr. Rathom with his host of secret agents had penetrated even into the German embassy at Washington! But something happened, nobody knew what. Mr. Rathom's narrative came to a sudden stop, and the "World's Work" said no more about it. It was not until several years later that the truth was revealed; the United States Secret Service authorities had objected to being represented as a collection of "boobs," and had forced Mr. Rathom to a showdown. Not merely had they made him stop the publication of his articles; they had made him sign an elaborate document, in which he admitted that a good part of his material was the product of his own imagination, and the rest had been furnished him by the Bohemian National Alliance, and the Croatian and Serbian national societies, and other anti-German and anti-Austrian groups in America! I quote you just one sentence of this document, in order that you may observe the nature of a worm when it wriggles:

I feel that the general public opinion, which has rather unfortunately credited us with the actual bringing to justice of German spies and malefactors, has been misdirected to the extent that our only possible claim to valuable constructive work in the past three and one-half years ought in fairness to be restricted to the educational value of our combined efforts, and the newspaper enterprise which produced a great number of stories printed in our newspapers.

And then follow twenty-eight long paragraphs, in which Mr. Rathom admits in detail the falsehoods in the "stories" he published, and winds up by agreeing to make no more public addresses during the war! Also, one ought not deny the honor of mention to Mr. James M.

Beck, corporation lawyer and amateur patriot. Mr. Beck holds three honorary degrees from American universities, and is described to me by a university professor as "the most notorious high-brow ass in the country." He travels about making commencement orations in our colleges, and clamoring for the casting out of professors who fail in loyalty to the plutocracy. If you want to know just how foolish one of these hundred percenters can make himself in public, read the controversy of Mr. Beck with Professor Frankfurter of the Harvard Law School concerning the Mooney case, published in the "New Republic" for January 18, 1922.

Another hundred percenter who is much concerned with our education is a leading corporation lawyer of Denver, Mr. Charles R. Brock, one of the grand dukes of Denver University, where we studied the career of Chancellor Buchtel. Mr. Brock is attorney for the "Big Four" utility corporations, which have run the city government of Denver for a generation; his partner was for a long time chairman of the infinitely corrupt Democratic party of Colorado. So Mr. Brock is terribly afraid of Socialists, and last spring I find him delivering a tirade against them to the young ladies of the most exclusive finishing school in Denver. Also he published in the Denver "Post" an attack upon President Thomas of Bryn Mawr, because of her radicalism. We shall have an inside glimpse at Miss Thomas's activities before long, and discover the truly comical cautiousness of her "radicalism."

It seems to trouble these corporation gentlemen especially that women should be venturing to think; they get after the women's colleges again and again. Thus, some years ago, the head of a woman's college got a letter from a high-up interlocking trustee, informing him that it had been discovered that twenty girls in that institution had formed a Socialist group, and that the trustee proposed to take action unless this group was broken up. The president of Wellesley received a letter from a prominent successful son, stating that he had learned that two members of the faculty had voted for Debs! At Vassar they pretend to permit freedom of discussion, but they limit the Socialist organization to two speakers a year, while they place no restriction upon the number of speakers brought

in by the Christian Association. A lecture by Albert
Rhys Williams was canceled, upon action of the trustees, after that friend of the Russian people had given
his testimony before the Overman committee of the
United States Senate. A professor at another woman's
college—she will not permit me to name the place—told
me a funny story of how the president was visited by a
hundred percent banker, who frightened her with the tidings that he had unearthed "radical activities" among the
faculty, and proposed to take action about it before the
trustees. He had the "goods" in his pocket, he said; and
after some persuasion, he consented to produce the
"goods"—which proved to consist of a letter from a
parent, reporting one of the professors as advising a girl
to read "those Bolshevist and Anarchist magazines, the
'Survey' and the 'New Republic'!"

CHAPTER LXXXII

THE HELEN GHOULS

I have reserved for a separate chapter our most
active anti-socialist organization, the National Civic Federation, a combination of class-conscious capitalists such
as Elbert H. Gary and Alton B. Parker, with high-
salaried labor leaders who have sold out their class. Once
a year these labor leaders are honored with an elaborate
banquet in New York City, where they listen to patriotic
speeches from the wholesale corrupters of our public life.
This National Civic Federation has a special department,
headed by Condé B. Pallen, a Catholic lecturer, the "Committee for the Study of Revolutionary Movements." It
runs an elaborate system of espionage, and is perhaps the
greatest single agency for the brow-beating of college
professors.

I had special opportunity to observe the workings of
this enterprise, because I served for ten years on the
executive committee of the Intercollegiate Socialist Society, which used to receive the special attention of Mr.
Ralph M. Easley, secretary of the Federation. This gentleman subscribed for six copies of our little monthly
magazine, and used to quote extracts from it as a means
of terrifying his backers into parting with their cash.

He would list the names of the professors and students whom we mentioned, and would stir up college presidents and trustees and local business men and newspaper editors against them. Some tragedies resulted from this; and often it happened that professors and students lost interest in our work, and offered no explanation.

The most prominent of the backers of this Federation has been Mrs. Finley J. Shepard, née Helen Gould; one of the half dozen children of Jay Gould, the old-time railroad wrecker and Wall Street gambler. His other children turned out wasters and wantons, but Helen was a woman of kind heart, who gave much money to charity, and was the darling of the New York newspapers in the days of my childhood. She married one of her employes, an official in the Gould railroads, and now she has swallowed whole the goblin stories of those who live by scaring rich people into putting up their money for class propaganda.

I do not mean to say that there are not men and women among the "reds" who would be glad to overthrow the American government and abolish the constitution, but I say that such people can only be met and overcome by free discussion, based upon an honest resolve to bring social justice into the world. Also, I say that the peril to our land which these "reds" represent is not one per cent of that represented by the big business criminals who run the National Civic Federation. I say furthermore that the constitution of the United States and the good name and credit of our country will not suffer as much damage from the propaganda of Lenin and Trotsky in a hundred years as they have suffered from the system of corruption and terrorism instituted by Ralph M. Easley and Condé B. Pallen with the money of Helen Gould Shepard.

When I was in New York I met a man who declared that he had been present at a luncheon-party, at which Mrs. Shepard stated that she had pledged her entire fortune to the stamping out of radicalism from our colleges. She was maintaining an organization for the carrying on of "investigations" into the teaching of social questions, and the ousting of those who taught unsound ideas. Within the last year Mrs. Shepard herself had caused the ousting of two such men. I did not want to repeat these statements without giving Mrs. Shepard an opportunity to confirm or deny them, so I wrote her a polite note, asking for an interview. This note was not answered, and a couple of months later I wrote a detailed letter, in which I stated what I had learned from several sources, and asked her to correct the statements if they were false. I pointed out that when persons of great wealth spend their money for propaganda, they enter a field which is of public concern, and the public has a right to be informed as to what they are doing. This letter likewise remained unanswered, so I take is as fair to assume that Mrs. Shepard admits the truth of the statements quoted above.

In these activities she is earnestly supported by her husband, who is a trustee of the University of Jabbergrab, and last spring was serving on a committee appointed by the state superintendent of education to browbeat the school teachers of the city who were suspected of unorthodox ideas. The sessions of this committee were secret, so I was not able to observe Mr. Shepard functioning. I have, however, a pretty good picture of the Shepard family life, in a letter from a well-known Methodist clergyman, who was invited to a dinner-party at the home of Mr. and Mrs. Shepard. Their conversation was devoted almost exclusively to "the intellectuals," whom Mrs. Shepard "held responsible for the present disturbance in the social order." She gave her guest the Lusk committee report—six large volumes, in the index of which the author of "The Goose-step" is listed as "a violent literary Socialist." Also, she gave him two books attacking modern ideas in religion—which books are published and distributed upon her bounty. Said Mr. Shepard: "It is the business of the preacher to preach salvation and let industry alone. When men are converted they will apply the gospel to business. My father was a preacher. What did he know about business?" Mr. Shepard characterized Judge Gary as "the savior of the country"; and Mrs. Shepard declared that "the Union Theological Seminary is the greatest menace to New York City today." Says the clergyman: "I came away with the idea well driven home, that the social Gospel is Socialism; that Socialism is Bolshevism; that Bolshevism is Atheism; and that nothing but the pure individualistic Gospel can save the nation and the world."

You may judge from this that it is not a diverting experience to be invited to a dinner-party at the home of the Shepards. I have before me another document, which indicates that it is a still less diverting experience to be invited to a cemetery with Mr. and Mrs. Shepard. This document is a four-page leaflet, containing an address signed, "Helen Gould Shepard," and headed as follows:

At the Graves of John More and Betty Taylor, His Wife
The Cemetery, Roxbury, New York
August 31, 1920

Cousins of the More Family:
We are here today to honor the memory of our ancestors, John More and Betty Taylor, his wife, who came from Scotland in 1722 and settled in the Catskill Mountains, then a very wild region.

The little speech goes on for three paragraphs, to tell about the virtues of the John Mores; after which, for five paragraphs is proceeds to implore the cousins of the More family not to fall victims to the evil and insidious modern "isms" which are "threatening to carry us on to utter catastrophe unless the Christians of the nation awaken." Imagine, if you can, this poor, good-hearted, feeble-minded rich lady reading a memorial oration at the graves of her ancestors, and devoting one-fourth of her time to reciting the bugaboo-stories sent out in the begging letters of the National Civic Federation! Hear a sample paragraph:

The forces of autocratic barbarism are not confined to the Socialists, Anarchists and I. W. W.'s, but the cause of Lenine is more actively furthered either frankly or by indirection by radical, pseudo-intellectual writers, editors, professors, teachers and clergymen in our newspapers, magazines, colleges, schools and churches, and in some of these the enemies of democratic government are found to hold the very highest positions.

You will say that this is ridiculous, and you may say that it is negligible; but I assure you that nothing is negligible in America that has money. The wage-slaves of the railroads of the United States furnish millions of dollars every year for Mrs. Shepard to use in circulating such drivel, and subsidizing professional intriguers and character-assassins. I presume that Mrs. Shepard is a tender-hearted woman, who would be incapable of killing a mouse with her own hands. History reports the same thing of Queen Mary; but that did not keep her from causing Protestants to be burned at the stake. Moved by religious terrors and class arrogance Mrs. Shepard considers herself justified in setting in motion machinery for destroying the careers of men whose only offense is that they resent social oppression, and venture here and there to raise a feeble voice against it.

I have before me a letter from one such man, who has been blacklisted by the National Civic Federation, and in consequence has been hounded from college to college throughout the United States; I submit him as an exhibit of Mrs. Shepard's achievements, a scalp which she wears at her belt. Or perhaps I might call him a series of scalps, since the poor man has lost his job ten times in sixteen years. I refrain from giving his name, at his request; he says: "I am perfectly capable of accumulating enough notoriety for myself without any professional assistance."

He goes on to tell about his adventures, one after another. He was on the faculty of the Florida State College for Women, and was very successful as a teacher, but it began to be noticed that his students developed Socialist opinions, and the local newspapers took up the case, and the board of trustees fired him, in spite of the protest of the students. Then he went to Lenox College in Iowa, a town which had elected a Socialist mayor. "In the spring the president called me in and told me that he did not want me to think they had decided to drop me, but they made no move toward holding me for another year, so I got another job." He went to Maryville College in Tennessee, and at the end of the second year "monied people in the East objected to my writings"; so he was dropped. Next he was dropped at Clark University, on account of his opposition to the war. He went to the University of Kentucky, and after a year of teaching was invited to give a lecture on Russia by the college Y. M. C. A. "The head of the department said it would be as much as his job was worth to recommend me for reappointment, and that the same would be true of the dean and the president; so I was not reappointed." That was the summer of 1919, and he went to DePauw, but before he got started the Chicago "Tribune" got after him, so that he was "out of a job before entering upon it."

The curious thing about all these experiences is how little the professor himself realized the significance of them. He wrote me: "My record does not seem to occasion special suspicion!" Again he said: "There is no organized system of control by privilege over American education!" As it happens, I was behind the scenes in New York, and heard some mention of this same professor's name. Some day we shall have a government in this country which will indict the heads of the National Civic Federation for criminal conspiracy, and then we may take a turn at looking into their papers, and this professor may learn why it was that the heads of so many colleges suddenly discovered that it would be as much as their jobs were worth to recommend him for promotion!

P. S.—It is interesting to note that only three months later this young professor had grown wiser. He wrote to me again, as follows:

I have been thinking that I might have to revise my letter to you in one point. I said I had never encountered anything like a black-list. Now I am not so sure. I had to hunt another job this year (just why I am not perfectly sure), but failed in my efforts to land anything suitable. A certain proportion of the institutions to which I applied answered in such a way as aroused no suspicion of anything ulterior. A good many did not answer at all, or else merely returned my material. I have a notion that some of them have me spotted. In one case where I was asked to apply in person, the case was closed in a dubious way, etc.

We have one supremely successful organization for standardizing the thoughts and morals of America, the Ku Klux Klan. The reason for its success is that its members dress themselves in night-gowns and white hoods, and its leaders call themselves Grand Goblins and Imperial Kleagles. These symbols and names of terror have proven so effective, that I wonder the idea is not taken up by the secret agents and scandal-hounds of the National Civic Federation's "Committee for Study of Revolutionary Movements." I offer the suggestion for what it is worth; let them name themselves the Helen Ghouls, and let Mr. Condé B. Pallen be known as the Shepard's Watch-dog, and Mr. Ralph M. Easley as the Shepard's Crook! I must not suggest this latter name without definite reason, so I set aside the next chapter to show you

by what devious devices Mr. Easley does his work of
destroying the reputation of educators who fail to recognize his plutocratic authority.

CHAPTER LXXXIII

THE SHEPARD'S CROOK

There is at Annandale, New York, an Episcopal
church institution called St. Stephen's College, having as
its president the Reverend Bernard Iddings Bell, who
was dean of the cathedral at Fond-du-lac, Wisconsin, for
five years, and chaplain of the Great Lakes Naval Training Station during the war. President Bell is a former
Socialist, who resigned from the Church Socialist Fellowship at the outbreak of the war, but has not abandoned
his belief that the way to confute error is to understand
it and tell the truth about it, instead of to lie about it and
repress it by force.

Immediately after the war the National Civic Federation invited Bishop Burch of the Episcopal diocese of
New York to send delegates to a conference on labor
conditions, and President Bell was asked to become one
of the delegates; he declined, and wrote Bishop Burch
advising him not to send any delegates, "since to do so
would be to tie up the church officially with an organization which is suspect among most social workers of
responsibility and reliability." As a result of this advice,
Bishop Burch sent no delegates.

Shortly afterwards word of this came to Mr. Ralph
M. Easley, and he was furiously incensed against President Bell. He met President MacCracken of Vassar
College at a dinner-party, and "in a most violent and unrestrained manner" announced that he was going to "get
this man Bell"; St. Stephen's College was "full of Bolshevism," etc. From various other people word came to
President Bell that Mr. Easley was attacking St. Steph-
en's, "in the same violent and unrestrained manner, selecting especially those persons who were liable to make
financial contributions to the college." President Bell
thereupon wrote Mr. Easley a very courteous letter, explaining that he was under an entire misapprehension concerning St. Stephen's, and inviting him to come there

and make an investigation of the place, and incidentally to explain the Civic Federation's work to the students. Mr. Easley replied that he could not come at once, but would take up the matter later. He never did take it up, nor did he ever accept the invitation several times repeated by President Bell during the controversy which followed.

What Mr. Easley did was to publish in the "National Civic Federation Review" for January, 1920, what President Bell described as "a vituperative article, based on false information and illegitimate deductions." These words were used by President Bell in a letter to Judge Alton B. Parker, president of the Civic Federation. Said President Bell: "I do not believe that the Civic Federation stands by this kind of thing, and I think it is high time that someone takes your publication in hand and teaches it the principles of honest journalism." President Bell went on to express his confidence in Judge Parker's belief in honesty and fair play; but apparently his confidence was misplaced, for Judge Parker never answered this letter, nor any other letter on the subject of the misdeeds of Mr. Easley. What Judge Parker did was to show President Bell's letter, "with violent indignation," to the general counsel of the Metropolitan Life Insurance Company, in the Metropolitan Club of New York, known as the "Millionaires." He was surprised to learn that this gentleman was a trustee of St. Stephen's, and that he stood by President Bell. The trustee undertook to obtain from President Bell a detailed statement of the falsehoods in Mr. Easley's article. So President Bell wrote to his trustee, pointing out a series of ten false statements and inferences in Mr. Easley's attack upon the college. I don't suppose the reader will wish to go into these details; suffice it to say that the clergyman proved his case thoroughly, and that his bill of complaint traveled by way of the trustee and Judge Parker to Mr. Easley, who wrote to President Bell, stating that he was turning the whole correspondence over "to a committee composed of members of the Protestant Episcopal Church who are interesting themselves in the subject of the extent to which the revolutionary forces have permeated that church."

This committee consisted of an obscure lawyer by

the name of Townsend, an Episcopal clergyman by the
name of Carstensen, and Mr. Everett P. Wheeler, a New
York lawyer, whose excuse is that he is eighty-two years
of age. Dr. Carstensen was courteous enough to advise
President Bell that he was serving on this committee, and
asked that an anti-Bolshevist army officer should be permitted to address the students of St. Stephen's College—
which request President Bell cheerfully granted.

About this time happened one of the those mysterious
things which may always be counted upon to happen
when you are dealing with the Helen Ghouls and the
Shepard's Crooks. Somehow or other the news of the
affair gets to the capitalist press; somehow the capitalist
press comes into possession of the complete documents—
of one side of the case! This time it was the New York
"World" which learned that a committee of the National
Civic Federation was preparing a report on Bolshevism
at St. Stephen's, and the "World" published this report
upon its front page. Dr. Carstensen, who in the meantime had visited St. Stephen's, wrote to President Bell
that he had refused to sign the report. He added that
the report was about to be issued officially by the National
Civic Federation; to which President Bell replied, expressing doubt that the report would be officially issued.
The publication in the New York "World" had raised a
storm among the supporters of St. Stephen's; and, said
President Bell, "Easley is not fond of making charges
the responsibility for which he cannot easily disavow,
when he discovers that he has done something unpopular."

Sure enough, when one of the trustees of the National
Civic Federation came out in the "World" supporting
President Bell, Mr. Easley suddenly stepped from under!
He publicly denied that he had anything to do with the
attack on St. Stephen's, and declared that the committee
had no connection with the National Civic Federation,
but that the members of the committee alone were responsible for what they had done! Imagine, if you can,
the chagrin of poor Mr. Eighty-two-year-old Everett P.
Wheeler! Mr. Wheeler wrote to President Bell to explain that he had nothing to do with the publication, that
he had protested against it to the New York "World,"
and that he considered it "a shameful abuse by a great

newspaper." The purpose of the committee, said Mr. Wheeler, had been to act toward President Bell "as Christian brethren, and to give you every opportunity to explain your position. We are not without hope that we may convince you that you have erred."

So you can see what has happened; poor Mr. Wheeler blames the New York "World," but his aged mind does not go back to the question of who supplied the "World" with the data of which it made use. Who was it, do you think? Was it the Shepard's Crook, employing the name and reputation of an aged dotard, once a vigorous reformer, as a means to assail a liberal teacher and clergyman? Telling Mr. Wheeler that he is serving on a committee of the National Civic Federation, and that the purpose of this committee is to prepare an appeal to President Bell, in the hope of convincing him that he has erred; and then secretly permitting this confidential material to reach the New York "World"; and finally when he sees that his charges have overshot the mark, disavowing his aged tool, and leaving him exposed to public contempt!

I conclude with President Bell's summary of what this story shows about Mr. Ralph M. Easley:

1. His willingness to attack an institution and a person because of personal bias, and to involve the National Civic Federation in the task of pulling his personal chestnuts out of the fire.

2. The absurdity of his contention that his society has never attacked individuals.

3. His absolute lack of courtesy in correspondence.

4. His willingness to circulate sub rosa information about people whom he does not like, and when caught at it to deny responsibility in the name of himself and of his Federation.

5. His using of other people for his purposes, telling them only what he wishes of the controversies in which he seeks to engage their aid. This is especially plain in his refusal to tell the committee headed by Mr. Wheeler that this college was welcoming investigation and that it had invited him to investigate for himself or send others to investigate. If Mr. Wheeler had known all this it would have thrown an entirely different emphasis upon the whole situation.

CHAPTER LXXXIV

CITIES OF REFUGE

The reader will be ready by this time with the question: are there no free colleges whatever in America, no institutions of higher learning where truth is sought and respected? There are a few, and we have now to give them credit.

We have heard Mrs. Helen Gould Shepard declaring at her dinner-table that "the Union Theological Seminary is the greatest menace to New York City today." Translated into commonsense, this means that there are professors at this institution who have come to realize the futility of basing the moral standards of mankind upon a literal acceptance of fairy stories, the product of the child-mind of the race; also who have read the words of Jesus about the impossibility of serving both God and Mammon.

Among these revolutionary theologians is Harry F. Ward, secretary of the Social Service Federation of the Methodist church. Dr. Ward was active in protest against the crimes of Judge Gary during the recent steel strike, and as a result fell victim to the Helen Ghouls. A man called upon him, being obviously not of the idealist type, but representing himself as a lecturer on Bolshevism, wishing to verify certain facts. After a brief conversation Dr. Ward gave the man a "calling-down," telling him that he was utterly ignorant of the subject with which he pretended to deal. Not long afterwards Dr. Ward learned of a document, issued by the National Civic Federation, but bearing no name, and accompanied by a request for its return after reading. It was being submitted to open shop employers and propagandists, and used as a means of money-getting: an alleged interview with Ward, in which he was represented as having said that Christianity would soon pass away, and Bolshevism take its place; the full absurdity of which statement you could not realize unless you had the fortune to know this passionately earnest Christian clergyman. Ward had mentioned a young Y. M. C. A. man named Hecker, as one who had first-hand knowledge of the Seattle strike, and this document named Hecker, and was used to procure his discharge. It was also used to bar Jerome Davis from Chautauqua platforms. When a committee of the Inter-church Federation called upon Judge Gary, they found the document on his desk, and he quoted from it liberally. Also it was in the hands of Chancellor Buchtel of Denver University when he barred Harry Ward from speaking. So far extends the reach of the Shepard's Crook!

There are other places in the country in which the revolutionary leaven of Jesus is working. There is the Berkeley Divinity School at Middletown, Connecticut, a place of open-mindedness and fine idealism, presided over by Dean W. P. Ladd. Wild rumors were spread concerning Bolshevist activities, and the grand duke of the trustees, Mr. Nettleton, president of the New Haven Gas Company, took up the fight. One of the charges was that the dean belonged to the Church League for Industrial Democracy—among whose members are fifteen bishops of the Episcopal church! The investigating committee of the trustees decided that it was unwise for the dean and members of the faculty to belong to this organization. They qualified their statement, "in the present state of the public mind, and from the standpoint of the citizen of the world"; to which Dean Ladd makes the pungent comment: "One would have thought that even a citizen of the world would prefer that a member of the faculty of a Christian divinity school should regulate his conduct, not with reference to the world and the prevailing state of the public mind, but according to the principles of the religion which he professes." Also the committee laid down the rule: "We cannot for a moment permit any action or influence of theirs (the faculty), as teachers, which would seem to develop Socialism as a political idea." And further, the committee laid down the rule: "What the teachings of the School shall be and how they shall be taught, and under what influences the students shall live are matters for (the trustees), if not entirely, at least in co-operation with the dean and the faculty."

Dean Ladd issued a counter statement, in which he frankly and completely differs from this policy, and declares that he will not follow it. He says:

I cannot while I remain dean of the School be a party to a policy so entirely at variance with my own judgment and conviction of what is right. The Berkeley Divinity School is, of course, desperately in need of money. And trustees and others have repeatedly said that no money will be forthcoming so long as our present policy continues. I hope this is not so. But if the School has to die in a losing fight for a policy, one feature of which is to try to make justice and love the controlling motive in all social conditions, I am quite ready to say, with Bishop Brewster, "Then let it die!" Better so to die than to live on prosperously in an attitude of subservience and compromise.

The school still lives; but you may judge the drawing-power of social idealism in America today by the fact that it has only fifteen students. It has to exist by gifts, because its trustees invested most of its funds in the shares of the New Haven Railroad!

Also at Oberlin, Ohio, is an old college under religious auspices, struggling hard to preserve the high traditions of its abolitionist founders. From its beginning in 1833 it admitted women and Negroes, and its internal affairs have always been controlled by its faculty. Appointments are made by the faculty and ratified by the trustees, and so far the trustees have behaved themselves. During the war they tried to drive out a professor on the ground that he was pro-German, but they were only able to get one faculty vote for the proposal, and so were forced to drop it. A professor at Oberlin writes me that the faculty is conservative, as in all other colleges, and they naturally try to appoint only those who conform; "but if a mistake is made there is never a thing said to coerce his freedom in the class or out." As a consequence, this professor has ventured to advise his classes to read "The Brass Check." When the librarian declared that the library had no funds with which to subscribe to the New York "Call," the professor of Hebrew advised him to take the money from the "Old Testament fund," explaining quite correctly that "the Old Testament is a book of prophecy."

Also, in Denver is the Iliff School of Theology of the Methodist church, where several young professors are following the example of the dangerous Harry Ward. When Ward was barred from speaking by Chancellor Buchtel, they brought him across the street and triumphantly listened to his message. When I came to Denver they welcomed me in a church, and told me the story of their struggle against the infinite corruption enthroned in Denver politics, and worshipped in Denver churches.

And then, I must not overlook the Y. M. C. A. College, located at Springfield, Massachusetts, which through some freak of chance has secured a phenomenal president in L. L. Doggett, who brought his old Oberlin professor, Ballantine, to teach some truth about the Bible, and thus caused anguish to the orthodox. The war brought President Doggett to the conclusion that the world cannot be saved by prayer and Indian clubs, and he went abroad and got into touch with the London School of Economics, and other European progressives, and came back and founded an "industrial course," in the face of bitter opposition from a solemn, prayerful and gymnastic faculty. The pious morons in the Association are fighting him tooth and nail, and have, of course, curtailed their gifts to the college. President Doggett has taken up an endowment campaign of his own, and I cheerfully give him this "boost," though I fear it may do him more harm than good!

This part of my story would not be complete unless I paid tribute to the Church League for Industrial Democracy, and to the tireless services of Richard W. Hogue, an Episcopal clergyman who was kicked out of his church and his open forum in Baltimore, and now travels over the country, gathering groups of theological students and Y. M. C. A. workers, and preaching to them the real gospel of the crucified proletarian. He tells me that he finds increasing welcome; he tells of several little colleges throughout the Middle West, whose faculties—and in one or two cases, the presidents—believe in free discussion, and have given him a hearing.

Also, there is one free law school in America—at Harvard. We have seen Dean Pound and Professors Frankfurter, Sayre and Chafee taking a bold stand for freedom of speech. These men fearlessly teach the evolution of law, and suggest to their students the possibility of improvement in American institutions. Thus, from the last report of Dean Pound I quote a few scattered sentences, just to give you an idea of the tone:

A clear body of law has grown up already as the result of the experience of a generation in the Interstate Commerce Commission, a body of law is forming under our eyes through the administration of workmen's compensation acts by industrial commissions, and the exigencies of general peace and good order, if nothing else, must lead before long to a new body of law governing industrial disputes. . . . . Collective bargaining is likely to compel us to think over again the whole subject of juristic personality in Anglo-American law. Criminal law and procedure call for the best efforts of thoroughly trained common-law lawyers acquainted with the social science of today. . . . . For much that we have had to study and to teach in the immediate past is already yielding in importance to these new elements in the legal system. Much of our nineteenth-century law will presently be as obsolete as the learning of real actions and of the feudal law of estates in land which held so large a place in the curriculum of the Law School a century ago, or the elaborate and involved procedural law which was so important fifty years later, or the pedantic law of bailments which has given way to a modern doctrine of the obligations of public service.

Needless to say, such utterances as this, from such a source, are the cause of continually increasing distress to the legal retainers of our plutocracy!

Also, there is a New England college of considerable reputation, whose president has taken a firm stand for open-mindedness, and that is Amherst. President Meikeljohn was one of the live men who got out of Brown when it began to die. He is now trying to make one small college in which young men are taught to think, instead of just to believe in dogmas. He is in the midst of a fight with reactionary trustees; in 1920 they asked for his resignation, but he consulted a lawyer and told them they had no authority in the premises. He is still in office, for how long I do not know.

Also, there is Swarthmore, in Pennsylvania, in which some professors are making a brave struggle. This is an old co-educational institution established by the Quakers, a sect which had more than its share of persecution, and took pains to provide for freedom of opinion. But now the Quakers have become rich, and there is a new kind of persecution in the world, and shall they permit freedom of opinion about special privilege? That Swarthmore has not been entirely liberal, you may judge from the fact that its most conspicuous graduates are Governor Sproul of Pennsylvania, who smashed the steel strike with his Cossacks, and Attorney-General Palmer, who killed and buried the constitution of the United States. The thousands of alleged radicals and helpless foreigners who had their heads cracked by Mr. Palmer's thugs will appreciate the gay humor of the fact that this gentleman is a devout and active Quaker!

Governor Sproul gave to Swarthmore an astronomical observatory; the stars are a long way off, and the governor is not afraid of anything that might be discovered there. But Professor Robert C. Brooks of Swarthmore put his sociological telescope upon Delaware County, in which the college is located, and drew a diagram of the "jury wheel system," whereby the big political crooks managed to keep themselves out of jail. Certain men of wealth came to the president of Swarthmore, saying: "Here we have given five millions, and we can't do it with a man like Brooks running round and stirring up trouble"; so the president had a "frank talk" with Professor Brooks.

Nevertheless, some professors are holding on both to their convictions and their jobs, and so the place is regarded as a "hot-bed." There is a professor of philosophy, who is using modern literature as a door to Plato, and tells the students to read "Man and Superman" and "The Spoon River Anthology." He got from this experiment a lively response; some of the boys and girls were shocked, but they asked questions, and presently began to think for themselves, and discovered that thinking is a thrilling experience. I am told that the librarian of the college stays shocked. Never before had he heard of students in college being taught from a book like "The Spoon River Anthology."

There is also one state institution which deserves mention—the University of North Carolina, sometimes called the "Wisconsin of the South." Richard Hogue tells me that he was permitted to explain the meaning of industrial democracy to the students of this institution. I wrote one of the professors and received from him a letter, assuring me that here was a place, having some twenty-five hundred students, which was both free and democratic. I thought I would test the matter a little, so I asked him whether a professor who was an avowed Socialist would be tolerated, and whether the modern Socialist movement was adequately explained to the students. My correspondent replied that he himself was a "Christian Socialist," but that he did not mean "as Bouck White sees it, or even as Ward sees it." He adds: "My experience is that the destructive radical is a chap with a screw loose somewhere—with a twist in his intelligence or with an excess of inflammable emotion. Oftimes he has intellect and courage, but is emotionally unbalanced, like Scott Nearing, for instance. Or he is intelligent and deliberately destructive like Foster." In comment on the above I will merely state my own opinion; first, that Scott Nearing is the ablest economist in the United States today; and second, that William Z. Foster is a very constructive force in the American labor movement.

I have letters from several other professors, who are sure that their institutions are free, and I tested them also with these questions. You will be amused to know that one of them was a professor at the University of Pennsylvania! He stated that professors known to be Socialists would be permitted to teach "as scientific scholars. I suppose if they devoted their time to propaganda they would properly be eliminated." Of course no mention is made of the many professors at the University of Pennsylvania who devote their time to capitalist propaganda—such as for example, Meade, Conway, Hess, Johnson and Huebner.

Some of the professors who seceded from Columbia University, including James Harvey Robinson, Charles A. Beard and Thorstein Veblen, organized a free institution known as the New School for Social Research; it was to cater to students who really wished to study, and to dispense with all the flummeries, including examinations and degrees. The enterprise has not proved a financial success, for a peculiar reason. The capitalist system does not permit people to study for the luxury of possessing knowledge; the purpose of study is to earn a living, and to that end you have to have a certificate that you have studied. In other words, you must go to an institution which fits as a cog in the educational machine. The New School for Social Research has on its teaching staff half a dozen of the best minds in America, and its purpose is really to teach people to think; therefore I give it a free "boost," and advise you that its address is 465 West 23rd Street, New York.

There was another free college in America; it didn't last long, but I mention it because it was a gallant effort, and offers a model for the future. It was known as Wire

City College, and had a beautiful location in a big house high up on the banks of the Missouri River at Leavenworth, Kansas. Its professors, and likewise its students, were military prisoners of the United States government, and they proceeded to organize themselves, forming a really free college, governed by its students and faculty. All the teachers were elected by the students, and ran the class until they were deposed; all the papers were voluntary, there were no examinations, and—most vital this difference from other colleges—all the students studied.

There was a secret library of three hundred radical books, in addition to the prison library of seven thousand respectable books. The library reading room was the lavatory. There were lectures every evening from seven to eight; on Monday English was taught by H. Austin Simons, a former reporter for the Hearst newspapers; on Tuesday logic was taught by Carl Haessler, now managing editor of the Federated Press; on Wednesday economics was taught by Carlton Rodolf, secretary of the Marx Institute of New York. (His students decided that he was too technical, so they fired him.) There was also Clark Getts, later connected with the Federated Press. On Thursday biology was taught by George Schmieder, former high school teacher and graduate of the University of Pennsylvania; on Friday philosophy was taught by Haessler; and on Saturday there were discussions.

The college published a paper, the "Wire City Weekly," also a bulletin, clandestinely made on prison typewriters; the time-schedules were printed by a conscientious objector in the prison printery. The institution was conducted for several months, until finally the authorities found out about it, and almost the entire faculty was kidnapped and carried off to Alcatraz Island, and almost the entire student body to Fort Douglas, Utah. So far as I know, this is the only college in America which has thus been dealt with; but no doubt the interlocking directorate has made note of the plan, and if free colleges should continue to spring up, we shall get used to the wholesale disappearance of college faculties and students.

CHAPTER LXXXV

THE ACADEMIC RABBITS

There are, of course, a large number of individual professors in institutions of higher learning who take their stand for what they believe to be the truth, and risk their jobs and chances of promotion. I have mentioned the existence of eight "renommir professoren." At Wellesley is Vida Scudder, who "gets by" because she is a devout Episcopalian; also Professor Ellen Hayes, who "gets by" because she is old, and because she teaches astronomy. These reasons are not my guesses, but were the statements of the president of the college, when she was asked at a women's club in Denver why she kept a notorious Socialist and labor agitator on her faculty.

Professor Hayes got this reputation by running for office on the Socialist party ticket; I visited her on my trip, and heard some funny stories. Here is one of the sweetest and most lovable old ladies you ever met, who is not mealy-mouthed about her belief in the right and destiny of the workers to control the world's industry for their own benefit. She deliberately lives in a working-class neighborhood—with rather comical results. Her neighbors are in awe of her, because she is a college professor, and a little afraid of her, because of her bad reputation; the one way she might get to know them, through the church, is not available, because Professor Hayes is a scientist.

On the other side of the continent is Guido Marx of Stanford, who shamelessly avows his sympathy with the co-operative movement, and likewise with faculty control of universities. Professor Marx, it is amusing to notice, teaches mechanical engineering, a subject almost as safe as the stars. If there is a single professor in the United States who teaches political economy and admits himself a Socialist, that professor is a needle which I have been unable to find in our academic hay-stack.

Of course there are many radicals who conceal their views, and judiciously try to open the minds of their students without putting any label upon themselves. I have told in "The Profits of Religion" about Jowett at Oxford, who got by with the Apostles' Creed whenever he had to recite it in public, by inserting the words "used to" between the words "I believe," saying the inserted words under his breath, thus: "I *used to* believe in the Father, the Son, and the Holy Ghost." I encountered several college professors who .have equally ingenious devices for salving their consciences in their unhappy situation. I might terrify the plutocratic world by stating that I know two presidents of small colleges in the United States, who in their own homes and among their trusted friends are real "reds." One of them, a young man recently appointed, was asked by his assembled trustees: "What are your views on property questions?" He answered, with an easy smile: "I fear I am far too conservative for a man of thirty-seven"—and he got by with that! The other one is head of a woman's college, and was asked by her trustees: "Are you a Socialist?" She said to me: "I could answer no with a perfectly good conscience, for I had just made up my mind that I am a convert to the Soviet form of political and industrial organization!"

Of course, it is perfectly possible to teach modern ideas without the labels, and to open the minds of your students by seeing that they hear both sides of every case. If you avoid the extremely crucial questions, such as the I. W. W. and Russia, you can get by with this in the majority of institutions, especially if you eschew outside activities and never get into the newspapers. Many professors are doing this, others have tried and slipped up, and have sacrificed promotion and security. Many professors are rovers in the academic world, staying in one place for two or three years, and when they are not able to stand it any more, moving on. There is an infinite variety of degrees and shadings in such cases; conditions differ with institutions, and with subjects taught, and with individual teachers. Some "get away" with what others dare not attempt. Some spoil their chances by bad manners or bad judgment; and, of course, many others are accused of doing this. You will seldom find a fight over a question of academic freedom where there are not other factors present or alleged, personal weaknesses or eccentricities. It is always easy to find defects in the characters and temperaments of persons whose ideas are offensive to us.

Likewise, of course, it is easy to find excuses for seeking the safest way, and holding on to our jobs. The psychoanalysts have a useful word for mental processes of this sort—they are "rationalizations"; and the masters of our educational system have provided an elaborate set of "rationalizations" for college professors who wish to avoid the painful duty of being heroes. They will be loyal to the institution and to their colleagues. They will be scholars and not propagandists. They will be judicious, instead of being "emotionally unbalanced, like Scott Nearing." They will argue that their specialty is one of unusual importance, and they are privileged beings, set apart to work at that. Or they will plead that social evolution takes a long time, and that every man's first duty is to look out for his wife and children. These, too, are phrases which I heard over and over again, and they reveal the psychology of the academic rabbits. You will perhaps be interested to meet one of these rabbits, so here is part of a letter written by a professor in a large college in New York City:

I do not believe that there is a single group of "special privilege." The human race is made up of people who are looking after their own interests first—some with energy and ability, some with weakness and folly, but not with less singleness of purpose. All such groups, in so far as they have ability enough, want to control education and all other group activities in their interest. This is perfectly natural. . . . . Of course the big book corporations work for the promotion of their friends just as you and I do. If they put bad people into the schools and colleges it is the fault of the employing agencies.

Before I conclude this chapter I ought to mention one hopeful incident which happened at Lafayette College, a religious institution located at Easton, Pennsylvania. The president of this institution, MacCracken, is a product of the University of Jabbergrab; he was professor of politics there for twelve years, and has five honorary degrees. He has as the grand duke of his trustees the president of the Hazleton National Bank and the Hazleton Iron Works; and as first assistant he has Mr. Fred Morgan Kirby, president of the Woolworth stores, also of a bank and a railroad; a high-up interlocking director in railroads, lumber, insurance, gas and electricity. Mr. Kirby decided that he did not like modern ideas, so he gave a hundred thousand dollars to Lafayette, to furnish a salary of seven thousand a year for the teaching of "civil rights"; very carefully laying down his definition—"those absolute rights of persons, such as . . . . the right to acquire and enjoy property as regulated and protected by law." Also he declared his purpose:

> That the fallacies of Socialism and kindred theories and practises which tend to hamper and discourage and throttle individual effort, and individual energy, may be exposed and avoided . . . . . with a firm belief that the protection of the civil rights of individuals has contributed greatly to the advancement of the nation and that the encroachments, and threatened encroachments on these rights will imperil the country, and destroy the prosperity and happiness of our people, I, Fred Morgan Kirby, give to Lafayette College, etc.

These are high-sounding legal phrases, and we shall understand the situation better if we put them into plain business English, as follows:

> I, Fred Morgan Kirby, having become owner of a chain of hundreds of stores throughout the United States, and wishing to have my descendants own these stores forever, seek to provide that the wage-slaves who work in these stores shall never organize, but shall come to be hired as individuals under the competitive-wage system. To this end I wish to hire a man to teach in a college that any proposition to have the Woolworth stores owned by the public, or democratically run by the people who work in the stores, will imperil the country and destroy the prosperity and happiness of America.

Mr. Kirby thought that seven thousand a year ought to buy a real high-up professor of political science, and his college president invited a young professor of a leading university, who asks me to omit his name in telling the story. This professor boldly asked for an opportunity to discuss the question with Mr. Kirby himself, so they sat down to luncheon, the grand duke and his university president and this young supposed-to-be rabbit. The supposed-to-be rabbit suggested that it might not be quite fair to lay down to a man of science exactly what he should teach forever after; which surprised Mr. Kirby, and rather hurt his feelings. He said that when he hired a salesman, he told him what to say and how to say it. Mr. Kirby is a nice, amiable old business gentleman, and he asked, plaintively: "Why can't I employ a college professor to sell my opinions?" The professor, who is a lawyer, said that he should be very glad to become Mr. Kirby's attorney if invited. He would give up teaching work and advocate Mr. Kirby's ideas—only the fee which Mr. Kirby offered was insufficient for a lawyer, and he would regard that merely as a retaining fee. Then the professor turned to President Mac-Cracken, asking him if he did not think that possibly the terms of the bequest might have a tendency to control the opinions of the professor who accepted the chair. President MacCracken answered naively that he had never thought of that. Such a dear, innocent college president—he had given an honorary degree to A. Mitchell Palmer only a year before this!

The deal with this professor did not go through, and—here is the significant part of the story—President MacCracken asked one university after another to recommend a man for that chair, and not one would do it; not one economist of standing could be found who would accept seven thousand dollars a year to become the salesman of Mr. Kirby's ideas! In the end they had to take an obscure lawyer from Washington, whom no one had ever heard of before, or has ever heard of since. That is encouraging—except for the poor students at Lafayette, who are innocently swallowing Mr. Kirby's poison!

CHAPTER LXXXVI

WORKERS' EDUCATION

We come now to one of the most important aspects of American education, the movement of the workers to take charge of their own minds. We have surveyed the field, and seen that our great universities and small colleges, with negligibly few exceptions, represent education of the people by the plutocracy for the plutocracy. As the class struggle intensifies, it naturally occurs to the exploited classes to have an educational system of their own, to be run by them for their own benefit. This is the movement known as Workers' Education.

I have been protesting in this book against class control of thinking. So the average American reader will be moved to say: "You object to capitalist class education, but now you are going to favor working class education!" There are a few words to be said on this subject before we enter the workers' colleges.

Let us assume for a moment that, human nature being what it is, and the forces of capitalism being what they are, we have to have some kind of class control of education. Which would be preferable, capitalist class education or working class education? The first point in reply is that the workers outnumber the capitalists in our society by a hundred to one; education for the benefit of the workers would be, therefore, education for the benefit of a hundred times as many people. The next point is that the workers extend to all capitalists a cordial invitation to become workers; whereas the capitalists extend no such invitation to the workers. They may, of course, do it in Fourth of July speeches and political campaign platforms, but in everyday life they do everything possible to keep the workers from becoming capitalists, and compel them to remain workers. If the capitalists were to accept the invitation of the workers and become workers, we should have classes abolished in our society, and our workers' education would be education for the benefit of all.

For this reason the program of the workers is generous and free, whereas that of the capitalists is selfish and repressive. The worker is able to face the truth, while the capitalist dares not face it. The worker has everything to gain by the truth, while the capitalist has everything to lose. So it happens that if you compare workers' colleges with capitalist colleges, you invariably find this difference: the workers' college believes in free discussion, and will hear anybody argue about any question; whereas the capitalist college fears free discussion, and invents a hundred pretexts to keep the other side from being heard. I have shown you everywhere throughout the country representatives of the working class being denied an opportunity to present their point of view to the students in capitalist colleges. I have never heard of a capitalist being denied an opportunity to explain his point of view to the students of workers' colleges; on the contrary, I have known of many cases of capitalists, or representatives of capitalism, being invited to debate, and finding some excuse to decline the invitation.

In the above discussion I am using the word "workers" in the intelligent, revolutionary sense. I do not mean the men who dig ditches or who run machines; I mean workers of hand or brain, all those men and women who do the useful and necessary work of the world, whether it be digging ditches or surveying them, tending machines or inventing them, sweeping out the buildings of a college, or teaching in its class-rooms, or determining its policies. I am using the term workers in contradistinction to the owners, those who live by monopolizing the means whereby other men live, and exacting from the others a tribute for the right to work. Also, I should explain that when I speak of labor, I do not mean the old-style labor unions which hold the field today. I perfectly well understand that they are products of capitalism, animated by the greeds and jealousies of the profit system. Little by little, however, these labor unions are forced to widen their boundaries, to combine and take in larger groups of the workers; and at the same time they broaden their ideals, and approach the revolutionary point of view, which understands by social justice the right of all workers to access to the sources of wealth, and understands by freedom the right of all men to agitate, educate and organize for a society in which no man exploits his fellows.

In college after college we have seen the brains of the working class stolen away from them; we have seen young men and women who come from the working class, and who should fight for their class and save it, being seduced by the dress-suit bribe, the flummeries and snobberies of academic life, and becoming traitors to their class, betrayers and even murderers of their class. So come the organized workers to save their own; to teach their sons and daughters, first, class loyalty, and through that, loyalty to truth and social justice. Such is the meaning of Workers' Education.

We have seen the capitalist college reveal its true colors on many occasions; but never does it reveal it more plainly than when the workers proceed to organize their own educational system. I have shown you Professor Egbert, Director of University Extension and Director of the School of Business of Columbia University, displaying himself to the extent of three columns in the New York "Times," announcing that "workers' education has virtually broken down in America." But the interlocking professors do not content themselves with lying about labor education in the capitalist press; they and their masters intrigue against it, they boycott it, they turn loose their slander factories, their Helen Ghouls and "hundred percent" mobs against it. We have seen the typewriters and the teachers of the Rand School of Social Science being thrown down the stairs. We shall see professors of capitalist colleges being, figuratively speaking, thrown down the stairs for venturing to help in labor education.

Let us take, for example, the experience of the Workers' College of Minneapolis, narrated in an affidavit by E. H. H. Holman, chairman of the education committee of some of the labor unions. The Workers' College of Minneapolis laid down a very moderate program:

It is hereby proposed to organize an educational program for the workers of Minneapolis, under their own control, through which such educational work will be undertaken as will better fit them to serve society through a wider comprehension of social problems, through an understanding of the technique of industrial production, and through a better knowledge of the labor problem in general, thus to be in position to act effectively in the solution of pressing problems that grip the world today.

Not such a bad statement, you may concede. This statement was adopted in December, 1920, and classes were organized, among them a class in public speaking. Professor T. P. Beyer of Hamline University was asked to take charge of this class, and he did so. There were protests in the newspapers of the Twin Cities, and several of the interlocking regents of Hamline gave newspaper interviews registering their indignation. It had been stated in the contract with Professor Beyer that he was not expected "to advocate any theories or further any propaganda." Nevertheless, the grand dukes of Hamline spoke, and Professor Beyer withdrew. Shortly afterwards Mr. Holman happened to meet President Kerfoot of Hamline University, a Methodist clergyman holding three honorary degrees; and this gentleman said that "it would never do" to have one of his professors linked up with radicals. "Those who contribute the money to support Hamline would never stand for it."

Again in Topeka, Kansas, the labor men were conducting an open forum, and considering the project for a labor college. Some of the professors from Washburn College took to attending this forum, and meeting these labor leaders. The interlocking newspapers made a scandal out of it, the intrigue being conducted by the secretary of the Merchants and Manufacturers' Association, who was maintaining a black-list against union men. One of the professors at Washburn College received a threatening letter; it was supposed to have come from the labor group, but manifestly it came from this "M & M" agent, or some of his spies. Anyway, the Washburn College professors were compelled to cease attending the open forum.

In Denver the president of the newly organized labor college applied for the use of some of the high school buildings, in the evening. The request was turned down, on the ground that the college was too radical; if the authorities allowed working-class people to meet in the schools, they must also allow the capitalists to meet. In Denver, you see, they have never opened the schools for free discussion, or for teaching the people anything except what the politicians approve. In this case the school authorities said that they would allow the use of the rooms, provided they were allowed to appoint the instructors!

Johns Hopkins University moved out to its magnificent new site at Homewood, which it had obtained by the selling of its soul. The old buildings were left in Baltimore, and the Reverend Richard Hogue, secretary of the Church League for Industrial Democracy, applied for the use of one of the buildings. They had actually begun meeting, under the direction of one of the professors, but the university put them out by order of the trustees. The "hundred percenters" who superintend education in Baltimore call themselves the George Washington Society, and they bitterly attacked one Johns Hopkins professor for taking part in a labor college, and demanded that he be forced out of Johns Hopkins.

You may be interested to know how it comes about that a young professor in one of our most prosperous and important universities happened to be espousing the cause of self-education by the workers. This young professor at the outbreak of the war was a reporter for the Richmond "News-Leader," and a strike was threatened in the Richmond plant of the American Locomotive Company. The basis of the strike was the refusal of the company officials to comply with the regulations of the War Labor Board; and the young reporter wrote the facts, and his newspaper published them, to the great indignation of the interlocking directorate. In the midst of the controversy a stranger turned up—we will call him Brown—producing credentials from the New York "World." He pretended to be sympathetic to the union men, and diligently sought information concerning them. The "News-Leader" became suspicious, and telegraphed to the New York "World," and the answer came, "Brown is all right."

So Brown continued his operations for a few days longer. He suggested to the young reporter a wonderful plan to get the facts about what the company was doing; he and the reporter were to bribe the book-keeper, and break into the company offices at night! Such temptations arise now and then in the lives of newspapermen, and if it is information against labor unions you are seeking, you may employ such methods. But this reporter knew that you cannot commit burglaries against big business, and his paper investigated further, and discovered that Brown was a secret agent of the American Locomotive Company, operating under the protection of the New York "World"! The young professor suggested that this story would fit in "The Brass Check"; but it seems to me that it does very well in this place—showing how a college professor who leaves the shelter of the cloister is forced to revise his formulas concerning large scale capitalist industry!

CHAPTER LXXXVII

THE SPIDER AND THE FLY

We have noted Professor Egbert of the University of J. P. Morgan & Company, advising the workers to avail themselves of the existing college system—in other words, to let the capitalists do their educating for them. "Won't you walk into my parlor? said the spider to the fly." Just what labor education turns into when it is superintended by the existing educational authorities was amus-

ingly demonstrated at Bryn Mawr, a very aristocratic
college for women located near Philadelphia, and having
the president of an insurance company for its treasurer,
and for its grand duke the president of a steel company
and a trust company, vice-president of a national bank
and director of a sugar company.

We have seen President Thomas of Bryn Mawr
branded in the Denver "Post" as a dangerous radical, and
we now discover the basis of the charge; she started a
movement to educate working girls! The idea was that
the brightest and most promising members of labor unions
should come to Bryn Mawr in the summer and be taught
by professors from various colleges. This, of course,
was a step in the right direction, and I have no desire
to belittle it; though I should have liked to see the further
provision that at the same time the young ladies of Bryn
Mawr should take the places of the working girls in the
factories.

I have no doubt whatever that this experiment was
well meant; but in its working out it revealed the impossibility of honesty under our present class system. In
raising money it was set forth that the purpose of the
plan was to bring the working girls into touch with the
cultured classes and break down the spirit of class con-
sciousness. Then, after the money was got, it was necessary to get the girls; and so the unions were told that the
purpose of the plan was to make the girls into more
efficient and capable leaders of unions.

Bryn Mawr has received a heavy endowment from
John D. Rockefeller; a hall is named for him, and also a
gateway. The organizers of the summer school were
getting up a prospectus telling of the plan, and they put
on the cover a photograph, with the name "Rockefeller
Gateway." But at the last moment it occurred to someone that this might not look well to the unions, so the
label "Rockefeller" was left off, and the photograph went
out with the caption, "A Gateway."

I met three different professors who were invited to
come to Bryn Mawr and teach at this summer session;
one of them, Professor H. W. L. Dana, whom we saw
turned out of Columbia University as a scapegoat for the
pacifism of Nicholas Miraculous. Professor Dana had an
interview with President Thomas, in which the terms of

the engagement were laid down to him. There were to be no social relationships with the working girls, no tennis dates, no activities outside the classes. His subject was to be literature, and he was to avoid dangerous writers, such as Morris, Whitman and Ruskin; he was to teach literature as art, and not as part of the labor movement.

On the train going home, Professor Dana decided that his academic dignity had been infringed upon; therefore he sent a telegram to President Thomas, saying that he was unable to agree to the terms. He sent a copy of this telegram to Rose Schneiderman, one of the working class leaders who had been charged with selecting the girls: the effect of which procedure was instant collapse on the part of President Thomas. She wrote saying that Professor Dana had entirely misunderstood her, she had not intended anything of the sort. Dana had asked that there should be student representation on the board controlling the experiment, and President Thomas now said that she had had that idea in mind all along. So they provided a system of student representation, with an open vote, and the balance of power in the hands of Bryn Mawr graduates, who were helping at the summer school with the title of "tutors." A harmless working girl, not a trades unionist, was selected as representative of the girls.

The union girls, of course, understood perfectly what was being done to them; they would smile to Professor Dana and say: "You must remember, they aren't used to democracy. You must be gentle with them. You see, they haven't suffered." (Stop and think about that beautiful phrase!). The "tutors" would gossip among themselves, telling about funny mistakes which the working girls had made, such as not knowing to what century Shakespeare belonged. They would correct the table manners of the girls—and without ever thinking that the girls also had secret laughter over the mistakes of the "tutors." Thus, some tutor had asked: "What do the letters A. F. of L. stand for?"—which seemed to the working girls quite as important a matter as the date of Shakespeare's birth. One of the tutors asked: "Is the International Ladies' Garment Workers' Union the same as the Third International?"—and that seemed the funniest thing in the world to these union girls.

More serious matters arose quickly; for you see, these

girls have convictions, and take them just as seriously as
Bryn Mawr girls take their table manners.   The first
thing they did was to go to the chambermaids and discover
that these women there were working twelve and fourteen hours a day.   They proceeded to organize the women,
and the college authorities were confronted with a demand
for an eight-hour day—which they granted! They granted
a number of other things before they got through. Teaching economics and social science to union girls was quite
a different matter from teaching it to the daughters of
the leisure class.   In the winter time Bryn Mawr professors can get by with formulas, but in these summer
months they had to come down to brass tacks; for to these
girls an economic theory meant some particular place,
some particular set of circumstances: "When I was in
such and such a shop," or, "When I was on strike in
New York!"   This made an entirely new thing out of
the subject of economics.

Also, it made a new thing out of literature.   Professor Dana was selected to read poetry to the girls at
chapel, and poetry, as we know, is an important source
of culture.   Dana read one or two poems on Russia,
at which the dean in charge seemed shocked.   She asked
him to read poems at least a hundred years old.   Dana
thought it over, and answered that he would do so, and
next morning he read in chapel two poems which were
exactly a hundred years old—Shelley's "Mask of Anarchy," and his

> Men of England, wherefore plow
> For the lords who lay ye low?

This Bryn Mawr experiment was repeated last summer, with much hurrah in the newspapers; but needless
to say, Harry Dana was not one of the teachers, and
neither was a woman professor who proved too sympathetic to the working girls.   Also a Bryn Mawr teacher,
who "got the vision" from the girls, and prepared to
teach some of them in the winter time, was omitted this
year.   Nevertheless, the leaven works, and two of the
"tutors," Bryn Mawr students, were arrested during the
summer school term while picketing a clothing shop in
Philadelphia, during a strike by the Amalgamated Clothing Workers.   Once let the rich girls realize what the

poor girls suffer, and some of the rich girls will protest!

I had a pleasant experience in Cambridge. I was guest in a home which is the shrine of pilgrims from all over the United States—that of New England's favorite poet and Cambridge's most eminent citizen, Henry Wadsworth Longfellow. Here lives the poet's grandson, who is also a grandson of Richard Henry Dana, a born teacher, and incidentally a warm-hearted and most lovable man. Nicholas Murray Butler has not invited him back to Columbia; nor has it occurred to President Lowell to invite him to step around the corner from his home and lecture on the literature of social protest to Harvard students. Nevertheless, Harry Dana has found some teaching to do; he travels over to the Boston Labor College, and teaches workingmen. One Sunday morning I attended a committee meeting of this institution—several college professors and several labor leaders, conspiring in the home of the poet Longfellow to overturn academic authority in the United States!

Then I traveled across the continent to my home in Pasadena, and found that Professor John Scott had been kicked out of the Pasadena High School in the interests of one hundred percent reaction, and with the help of progressive labor leaders had started a workers' college in Los Angeles. So it goes, in one city after another; any time a group of labor men want to save the brains of their young people, they can find a kicked-out professor; and any time a kicked-out professor is willing to cultivate his self-respect on a little oatmeal, he can manage to get together a group of class-conscious labor men, and can greatly increase his influence and effectiveness. When Dana was fired from Columbia, he lectured to classes of six and eight hundred people at the Rand School; while Scott Nearing assures me that continuously during the eight years since he parted from the University of Pennsylvania, he has had not merely larger audiences, but more serious and more interesting audiences.

CHAPTER LXXXVIII

THE WORKERS' COLLEGES

I begin this chapter by telling you about a very pleasant enterprise, the resident college which has just been started by the labor education movement, the Brookwood School at Katonah, New York. Brookwood is a co-educational college, with a two years' course and a year of post-graduate work. Its aims are set forth as follows:

> Brookwood aims to train economists, statisticians, journalists, writers and teachers, organizers, workers and speakers, for the labor and farmer movements in order that these movements may have people coming from their own ranks, with their own point of view, who are fully capable by training and knowledge of exercising a genuine statesmanship.

Brookwood was organized by Toscan Bennett, a reformed corporation lawyer, and his wife, a reformed suffragette. They purchased a farm, with a beautiful old colonial building, and this summer, while I am writing a book, they are working on new dormitories—and I wish I might be there! If you want to find in this ugly and greedy world a place where the true spirit of comradeship prevails, where men and women, middle-aged and young, consecrate themselves with fervor, and also with fun, to the service of freedom and social justice, take my advice and pay a visit to Brookwood.

The clothing workers' unions in New York and the coal miners in Pennsylvania furnish most of the pupils, and pay a part of their expenses. They are taught by the customary outfit of kicked-out college professors and school teachers. There is Josephine Colby, who organized the teachers of Fresno, California, and was separated from her position by a superintendent who stated in the newspapers that he didn't believe in using arguments in dealing with union school teachers, the thing to use was a baseball bat. Also there is David Saposs, who was in a student revolt at the University of Wisconsin, when the working students organized and got the business manager of the university fired; as a result, Saposs was told that it would do him no good to get a degree, as he would not be recommended for a teaching position! Also there is A. J. Muste, a reformed Quaker clergyman, who has received a quite unique training for his career as labor educator. I first heard of him as a theological student, through a little mimeographed circular, "Towards a New Preaching Order." He and a group of three or four young men proposed to go out into the world in the old apostolic fashion, without scrip or purse, and bring capitalism to its knees by moral fervor. It was a most eloquent piece of writing, and I marked this young clergyman for a career. Next I heard of him in the Lawrence textile strike of 1919; his "preaching order" was trying its eloquence upon the president of the Woolen Trust, who came within an ace of going to prison, upon the charge of having had dynamite planted in the homes of non-union workers, as a means of discrediting the strikers. Mr. Wood did not yield to young Muste's apostolic fervor; on the contrary, he had his Cossacks ride the young clergyman down on the sidewalk, and pound him over the head with their clubs and finally throw him into jail. So Mr. Muste preached to the strikers, and following the best apostolic precedents, started a soup kitchen for them, performing the miracle of the loaves and fishes with the help of checks from a few good angels scattered over the country. After he had got through with that strike, he was a trained labor scholar and ready to teach literature in a workers' college!

Four years ago there were only two or three labor colleges in the United States, all of them in New York City; now there are six in the state of Pennsylvania alone. A bulletin of the United States Bureau of Labor, published in June, 1921, "Education of Adult Working Classes," lists twenty-four such institutions, in places as widely scattered as Washington, Pittsburgh, Rochester, Cleveland, Detroit, St. Paul, Minneapolis, Duluth and Seattle. The auspices under which these schools are organized are: central labor unions, five; local unions, five; international unions, five; State federations, seven; Socialist and radical groups, one; the Women's Trade-Union League, one.

Mr. Paul Blanshard, secretary of the Rochester Labor College, gives me an interesting account of one such institution, and the vicissitudes of a would-be teacher. Mr. Blanshard got his training in class-consciousness during the textile strike at Utica several years ago; he tried to start some classes for foreigners in English, and the interlocking newspapers took him up, and all Utica read that he was starting "a school in Bolshevism"! The Lusk committee went after him—on the testimony of a police captain who was later released from the force under grave suspicion; also of a detective in the employ of the Helen Ghouls. Mr. Blanshard, of course, was not given a hearing, and the scare headlines in the newspapers frightened away all his pupils.

But the Amalgamated Clothing Workers are powerful in Rochester, and are not so easily frightened; they joined with thirteen other unions to make a college for Mr. Blanshard to run. They make a contribution of one cent per month for each member, a total income of seven hundred dollars a year—which no doubt looks extremely small to Professor Egbert of Columbia University, which has seven millions a year. Nevertheless, on this income the college has weekly educational mass meetings, addressed by the livest men in the country, and attended by some fifteen hundred workers; it publishes a four-page educational bulletin every week, and has classes in unionism and public speaking, in English, in current events, in economics, and in labor problems.

That is a glimpse at one city; and you will find the same thing happening in all the others. In Portland, Oregon, the college meets in the Labor Temple, and the Central Labor Council assesses one-twelfth of its total revenue to save its brains for its own uses. In New York City two of the greatest unions, the International Ladies' Garment Workers and the Amalgamated Clothing Workers, have established educational departments, and are carrying out elaborate programs for the benefit of their members. The I. L. G. W. U. has eight "unity centers" in New York public schools, with classes in English, the teachers assigned by the Board of Education. It arranges independent courses in the labor movement, economics, psychology, literature, music, health, etc. Its "Workers' University" meets in the Washington Irving High School, with courses in about twenty subjects, and a registration of three hundred students. Also there is an extension department, which arranges for lectures, concerts, and classes of all sorts at the headquarters of the various local unions. There are branches of this enterprise in Cleveland and Philadelphia, and the whole thing is the growth of only four years.

In order to realize the deliberate dishonesty of Professor Egbert's statement that "labor education has virtually broken down in America," you should have attended a conference called by the Workers' Education Bureau of America, organized in connection with the New School for Social Research in New York City, for the purpose of co-ordinating these labor colleges, and furnishing them with literature and text-books. This conference was held April 22 and 23, 1922, just one month before Professor Egbert's three columns of treachery were featured in the New York "Times." Here were eager delegates, teachers and students, addressed by speakers as wide apart in their views as Samuel Gompers, James Maurer, Charles A. Beard and Benjamin Schlesinger. I will list the subjects discussed at one of the sessions, dealing with "Teaching Methods in Workers' Education"—this just to give you an idea of the breadth of view and practical grip of the movement: "The Forum," "The Debate," "School-room Methods," "Discussion Methods," "Health Education," "Methods of Health Education," "The Teaching of Economics," "Journalism," "Mass Education," "Educational Aspects of Work," "Correspondence Education," "Text Books," "Public Discussion," "Trade Union Meetings," "Problems of Adult Instruction."

Also this Workers' Education Bureau is publishing a series of volumes, entitled "The Workers' Bookshelf," to serve as text-books in the labor colleges. They are the kind of books I believe in, for they cost only fifty cents a volume. In the "Labor Age," New York, you will find much news about these movements. Also you should know something about the work in England, where it is twenty years old, and has grown to be the brains and fighting spirit of the British labor movement. The story is told in "An Adventure in Working Class Education," by Albert Mansbridge, founder and general secretary of the Workers' Educational Association of Great Britain. The radicals who are making over the mind of British labor have a magazine, the "Plebs," which American students ought to see.

30

Teaching at these workers' colleges is a very different matter from being an old-line college professor. Here you have students who really want to study. You are back in the twelfth century when five thousand men thronged to Paris and sat on the hillside to listen to Abelard and dispute with him. You are back in the old days in America, when a college was "a student sitting one end of a log and Mark Hopkins on the other end." You are dealing with students who, while they may be painfully deficient in book learning, have acquired much knowledge of life, and are accustomed to assert their point of view. It does not occur to them to defer to authority; they only defer to facts, and you have to produce the facts and convince them. Many times the teacher will find that he himself has become a student, and all college professors who have tried the adventure agreed in testifying how exhilarating they find this.

Labor education offers to the college professor a semi-respectable way to get into contact with the real world. So I plead with professors who read this book to avail themselves of the opportunities existing—or if there are none in their neighborhood, to get busy and make some. I am told of one professor in Pennsylvania who used to travel about from town to town teaching labor groups, a class each night in a different town. That is real adventure, and it lies right at the gates of all our institutions of higher learning. Try it for a year or two, and you may find that you have built up a clientele, and no longer have to shiver in your boots when you hear a rumor that one of your trustees has asked whether it is true that you are a Bolshevik!

CHAPTER LXXXIX

THE PROFESSORS' UNION

The labor movement at its present stage can, of course, not support all the college professors who would like to be free, so it becomes necessary to seek another remedy. This remedy is obvious; the college professor must do what the labor men are doing—agitate, educate, organize. The formula, "In union there is strength," applies to brain workers precisely as to hand workers. You would think the brain workers ought to have the brains to realize this, but they do not, for the reason that their class prejudices stand in the way, the anarchist attitude which goes with the intellectual life. So it comes about that college professors are only two or three percent organized, while coal miners are sixty or seventy percent organized, and garment workers and railway men from ninety to a hundred percent organized.

The union of our higher educators is known as the American Association of University Professors, and we have seen it at work in a number of institutions. It has a total membership of five thousand, among a possible membership of some two hundred thousand. Thus two or three percent of higher educators pay the cost and bear the burden of representing the whole group. They publish a quarterly bulletin from their headquarters at 222 Charles River Road, Cambridge, Massachusetts, and investigate cases of infringement of academic freedom, and work out constructive programs of faculty control. I have quoted extracts from their reports, the accuracy and honesty of which have never been successfully challenged. So far as this work goes it is excellent, but it represents only a feeble start upon the way.

What spoils the usefulness of the professors' association is precisely that feeling of class superiority, which makes them as fat rabbits to the plutocracy. The first aim of the association has apparently been to distinguish itself from labor unions, whereas the fact is that it is a labor union, an organization of intellectual proletarians, who have nothing but their brain-power to sell. Instructors at the University of California begin on a salary of a hundred and fifty dollars a month, at the University of Chicago on a hundred and thirty-three dollars a month, at the University of Illinois the same, at Yale and Michigan on a hundred and twenty-five, and at Harvard for salaries as low as fifty and one hundred a month—this for the glory of a Harvard record! Men who have to keep their families, and dress as gentlemen, and purchase the tools of a highly specialized trade upon such pay are proletarians, and the bulk of them will remain proletarians all their lives, and the quicker they realize it the better for them. Even though their salaries be raised, and they be put in position to acquire a home and a few investments, they remain dependent for the things they value most upon an exploiting class, which dominates the industry of the country, and therefore inevitably dominates its thought.

This being the case, the college professor's freedom is bound up with the freedom of the working class. He may protest to the end of time, but his status will remain the same, until the plutocratic empire is overthrown and industrial democracy takes its place. After that, the status of the professor, as of all intellectual workers, will rest in the hands of labor—and this is something which is coming, regardless of anything the professor can do. Such being the case, it would seem sensible for him to study the labor movement and take his place in it—not merely in his own interest, but in the interest of the intellectual life. I have shown you in the labor colleges working-class leaders co-operating with college professors; and the significance of this is not merely that educational men are helping the industrial revolution; it is that the new forces which are preparing to take control of society are coming to understand what the intellectual life means, and learning to trust those who live that life. This is something the importance of which no one can exaggerate; and so I point out to those college professors who shut themselves up in their shell of academic snobbery, that the time is coming, and coming soon, when they will have cause to wish that they had not been quite so haughtily indifferent to the heartbreak of the poor.

I have on my desk an interesting letter from a Stanford professor, discussing a problem in etiquette which I submitted to him: the story of a young Columbia instructor who refused to obey the casual command of Nicholas Miraculous and escort old Pierpont Morgan to his car. Says the Stanford professor:

As I view it, the essence of wage-slavery lies in the acceptance (on both sides) of the assumption that the man who happens to "pay" the wages for work done thereby attains a right to dictate in the fields of all other thoughts and acts of the employe. This is passively so generally accepted that I have always refused to consider myself in the light of an employe of the president and board, but rather as a co-worker in a mutual administration of a trust in which they have their part and I have mine—and this despite the fact that they have the undoubted legal power to "dismiss" me and I have not that to dismiss them, this being merely one of the differentiations of function in the administration of the trust. Authority is an insidious thing. Few can possess it without being ruined, and I never heard that Butler was among the exceptions.

This, you will admit, is the dignified attitude of a scholar; and I have no doubt that many college professors seek to maintain that attitude. All I can do is to tell them how they seem to me—as men swimming against a powerful current, and it is only a question of time before their energy gives out and they move the way everything else is moving. An individual may hold out, his prestige enabling him to be regarded as a harmless eccentric; but the young man who tries to take such an attitude will go out and write life insurance or make wash-boards.

The effect of economic inferiority is inescapable and automatic; it produces a psychology of submission, it produces a set of customs and manners based upon that, and Mrs. Partington, who tried to sweep back the sea with her broom, was no more foolish than the college professor who imagines that he can have an institution with wealthy trustees dominating its financial existence, and preserve in that institution a real respect for the intellectual life, or a real democratic relationship between the trustees and their hired servants.

If this be true, then the dignity of the intellectual worker depends upon the establishment of industrial democracy; freedom for the college professor awaits the overthrow of the plutocratic empire. And since the only force in our society which can achieve that overthrow is labor, it follows that the college professor's hopes are bound up with the movement of the workers for freedom. A college professor who imagines that he can work for faculty control and academic independence, while at the same time remaining a conservative in his political and economic ideas, is simply a man with water-tight compartments in his brain.

The forces of industrialism compel the worker to organize in larger and larger units, and to take into solidarity a wider and wider proportion of the population. Exactly the same forces are compelling the college professor, first to realize himself as a class, and second, to study the movements of other workers for freedom, to become more sympathetic toward them, and more identified with them in interest and action. College professors must join their own union; they must set before themselves the same goal as miners and railwaymen—to organize one hundred per cent of their trade, and develop a spirit of class loyalty and class discipline. I have shown you the indignities endured by college professors, and how pitifully they submit and hold on to their jobs; I have shown you individuals and groups unceremoniously kicked out, and obediently going out and seeking for new jobs. Perhaps it never occurred to you to notice what was lacking—I have not been able to tell about a single strike of college professors in America! There have been several cases of student strikes—the young are impulsive, so that it has been possible for them to act like human beings; but if there has ever been a group of college professors in the United States who have banded themselves together and said: "If one of us goes, all of us go," I have not been able to learn of that instance.

No, college professors are like actors; they have their individual idiosyncrasies, their jealousies and personal superiorities. They do not think of themselves as a class; each one thinks of himself as something impossible to duplicate. An official of a school-teacher's union remarked to me that the price of a teacher is fifty dollars— meaning thereby that an increase of that amount in salaries would cause a group of teachers to foreswear their union and place themselves at the mercy of a school-board. Just what is the price of a college professor I do not know, but I could cite thousands of cases of men who should have stood by a colleague in some flagrant case of oppression, but who stayed on and got rewarded for loyalty to their masters.

The all-important fact in the situation is this; any time the college professors of America get ready to take control of their own destinies, and of the intellectual life of their institutions, they can do it. There is not a college or university in the United States today which could resists the demands of its faculty a hundred percent organized and meaning business. Even Nicholas Murray Butler would bow his haughty head if the faculty of Columbia should rise up and demand for that plutocratic empire a system of constitutional government. Chancellor

Day may pound on the table and tell his faculty that he could replace them in an hour and a half, but he would find that he could not replace them in a century and a half—especially if they took another leaf out of the note-book of labor, and set pickets at the gates of Heaven! When the college professors of America get ready to go on strike, they will have their reasons and their program; they will put these before the student-body and before their colleagues in other institutions; nor will they be so easy to intimidate with policemen's clubs and court injunctions as are the wage-slaves of factories and mines!

A humble beginning has been made. The American Federation of Teachers, which is a labor union, affiliated with the American Federation of Labor, has a local, No. 120, at the University of Montana. This union was a result of the Levine case, and it comprises practically the entire faculty. There is a similar local at the University of North Dakota, a consequence of the class struggle there. And in New York City is the Teachers' Union of New York No. 5, which includes a number of social minded college men, including Dewey of Columbia, Ward of the Union Theological Seminary, and Overstreet and Stairs of the College of the City of New York. The president of the American Federation of Teachers writes me:

We have had a few other collegiate and university locals but they did not prove very long-lived, and it was very difficult for us to get detailed reasons for their decline. I presume fear would account for most of them.

CHAPTER XC

THE PROFESSORS' STRIKE

The final purpose of this book, you will now realize, is to bring about a strike of college professors. The next question to be considered is, what are the principles upon which this strike shall be based?

First and foremost, the question of tenure; which is exactly the same thing as the claim of the worker to security in his job. The college professor must not forfeit his standing except for cause, and upon due and reasonable notice. He must have the right which every criminal possesses, of knowing what are the charges against him, and of having a hearing in which he is confronted by his accusers, and given the right to cross-question them, and to answer their charges and prove them false if he can. The decision in his case must rest, not with his masters and exploiters, but with his fellow-workers; in other words, the ancient right embodied in Magna Carta, to be tried by a jury of his peers. These rights are elemental; there can be no freedom, no dignity or self-respect for any man who does not possess them. They are possessed by scholars in all other civilized countries; it is only in our sweet land of liberty that scholars are slaves. Says James McKeen Cattell:

> That a professor's salary should depend on the favor of a president, or that he should be dismissed without a hearing by a president with the consent of an absentee board of trustees, is a state of affairs not conceivable in an English or a German university.

The reason for this anomaly is that the American college has not been organized on the principles of American government, but on those of American business; the college is not a state, but a factory. I have compared Columbia and Minnesota to department-stores and Clark and Johns Hopkins to Ford factories; and in so doing I was not merely calling names, but making a diagnosis. They are organized upon that basis, and run upon that basis, and the problem of changing them is simply one of the problems of Americanization. The college must become a democratic republic, run by its citizens and workers.

That brings us to the second demand of the college professor; not merely must he have security in his job, he must have collective control of that job, he must say how the college shall be conducted, and what higher education shall be. That means that he must take from the trustees, and from their hired man, the president, the greater part of their present functions.

I say democracy in education, and you have a vision of a great university turned into a debating society, all the time which should be spent in "getting things done" being devoted to squabbling and bickering among various factions and cliques of the faculty. That will happen sometimes, inevitably; it is one of the incidentals of all

beginnings of democracy to function. But we have been
trying out democracy in this country for three centuries,
and we do not have to begin all over again with the
blunders of our childhood. We know today what a constitution is; we understand the differences among the three
functions of government, the legislative, the executive,
and the judicial; we understand how an executive can be
democratically chosen, and given authority for a reasonable period of time, and loyally obeyed for that time. We
understand how it is possible to have a thorough and free
democratic discussion of policy, and to decide by majority
vote, and then to carry out the will of the majority. If
we do not know how to do these things, the students will
teach us, for they are accustomed every year to organize
a football team, and to thresh out its policies, and elect
a captain, and then do what he says. On the football
field they do not stop to argue about signals; they play
the game.

The question of a constitution for universities is one
of detail; you will find a very thorough exposition of it
in Professor Cattell's book, "University Control." Professor J. E. Kirkpatrick of the University of Michigan
has worked out practical suggestions. Also the matter is
being frequently discussed in "School and Society," and
in the bulletins of the professors' association. We have
not the space in this book for anything but a brief statement. It is a problem of reconciling the rights of many
different groups, which perform many different functions.
The largest single group upon the board of a college
should obviously be the faculty, who know most about
the institution, and have its interests most at heart. The
alumni should be represented, for their interest is real,
and their services will became more valuable as colleges
become democratic, and as the spirit of class is broken in
our society. Likewise the students are entitled to representation, especially the upper classes, which have come
to know the institution. If the purpose of the college
is to train men to live and serve in a democracy, then
manifestly there should be democracy in their training;
they should be given encouragement to discuss their own
needs and purposes, to arrive at collective agreements,
and to make their will effective

So long as we have a system of private ownership

of natural resources, we shall of course have to have trustees who represent money interests. But we should endeavor to pare down the powers of this special privilege group as much as possible; and especially all faculty members should set their face against the idea of any interference with teaching, or with the opinions or outside activities of the faculty, by monied men who represent ownership and not service in the institution.

You have followed me from college to college, listing the grand dukes and the interlocking directors, and you have thought perhaps that I condemn these men because they are rich, and consider that people who have money are ipso facto unfit to have anything to do with education. All I can answer is that I number among my friends some rich people, who are ardently striving to abolish special privilege from the world; and if any rich man wants to come into a college and work for faculty control and academic freedom, for the right of service and true scholarship to guide our education, I will bid that man welcome, and will promise to make no complaint because he happens to be president of six national banks, director of eight railroads, ten steel companies and a dozen pickle factories and sausage mills. The world for which I am working is a world of freedom and fair play; my kingdom of heaven is open to all, and any man may do his part to make it real on earth. All that I insist is that the rich man shall renounce his class and his class interests; he shall turn traitor to that predatory group which now controls our country and its thinking.

I do not expect many of the interlocking trustees to accept this invitation. I do expect, however, that developments in our public affairs will force a constantly increasing number of college professors to realize the intolerable nature of their present position, and to take up the work of educating their colleagues and the general public. These men will come to realize the broad nature of their task; how the roots of our academic problem go down into the very deeps of our political and economic life. The need of the college professor is one with the need of the citizen and the worker; and so, when you agitate for academic democracy and freedom of teaching, you are educating the community and taking your part in that class struggle which is the dominant fact of our time.

You will find that the struggle calls for its heroes and its martyrs, in üniversities as in factories and mines. To college professors who read this book—and especially the young ones—I say: what is life without a little adventure? You will not starve; no educated man need starve in America, if he keeps command of his inner forces, and uses but a small quantity of that shrewdness with which his enemies are so well provided. And surely it is not too much to ask that among the two hundred thousand instructors in American colleges there should arise just a few who are capable of combining intelligence and self-sacrifice!

What are you? You teach history, perhaps; you handle the bones of dead heroes, the ashes of martyrs are the stuff with which you work. Or you teach literature; the spirits of thousands of idealists come to your study, and cry out to you in your dreams. Or perhaps you are a scientist; if so, remind yourself how Socrates drank the hemlock cup with dignity, in order that men might be free to use their reason; how Galileo was tortured in a dungeon, in order that modern science might be born. Is it then too much to ask that you should risk your monthly pay check, to save the minds of the young men and women of our time? Think of these things, the next time you are summoned by your dean for a scolding, and tell him that a college professor remains an American citizen, and that he does not sell all his brains for two or three hundred dollars a month!

I ask for a little personal boldness, also a little for your institution. What if the new endowment does not come, and you cannot get the new buildings you had hoped for? The best work of men's brains has been done in garrets, and not in marble halls. Remember the glorious example of Johns Hopkins and Clark in the old days! It is really possible for a university to remain small, and for everybody in it to starve along and serve the unfolding spirit of man. You do not know the possibilities of sacrifice that lie in a group of scholars and thinkers until you try; even your students would be willing to work and earn money for their institution, if it were put up to them as a new crusade. Yes, and you would find here and there an alumnus who would understand and help. I do not urge that you should refuse money when it is offered on honest terms; all I mean is that you should make plain your policy, that money has no voice in the control of the institution, which knows but one loyalty—to the truth—and but one instrument—the open mind—and but one method—investigation and free discussion. Say to your would-be benefactors: we are educators; we know what the pursuit of knowledge is, and we teach it; if you wish to help in that, well and good; otherwise we go our way alone. I conclude this chapter with three stanzas written by Ralph Chaplin, one of America's greatest poets, whom the United States government has held in prison for the last five years, and plans to hold for fifteen years longer, on account of his political opinions.

> Mourn not the dead that in the cool earth lie—
>   Dust unto dust—
> The calm, sweet earth that mothers all who die
>   As all men must.
>
> Mourn not your captive comrades who must dwell—
>   Too strong to strive—
> Within each steel-bound coffin of a cell,
>   Buried alive.
>
> But rather mourn the apathetic throng—
>   The cowed and meek—
> Who see the world's great anguish and its wrong
>   And dare not speak!

CHAPTER XCI

EDUCATING THE EDUCATORS

There is another group in the colleges which must help to reform them, and that is the students. I have already shown that the student-body alone cannot dominate a college for any length of time; but in the student body is always a little group of thinking men, and these constitute a leaven which can work mighty changes in a great mass of solid dough.

The first organized effort of college students to educate themselves, and incidentally to educate their educators, was the Intercollegiate Socialist Society, which was founded by the writer some eighteen years ago. That was after I had come out from nine years of college and university life without knowing that the modern Socialist movement existed; I resolved to do what I could to make it less easy for the plutocracy to accomplish that feat in future. Some twenty or thirty people got together in New York City, and elected Jack London as president, and he delivered his famous address, "Revolution," within the shuddering walls of the Universities of California, Chicago, Harvard and Yale. We were careful to specify our purpose: "to promote an intelligent interest in the study of Socialism"; but even with that moderate statement, only a few institutions would let us in under our own evil name, and we had to disguise ourselves as liberal societies, and open forums, and social science clubs.

The name Socialism became so unpopular during the recent flood-tide of patriotism, that the organization has now called itself the League for Industrial Democracy. It has as its directors the Reverend Norman Thomas, editor of "The World Tomorrow," and Harry Laidler, author of an excellent text-book, which ought to be used in every college, "Socialism in Thought and Action." The purpose of the league is declared to be "education for a new social order, based on production for use and not for profit." It undertakes "research work, the development of pamphlet literature, and the thinking through of concrete problems of social ownership." The president is Professor Robert Morss Lovett of the University of Chicago, and the vice-presidents are Charles P. Steinmetz, Evans Clark, Florence Kelley and Arthur Gleason. The league holds a winter convention in New York and a summer conference lasting a week, at Camp Tamiment, belonging to the Rand School. The address of the league is 70 Fifth Avenue, New York.

Recently another student organization has entered the field, the National Student Forum, product of the labors of a group of young Harvard liberals, with John Rothschild as secretary. They publish a fortnightly paper, "The New Student," at 2929 Broadway, New York; they have drawn up a "preamble," which is so much to the point that I quote it in full:

"Realizing that these are times of rapid social change, the liberal spirited students of America are building this organization as an instrument of orderly progress.

"It is apparent to them that if the social changes now in process are to proceed sanely, those whose education is fitting them for positions of leadership must be better informed than hitherto regarding the contemporary affairs of the world in which they live. The students who founded The National Student Forum are aware that already in almost every institution of learning there is a group of students whose interest in social problems has brought them together into some local organization. It is their belief that to be of influence in the student life of America the scattered groups must effect an association through which they may learn from one another's experience, and publicly share the search for new light.

"With this in mind they have founded and now maintain The National Student Forum. They dedicate this organization to the cultivation of the scientifically inquiring mind; they declare it unbiased in any particular controversy, yet permitting within itself the expression of every bias; they declare its one principle to be freedom of expression, for they realize that without intellectual liberty the students of America cannot attain the completeness of vision and the social understanding which will enable them to be effective in the progress of the community."

As an illustration of the activities of this group I mention that the Harvard Liberal Club, during the year 1922, had sixty luncheon speakers in five months, including such radicals as Clark Getts, Lincoln Steffens, Florence Kelley, Raymond Robins, Frank Tannenbaum, Roger Baldwin, Percy Mackaye, Clare Sheridan, Norman Angell, and W. E. B. Dubois; properly balanced by a group of respectable people, including Admiral Sims, Hamilton Holt, President Eliot, and a nephew of Lord Bryce. What it means to the students of one of our universities to have such a corrective to the provincialism of its curriculum is something which only the students themselves can tell you, after they have had a chance to notice the difference. They come with bright eyes and eager faces, they listen and applaud, and they stay for hours to ask questions. They go away, knowing at least this much: that there are ideas in the world which are not tedious and dusty, and that the free use of the intellectual faculties can be as interesting as fraternity gossip and waving flags at gladiatorial combats.

So to the little group who come from free-thinking homes, or from the working classes, and do not mean to sell out their own people, I say: face the gales of ridicule and scolding, and see to it that while you are in college the students become acquainted with modern ideas. Get together a little group, and invite in speakers of all shades of opinion, and if the radical ones are barred, make an issue of it, and agitate for freedom of discussion. Join with those members of the faculty who are sympathetic to your point of view, extend their influence among the student-body, and back them up in controversies with the administration. Constitute yourself a ferment and leaven the dough-heads! I do not mean by this that you should be "fresh," or should go out of your way to seek trouble. Take the time to study, and know what you are talking about, so that when you take a position you will not be easily put down. When you have really studied and thought, then do not be afraid of being laughed at; for you will surely never do anything new or worthwhile in your life without being laughed at by fools and idlers.

Choose the big issues, and choose men and women who really have something to bring to the student-body. You will find them nearly always willing to come—all except the conservatives; but invite these also, and keep after them, and advertise the fact that you have done it. You have nothing to fear from their arguments, however masterful may be their air; we can handle them, I promise you—I have been through the whole question from A to Z, I have read the best that the opposition has to produce, and they cannot refute the claims of the workers for freedom, for social justice, and for light. If I had only one message to give to college students, it would be this: there exists in the modern revolutionary movement a vast treasure of idealism and inspiration, which your elders seek by every means in their power to keep from you. This treasure is your birthright, and to make it yours is your life's great success.

That they cannot answer the arguments of the social rebels, is something which the League of the Old Men knows perfectly well, and that is why they are afraid of us. In the literature of the Better America Federation of California it is again and again admitted that the immature minds of the young cannot be trusted to resist the temptations of idealism; if they meet these beautiful-sounding ideas they adopt them—and so they must be kept from knowing that the ideas exist! The soundness of this fear has been proven, wherever free discussion has been tried out. For example, in the state of Colorado, one of the great centers of metal mining and corruption in our country, the various colleges organized a State League for Debating, and they held a debate on the "open shop," and one of the teachers reported to me the results. There were eleven members of the "team," and they came from the homes of the employing classes, and everyone of them believed in the "American plan." At the end of the debate two were in doubt and nine opposed to the plan! Another team consisted of four women, and three of these were converted.

There is another interesting college movement, which has taken its rise in the West, under the leadership of B. M. Cherrington, a young Y. M. C. A. worker of the new type, who has seen the light and is preaching the social gospel. This organization is taking college students out into industry in the summer-time, not merely to earn money, but to learn the facts about labor conditions, and to understand them. The students are required to read books on the subject, and to prepare papers on what they have found. There was a street railway strike, in which more than sixty persons were shot. The students attended the conferences over this strike, and heard both sides presented. At the end of the summer's work they held a convention and drew up a statement, as follows:

"Having been associated, under the leadership of men of high ideals and Christian motives, for the purpose of intensive study of the human factor in industry, and having, as a result, come to a realization of the present seriousness and possible disastrous results of the turmoil and unrest which is now gripping the industrial world; and further realizing that those who are to become the business, professional and political leaders of tomorrow, the present college men, are, through lack of knowledge of and interest in these conditions, not only neglecting a vital part of their education, but are actually committing an injustice against humanity in failing to prepare themselves to meet the inevitable crisis, we, the members of the Denver Summer Study Group of 1920, undertake to expand that organization under the name "The Collegiate Industrial Research Movement."

The same thing is being done by the Young Women's Christian Association. There was a movement of this kind under the direction of Miss Caroline Goforth, and I heard an interesting story about one of the girls, who was running an elevator, and had her foot caught and injured. She was dressed like a "lady," and looked like one, and the surgeon took her for a passenger, and was courteous and helpful—until he discovered that she was an employe, when he became abrupt and negligent. Our interlocking newspapers profess to wonder at the existence of "parlor Bolshevists" and "pink tea Socialists," and may be interested to know how such creatures are made. Here was one made in a few minutes, by sharing the actual bitter experience of the workers!

I have narrated how the working class students at Bryn Mawr proceeded to unionize the "help" at that college. This is another work which liberal students may undertake with profit at many American colleges and universities. I have already referred to the experience of a group of students who set out ten years ago to reform conditions of labor at the University of Wisconsin. They organized an industrial union of all working students; the university authorities tried to break it up, and threatened to expel a group of forty active students from their jobs—and therefore from the university. They locked out a hundred and fifty from the University Commons. But the students succeeded in getting publicity; they brought in labor organizers, who surveyed the working conditions, and showed up the graft in the running of the university dining-rooms, the purchasing of milk and other supplies. They showed that two carloads of potatoes had been allowed to rot, that a car of apples had been allowed to freeze; also that the university was working girls in violation of the state industrial law.

The interlocking regents were called in, and also the board of visitors, and there was great excitement. One of the students reminded President Van Hise that the Milwaukee Trades and Labor Assembly controlled a

31

hundred and fifty thousand votes; which apparently produced the effect intended, for the business manager of the university retired. The interlocking trustees showed their appreciation of his fidelity to the principles of exploitation by immediately calling him to become president of Tufts College! Tufts gave him an honorary degree, and Brown and Clark followed suit, and now he is chairman of the Massachusetts Security League!

CHAPTER XCII

THE LEAGUE OF YOUTH

I have ventured to suggest student representation on boards controlling our colleges; and perhaps you thought I was showing too much confidence in student wisdom. Fortunately I can show you a few places where students are beginning to take up the problems of their own educating, and to find fault with the courses served out to them by the interlocking directorate. For example, Mt. Holyoke, a woman's college with a thousand students, located at South Hadley, Massachusetts; they have organized the "Mt. Holyoke College Community," governed entirely by committees of students and faculty. I note that they are fully aware of the various functions of government, and how to make a democracy work. They have arranged "an executive body consisting of the acting President of the College Community (a student) and the presidents of various student and faculty organizations; a legislative body consisting of one member for every fifteen students and one for every five members of the faculty; and a judicial body consisting of five students and two members of the faculty." Also these students have organized a committee on the curriculum, and three hundred and forty of them have reported "a strong demand for the elimination of required Latin and mathematics, and for the requirement of physiology and economics; also for modern government and hygiene."

More significant yet, the students of Barnard have got busy, right under the nose of Nicholas Miraculous! They organized a committee on their own initiative, and have constructed an "ideal" curriculum. Listen to what these progressive young ladies purpose requiring of freshmen:

a course on the history of mankind, counting ten points, "a synthetic survey course designed to bring out the chief aspects of man's relation to his environment by tracing present conditions and tendencies to historic processes; the physical nature of the universe . . . . man as a product of evolution . . . . the early history of man . . . . the concept of culture . . . . the historical processes leading to present cultural conditions . . . . modern problems, political, economic and social." Next they want a course, counting six points, in human biology and psychology, "giving an outline of human development and distribution on earth, man in relation to his nearest kin, a survey of human powers and functions, an introduction to general biology, the structure of the human body, outlines of embryology, functions of the body and their inter-relationships"—and laboratory work on all these problems. Also—imagine young ladies actually putting such things on paper!—they ask for:

"Specific human development of the sex-reproductive-child bearing function.

    a. "The facts of structure, functions, development and hygiene of the sex and reproductive apparatus of the male and female.

    b. "The outstanding facts of maternity and paternity.

    c. "Effects of sex on individual human development from fertilization to maturity.

    d. "The nature and power of the sex impulse.

    e. "The gradually developed sex controls imposed on the individual by society.

    f. "The pathological effects of perverse and unsocial uses of sex in society.

    g. "The facts underlying a satisfactory adjustment in marriage and homemaking."

Also they want a course in "general mathematical analysis," counting six points; "the technique of expression," counting two points; and "English literature," counting six points, with the aim "to present literature as an aspect of life; the emphasis throughout is therefore on subject matter rather than on technical or historical problems."

Yes; and also these young ladies of Barnard have taken up the problem of having Nicholas Miraculous tell them whom they may listen to. It was declared to them that the good repute of the college must be preserved, and after an argument they submitted to that imposition; but one thing they laid down very emphatically—they want the college authorities to give up the idea of protecting their tender young minds! As they put it:

"Resolved, that it is the feeling of the Student Council:

"That there is nothing gained in shielding students during four years from problems and ideas they must face during the rest of their life, and

"That if they are considered incapable of rational judgment upon theories presented to them, the solution lies in further training in scientific method rather than in quarantine from ideas, and

"That a reputation for fearless open-mindedness is more to be desired for an academic institution than material prosperity."

Also the Harvard students are waking up, under the influence of the Liberal Club. They have been discussing the subject of education, calling in various professors and deans to address them, and last spring the members of the corporation and the board of overseers were the guests of the club, to consider inaugurating the English tutorial system at Harvard. Also Harvard has a co-operative society, with three students upon its board of directors, and the Barnard students are planning a co-operative book-store, to be run entirely by themselves.

Such things as this have a way of spreading; they are spreading rapidly in Germany, where there is a movement of insurgent youth, taking steps to form a "World League of Youth," to make over the thinking and the social life of mankind. You will no doubt admit that the youth of Germany have justification for being discontented with the management of their Fatherland. Let me quote from their manifesto:

"Comrades! We are united in the hatred of the institutions of our social life and of our time. We ask ourselves: Whose fault are these institutions, this civilization? On whose conscience rest these political systems, these schools, these churches, these politics, these newspaper and so much else? The 'adult' people. . . . ."

Again, here is a statement from one of the leaders of this new and vitally important movement:

"The unifying characteristic, indeed the only sense of the youth movement is this: we no longer want to obey laws, coercions, customs that come to us from the outside and that have aims without a living, inner meaning to ourselves. We want to form our lives in accordance with laws that are within us, laws toward which alone we feel a responsibility."

Our own country has been more fortunate than Germany; we have still a great measure of prosperity, we are not yet in the pit of hell with Central Europe. But we are sliding, and sliding fast, and those who run our country do not know how to stop the process. I have shown you the League of the Old Men, suppressing thought and wrecking the world; and now here is the answer—the League of Youth! The Old Men were raised in the old order, their thinking is bound by its limitations. But we, the youth of the world, live in a new age, and have new problems to deal with. We cannot well do worse than our elders have done; we may very easily do better. Since we have longer to live in this world than our elders, we have surely the right to save it if we can!

CHAPTER XCIII

THE OPEN FORUM

I am writing in a time of reaction, but already the streaks of dawn are beginning to show. We are soon to witness the social revolution in Western Europe, and it will not be possible to keep these ideas from stirring the minds of young America. Our politics will change, and with that change will come freedom in our state universities, and the privately endowed institutions will be forced to come along. Just what will happen in the great centers of snobbery, such as Columbia and Princeton and Pennsylvania, I do not attempt to predict; perhaps their faculties will wake up and take control of their own destinies, or perhaps we shall see in our political life some violent revolutionary change, which will sweep the plutocratic endowments out of existence all at once. I am not advocating such a procedure, but I see our ruling classes doing everything in their power to force it, and if their efforts should succeed, we may see very quick reforms in American higher education.

What is it that I want? What should I do if I had my own unhampered way? Should I kick out all the reactionary professors, and turn Columbia and Princeton and Pennsylvania into Socialist propaganda clubs? If I could have my way, I should not commit a single violation of the principles of academic freedom for which I have pleaded in this book. The trustees and the presidents should of course be laid on the shelf, for these are administrative officials, and properly removable when a change of policy is desired. This would apply equally to the deans as administrators; but so far as the teachers are concerned, I would do them the honor to set them free, and plead with them to open their eyes to the new dawn of social justice. Just as there are thousands of members of the clergy who would jump up with a shout if they knew they could cease preaching fairy tales without losing their jobs, so there are thousands of college professors who would consider the truth if it were presented to them, and would teach it if they were encouraged.

As for the aged-minded ones—what I should do with them is to compete them out of business. I really believe in truth, and in the power of truth to confute error; I take my stand on the sentence of Wendell Phillips: "If anything cannot stand the truth, let it crack." What I ask is free discussion; what I want in the colleges is that both faculty and students should have opportunity to hear all sides of all questions, and especially those questions which lie at the heart of the great class struggle of our time. What I should do to the college would be to introduce a few live young professors who know modern ideas, and would lecture on modern books and modern political movements, explaining the revolutionary spirit which is vitalizing history, philosophy, religion and art. You would see in a year or two how the students thronged to these live men, and how the old men would have to wake up and fight for their prestige.

This is the plan of the open forum, and I urge groups of young professors and students everywhere to take their

stand on that. We desperately need men to lift their
voices in this cause just now, for in the last eight bitter
years the American people have shown that they have no
idea what free speech means—no trace of such an idea!
We sent one or two thousand men to jail for the crime
of expressing unpopular opinion; as I write, four years
after the armistice, we are still holding seventy-six such
men in torment, and the great mass of authority which
controls our politics, our press and our pulpits shows that
it has no conception whatever of the right of a man to
advocate an unpopular belief, or of the danger to society
involved in the crushing of minority opinion.

It is not too much to say that in America today it is
a general and firmly held conviction that to believe and
teach certain ideas is a crime. And from where shall
we expect opposition to this survival of savagery among
us, if not from our universities, which are supposed to
be dedicated to the search for truth? It is the shame of
our time that our colleges and universities have been silent
while freedom of opinion has been strangled in America.
Right here is the crucial issue, here is where the call for
academic heroes and martyrs goes out. The few of us
who believe in the truth have an organization, which will
back you and furnish you with ammunition in this fight;
if you do not know its literature, write to the American
Civil Liberties Union, New York City.

I have heard the arguments of the reactionaries, their
cries of horror at the idea that the sensitive minds of the
young should be exposed to the corruption of vicious
and incendiary ideas. To this the answer is plain: if
any parent wants to keep his child from thinking, there
is no law to deny him this power, but he should keep
that child at home, and not send it to an institution
which exists for the purpose of training young men and
women to use the faculties of the mind. Colleges and universities are places, or should be places, for those who
wish to think; and for any institution making such a
pretense there can be but one rule of procedure, which
is that all ideas are given a hearing and tried out in the
furnace of controversy.

I am aware, of course, that there are lunatics in the
world, and an infinite variety of cranks and bores—my
mail is burdened with their writings, and they keep my

door bell buzzing. I do not mean to say that college platforms should be turned over to such people; what I do say is, that whenever any considerable group of thinking people claim to have important new ideas to teach the world, they should be given a hearing in colleges, and if their ideas are unsound, let it be the business of the college to produce some one on the same platform to expose that unsoundness. The one thing that should never be heard inside college walls, or in connection with college policy, is that ideas should be suppressed because they are "dangerous"—because, in other words, they might win converts if they were given a hearing!

I met on my journey a horrified university trustee, who exclaimed: "What! You would permit anarchists and I. W. W.'s to speak at our institution?"

My answer was a counter-question: "Do you think that anarchism is right, or that it is wrong?"

The answer was: "Wrong!"

"Then," I said, "why are you afraid to hear it?"

"I am not afraid for myself, but when you are dealing with young minds"—and there you are; we must protect the minds of the young! It is hard for the old to realize that the young may have older minds, having grown up in a world with better means of thinking and of spreading ideas.

We deported Emma Goldman, and thought we had thereby prevented the spread of anarchism; which shows that whatever else our colleges and universities have done, they have not taught us the psychology of martyrdom. I agree with the university trustee in thinking that anarchism is wrong—at least for a hundred years or so; but my way of handling Emma Goldman would have been to run her on a lecture tour in every American college and university, in a debate with some thoroughly trained expert in the history of social evolution. I would have let all the students hear her, and keep her until midnight answering questions; so, if there was truth in her views it would have spread, and if there was error the students would have been inoculated against it for life.

Some years ago I wrote that I should like to send every clergyman in the United States to jail for a week; this not out of any ill will for the church, but as a step toward prison reform. In the same way I should like to see our college students go to jail; or barring that, I should like to have the prisoners come to the colleges, to tell the students how men become criminals, and what society could do about it. Some of the most interesting men I ever met were criminals, and others were tramps, and others were social revolutionists. I should like to see all college students go to work in factories, and I should like to see the leaders of labor, both conservatives and radicals, brought to the colleges to tell the students about industrial problems. Let the employers come also—both sides would be more careful of their facts if they knew they had to present them before a jury of wide-awake students and highly trained faculty members. What a service the college might perform, in toning down the bitterness of the class struggle, if the faculty made it their business to invite both sides in every labor dispute to come and justify themselves; if the faculty would keep at it, and accept no refusal, but "smoke out" the arrogant ones, who take, either publicly or privately, the old-style attitude of "the public be damned!"

That is my program for colleges—to discuss the vital ideas, the subjects that men are arguing and fighting over, the problems that must be solved if our society is not to be rent by civil war. Everybody is interested in these questions, old and young, rich and poor, high and low, and if you deal with them you solve several vexing problems at once. You solve the problem of getting students to study, and also the problem of student morals; you turn your college from a country club to which elegant young gentlemen come to wear good clothes and play games, and more or less in secret to drink and carouse—you turn it from that into a place where ideas are taken seriously, and the young learn the use of the most wonderful tool that the human race has so far developed, that of experimental science.

When you understand this weapon and its powers, you are no longer afraid of the specters and the goblins, the dragons and devils and other monsters which haunted the imagination of our racial childhood. You know; you know precisely, and you know certainly, and so you are free from fear; you go out into life as a young warrior with an enchanted sword, all powerful against all enemies. To forge that sword and train you in the care of it and the use of it—that is the true task of our institutions of higher education. To that end the call goes out to all men and women, who have learned to believe in reason, and wish to have it vindicated and used in the world. Our educational system today is in the hands of its last organized enemy, which is class greed and selfishness based upon economic privilege. To slay that monster is to set free all the future. If this book helps to make clear the issue, and to bring fresh recruits to the army of emancipation, its purpose will be served and its author will be content.

It was my original intention to write a book dealing with our whole educational system; but as you have seen, the mass of material dealing with colleges alone proved sufficient to make a full-sized book. It is my purpose to follow this with a second volume, dealing with the public schools, and entitled "The Goslings."

INDEX

Roman numerals refer to chapters, Arabic numerals to pages.
Names of colleges and universities are in italics.

479

W. B. C.

They Call Me Carpenter

By UPTON SINCLAIR

WOULD you like to meet Jesus? Would you care to walk down Broadway with him in the year 1922? What would he order for dinner in a lobster palace? What would he do in a beauty parlor? What would he make of a permanent wave? What would he say to Mary Magna, million dollar queen of the movies? And how would he greet the pillars of St. Bartholomew's Church? How would he behave at strike headquarters? What would he say at a mass meeting of the "reds"? And what would the American Legion do to him?

From the "Survey":

"Upton Sinclair has a reputation for rushing in where angels fear to tread. He has done it again and, artist that he is, has mastered the most difficult theme with ease and sureness. That the figure of Jesus is woven into a novel which is glorious fun, in itself will shock many people. But the graphic arts have long been given the liberty of treating His life in a contemporary setting—why not the novelist?

"Heywood Broun and other critics notwithstanding, it must be stated that Sinclair has treated the figure of Christ with a reverence far more sincere than that of writings in which His presence is shrouded in pseudo-mystic inanity. By an artistry borrowed from the technique of modern expressionist fiction, he has combined downright realism with an extravagant imaginativeness in which the appearance of Christ is no more improper than it is in the actual dreams of hundreds of thousands of devout Christians.

"Like all of Sinclair's writings, this book is, of course, a Socialist tract; but here—in a spirit which entirely destroys Mr. Broun's charge that he has made Christ the spokesman of one class—he is unmerciful in his exposure of the sins of the poor as well as of the rich, and directs at the comrades in radical movements a sermon which every churchman will gladly endorse.

"It is not necessary to recommend a book that will find its way into thousands of homes. Incidentally one wonders how a story so colloquially American—Mr. Broun considers this bad taste—can possibly be translated into the Hungarian, the Chinese and the dozen or so other languages in which Sinclair's books are devoured by the common people of the world."

Single copy, cloth, $1.50; paper, $1.00, postpaid.

UPTON SINCLAIR, Los Angeles (West Branch), Calif.

A New Novel by Upton Sinclair

100%

THE STORY OF A PATRIOT

WOULD you like to go behind the scenes and see the "invisible government" of your country saving you from the Bolsheviks and the Reds? Would you like to meet the secret agents and provocateurs of "Big Business," to know what they look like, how they talk and what they are doing to make the world safe for democracy? Several of these gentlemen have been haunting the home of Upton Sinclair during the past three years and he has had the idea of turning the tables and investigating the investigators. He has put one of them, Peter Gudge by name, into a book, together with Peter's lady-loves, and his wife, and his boss and a whole group of his fellow-agents and their employers.

The hero of this book is a red-blooded, 100% American, a "he-man" and no mollycoddle. He begins with the Mooney case, and goes through half a dozen big cases of which you have heard. His story is a fact-story of America from 1916 to 1920, and will make a bigger sensation than "The Jungle." Albert Rhys Williams, author of "Lenin" and "In the Claws of the German Eagle," read the MS. and wrote:

"This is the first novel of yours that I have read through with real interest. It is your most timely work, and is bound to make a sensation. I venture that you will have even more trouble than you had with 'The Brass Check'—in getting the books printed fast enough."

Cloth, Price, $1.50

UPTON SINCLAIR
Los Angeles (West Branch), California

Concerning
The Jungle

Not since Byron awoke one morning to find himself famous has there been such an example of world-wide celebrity won in a day by a book as has come to Upton Sinclair.—*New York Evening World.*

It is a book that does for modern industrial slavery what "Uncle Tom's Cabin" did for black slavery. But the work is done far better and more accurately in "The Jungle" than in "Uncle Tom's Cabin."—*Arthur Brisbane in the New York Evening Journal.*

I never expected to read a serial. I am reading *"The Jungle,"* and I should be afraid to trust myself to tell how it affects me. It is a great work. I have a feeling that you yourself will be dazed some day by the excitement about it. It is impossible that such a power should not be felt. It is so simple, so true, so tragic and so human. It is so eloquent, and yet so exact. I must restrain myself or you may misunderstand.—*David Graham Phillips.*

In this fearful story the horrors of industrial slavery are as vividly drawn as if by lightning. It marks an epoch in revolutionary literature.—*Eugene V. Debs.*

Mr. Heinemann isn't a man to bungle;
He's published a book which is called "The Jungle."
It's written by Upton Sinclair, who
Appears to have heard a thing or two
About Chicago and what men do
Who live in that city—a loathsome crew.
It's there that the stockyards reek with blood,
And the poor man dies, as he lives, in mud;
The Trusts are wealthy beyond compare,
And the bosses are all triumphant there,
And everything rushes without a skid
To be plunged in a hell which has lost its lid.
For a country where things like that are done
There's just one remedy, only one,
A latter-day Upton Sinclairism
Which the rest of us know as Socialism.
Here's luck to the book! It will make you cower,
For it's written with wonderful, thrilling power.
It grips your throat with a grip Titanic,
And scatters shams with a force volcanic.
Go buy the book, for I judge you need it,
And when you have bought it, read it, read it.
                              —*Punch (London).*

www.ingramcontent.com/pod-product-compliance
Lightning Source LLC
Chambersburg PA
CBHW081323090726
47907CB00010B/2354